THE SHIPWRECK COLLECTION

The Shipwreck Collection
Crusoe, Swift, Stevenson & Wells

Robinson Crusoe
Defoe, Daniel, 1660 – 1731
First Published by W. Taylor in 1719
Gulliver's Travels
Swift, Jonathan 1667 – 1745
First Published by Benjamin Motte in 1726
Treasure Island
Stevenson, Robert Louis 1850 – 1894
First Published by J Cassell & Co. in 1883
The Island of Doctor Moreau
Wells, H.G., 1866 – 1946
First Published by Heinemann,
Stone & Kimball in 1896

Mailing address:
Engage Books
PO BOX 4608
Main Station Terminal
349 West Georgia Street
Vancouver, BC
Canada, V6B 4A1

www.engagebooks.com

Cover design by: A.R. Roumanis

Text set in Minion Pro. Chapter headings set in News Gothic Standard.

ISBN: 978-1-77476-230-1

FIRST EDITION / FIRST PRINTING

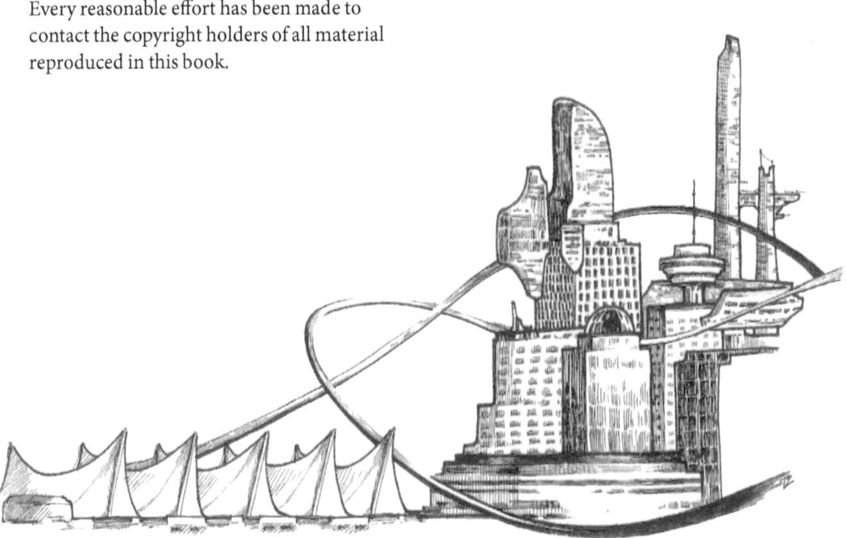

THE SHIPWRECK COLLECTION

DANIEL DEFOE

ROBINSON CRUSOE

JONATHAN SWIFT

GULLIVER'S TRAVELS

ROBERT L. STEVENSON

TREASURE ISLAND

H. G. WELLS

THE ISLAND OF DR MOREAU

VANCOUVER:
ENGAGE BOOKS
2021

CONTENTS

ROBINSON CRUSOE

1726 illustration by W. Mears & T. Woodward

CONTENTS

CHAPTER ONE

Start in Life

I WAS BORN IN THE YEAR 1632, in the city of York, of a good family, though not of that country, my father being a foreigner of Bremen, who settled first at Hull. He got a good estate by merchandise, and leaving off his trade, lived afterwards at York, from whence he had married my mother, whose relations were named Robinson, a very good family in that country, and from whom I was called Robinson Kreutznaer; but, by the usual corruption of words in England, we are now called – nay we call ourselves and write our name – Crusoe; and so my companions always called me.

I had two elder brothers, one of whom was Lieutenant-Colonel to an English regiment of Foot in Flanders, formerly commanded by the famous Colonel Lockhart, and was killed at the battle near Dunkirk against the Spaniards. What became of my second brother I never knew, any more than my father or mother knew what became of me.

Being the third son of the family and not bred to any trade, my head began to be filled very early with rambling thoughts. My father, who was very ancient, had given me a competent share of learning, as far as house-education and a country free school generally go, and designed me for the law; but I would be satisfied with nothing but going to sea; and my inclination to this led me so strongly against the will, nay, the commands of my father, and against all the entreaties and persuasions of my mother and other friends, that there seemed to be something fatal in that propensity of nature, tending directly to the life of misery which was to befall me.

My father, a wise and grave man, gave me serious and excellent counsel against what he foresaw was my design. He called me one morning into his chamber, where he was confined by the gout, and expostulated very warmly with me upon this subject. He asked me what reasons, more than a mere wandering inclination, I had for leaving father's house and my native country, where I might be well introduced, and had a prospect of raising my fortune by application and industry, with a life of ease and pleasure. He told me it was men of desperate fortunes on one hand, or of aspiring, superior fortunes on the other, who went abroad upon adventures, to rise by enterprise, and make themselves famous in undertakings of a nature out of the common road; that these things were all either too far above me or too far below me; that mine was the middle state, or what might be called the upper station of low life, which he had found, by long experience, was the best state in the world, the most suited to human happiness, not exposed to the miseries and hardships, the labour and sufferings of the mechanic part of mankind, and not embarrassed with the pride, luxury, ambition, and envy of the upper part of mankind. He told me I might judge of the happiness of this state by this one thing – *viz.* that this was the state of life which all other people envied; that kings have frequently lamented the miserable consequence of being born to great things, and wished they had been placed in the middle of the two extremes, between the mean and the great; that the wise man gave his testimony to this, as the standard of felicity, when he prayed to have neither poverty nor riches.

He bade me observe it, and I should always find that the calamities of life were shared among the upper and lower part of mankind, but that the middle station had the fewest disasters, and was not exposed to so many vicissitudes as the higher or lower part of mankind; nay, they were not subjected to so many distempers and uneasinesses, either of body or mind, as those were who, by vicious living, luxury, and extravagances on the one hand, or by hard labour, want of necessaries, and mean or insufficient diet on the other hand, bring distemper upon themselves by the natural consequences of their way of living; that the middle station of life was calculated for all kind of virtue and all kind of enjoyments; that peace and plenty were the handmaids of a middle fortune; that temperance, moderation, quietness, health, society, all agreeable diversions, and all desirable pleasures, were the blessings attending the middle station of life; that this way men went silently and smoothly through the world, and comfortably out of it, not embarrassed with the labours of the hands or of the head, not sold to a life of slavery for daily bread, nor harassed with perplexed circumstances, which rob the soul of peace and the body of rest, nor enraged with the passion of envy, or the secret burning lust of ambition for great things; but, in easy circumstances, sliding gently through the world, and sensibly tasting the sweets of living, without the bitter; feeling that they are happy, and learning by every day's experience to know it more sensibly,

After this he pressed me earnestly, and in the most affectionate manner, not to play the young man, nor to precipitate myself into miseries which nature, and the station of life I was born in, seemed to have provided against; that I was under no necessity of seeking my bread; that he would do well for me, and endeavour to enter me fairly into the station of life which he had just been recommending to me; and that if I was not very easy and happy in the world, it must be my mere fate or fault that must hinder it; and that he should have nothing to answer for, having thus discharged his duty in warning me against measures which he knew would be to my hurt; in a word, that as he would do very kind things for me if I would stay and settle at home as he directed, so he would not have so much hand in my misfortunes as to give me any encouragement to go away; and to close all, he told me I had my elder brother for an example, to whom he had used the same earnest persuasions to keep him from going into the Low Country wars, but could not prevail, his young desires prompting him to run into the army, where he was killed; and though he said he would not cease to pray for me, yet he would venture to say to me, that if I did take this foolish step, God would not bless me, and I should have leisure hereafter to reflect upon having neglected his counsel when there might be none to assist in my recovery.

I observed in this last part of his discourse, which was truly prophetic, though I suppose my father did not know it to be so himself – I say, I observed the tears run down his face very plentifully, especially when he spoke of my brother who was killed: and that when he spoke of my having leisure to repent, and none to assist me, he was so moved that he broke off the discourse, and told me his heart was so full he could say no more to me.

I was sincerely affected with this discourse, and, indeed, who could be otherwise? and I resolved not to think of going abroad any more, but to settle at home according to my father's desire. But alas! a few days wore it all off; and, in short, to prevent any of my father's further importunities, in a few weeks after I resolved to run quite away from him. However, I did not act quite so hastily as the first heat of my resolution prompted; but I took my mother at a time when I thought her a little more pleasant than ordinary, and told her that my thoughts were so entirely bent upon seeing the world that I should never settle to anything with resolution enough to go through with it, and my father had better give me his consent than force me to go without it; that I was now eighteen years old, which was too late to go apprentice to a trade or clerk to an attorney; that I was sure if I did I should never serve out my time, but I should certainly run away from my Master before my time was out, and go to sea; and if she would speak to my father to let me go one voyage abroad, if I came home again, and did not like it, I would go no more; and I would promise, by a double diligence, to recover the time that I had lost.

This put my mother into a great passion; she told me she knew it would be to no purpose to speak to my father upon any such subject; that he knew too well what was my interest to give his consent to anything so much for my hurt; and that she wondered how I could think of any such thing after the discourse I had had with my father, and such kind and tender expressions as she knew my father had used to me; and that, in short, if I would ruin myself, there was no help for me; but I might depend I should never have their consent to it; that for her part she would not have so much hand in my destruction; and I should never have it to say that my mother was willing when my father was not.

Though my mother refused to move it to my father, yet I heard afterwards that she reported all the discourse to him, and that my father, after showing a great concern at it, said to her, with a sigh, "That boy might be happy if he would stay at home; but if he goes abroad, he will be the most miserable wretch that ever was born: I can give no consent to it."

It was not till almost a year after this that I broke loose, though, in the meantime, I continued obstinately deaf to all proposals of settling to business, and frequently expostulated with my father and mother about their being so positively determined against what they knew my inclinations prompted me to. But being one day at Hull, where I went casually, and without any purpose of making an elopement at that time; but, I say, being there, and one of my companions being about to sail to London in his father's ship, and prompting me to go with them with the common allurement of seafaring men, that it should cost me nothing for my passage, I consulted neither father nor mother any more, nor so much as sent them word of it; but leaving them to hear of it as they might, without asking God's blessing or my father's, without any consideration of circumstances or consequences, and in an ill hour, God knows, on the 1st of September 1651, I went on board a ship bound for London. Never any young adventurer's misfortunes, I believe, began sooner, or continued longer than mine. The ship was no sooner out of the Humber than the wind began to blow and the sea to rise in a most frightful manner; and, as I had never been at sea before, I was most inexpressibly sick in body and terrified in mind. I began now seriously to reflect upon what I had done, and how justly I was overtaken by the judgment of Heaven for my wicked leaving my father's house, and abandoning my duty. All the good counsels of my parents, my father's tears and my mother's entreaties, came now fresh into my mind; and my conscience, which was not yet come to the pitch of hardness to which it has since, reproached me with the contempt of advice, and the breach of my duty to God and my father.

All this while the storm increased, and the sea went very high, though nothing like what I have seen many times since; no, nor what I saw a few days after; but it was enough to affect me then, who was but a young sailor, and had never known anything of the matter. I expected every wave would have swallowed us up, and that every time the ship fell down, as I thought it did, in the trough or hollow of the sea, we should never rise more; in this agony of mind, I made many vows and resolutions that if it would please God to spare my life in this one voyage, if ever I got once my foot upon dry land again, I would go directly home to my father, and never set it into a ship again while I lived; that I would take his advice, and never run myself into such miseries as these any more. Now I saw plainly the goodness of his observations about the middle station of life, how easy, how comfortably he had lived all his days, and never had been exposed to tempests at sea or troubles on shore; and I resolved that I would, like a true repenting prodigal, go home to my father.

These wise and sober thoughts continued all the while the storm lasted, and indeed some time after; but the next day the wind was abated, and the sea calmer, and I began to be a little inured to it; however, I was very grave for all that day, being also a little sea-sick still; but towards night the weather cleared up, the wind was quite over, and a charming fine evening followed; the sun went down perfectly clear, and rose so the next morning; and having little or no wind, and a smooth sea, the sun shining upon it, the sight was, as I thought, the most delightful that ever I saw.

I had slept well in the night, and was now no more sea-sick, but very cheerful, looking with wonder upon the sea that was so rough and terrible the day before, and could be so calm and so pleasant in so little a time after. And now, lest my good resolutions should continue, my companion, who had enticed me away, comes to me; "Well, Bob," says he, clapping me upon the shoulder, "how do you do after it? I warrant you were frighted, wer'n't you, last night, when it blew but a capful of wind?" "A capful d'you call it?" said I; "'twas a terrible storm." "A storm, you fool you," replies he; "do you call that a storm? why, it was nothing at all; give us but a good ship and sea-room, and we think nothing of such a squall of wind as that; but you're but a fresh-water sailor, Bob. Come, let us make a bowl of punch, and we'll forget all that; d'ye see what charming weather 'tis now?" To make short this sad part of my story, we went the way of all sailors; the punch was made and I was made half drunk with it: and in that one night's wickedness I drowned all my repentance, all my reflections upon my past conduct, all my resolutions for the future. In a word, as the sea was returned to its smoothness of surface and settled calmness by the abatement of that storm, so the hurry of my thoughts being over, my fears and apprehensions of being swallowed up by the sea being forgotten, and the current of my former desires returned, I entirely forgot the vows and promises that I made in my distress. I found, indeed, some intervals of reflection; and the serious thoughts did, as it were, endeavour to return again sometimes; but I shook them off, and roused myself from them as it were from a distemper, and applying myself to drinking and company, soon mastered the return of those fits – for so I called them; and I had in five or six days got as complete a victory over conscience as any young fellow that resolved not to be troubled with it could desire. But I was to have another trial for it still; and Providence, as in such cases generally it does, resolved to leave me entirely without excuse; for if I would not take this for a deliverance, the next was to be such a one as the worst and most hardened wretch among us would confess both the danger and the mercy of.

The 6th day of our being at sea we came into Yarmouth Roads; the wind having been contrary and the weather calm, we had made but little way since the storm. Here we were obliged to come to an anchor, and here we lay, the wind continuing contrary – *viz.* at south-west – for seven or eight days, during which time a great many ships from Newcastle came into the same Roads, as the common harbour where the ships might wait for a wind for the river.

We had not, however, rid here so long but we should have tided it up the river, but that the wind blew too fresh, and after we had lain four or five days, blew very hard. However, the Roads being reckoned as good as a harbour, the anchorage good, and our ground-tackle very strong, our men were unconcerned, and not in the least apprehensive of danger, but spent the time in rest and mirth, after the manner of the sea; but the eighth day, in the morning, the wind increased, and we had all hands at work to strike our topmasts, and make everything snug and close, that the ship might ride as easy as possible. By noon the sea went very high indeed, and our ship rode forecastle in, shipped several seas, and we thought once or twice our anchor had come home; upon which our Master ordered out the sheet-anchor, so that we rode with two anchors ahead, and the cables veered out to the bitter end.

By this time it blew a terrible storm indeed; and now I began to see terror and amazement in the faces even of the seamen themselves. The

Master, though vigilant in the business of preserving the ship, yet as he went in and out of his cabin by me, I could hear him softly to himself say, several times, "Lord be merciful to us! we shall be all lost! we shall be all undone!" and the like. During these first hurries I was stupid, lying still in my cabin, which was in the steerage, and cannot describe my temper: I could ill resume the first penitence which I had so apparently trampled upon and hardened myself against: I thought the bitterness of death had been past, and that this would be nothing like the first; but when the Master himself came by me, as I said just now, and said we should be all lost, I was dreadfully frighted. I got up out of my cabin and looked out; but such a dismal sight I never saw: the sea ran mountains high, and broke upon us every three or four minutes; when I could look about, I could see nothing but distress round us; two ships that rode near us, we found, had cut their masts by the board, being deep laden; and our men cried out that a ship which rode about a mile ahead of us was foundered. Two more ships, being driven from their anchors, were run out of the Roads to sea, at all adventures, and that with not a mast standing. The light ships fared the best, as not so much labouring in the sea; but two or three of them drove, and came close by us, running away with only their spritsail out before the wind.

Towards evening the Mate and boatswain begged the Master of our ship to let them cut away the fore-mast, which he was very unwilling to do; but the boatswain protesting to him that if he did not the ship would founder, he consented; and when they had cut away the fore-mast, the main-mast stood so loose, and shook the ship so much, they were obliged to cut that away also, and make a clear deck.

Any one may judge what a condition I must be in at all this, who was but a young sailor, and who had been in such a fright before at but a little. But if I can express at this distance the thoughts I had about me at that time, I was in tenfold more horror of mind upon account of my former convictions, and the having returned from them to the resolutions I had wickedly taken at first, than I was at death itself; and these, added to the terror of the storm, put me into such a condition that I can by no words describe it. But the worst was not come yet; the storm continued with such fury that the seamen themselves acknowledged they had never seen a worse. We had a good ship, but she was deep laden, and wallowed in the sea, so that the seamen every now and then cried out she would founder. It was my advantage in one respect, that I did not know what they meant by founder till I inquired. However, the storm was so violent that I saw, what is not often seen, the Master, the boatswain, and some others more sensible than the rest, at their prayers, and expecting every moment when the ship would go to the bottom. In the middle of the night, and under all the rest of our distresses, one of the men that had been down to see cried out we had sprung a leak; another said there was four feet water in the hold. Then all hands were called to the pump. At that word, my heart, as I thought, died within me: and I fell backwards upon the side of my bed where I sat, into the cabin. However, the men roused me, and told me that I, that was able to do nothing before, was as well able to pump as another; at which I stirred up and went to the pump, and worked very heartily. While this was doing the Master, seeing some light colliers, who, not able to ride out the storm were obliged to slip and run away to sea, and would come near us, ordered to fire a gun as a signal of distress. I, who knew nothing what they meant, thought the ship had broken, or some dreadful thing happened. In a word, I was so surprised that I fell down in a swoon. As this was a time when everybody had his own life to think of, nobody minded me, or what was become of me; but another man stepped up to the pump, and thrusting me aside with his foot, let me lie, thinking I had been dead; and it was a great while before I came to myself.

We worked on; but the water increasing in the hold, it was apparent that the ship would founder; and though the storm began to abate a little, yet it was not possible she could swim till we might run into any port; so the Master continued firing guns for help; and a light ship, who had rid it out just ahead of us, ventured a boat out to help us. It was with the utmost hazard the boat came near us; but it was impossible for us to get on board, or for the boat to lie near the ship's side, till at last the men rowing very heartily, and venturing their lives to save ours, our men cast them a rope over the stern with a buoy to it, and then veered it out a great length, which they, after much labour and hazard, took hold of, and we hauled them close under our stern, and got all into their boat. It was to no purpose for them or us, after we were in the boat, to think of reaching their own ship; so all agreed to let her drive, and only to pull her in towards shore as much as we could; and our Master promised them, that if the boat was staved upon shore, he would make it good to their Master: so partly rowing and partly driving, our boat went away to the northward, sloping towards the shore almost as far as Winterton Ness.

We were not much more than a quarter of an hour out of our ship till we saw her sink, and then I understood for the first time what was meant by a ship foundering in the sea. I must acknowledge I had hardly eyes to look up when the seamen told me she was sinking; for from the moment that they rather put me into the boat than that I might be said to go in, my heart was, as it were, dead within me, partly with fright, partly with horror of mind, and the thoughts of what was yet before me.

While we were in this condition – the men yet labouring at the oar to bring the boat near the shore – we could see (when, our boat mounting the waves, we were able to see the shore) a great many people running along the strand to assist us when we should come near; but we made but slow way towards the shore; nor were we able to reach the shore till, being past the lighthouse at Winterton, the shore falls off to the westward towards Cromer, and so the land broke off a little the violence of the wind. Here we got in, and though not without much difficulty, got all safe on shore, and walked afterwards on foot to Yarmouth, where, as unfortunate men, we were used with great humanity, as well by the magistrates of the town, who assigned us good quarters, as by particular merchants and owners of ships, and had money given us sufficient to carry us either to London or back to Hull as we thought fit.

Had I now had the sense to have gone back to Hull, and have gone home, I had been happy, and my father, as in our blessed Saviour's parable, had even killed the fatted calf for me; for hearing the ship I went away in was cast away in Yarmouth Roads, it was a great while before he had any assurances that I was not drowned.

But my ill fate pushed me on now with an obstinacy that nothing could resist; and though I had several times loud calls from my reason and my more composed judgment to go home, yet I had no power to do it. I know not what to call this, nor will I urge that it is a secret overruling decree, that hurries us on to be the instruments of our own destruction, even though it be before us, and that we rush upon it with our eyes open. Certainly, nothing but some such decreed unavoidable misery, which it was impossible for me to escape, could have pushed me forward against the calm reasonings and persuasions of my most retired thoughts, and against two such visible instructions as I had met with in my first attempt.

My comrade, who had helped to harden me before, and who was the Master's son, was now less forward than I. The first time he spoke to me after we were at Yarmouth, which was not till two or three days, for we were separated in the town to several quarters; I say, the first time he saw me, it appeared his tone was altered; and, looking very melancholy, and shaking his head, he asked me how I did, and telling his father who I was, and how I had come this voyage only for a trial, in order to go further abroad, his father, turning to me with a very grave and concerned tone "Young man," says he, "you ought never to go to sea any more; you ought to take this for a plain and visible token that you are not to be a seafaring man." "Why, sir," said I, "will you go to sea no more?" "That is another case," said he; "it is my calling, and therefore my duty; but as you made this voyage on trial, you see what a taste Heaven has given you of what you are to expect if you persist. Perhaps this has all befallen us on your account, like Jonah in the ship of Tarshish. Pray," continues he, "what are you; and on what account did you go to sea?" Upon that I told him some of my story; at the end of which he burst out into a strange kind of passion: "What had I done," says he, "that such an unhappy wretch should come into my ship? I would not set my foot in the same ship with thee again for 1,000 pounds." This indeed was, as I said, an excursion of his spirits, which were yet agitated by the sense of his loss, and was farther than he could have authority to go. However, he afterwards talked very gravely to me, exhorting me to go back to my father, and not tempt Providence to my ruin, telling me I might see a visible hand of Heaven against me. "And, young man," said he, "depend upon it, if you do not go back, wherever you go, you will meet with nothing but disasters and disappointments, till your father's words are fulfilled upon you."

We parted soon after; for I made him little answer, and I saw him no more; which way he went I knew not. As for me, having some money in my pocket, I travelled to London by land; and there, as well as on the road, had many struggles with myself what course of life I should take, and whether I should go home or to sea.

As to going home, shame opposed the best motions that offered to my thoughts, and it immediately occurred to me how I should be laughed at among the neighbours, and should be ashamed to see, not my father and mother only, but even everybody else; from whence I have since often observed, how incongruous and irrational the common temper of mankind is, especially of youth, to that reason which ought to guide them in such cases – *viz.* that they are not ashamed to sin, and yet are ashamed to repent; not ashamed of the action for which they ought justly to be esteemed fools, but are ashamed of the returning, which only can make them be esteemed wise men.

In this state of life, however, I remained some time, uncertain what measures to take, and what course of life to lead. An irresistible reluctance continued to going home; and as I stayed away a while, the remembrance of the distress I had been in wore off, and as that abated, the little motion I had in my desires to return wore off with it, till at last I quite laid aside the thoughts of it, and looked out for a voyage.

CHAPTER TWO

Slavery and Escape

THAT EVIL INFLUENCE WHICH CARRIED me first away from my father's house – which hurried me into the wild and indigested notion of raising my fortune, and that impressed those conceits so forcibly upon me as to make me deaf to all good advice, and to the entreaties and even the commands of my father – I say, the same influence, whatever it was, presented the most unfortunate of all enterprises to my view; and I went on board a vessel bound to the coast of Africa; or, as our sailors vulgarly called it, a voyage to Guinea.

It was my great misfortune that in all these adventures I did not ship myself as a sailor; when, though I might indeed have worked a little harder than ordinary, yet at the same time I should have learnt the duty and office of a fore-mast man, and in time might have qualified myself for a Mate or Lieutenant, if not for a Master. But as it was always my fate to choose for the worse, so I did here; for having money in my pocket and good clothes upon my back, I would always go on board in the habit of a gentleman; and so I neither had any business in the ship, nor learned to do any.

It was my lot first of all to fall into pretty good company in London, which does not always happen to such loose and misguided young fellows as I then was; the devil generally not omitting to lay some snare for them very early; but it was not so with me. I first got acquainted with the master of a ship who had been on the coast of Guinea; and who, having had very good success there, was resolved to go again. This Captain taking a fancy to my conversation, which was not at all disagreeable at that time, hearing me say I had a mind to see the world, told me if I would go the voyage with him I should be at no expense; I should be his messmate and his companion; and if I could carry anything with me, I should have all the advantage of it that the trade would admit; and perhaps I might meet with some encouragement.

I embraced the offer; and entering into a strict friendship with this Captain, who was an honest, plain-dealing man, I went the voyage with him, and carried a small adventure with me, which, by the disinterested honesty of my friend the Captain, I increased very considerably; for I carried about 40 pounds in such toys and trifles as the Captain directed me to buy. These 40 pounds I had mustered together by the assistance of some of my relations whom I corresponded with; and who, I believe, got my father, or at least my mother, to contribute so much as that to my first adventure.

This was the only voyage which I may say was successful in all my adventures, which I owe to the integrity and honesty of my friend the Captain; under whom also I got a competent knowledge of the mathematics and the rules of navigation, learned how to keep an account of the ship's course, take an observation, and, in short, to understand some things that were needful to be understood by a sailor; for, as he took delight to instruct me, I took delight to learn; and, in a word, this voyage made me both a sailor and a merchant; for I brought home 5 pounds 9 ounces of gold-dust for my adventure, which yielded me in London, at my return, almost 300 pounds; and this filled me with those aspiring thoughts which have since so completed my ruin.

Yet even in this voyage I had my misfortunes too; particularly, that I was continually sick, being thrown into a violent calenture by the excessive heat of the climate; our principal trading being upon the coast, from latitude of 15 degrees north even to the line itself.

I was now set up for a Guinea trader; and my friend, to my great misfortune, dying soon after his arrival, I resolved to go the same voyage again, and I embarked in the same vessel with one who was his Mate in the former voyage, and had now got the command of the ship. This was the unhappiest voyage that ever man made; for though I did not carry quite 100 pounds of my new-gained wealth, so that I had 200 pounds left, which I had lodged with my friend's widow, who was very just to me, yet I fell into terrible misfortunes. The first was this: our ship making her course towards the Canary Islands, or rather between those islands and the African shore, was surprised in the grey of the morning by a Turkish rover of Sallee, who gave chase to us with all the sail she could make. We crowded also as much canvas as our yards would spread, or our masts carry, to get clear; but finding the pirate gained upon us, and would certainly come up with us in a few hours, we prepared to fight; our ship having 12 guns, and the rogue 18. About three in the afternoon he came up with us, and bringing to, by mistake, just athwart our quarter, instead of athwart our stern, as he intended, we brought 8 of our guns to bear on that side, and poured in a broadside upon him, which made him sheer off again, after returning our fire, and pouring in also his small shot from near 200 men which he had on board. However, we had not a man touched, all our men keeping close. He prepared to attack us again, and we to defend ourselves. But laying us on board the next time upon our other quarter, he entered 60 men upon our decks, who immediately fell to cutting and hacking the sails and rigging. We plied them with small shot, half-pikes, powder-chests, and such like, and cleared our deck of them twice. However, to cut short this melancholy part of our story, our ship being disabled, and three of our men killed, and eight wounded, we were obliged to yield, and were carried all prisoners into Sallee, a port belonging to the Moors.

The usage I had there was not so dreadful as at first I apprehended; nor was I carried up the country to the Emperor's court, as the rest of our men were, but was kept by the Captain of the rover as his proper prize, and made his slave, being young and nimble, and fit for his business. At this surprising change of my circumstances, from a merchant to a miserable slave, I was perfectly overwhelmed; and now I looked back upon my father's prophetic discourse to me, that I should be miserable and have none to relieve me, which I thought was now so effectually brought to pass that I could not be worse; for now the hand of Heaven had overtaken me, and I was undone without redemption; but, alas! this was but a taste of the misery I was to go through, as will appear in the sequel of this story.

As my new Patron, or Master, had taken me home to his house, so I was in hopes that he would take me with him when he went to sea again, believing that it would some time or other be his fate to be taken by a Spanish or Portugal man-of-war; and that then I should be set at liberty. But this hope of mine was soon taken away; for when he went to sea, he left me on shore to look after his little garden, and do the common drudgery of slaves about his house; and when he came home again from his cruise, he ordered me to lie in the cabin to look after the ship.

Here I meditated nothing but my escape, and what method I might take to effect it, but found no way that had the least probability in it; nothing presented to make the supposition of it rational; for I had nobody to communicate it to that would embark with me – no fellow-slave, no Englishman, Irishman, or Scotchman there but myself; so that for two years, though I often pleased myself with the imagination, yet I never had the least encouraging prospect of putting it in practice.

After about two years, an odd circumstance presented itself, which put the old thought of making some attempt for my liberty again in my head. My Patron lying at home longer than usual without fitting out his ship, which, as I heard, was for want of money, he used constantly, once or twice a week, sometimes oftener if the weather was fair, to take the ship's pinnace and go out into the road a-fishing; and as he always took me and young Maresco with him to row the boat, we made him very merry, and I proved very dexterous in catching fish; insomuch that sometimes he would send me with a Moor, one of his kinsmen, and the youth – the Maresco, as they called him – to catch a dish of fish for him.

It happened one time, that going a-fishing in a calm morning, a fog rose so thick that, though we were not half a league from the shore, we lost sight of it; and rowing we knew not whither or which way, we laboured all day, and all the next night; and when the morning came we found we had pulled off to sea instead of pulling in for the shore; and that we were at least two leagues from the shore. However, we got well in again, though with a great deal of labour and some danger; for the wind began to blow pretty fresh in the morning; but we were all very hungry.

But our Patron, warned by this disaster, resolved to take more care of himself for the future; and having lying by him the longboat of our English ship that he had taken, he resolved he would not go a-fishing any more without a compass and some provision; so he ordered the carpenter of his ship, who also was an English slave, to build a little state-room, or cabin, in the middle of the long-boat, like that of a barge, with a place to stand behind it to steer, and haul home the main-sheet; the room before for a hand or two to stand and work the sails. She sailed with what we call a shoulder-of-mutton sail; and the boom jibed over the top of the cabin, which lay very snug and low, and had in it room for him to lie, with a slave or two, and a table to eat on, with some small lockers to put in some bottles of such liquor as he thought fit to drink; and his bread, rice, and coffee.

We went frequently out with this boat a-fishing; and as I was most dexterous to catch fish for him, he never went without me. It happened that he had appointed to go out in this boat, either for pleasure or for fish, with two or three Moors of some distinction in that place, and for whom he had provided extraordinarily, and had, therefore, sent on board the boat overnight a larger store of provisions than ordinary; and had ordered me to get ready three fuzees with powder and shot, which were on board his ship, for that they designed some sport of fowling as well as fishing.

I got all things ready as he had directed, and waited the next morning with the boat washed clean, her ancient and pendants out, and everything to accommodate his guests; when by-and-by my Patron came on board alone, and told me his guests had put off going from some business that fell out, and ordered me, with the man and boy, as usual, to go out with the boat and catch them some fish, for that his friends were to sup at his house, and commanded that as soon as I got some fish I should bring it home to his house; all which I prepared to do.

This moment my former notions of deliverance darted into my thoughts, for now I found I was likely to have a little ship at my command; and my Master being gone, I prepared to furnish myself, not for fishing business, but for a voyage; though I knew not, neither did I so much as consider, whither I should steer – anywhere to get out of that place was my desire.

My first contrivance was to make a pretence to speak to this Moor, to get something for our subsistence on board; for I told him we must not presume to eat of our Patron's bread. He said that was true; so he brought a large basket of rusk or biscuit, and three jars of fresh water, into the boat. I knew where my Patron's case of bottles stood, which it was evident, by the make, were taken out of some English prize, and I conveyed them into the boat while the Moor was on shore, as if they had been there before for our Master. I conveyed also a great lump of beeswax into the boat, which weighed about half a hundred-weight, with a parcel of twine or thread, a hatchet, a saw, and a hammer, all of which were of great use to us afterwards, especially the wax, to make candles. Another trick I tried upon him, which he innocently came into also: his name was Ismael, which they call Muley, or Moely; so I called to him – "Moely," said I, "our Patron's guns are on board the boat; can you not get a little powder and shot? It may be we may kill some alcamies (a fowl like our curlews) for ourselves, for I know he keeps the gunner's stores in the ship." "Yes," says he, "I'll bring some;" and accordingly he brought a great leather pouch, which held a pound and a half of powder, or rather more; and another with shot, that had 5 or 6 pounds, with some bullets, and put all into the boat. At the same time I had found some powder of my Master's in the great cabin, with which I filled one of the large bottles in the case, which was almost empty, pouring what was in it into another; and thus furnished with everything needful, we sailed out of the port to fish. The castle, which is at the entrance of the port, knew who we were, and took no notice of us; and we were not above a mile out of the port before we hauled in our sail and set us down to fish. The wind blew from the N.N.E., which was contrary to my desire, for had it blown southerly I had been sure to have made the coast of Spain, and at least reached to the bay of Cadiz; but my resolutions were, blow which way it would, I would be gone from that horrid place where I was, and leave the rest to fate.

After we had fished some time and caught nothing – for when I had fish on my hook I would not pull them up, that he might not see them – I said to the Moor, "This will not do; our Master will not be thus served; we must stand farther off." He, thinking no harm, agreed, and being in the head of the boat, set the sails; and, as I had the helm, I ran the boat out near a league farther, and then brought her to, as if I would fish; when, giving the boy the helm, I stepped forward to where the Moor was, and making as if I stooped for something behind him, I took him by surprise with my arm under his waist, and tossed him clear overboard into the sea. He rose immediately, for he swam like a cork, and called to me, begged to be taken in, told me he would go all over the world with me. He swam so strong after the boat that he would have reached me very quickly, there being but little wind; upon which I stepped into the cabin, and fetching one of the fowling-pieces, I presented it at him, and told him I had done him no hurt, and if he would be quiet I would do him none. "But," said I, "you swim well enough to reach to the shore, and the sea is calm; make the best of your way to shore, and I will do you no harm; but if you come near the boat I'll shoot you through the head, for I am resolved to have my liberty;" so he turned himself about, and swam for the shore, and I make no doubt but he reached it with ease, for he was an excellent swimmer.

I could have been content to have taken this Moor with me, and have drowned the boy, but there was no venturing to trust him. When he was gone, I turned to the boy, whom they called Xury, and said to him, "Xury, if you will be faithful to me, I'll make you a great man; but if you will not stroke your face to be true to me" – that is, swear by Mahomet and his father's beard – "I must throw you into the sea too." The boy smiled in my face, and spoke so innocently that I could not distrust him, and swore to be faithful to me, and go all over the world with me.

While I was in view of the Moor that was swimming, I stood out directly to sea with the boat, rather stretching to windward, that they might think me gone towards the Straits' mouth (as indeed any one that had been in their wits must have been supposed to do): for who would have supposed we were sailed on to the southward, to the truly Barbarian coast, where whole nations of negroes were sure to surround us with their canoes and destroy us; where we could not go on shore but we should be devoured by savage beasts, or more merciless savages of human kind.

But as soon as it grew dusk in the evening, I changed my course, and steered directly south and by east, bending my course a little towards the east, that I might keep in with the shore; and having a fair, fresh gale of wind, and a smooth, quiet sea, I made such sail that I believe by the next day, at three o'clock in the afternoon, when I first made the land, I could not be less than 150 miles south of Sallee; quite beyond the Emperor of Morocco's dominions, or indeed of any other king thereabouts, for we saw no people.

Yet such was the fright I had taken of the Moors, and the dreadful apprehensions I had of falling into their hands, that I would not stop, or go on shore, or come to an anchor; the wind continuing fair till I had sailed in that manner five days; and then the wind shifting to the southward, I concluded also that if any of our vessels were in chase of me, they also would now give over; so I ventured to make to the coast, and came to an anchor in the mouth of a little river, I knew not what, nor where, neither what latitude, what country, what nation, or what river. I neither saw, nor desired to see any people; the principal thing I wanted was fresh water. We came into this creek in the evening, resolving to swim on shore as soon as it was dark, and discover the country; but as soon as it was quite dark, we heard such dreadful noises of the barking, roaring, and howling of wild creatures, of we knew not what kinds, that the poor boy was ready to die with fear, and begged of me not to go on shore till day. "Well, Xury," said I, "then I won't; but it may be that we may see men by day, who will be as bad to us as those lions." "Then we give them the shoot gun," says Xury, laughing, "make them run wey." Such English Xury spoke by conversing among us slaves. However, I was glad to see the boy so cheerful, and I gave him a dram (out of our Patron's case of bottles) to cheer him up. After all, Xury's advice was good, and I took it; we dropped our little anchor, and lay still all night; I say still, for we slept none; for in two or three hours we saw vast great creatures (we knew not what to call them) of many sorts, come down to the sea-shore and run into the water, wallowing and washing themselves for the pleasure of cooling themselves; and they made such hideous howlings and yellings, that I never indeed heard the like.

Xury was dreadfully frighted, and indeed so was I too; but we were both more frighted when we heard one of these mighty creatures come swimming towards our boat; we could not see him, but we might hear him by his blowing to be a monstrous huge and furious beast. Xury said it was a lion, and it might be so for aught I know; but poor Xury cried to me to weigh the anchor and row away; "No," says I, "Xury; we can slip our cable, with the buoy to it, and go off to sea; they cannot follow us far." I had no sooner said so, but I perceived the creature (whatever it was) within two oars' length, which something surprised me; however, I immediately stepped to the cabin door, and taking up my gun, fired at him; upon which he immediately turned about and swam towards the shore again.

But it is impossible to describe the horrid noises, and hideous cries and howlings that were raised, as well upon the edge of the shore as higher within the country, upon the noise or report of the gun, a thing I have some reason to believe those creatures had never heard before: this convinced me that there was no going on shore for us in the night on that coast, and how to venture on shore in the day was another question too; for to have fallen into the hands of any of the savages had been as bad as to have fallen into the hands of the lions and tigers; at least we were equally apprehensive of the danger of it.

Be that as it would, we were obliged to go on shore somewhere or other for water, for we had not a pint left in the boat; when and where to get to it was the point. Xury said, if I would let him go on shore with one of the jars, he would find if there was any water, and bring some to me. I asked him why he would go? why I should not go, and he stay in the boat? The boy answered with so much affection as made me love him ever after. Says he, "If wild mans come, they eat me, you go wey." "Well, Xury," said I, "we will both go and if the wild mans come, we will kill them, they shall eat neither of us." So I gave Xury a piece of rusk bread to eat, and a dram out of our Patron's case of bottles which I mentioned before; and we hauled the boat in as near the shore as we thought was proper, and so waded on shore, carrying nothing but our arms and two jars for water.

I did not care to go out of sight of the boat, fearing the coming of canoes with savages down the river; but the boy seeing a low place about a mile up the country, rambled to it, and by-and-by I saw him come running towards me. I thought he was pursued by some savage, or frighted with some wild beast, and I ran forward towards him to help him; but when I came nearer to him I saw something hanging over his shoulders, which was a creature that he had shot, like a hare, but different in colour, and longer legs; however, we were very glad of it, and it was very good meat; but the great joy that poor Xury came with, was to tell me he had found good water and seen no wild mans.

But we found afterwards that we need not take such pains for water, for a little higher up the creek where we were we found the water fresh when the tide was out, which flowed but a little way up; so we filled our jars, and feasted on the hare he had killed, and prepared to go on our way, having seen no footsteps of any human creature in that part of the country.

As I had been one voyage to this coast before, I knew very well that the islands of the Canaries, and the Cape de Verde Islands also, lay not far off from the coast. But as I had no instruments to take an observation to know what latitude we were in, and not exactly knowing, or at least remembering, what latitude they were in, I knew not where to look for them, or when to stand off to sea towards them; otherwise I might now easily have found some of these islands. But my hope was, that if I stood along this coast till I came to that part where the English traded, I should find some of their vessels upon their usual design of trade, that would relieve and take us in.

By the best of my calculation, that place where I now was must be that country which, lying between the Emperor of Morocco's dominions and the negroes, lies waste and uninhabited, except by wild beasts; the negroes having abandoned it and gone farther south for fear of the Moors, and the Moors not thinking it worth inhabiting by reason of its barrenness; and indeed, both forsaking it because of the prodigious number of tigers, lions, leopards, and other furious creatures which harbour there; so that the Moors use it for their hunting only, where they go like an army, two or three thousand men at a time; and indeed for near a hundred miles together upon this coast we saw nothing but a waste, uninhabited country by day, and heard nothing but howlings and roaring of wild beasts by night.

Once or twice in the daytime I thought I saw the Pico of Teneriffe, being the high top of the Mountain Teneriffe in the Canaries, and had a great mind to venture out, in hopes of reaching thither; but having tried twice, I was forced in again by contrary winds, the sea also going too high for my little vessel; so, I resolved to pursue my first design, and keep along the shore.

Several times I was obliged to land for fresh water, after we had left this place; and once in particular, being early in morning, we came to an anchor under a little point of land, which was pretty high; and the tide beginning to flow, we lay still to go farther in. Xury, whose eyes were more about him than it seems mine were, calls softly to me, and tells me that we had best go farther off the shore; "For," says he, "look, yonder lies a dreadful monster on the side of that hillock, fast asleep." I looked where he pointed, and saw a dreadful monster indeed, for it was a terrible, great lion that lay on the side of the shore, under the shade of a piece of the hill that hung as it were a little over him. "Xury," says I, "you shall on shore and kill him." Xury, looked frighted, and said, "Me kill! he eat me at one mouth!" – one mouthful he meant. However, I said no more to the boy, but bade him lie still, and I took our biggest gun, which was almost musket-bore, and loaded it with a good charge of powder, and with two slugs, and laid it down; then I loaded another gun with two bullets; and the third (for we had three pieces) I loaded with five smaller bullets. I took the best aim I could with the first piece to have shot him in the head, but he lay so with his leg raised a little above his nose, that the slugs hit his leg about the knee and broke the bone. He started up, growling at first, but finding his leg broken, fell down again; and then got upon three legs, and gave the most hideous roar that ever I heard. I was a little surprised that I had not hit him on the head; however, I took up the second piece immediately, and though he began to move off, fired again, and shot him in the head, and had the pleasure to see him drop and make but little noise, but lie struggling for life. Then Xury took heart, and would have me let him go on shore. "Well, go," said I: so the boy jumped into the water and taking a little gun in one hand, swam to shore with the other hand, and coming close to the creature, put the muzzle of the piece to his ear, and shot him in the head again, which dispatched him quite.

This was game indeed to us, but this was no food; and I was very sorry to lose three charges of powder and shot upon a creature that was good for nothing to us. However, Xury said he would have some of him; so he comes on board, and asked me to give him the hatchet. "For what, Xury?" said I. "Me cut off his head," said he. However, Xury could not cut off his head, but he cut off a foot, and brought it with him, and it was a monstrous great one.

I bethought myself, however, that, perhaps the skin of him might, one way or other, be of some value to us; and I resolved to take off his skin if I could. So Xury and I went to work with him; but Xury was much the better workman at it, for I knew very ill how to do it. Indeed, it took us both up the whole day, but at last we got off the hide of him, and spreading it on the top of our cabin, the sun effectually dried it in two days' time, and it afterwards served me to lie upon.

1726 illustration by W. Mears & T. Woodward

CHAPTER THREE

Wrecked on a Desert Island

After this stop, we made on to the southward continually for ten or twelve days, living very sparingly on our provisions, which began to abate very much, and going no oftener to the shore than we were obliged to for fresh water. My design in this was to make the river Gambia or Senegal, that is to say anywhere about the Cape de Verde, where I was in hopes to meet with some European ship; and if I did not, I knew not what course I had to take, but to seek for the islands, or perish there among the negroes. I knew that all the ships from Europe, which sailed either to the coast of Guinea or to Brazil, or to the East Indies, made this cape, or those islands; and, in a word, I put the whole of my fortune upon this single point, either that I must meet with some ship or must perish.

When I had pursued this resolution about ten days longer, as I have said, I began to see that the land was inhabited; and in two or three places, as we sailed by, we saw people stand upon the shore to look at us; we could also perceive they were quite black and naked. I was once inclined to have gone on shore to them; but Xury was my better counsellor, and said to me, "No go, no go." However, I hauled in nearer the shore that I might talk to them, and I found they ran along the shore by me a good way. I observed they had no weapons in their hand, except one, who had a long slender stick, which Xury said was a lance, and that they could throw them a great way with good aim; so I kept at a distance, but talked with them by signs as well as I could; and particularly made signs for something to eat: they beckoned to me to stop my boat, and they would fetch me some meat. Upon this I lowered the top of my sail and lay by, and two of them ran up into the country, and in less than half-an-hour came back, and brought with them two pieces of dried flesh and some corn, such as is the produce of their country; but we neither knew what the one or the other was; however, we were willing to accept it, but how to come at it was our next dispute, for I would not venture on shore to them, and they were as much afraid of us; but they took a safe way for us all, for they brought it to the shore and laid it down, and went and stood a great way off till we fetched it on board, and then came close to us again.

We made signs of thanks to them, for we had nothing to make them amends; but an opportunity offered that very instant to oblige them wonderfully; for while we were lying by the shore came two mighty creatures, one pursuing the other (as we took it) with great fury from the mountains towards the sea; whether it was the male pursuing the female, or whether they were in sport or in rage, we could not tell, any more than we could tell whether it was usual or strange, but I believe it was the latter; because, in the first place, those ravenous creatures seldom appear but in the night; and, in the second place, we found the people terribly frighted, especially the women. The man that had the lance or dart did not fly from them, but the rest did; however, as the two creatures ran directly into the water, they did not offer to fall upon any of the negroes, but plunged themselves into the sea, and swam about, as if they had come for their diversion; at last one of them began to come nearer our boat than at first I expected; but I lay ready for him, for I had loaded my gun with all possible expedition, and bade Xury load both the others. As soon as he came fairly within my reach, I fired, and shot him directly in the head; immediately he sank down into the water, but rose instantly, and plunged up and down, as if he were struggling for life, and so indeed he was; he immediately made to the shore; but between the wound, which was his mortal hurt, and the strangling of the water, he died just before he reached the shore.

It is impossible to express the astonishment of these poor creatures at the noise and fire of my gun: some of them were even ready to die for fear, and fell down as dead with the very terror; but when they saw the creature dead, and sunk in the water, and that I made signs to them to come to the shore, they took heart and came, and began to search for the creature. I found him by his blood staining the water; and by the help of a rope, which I slung round him, and gave the negroes to haul, they dragged him on shore, and found that it was a most curious leopard, spotted, and fine to an admirable degree; and the negroes held up their hands with admiration, to think what it was I had killed him with.

The other creature, frighted with the flash of fire and the noise of the gun, swam on shore, and ran up directly to the mountains from whence they came; nor could I, at that distance, know what it was. I found quickly the negroes wished to eat the flesh of this creature, so I was willing to have them take it as a favour from me; which, when I made signs to them that they might take him, they were very thankful for. Immediately they fell to work with him; and though they had no knife, yet, with a sharpened piece of wood, they took off his skin as readily, and much more readily, than we could have done with a knife. They offered me some of the flesh, which I declined, pointing out that I would give it them; but made signs for the skin, which they gave me very freely, and brought me a great deal more of their provisions, which, though I did not understand, yet I accepted. I then made signs to them for some water, and held out one of my jars to them, turning it bottom upward, to show that it was empty, and that I wanted to have it filled. They called immediately to some of their friends, and there came two women, and brought a great vessel made of earth, and burnt, as I supposed, in the sun, this they set down to me, as before, and I sent Xury on shore with my jars, and filled them all three. The women were as naked as the men.

I was now furnished with roots and corn, such as it was, and water; and leaving my friendly negroes, I made forward for about eleven days more, without offering to go near the shore, till I saw the land run out a great length into the sea, at about the distance of four or five leagues before me; and the sea being very calm, I kept a large offing to make this point. At length, doubling the point, at about two leagues from the land, I saw plainly land on the other side, to seaward; then I concluded, as it was most certain indeed, that this was the Cape de Verde, and those the islands called, from thence, Cape de Verde Islands. However, they were at a great distance, and I could not well tell what I had best to do; for if I should be taken with a fresh of wind, I might neither reach one or other.

In this dilemma, as I was very pensive, I stepped into the cabin and sat down, Xury having the helm; when, on a sudden, the boy cried out, "Master, Master, a ship with a sail!" and the foolish boy was frighted out of his wits, thinking it must needs be some of his Master's ships sent to pursue us, but I knew we were far enough out of their reach. I jumped out of the cabin, and immediately saw, not only the ship, but that it was a Portuguese ship; and, as I thought, was bound to the coast of Guinea, for negroes. But, when I observed the course she steered, I was soon convinced they were bound some other way, and did not design to come any nearer to the shore; upon which I stretched out to sea as much as I could, resolving to speak with them if possible.

With all the sail I could make, I found I should not be able to come in their way, but that they would be gone by before I could make any signal to them: but after I had crowded to the utmost, and began to despair, they, it seems, saw by the help of their glasses that it was some

European boat, which they supposed must belong to some ship that was lost; so they shortened sail to let me come up. I was encouraged with this, and as I had my Patron's ancient on board, I made a waft of it to them, for a signal of distress, and fired a gun, both which they saw; for they told me they saw the smoke, though they did not hear the gun. Upon these signals they very kindly brought to, and lay by for me; and in about three hours; time I came up with them.

They asked me what I was, in Portuguese, and in Spanish, and in French, but I understood none of them; but at last a Scotch sailor, who was on board, called to me: and I answered him, and told him I was an Englishman, that I had made my escape out of slavery from the Moors, at Sallee; they then bade me come on board, and very kindly took me in, and all my goods.

It was an inexpressible joy to me, which any one will believe, that I was thus delivered, as I esteemed it, from such a miserable and almost hopeless condition as I was in; and I immediately offered all I had to the Captain of the ship, as a return for my deliverance; but he generously told me he would take nothing from me, but that all I had should be delivered safe to me when I came to the Brazils. "For," says he, "I have saved your life on no other terms than I would be glad to be saved myself: and it may, one time or other, be my lot to be taken up in the same condition. Besides," said he, "when I carry you to the Brazils, so great a way from your own country, if I should take from you what you have, you will be starved there, and then I only take away that life I have given. No, no," says he: "Seignior Inglese" (Mr. Englishman), "I will carry you thither in charity, and those things will help to buy your subsistence there, and your passage home again."

As he was charitable in this proposal, so he was just in the performance to a tittle; for he ordered the seamen that none should touch anything that I had: then he took everything into his own possession, and gave me back an exact inventory of them, that I might have them, even to my three earthen jars.

As to my boat, it was a very good one; and that he saw, and told me he would buy it of me for his ship's use; and asked me what I would have for it? I told him he had been so generous to me in everything that I could not offer to make any price of the boat, but left it entirely to him: upon which he told me he would give me a note of hand to pay me 80 pieces of eight for it at Brazil; and when it came there, if any one offered to give more, he would make it up. He offered me also 60 pieces of eight more for my boy Xury, which I was loath to take; not that I was unwilling to let the Captain have him, but I was very loath to sell the poor boy's liberty, who had assisted me so faithfully in procuring my own. However, when I let him know my reason, he owned it to be just, and offered me this medium, that he would give the boy an obligation to set him free in ten years, if he turned Christian: upon this, and Xury saying he was willing to go to him, I let the Captain have him.

We had a very good voyage to the Brazils, and I arrived in the Bay de Todos los Santos, or All Saints' Bay, in about twenty-two days after. And now I was once more delivered from the most miserable of all conditions of life; and what to do next with myself I was to consider.

The generous treatment the Captain gave me I can never enough remember: he would take nothing of me for my passage, gave me 20 ducats for the leopard's skin, and forty for the lion's skin, which I had in my boat, and caused everything I had in the ship to be punctually delivered to me; and what I was willing to sell he bought of me, such as the case of bottles, two of my guns, and a piece of the lump of beeswax – for I had made candles of the rest: in a word, I made about 220 pieces of eight of all my cargo; and with this stock I went on shore in the Brazils.

I had not been long here before I was recommended to the house of a good honest man like himself, who had an *Ingenio*, as they call it (that is, a plantation and a sugar-house). I lived with him some time, and acquainted myself by that means with the manner of planting and making of sugar; and seeing how well the planters lived, and how they got rich suddenly, I resolved, if I could get a licence to settle there, I would turn planter among them: resolving in the meantime to find out some way to get my money, which I had left in London, remitted to me. To this purpose, getting a kind of letter of naturalization, I purchased as much land that was uncured as my money would reach, and formed a plan for my plantation and settlement; such a one as might be suitable to the stock which I proposed to myself to receive from England.

I had a neighbour, a Portuguese, of Lisbon, but born of English parents, whose name was Wells, and in much such circumstances as I was. I call him my neighbour, because his plantation lay next to mine, and we went on very sociably together. My stock was but low, as well as his; and we rather planted for food than anything else, for about two years. However, we began to increase, and our land began to come into order; so that the third year we planted some tobacco, and made each of us a large piece of ground ready for planting canes in the year to come. But we both wanted help; and now I found, more than before, I had done wrong in parting with my boy Xury.

But, alas! for me to do wrong that never did right, was no great wonder. I hail no remedy but to go on: I had got into an employment quite remote to my genius, and directly contrary to the life I delighted in, and for which I forsook my father's house, and broke through all his good advice. Nay, I was coming into the very middle station, or upper degree of low life, which my father advised me to before, and which, if I resolved to go on with, I might as well have stayed at home, and never have fatigued myself in the world as I had done; and I used often to say to myself, I could have done this as well in England, among my friends, as have gone 5,000 miles off to do it among strangers and savages, in a wilderness, and at such a distance as never to hear from any part of the world that had the least knowledge of me.

In this manner I used to look upon my condition with the utmost regret. I had nobody to converse with, but now and then this neighbour; no work to be done, but by the labour of my hands; and I used to say, I lived just like a man cast away upon some desolate island, that had nobody there but himself. But how just has it been – and how should all men reflect, that when they compare their present conditions with others that are worse, Heaven may oblige them to make the exchange, and be convinced of their former felicity by their experience – I say, how just has it been, that the truly solitary life I reflected on, in an island of mere desolation, should be my lot, who had so often unjustly compared it with the life which I then led, in which, had I continued, I had in all probability been exceeding prosperous and rich.

I was in some degree settled in my measures for carrying on the plantation before my kind friend, the Captain of the ship that took me up at sea, went back – for the ship remained there, in providing his lading and preparing for his voyage, nearly three months – when telling him what little stock I had left behind me in London, he gave me this friendly and sincere advice: – "Seignior Inglese," says he (for so he always called me), "if you will give me letters, and a procuration in form to me, with orders to the person who has your money in London to send your effects to Lisbon, to such persons as I shall direct, and in such goods as are proper for this country, I will bring you the produce of them, God willing, at my return; but, since human affairs are all subject to changes and disasters, I would have you give orders but for 100 pounds sterling, which, you say, is half your stock, and let the hazard be run for the first; so that, if it come safe, you may order the rest the same way, and, if it miscarry, you may have the other half to have recourse to for your supply."

This was so wholesome advice, and looked so friendly, that I could not but be convinced it was the best course I could take; so I accordingly prepared letters to the gentlewoman with whom I had left my money, and a procuration to the Portuguese Captain, as he desired.

I wrote the English Captain's widow a full account of all my adventures – my slavery, escape, and how I had met with the Portuguese Captain at sea, the humanity of his behaviour, and what condition I was now in, with all other necessary directions for my supply; and when this honest Captain came to Lisbon, he found means, by some of the English merchants there, to send over, not the order only, but a full account of my story to a merchant in London, who represented it effectually to her; whereupon she not only delivered the money, but out of her own pocket sent the Portugal Captain a very handsome present for his humanity and charity to me.

The merchant in London, vesting this hundred pounds in English goods, such as the Captain had written for, sent them directly to him at Lisbon, and he brought them all safe to me to the Brazils; among which, without my direction (for I was too young in my business to think of them), he had taken care to have all sorts of tools, ironwork, and utensils necessary for my plantation, and which were of great use to me.

When this cargo arrived I thought my fortune made, for I was surprised with the joy of it; and my stood steward, the Captain, had laid out the 5 pounds, which my friend had sent him for a present for himself, to purchase and bring me over a servant, under bond for six years' service, and would not accept of any consideration, except a little tobacco, which I would have him accept, being of my own produce.

Neither was this all; for my goods being all English manufacture, such as cloth, stuffs, baize, and things particularly valuable and desirable in the country, I found means to sell them to a very great advantage; so that I might say I had more than four times the value of my first cargo, and was now infinitely beyond my poor neighbour – I mean in the advancement of my plantation; for the first thing I did, I bought me a negro slave, and an European servant also – I mean another besides that which the Captain brought me from Lisbon.

But as abused prosperity is oftentimes made the very means of our greatest adversity, so it was with me. I went on the next year with great success in my plantation: I raised 50 great rolls of tobacco on my own ground, more than I had disposed of for necessaries among my neighbours; and these 50 rolls, being each of above a hundredweight, were well cured, and laid by against the return of the fleet from Lisbon: and now increasing in business and wealth, my head began to be full of projects and undertakings beyond my reach; such as are, indeed, often the ruin of the best heads in business. Had I continued in the station I was now in, I had room for all the happy things to have yet befallen me for which my father so earnestly recommended a quiet, retired life, and of which he had so sensibly described the middle station of life to be full of; but other things attended me, and I was still to be the wilful agent of all my own miseries; and particularly, to increase my fault, and double the reflections upon myself, which in my future sorrows I should have leisure to make, all these miscarriages were procured by my apparent obstinate adhering to my foolish inclination of wandering abroad, and pursuing that inclination, in contradiction to the clearest views of doing myself good in a fair and plain pursuit of those prospects, and those measures of life, which nature and Providence concurred to present me with, and to make my duty.

As I had once done thus in my breaking away from my parents, so I could not be content now, but I must go and leave the happy view I had of being a rich and thriving man in my new plantation, only to pursue a rash and immoderate desire of rising faster than the nature of the thing admitted; and thus I cast myself down again into the deepest gulf of human misery that ever man fell into, or perhaps could be consistent with life and a state of health in the world.

To come, then, by the just degrees to the particulars of this part of my story. You may suppose, that having now lived almost four years in the Brazils, and beginning to thrive and prosper very well upon my plantation, I had not only learned the language, but had contracted acquaintance and friendship among my fellow-planters, as well as among the merchants at St. Salvador, which was our port; and that, in my discourses among them, I had frequently given them an account of my two voyages to the coast of Guinea: the manner of trading with the negroes there, and how easy it was to purchase upon the coast for trifles – such as beads, toys, knives, scissors, hatchets, bits of glass, and the like – not only gold-dust, Guinea grains, elephants' teeth, &c. but negroes, for the service of the Brazils, in great numbers.

They listened always very attentively to my discourses on these heads, but especially to that part which related to the buying of negroes, which was a trade at that time, not only not far entered into, but, as far as it was, had been carried on by the Assiento's, or permission of the kings of Spain and Portugal, and engrossed in the public stock: so that few negroes were bought, and these excessively dear.

It happened, being in company with some merchants and planters of my acquaintance, and talking of those things very earnestly, three of them came to me next morning, and told me they had been musing very much upon what I had discoursed with them of the last night, and they came to make a secret proposal to me; and, after enjoining me to secrecy, they told me that they had a mind to fit out a ship to go to Guinea; that they had all plantations as well as I, and were straitened for nothing so much as servants; that as it was a trade that could not be carried on, because they could not publicly sell the negroes when they came home, so they desired to make but one voyage, to bring the negroes on shore privately, and divide them among their own plantations; and, in a word, the question was whether I would go their supercargo in the ship, to manage the trading part upon the coast of Guinea; and they offered me that I should have my equal share of the negroes, without providing any part of the stock.

This was a fair proposal, it must be confessed, had it been made to any one that had not had a settlement and a plantation of his own to look after, which was in a fair way of coming to be very considerable, and with a good stock upon it; but for me, that was thus entered and established, and had nothing to do but to go on as I had begun, for three or four years more, and to have sent for the other 100 pounds from England; and who in that time, and with that little addition, could scarce have failed of being worth three or four thousand pounds sterling, and that increasing too – for me to think of such a voyage was the most preposterous thing that ever man in such circumstances could be guilty of.

But I, that was born to be my own destroyer, could no more resist the offer than I could restrain my first rambling designs when my father' good counsel was lost upon me. In a word, I told them I would go with all my heart, if they would undertake to look after my plantation in my absence, and would dispose of it to such as I should direct, if I miscarried. This they all engaged to do, and entered into writings or covenants to do so; and I made a formal will, disposing of my plantation and effects in case of my death, making the Captain of the ship that had saved my life, as before, my universal heir, but obliging him to dispose of my effects as I had directed in my will; one half of the produce being to himself, and the other to be shipped to England.

In short, I took all possible caution to preserve my effects and to keep up my plantation. Had I used half as much prudence to have looked into my own interest, and have made a judgment of what I ought to have done and not to have done, I had certainly never gone away from so prosperous an undertaking, leaving all the probable views of a thriving circumstance, and gone upon a voyage to sea, attended with all its common hazards, to say nothing of the reasons I had to expect particular misfortunes to myself.

But I was hurried on, and obeyed blindly the dictates of my fancy rather than my reason; and, accordingly, the ship being fitted out, and the cargo furnished, and all things done, as by agreement, by my partners in the voyage, I went on board in an evil hour, the 1st September 1659, being the same day eight years that I went from my father and mother at Hull, in order to act the rebel to their authority, and the fool to my own interests.

Our ship was about 120 tons burden, carried 6 guns and 14 men, besides the Master, his boy, and myself. We had on board no large cargo of goods, except of such toys as were fit for our trade with the negroes, such as beads, bits of glass, shells, and other trifles, especially little looking-glasses, knives, scissors, hatchets, and the like.

The same day I went on board we set sail, standing away to the northward upon our own coast, with design to stretch over for the African coast when we came about 10 or 12 degrees of northern latitude, which, it seems, was the manner of course in those days. We had very good weather, only excessively hot, all the way upon our own coast, till we came to the height of Cape St. Augustino; from whence, keeping further off at sea, we lost sight of land, and steered as if we were bound for the isle Fernando de Noronha, holding our course N.E. by N., and leaving those isles on the east. In this course we passed the line in about twelve days' time, and were, by our last observation, in 7 degrees 22 minutes northern latitude, when a violent tornado, or hurricane, took us quite out of our knowledge. It began from the south-east, came about to the north-west, and then settled in the north-east; from whence it blew in such a terrible manner, that for twelve days together we could do nothing but drive, and, scudding away before it, let it carry us whither fate and the fury of the winds directed; and, during these twelve days, I need not say that I expected every day to be swallowed up; nor, indeed, did any in the ship expect to save their lives.

In this distress we had, besides the terror of the storm, one of our men die of the calenture, and one man and the boy washed overboard. About the twelfth day, the weather abating a little, the Master made an observation as well as he could, and found that he was in about 11 degrees north latitude, but that he was 22 degrees of longitude difference west from Cape St. Augustino; so that he found he was upon the coast of Guiana, or the north part of Brazil, beyond the river Amazon, toward that of the river Orinoco, commonly called the Great River; and began to consult with me what course he should take, for the ship was leaky, and very much disabled, and he was going directly back to the coast of Brazil.

I was positively against that; and looking over the charts of the sea-coast of America with him, we concluded there was no inhabited country for us to have recourse to till we came within the circle of the Caribbee Islands, and therefore resolved to stand away for Barbadoes; which, by keeping off at sea, to avoid the indraft of the Bay or Gulf of Mexico, we might easily perform, as we hoped, in about fifteen days' sail; whereas we could not possibly make our voyage to the coast of Africa without some assistance both to our ship and to ourselves.

With this design we changed our course, and steered away N.W. by W., in order to reach some of our English islands, where I hoped for relief. But our voyage was otherwise determined; for, being in the latitude of 12 degrees 18 minutes, a second storm came upon us, which carried us away with the same impetuosity westward, and drove us so out of the way of all human commerce, that, had all our lives been saved as to the sea, we were rather in danger of being devoured by savages than ever returning to our own country.

In this distress, the wind still blowing very hard, one of our men early in the morning cried out, "Land!" and we had no sooner run out of the cabin to look out, in hopes of seeing whereabouts in the world we were, than the ship struck upon a sand, and in a moment her motion being so stopped, the sea broke over her in such a manner that we expected we should all have perished immediately; and we were immediately driven into our close quarters, to shelter us from the very foam and spray of the sea.

It is not easy for any one who has not been in the like condition to describe or conceive the consternation of men in such circumstances. We knew nothing where we were, or upon what land it was we were driven – whether an island or the main, whether inhabited or not inhabited. As the rage of the wind was still great, though rather less than at first, we could not so much as hope to have the ship hold many minutes without breaking into pieces, unless the winds, by a kind of miracle, should turn immediately about. In a word, we sat looking upon one another, and expecting death every moment, and every man, accordingly, preparing for another world; for there was little or nothing more for us to do in this. That which was our present comfort, and all the comfort we had, was that, contrary to our expectation, the ship did not break yet, and that the Master said the wind began to abate.

Now, though we thought that the wind did a little abate, yet the ship having thus struck upon the sand, and sticking too fast for us to expect her getting off, we were in a dreadful condition indeed, and had nothing to do but to think of saving our lives as well as we could. We had a boat at our stern just before the storm, but she was first staved by dashing against the ship's rudder, and in the next place she broke away, and either sunk or was driven off to sea; so there was no hope from her. We had another boat on board, but how to get her off into the sea was a doubtful thing. However, there was no time to debate, for we fancied that the ship would break in pieces every minute, and some told us she was actually broken already.

In this distress the Mate of our vessel laid hold of the boat, and with the help of the rest of the men got her slung over the ship's side; and getting all into her, let go, and committed ourselves, being 11 in number, to God's mercy and the wild sea; for though the storm was abated considerably, yet the sea ran dreadfully high upon the shore, and might be well called *Den wild Zee*, as the Dutch call the sea in a storm.

And now our case was very dismal indeed; for we all saw plainly that the sea went so high that the boat could not live, and that we should be inevitably drowned. As to making sail, we had none, nor if we had could we have done anything with it; so we worked at the oar towards the land, though with heavy hearts, like men going to execution; for we all knew that when the boat came near the shore she would be dashed in a thousand pieces by the breach of the sea. However, we committed our souls to God in the most earnest manner; and the wind driving us towards the shore, we hastened our destruction with our own hands, pulling as well as we could towards land.

What the shore was, whether rock or sand, whether steep or shoal, we knew not. The only hope that could rationally give us the least shadow of expectation was, if we might find some bay or gulf, or the mouth of some river, where by great chance we might have run our boat in, or got under the lee of the land, and perhaps made smooth water. But there was nothing like this appeared; but as we made nearer and nearer the shore, the land looked more frightful than the sea.

After we had rowed, or rather driven about a league and a half, as we reckoned it, a raging wave, mountain-like, came rolling astern of us, and plainly bade us expect the coup de gras. It took us with such a fury, that it overset the boat at once; and separating us as well from the boat as from one another, gave us no time to say, "O God!" for we were all swallowed up in a moment.

Nothing can describe the confusion of thought which I felt when I sank into the water; for though I swam very well, yet I could not deliver myself from the waves so as to draw breath, till that wave having driven me, or rather carried me, a vast way on towards the shore, and having spent itself, went back, and left me upon the land almost dry, but half dead with the water I took in. I had so much presence of mind, as well as breath left, that seeing myself nearer the mainland than I expected, I got upon my feet, and endeavoured to make on towards the land as fast as I could before another wave should return and take me up again; but I soon found it was impossible to avoid it; for I saw the sea come after me as high as a great hill, and as furious as an enemy, which I had no means or strength to contend with: my business was to hold my breath, and raise myself upon the water if I could; and so, by swimming, to preserve my breathing, and pilot myself towards the shore, if possible, my greatest concern now being that the sea, as it would carry me a great way towards the shore when it came on, might not carry me back again with it when it gave back towards the sea.

The wave that came upon me again buried me at once 20 or 30 feet deep in its own body, and I could feel myself carried with a mighty force and swiftness towards the shore – a very great way; but I held my breath, and assisted myself to swim still forward with all my might. I was ready to burst with holding my breath, when, as I felt myself rising up, so, to my immediate relief, I found my head and hands shoot out above the surface of the water; and though it was not two seconds of time that I could keep myself so, yet it relieved me greatly, gave me breath, and new courage. I was covered again with water a good while, but not so long but I held it out; and finding the water had spent itself, and began to return, I struck forward against the return of the waves, and felt ground again with my feet. I stood still a few moments to recover breath, and till the waters went from me, and then took to my heels and ran with what strength I had further towards the shore. But neither would this deliver me from the fury of the sea, which came pouring in after me again; and twice more I was lifted up by the waves and carried forward as before, the shore being very flat.

The last time of these two had well-nigh been fatal to me, for the sea having hurried me along as before, landed me, or rather dashed me, against a piece of rock, and that with such force, that it left me senseless, and indeed helpless, as to my own deliverance; for the blow taking my side and breast, beat the breath as it were quite out of my body; and had it returned again immediately, I must have been strangled in the water; but I recovered a little before the return of the waves, and seeing I should be covered again with the water, I resolved to hold fast by a piece of the rock, and so to hold my breath, if possible, till the wave went back. Now, as the waves were not so high as at first, being nearer land, I held my hold till the wave abated, and then fetched another run, which brought me so near the shore that the next wave, though it went over me, yet did not so swallow me up as to carry me away; and the next run I took, I got to the mainland, where, to my great comfort, I clambered up the cliffs of the shore and sat me down upon the grass, free from danger and quite out of the reach of the water.

I was now landed and safe on shore, and began to look up and thank God that my life was saved, in a case wherein there was some minutes before scarce any room to hope. I believe it is impossible to express, to the life, what the ecstasies and transports of the soul are, when it is so saved, as I may say, out of the very grave: and I do not wonder now at the custom, when a malefactor, who has the halter about his neck, is tied up, and just going to be turned off, and has a reprieve brought to him – I say, I do not wonder that they bring a surgeon with it, to let him blood that very moment they tell him of it, that the surprise may not drive the animal spirits from the heart and overwhelm him.

"For sudden joys, like griefs, confound at first."

I walked about on the shore lifting up my hands, and my whole being, as I may say, wrapped up in a contemplation of my deliverance; making a thousand gestures and motions, which I cannot describe; reflecting upon all my comrades that were drowned, and that there should not be one soul saved but myself; for, as for them, I never saw them afterwards, or any sign of them, except three of their hats, one cap, and two shoes that were not fellows.

I cast my eye to the stranded vessel, when, the breach and froth of the sea being so big, I could hardly see it, it lay so far of; and considered, Lord! how was it possible I could get on shore?

After I had solaced my mind with the comfortable part of my condition, I began to look round me, to see what kind of place I was in, and what was next to be done; and I soon found my comforts abate, and that, in a word, I had a dreadful deliverance; for I was wet, had no clothes to shift me, nor anything either to eat or drink to comfort me; neither did I see any prospect before me but that of perishing with hunger or being devoured by wild beasts; and that which was particularly afflicting to me was, that I had no weapon, either to hunt and kill any creature for my sustenance, or to defend myself against any other creature that might desire to kill me for theirs. In a word, I had nothing about me but a knife, a tobacco-pipe, and a little tobacco in a box. This was all my provisions; and this threw me into such terrible agonies of mind, that for a while I ran about like a madman. Night coming upon me, I began with a heavy heart to consider what would be my lot if there were any ravenous beasts in that country, as at night they always come abroad for their prey.

All the remedy that offered to my thoughts at that time was to get up into a thick bushy tree like a fir, but thorny, which grew near me, and where I resolved to sit all night, and consider the next day what death I should die, for as yet I saw no prospect of life. I walked about a furlong from the shore, to see if I could find any fresh water to drink, which I did, to my great joy; and having drank, and put a little tobacco into my mouth to prevent hunger, I went to the tree, and getting up into it, endeavoured to place myself so that if I should sleep I might not fall. And having cut me a short stick, like a truncheon, for my defence, I took up my lodging; and having been excessively fatigued, I fell fast asleep, and slept as comfortably as, I believe, few could have done in my condition, and found myself more refreshed with it than, I think, I ever was on such an occasion.

CHAPTER FOUR

First Weeks on the Island

WHEN I WAKED IT WAS BROAD DAY, the weather clear, and the storm abated, so that the sea did not rage and swell as before. But that which surprised me most was, that the ship was lifted off in the night from the sand where she lay by the swelling of the tide, and was driven up almost as far as the rock which I at first mentioned, where I had been so bruised by the wave dashing me against it. This being within about a mile from the shore where I was, and the ship seeming to stand upright still, I wished myself on board, that at least I might save some necessary things for my use.

When I came down from my apartment in the tree, I looked about me again, and the first thing I found was the boat, which lay, as the wind and the sea had tossed her up, upon the land, about two miles on my right hand. I walked as far as I could upon the shore to have got to her; but found a neck or inlet of water between me and the boat which was about half a mile broad; so I came back for the present, being more intent upon getting at the ship, where I hoped to find something for my present subsistence.

A little after noon I found the sea very calm, and the tide ebbed so far out that I could come within a quarter of a mile of the ship. And here I found a fresh renewing of my grief; for I saw evidently that if we had kept on board we had been all safe – that is to say, we had all got safe on shore, and I had not been so miserable as to be left entirety destitute of all comfort and company as I now was. This forced tears to my eyes again; but as there was little relief in that, I resolved, if possible, to get to the ship; so I pulled off my clothes – for the weather was hot to extremity – and took the water. But when I came to the ship my difficulty was still greater to know how to get on board; for, as she lay aground, and high out of the water, there was nothing within my reach to lay hold of. I swam round her twice, and the second time I spied a small piece of rope, which I wondered I did not see at first, hung down by the fore-chains so low, as that with great difficulty I got hold of it, and by the help of that rope I got up into the forecastle of the ship. Here I found that the ship was bulged, and had a great deal of water in her hold, but that she lay so on the side of a bank of hard sand, or, rather earth, that her stern lay lifted up upon the bank, and her head low, almost to the water. By this means all her quarter was free, and all that was in that part was dry; for you may be sure my first work was to search, and to see what was spoiled and what was free. And, first, I found that all the ship's provisions were dry and untouched by the water, and being very well disposed to eat, I went to the bread room and filled my pockets with biscuit, and ate it as I went about other things, for I had no time to lose. I also found some rum in the great cabin, of which I took a large dram, and which I had, indeed, need enough of to spirit me for what was before me. Now I wanted nothing but a boat to furnish myself with many things which I foresaw would be very necessary to me.

It was in vain to sit still and wish for what was not to be had; and this extremity roused my application. We had several spare yards, and two or three large spars of wood, and a spare topmast or two in the ship; I resolved to fall to work with these, and I flung as many of them overboard as I could manage for their weight, tying every one with a rope, that they might not drive away. When this was done I went down the ship's side, and pulling them to me, I tied four of them together at both ends as well as I could, in the form of a raft, and laying two or three short pieces of plank upon them crossways, I found I could walk upon it very well, but that it was not able to bear any great weight, the pieces being too light. So I went to work, and with a carpenter's saw I cut a spare topmast into three lengths, and added them to my raft, with a great deal of labour and pains. But the hope of furnishing myself with necessaries encouraged me to go beyond what I should have been able to have done upon another occasion.

My raft was now strong enough to bear any reasonable weight. My next care was what to load it with, and how to preserve what I laid upon it from the surf of the sea; but I was not long considering this. I first laid all the planks or boards upon it that I could get, and having considered well what I most wanted, I got three of the seamen's chests, which I had broken open, and emptied, and lowered them down upon my raft; the first of these I filled with provisions – *viz.* bread, rice, 3 Dutch cheeses, 5 pieces of dried goat's flesh (which we lived much upon), and a little remainder of European corn, which had been laid by for some fowls which we brought to sea with us, but the fowls were killed. There had been some barley and wheat together; but, to my great disappointment, I found afterwards that the rats had eaten or spoiled it all. As for liquors, I found several, cases of bottles belonging to our skipper, in which were some cordial waters; and, in all, about 5 or 6 gallons of rack. These I stowed by themselves, there being no need to put them into the chest, nor any room for them. While I was doing this, I found the tide begin to flow, though very calm; and I had the mortification to see my coat, shirt, and waistcoat, which I had left on the shore, upon the sand, swim away. As for my breeches, which were only linen, and open-kneed, I swam on board in them and my stockings. However, this set me on rummaging for clothes, of which I found enough, but took no more than I wanted for present use, for I had others things which my eye was more upon – as, first, tools to work with on shore. And it was after long searching that I found out the carpenter's chest, which was, indeed, a very useful prize to me, and much more valuable than a shipload of gold would have been at that time. I got it down to my raft, whole as it was, without losing time to look into it, for I knew in general what it contained.

My next care was for some ammunition and arms. There were two very good fowling-pieces in the great cabin, and two pistols. These I secured first, with some powder-horns and a small bag of shot, and two old rusty swords. I knew there were three barrels of powder in the ship, but knew not where our gunner had stowed them; but with much search I found them, two of them dry and good, the third had taken water. Those two I got to my raft with the arms. And now I thought myself pretty well freighted, and began to think how I should get to shore with them, having neither sail, oar, nor rudder; and the least capful of wind would have overset all my navigation.

I had three encouragements – first, a smooth, calm sea; secondly, the tide rising, and setting in to the shore; thirdly, what little wind there was blew me towards the land. And thus, having found two or three broken oars belonging to the boat – and, besides the tools which were in the chest, I found two saws, an axe, and a hammer; with this cargo I put to sea. For a mile or thereabouts my raft went very well, only that I found it drive a little distant from the place where I had landed before; by which I perceived that there was some indraft of the water, and consequently I hoped to find some creek or river there, which I might make use of as a port to get to land with my cargo.

As I imagined, so it was. There appeared before me a little opening of the land, and I found a strong current of the tide set into it; so I guided my raft as well as I could, to keep in the middle of the stream.

But here I had like to have suffered a second shipwreck, which, if I had, I think verily would have broken my heart; for, knowing nothing of the coast, my raft ran aground at one end of it upon a shoal, and not being aground at the other end, it wanted but a little that all my cargo had slipped off towards the end that was afloat, and so fallen into the water. I did my utmost, by setting my back against the chests, to keep them in their places, but could not thrust off the raft with all my strength; neither durst I stir from the posture I was in; but holding up the chests with all my might, I stood in that manner near half-an-hour, in which time the rising of the water brought me a little more upon a level; and a little after, the water still-rising, my raft floated again, and I thrust her off with the oar I had into the channel, and then driving up higher, I at length found myself in the mouth of a little river, with land on both sides, and a strong current of tide running up. I looked on both sides for a proper place to get to shore, for I was not willing to be driven too high up the river: hoping in time to see some ships at sea, and therefore resolved to place myself as near the coast as I could.

At length I spied a little cove on the right shore of the creek, to which with great pain and difficulty I guided my raft, and at last got so near that, reaching ground with my oar, I could thrust her directly in. But here I had like to have dipped all my cargo into the sea again; for that shore lying pretty steep – that is to say sloping – there was no place to land, but where one end of my float, if it ran on shore, would lie so high, and the other sink lower, as before, that it would endanger my cargo again. All that I could do was to wait till the tide was at the highest, keeping the raft with my oar like an anchor, to hold the side of it fast to the shore, near a flat piece of ground, which I expected the water would flow over; and so it did. As soon as I found water enough – for my raft drew about a foot of water – I thrust her upon that flat piece of ground, and there fastened or moored her, by sticking my two broken oars into the ground, one on one side near one end, and one on the other side near the other end; and thus I lay till the water ebbed away, and left my raft and all my cargo safe on shore.

My next work was to view the country, and seek a proper place for my habitation, and where to stow my goods to secure them from whatever might happen. Where I was, I yet knew not; whether on the continent or on an island; whether inhabited or not inhabited; whether in danger of wild beasts or not. There was a hill not above a mile from me, which rose up very steep and high, and which seemed to overtop some other hills, which lay as in a ridge from it northward. I took out one of the fowling-pieces, and one of the pistols, and a horn of powder; and thus armed, I travelled for discovery up to the top of that hill, where, after I had with great labour and difficulty got to the top, I saw any fate, to my great affliction – *viz.* that I was in an island environed every way with the sea: no land to be seen except some rocks, which lay a great way off; and two small islands, less than this, which lay about three leagues to the west.

I found also that the island I was in was barren, and, as I saw good reason to believe, uninhabited except by wild beasts, of whom, however, I saw none. Yet I saw abundance of fowls, but knew not their kinds; neither when I killed them could I tell what was fit for food, and what not. At my coming back, I shot at a great bird which I saw sitting upon a tree on the side of a great wood. I believe it was the first gun that had been fired there since the creation of the world. I had no sooner fired, than from all parts of the wood there arose an innumerable number of fowls, of many sorts, making a confused screaming and crying, and every one according to his usual note, but not one of them of any kind that I knew. As for the creature I killed, I took it to be a kind of hawk, its colour and beak resembling it, but it had no talons or claws more than common. Its flesh was carrion, and fit for nothing.

Contented with this discovery, I came back to my raft, and fell to work to bring my cargo on shore, which took me up the rest of that day. What to do with myself at night I knew not, nor indeed where to rest, for I was afraid to lie down on the ground, not knowing but some wild beast might devour me, though, as I afterwards found, there was really no need for those fears.

However, as well as I could, I barricaded myself round with the chest and boards that I had brought on shore, and made a kind of hut for that night's lodging. As for food, I yet saw not which way to supply myself, except that I had seen two or three creatures like hares run out of the wood where I shot the fowl.

I now began to consider that I might yet get a great many things out of the ship which would be useful to me, and particularly some of the rigging and sails, and such other things as might come to land; and I resolved to make another voyage on board the vessel, if possible. And as I knew that the first storm that blew must necessarily break her all in pieces, I resolved to set all other things apart till I had got everything out of the ship that I could get. Then I called a council – that is to say in my thoughts – whether I should take back the raft; but this appeared impracticable: so I resolved to go as before, when the tide was down; and I did so, only that I stripped before I went from my hut, having nothing on but my checquered shirt, a pair of linen drawers, and a pair of pumps on my feet.

I got on board the ship as before, and prepared a second raft; and, having had experience of the first, I neither made this so unwieldy, nor loaded it so hard, but yet I brought away several things very useful to me; as first, in the carpenters stores I found two or three bags full of nails and spikes, a great screw-jack, a dozen or two of hatchets, and, above all, that most useful thing called a grindstone. All these I secured, together with several things belonging to the gunner, particularly two or three iron crows, and two barrels of musket bullets, seven muskets, another fowling-piece, with some small quantity of powder more; a large bagful of small shot, and a great roll of sheet-lead; but this last was so heavy, I could not hoist it up to get it over the ship's side.

Besides these things, I took all the men's clothes that I could find, and a spare fore-topsail, a hammock, and some bedding; and with this I loaded my second raft, and brought them all safe on shore, to my very great comfort.

I was under some apprehension, during my absence from the land, that at least my provisions might be devoured on shore: but when I came back I found no sign of any visitor; only there sat a creature like a wild cat upon one of the chests, which, when I came towards it, ran away a little distance, and then stood still. She sat very composed and unconcerned, and looked full in my face, as if she had a mind to be acquainted with me. I presented my gun at her, but, as she did not understand it, she was perfectly unconcerned at it, nor did she offer to stir away; upon which I tossed her a bit of biscuit, though by the way, I was not very free of it, for my store was not great: however, I spared her a bit, I say, and she went to it, smelled at it, and ate it, and looked (as if pleased) for more; but I thanked her, and could spare no more: so she marched off.

Having got my second cargo on shore – though I was fain to open the barrels of powder, and bring them by parcels, for they were too heavy, being large casks – I went to work to make me a little tent with the sail and some poles which I cut for that purpose: and into this tent I brought everything that I knew would spoil either with rain or sun; and I piled all the empty chests and casks up in a circle round the tent, to fortify it from any sudden attempt, either from man or beast.

When I had done this, I blocked up the door of the tent with some boards within, and an empty chest set up on end without; and spreading one of the beds upon the ground, laying my two pistols just at my head, and my gun at length by me, I went to bed for the first time, and slept very quietly all night, for I was very weary and heavy; for the night before I had slept little, and had laboured very hard all day to fetch all those things from the ship, and to get them on shore.

I had the biggest magazine of all kinds now that ever was laid up, I believe, for one man: but I was not satisfied still, for while the ship sat upright in that posture, I thought I ought to get everything out of her that I could; so every day at low water I went on board, and brought away something or other; but particularly the third time I went I brought away as much of the rigging as I could, as also all the small ropes and rope-twine I could get, with a piece of spare canvas, which was to mend the sails upon occasion, and the barrel of wet gunpowder. In a word, I brought away all the sails, first and last; only that I was fain to cut them in pieces, and bring as much at a time as I could, for they were no more useful to be sails, but as mere canvas only.

But that which comforted me more still, was, that last of all, after I had made five or six such voyages as these, and thought I had nothing more to expect from the ship that was worth my meddling with – I say, after all this, I found a great hogshead of bread, three large runlets of rum, or spirits, a box of sugar, and a barrel of fine flour; this was surprising to me, because I had given over expecting any more provisions, except what was spoiled by the water. I soon emptied the hogshead of the bread, and wrapped it up, parcel by parcel, in pieces of the sails, which I cut out; and, in a word, I got all this safe on shore also.

The next day I made another voyage, and now, having plundered the ship of what was portable and fit to hand out, I began with the cables. Cutting the great cable into pieces, such as I could move, I got two cables and a hawser on shore, with all the ironwork I could get; and having cut down the spritsail-yard, and the mizzen-yard, and everything I could, to make a large raft, I loaded it with all these heavy goods, and came away. But my good luck began now to leave me; for this raft was so unwieldy, and so overladen, that, after I had entered the little cove where I had landed the rest of my goods, not being able to guide it so handily as I did the other, it overset, and threw me and all my cargo into the water. As for myself, it was no great harm, for I was near the shore; but as to my cargo, it was a great part of it lost, especially the iron, which I expected would have been of great use to me; however, when the tide was out, I got most of the pieces of the cable ashore, and some of the iron, though with infinite labour; for I was fain to dip for it into the water, a work which fatigued me very much. After this, I went every day on board, and brought away what I could get.

I had been now thirteen days on shore, and had been eleven times on board the ship, in which time I had brought away all that one pair of hands could well be supposed capable to bring; though I believe verily, had the calm weather held, I should have brought away the whole ship, piece by piece. But preparing the twelfth time to go on board, I found the wind began to rise: however, at low water I went on board, and though I thought I had rummaged the cabin so effectually that nothing more could be found, yet I discovered a locker with drawers in it, in one of which I found two or three razors, and one pair of large scissors, with some ten or a dozen of good knives and forks: in another I found about 36 pounds value in money – some European coin, some Brazil, some pieces of eight, some gold, and some silver.

I smiled to myself at the sight of this money: "O drug!" said I, aloud, "what art thou good for? Thou art not worth to me – no, not the taking off the ground; one of those knives is worth all this heap; I have no manner of use for thee – e'en remain where thou art, and go to the bottom as a creature whose life is not worth saving." However, upon second thoughts I took it away; and wrapping all this in a piece of canvas, I began to think of making another raft; but while I was preparing this, I found the sky overcast, and the wind began to rise, and in a quarter of an hour it blew a fresh gale from the shore. It presently occurred to me that it was in vain to pretend to make a raft with the wind offshore; and that it was my business to be gone before the tide of flood began, otherwise I might not be able to reach the shore at all. Accordingly, I let myself down into the water, and swam across the channel, which lay between the ship and the sands, and even that with difficulty enough, partly with the weight of the things I had about me, and partly the roughness of the water; for the wind rose very hastily, and before it was quite high water it blew a storm.

But I had gotten home to my little tent, where I lay, with all my wealth about me, very secure. It blew very hard all night, and in the morning, when I looked out, behold, no more ship was to be seen! I was a little surprised, but recovered myself with the satisfactory reflection that I had lost no time, nor abated any diligence, to get everything out of her that could be useful to me; and that, indeed, there was little left in her that I was able to bring away, if I had had more time.

I now gave over any more thoughts of the ship, or of anything out of her, except what might drive on shore from her wreck; as, indeed, divers pieces of her afterwards did; but those things were of small use to me.

My thoughts were now wholly employed about securing myself against either savages, if any should appear, or wild beasts, if any were in the island; and I had many thoughts of the method how to do this, and what kind of dwelling to make – whether I should make me a cave in the earth, or a tent upon the earth; and, in short, I resolved upon both; the manner and description of which, it may not be improper to give an account of.

I soon found the place I was in was not fit for my settlement, because it was upon a low, moorish ground, near the sea, and I believed it would not be wholesome, and more particularly because there was no fresh water near it; so I resolved to find a more healthy and more convenient spot of ground.

I consulted several things in my situation, which I found would he proper for me: First, health and fresh water, I just now mentioned; secondly, shelter from the heat of the sun; thirdly, security from ravenous creatures, whether man or beast; fourthly, a view to the sea, that if God sent any ship in sight, I might not lose any advantage for my deliverance, of which I was not willing to banish all my expectation yet.

In search of a place proper for this, I found a little plain on the side of a rising hill, whose front towards this little plain was steep as a houseside, so that nothing could come down upon me from the top. On the one side of the rock there was a hollow place, worn a little way in, like the entrance or door of a cave but there was not really any cave or way into the rock at all.

On the flat of the green, just before this hollow place, I resolved to pitch my tent. This plain was not above a hundred yards broad, and about twice as long, and lay like a green before my door; and, at the end of it, descended irregularly every way down into the low ground by the seaside. It was on the N.N.W. side of the hill; so that it was sheltered from the heat every day, till it came to a W. and by S. sun, or thereabouts, which, in those countries, is near the setting.

Before I set up my tent I drew a half-circle before the hollow place, which took in about ten yards in its semi-diameter from the rock, and twenty yards in its diameter from its beginning and ending.

In this half-circle I pitched two rows of strong stakes, driving them into the ground till they stood very firm like piles, the biggest end being out of the ground above five feet and a half, and sharpened on the top. The two rows did not stand above six inches from one another.

Then I took the pieces of cable which I had cut in the ship, and laid them in rows, one upon another, within the circle, between these two rows of stakes, up to the top, placing other stakes in the inside, leaning against them, about two feet and a half high, like a spur to a post; and this fence was so strong, that neither man nor beast could get into it or over it. This cost me a great deal of time and labour, especially to cut the piles in the woods, bring them to the place, and drive them into the earth.

The entrance into this place I made to be, not by a door, but by a short ladder to go over the top; which ladder, when I was in, I lifted over after me; and so I was completely fenced in and fortified, as I thought, from all the world, and consequently slept secure in the night, which otherwise I could not have done; though, as it appeared afterwards, there was no need of all this caution from the enemies that I apprehended danger from.

Into this fence or fortress, with infinite labour, I carried all my riches, all my provisions, ammunition, and stores, of which you have the account above; and I made a large tent, which to preserve me from the rains that in one part of the year are very violent there, I made double – one smaller tent within, and one larger tent above it; and covered the uppermost with a large tarpaulin, which I had saved among the sails.

And now I lay no more for a while in the bed which I had brought on shore, but in a hammock, which was indeed a very good one, and belonged to the Mate of the ship.

Into this tent I brought all my provisions, and everything that would spoil by the wet; and having thus enclosed all my goods, I made up the entrance, which till now I had left open, and so passed and repassed, as I said, by a short ladder.

When I had done this, I began to work my way into the rock, and bringing all the earth and stones that I dug down out through my tent, I laid them up within my fence, in the nature of a terrace, so that it raised the ground within about a foot and a half; and thus I made me a cave, just behind my tent, which served me like a cellar to my house.

It cost me much labour and many days before all these things were brought to perfection; and therefore I must go back to some other things which took up some of my thoughts. At the same time it happened, after I had laid my scheme for the setting up my tent, and making the cave, that a storm of rain falling from a thick, dark cloud, a sudden flash of lightning happened, and after that a great clap of thunder, as is naturally the effect of it. I was not so much surprised with the lightning as I was with the thought which darted into my mind as swift as the lightning itself – Oh, my powder! My very heart sank within me when I thought that, at one blast, all my powder might be destroyed; on which, not my defence only, but the providing my food, as I thought, entirely depended. I was nothing near so anxious about my own danger, though, had the powder took fire, I should never have known who had hurt me.

Such impression did this make upon me, that after the storm was over I laid aside all my works, my building and fortifying, and applied myself to make bags and boxes, to separate the powder, and to keep it a little and a little in a parcel, in the hope that, whatever might come, it might not all take fire at once; and to keep it so apart that it should not be possible to make one part fire another. I finished this work in about a fortnight; and I think my powder, which in all was about 240 pounds weight, was divided in not less than a hundred parcels. As to the barrel that had been wet, I did not apprehend any danger from that; so I placed it in my new cave, which, in my fancy, I called my kitchen; and the rest I hid up and down in holes among the rocks, so that no wet might come to it, marking very carefully where I laid it.

In the interval of time while this was doing, I went out once at least every day with my gun, as well to divert myself as to see if I could kill anything fit for food; and, as near as I could, to acquaint myself with what the island produced. The first time I went out, I presently discovered that there were goats in the island, which was a great satisfaction to me; but then it was attended with this misfortune to me – *viz.* that they were so shy, so subtle, and so swift of foot, that it was the most difficult thing in the world to come at them; but I was not discouraged at this, not doubting but I might now and then shoot one, as it soon happened; for after I had found their haunts a little, I laid wait in this manner for them: I observed if they saw me in the valleys, though they were upon the rocks, they would run away, as in a terrible fright; but if they were feeding in the valleys, and I was upon the rocks, they took no notice of me; from whence I concluded that, by the position of their optics, their sight was so directed downward that they did not readily see objects that were above them; so afterwards I took this method – I always climbed the rocks first, to get above them, and then had frequently a fair mark.

The first shot I made among these creatures, I killed a she-goat, which had a little kid by her, which she gave suck to, which grieved me heartily; for when the old one fell, the kid stood stock still by her, till I came and took her up; and not only so, but when I carried the old one with me, upon my shoulders, the kid followed me quite to my enclosure; upon which I laid down the dam, and took the kid in my arms, and

1903 illustration by John Ward Dunsmore

carried it over my pale, in hopes to have bred it up tame; but it would not eat; so I was forced to kill it and eat it myself. These two supplied me with flesh a great while, for I ate sparingly, and saved my provisions, my bread especially, as much as possibly I could.

Having now fixed my habitation, I found it absolutely necessary to provide a place to make a fire in, and fuel to burn: and what I did for that, and also how I enlarged my cave, and what conveniences I made, I shall give a full account of in its place; but I must now give some little account of myself, and of my thoughts about living, which, it may well be supposed, were not a few.

I had a dismal prospect of my condition; for as I was not cast away upon that island without being driven, as is said, by a violent storm, quite out of the course of our intended voyage, and a great way, *viz.* some hundreds of leagues, out of the ordinary course of the trade of mankind, I had great reason to consider it as a determination of Heaven, that in this desolate place, and in this desolate manner, I should end my life. The tears would run plentifully down my face when I made these reflections; and sometimes I would expostulate with myself why Providence should thus completely ruin His creatures, and render them so absolutely miserable; so without help, abandoned, so entirely depressed, that it could hardly be rational to be thankful for such a life.

But something always returned swift upon me to check these thoughts, and to reprove me; and particularly one day, walking with my gun in my hand by the seaside, I was very pensive upon the subject of my present condition, when reason, as it were, expostulated with me the other way, thus: "Well, you are in a desolate condition, it is true; but, pray remember, where are the rest of you? Did not you come, eleven of you in the boat? Where are the ten? Why were they not saved, and you lost? Why were you singled out? Is it better to be here or there?" And then I pointed to the sea. All evils are to be considered with the good that is in them, and with what worse attends them.

Then it occurred to me again, how well I was furnished for my subsistence, and what would have been my case if it had not happened (which was a hundred thousand to one) that the ship floated from the place where she first struck, and was driven so near to the shore that I had time to get all these things out of her; what would have been my case, if I had been forced to have lived in the condition in which I at first came on shore, without necessaries of life, or necessaries to supply and procure them? "Particularly," said I, aloud (though to myself), "what should I have done without a gun, without ammunition, without any tools to make anything, or to work with, without clothes, bedding, a tent, or any manner of covering?" and that now I had all these to sufficient quantity, and was in a fair way to provide myself in such a manner as to live without my gun, when my ammunition was spent: so that I had a tolerable view of subsisting, without any want, as long as I lived; for I considered from the beginning how I would provide for the accidents that might happen, and for the time that was to come, even not only after my ammunition should be spent, but even after my health and strength should decay.

I confess I had not entertained any notion of my ammunition being destroyed at one blast – I mean my powder being blown up by lightning; and this made the thoughts of it so surprising to me, when it lightened and thundered, as I observed just now.

And now being about to enter into a melancholy relation of a scene of silent life, such, perhaps, as was never heard of in the world before, I shall take it from its beginning, and continue it in its order. It was by my account the 30th of September, when, in the manner as above said, I first set foot upon this horrid island; when the sun, being to us in its autumnal equinox, was almost over my head; for I reckoned myself, by observation, to be in the latitude of 9 degrees 22 minutes north of the line.

After I had been there about ten or twelve days, it came into my thoughts that I should lose my reckoning of time for want of books, and pen and ink, and should even forget the Sabbath days; but to prevent this, I cut with my knife upon a large post, in capital letters – and making it into a great cross, I set it up on the shore where I first landed – "I came on shore here on the 30th September 1659."

Upon the sides of this square post I cut every day a notch with my knife, and every seventh notch was as long again as the rest, and every first day of the month as long again as that long one; and thus I kept my calendar, or weekly, monthly, and yearly reckoning of time.

In the next place, we are to observe that among the many things which I brought out of the ship, in the several voyages which, as above mentioned, I made to it, I got several things of less value, but not at all less useful to me, which I omitted setting down before; as, in particular, pens, ink, and paper, several parcels in the Captain's, Mate's, gunner's and carpenter's keeping; three or four compasses, some mathematical instruments, dials, perspectives, charts, and books of navigation, all which I huddled together, whether I might want them or no; also, I found three very good Bibles, which came to me in my cargo from England, and which I had packed up among my things; some Portuguese books also; and among them two or three Popish prayer-books, and several other books, all which I carefully secured. And I must not forget that we had in the ship a dog and two cats, of whose eminent history I may have occasion to say something in its place; for I carried both the cats with me; and as for the dog, he jumped out of the ship of himself, and swam on shore to me the day after I went on shore with my first cargo, and was a trusty servant to me many years; I wanted nothing that he could fetch me, nor any company that he could make up to me; I only wanted to have him talk to me, but that would not do. As I observed before, I found pens, ink, and paper, and I husbanded them to the utmost; and I shall show that while my ink lasted, I kept things very exact, but after that was gone I could not, for I could not make any ink by any means that I could devise.

And this put me in mind that I wanted many things notwithstanding all that I had amassed together; and of these, ink was one; as also a spade, pickaxe, and shovel, to dig or remove the earth; needles, pins, and thread; as for linen, I soon learned to want that without much difficulty.

This want of tools made every work I did go on heavily; and it was near a whole year before I had entirely finished my little pale, or surrounded my habitation. The piles, or stakes, which were as heavy as I could well lift, were a long time in cutting and preparing in the woods, and more, by far, in bringing home; so that I spent sometimes two days in cutting and bringing home one of those posts, and a third day in driving it into the ground; for which purpose I got a heavy piece of wood at first, but at last bethought myself of one of the iron crows; which, however, though I found it, made driving those posts or piles very laborious and tedious work. But what need I have been concerned at the tediousness of anything I had to do, seeing I had time enough to do it in? nor had I any other employment, if that had been over, at least that I could foresee, except the ranging the island to seek for food, which I did, more or less, every day.

I now began to consider seriously my condition, and the circumstances I was reduced to; and I drew up the state of my affairs in writing, not so much to leave them to any that were to come after me – for I was likely to have but few heirs – as to deliver my thoughts from daily poring over them, and afflicting my mind; and as my reason began now to Master my despondency, I began to comfort myself as well as I could, and to set the good against the evil, that I might have something to distinguish my case from worse; and I stated very impartially, like debtor and creditor, the comforts I enjoyed against the miseries I suffered, thus:

EVIL	GOOD
I am cast upon a horrible, desolate island, void of all hope of recovery.	*But I am alive; and not drowned, as all my ship's company were.*
I am singled out and separated, as it were, from all the world, to be miserable.	*But I am singled out, too, from all the ship's crew, to be spared from death; and He that miraculously saved me from death can deliver me from this condition.*
I am divided from mankind – a solitaire; one banished from human society.	*But I am not starved, and perishing on a barren place, affording no sustenance.*
I have no clothes to cover me.	*But I am in a hot climate, where, if I had clothes, I could hardly wear them.*
I am without any defence, or means to resist any violence of man or beast.	*But I am cast on an island where I see no wild beasts to hurt me, as I saw on the coast of Africa; and what if I had been shipwrecked there?*
I have no soul to speak to or relieve me.	*But God wonderfully sent the ship in near enough to the shore, that I have got out as many necessary things as will either supply my wants or enable me to supply myself, even as long as I live.*

Upon the whole, here was an undoubted testimony that there was scarce any condition in the world so miserable but there was something negative or something positive to be thankful for in it; and let this stand as a direction from the experience of the most miserable of all conditions in this world: that we may always find in it something to comfort ourselves from, and to set, in the description of good and evil, on the credit side of the account.

Having now brought my mind a little to relish my condition, and given over looking out to sea, to see if I could spy a ship – I say, giving over these things, I begun to apply myself to arrange my way of living, and to make things as easy to me as I could.

I have already described my habitation, which was a tent under the side of a rock, surrounded with a strong pale of posts and cables: but I might now rather call it a wall, for I raised a kind of wall up against it of turfs, about two feet thick on the outside; and after some time (I think it was a year and a half) I raised rafters from it, leaning to the rock, and thatched or covered it with boughs of trees, and such things as I could get, to keep out the rain; which I found at some times of the year very violent.

I have already observed how I brought all my goods into this pale, and into the cave which I had made behind me. But I must observe, too, that at first this was a confused heap of goods, which, as they lay in no order, so they took up all my place; I had no room to turn myself: so I set myself to enlarge my cave, and work farther into the earth; for it was a loose sandy rock, which yielded easily to the labour I bestowed on it: and so when I found I was pretty safe as to beasts of prey, I worked sideways, to the right hand, into the rock; and then, turning to the right again, worked quite out, and made me a door to come out on the outside of my pale or fortification. This gave me not only egress and regress, as it was a back way to my tent and to my storehouse, but gave me room to store my goods.

And now I began to apply myself to make such necessary things as I found I most wanted, particularly a chair and a table; for without these I was not able to enjoy the few comforts I had in the world; I could not write or eat, or do several things, with so much pleasure without a table: so I went to work. And here I must needs observe, that as reason is the substance and origin of the mathematics, so by stating and squaring everything by reason, and by making the most rational judgment of things, every man may be, in time, Master of every mechanic art. I had never handled a tool in my life; and yet, in time, by labour, application, and contrivance, I found at last that I wanted nothing but I could have made it, especially if I had had tools. However, I made abundance of things, even without tools; and some with no more tools than an adze and a hatchet, which perhaps were never made that way before, and that with infinite labour. For example, if I wanted a board, I had no other way but to cut down a tree, set it on an edge before me, and hew it flat on either side with my axe, till I brought it to be thin as a plank, and then dub it smooth with my adze. It is true, by this method I could make but one board out of a whole tree; but this I had no remedy for but patience, any more than I had for the prodigious deal of time and labour which it took me up to make a plank or board: but my time or labour was little worth, and so it was as well employed one way as another.

However, I made me a table and a chair, as I observed above, in the first place; and this I did out of the short pieces of boards that I brought on my raft from the ship. But when I had wrought out some boards as above, I made large shelves, of the breadth of a foot and a half, one over another all along one side of my cave, to lay all my tools, nails and ironwork on; and, in a word, to separate everything at large into their places, that I might come easily at them. I knocked pieces into the wall of the rock to hang my guns and all things that would hang up; so that, had my cave been to be seen, it looked like a general magazine of all necessary things; and had everything so ready at my hand, that it was a great pleasure to me to see all my goods in such order, and especially to find my stock of all necessaries so great.

And now it was that I began to keep a journal of every day's employment; for, indeed, at first I was in too much hurry, and not only hurry as to labour, but in too much discomposure of mind; and my journal would have been full of many dull things; for example, I must have said thus: "30th. – After I had got to shore, and escaped drowning, instead of being thankful to God for my deliverance, having first vomited, with the great quantity of salt water which had got into my stomach, and recovering myself a little, I ran about the shore wringing my hands and beating my head and face, exclaiming at my misery, and crying out, 'I was undone, undone!' till, tired and faint, I was forced to lie down on the ground to repose, but durst not sleep for fear of being devoured."

Some days after this, and after I had been on board the ship, and got all that I could out of her, yet I could not forbear getting up to the top of a little mountain and looking out to sea, in hopes of seeing a ship; then fancy at a vast distance I spied a sail, please myself with the hopes of it, and then after looking steadily, till I was almost blind, lose it quite, and sit down and weep like a child, and thus increase my misery by my folly.

But having gotten over these things in some measure, and having settled my household staff and habitation, made me a table and a chair, and all as handsome about me as I could, I began to keep my journal; of which I shall here give you the copy (though in it will be told all these particulars over again) as long as it lasted; for having no more ink, I was forced to leave it off.

CHAPTER FIVE

Builds a House – The Journal

SEPTEMBER 30, 1659. – I, poor miserable Robinson Crusoe, being shipwrecked during a dreadful storm in the offing, came on shore on this dismal, unfortunate island, which I called "The Island of Despair"; all the rest of the ship's company being drowned, and myself almost dead.

All the rest of the day I spent in afflicting myself at the dismal circumstances I was brought to – *viz.* I had neither food, house, clothes, weapon, nor place to fly to; and in despair of any relief, saw nothing but death before me – either that I should be devoured by wild beasts, murdered by savages, or starved to death for want of food. At the approach of night I slept in a tree, for fear of wild creatures; but slept soundly, though it rained all night.

OCTOBER 1. – In the morning I saw, to my great surprise, the ship had floated with the high tide, and was driven on shore again much nearer the island; which, as it was some comfort, on one hand – for, seeing her set upright, and not broken to pieces, I hoped, if the wind abated, I might get on board, and get some food and necessaries out of her for my relief – so, on the other hand, it renewed my grief at the loss of my comrades, who, I imagined, if we had all stayed on board, might have saved the ship, or, at least, that they would not have been all drowned as they were; and that, had the men been saved, we might perhaps have built us a boat out of the ruins of the ship to have carried us to some other part of the world. I spent great part of this day in perplexing myself on these things; but at length, seeing the ship almost dry, I went upon the sand as near as I could, and then swam on board. This day also it continued raining, though with no wind at all.

From the 1st of OCTOBER to the 24th. – All these days entirely spent in many several voyages to get all I could out of the ship, which I brought on shore every tide of flood upon rafts. Much rain also in the days, though with some intervals of fair weather; but it seems this was the rainy season.

OCT. 20. – I overset my raft, and all the goods I had got upon it; but, being in shoal water, and the things being chiefly heavy, I recovered many of them when the tide was out.

OCT. 25. – It rained all night and all day, with some gusts of wind; during which time the ship broke in pieces, the wind blowing a little harder than before, and was no more to be seen, except the wreck of her, and that only at low water. I spent this day in covering and securing the goods which I had saved, that the rain might not spoil them.

OCT. 26. – I walked about the shore almost all day, to find out a place to fix my habitation, greatly concerned to secure myself from any attack in the night, either from wild beasts or men. Towards night, I fixed upon a proper place, under a rock, and marked out a semicircle for my encampment; which I resolved to strengthen with a work, wall, or fortification, made of double piles, lined within with cables, and without with turf.

From the 26th to the 30th I worked very hard in carrying all my goods to my new habitation, though some part of the time it rained exceedingly hard.

The 31st, in the morning, I went out into the island with my gun, to seek for some food, and discover the country; when I killed a she-goat, and her kid followed me home, which I afterwards killed also, because it would not feed.

NOVEMBER 1. – I set up my tent under a rock, and lay there for the first night; making it as large as I could, with stakes driven in to swing my hammock upon.

NOV. 2. – I set up all my chests and boards, and the pieces of timber which made my rafts, and with them formed a fence round me, a little within the place I had marked out for my fortification.

NOV. 3. – I went out with my gun, and killed two fowls like ducks, which were very good food. In the afternoon went to work to make me a table.

NOV. 4. – This morning I began to order my times of work, of going out with my gun, time of sleep, and time of diversion – *viz.* every morning I walked out with my gun for 2 or 3 hours, if it did not rain; then employed myself to work till about 11 o'clock; then eat what I had to live on; and from 12 to 2 I lay down to sleep, the weather being excessively hot; and then, in the evening, to work again. The working part of this day and of the next were wholly employed in making my table, for I was yet but a very sorry workman, though time and necessity made me a complete natural mechanic soon after, as I believe they would do any one else.

Nov. 5. – This day went abroad with my gun and my dog, and killed a wild cat; her skin pretty soft, but her flesh good for nothing; every creature that I killed I took of the skins and preserved them. Coming back by the sea-shore, I saw many sorts of sea-fowls, which I did not understand; but was surprised, and almost frightened, with two or three seals, which, while I was gazing at, not well knowing what they were, got into the sea, and escaped me for that time.

Nov. 6. – After my morning walk I went to work with my table again, and finished it, though not to my liking; nor was it long before I learned to mend it.

Nov. 7. – Now it began to be settled fair weather. The 7th, 8th, 9th, 10th, and part of the 12th (for the 11th was Sunday) I took wholly up to make me a chair, and with much ado brought it to a tolerable shape, but never to please me; and even in the making I pulled it in pieces several times.

Note. – I soon neglected my keeping Sundays; for, omitting my mark for them on my post, I forgot which was which.

Nov. 13. – This day it rained, which refreshed me exceedingly, and cooled the earth; but it was accompanied with terrible thunder and lightning, which frightened me dreadfully, for fear of my powder. As soon as it was over, I resolved to separate my stock of powder into as many little parcels as possible, that it might not be in danger.

Nov. 14, 15, 16. – These three days I spent in making little square chests, or boxes, which might hold about a pound, or two pounds at most, of powder; and so, putting the powder in, I stowed it in places as secure and remote from one another as possible. On one of these three days I killed a large bird that was good to eat, but I knew not what to call it.

Nov. 17. – This day I began to dig behind my tent into the rock, to make room for my further conveniency.

Note. – Three things I wanted exceedingly for this work – *viz.* a pickaxe, a shovel, and a wheelbarrow or basket; so I desisted from my work, and began to consider how to supply that want, and make me some tools. As for the pickaxe, I made use of the iron crows, which were proper enough, though heavy; but the next thing was a shovel or spade; this was so absolutely necessary, that, indeed, I could do nothing effectually without it; but what kind of one to make I knew not.

Nov. 18. – The next day, in searching the woods, I found a tree of that wood, or like it, which in the Brazils they call the iron-tree, for its exceeding hardness. Of this, with great labour, and almost spoiling my axe, I cut a piece, and brought it home, too, with difficulty enough, for it was exceeding heavy. The excessive hardness of the wood, and my having no other way, made me a long while upon this machine, for I worked it effectually by little and little into the form of a shovel or spade; the handle exactly shaped like ours in England, only that the board part having no iron shod upon it at bottom, it would not last me so long; however, it served well enough for the uses which I had occasion to put it to; but never was a shovel, I believe, made after that fashion, or so long in making.

I was still deficient, for I wanted a basket or a wheelbarrow. A basket I could not make by any means, having no such things as twigs that would bend to make wicker-ware – at least, none yet found out; and as to a wheelbarrow, I fancied I could make all but the wheel; but that I had no notion of; neither did I know how to go about it; besides, I had no possible way to make the iron gudgeons for the spindle or axis of the wheel to run in; so I gave it over, and so, for carrying away the earth which I dug out of the cave, I made me a thing like a hodd which the labourers carry mortar in when they serve the bricklayers. This was not so difficult to me as the making the shovel: and yet this and the shovel, and the attempt which I made in vain to make a wheelbarrow, took me up no less than four days – I mean always excepting my morning walk with my gun, which I seldom failed, and very seldom failed also bringing home something fit to eat.

Nov. 23. – My other work having now stood still, because of my making these tools, when they were finished I went on, and working every day, as my strength and time allowed, I spent eighteen days entirely in widening and deepening my cave, that it might hold my goods commodiously.

Note. – During all this time I worked to make this room or cave spacious enough to accommodate me as a warehouse or magazine, a kitchen, a dining-room, and a cellar. As for my lodging, I kept to the tent; except that sometimes, in the wet season of the year, it rained so hard that I could not keep myself dry, which caused me afterwards to cover all my place within my pale with long poles, in the form of rafters, leaning against the rock, and load them with flags and large leaves of trees, like a thatch.

December 10. – I began now to think my cave or vault finished, when on a sudden (it seems I had made it too large) a great quantity of earth fell down from the top on one side; so much that, in short, it frighted me, and not without reason, too, for if I had been under it, I had never wanted a gravedigger. I had now a great deal of work to do over again, for I had the loose earth to carry out; and, which was of more importance, I had the ceiling to prop up, so that I might be sure no more would come down.

Dec. 11. – This day I went to work with it accordingly, and got two shores or posts pitched upright to the top, with two pieces of boards across over each post; this I finished the next day; and setting more posts up with boards, in about a week more I had the roof secured, and the posts, standing in rows, served me for partitions to part off the house.

Dec. 17. – From this day to the 20th I placed shelves, and knocked up nails on the posts, to hang everything up that could be hung up; and now I began to be in some order within doors.

Dec. 20. – Now I carried everything into the cave, and began to furnish my house, and set up some pieces of boards like a dresser, to order my victuals upon; but boards began to be very scarce with me; also, I made me another table.

Dec. 24. – Much rain all night and all day. No stirring out.

Dec. 25. – Rain all day.

Dec. 26. – No rain, and the earth much cooler than before, and pleasanter.

Dec. 27. – Killed a young goat, and lamed another, so that I caught it and led it home in a string; when I had it at home, I bound and splintered up its leg, which was broke.

N.B. – I took such care of it that it lived, and the leg grew well and as strong as ever; but, by my nursing it so long, it grew tame, and fed upon the little green at my door, and would not go away. This was the first time that I entertained a thought of breeding up some tame creatures, that I might have food when my powder and shot was all spent.

Dec. 28,29,30,31. – Great heats, and no breeze, so that there was no stirring abroad, except in the evening, for food; this time I spent in putting all my things in order within doors.

January 1. – Very hot still: but I went abroad early and late with my gun, and lay still in the middle of the day. This evening, going farther into the valleys which lay towards the centre of the island, I found there were plenty of goats, though exceedingly shy, and hard to come at; however, I resolved to try if I could not bring my dog to hunt them down.

Jan. 2. – Accordingly, the next day I went out with my dog, and set him upon the goats, but I was mistaken, for they all faced about upon the dog, and he knew his danger too well, for he would not come near them.

Jan. 3. – I began my fence or wall; which, being still jealous of my being attacked by somebody, I resolved to make very thick and strong.

N.B. – This wall being described before, I purposely omit what was said in the journal; it is sufficient to observe, that I was no less time than from the 2nd of January to the 14th of April working, finishing, and perfecting this wall, though it was no more than about 24 yards in length, being a half-circle from one place in the rock to another place, about 8 yards from it, the door of the cave being in the centre behind it.

All this time I worked very hard, the rains hindering me many days, nay, sometimes weeks together; but I thought I should never be perfectly secure till this wall was finished; and it is scarce credible what inexpressible labour everything was done with, especially the bringing piles out of the woods and driving them into the ground; for I made them much bigger than I needed to have done.

When this wall was finished, and the outside double fenced, with a turf wall raised up close to it, I perceived myself that if any people were to come on shore there, they would not perceive anything like a habitation; and it was very well I did so, as may be observed hereafter, upon a very remarkable occasion.

During this time I made my rounds in the woods for game every day when the rain permitted me, and made frequent discoveries in these walks of something or other to my advantage; particularly, I found a kind of wild pigeons, which build, not as wood-pigeons in a tree, but rather as house-pigeons, in the holes of the rocks; and taking some young ones, I endeavoured to breed them up tame, and did so; but when they grew older they flew away, which perhaps was at first for want of feeding them, for I had nothing to give them; however, I frequently found their nests, and got their young ones, which were very good meat. And now, in the managing my household affairs, I found myself wanting in many things, which I thought at first it was impossible for me to make; as, indeed, with some of them it was: for instance, I could never make a cask to be hooped. I had a small runlet or two, as I observed before; but I could never arrive at the capacity of making one by them, though I spent many weeks about it; I could neither put in the heads, or join the staves so true to one another as to make them hold water; so I gave that also over. In the next place, I was at a great loss for candles; so that as soon as ever it was dark, which was generally by seven o'clock, I was obliged to go to bed. I remembered the lump of beeswax with which I made candles in my African adventure; but I had none of that now; the only remedy I had was, that when I had killed a goat I saved the tallow, and with a little dish made of clay, which I baked in the sun, to which I added a wick of some oakum, I made me a lamp; and this gave me light, though not a clear, steady light, like a candle. In the middle of all my labours it happened that, rummaging my things, I found a little bag which, as I hinted before, had been filled with corn for the feeding of poultry – not for this voyage, but before, as I suppose, when the ship came from Lisbon. The little remainder of corn that had been in the bag was all devoured by the rats, and I saw nothing in the bag but husks and dust; and being willing to have the bag for some other use (I think it was to put powder in, when I divided it for fear of the lightning, or some such use), I shook the husks of corn out of it on one side of my fortification, under the rock.

It was a little before the great rains just now mentioned that I threw this stuff away, taking no notice, and not so much as remembering that I had thrown anything there, when, about a month after, or thereabouts, I saw some few stalks of something green shooting out of the ground, which I fancied might be some plant I had not seen; but I was surprised, and perfectly astonished, when, after a little longer time, I saw about 10 or 12 ears come out, which were perfect green barley, of the same kind as our European – nay, as our English barley.

It is impossible to express the astonishment and confusion of my thoughts on this occasion. I had hitherto acted upon no religious foundation at all; indeed, I had very few notions of religion in my head, nor had entertained any sense of anything that had befallen me otherwise than as chance, or, as we lightly say, what pleases God, without so much as inquiring into the end of Providence in these things, or His order in governing events for the world. But after I saw barley grow there, in a climate which I knew was not proper for corn, and especially that I knew not how it came there, it startled me strangely, and I began to suggest that God had miraculously caused His grain to grow without any help of seed sown, and that it was so directed purely for my sustenance on that wild, miserable place.

This touched my heart a little, and brought tears out of my eyes, and I began to bless myself that such a prodigy of nature should happen upon my account; and this was the more strange to me, because I saw near it still, all along by the side of the rock, some other straggling stalks, which proved to be stalks of rice, and which I knew, because I had seen it grow in Africa when I was ashore there.

I not only thought these the pure productions of Providence for my support, but not doubting that there was more in the place, I went all over that part of the island, where I had been before, peering in every corner, and under every rock, to see for more of it, but I could not find any. At last it occurred to my thoughts that I shook a bag of chickens' meat out in that place; and then the wonder began to cease; and I must confess my religious thankfulness to God's providence began to abate, too, upon the discovering that all this was nothing but what was common; though I ought to have been as thankful for so strange and unforeseen a providence as if it had been miraculous; for it was really the work of Providence to me, that should order or appoint that 10 or 12 grains of corn should remain unspoiled, when the rats had destroyed all the rest, as if it had been dropped from heaven; as also, that I should throw it out in that particular place, where, it being in the shade of a high rock, it sprang up immediately; whereas, if I had thrown it anywhere else at that time, it had been burnt up and destroyed.

I carefully saved the ears of this corn, you may be sure, in their season, which was about the end of June; and, laying up every corn, I resolved to sow them all again, hoping in time to have some quantity sufficient to supply me with bread. But it was not till the fourth year that I could allow myself the least grain of this corn to eat, and even then but sparingly, as I shall say afterwards, in its order; for I lost all that I sowed the first season by not observing the proper time; for I sowed it just before the dry season, so that it never came up at all, at least not as it would have done; of which in its place.

Besides this barley, there were, as above, 20 or 30 stalks of rice, which I preserved with the same care and for the same use, or to the same purpose – to make me bread, or rather food; for I found ways to cook it without baking, though I did that also after some time.

But to return to my Journal.

I worked excessive hard these three or four months to get my wall done; and the 14th of April I closed it up, contriving to go into it, not by a door but over the wall, by a ladder, that there might be no sign on the outside of my habitation.

APRIL 16. – I finished the ladder; so I went up the ladder to the top, and then pulled it up after me, and let it down in the inside. This was a complete enclosure to me; for within I had room enough, and nothing could come at me from without, unless it could first mount my wall.

The very next day after this wall was finished I had almost had all my labour overthrown at once, and myself killed. The case was thus: As I was busy in the inside, behind my tent, just at the entrance into my cave, I was terribly frighted with a most dreadful, surprising thing indeed; for all on a sudden I found the earth come crumbling down from the roof of my cave, and from the edge of the hill over my head, and two of the posts I had set up in the cave cracked in a frightful manner. I was heartily scared; but thought nothing of what was really the cause, only thinking that the top of my cave was fallen in, as some of it had done before: and for fear I should be buried in it I ran forward to my ladder, and not thinking myself safe there neither, I got over my wall for fear of the pieces of the hill, which I expected might roll down upon me. I had no sooner stepped down upon the firm ground, than I plainly saw it was a terrible earthquake, for the ground I stood on shook three times at about eight minutes' distance, with three such shocks as would have overturned the strongest building that could be supposed to have stood on the earth; and a great piece of the top of a rock which stood about half a mile from me next the sea fell down with such a terrible noise as I never heard in all my life. I perceived also the very sea was put into violent motion by it; and I believe the shocks were stronger under the water than on the island.

I was so much amazed with the thing itself, having never felt the like, nor discoursed with any one that had, that I was like one dead or stupefied; and the motion of the earth made my stomach sick, like one that was tossed at sea; but the noise of the falling of the rock awakened me, as it were, and rousing me from the stupefied condition I was in, filled me with horror; and I thought of nothing then but the hill falling upon my tent and all my household goods, and burying all at once; and this sunk my very soul within me a second time.

After the third shock was over, and I felt no more for some time, I began to take courage; and yet I had not heart enough to go over my wall again, for fear of being buried alive, but sat still upon the ground greatly cast down and disconsolate, not knowing what to do. All this while I had not the least serious religious thought; nothing but the common "Lord have mercy upon me!" and when it was over that went away too.

While I sat thus, I found the air overcast and grow cloudy, as if it would rain. Soon after that the wind arose by little and little, so that in less than half-an-hour it blew a most dreadful hurricane; the sea was all on a sudden covered over with foam and froth; the shore was covered with the breach of the water, the trees were torn up by the roots, and a terrible storm it was. This held about three hours, and then began to abate; and in two hours more it was quite calm, and began to rain very hard. All this while I sat upon the ground very much terrified and dejected; when on a sudden it came into my thoughts, that these winds and rain being the consequences of the earthquake, the earthquake itself was spent and over, and I might venture into my cave again. With this thought my spirits began to revive; and the rain also helping to persuade me, I went in and sat down in my tent. But the rain was so violent that my tent was ready to be beaten down with it; and I was forced to go into my cave, though very much afraid and uneasy, for fear it should fall on my head. This violent rain forced me to a new work – *viz.* to cut a hole through my new fortification, like a sink, to let the water go out, which would else have flooded my cave. After I had been in my cave for some time, and found still no more shocks of the earthquake follow, I began to be more composed. And now, to support my spirits, which indeed wanted it very much, I went to my little store, and took a small sup of rum; which, however, I did then and always very sparingly, knowing I could have no more when that was gone. It continued raining all that night and great part of the next day, so that I could not stir abroad; but my mind being more composed, I began to think of what I had best do; concluding that if the island was subject to these earthquakes, there would be no living for me in a cave, but I must consider of building a little hut in an open place which I might surround with a wall, as I had done here, and so make myself secure from wild beasts or men; for I concluded, if I stayed where I was, I should certainly one time or other be buried alive.

With these thoughts, I resolved to remove my tent from the place where it stood, which was just under the hanging precipice of the hill; and which, if it should be shaken again, would certainly fall upon my tent; and I spent the two next days, being the 19th and 20th of April, in contriving where and how to remove my habitation. The fear of being swallowed up alive made me that I never slept in quiet; and yet the apprehension of lying abroad without any fence was almost equal to it; but still, when I looked about, and saw how everything was put in order, how pleasantly concealed I was, and how safe from danger, it made me very loath to remove. In the meantime, it occurred to me that it would require a vast deal of time for me to do this, and that I must be contented to venture where I was, till I had formed a camp for myself, and had secured it so as to remove to it. So with this resolution I composed myself for a time, and resolved that I would go to work with all speed to build me a wall with piles and cables, &c. in a circle, as before, and set my tent up in it when it was finished; but that I would venture to stay where I was till it was finished, and fit to remove. This was the 21st.

April 22. – The next morning I begin to consider of means to put this resolve into execution; but I was at a great loss about my tools. I had three large axes, and abundance of hatchets (for we carried the hatchets for traffic with the Indians); but with much chopping and cutting knotty hard wood, they were all full of notches, and dull; and though I had a grindstone, I could not turn it and grind my tools too. This cost me as much thought as a statesman would have bestowed upon a grand point of politics, or a judge upon the life and death of a man. At length I contrived a wheel with a string, to turn it with my foot, that I might have both my hands at liberty.

Note. – I had never seen any such thing in England, or at least, not to take notice how it was done, though since I have observed, it is very common there; besides that, my grindstone was very large and heavy. This machine cost me a full week's work to bring it to perfection.

April 28, 29. – These two whole days I took up in grinding my tools, my machine for turning my grindstone performing very well.

April 30. – Having perceived my bread had been low a great while, now I took a survey of it, and reduced myself to one biscuit cake a day, which made my heart very heavy.

May 1. – In the morning, looking towards the sea side, the tide being low, I saw something lie on the shore bigger than ordinary, and it looked like a cask; when I came to it, I found a small barrel, and two or three pieces of the wreck of the ship, which were driven on shore by the late hurricane; and looking towards the wreck itself, I thought it seemed to lie higher out of the water than it used to do. I examined the barrel which was driven on shore, and soon found it was a barrel of gunpowder; but it had taken water, and the powder was caked as hard as a stone; however, I rolled it farther on shore for the present, and went on upon the sands, as near as I could to the wreck of the ship, to look for more.

CHAPTER SIX

Ill and Conscience-Stricken

WHEN I CAME DOWN TO THE SHIP I found it strangely removed. The forecastle, which lay before buried in sand, was heaved up at least six feet, and the stern, which was broke in pieces and parted from the rest by the force of the sea, soon after I had left rummaging her, was tossed as it were up, and cast on one side; and the sand was thrown so high on that side next her stern, that whereas there was a great place of water before, so that I could not come within a quarter of a mile of the wreck without swimming I could now walk quite up to her when the tide was out. I was surprised with this at first, but soon concluded it must be done by the earthquake; and as by this violence the ship was more broke open than formerly, so many things came daily on shore, which the sea had loosened, and which the winds and water rolled by degrees to the land.

This wholly diverted my thoughts from the design of removing my habitation, and I busied myself mightily, that day especially, in searching whether I could make any way into the ship; but I found nothing was to be expected of that kind, for all the inside of the ship was choked up with sand. However, as I had learned not to despair of anything, I resolved to pull everything to pieces that I could of the ship, concluding that everything I could get from her would be of some use or other to me.

MAY 3. – I began with my saw, and cut a piece of a beam through, which I thought held some of the upper part or quarter-deck together, and when I had cut it through, I cleared away the sand as well as I could from the side which lay highest; but the tide coming in, I was obliged to give over for that time.

May 4. – I went a-fishing, but caught not one fish that I durst eat of, till I was weary of my sport; when, just going to leave off, I caught a young dolphin. I had made me a long line of some rope-yarn, but I had no hooks; yet I frequently caught fish enough, as much as I cared to eat; all which I dried in the sun, and ate them dry.

May 5. – Worked on the wreck; cut another beam asunder, and brought three great fir planks off from the decks, which I tied together, and made to float on shore when the tide of flood came on.

May 6. – Worked on the wreck; got several iron bolts out of her and other pieces of ironwork. Worked very hard, and came home very much tired, and had thoughts of giving it over.

May 7. – Went to the wreck again, not with an intent to work, but found the weight of the wreck had broke itself down, the beams being cut; that several pieces of the ship seemed to lie loose, and the inside of the hold lay so open that I could see into it; but it was almost full of water and sand.

May 8. – Went to the wreck, and carried an iron crow to wrench up the deck, which lay now quite clear of the water or sand. I wrenched open two planks, and brought them on shore also with the tide. I left the iron crow in the wreck for next day.

May 9. – Went to the wreck, and with the crow made way into the body of the wreck, and felt several casks, and loosened them with the crow, but could not break them up. I felt also a roll of English lead, and could stir it, but it was too heavy to remove.

May 10-14. – Went every day to the wreck; and got a great many pieces of timber, and boards, or plank, and two or three hundredweight of iron.

May 15. – I carried two hatchets, to try if I could not cut a piece off the roll of lead by placing the edge of one hatchet and driving it with the other; but as it lay about a foot and a half in the water, I could not make any blow to drive the hatchet.

May 16. – It had blown hard in the night, and the wreck appeared more broken by the force of the water; but I stayed so long in the woods, to get pigeons for food, that the tide prevented my going to the wreck that day.

May 17. – I saw some pieces of the wreck blown on shore, at a great distance, near two miles off me, but resolved to see what they were, and found it was a piece of the head, but too heavy for me to bring away.

May 24. – Every day, to this day, I worked on the wreck; and with hard labour I loosened some things so much with the crow, that the first flowing tide several casks floated out, and two of the seamen's chests;

but the wind blowing from the shore, nothing came to land that day but pieces of timber, and a hogshead, which had some Brazil pork in it; but the salt water and the sand had spoiled it. I continued this work every day to the 15th of June, except the time necessary to get food, which I always appointed, during this part of my employment, to be when the tide was up, that I might be ready when it was ebbed out; and by this time I had got timber and plank and ironwork enough to have built a good boat, if I had known how; and also I got, at several times and in several pieces, near one hundredweight of the sheet lead.

June 16. – Going down to the seaside, I found a large tortoise or turtle. This was the first I had seen, which, it seems, was only my misfortune, not any defect of the place, or scarcity; for had I happened to be on the other side of the island, I might have had hundreds of them every day, as I found afterwards; but perhaps had paid dear enough for them.

June 17. – I spent in cooking the turtle. I found in her three-score eggs; and her flesh was to me, at that time, the most savoury and pleasant that ever I tasted in my life, having had no flesh, but of goats and fowls, since I landed in this horrid place.

June 18. – Rained all day, and I stayed within. I thought at this time the rain felt cold, and I was something chilly; which I knew was not usual in that latitude.

June 19. – Very ill, and shivering, as if the weather had been cold.

June 20. – No rest all night; violent pains in my head, and feverish.

June 21. – Very ill; frighted almost to death with the apprehensions of my sad condition – to be sick, and no help. Prayed to God, for the first time since the storm off Hull, but scarce knew what I said, or why, my thoughts being all confused.

June 22. – A little better; but under dreadful apprehensions of sickness.

June 22. – Very bad again; cold and shivering, and then a violent headache.

June 24. – Much better.

June 25. – An ague very violent; the fit held me seven hours; cold fit and hot, with faint sweats after it.

June 26. – Better; and having no victuals to eat, took my gun, but found myself very weak. However, I killed a she-goat, and with much difficulty got it home, and broiled some of it, and ate, I would fain have stewed it, and made some broth, but had no pot.

June 27. – The ague again so violent that I lay a-bed all day, and neither ate nor drank. I was ready to perish for thirst; but so weak, I had not strength to stand up, or to get myself any water to drink. Prayed to God again, but was light-headed; and when I was not, I was so ignorant that I knew not what to say; only I lay and cried, "Lord, look upon me! Lord, pity me! Lord, have mercy upon me!" I suppose I did nothing else for two or three hours; till, the fit wearing off, I fell asleep, and did not wake till far in the night. When I awoke, I found myself much refreshed, but weak, and exceeding thirsty. However, as I had no water in my habitation, I was forced to lie till morning, and went to sleep again. In this second sleep I had this terrible dream: I thought that I was sitting on the ground, on the outside of my wall, where I sat when the storm blew after the earthquake, and that I saw a man descend from a great black cloud, in a bright flame of fire, and light upon the ground. He was all over as bright as a flame, so that I could but just bear to look towards him; his countenance was most inexpressibly dreadful, impossible for words to describe. When he stepped upon the ground with his feet, I thought the earth trembled, just as it had done before in the earthquake, and all the air looked, to my apprehension, as if it had been filled with flashes of fire. He was no sooner landed upon the earth, but he moved forward towards me, with a long spear or weapon in his hand, to kill me; and when he came to a rising ground, at some distance, he spoke to me – or I heard a voice so terrible that it is impossible to express the terror of it. All that I can say I understood was this: "Seeing all these things have not brought thee to repentance, now thou shalt die;" at which words, I thought he lifted up the spear that was in his hand to kill me.

No one that shall ever read this account will expect that I should be able to describe the horrors of my soul at this terrible vision. I mean, that even while it was a dream, I even dreamed of those horrors. Nor is it any more possible to describe the impression that remained upon my mind when I awaked, and found it was but a dream.

I had, alas! no divine knowledge. What I had received by the good instruction of my father was then worn out by an uninterrupted series, for eight years, of seafaring wickedness, and a constant conversation with none but such as were, like myself, wicked and profane to the last degree. I do not remember that I had, in all that time, one thought that so much as tended either to looking upwards towards God, or inwards towards a reflection upon my own ways; but a certain stupidity of soul, without desire of good, or conscience of evil, had entirely overwhelmed me; and I was all that the most hardened, unthinking, wicked creature among our common sailors can be supposed to be; not having the least sense, either of the fear of God in danger, or of thankfulness to God in deliverance.

In the relating what is already past of my story, this will be the more easily believed when I shall add, that through all the variety of miseries that had to this day befallen me, I never had so much as one thought of it being the hand of God, or that it was a just punishment for my sin – my rebellious behaviour against my father – or my present sins, which were great – or so much as a punishment for the general course of my wicked life. When I was on the desperate expedition on the desert shores of Africa, I never had so much as one thought of what would become of me, or one wish to God to direct me whither I should go, or to keep me from the danger which apparently surrounded me, as well from voracious creatures as cruel savages. But I was merely thoughtless of a God or a Providence, acted like a mere brute, from the principles of nature, and by the dictates of common sense only, and, indeed, hardly that. When I was delivered and taken up at sea by the Portugal Captain, well used, and dealt justly and honourably with, as well as charitably, I had not the least thankfulness in my thoughts. When, again, I was shipwrecked, ruined, and in danger of drowning on this island, I was as far from remorse, or looking on it as a judgment. I only said to myself often, that I was an unfortunate dog, and born to be always miserable.

It is true, when I got on shore first here, and found all my ship's crew drowned and myself spared, I was surprised with a kind of ecstasy, and some transports of soul, which, had the grace of God assisted, might have come up to true thankfulness; but it ended where it began, in a mere common flight of joy, or, as I may say, being glad I was alive, without the least reflection upon the distinguished goodness of the hand which had preserved me, and had singled me out to be preserved when all the rest were destroyed, or an inquiry why Providence had been thus merciful unto me. Even just the same common sort of joy which seamen generally have, after they are got safe ashore from a shipwreck, which they drown all in the next bowl of punch, and forget almost as soon as it is over; and all the rest of my life was like it. Even when I was afterwards, on due consideration, made sensible of my condition, how I was cast on this dreadful place, out of the reach of human kind, out of all hope of relief, or prospect of redemption, as soon as I saw but a prospect of living and that I should not starve and perish for hunger, all the sense of my affliction wore off; and I began to be very easy, applied myself to the works proper for my preservation and supply, and was far enough from being afflicted at my condition, as a judgment from heaven, or as the hand of God against me: these were thoughts which very seldom entered my head.

The growing up of the corn, as is hinted in my Journal, had at first some little influence upon me, and began to affect me with seriousness, as long as I thought it had something miraculous in it; but as soon as ever that part of the thought was removed, all the impression that was raised from it wore off also, as I have noted already.

Even the earthquake, though nothing could be more terrible in its nature, or more immediately directing to the invisible Power which alone directs such things, yet no sooner was the first fright over, but the impression it had made went off also. I had no more sense of God or His judgments – much less of the present affliction of my circumstances being from His hand – than if I had been in the most prosperous condition of life.

But now, when I began to be sick, and a leisurely view of the miseries of death came to place itself before me; when my spirits began to sink under the burden of a strong distemper, and nature was exhausted with the violence of the fever; conscience, that had slept so long, began to awake, and I began to reproach myself with my past life, in which I had so evidently, by uncommon wickedness, provoked the justice of God to lay me under uncommon strokes, and to deal with me in so vindictive a manner.

These reflections oppressed me for the second or third day of my distemper; and in the violence, as well of the fever as of the dreadful reproaches of my conscience, extorted some words from me like praying to God, though I cannot say they were either a prayer attended with desires or with hopes: it was rather the voice of mere fright and distress. My thoughts were confused, the convictions great upon my mind, and the horror of dying in such a miserable condition raised vapours into my head with the mere apprehensions; and in these hurries of my soul I knew not what my tongue might express. But it was rather exclamation, such as, "Lord, what a miserable creature am I! If I should be sick, I shall certainly die for want of help; and what will become of me!" Then the tears burst out of my eyes, and I could say no more for a good while.

In this interval the good advice of my father came to my mind, and presently his prediction, which I mentioned at the beginning of this story – *viz.* that if I did take this foolish step, God would not bless me, and I would have leisure hereafter to reflect upon having neglected his counsel when there might be none to assist in my recovery. "Now," said I, aloud, "my dear father's words are come to pass; God's justice has overtaken me, and I have none to help or hear me. I rejected the voice of Providence, which had mercifully put me in a posture or station of life wherein I might have been happy and easy; but I would neither see it myself nor learn to know the blessing of it from my parents. I left them to mourn over my folly, and now I am left to mourn under the consequences of it. I abused their help and assistance, who would have lifted me in the world, and would have made everything easy to me; and now I have difficulties to struggle with, too great for even nature itself to support, and no assistance, no help, no comfort, no advice."

Then I cried out, "Lord, be my help, for I am in great distress." This was the first prayer, if I may call it so, that I had made for many years. But to return to my Journal.

June 28. – Having been somewhat refreshed with the sleep I had had, and the fit being entirely off, I got up; and though the fright and terror of my dream was very great, yet I considered that the fit of the ague would return again the next day, and now was my time to get something to refresh and support myself when I should be ill; and the first thing I did, I filled a large square case-bottle with water, and set it upon my table, in reach of my bed; and to take off the chill or aguish disposition of the water, I put about a quarter of a pint of rum into it, and mixed them together. Then I got me a piece of the goat's flesh and broiled it on the coals, but could eat very little. I walked about, but was very weak, and withal very sad and heavy-hearted under a sense of my miserable condition, dreading, the return of my distemper the next day. At night I made my supper of three of the turtle's eggs, which I roasted in the ashes, and ate, as we call it, in the shell, and this was the first bit of meat I had ever asked God's blessing to, that I could remember, in my whole life.

After I had eaten I tried to walk, but found myself so weak that I could hardly carry a gun, for I never went out without that; so I went but a little way, and sat down upon the ground, looking out upon the sea, which was just before me, and very calm and smooth. As I sat here some such thoughts as these occurred to me: What is this earth and sea, of which I have seen so much? Whence is it produced? And what am I, and all the other creatures wild and tame, human and brutal? Whence are we? Sure we are all made by some secret Power, who formed the earth and sea, the air and sky. And who is that? Then it followed most naturally, it is God that has made all. Well, but then it came on strangely, if God has made all these things, He guides and governs them all, and all things that concern them; for the power that could make all things must certainly have power to guide and direct them. If so, nothing can happen in the great circuit of His works, either without His knowledge or appointment.

And if nothing happens without His knowledge, He knows that I am here, and am in this dreadful condition; and if nothing happens without His appointment, He has appointed all this to befall me. Nothing occurred to my thought to contradict any of these conclusions, and therefore it rested upon me with the greater force, that it must needs be that God had appointed all this to befall me; that I was brought into this miserable circumstance by His direction, He having the sole power, not of me only, but of everything that happened in the world. Immediately it followed: Why has God done this to me? What have I done to be thus used? My conscience presently checked me in that inquiry, as if I had blasphemed, and methought it spoke to me like a voice: "Wretch! dost thou ask what thou hast done? Look back upon a dreadful misspent life, and ask thyself what thou hast not done? Ask, why is it that thou wert not long ago destroyed? Why wert thou not drowned in Yarmouth Roads; killed in the fight when the ship was taken by the Sallee man-of-war; devoured by the wild beasts on the coast of Africa; or drowned here, when all the crew perished but thyself? Dost thou ask, what have I done?"

I was struck dumb with these reflections, as one astonished, and had not a word to say – no, not to answer to myself, but rose up pensive and sad, walked back to my retreat, and went up over my wall, as if I had been going to bed; but my thoughts were sadly disturbed, and I had no inclination to sleep; so I sat down in my chair, and lighted my lamp, for it began to be dark. Now, as the apprehension of the return of my distemper terrified me very much, it occurred to my thought that the Brazilians take no physic but their tobacco for almost all distempers, and I had a piece of a roll of tobacco in one of the chests, which was quite cured, and some also that was green, and not quite cured.

I went, directed by Heaven no doubt; for in this chest I found a cure both for soul and body. I opened the chest, and found what I looked for, the tobacco; and as the few books I had saved lay there too, I took out one of the Bibles which I mentioned before, and which to this time I had not found leisure or inclination to look into. I say, I took it out, and brought both that and the tobacco with me to the table.

What use to make of the tobacco I knew not, in my distemper, or whether it was good for it or no: but I tried several experiments with it, as if I was resolved it should hit one way or other. I first took a piece of leaf, and chewed it in my mouth, which, indeed, at first almost stupefied my brain, the tobacco being green and strong, and that I had not been much used to. Then I took some and steeped it an hour or two in some rum, and resolved to take a dose of it when I lay down; and lastly, I burnt some upon a pan of coals, and held my nose close over the smoke of it as long as I could bear it, as well for the heat as almost for suffocation.

In the interval of this operation I took up the Bible and began to read; but my head was too much disturbed with the tobacco to bear reading, at least at that time; only, having opened the book casually, the first words that occurred to me were these, "Call on Me in the day of trouble, and I will deliver thee, and thou shalt glorify Me."

These words were very apt to my case, and made some impression upon my thoughts at the time of reading them, though not so much as they did afterwards; for, as for being delivered, the word had no sound, as I may say, to me; the thing was so remote, so impossible in my apprehension of things, that I began to say, as the children of Israel did when they were promised flesh to eat, "Can God spread a table in the wilderness?" so I began to say, "Can God Himself deliver me from this place?" And as it was not for many years that any hopes appeared, this prevailed very often upon my thoughts; but, however, the words made a great impression upon me, and I mused upon them very often. It grew now late, and the tobacco had, as I said, dozed my head so much that I inclined to sleep; so I left my lamp burning in the cave, lest I should want anything in the night, and went to bed. But before I lay down, I did what I never had done in all my life – I kneeled down, and prayed to God to fulfil the promise to me, that if I called upon Him in the day of trouble, He would deliver me. After my broken and imperfect prayer was over, I drank the rum in which I had steeped the tobacco, which was so strong and rank of the tobacco that I could scarcely get it down; immediately upon this I went to bed. I found presently it flew up into my head violently; but I fell into a sound sleep, and waked no more till, by the sun, it must necessarily be near three o'clock in the afternoon the next day – nay, to this hour I am partly of opinion that I slept all the next day and night, and till almost three the day after; for otherwise I know not how I should lose a day out of my reckoning in the days of the week, as it appeared some years after I had done; for if I had lost it by crossing and recrossing the line, I should have lost more than one day; but certainly I lost a day in my account, and never knew which way. Be that, however, one way or the other, when I awaked I found myself exceedingly refreshed, and my spirits lively and cheerful; when I got up I was stronger than I was the day before, and my stomach better, for I was hungry; and, in short, I had no fit the next day, but continued much altered for the better. This was the 29th.

The 30th was my well day, of course, and I went abroad with my gun, but did not care to travel too far. I killed a sea-fowl or two, something like a brandgoose, and brought them home, but was not very forward to eat them; so I ate some more of the turtle's eggs, which were very good. This evening I renewed the medicine, which I had supposed did me good the day before – the tobacco steeped in rum; only I did not take so much as before, nor did I chew any of the leaf, or hold my head over the smoke; however, I was not so well the next day, which was the first of July, as I hoped I should have been; for I had a little spice of the cold fit, but it was not much.

July 2. – I renewed the medicine all the three ways; and dosed myself with it as at first, and doubled the quantity which I drank.

July 3. – I missed the fit for good and all, though I did not recover my full strength for some weeks after. While I was thus gathering strength, my thoughts ran exceedingly upon this Scripture, "I will deliver thee"; and the impossibility of my deliverance lay much upon my mind, in bar of my ever expecting it; but as I was discouraging myself with such thoughts, it occurred to my mind that I pored so much upon my deliverance from the main affliction, that I disregarded the deliverance I had received, and I was as it were made to ask myself such questions as these – *viz.* Have I not been delivered, and wonderfully too, from sickness – from the most distressed condition that could be, and that was so frightful to me, and what notice had I taken of it? Had I done my part? God had delivered me, but I had not glorified Him – that is to say, I had not owned and been thankful for that as a deliverance; and how could I expect greater deliverance? This touched my heart very much; and immediately I knelt down and gave God thanks aloud for my recovery from my sickness.

July 4. – In the morning I took the Bible; and beginning at the New Testament, I began seriously to read it, and imposed upon myself to read a while every morning and every night; not tying myself to the number of chapters, but long as my thoughts should engage me. It was not long after I set seriously to this work till I found my heart more deeply and sincerely affected with the wickedness of my past life. The impression of my dream revived; and the words, "All these things have not brought thee to repentance," ran seriously through my thoughts. I was earnestly begging of God to give me repentance, when it happened providentially, the very day, that, reading the Scripture, I came to these words: "He is exalted a Prince and a Saviour, to give repentance and to give remission." I threw down the book; and with my heart as well as my hands lifted up to heaven, in a kind of ecstasy of joy, I cried out aloud, "Jesus, thou son of David! Jesus, thou exalted Prince and Saviour! give me repentance!" This was the first time I could say, in the true sense of the words, that I prayed in all my life; for now I prayed with a sense of my condition, and a true Scripture view of hope, founded on the encouragement of the Word of God; and from this time, I may say, I began to hope that God would hear me.

Now I began to construe the words mentioned above, "Call on Me, and I will deliver thee," in a different sense from what I had ever done before; for then I had no notion of anything being called deliverance, but my being delivered from the captivity I was in; for though I was indeed at large in the place, yet the island was certainly a prison to me, and that in the worse sense in the world. But now I learned to take it in another sense: now I looked back upon my past life with such horror, and my sins appeared so dreadful, that my soul sought nothing of God but deliverance from the load of guilt that bore down all my comfort. As for my solitary life, it was nothing. I did not so much as pray to be delivered from it or think of it; it was all of no consideration in comparison to this. And I add this part here, to hint to whoever shall read it, that whenever they come to a true sense of things, they will find deliverance from sin a much greater blessing than deliverance from affliction.

But, leaving this part, I return to my Journal.

My condition began now to be, though not less miserable as to my way of living, yet much easier to my mind: and my thoughts being directed, by a constant reading the Scripture and praying to God, to things of a higher nature, I had a great deal of comfort within, which till now I knew nothing of; also, my health and strength returned, I bestirred myself to furnish myself with everything that I wanted, and make my way of living as regular as I could.

From the 4th of July to the 14th I was chiefly employed in walking about with my gun in my hand, a little and a little at a time, as a man that was gathering up his strength after a fit of sickness; for it is hardly to be imagined how low I was, and to what weakness I was reduced. The application which I made use of was perfectly new, and perhaps which had never cured an ague before; neither can I recommend it to any to practise, by this experiment: and though it did carry off the fit, yet it rather contributed to weakening me; for I had frequent convulsions in my nerves and limbs for some time. I learned from it also this, in particular, that being abroad in the rainy season was the most pernicious thing to my health that could be, especially in those rains which came attended with storms and hurricanes of wind; for as the rain which came in the dry season was almost always accompanied with such storms, so I found that rain was much more dangerous than the rain which fell in September and October.

CHAPTER SEVEN

Agricultural Experience

I HAD NOW BEEN IN THIS UNHAPPY ISLAND above ten months. All possibility of deliverance from this condition seemed to be entirely taken from me; and I firmly believe that no human shape had ever set foot upon that place. Having now secured my habitation, as I thought, fully to my mind, I had a great desire to make a more perfect discovery of the island, and to see what other productions I might find, which I yet knew nothing of.

It was on the 15th of July that I began to take a more particular survey of the island itself. I went up the creek first, where, as I hinted, I brought my rafts on shore. I found after I came about two miles up, that the tide did not flow any higher, and that it was no more than a little brook of running water, very fresh and good; but this being the dry season, there was hardly any water in some parts of it – at least not enough to run in any stream, so as it could be perceived. On the banks of this brook I found many pleasant savannahs or meadows, plain, smooth, and covered with grass; and on the rising parts of them, next to the higher grounds, where the water, as might be supposed, never overflowed, I found a great deal of tobacco, green, and growing to a great and very strong stalk. There were divers other plants, which I had no notion of or understanding about, that might, perhaps, have virtues of their own, which I could not find out. I searched for the cassava root, which the Indians, in all that climate, make their bread of, but I could find none. I saw large plants of aloes, but did not understand them. I saw several sugar-canes, but wild, and, for want of cultivation, imperfect. I contented myself with these discoveries for this time, and came back, musing with myself what course I might take to know the virtue and goodness of any of the fruits or plants which I should discover, but could bring it to no conclusion; for, in short, I had made so little observation while I was in the Brazils, that I knew little of the plants in the field; at least, very little that might serve to any purpose now in my distress.

The next day, the 16th, I went up the same way again; and after going something further than I had gone the day before, I found the brook and the savannahs cease, and the country become more woody than before. In this part I found different fruits, and particularly I found melons upon the ground, in great abundance, and grapes upon the trees. The vines had spread, indeed, over the trees, and the clusters of grapes were just now in their prime, very ripe and rich. This was a surprising discovery, and I was exceeding glad of them; but I was warned by my experience to eat sparingly of them; remembering that when I was ashore in Barbary, the eating of grapes killed several of our Englishmen, who were slaves there, by throwing them into fluxes and fevers. But I found an excellent use for these grapes; and that was, to cure or dry them in the sun, and keep them as dried grapes or raisins are kept, which I thought would be, as indeed they were, wholesome and agreeable to eat when no grapes could be had.

I spent all that evening there, and went not back to my habitation; which, by the way, was the first night, as I might say, I had lain from home. In the night, I took my first contrivance, and got up in a tree, where I slept well; and the next morning proceeded upon my discovery; travelling nearly four miles, as I might judge by the length of the valley, keeping still due north, with a ridge of hills on the south and north side of me. At the end of this march I came to an opening where the country seemed to descend to the west; and a little spring of fresh water, which issued out of the side of the hill by me, ran the other way, that is, due east; and the country appeared so fresh, so green, so flourishing, everything being in a constant verdure or flourish of spring that it looked like a planted garden. I descended a little on the side of that delicious vale, surveying it with a secret kind of pleasure, though mixed with my other afflicting thoughts, to think that this was all my own; that I was king and lord of all this country indefensibly, and had a right of possession; and if I could convey it, I might have it in inheritance as completely as any lord of a manor in England. I saw here abundance of cocoa trees, orange, and lemon, and citron trees; but all wild, and very few bearing any fruit, at least not then. However, the green limes that I gathered were not only pleasant to eat, but very wholesome; and I mixed their juice afterwards with water, which made it very wholesome, and very cool and refreshing. I found now I had business enough to gather and carry home; and I resolved to lay up a store as well of grapes as limes and lemons, to furnish myself for the wet season, which I knew was approaching. In order to do this, I gathered a great heap of grapes in one place, a lesser heap in another place, and a great parcel of limes and lemons in another place; and taking a few of each with me, I travelled homewards; resolving to come again, and bring a bag or sack, or what I could make, to carry the rest home. Accordingly, having spent three days in this journey, I came home (so I must now call my tent and my cave); but before I got thither the grapes were spoiled; the richness of the fruit and the weight of the juice having broken them and bruised them, they were good for little or nothing; as to the limes, they were good, but I could bring but a few.

The next day, being the 19th, I went back, having made me two small bags to bring home my harvest; but I was surprised, when coming to my heap of grapes, which were so rich and fine when I gathered them, to find them all spread about, trod to pieces, and dragged about, some here, some there, and abundance eaten and devoured. By this I concluded there were some wild creatures thereabouts, which had done this; but what they were I knew not. However, as I found there was no laying them up on heaps, and no carrying them away in a sack, but that one way they would be destroyed, and the other way they would be crushed with their own weight, I took another course; for I gathered a large quantity of the grapes, and hung them trees, that they might cure and dry in the sun; and as for the limes and lemons, I carried as many back as I could well stand under.

When I came home from this journey, I contemplated with great pleasure the fruitfulness of that valley, and the pleasantness of the situation; the security from storms on that side of the water, and the wood: and concluded that I had pitched upon a place to fix my abode which was by far the worst part of the country. Upon the whole, I began to consider of removing my habitation, and looking out for a place equally safe as where now I was situate, if possible, in that pleasant, fruitful part of the island.

This thought ran long in my head, and I was exceeding fond of it for some time, the pleasantness of the place tempting me; but when I came to a nearer view of it, I considered that I was now by the seaside, where it was at least possible that something might happen to my advantage, and, by the same ill fate that brought me hither might bring some other unhappy wretches to the same place; and though it was scarce probable that any such thing should ever happen, yet to enclose myself among the hills and woods in the centre of the island was to anticipate my bondage, and to render such an affair not only improbable, but impossible; and that therefore I ought not by any means to remove. However, I was so enamoured of this place, that I spent much of my time there for the whole of the remaining part of the month of July; and though upon second thoughts, I resolved not to remove, yet I built me a little kind of a bower, and surrounded it at a distance with a strong fence, being a double hedge, as high as I could reach, well staked and filled between with brushwood; and here I lay very secure, sometimes two or three nights together; always going over it with a ladder; so that I fancied now I had my country house and my sea-coast house; and this work took me up to the beginning of August.

I had but newly finished my fence, and began to enjoy my labour, when the rains came on, and made me stick close to my first habitation; for though I had made me a tent like the other, with a piece of a sail, and spread it very well, yet I had not the shelter of a hill to keep me from storms, nor a cave behind me to retreat into when the rains were extraordinary.

About the beginning of August, as I said, I had finished my bower, and began to enjoy myself. The 3rd of August, I found the grapes I had hung up perfectly dried, and, indeed, were excellent good raisins of the sun; so I began to take them down from the trees, and it was very happy that I did so, for the rains which followed would have spoiled them, and I had lost the best part of my winter food; for I had above 200 large bunches of them. No sooner had I taken them all down, and carried the most of them home to my cave, than it began to rain; and from hence, which was the 14th of August, it rained, more or less, every day till the middle of October; and sometimes so violently, that I could not stir out of my cave for several days.

In this season I was much surprised with the increase of my family; I had been concerned for the loss of one of my cats, who ran away from me, or, as I thought, had been dead, and I heard no more tidings of her till, to my astonishment, she came home about the end of August with three kittens. This was the more strange to me because, though I had killed a wild cat, as I called it, with my gun, yet I thought it was quite a different kind from our European cats; but the young cats were the same kind of house-breed as the old one; and both my cats being females, I thought it very strange. But from these three cats I afterwards came to be so pestered with cats that I was forced to kill them like vermin or wild beasts, and to drive them from my house as much as possible.

From the 14th of August to the 26th, incessant rain, so that I could not stir, and was now very careful not to be much wet. In this confinement, I began to be straitened for food: but venturing out twice, I one day killed a goat; and the last day, which was the 26th, found a very large tortoise, which was a treat to me, and my food was regulated thus: I ate a bunch of raisins for my breakfast; a piece of the goat's flesh, or of the turtle, for my dinner, broiled – for, to my great misfortune, I had no vessel to boil or stew anything; and two or three of the turtle's eggs for my supper.

During this confinement in my cover by the rain, I worked daily two or three hours at enlarging my cave, and by degrees worked it on towards one side, till I came to the outside of the hill, and made a door or way out, which came beyond my fence or wall; and so I came in and out this way. But I was not perfectly easy at lying so open; for, as I had managed myself before, I was in a perfect enclosure; whereas now I thought I lay exposed, and open for anything to come in upon me; and yet I could not perceive that there was any living thing to fear, the biggest creature that I had yet seen upon the island being a goat.

September 30. – I was now come to the unhappy anniversary of my landing. I cast up the notches on my post, and found I had been on shore 365 days. I kept this day as a solemn fast, setting it apart for religious exercise, prostrating myself on the ground with the most serious humiliation, confessing my sins to God, acknowledging His righteous judgments upon me, and praying to Him to have mercy on me through Jesus Christ; and not having tasted the least refreshment for twelve hours, even till the going down of the sun, I then ate a biscuit-cake and a bunch of grapes, and went to bed, finishing the day as I began it. I had all this time observed no Sabbath day; for as at first I had no sense of religion upon my mind, I had, after some time, omitted to distinguish the weeks, by making a longer notch than ordinary for the Sabbath day, and so did not really know what any of the days were; but now, having cast up the days as above, I found I had been there a year; so I divided it into weeks, and set apart every 7th day for a Sabbath; though I found at the end of my account I had lost a day or two in my reckoning. A little after this, my ink began to fail me, and so I contented myself to use it more sparingly, and to write down only the most remarkable events of my life, without continuing a daily memorandum of other things.

The rainy season and the dry season began now to appear regular to me, and I learned to divide them so as to provide for them accordingly; but I bought all my experience before I had it, and this I am going to relate was one of the most discouraging experiments that I made.

I have mentioned that I had saved the few ears of barley and rice, which I had so surprisingly found spring up, as I thought, of themselves, and I believe there were about 30 stalks of rice, and about 20 of barley; and now I thought it a proper time to sow it, after the rains, the sun being in its southern position, going from me. Accordingly, I dug up a piece of ground as well as I could with my wooden spade, and dividing it into two parts, I sowed my grain; but as I was sowing, it casually occurred to my thoughts that I would not sow it all at first, because I did not know when was the proper time for it, so I sowed about two-thirds of the seed, leaving about a handful of each. It was a great comfort to me afterwards that I did so, for not one grain of what I sowed this time came to anything: for the dry months following, the earth having had no rain after the seed was sown, it had no moisture to assist its growth, and never came up at all till the wet season had come again, and then it grew as if it had been but newly sown. Finding my first seed did not grow, which I easily imagined was by the drought, I sought for a moister piece of ground to make another trial in, and I dug up a piece of ground near my new bower, and sowed the rest of my seed in February, a little before the vernal equinox; and this having the rainy months of March and April to water it, sprung up very pleasantly, and yielded a very good crop; but having part of the seed left only, and not daring to sow all that I had, I had but a small quantity at last, my whole crop not amounting to above half a peck of each kind. But by this experiment I was made Master of my business, and knew exactly when the proper season was to sow, and that I might expect two seed-times and two harvests every year.

While this corn was growing I made a little discovery, which was of use to me afterwards. As soon as the rains were over, and the weather began to settle, which was about the month of November, I made a visit up the country to my bower, where, though I had not been some months, yet I found all things just as I left them. The circle or double hedge that I had made was not only firm and entire, but the stakes which I had cut out of some trees that grew thereabouts were all shot out and grown with long branches, as much as a willow-tree usually shoots the first year after lopping its head. I could not tell what tree to call it that these stakes were cut from. I was surprised, and yet very well pleased, to see the young trees grow; and I pruned them, and led them up to grow as much alike as I could; and it is scarce credible how beautiful a figure they grew into in three years; so that though the hedge made a circle of about 25 yards in diameter, yet the trees, for such I might now call them, soon covered it, and it was a complete shade, sufficient to lodge under all the dry season. This made me resolve to cut some more stakes, and make me a hedge like this, in a semi-circle round my wall

(I mean that of my first dwelling), which I did; and placing the trees or stakes in a double row, at about 8 yards distance from my first fence, they grew presently, and were at first a fine cover to my habitation, and afterwards served for a defence also, as I shall observe in its order.

I found now that the seasons of the year might generally be divided, not into summer and winter, as in Europe, but into the rainy seasons and the dry seasons, which were generally thus: – The half of February, the whole of March, and the half of April – rainy, the sun being then on or near the equinox.

The half of April, the whole of May, June, and July, and the half of August – dry, the sun being then to the north of the line.

The half of August, the whole of September, and the half of October rainy, the sun being then come back.

The half of October, the whole of November, December, and January, and the half of February – dry, the sun being then to the south of the line.

The rainy seasons sometimes held longer or shorter as the winds happened to blow, but this was the general observation I made. After I had found by experience the ill consequences of being abroad in the rain, I took care to furnish myself with provisions beforehand, that I might not be obliged to go out, and I sat within doors as much as possible during the wet months. This time I found much employment, and very suitable also to the time, for I found great occasion for many things which I had no way to furnish myself with but by hard labour and constant application; particularly I tried many ways to make myself a basket, but all the twigs I could get for the purpose proved so brittle that they would do nothing. It proved of excellent advantage to me now, that when I was a boy, I used to take great delight in standing at a basket-maker's, in the town where my father lived, to see them make their wicker-ware; and being, as boys usually are, very officious to help, and a great observer of the manner in which they worked those things, and sometimes lending a hand, I had by these means full knowledge of the methods of it, and I wanted nothing but the materials, when it came into my mind that the twigs of that tree from whence I cut my stakes that grew might possibly be as tough as the sallows, willows, and osiers in England, and I resolved to try. Accordingly, the next day I went to my country house, as I called it, and cutting some of the smaller twigs, I found them to my purpose as much as I could desire; whereupon I came the next time prepared with a hatchet to cut down a quantity, which I soon found, for there was great plenty of them. These I set up to dry within my circle or hedge, and when they were fit for use I carried them to my cave; and here, during the next season, I employed myself in making, as well as I could, a great many baskets, both to carry earth or to carry or lay up anything, as I had occasion; and though I did not finish them very handsomely, yet I made them sufficiently serviceable for my purpose; thus, afterwards, I took care never to be without them; and as my wicker-ware decayed, I made more, especially strong, deep baskets to place my corn in, instead of sacks, when I should come to have any quantity of it.

Having mastered this difficulty, and employed a world of time about it, I bestirred myself to see, if possible, how to supply two wants. I had no vessels to hold anything that was liquid, except two runlets, which were almost full of rum, and some glass bottles, some of the common size, and others which were case bottles, square, for the holding of water, spirits, &c. I had not so much as a pot to boil anything, except a great kettle, which I saved out of the ship, and which was too big for such as I desired it – *viz.* to make broth, and stew a bit of meat by itself. The second thing I fain would have had was a tobacco-pipe, but it was impossible to me to make one; however, I found a contrivance for that, too, at last. I employed myself in planting my second rows of stakes or piles, and in this wicker-working all the summer or dry season, when another business took me up more time than it could be imagined I could spare.

CHAPTER EIGHT

Surveys His Position

I MENTIONED BEFORE THAT I HAD a great mind to see the whole island, and that I had travelled up the brook, and so on to where I built my bower, and where I had an opening quite to the sea, on the other side of the island. I now resolved to travel quite across to the sea-shore on that side; so, taking my gun, a hatchet, and my dog, and a larger quantity of powder and shot than usual, with two biscuit-cakes and a great bunch of raisins in my pouch for my store, I began my journey. When I had passed the vale where my bower stood, as above, I came within view of the sea to the west, and it being a very clear day, I fairly descried land - whether an island or a continent I could not tell; but it lay very high, extending from the W. to the W.S.W. at a very great distance; by my guess it could not be less than 15 or 20 leagues off.

I could not tell what part of the world this might be, otherwise than that I knew it must be part of America, and, as I concluded by all my observations, must be near the Spanish dominions, and perhaps was all inhabited by savages, where, if I had landed, I had been in a worse condition than I was now; and therefore I acquiesced in the dispositions of Providence, which I began now to own and to believe ordered everything for the best; I say I quieted my mind with this, and left off afflicting myself with fruitless wishes of being there.

Besides, after some thought upon this affair, I considered that if this land was the Spanish coast, I should certainly, one time or other, see some vessel pass or repass one way or other; but if not, then it was the savage coast between the Spanish country and Brazils, where are found the worst of savages; for they are cannibals or men-eaters, and fail not to murder and devour all the human bodies that fall into their hands.

With these considerations, I walked very leisurely forward. I found that side of the island where I now was much pleasanter than mine – the open or savannah fields sweet, adorned with flowers and grass, and full of very fine woods. I saw abundance of parrots, and fain I would have caught one, if possible, to have kept it to be tame, and taught it to speak to me. I did, after some painstaking, catch a young parrot, for I knocked it down with a stick, and having recovered it, I brought it home; but it was some years before I could make him speak; however, at last I taught him to call me by name very familiarly. But the accident that followed, though it be a trifle, will be very diverting in its place.

I was exceedingly diverted with this journey. I found in the low grounds hares (as I thought them to be) and foxes; but they differed greatly from all the other kinds I had met with, nor could I satisfy myself to eat them, though I killed several. But I had no need to be venturous, for I had no want of food, and of that which was very good too, especially these three sorts, *viz.* goats, pigeons, and turtle, or tortoise, which added to my grapes, Leaden-hall market could not have furnished a table better than I, in proportion to the company; and though my case was deplorable enough, yet I had great cause for thankfulness that I was not driven to any extremities for food, but had rather plenty, even to dainties.

I never travelled in this journey above two miles outright in a day, or thereabouts; but I took so many turns and re-turns to see what discoveries I could make, that I came weary enough to the place where I resolved to sit down all night; and then I either reposed myself in a tree, or surrounded myself with a row of stakes set upright in the ground, either from one tree to another, or so as no wild creature could come at me without waking me.

As soon as I came to the sea-shore, I was surprised to see that I had taken up my lot on the worst side of the island, for here, indeed, the shore was covered with innumerable turtles, whereas on the other side I had found but three in a year and a half. Here was also an infinite number of fowls of many kinds, some which I had seen, and some which I had not seen before, and many of them very good meat, but such as I knew not the names of, except those called penguins.

I could have shot as many as I pleased, but was very sparing of my powder and shot, and therefore had more mind to kill a she-goat if I could, which I could better feed on; and though there were many goats here, more than on my side the island, yet it was with much more difficulty that I could come near them, the country being flat and even, and they saw me much sooner than when I was on the hills.

I confess this side of the country was much pleasanter than mine; but yet I had not the least inclination to remove, for as I was fixed in my habitation it became natural to me, and I seemed all the while I was here to be as it were upon a journey, and from home. However, I travelled along the shore of the sea towards the east, I suppose about 12 miles, and then setting up a great pole upon the shore for a mark, I concluded I would go home again, and that the next journey I took should be on the other side of the island east from my dwelling, and so round till I came to my post again.

I took another way to come back than that I went, thinking I could easily keep all the island so much in my view that I could not miss finding my first dwelling by viewing the country; but I found myself mistaken, for being come about two or three miles, I found myself descended into a very large valley, but so surrounded with hills, and those hills covered with wood, that I could not see which was my way by any direction but that of the sun, nor even then, unless I knew very well the position of the sun at that time of the day. It happened, to my further misfortune, that the weather proved hazy for three or four days while I was in the valley, and not being able to see the sun, I wandered about very uncomfortably, and at last was obliged to find the seaside, look for my post, and come back the same way I went: and then, by easy journeys, I turned homeward, the weather being exceeding hot, and my gun, ammunition, hatchet, and other things very heavy.

In this journey my dog surprised a young kid, and seized upon it; and I, running in to take hold of it, caught it, and saved it alive from the dog. I had a great mind to bring it home if I could, for I had often been musing whether it might not be possible to get a kid or two, and so raise a breed of tame goats, which might supply me when my powder and shot should be all spent. I made a collar for this little creature, and with a string, which I made of some rope-yam, which I always carried about me, I led him along, though with some difficulty, till I came to my bower, and there I enclosed him and left him, for I was very impatient to be at home, from whence I had been absent above a month.

I cannot express what a satisfaction it was to me to come into my old hutch, and lie down in my hammock-bed. This little wandering journey, without settled place of abode, had been so unpleasant to me, that my own house, as I called it to myself, was a perfect settlement to me compared to that; and it rendered everything about me so comfortable, that I resolved I would never go a great way from it again while it should be my lot to stay on the island.

I reposed myself here a week, to rest and regale myself after my long journey; during which most of the time was taken up in the weighty affair of making a cage for my Poll, who began now to be a mere domestic, and to be well acquainted with me. Then I began to think of the poor kid which I had penned in within my little circle, and resolved to go and fetch it home, or give it some food; accordingly I went, and found it where I left it, for indeed it could not get out, but was almost starved for want of food. I went and cut boughs of trees, and branches of such shrubs as I could find, and threw it over, and having fed it, I tied it as I did before, to lead it away; but it was so tame with being hungry, that I had no need to have tied it, for it followed me like a dog: and as I continually fed it, the creature became so loving, so gentle, and so fond, that it became from that time one of my domestics also, and would never leave me afterwards.

The rainy season of the autumnal equinox was now come, and I kept the 30th of September in the same solemn manner as before, being the anniversary of my landing on the island, having now been there two years, and no more prospect of being delivered than the first day I came there, I spent the whole day in humble and thankful acknowledgments of the many wonderful mercies which my solitary condition was attended with, and without which it might have been infinitely more miserable. I gave humble and hearty thanks that God had been pleased to discover to me that it was possible I might be more happy in this solitary condition than I should have been in the liberty of society, and in all the pleasures of the world; that He could fully make up to me the deficiencies of my solitary state, and the want of human society, by His presence and the communications of His grace to my soul; supporting, comforting, and encouraging me to depend upon His providence here, and hope for His eternal presence hereafter.

It was now that I began sensibly to feel how much more happy this life I now led was, with all its miserable circumstances, than the wicked, cursed, abominable life I led all the past part of my days; and now I changed both my sorrows and my joys; my very desires altered, my affections changed their gusts, and my delights were perfectly new from what they were at my first coming, or, indeed, for the two years past.

Before, as I walked about, either on my hunting or for viewing the country, the anguish of my soul at my condition would break out upon me on a sudden, and my very heart would die within me, to think of the woods, the mountains, the deserts I was in, and how I was a prisoner, locked up with the eternal bars and bolts of the ocean, in an uninhabited wilderness, without redemption. In the midst of the greatest composure of my mind, this would break out upon me like a storm, and make me wring my hands and weep like a child. Sometimes it would take me in the middle of my work, and I would immediately sit down and sigh, and look upon the ground for an hour or two together; and this was still worse to me, for if I could burst out into tears, or vent myself by words, it would go off, and the grief, having exhausted itself, would abate.

But now I began to exercise myself with new thoughts: I daily read the word of God, and applied all the comforts of it to my present state. One morning, being very sad, I opened the Bible upon these words, "I will never, never leave thee, nor forsake thee." Immediately it occurred that these words were to me; why else should they be directed in such a manner, just at the moment when I was mourning over my condition, as one forsaken of God and man? "Well, then," said I, "if God does not forsake me, of what ill consequence can it be, or what matters it, though the world should all forsake me, seeing on the other hand, if I had all the world, and should lose the favour and blessing of God, there would be no comparison in the loss?"

From this moment I began to conclude in my mind that it was possible for me to be more happy in this forsaken, solitary condition than it was probable I should ever have been in any other particular state in the world; and with this thought I was going to give thanks to God for bringing me to this place. I know not what it was, but something shocked my mind at that thought, and I durst not speak the words. "How canst thou become such a hypocrite," said I, even audibly, "to pretend to be thankful for a condition which, however thou mayest endeavour to be contented with, thou wouldst rather pray heartily to be delivered from?" So I stopped there; but though I could not say I thanked God for being there, yet I sincerely gave thanks to God for opening my eyes, by whatever afflicting providences, to see the former condition of my life, and to mourn for my wickedness, and repent. I never opened the Bible, or shut it, but my very soul within me blessed God for directing my friend in England, without any order of mine, to pack it up among my goods, and for assisting me afterwards to save it out of the wreck of the ship.

Thus, and in this disposition of mind, I began my third year; and though I have not given the reader the trouble of so particular an account of my works this year as the first, yet in general it may be observed that I was very seldom idle, but having regularly divided my time according to the several daily employments that were before me, such as: first, my duty to God, and the reading the Scriptures, which I constantly set apart some time for thrice every day; secondly, the going abroad with my gun for food, which generally took me up three hours in every morning, when it did not rain; thirdly, the ordering, cutting, preserving, and cooking what I had killed or caught for my supply; these took up great part of the day. Also, it is to be considered, that in the middle of the day, when the sun was in the zenith, the violence of the heat was too great to stir out; so that about four hours in the evening was all the time I could be supposed to work in, with this exception, that sometimes I changed my hours of hunting and working, and went to work in the morning, and abroad with my gun in the afternoon.

To this short time allowed for labour I desire may be added the exceeding laboriousness of my work; the many hours which, for want of tools, want of help, and want of skill, everything I did took up out of my time. For example, I was full two and forty days in making a board for a long shelf, which I wanted in my cave; whereas, two sawyers, with their tools and a saw-pit, would have cut six of them out of the same tree in half a day.

My case was this: it was to be a large tree which was to be cut down, because my board was to be a broad one. This tree I was three days in cutting down, and two more cutting off the boughs, and reducing it to a log or piece of timber. With inexpressible hacking and hewing I reduced both the sides of it into chips till it began to be light enough to move; then I turned it, and made one side of it smooth and flat as a board from end to end; then, turning that side downward, cut the other side till I brought the plank to be about three inches thick, and smooth on both sides. Any one may judge the labour of my hands in such a piece of work; but labour and patience carried me through that, and many other things. I only observe this in particular, to show the reason why so much of my time went away with so little work – *viz.* that what might be a little to be done with help and tools, was a vast labour and required a prodigious time to do alone, and by hand. But notwithstanding this, with patience and labour I got through everything that my circumstances made necessary to me to do, as will appear by what follows.

I was now, in the months of November and December, expecting my crop of barley and rice. The ground I had manured and dug up for them was not great; for, as I observed, my seed of each was not above the quantity of half a peck, for I had lost one whole crop by sowing in the dry season. But now my crop promised very well, when on a sudden I found I was in danger of losing it all again by enemies of several sorts, which it was scarcely possible to keep from it; as, first, the goats, and wild creatures which I called hares, who, tasting the sweetness of the blade, lay in it night and day, as soon as it came up, and eat it so close, that it could get no time to shoot up into stalk.

This I saw no remedy for but by making an enclosure about it with a hedge; which I did with a great deal of toil, and the more, because it required speed. However, as my arable land was but small, suited to my crop, I got it totally well fenced in about three weeks' time; and shooting some of the creatures in the daytime, I set my dog to guard it in the night, tying him up to a stake at the gate, where he would stand and bark all night long; so in a little time the enemies forsook the place, and the corn grew very strong and well, and began to ripen apace.

But as the beasts ruined me before, while my corn was in the blade, so the birds were as likely to ruin me now, when it was in the ear; for, going along by the place to see how it throve, I saw my little crop surrounded with fowls, of I know not how many sorts, who stood, as it were, watching till I should be gone. I immediately let fly among them, for I always had my gun with me. I had no sooner shot, but there rose up a little cloud of fowls, which I had not seen at all, from among the corn itself.

This touched me sensibly, for I foresaw that in a few days they would devour all my hopes; that I should be starved, and never be able to raise a crop at all; and what to do I could not tell; however, I resolved not to lose my corn, if possible, though I should watch it night and day. In the first place, I went among it to see what damage was already done, and found they had spoiled a good deal of it; but that as it was yet too green for them, the loss was not so great but that the remainder was likely to be a good crop if it could be saved.

I stayed by it to load my gun, and then coming away, I could easily see the thieves sitting upon all the trees about me, as if they only waited till I was gone away, and the event proved it to be so; for as I walked off, as if I was gone, I was no sooner out of their sight than they dropped down one by one into the corn again. I was so provoked, that I could not have patience to stay till more came on, knowing that every grain that they ate now was, as it might be said, a peck-loaf to me in the consequence; but coming up to the hedge, I fired again, and killed three of them. This was what I wished for; so I took them up, and served them as we serve notorious thieves in England – hanged them in chains, for a terror to others. It is impossible to imagine that this should have such an effect as it had, for the fowls would not only not come at the corn, but, in short, they forsook all that part of the island, and I could never see a bird near the place as long as my scarecrows hung there. This I was very glad of, you may be sure, and about the latter end of December, which was our second harvest of the year, I reaped my corn.

I was sadly put to it for a scythe or sickle to cut it down, and all I could do was to make one, as well as I could, out of one of the broadswords, or cutlasses, which I saved among the arms out of the ship. However, as my first crop was but small, I had no great difficulty to cut it down; in short, I reaped it in my way, for I cut nothing off but the ears, and carried it away in a great basket which I had made, and so rubbed it out with my hands; and at the end of all my harvesting, I found that out of my half-peck of seed I had near two bushels of rice, and about two bushels and a half of barley; that is to say, by my guess, for I had no measure at that time.

However, this was a great encouragement to me, and I foresaw that, in time, it would please God to supply me with bread. And yet here I was perplexed again, for I neither knew how to grind or make meal of my corn, or indeed how to clean it and part it; nor, if made into meal, how to make bread of it; and if how to make it, yet I knew not how to bake it. These things being added to my desire of having a good quantity for store, and to secure a constant supply, I resolved not to taste any of this crop but to preserve it all for seed against the next season; and in the meantime to employ all my study and hours of working to accomplish this great work of providing myself with corn and bread.

It might be truly said, that now I worked for my bread. I believe few people have thought much upon the strange multitude of little things necessary in the providing, producing, curing, dressing, making, and finishing this one article of bread.

I, that was reduced to a mere state of nature, found this to my daily discouragement; and was made more sensible of it every hour, even after I had got the first handful of seed-corn, which, as I have said, came up unexpectedly, and indeed to a surprise.

First, I had no plough to turn up the earth – no spade or shovel to dig it. Well, this I conquered by making me a wooden spade, as I observed before; but this did my work but in a wooden manner; and though it cost me a great many days to make it, yet, for want of iron, it not only wore out soon, but made my work the harder, and made it be performed much worse. However, this I bore with, and was content to work it out with patience, and bear with the badness of the performance. When the corn was sown, I had no harrow, but was forced to go over it myself, and drag a great heavy bough of a tree over it, to scratch it, as it may be called, rather than rake or harrow it. When it was growing, and grown, I have observed already how many things I wanted to fence it, secure it, mow or reap it, cure and carry it home, thrash, part it from the chaff, and save it. Then I wanted a mill to grind it, sieves to dress it, yeast and salt to make it into bread, and an oven to bake it; but all these things I did without, as shall be observed; and yet the corn was an inestimable comfort and advantage to me too. All this, as I said, made everything laborious and tedious to me; but that there was no help for. Neither was my time so much loss to me, because, as I had divided it, a certain part of it was every day appointed to these works; and as I had resolved to use none of the corn for bread till I had a greater quantity by me, I had the next six months to apply myself wholly, by labour and invention, to furnish myself with utensils proper for the performing all the operations necessary for making the corn, when I had it, fit for my use.

CHAPTER NINE

A Boat

But first I was to prepare more land, for I had now seed enough to sow above an acre of ground. Before I did this, I had a week's work at least to make me a spade, which, when it was done, was but a sorry one indeed, and very heavy, and required double labour to work with it. However, I got through that, and sowed my seed in two large flat pieces of ground, as near my house as I could find them to my mind, and fenced them in with a good hedge, the stakes of which were all cut off that wood which I had set before, and knew it would grow; so that, in a year's time, I knew I should have a quick or living hedge, that would want but little repair. This work did not take me up less than three months, because a great part of that time was the wet season, when I could not go abroad. Within-doors, that is when it rained and I could not go out, I found employment in the following occupations – always observing, that all the while I was at work I diverted myself with talking to my parrot, and teaching him to speak; and I quickly taught him to know his own name, and at last to speak it out pretty loud, "Poll," which was the first word I ever heard spoken in the island by any mouth but my own. This, therefore, was not my work, but an assistance to my work; for now, as I said, I had a great employment upon my hands, as follows: I had long studied to make, by some means or other, some earthen vessels, which, indeed, I wanted sorely, but knew not where to come at them. However, considering the heat of the climate, I did not doubt but if I could find out any clay, I might make some pots that might, being dried in the sun, be hard enough and strong enough to bear handling, and to hold anything that was dry, and required to be kept so; and as this was necessary in the preparing corn, meal, &c. which was the thing I was doing, I resolved to make some as large as I could, and fit only to stand like jars, to hold what should be put into them.

It would make the reader pity me, or rather laugh at me, to tell how many awkward ways I took to raise this paste; what odd, misshapen, ugly things I made; how many of them fell in and how many fell out, the clay not being stiff enough to bear its own weight; how many cracked by the over-violent heat of the sun, being set out too hastily; and how many fell in pieces with only removing, as well before as after they were dried; and, in a word, how, after having laboured hard to find the clay – to dig it, to temper it, to bring it home, and work it – I could not make above two large earthen ugly things (I cannot call them jars) in about two months' labour.

However, as the sun baked these two very dry and hard, I lifted them very gently up, and set them down again in two great wicker baskets, which I had made on purpose for them, that they might not break; and as between the pot and the basket there was a little room to spare, I stuffed it full of the rice and barley straw; and these two pots being to stand always dry I thought would hold my dry corn, and perhaps the meal, when the corn was bruised.

Though I miscarried so much in my design for large pots, yet I made several smaller things with better success; such as little round pots, flat dishes, pitchers, and pipkins, and any things my hand turned to; and the heat of the sun baked them quite hard.

But all this would not answer my end, which was to get an earthen pot to hold what was liquid, and bear the fire, which none of these could do. It happened after some time, making a pretty large fire for cooking my meat, when I went to put it out after I had done with it, I found a broken piece of one of my earthenware vessels in the fire, burnt as hard as a stone, and red as a tile. I was agreeably surprised to see it, and said to myself, that certainly they might be made to burn whole, if they would burn broken.

This set me to study how to order my fire, so as to make it burn some pots. I had no notion of a kiln, such as the potters burn in, or of glazing them with lead, though I had some lead to do it with; but I placed three large pipkins and two or three pots in a pile, one upon another, and placed my firewood all round it, with a great heap of embers under them. I plied the fire with fresh fuel round the outside and upon the top, till I saw the pots in the inside red-hot quite through, and observed that they did not crack at all. When I saw them clear red, I let them stand in that heat about five or six hours, till I found one of them, though it did not crack, did melt or run; for the sand which was mixed with the clay melted by the violence of the heat, and would have run into glass if I had gone on; so I slacked my fire gradually till the pots began to abate of the red colour; and watching them all night, that I might not let the fire abate too fast, in the morning I had three very good (I will not say handsome) pipkins, and two other earthen pots, as hard burnt as could be desired, and one of them perfectly glazed with the running of the sand.

After this experiment, I need not say that I wanted no sort of earthenware for my use; but I must needs say as to the shapes of them, they were very indifferent, as any one may suppose, when I had no way of making them but as the children make dirt pies, or as a woman would make pies that never learned to raise paste.

No joy at a thing of so mean a nature was ever equal to mine, when I found I had made an earthen pot that would bear the fire; and I had hardly patience to stay till they were cold before I set one on the fire again with some water in it to boil me some meat, which it did admirably well; and with a piece of a kid I made some very good broth, though I wanted oatmeal, and several other ingredients requisite to make it as good as I would have had it been.

My next concern was to get me a stone mortar to stamp or beat some corn in; for as to the mill, there was no thought of arriving at that perfection of art with one pair of hands. To supply this want, I was at a great loss; for, of all the trades in the world, I was as perfectly unqualified for a stone-cutter as for any whatever; neither had I any tools to go about it with. I spent many a day to find out a great stone big enough to cut hollow, and make fit for a mortar, and could find none at all, except what was in the solid rock, and which I had no way to dig or cut out; nor indeed were the rocks in the island of hardness sufficient, but were all of a sandy, crumbling stone, which neither would bear the weight of a heavy pestle, nor would break the corn without filling it with sand. So, after a great deal of time lost in searching for a stone, I gave it over, and resolved to look out for a great block of hard wood, which I found, indeed, much easier; and getting one as big as I had strength to stir, I rounded it, and formed it on the outside with my axe and hatchet, and then with the help of fire and infinite labour, made a hollow place in it, as the Indians in Brazil make their canoes. After this, I made a great heavy pestle or beater of the wood called the iron-wood; and this I prepared and laid by against I had my next crop of corn, which I proposed to myself to grind, or rather pound into meal to make bread.

My next difficulty was to make a sieve or search, to dress my meal, and to part it from the bran and the husk; without which I did not see it possible I could have any bread. This was a most difficult thing even to think on, for to be sure I had nothing like the necessary thing to make it – I mean fine thin canvas or stuff to search the meal through. And here I was at a full stop for many months; nor did I really know what to do. Linen I had none left but what was mere rags; I had goat's hair, but neither knew how to weave it or spin it; and had I known how, here were no tools to work it with. All the remedy that I found for this was, that at last I did remember I had, among the seamen's clothes which were saved out of the ship, some neckcloths of calico or muslin; and with some pieces of these I made three small sieves proper enough for the work; and thus I made shift for some years: how I did afterwards, I shall show in its place.

The baking part was the next thing to be considered, and how I should make bread when I came to have corn; for first, I had no yeast. As to that part, there was no supplying the want, so I did not concern myself much about it. But for an oven I was indeed in great pain. At length I found out an experiment for that also, which was this: I made some earthen-vessels very broad but not deep, that is to say, about two feet diameter, and not above nine inches deep. These I burned in the fire, as I had done the other, and laid them by; and when I wanted to bake, I made a great fire upon my hearth, which I had paved with some square tiles of my own baking and burning also; but I should not call them square.

When the firewood was burned pretty much into embers or live coals, I drew them forward upon this hearth, so as to cover it all over, and there I let them lie till the hearth was very hot. Then sweeping away all the embers, I set down my loaf or loaves, and whelming down the earthen pot upon them, drew the embers all round the outside of the pot, to keep in and add to the heat; and thus as well as in the best oven in the world, I baked my barley-loaves, and became in little time a good pastry-cook into the bargain; for I made myself several cakes and puddings of the rice; but I made no pies, neither had I anything to put into them supposing I had, except the flesh either of fowls or goats.

It need not be wondered at if all these things took me up most part of the third year of my abode here; for it is to be observed that in the intervals of these things I had my new harvest and husbandry to manage; for I reaped my corn in its season, and carried it home as well as I could, and laid it up in the ear, in my large baskets, till I had time to rub it out, for I had no floor to thrash it on, or instrument to thrash it with.

And now, indeed, my stock of corn increasing, I really wanted to build my barns bigger; I wanted a place to lay it up in, for the increase of the corn now yielded me so much, that I had of the barley about 20 bushels, and of the rice as much or more; insomuch that now I resolved to begin to use it freely; for my bread had been quite gone a great while; also I resolved to see what quantity would be sufficient for me a whole year, and to sow but once a year.

Upon the whole, I found that the forty bushels of barley and rice were much more than I could consume in a year; so I resolved to sow just the same quantity every year that I sowed the last, in hopes that such a quantity would fully provide me with bread, &c.

All the while these things were doing, you may be sure my thoughts ran many times upon the prospect of land which I had seen from the other side of the island; and I was not without secret wishes that I were on shore there, fancying that, seeing the mainland, and an inhabited country, I might find some way or other to convey myself further, and perhaps at last find some means of escape.

But all this while I made no allowance for the dangers of such an undertaking, and how I might fall into the hands of savages, and perhaps such as I might have reason to think far worse than the lions and tigers of Africa: that if I once came in their power, I should run a hazard of more than a thousand to one of being killed, and perhaps of being eaten; for I had heard that the people of the Caribbean coast were cannibals or man-eaters, and I knew by the latitude that I could not be far from that shore. Then, supposing they were not cannibals, yet they might kill me, as many Europeans who had fallen into their hands had been served, even when they had been ten or twenty together – much more I, that was but one, and could make little or no defence; all these things, I say, which I ought to have considered well; and did come into my thoughts afterwards, yet gave me no apprehensions at first, and my head ran mightily upon the thought of getting over to the shore.

Now I wished for my boy Xury, and the long-boat with shoulder-of-mutton sail, with which I sailed above a thousand miles on the coast of Africa; but this was in vain: then I thought I would go and look at our ship's boat, which, as I have said, was blown up upon the shore a great way, in the storm, when we were first cast away. She lay almost where she did at first, but not quite; and was turned, by the force of the waves and the winds, almost bottom upward, against a high ridge of beachy, rough sand, but no water about her. If I had had hands to have refitted her, and to have launched her into the water, the boat would have done well enough, and I might have gone back into the Brazils with her easily enough; but I might have foreseen that I could no more turn her and set her upright upon her bottom than I could remove the island; however, I went to the woods, and cut levers and rollers, and brought them to the boat resolving to try what I could do; suggesting to myself that if I could but turn her down, I might repair the damage she had received, and she would be a very good boat, and I might go to sea in her very easily.

I spared no pains, indeed, in this piece of fruitless toil, and spent, I think, three or four weeks about it; at last finding it impossible to heave it up with my little strength, I fell to digging away the sand, to undermine it, and so to make it fall down, setting pieces of wood to thrust and guide it right in the fall.

But when I had done this, I was unable to stir it up again, or to get under it, much less to move it forward towards the water; so I was forced to give it over; and yet, though I gave over the hopes of the boat, my desire to venture over for the main increased, rather than decreased, as the means for it seemed impossible.

This at length put me upon thinking whether it was not possible to make myself a canoe, or periagua, such as the natives of those climates make, even without tools, or, as I might say, without hands, of the trunk of a great tree. This I not only thought possible, but easy, and pleased myself extremely with the thoughts of making it, and with my having much more convenience for it than any of the negroes or Indians; but not at all considering the particular inconveniences which I lay under more than the Indians did – *viz.* want of hands to move it, when it was made, into the water – a difficulty much harder for me to surmount than all the consequences of want of tools could be to them; for what was it to me, if when I had chosen a vast tree in the woods, and with much trouble cut it down, if I had been able with my tools to hew and dub the outside into the proper shape of a boat, and burn or cut out the inside to make it hollow, so as to make a boat of it – if, after all this, I must leave it just there where I found it, and not be able to launch it into the water?

One would have thought I could not have had the least reflection upon my mind of my circumstances while I was making this boat, but I should have immediately thought how I should get it into the sea; but my thoughts were so intent upon my voyage over the sea in it, that I never once considered how I should get it off the land: and it was really, in its own nature, more easy for me to guide it over 45 miles of sea than about 45 fathoms of land, where it lay, to set it afloat in the water.

I went to work upon this boat the most like a fool that ever man did who had any of his senses awake. I pleased myself with the design, without determining whether I was ever able to undertake it; not but that the difficulty of launching my boat came often into my head; but I put a stop to my inquiries into it by this foolish answer which I gave myself – "Let me first make it; I warrant I will find some way or other to get it along when it is done."

This was a most preposterous method; but the eagerness of my fancy prevailed, and to work I went. I felled a cedar-tree, and I question much whether Solomon ever had such a one for the building of the Temple of Jerusalem; it was 5 feet 10 inches diameter at the lower part next the stump, and 4 feet 11 inches diameter at the end of 22 feet; after which it lessened for a while, and then parted into branches. It was not without infinite labour that I felled this tree; I was twenty days hacking and hewing at it at the bottom; I was fourteen more getting the branches and limbs and the vast spreading head cut off, which I hacked and hewed through with axe and hatchet, and inexpressible labour; after this, it cost me a month to shape it and dub it to a proportion, and to something like the bottom of a boat, that it might swim upright as it ought to do. It cost me near three months more to clear the inside, and work it out so as to make an exact boat of it; this I did, indeed, without fire, by mere mallet and chisel, and by the dint of hard labour, till I had brought it to be a very handsome periagua, and big enough to have carried six-and-twenty men, and consequently big enough to have carried me and all my cargo.

When I had gone through this work I was extremely delighted with it. The boat was really much bigger than ever I saw a canoe or periagua, that was made of one tree, in my life. Many a weary stroke it had cost, you may be sure; and had I gotten it into the water, I make no question, but I should have begun the maddest voyage, and the most unlikely to be performed, that ever was undertaken.

But all my devices to get it into the water failed me; though they cost me infinite labour too. It lay about 100 yards from the water, and not more; but the first inconvenience was, it was up hill towards the creek. Well, to take away this discouragement, I resolved to dig into the surface of the earth, and so make a declivity: this I began, and it cost me a prodigious deal of pains (but who grudge pains who have their deliverance in view?); but when this was worked through, and this difficulty managed, it was still much the same, for I could no more stir the canoe than I could the other boat. Then I measured the distance of ground, and resolved to cut a dock or canal, to bring the water up to the canoe, seeing I could not bring the canoe down to the water. Well, I began this work; and when I began to enter upon it, and calculate how deep it was to be dug, how broad, how the stuff was to be thrown out,

I found that, by the number of hands I had, being none but my own, it must have been ten or twelve years before I could have gone through with it; for the shore lay so high, that at the upper end it must have been at least 20 feet deep; so at length, though with great reluctancy, I gave this attempt over also.

This grieved me heartily; and now I saw, though too late, the folly of beginning a work before we count the cost, and before we judge rightly of our own strength to go through with it.

In the middle of this work I finished my fourth year in this place, and kept my anniversary with the same devotion, and with as much comfort as ever before; for, by a constant study and serious application to the Word of God, and by the assistance of His grace, I gained a different knowledge from what I had before. I entertained different notions of things. I looked now upon the world as a thing remote, which I had nothing to do with, no expectations from, and, indeed, no desires about: in a word, I had nothing indeed to do with it, nor was ever likely to have, so I thought it looked, as we may perhaps look upon it hereafter – *viz.* as a place I had lived in, but was come out of it; and well might I say, as Father Abraham to Dives, "Between me and thee is a great gulf fixed."

In the first place, I was removed from all the wickedness of the world here; I had neither the lusts of the flesh, the lusts of the eye, nor the pride of life. I had nothing to covet, for I had all that I was now capable of enjoying; I was lord of the whole manor; or, if I pleased, I might call myself king or Emperor over the whole country which I had possession of: there were no rivals; I had no competitor, none to dispute sovereignty or command with me: I might have raised ship-loadings of corn, but I had no use for it; so I let as little grow as I thought enough for my occasion. I had tortoise or turtle enough, but now and then one was as much as I could put to any use: I had timber enough to have built a fleet of ships; and I had grapes enough to have made wine, or to have cured into raisins, to have loaded that fleet when it had been built.

But all I could make use of was all that was valuable: I had enough to eat and supply my wants, and what was all the rest to me? If I killed more flesh than I could eat, the dog must eat it, or vermin; if I sowed more corn than I could eat, it must be spoiled; the trees that I cut down were lying to rot on the ground; I could make no more use of them but for fuel, and that I had no occasion for but to dress my food.

In a word, the nature and experience of things dictated to me, upon just reflection, that all the good things of this world are no farther good to us than they are for our use; and that, whatever we may heap up to give others, we enjoy just as much as we can use, and no more. The most covetous, griping miser in the world would have been cured of the vice of covetousness if he had been in my case; for I possessed infinitely more than I knew what to do with. I had no room for desire, except it was of things which I had not, and they were but trifles, though, indeed, of great use to me. I had, as I hinted before, a parcel of money, as well gold as silver, about 36 pounds sterling. Alas! there the sorry, useless stuff lay; I had no more manner of business for it; and often thought with myself that I would have given a handful of it for a gross of tobacco-pipes; or for a hand-mill to grind my corn; nay, I would have given it all for a sixpenny-worth of turnip and carrot seed out of England, or for a handful of peas and beans, and a bottle of ink. As it was, I had not the least advantage by it or benefit from it; but there it lay in a drawer, and grew mouldy with the damp of the cave in the wet seasons; and if I had had the drawer full of diamonds, it had been the same case – they had been of no manner of value to me, because of no use.

I had now brought my state of life to be much easier in itself than it was at first, and much easier to my mind, as well as to my body. I frequently sat down to meat with thankfulness, and admired the hand of God's providence, which had thus spread my table in the wilderness. I learned to look more upon the bright side of my condition, and less upon the dark side, and to consider what I enjoyed rather than what I wanted; and this gave me sometimes such secret comforts, that I cannot express them; and which I take notice of here, to put those discontented people in mind of it, who cannot enjoy comfortably what God has given them, because they see and covet something that He has not given them. All our discontents about what we want appeared to me to spring from the want of thankfulness for what we have.

Another reflection was of great use to me, and doubtless would be so to any one that should fall into such distress as mine was; and this was, to compare my present condition with what I at first expected it would be; nay, with what it would certainly have been, if the good providence of God had not wonderfully ordered the ship to be cast up nearer to the shore, where I not only could come at her, but could bring what I got out of her to the shore, for my relief and comfort; without which, I had wanted for tools to work, weapons for defence, and gunpowder and shot for getting my food.

I spent whole hours, I may say whole days, in representing to myself, in the most lively colours, how I must have acted if I had got nothing out of the ship. How I could not have so much as got any food, except fish and turtles; and that, as it was long before I found any of them, I must have perished first; that I should have lived, if I had not perished, like a mere savage; that if I had killed a goat or a fowl, by any contrivance, I had no way to flay or open it, or part the flesh from the skin and the bowels, or to cut it up; but must gnaw it with my teeth, and pull it with my claws, like a beast.

These reflections made me very sensible of the goodness of Providence to me, and very thankful for my present condition, with all its hardships and misfortunes; and this part also I cannot but recommend to the reflection of those who are apt, in their misery, to say, "Is any affliction like mine?" Let them consider how much worse the cases of some people are, and their case might have been, if Providence had thought fit.

I had another reflection, which assisted me also to comfort my mind with hopes; and this was comparing my present situation with what I had deserved, and had therefore reason to expect from the hand of Providence. I had lived a dreadful life, perfectly destitute of the knowledge and fear of God. I had been well instructed by father and mother; neither had they been wanting to me in their early endeavours to infuse a religious awe of God into my mind, a sense of my duty, and what the nature and end of my being required of me. But, alas! falling early into the seafaring life, which of all lives is the most destitute of the fear of God, though His terrors are always before them; I say, falling early into the seafaring life, and into seafaring company, all that little sense of religion which I had entertained was laughed out of me by my messmates; by a hardened despising of dangers, and the views of death, which grew habitual to me by my long absence from all manner of opportunities to converse with anything but what was like myself, or to hear anything that was good or tended towards it.

So void was I of everything that was good, or the least sense of what I was, or was to be, that, in the greatest deliverances I enjoyed – such as my escape from Sallee; my being taken up by the Portuguese Master of the ship; my being planted so well in the Brazils; my receiving the cargo from England, and the like – I never had once the words "Thank God!" so much as on my mind, or in my mouth; nor in the greatest distress had I so much as a thought to pray to Him, or so much as to say, "Lord, have mercy upon me!" no, nor to mention the name of God, unless it was to swear by, and blaspheme it.

I had terrible reflections upon my mind for many months, as I have already observed, on account of my wicked and hardened life past; and when I looked about me, and considered what particular providences had attended me since my coming into this place, and how God had dealt bountifully with me – had not only punished me less than my iniquity had deserved, but had so plentifully provided for me – this gave me great hopes that my repentance was accepted, and that God had yet mercy in store for me.

With these reflections I worked my mind up, not only to a resignation to the will of God in the present disposition of my circumstances, but even to a sincere thankfulness for my condition; and that I, who was yet a living man, ought not to complain, seeing I had not the due punishment of my sins; that I enjoyed so many mercies which I had no reason to have expected in that place; that I ought never more to repine at my condition, but to rejoice, and to give daily thanks for that daily bread, which nothing but a crowd of wonders could have brought; that I ought to consider I had been fed even by a miracle, even as great as that of feeding Elijah by ravens, nay, by a long series of miracles; and that I could hardly have named a place in the uninhabitable part of the world where I could have been cast more to my advantage; a place where, as I had no society, which was my affliction on one hand, so I found no ravenous beasts, no furious wolves or tigers, to threaten my life; no venomous creatures, or poisons, which I might feed on to my hurt; no savages to murder and devour me. In a word, as my life was a life of sorrow one way, so it was a life of mercy another; and I wanted nothing to make it a life of comfort but to be able to make my sense of God's goodness to me, and care over me in this condition, be my daily consolation; and after I did make a just improvement on these things, I went away, and was no more sad. I had now been here so long that many things which I had brought on shore for my help were either quite gone, or very much wasted and near spent.

My ink, as I observed, had been gone some time, all but a very little, which I eked out with water, a little and a little, till it was so pale, it scarce left any appearance of black upon the paper. As long as it lasted I made use of it to minute down the days of the month on which any remarkable thing happened to me; and first, by casting up times past, I remembered that there was a strange concurrence of days in the various providences which befell me, and which, if I had been superstitiously inclined to observe days as fatal or fortunate, I might have had reason to have looked upon with a great deal of curiosity.

First, I had observed that the same day that I broke away from my father and friends and ran away to Hull, in order to go to sea, the same day afterwards I was taken by the Sallee man-of-war, and made a slave; the same day of the year that I escaped out of the wreck of that ship in Yarmouth Roads, that same day-year afterwards I made my escape from Sallee in a boat; the same day of the year I was born on – *viz.* the 30th of September, that same day I had my life so miraculously saved twenty-six years after, when I was cast on shore in this island; so that my wicked life and my solitary life began both on a day.

The next thing to my ink being wasted was that of my bread – I mean the biscuit which I brought out of the ship; this I had husbanded to the last degree, allowing myself but one cake of bread a-day for above a year; and yet I was quite without bread for near a year before I got any corn of my own, and great reason I had to be thankful that I had any at all, the getting it being, as has been already observed, next to miraculous.

My clothes, too, began to decay; as to linen, I had had none a good while, except some checquered shirts which I found in the chests of the other seamen, and which I carefully preserved; because many times I could bear no other clothes on but a shirt; and it was a very great help to me that I had, among all the men's clothes of the ship, almost three dozen of shirts. There were also, indeed, several thick watch-coats of the seamen's which were left, but they were too hot to wear; and though it is true that the weather was so violently hot that there was no need of clothes, yet I could not go quite naked – no, though I had been inclined to it, which I was not, nor could I abide the thought of it, though I was alone. The reason why I could not go naked was, I could not bear the heat of the sun so well when quite naked as with some clothes on; nay, the very heat frequently blistered my skin: whereas, with a shirt on, the air itself made some motion, and whistling under the shirt, was twofold cooler than without it. No more could I ever bring myself to go out in the heat of the sun without a cap or a hat; the heat of the sun, beating with such violence as it does in that place, would give me the headache presently, by darting so directly on my head, without a cap or hat on, so that I could not bear it; whereas, if I put on my hat it would presently go away.

Upon these views I began to consider about putting the few rags I had, which I called clothes, into some order; I had worn out all the waistcoats I had, and my business was now to try if I could not make jackets out of the great watch-coats which I had by me, and with such other materials as I had; so I set to work, tailoring, or rather, indeed, botching, for I made most piteous work of it. However, I made shift to make two or three new waistcoats, which I hoped would serve me a great while: as for breeches or drawers, I made but a very sorry shift indeed till afterwards.

I have mentioned that I saved the skins of all the creatures that I killed, I mean four-footed ones, and I had them hung up, stretched out with sticks in the sun, by which means some of them were so dry and hard that they were fit for little, but others were very useful. The first thing I made of these was a great cap for my head, with the hair on the outside, to shoot off the rain; and this I performed so well, that after I made me a suit of clothes wholly of these skins – that is to say, a waistcoat, and breeches open at the knees, and both loose, for they were rather wanting to keep me cool than to keep me warm. I must not omit to acknowledge that they were wretchedly made; for if I was a bad carpenter, I was a worse tailor. However, they were such as I made very good shift with, and when I was out, if it happened to rain, the hair of my waistcoat and cap being outermost, I was kept very dry.

After this, I spent a great deal of time and pains to make an umbrella; I was, indeed, in great want of one, and had a great mind to make one; I had seen them made in the Brazils, where they are very useful in the great heats there, and I felt the heats every jot as great here, and greater too, being nearer the equinox; besides, as I was obliged to be much abroad, it was a most useful thing to me, as well for the rains as the heats. I took a world of pains with it, and was a great while before I could make anything likely to hold: nay, after I had thought I had hit the way, I spoiled two or three before I made one to my mind: but at last I made one that answered indifferently well: the main difficulty I found was to make it let down. I could make it spread, but if it did not let down too, and draw in, it was not portable for me any way but just over my head, which would not do. However, at last, as I said, I made one to answer, and covered it with skins, the hair upwards, so that it cast off the rain like a pent-house, and kept off the sun so effectually, that I could walk out in the hottest of the weather with greater advantage than I could before in the coolest, and when I had no need of it could close it, and carry it under my arm

Thus I lived mighty comfortably, my mind being entirely composed by resigning myself to the will of God, and throwing myself wholly upon the disposal of His providence. This made my life better than sociable, for when I began to regret the want of conversation I would ask myself, whether thus conversing mutually with my own thoughts, and (as I hope I may say) with even God Himself, by ejaculations, was not better than the utmost enjoyment of human society in the world?

CHAPTER TEN

Tames Goats

I CANNOT SAY THAT AFTER THIS, for five years, any extraordinary thing happened to me, but I lived on in the same course, in the same posture and place, as before; the chief things I was employed in, besides my yearly labour of planting my barley and rice, and curing my raisins, of both which I always kept up just enough to have sufficient stock of one year's provisions beforehand; I say, besides this yearly labour, and my daily pursuit of going out with my gun, I had one labour, to make a canoe, which at last I finished: so that, by digging a canal to it of six feet wide and four feet deep, I brought it into the creek, almost half a mile. As for the first, which was so vastly big, for I made it without considering beforehand, as I ought to have done, how I should be able to launch it, so, never being able to bring it into the water, or bring the water to it, I was obliged to let it lie where it was as a memorandum to teach me to be wiser the next time: indeed, the next time, though I could not get a tree proper for it, and was in a place where I could not get the water to it at any less distance than, as I have said, near half a mile, yet, as I saw it was practicable at last, I never gave it over; and though I was near two years about it, yet I never grudged my labour, in hopes of having a boat to go off to sea at last.

However, though my little periagua was finished, yet the size of it was not at all answerable to the design which I had in view when I made the first; I mean of venturing over to the *Terra Firma*, where it was above forty miles broad; accordingly, the smallness of my boat assisted to put an end to that design, and now I thought no more of it. As I had a boat, my next design was to make a cruise round the island; for as I had been on the other side in one place, crossing, as I have already described it, over the land, so the discoveries I made in that little journey made me very eager to see other parts of the coast; and now I had a boat, I thought of nothing but sailing round the island.

For this purpose, that I might do everything with discretion and consideration, I fitted up a little mast in my boat, and made a sail too out of some of the pieces of the ship's sails which lay in store, and of which I had a great stock by me. Having fitted my mast and sail, and tried the boat, I found she would sail very well; then I made little lockers or boxes at each end of my boat, to put provisions, necessaries, ammunition, &c. into, to be kept dry, either from rain or the spray of the sea; and a little, long, hollow place I cut in the inside of the boat, where I could lay my gun, making a flap to hang down over it to keep it dry.

I fixed my umbrella also in the step at the stern, like a mast, to stand over my head, and keep the heat of the sun off me, like an awning; and thus I every now and then took a little voyage upon the sea, but never went far out, nor far from the little creek. At last, being eager to view the circumference of my little kingdom, I resolved upon my cruise; and accordingly I victualled my ship for the voyage, putting in two dozen of loaves (cakes I should call them) of barley-bread, an earthen pot full of parched rice (a food I ate a good deal of), a little bottle of rum, half a goat, and powder and shot for killing more, and two large watch-coats, of those which, as I mentioned before, I had saved out of the seamen's chests; these I took, one to lie upon, and the other to cover me in the night.

It was the 6th of November, in the 6th year of my reign – or my captivity, which you please – that I set out on this voyage, and I found it much longer than I expected; for though the island itself was not very large, yet when I came to the east side of it, I found a great ledge of rocks lie out about two leagues into the sea, some above water, some under it; and beyond that a shoal of sand, lying dry half a league more, so that I was obliged to go a great way out to sea to double the point.

When I first discovered them, I was going to give over my enterprise, and come back again, not knowing how far it might oblige me to go out to sea; and above all, doubting how I should get back again: so I came to an anchor; for I had made a kind of an anchor with a piece of a broken grappling which I got out of the ship.

Having secured my boat, I took my gun and went on shore, climbing up a hill, which seemed to overlook that point where I saw the full extent of it, and resolved to venture.

In my viewing the sea from that hill where I stood, I perceived a strong, and indeed a most furious current, which ran to the east, and even came close to the point; and I took the more notice of it because I saw there might be some danger that when I came into it I might be carried out to sea by the strength of it, and not be able to make the island again; and indeed, had I not got first upon this hill, I believe it would have been so; for there was the same current on the other side the island, only that it set off at a further distance, and I saw there was a strong eddy under the shore; so I had nothing to do but to get out of the first current, and I should presently be in an eddy.

I lay here, however, two days, because the wind blowing pretty fresh at E.S.E. and that being just contrary to the current, made a great breach of the sea upon the point: so that it was not safe for me to keep too close to the shore for the breach, nor to go too far off, because of the stream.

The third day, in the morning, the wind having abated overnight, the sea was calm, and I ventured: but I am a warning to all rash and ignorant pilots; for no sooner was I come to the point, when I was not even my boat's length from the shore, but I found myself in a great depth of water, and a current like the sluice of a mill; it carried my boat along with it with such violence that all I could do could not keep her so much as on the edge of it; but I found it hurried me farther and farther out from the eddy, which was on my left hand. There was no wind stirring to help me, and all I could do with my paddles signified nothing: and now I began to give myself over for lost; for as the current was on both sides of the island, I knew in a few leagues distance they must join again, and then I was irrecoverably gone; nor did I see any possibility of avoiding it; so that I had no prospect before me but of perishing, not by the sea, for that was calm enough, but of starving from hunger. I had, indeed, found a tortoise on the shore, as big almost as I could lift, and had tossed it into the boat; and I had a great jar of fresh water, that is to say, one of my earthen pots; but what was all this to being driven into the vast ocean, where, to be sure, there was no shore, no mainland or island, for a thousand leagues at least?

And now I saw how easy it was for the providence of God to make even the most miserable condition of mankind worse. Now I looked back upon my desolate, solitary island as the most pleasant place in the world and all the happiness my heart could wish for was to be but there again. I stretched out my hands to it, with eager wishes – "O happy desert!" said I, "I shall never see thee more. O miserable creature! Whither am I going?" Then I reproached myself with my unthankful temper, and that I had repined at my solitary condition; and now what would I give to be on shore there again! Thus, we never see the true state of our condition till it is illustrated to us by its contraries, nor know how to value what we enjoy, but by the want of it. It is scarcely possible to imagine the consternation I was now in, being driven from my beloved island (for so it appeared to me now to be) into the wide ocean, almost two leagues, and in the utmost despair of ever recovering it again. However, I worked hard till, indeed, my strength was almost exhausted, and kept my boat as much to the northward, that is, towards the side of the current which the eddy lay on, as possibly I could; when about noon, as the sun passed the meridian, I thought I felt a little breeze of wind in my face, springing up from S.S.E. This cheered my heart a little, and especially when, in about half-an-hour more, it blew a pretty gentle gale. By this time I had got at a frightful distance from the island, and had the least cloudy or hazy weather intervened, I had been undone another way, too; for I had no compass on board, and should never have known how to have steered towards the island, if I had but once lost sight of it; but the weather continuing clear, I applied myself to get up my mast again, and spread my sail, standing away to the north as much as possible, to get out of the current.

Just as I had set my mast and sail, and the boat began to stretch away, I saw even by the clearness of the water some alteration of the current was near; for where the current was so strong the water was foul; but perceiving the water clear, I found the current abate; and presently I found to the east, at about half a mile, a breach of the sea upon some rocks: these rocks I found caused the current to part again, and as the main stress of it ran away more southerly, leaving the rocks to the north-east, so the other returned by the repulse of the rocks, and made a strong eddy, which ran back again to the north-west, with a very sharp stream.

They who know what it is to have a reprieve brought to them upon the ladder, or to be rescued from thieves just going to murder them, or who have been in such extremities, may guess what my present surprise of joy was, and how gladly I put my boat into the stream of this eddy; and the wind also freshening, how gladly I spread my sail to it, running cheerfully before the wind, and with a strong tide or eddy underfoot.

This eddy carried me about a league on my way back again, directly towards the island, but about two leagues more to the northward than the current which carried me away at first; so that when I came near the island, I found myself open to the northern shore of it, that is to say, the other end of the island, opposite to that which I went out from.

When I had made something more than a league of way by the help of this current or eddy, I found it was spent, and served me no further. However, I found that being between two great currents – *viz.* that on the south side, which had hurried me away, and that on the north, which lay about a league on the other side; I say, between these two, in the wake of the island, I found the water at least still, and running no way; and having still a breeze of wind fair for me, I kept on steering directly for the island, though not making such fresh way as I did before.

About four o'clock in the evening, being then within a league of the island, I found the point of the rocks which occasioned this disaster stretching out, as is described before, to the southward, and casting off the current more southerly, had, of course, made another eddy to the north; and this I found very strong, but not directly setting the way my course lay, which was due west, but almost full north. However, having a fresh gale, I stretched across this eddy, slanting north-west; and in about an hour came within about a mile of the shore, where, it being smooth water, I soon got to land.

When I was on shore, God I fell on my knees and gave God thanks for my deliverance, resolving to lay aside all thoughts of my deliverance by my boat; and refreshing myself with such things as I had, I brought my boat close to the shore, in a little cove that I had spied under some trees, and laid me down to sleep, being quite spent with the labour and fatigue of the voyage.

I was now at a great loss which way to get home with my boat! I had run so much hazard, and knew too much of the case, to think of attempting it by the way I went out; and what might be at the other side (I mean the west side) I knew not, nor had I any mind to run any more ventures; so I resolved on the next morning to make my way westward along the shore, and to see if there was no creek where I might lay up my frigate in safety, so as to have her again if I wanted her. In about three miles or thereabouts, coasting the shore, I came to a very good inlet or bay, about a mile over, which narrowed till it came to a very little rivulet or brook, where I found a very convenient harbour for my boat, and where she lay as if she had been in a little dock made on purpose for her. Here I put in, and having stowed my boat very safe, I went on shore to look about me, and see where I was.

I soon found I had but a little passed by the place where I had been before, when I travelled on foot to that shore; so taking nothing out of my boat but my gun and umbrella, for it was exceedingly hot, I began my march. The way was comfortable enough after such a voyage as I had been upon, and I reached my old bower in the evening, where I found everything standing as I left it; for I always kept it in good order, being, as I said before, my country house.

I got over the fence, and laid me down in the shade to rest my limbs, for I was very weary, and fell asleep; but judge you, if you can, that read my story, what a surprise I must be in when I was awaked out of my sleep by a voice calling me by my name several times, "Robin, Robin, Robin Crusoe: poor Robin Crusoe! Where are you, Robin Crusoe? Where are you? Where have you been?"

I was so dead asleep at first, being fatigued with rowing, or part of the day, and with walking the latter part, that I did not wake thoroughly; but dozing thought I dreamed that somebody spoke to me; but as the voice continued to repeat, "Robin Crusoe, Robin Crusoe," at last I began to wake more perfectly, and was at first dreadfully frightened, and started up in the utmost consternation; but no sooner were my eyes open, but I saw my Poll sitting on the top of the hedge; and immediately knew that it was he that spoke to me; for just in such bemoaning language I had used to talk to him and teach him; and he had learned it so perfectly that he would sit upon my finger, and lay his bill close to my face and cry, "Poor Robin Crusoe! Where are you? Where have you been? How came you here?" and such things as I had taught him.

However, even though I knew it was the parrot, and that indeed it could be nobody else, it was a good while before I could compose myself. First, I was amazed how the creature got thither; and then, how he should just keep about the place, and nowhere else; but as I was well satisfied it could be nobody but honest Poll, I got over it; and holding out my hand, and calling him by his name, "Poll," the sociable creature came to me, and sat upon my thumb, as he used to do, and continued talking to me, "Poor Robin Crusoe! and how did I come here? and where had I been?" just as if he had been overjoyed to see me again; and so I carried him home along with me.

I had now had enough of rambling to sea for some time, and had enough to do for many days to sit still and reflect upon the danger I had been in. I would have been very glad to have had my boat again on my side of the island; but I knew not how it was practicable to get it about. As to the east side of the island, which I had gone round, I knew well enough there was no venturing that way; my very heart would shrink, and my very blood run chill, but to think of it; and as to the other side of the island, I did not know how it might be there; but supposing the current ran with the same force against the shore at the east as it passed by it on the other, I might run the same risk of being driven down the stream, and carried by the island, as I had been before of being carried away from it: so with these thoughts, I contented myself to be without any boat, though it had been the product of so many months' labour to make it, and of so many more to get it into the sea.

In this government of my temper I remained near a year; and lived a very sedate, retired life, as you may well suppose; and my thoughts being very much composed as to my condition, and fully comforted in resigning myself to the dispositions of Providence, I thought I lived really very happily in all things except that of society.

I improved myself in this time in all the mechanic exercises which my necessities put me upon applying myself to; and I believe I should, upon occasion, have made a very good carpenter, especially considering how few tools I had.

Besides this, I arrived at an unexpected perfection in my earthenware, and contrived well enough to make them with a wheel, which I found infinitely easier and better; because I made things round and shaped, which before were filthy things indeed to look on. But I think I was never more vain of my own performance, or more joyful for anything I found out, than for my being able to make a tobacco-pipe; and though it was a very ugly, clumsy thing when it was done, and only burned red, like other earthenware, yet as it was hard and firm, and would draw the smoke, I was exceedingly comforted with it, for I had been always used to smoke; and there were pipes in the ship, but I forgot them at first, not thinking there was tobacco in the island; and afterwards, when I searched the ship again, I could not come at any pipes.

In my wicker-ware also I improved much, and made abundance of necessary baskets, as well as my invention showed me; though not very handsome, yet they were such as were very handy and convenient for laying things up in, or fetching things home. For example, if I killed a goat abroad, I could hang it up in a tree, flay it, dress it, and cut it in pieces, and bring it home in a basket; and the like by a turtle; I could cut it up, take out the eggs and a piece or two of the flesh, which was enough for me, and bring them home in a basket, and leave the rest behind me. Also, large deep baskets were the receivers of my corn, which I always rubbed out as soon as it was dry and cured, and kept it in great baskets.

I began now to perceive my powder abated considerably; this was a want which it was impossible for me to supply, and I began seriously to consider what I must do when I should have no more powder; that is to say, how I should kill any goats. I had, as is observed in the third year of my being here, kept a young kid, and bred her up tame, and I was in hopes of getting a he-goat; but I could not by any means bring it to pass, till my kid grew an old goat; and as I could never find in my heart to kill her, she died at last of mere age.

But being now in the 11th year of my residence, and, as I have said, my ammunition growing low, I set myself to study some art to trap and snare the goats, to see whether I could not catch some of them alive; and particularly I wanted a she-goat great with young. For this purpose I made snares to hamper them; and I do believe they were more than once taken in them; but my tackle was not good, for I had no wire, and I always found them broken and my bait devoured. At length I resolved to try a pitfall; so I dug several large pits in the earth, in places where I had observed the goats used to feed, and over those pits I placed hurdles of my own making too, with a great weight upon them; and several times I put ears of barley and dry rice without setting the trap; and I could easily perceive that the goats had gone in and eaten up the corn, for I could see the marks of their feet. At length I set three traps in one night, and going the next morning I found them, all standing, and yet the bait eaten and gone; this was very discouraging. However, I altered my traps; and not to trouble you with particulars, going one morning to see my traps, I found in one of them a large old he-goat; and in one of the others three kids, a male and two females.

As to the old one, I knew not what to do with him; he was so fierce I durst not go into the pit to him; that is to say, to bring him away alive, which was what I wanted. I could have killed him, but that was not my business, nor would it answer my end; so I even let him out, and he ran away as if he had been frightened out of his wits. But I did not then know what I afterwards learned, that hunger will tame a lion. If I had let him stay three or four days without food, and then have carried him some water to drink and then a little corn, he would have been as tame as one of the kids; for they are mighty sagacious, tractable creatures, where they are well used.

However, for the present I let him go, knowing no better at that time: then I went to the three kids, and taking them one by one, I tied them with strings together, and with some difficulty brought them all home.

It was a good while before they would feed; but throwing them some sweet corn, it tempted them, and they began to be tame. And now I found that if I expected to supply myself with goats' flesh, when I had no powder or shot left, breeding some up tame was my only way, when, perhaps, I might have them about my house like a flock of sheep. But then it occurred to me that I must keep the tame from the wild, or else they would always run wild when they grew up; and the only way for this was to have some enclosed piece of ground, well fenced either with hedge or pale, to keep them in so effectually, that those within might not break out, or those without break in.

This was a great undertaking for one pair of hands yet, as I saw there was an absolute necessity for doing it, my first work was to find out a proper piece of ground, where there was likely to be herbage for them to eat, water for them to drink, and cover to keep them from the sun.

Those who understand such enclosures will think I had very little contrivance when I pitched upon a place very proper for all these (being a plain, open piece of meadow land, or savannah, as our people call it in the western colonies), which had two or three little drills of fresh water in it, and at one end was very woody – I say, they will smile at my forecast, when I shall tell them I began by enclosing this piece of ground in such a manner that, my hedge or pale must have been at least two miles about. Nor was the madness of it so great as to the compass, for if it was ten miles about, I was like to have time enough to do it in; but I did not consider that my goats would be as wild in so much compass as if they had had the whole island, and I should have so much room to chase them in that I should never catch them.

My hedge was begun and carried on, I believe, about 50 yards when this thought occurred to me; so I presently stopped short, and, for the beginning, I resolved to enclose a piece of about 150 yards in length, and 100 yards in breadth, which, as it would maintain as many as I should have in any reasonable time, so, as my stock increased, I could add more ground to my enclosure.

This was acting with some prudence, and I went to work with courage. I was about three months hedging in the first piece; and, till I had done it, I tethered the three kids in the best part of it, and used them to feed as near me as possible, to make them familiar; and very often I would go and carry them some ears of barley, or a handful of rice, and feed them out of my hand; so that after my enclosure was finished and I let them loose, they would follow me up and down, bleating after me for a handful of corn.

This answered my end, and in about a year and a half I had a flock of about twelve goats, kids and all; and in two years more I had three-and-forty, besides several that I took and killed for my food. After that, I enclosed five several pieces of ground to feed them in, with little pens to drive them to take them as I wanted, and gates out of one piece of ground into another.

But this was not all; for now I not only had goat's flesh to feed on when I pleased, but milk too – a thing which, indeed, in the beginning, I did not so much as think of, and which, when it came into my thoughts, was really an agreeable surprise, for now I set up my dairy, and had sometimes a gallon or two of milk in a day. And as Nature, who gives supplies of food to every creature, dictates even naturally how to make use of it, so I, that had never milked a cow, much less a goat, or seen butter or cheese made only when I was a boy, after a great many essays and miscarriages, made both butter and cheese at last, also salt (though I found it partly made to my hand by the heat of the sun upon some of the rocks of the sea), and never wanted it afterwards. How mercifully can our Creator treat His creatures, even in those conditions in which they seemed to be overwhelmed in destruction! How can He sweeten the bitterest providences, and give us cause to praise Him for dungeons and prisons! What a table was here spread for me in the wilderness, where I saw nothing at first but to perish for hunger!

CHAPTER ELEVEN

Finds Print of Man's Foot on the Sand

IT WOULD HAVE MADE A STOIC SMILE to have seen me and my little family sit down to dinner. There was my majesty the prince and lord of the whole island; I had the lives of all my subjects at my absolute command; I could hang, draw, give liberty, and take it away, and no rebels among all my subjects. Then, to see how like a king I dined, too, all alone, attended by my servants! Poll, as if he had been my favourite, was the only person permitted to talk to me. My dog, who was now grown old and crazy, and had found no species to multiply his kind upon, sat always at my right hand; and two cats, one on one side of the table and one on the other, expecting now and then a bit from my hand, as a mark of especial favour.

But these were not the two cats which I brought on shore at first, for they were both of them dead, and had been interred near my habitation by my own hand; but one of them having multiplied by I know not what kind of creature, these were two which I had preserved tame; whereas the rest ran wild in the woods, and became indeed troublesome to me at last, for they would often come into my house, and plunder me too, till at last I was obliged to shoot them, and did kill a great many; at length they left me. With this attendance and in this plentiful manner I lived; neither could I be said to want anything but society; and of that, some time after this, I was likely to have too much.

I was something impatient, as I have observed, to have the use of my boat, though very loath to run any more hazards; and therefore sometimes I sat contriving ways to get her about the island, and at other times I sat myself down contented enough without her. But I had a strange uneasiness in my mind to go down to the point of the island where, as I have said in my last ramble, I went up the hill to see how the shore lay, and how the current set, that I might see what I had to do: this inclination increased upon me every day, and at length I resolved to travel thither by land, following the edge of the shore. I did so; but had any one in England met such a man as I was, it must either have frightened him, or raised a great deal of laughter; and as I frequently stood still to look at myself, I could not but smile at the notion of my travelling through Yorkshire with such an equipage, and in such a dress. Be pleased to take a sketch of my figure, as follows.

I had a great high shapeless cap, made of a goat's skin, with a flap hanging down behind, as well to keep the sun from me as to shoot the rain off from running into my neck, nothing being so hurtful in these climates as the rain upon the flesh under the clothes.

I had a short jacket of goat's skin, the skirts coming down to about the middle of the thighs, and a pair of open-kneed breeches of the same; the breeches were made of the skin of an old he-goat, whose hair hung down such a length on either side that, like pantaloons, it reached to the middle of my legs; stockings and shoes I had none, but had made me a pair of some-things, I scarce knew what to call them, like buskins, to flap over my legs, and lace on either side like spatter-dashes, but of a most barbarous shape, as indeed were all the rest of my clothes.

I had on a broad belt of goat's skin dried, which I drew together with two thongs of the same instead of buckles, and in a kind of a frog on either side of this, instead of a sword and dagger, hung a little saw and a hatchet, one on one side and one on the other. I had another belt not so broad, and fastened in the same manner, which hung over my shoulder, and at the end of it, under my left arm, hung two pouches, both made of goat's skin too, in one of which hung my powder, in the other my shot. At my back I carried my basket, and on my shoulder my gun, and over my head a great clumsy, ugly, goat's-skin umbrella, but which, after all, was the most necessary thing I had about me next to my gun. As for my face, the colour of it was really not so mulatto-like as one might expect from a man not at all careful of it, and living within nine or ten degrees of the equinox. My beard I had once suffered to grow till it was about a quarter of a yard long; but as I had both scissors and razors sufficient, I had cut it pretty short, except what grew on my upper lip, which I had trimmed into a large pair of Mahometan whiskers, such as I had seen worn by some Turks at Sallee, for the Moors did not wear such, though the Turks did; of these moustachios, or whiskers, I will not say they were long enough to hang my hat upon them, but they were of a length and shape monstrous enough, and such as in England would have passed for frightful.

But all this is by-the-bye; for as to my figure, I had so few to observe me that it was of no manner of consequence, so I say no more of that. In this kind of dress I went my new journey, and was out five or six days. I travelled first along the sea-shore, directly to the place where I first brought my boat to an anchor to get upon the rocks; and having no boat now to take care of, I went over the land a nearer way to the same height that I was upon before, when, looking forward to the points of the rocks which lay out, and which I was obliged to double with my boat, as is said above, I was surprised to see the sea all smooth and quiet – no rippling, no motion, no current, any more there than in other places. I was at a strange loss to understand this, and resolved to spend some time in the observing it, to see if nothing from the sets of the tide had occasioned it; but I was presently convinced how it was – *viz.* that the tide of ebb setting from the west, and joining with the current of waters from some great river on the shore, must be the occasion of this current, and that, according as the wind blew more forcibly from the west or from the north, this current came nearer or went farther from the shore; for, waiting thereabouts till evening, I went up to the rock again, and then the tide of ebb being made, I plainly saw the current again as before, only that it ran farther off, being near half a league from the shore, whereas in my case it set close upon the shore, and hurried me and my canoe along with it, which at another time it would not have done.

This observation convinced me that I had nothing to do but to observe the ebbing and the flowing of the tide, and I might very easily bring my boat about the island again; but when I began to think of putting it in practice, I had such terror upon my spirits at the remembrance of the danger I had been in, that I could not think of it again with any patience, but, on the contrary, I took up another resolution, which was more safe, though more laborious – and this was, that I would build, or rather make, me another periagua or canoe, and so have one for one side of the island, and one for the other.

You are to understand that now I had, as I may call it, two plantations in the island – one my little fortification or tent, with the wall about it, under the rock, with the cave behind me, which by this time I had enlarged into several apartments or caves, one within another. One of these, which was the driest and largest, and had a door out beyond my wall or fortification – that is to say, beyond where my wall joined to the rock – was all filled up with the large earthen pots of which I have given an account, and with fourteen or fifteen great baskets, which would hold five or six bushels each, where I laid up my stores of provisions, especially my corn, some in the ear, cut off short from the straw, and the other rubbed out with my hand.

As for my wall, made, as before, with long stakes or piles, those piles grew all like trees, and were by this time grown so big, and spread so very much, that there was not the least appearance, to any one's view, of any habitation behind them.

Near this dwelling of mine, but a little farther within the land, and upon lower ground, lay my two pieces of corn land, which I kept duly cultivated and sowed, and which duly yielded me their harvest in its season; and whenever I had occasion for more corn, I had more land adjoining as fit as that.

Besides this, I had my country seat, and I had now a tolerable plantation there also; for, first, I had my little bower, as I called it, which I kept in repair – that is to say, I kept the hedge which encircled it in constantly fitted up to its usual height, the ladder standing always in the inside. I kept the trees, which at first were no more than stakes, but were now grown very firm and tall, always cut, so that they might spread and grow thick and wild, and make the more agreeable shade, which they did effectually to my mind. In the middle of this I had my tent always standing, being a piece of a sail spread over poles, set up for that purpose, and which never wanted any repair or renewing; and under this I had made me a squab or couch with the skins of the creatures I had killed, and with other soft things, and a blanket laid on them, such as belonged to our sea-bedding, which I had saved; and a great watch-coat to cover me. And here, whenever I had occasion to be absent from my chief seat, I took up my country habitation.

Adjoining to this I had my enclosures for my cattle, that is to say my goats, and I had taken an inconceivable deal of pains to fence and enclose this ground. I was so anxious to see it kept entire, lest the goats should break through, that I never left off till, with infinite labour, I had stuck the outside of the hedge so full of small stakes, and so near to one another, that it was rather a pale than a hedge, and there was scarce room to put a hand through between them; which afterwards, when those stakes grew, as they all did in the next rainy season, made the enclosure strong like a wall, indeed stronger than any wall.

This will testify for me that I was not idle, and that I spared no pains to bring to pass whatever appeared necessary for my comfortable support, for I considered the keeping up a breed of tame creatures thus at my hand would be a living magazine of flesh, milk, butter, and cheese for me as long as I lived in the place, if it were to be forty years; and that keeping them in my reach depended entirely upon my perfecting my enclosures to such a degree that I might be sure of keeping them together; which by this method, indeed, I so effectually secured, that when these little stakes began to grow, I had planted them so very thick that I was forced to pull some of them up again.

In this place also I had my grapes growing, which I principally depended on for my winter store of raisins, and which I never failed to preserve very carefully, as the best and most agreeable dainty of my whole diet; and indeed they were not only agreeable, but medicinal, wholesome, nourishing, and refreshing to the last degree.

As this was also about half-way between my other habitation and the place where I had laid up my boat, I generally stayed and lay here in my way thither, for I used frequently to visit my boat; and I kept all things about or belonging to her in very good order. Sometimes I went out in her to divert myself, but no more hazardous voyages would I go, scarcely ever above a stone's cast or two from the shore, I was so apprehensive of being hurried out of my knowledge again by the currents or winds, or any other accident. But now I come to a new scene of my life. It happened one day, about noon, going towards my boat, I was exceedingly surprised with the print of a man's naked foot on the shore, which was very plain to be seen on the sand. I stood like one thunderstruck, or as if I had seen an apparition. I listened, I looked round me, but I could hear nothing, nor see anything; I went up to a rising ground to look farther; I went up the shore and down the shore, but it was all one; I could see no other impression but that one. I went to it again to see if there were any more, and to observe if it might not be my fancy; but there was no room for that, for there was exactly the print of a foot – toes, heel, and every part of a foot. How it came thither I knew not, nor could I in the least imagine; but after innumerable fluttering thoughts, like a man perfectly confused and out of myself, I came home to my fortification, not feeling, as we say, the ground I went on, but terrified to the last degree, looking behind me at every two or three steps, mistaking every bush and tree, and fancying every stump at a distance to be a man. Nor is it possible to describe how many various shapes my affrighted imagination represented things to me in, how many wild ideas were found every moment in my fancy, and what strange, unaccountable whimsies came into my thoughts by the way.

When I came to my castle (for so I think I called it ever after this), I fled into it like one pursued. Whether I went over by the ladder, as first contrived, or went in at the hole in the rock, which I had called a door, I cannot remember; no, nor could I remember the next morning, for never frightened hare fled to cover, or fox to earth, with more terror of mind than I to this retreat.

1903 illustration by Williams

I slept none that night; the farther I was from the occasion of my fright, the greater my apprehensions were, which is something contrary to the nature of such things, and especially to the usual practice of all creatures in fear; but I was so embarrassed with my own frightful ideas of the thing, that I formed nothing but dismal imaginations to myself, even though I was now a great way off. Sometimes I fancied it must be the devil, and reason joined in with me in this supposition, for how should any other thing in human shape come into the place? Where was the vessel that brought them? What marks were there of any other footstep? And how was it possible a man should come there? But then, to think that Satan should take human shape upon him in such a place, where there could be no manner of occasion for it, but to leave the print of his foot behind him, and that even for no purpose too, for he could not be sure I should see it – this was an amusement the other way. I considered that the devil might have found out abundance of other ways to have terrified me than this of the single print of a foot; that as I lived quite on the other side of the island, he would never have been so simple as to leave a mark in a place where it was ten thousand to one whether I should ever see it or not, and in the sand too, which the first surge of the sea, upon a high wind, would have defaced entirely. All this seemed inconsistent with the thing itself and with all the notions we usually entertain of the subtlety of the devil.

Abundance of such things as these assisted to argue me out of all apprehensions of its being the devil; and I presently concluded then that it must be some more dangerous creature – *viz.* that it must be some of the savages of the mainland opposite who had wandered out to sea in their canoes, and either driven by the currents or by contrary winds, had made the island, and had been on shore, but were gone away again to sea; being as loath, perhaps, to have stayed in this desolate island as I would have been to have had them.

While these reflections were rolling in my mind, I was very thankful in my thoughts that I was so happy as not to be thereabouts at that time, or that they did not see my boat, by which they would have concluded that some inhabitants had been in the place, and perhaps have searched farther for me. Then terrible thoughts racked my imagination about their having found out my boat, and that there were people here; and that, if so, I should certainly have them come again in greater numbers and devour me; that if it should happen that they should not find me, yet they would find my enclosure, destroy all my corn, and carry away all my flock of tame goats, and I should perish at last for mere want.

Thus my fear banished all my religious hope, all that former confidence in God, which was founded upon such wonderful experience as I had had of His goodness; as if He that had fed me by miracle hitherto could not preserve, by His power, the provision which He had made for me by His goodness. I reproached myself with my laziness, that would not sow any more corn one year than would just serve me till the next season, as if no accident could intervene to prevent my enjoying the crop that was upon the ground; and this I thought so just a reproof, that I resolved for the future to have two or three years' corn beforehand; so that, whatever might come, I might not perish for want of bread.

How strange a checquer-work of Providence is the life of man! and by what secret different springs are the affections hurried about, as different circumstances present! To-day we love what to-morrow we hate; to-day we seek what to-morrow we shun; to-day we desire what to-morrow we fear, nay, even tremble at the apprehensions of. This was exemplified in me, at this time, in the most lively manner imaginable; for I, whose only affliction was that I seemed banished from human society, that I was alone, circumscribed by the boundless ocean, cut off from mankind, and condemned to what I call silent life; that I was as one whom Heaven thought not worthy to be numbered among the living, or to appear among the rest of His creatures; that to have seen one of my own species would have seemed to me a raising me from death to life, and the greatest blessing that Heaven itself, next to the supreme blessing of salvation, could bestow; I say, that I should now tremble at the very apprehensions of seeing a man, and was ready to sink into the ground at but the shadow or silent appearance of a man having set his foot in the island.

Such is the uneven state of human life; and it afforded me a great many curious speculations afterwards, when I had a little recovered my first surprise. I considered that this was the station of life the infinitely wise and good providence of God had determined for me; that as I could not foresee what the ends of Divine wisdom might be in all this, so I was not to dispute His sovereignty; who, as I was His creature, had an undoubted right, by creation, to govern and dispose of me absolutely as He thought fit; and who, as I was a creature that had offended Him, had likewise a judicial right to condemn me to what punishment He thought fit; and that it was my part to submit to bear His indignation, because I had sinned against Him. I then reflected, that as God, who was not only righteous but omnipotent, had thought fit thus to punish and afflict me, so He was able to deliver me: that if He did not think fit to do so, it was my unquestioned duty to resign myself absolutely and entirely to His will; and, on the other hand, it was my duty also to hope in Him, pray to Him, and quietly to attend to the dictates and directions of His daily providence,

These thoughts took me up many hours, days, nay, I may say weeks and months: and one particular effect of my cogitations on this occasion I cannot omit. One morning early, lying in my bed, and filled with thoughts about my danger from the appearances of savages, I found it discomposed me very much; upon which these words of the Scripture came into my thoughts, "Call upon Me in the day of trouble, and I will deliver thee, and thou shalt glorify Me." Upon this, rising cheerfully out of my bed, my heart was not only comforted, but I was guided and encouraged to pray earnestly to God for deliverance: when I had done praying I took up my Bible, and opening it to read, the first words that presented to me were, "Wait on the Lord, and be of good cheer, and He shall strengthen thy heart; wait, I say, on the Lord." It is impossible to express the comfort this gave me. In answer, I thankfully laid down the book, and was no more sad, at least on that occasion.

In the middle of these cogitations, apprehensions, and reflections, it came into my thoughts one day that all this might be a mere chimera of my own, and that this foot might be the print of my own foot, when I came on shore from my boat: this cheered me up a little, too, and I began to persuade myself it was all a delusion; that it was nothing else but my own foot; and why might I not come that way from the boat, as well as I was going that way to the boat? Again, I considered also that I could by no means tell for certain where I had trod, and where I had not; and that if, at last, this was only the print of my own foot, I had played the part of those fools who try to make stories of spectres and apparitions, and then are frightened at them more than anybody.

Now I began to take courage, and to peep abroad again, for I had not stirred out of my castle for three days and nights, so that I began to starve for provisions; for I had little or nothing within doors but some barley-cakes and water; then I knew that my goats wanted to be milked too, which usually was my evening diversion: and the poor creatures were in great pain and inconvenience for want of it; and, indeed, it almost spoiled some of them, and almost dried up their milk. Encouraging myself, therefore, with the belief that this was nothing but the print of one of my own feet, and that I might be truly said to start at my own shadow, I began to go abroad again, and went to my country house to milk my flock: but to see with what fear I went forward, how often I looked behind me, how I was ready every now and then to lay down my basket and run for my life, it would have made any one have thought I was haunted with an evil conscience, or that I had been lately most terribly frightened; and so, indeed, I had. However, I went down thus two or three days, and having seen nothing, I began to be a little bolder, and to think there was really nothing in it but my own imagination; but I could not persuade myself fully of this till I should go down to the shore again, and see this print of a foot, and measure it by my own, and see if there was any similitude or fitness, that I might be assured it was my own foot: but when I came to the place, first, it appeared evidently to me, that when I laid up my boat I could not possibly be on shore anywhere thereabouts; secondly, when I came to measure the mark with my own foot, I found my foot not so large by a great deal. Both these things filled my head with new imaginations, and gave me the vapours again to the highest degree, so that I shook with cold like one in an ague; and I went home again, filled with the belief that some man or men had been on shore there; or, in short, that the island was inhabited, and I might be surprised before I was aware; and what course to take for my security I knew not.

Oh, what ridiculous resolutions men take when possessed with fear! It deprives them of the use of those means which reason offers for their relief. The first thing I proposed to myself was, to throw down my enclosures, and turn all my tame cattle wild into the woods, lest the enemy should find them, and then frequent the island in prospect of the same or the like booty: then the simple thing of digging up my two corn-fields, lest they should find such a grain there, and still be prompted to frequent the island: then to demolish my bower and tent, that they might not see any vestiges of habitation, and be prompted to look farther, in order to find out the persons inhabiting.

These were the subject of the first night's cogitations after I was come home again, while the apprehensions which had so overrun my mind were fresh upon me, and my head was full of vapours. Thus, fear of danger is 10,000 times more terrifying than danger itself, when apparent to the eyes; and we find the burden of anxiety greater, by much, than the evil which we are anxious about: and what was worse than all this, I had not that relief in this trouble that from the resignation I used to practise I hoped to have. I looked, I thought, like Saul, who complained not only that the Philistines were upon him, but that God had forsaken him; for I did not now take due ways to compose my mind, by crying to God in my distress, and resting upon His providence, as I had done before, for my defence and deliverance; which, if I had done, I had at least been more cheerfully supported under this new surprise, and perhaps carried through it with more resolution.

This confusion of my thoughts kept me awake all night; but in the morning I fell asleep; and having, by the amusement of my mind, been as it were tired, and my spirits exhausted, I slept very soundly, and waked much better composed than I had ever been before. And now I began to think sedately; and, upon debate with myself, I concluded that this island (which was so exceedingly pleasant, fruitful, and no farther from the mainland than as I had seen) was not so entirely abandoned as I might imagine; that although there were no stated inhabitants who lived on the spot, yet that there might sometimes come boats off from the shore, who, either with design, or perhaps never but when they were driven by cross winds, might come to this place; that I had lived there fifteen years now and had not met with the least shadow or figure of any people yet; and that, if at any time they should be driven here, it was probable they went away again as soon as ever they could, seeing they had never thought fit to fix here upon any occasion; that the most I could suggest any danger from, was, from any casual accidental landing of straggling people from the main, who, as it was likely, if they were driven hither, were here against their wills, so they made no stay here, but went off again with all possible speed; seldom staying one night on shore, lest they should not have the help of the tides and daylight back again; and that, therefore, I had nothing to do but to consider of some safe retreat, in case I should see any savages land upon the spot.

Now, I began sorely to repent that I had dug my cave so large as to bring a door through again, which door, as I said, came out beyond where my fortification joined to the rock: upon maturely considering this, therefore, I resolved to draw me a second fortification, in the manner of a semicircle, at a distance from my wall, just where I had planted a double row of trees about twelve years before, of which I made mention: these trees having been planted so thick before, they wanted but few piles to be driven between them, that they might be thicker and stronger, and my wall would be soon finished. So that I had now a double wall; and my outer wall was thickened with pieces of timber, old cables, and everything I could think of, to make it strong; having in it seven little holes, about as big as I might put my arm out at. In the inside of this I thickened my wall to about ten feet thick with continually bringing earth out of my cave, and laying it at the foot of the wall, and walking upon it; and through the seven holes I contrived to plant the muskets, of which I took notice that I had got seven on shore out of the ship; these I planted like my cannon, and fitted them into frames, that held them like a carriage, so that I could fire all the seven guns in two minutes' time; this wall I was many a weary month in finishing, and yet never thought myself safe till it was done.

When this was done I stuck all the ground without my wall, for a great length every way, as full with stakes or sticks of the osier-like wood, which I found so apt to grow, as they could well stand; insomuch that I believe I might set in near 20,000 of them, leaving a pretty large space between them and my wall, that I might have room to see an enemy, and they might have no shelter from the young trees, if they attempted to approach my outer wall.

Thus in two years' time I had a thick grove; and in five or six years' time I had a wood before my dwelling, growing so monstrously thick and strong that it was indeed perfectly impassable: and no men, of what kind soever, could ever imagine that there was anything beyond it, much less a habitation. As for the way which I proposed to myself to go in and out (for I left no avenue), it was by setting two ladders, one to a part of the rock which was low, and then broke in, and left room to place another ladder upon that; so when the two ladders were taken down no man living could come down to me without doing himself mischief; and if they had come down, they were still on the outside of my outer wall.

Thus I took all the measures human prudence could suggest for my own preservation; and it will be seen at length that they were not altogether without just reason; though I foresaw nothing at that time more than my mere fear suggested to me.

CHAPTER TWELVE

A Cave Retreat

While this was doing, I was not altogether careless of my other affairs; for I had a great concern upon me for my little herd of goats: they were not only a ready supply to me on every occasion, and began to be sufficient for me, without the expense of powder and shot, but also without the fatigue of hunting after the wild ones; and I was loath to lose the advantage of them, and to have them all to nurse up over again.

For this purpose, after long consideration, I could think of but two ways to preserve them: one was, to find another convenient place to dig a cave underground, and to drive them into it every night; and the other was to enclose two or three little bits of land, remote from one another, and as much concealed as I could, where I might keep about half-a-dozen young goats in each place; so that if any disaster happened to the flock in general, I might be able to raise them again with little trouble and time: and this though it would require a good deal of time and labour, I thought was the most rational design.

Accordingly, I spent some time to find out the most retired parts of the island; and I pitched upon one, which was as private, indeed, as my heart could wish: it was a little damp piece of ground in the middle of the hollow and thick woods, where, as is observed, I almost lost myself once before, endeavouring to come back that way from the eastern part of the island. Here I found a clear piece of land, near three acres, so surrounded with woods that it was almost an enclosure by nature; at least, it did not want near so much labour to make it so as the other piece of ground I had worked so hard at.

I immediately went to work with this piece of ground; and in less than a month's time I had so fenced it round that my flock, or herd, call it which you please, which were not so wild now as at first they might be supposed to be, were well enough secured in it: so, without any further delay, I removed ten young she-goats and two he-goats to this piece, and when they were there I continued to perfect the fence till I had made it as secure as the other; which, however, I did at more leisure, and it took me up more time by a great deal. All this labour I was at the expense of, purely from my apprehensions on account of the print of a man's foot; for as yet I had never seen any human creature come near the island; and I had now lived two years under this uneasiness, which, indeed, made my life much less comfortable than it was before, as may be well imagined by any who know what it is to live in the constant snare of the fear of man. And this I must observe, with grief, too, that the discomposure of my mind had great impression also upon the religious part of my thoughts; for the dread and terror of falling into the hands of savages and cannibals lay so upon my spirits, that I seldom found myself in a due temper for application to my Maker; at least, not with the sedate calmness and resignation of soul which I was wont to do: I rather prayed to God as under great affliction and pressure of mind, surrounded with danger, and in expectation every night of being murdered and devoured before morning; and I must testify, from my experience, that a temper of peace, thankfulness, love, and affection, is much the more proper frame for prayer than that of terror and discomposure: and that under the dread of mischief impending, a man is no more fit for a comforting performance of the duty of praying to God than he is for a repentance on a sick-bed; for these discomposures affect the mind, as the others do the body; and the discomposure of the mind must necessarily be as great a disability as that of the body, and much greater; praying to God being properly an act of the mind, not of the body.

But to go on. After I had thus secured one part of my little living stock, I went about the whole island, searching for another private place to make such another deposit; when, wandering more to the west point of the island than I had ever done yet, and looking out to sea, I thought I saw a boat upon the sea, at a great distance. I had found a perspective glass or two in one of the seamen's chests, which I saved out of our ship, but I had it not about me; and this was so remote that I could not tell what to make of it, though I looked at it till my eyes were not able to hold to look any longer; whether it was a boat or not I do not know, but as I descended from the hill I could see no more of it, so I gave it over; only I resolved to go no more out without a perspective glass in my pocket. When I was come down the hill to the end of the island, where, indeed, I had never been before, I was presently convinced that the seeing the print of a man's foot was not such a strange thing in the island as I imagined:

and but that it was a special providence that I was cast upon the side of the island where the savages never came, I should easily have known that nothing was more frequent than for the canoes from the main, when they happened to be a little too far out at sea, to shoot over to that side of the island for harbour: likewise, as they often met and fought in their canoes, the victors, having taken any prisoners, would bring them over to this shore, where, according to their dreadful customs, being all cannibals, they would kill and eat them; of which hereafter.

When I was come down the hill to the shore, as I said above, being the S.W. point of the island, I was perfectly confounded and amazed; nor is it possible for me to express the horror of my mind at seeing the shore spread with skulls, hands, feet, and other bones of human bodies; and particularly I observed a place where there had been a fire made, and a circle dug in the earth, like a cockpit, where I supposed the savage wretches had sat down to their human feastings upon the bodies of their fellow-creatures.

I was so astonished with the sight of these things, that I entertained no notions of any danger to myself from it for a long while: all my apprehensions were buried in the thoughts of such a pitch of inhuman, hellish brutality, and the horror of the degeneracy of human nature, which, though I had heard of it often, yet I never had so near a view of before; in short, I turned away my face from the horrid spectacle; my stomach grew sick, and I was just at the point of fainting, when nature discharged the disorder from my stomach; and having vomited with uncommon violence, I was a little relieved, but could not bear to stay in the place a moment; so I got up the hill again with all the speed I could, and walked on towards my own habitation.

When I came a little out of that part of the island I stood still awhile, as amazed, and then, recovering myself, I looked up with the utmost affection of my soul, and, with a flood of tears in my eyes, gave God thanks, that had cast my first lot in a part of the world where I was distinguished from such dreadful creatures as these; and that, though I had esteemed my present condition very miserable, had yet given me so many comforts in it that I had still more to give thanks for than to complain of: and this, above all, that I had, even in this miserable condition, been comforted with the knowledge of Himself, and the hope of His blessing: which was a felicity more than sufficiently equivalent to all the misery which I had suffered, or could suffer.

In this frame of thankfulness I went home to my castle, and began to be much easier now, as to the safety of my circumstances, than ever I was before: for I observed that these wretches never came to this island in search of what they could get; perhaps not seeking, not wanting, or not expecting anything here; and having often, no doubt, been up the covered, woody part of it without finding anything to their purpose. I knew I had been here now almost eighteen years, and never saw the least footsteps of human creature there before; and I might be eighteen years more as entirely concealed as I was now, if I did not discover myself to them, which I had no manner of occasion to do; it being my only business to keep myself entirely concealed where I was, unless I found a better sort of creatures than cannibals to make myself known to. Yet I entertained such an abhorrence of the savage wretches that I have been speaking of, and of the wretched, inhuman custom of their devouring and eating one another up, that I continued pensive and sad, and kept close within my own circle for almost two years after this: when I say my own circle, I mean by it my three plantations – *viz.* my castle, my country seat (which I called my bower), and my enclosure in the woods: nor did I look after this for any other use than an enclosure for my goats; for the aversion which nature gave me to these hellish wretches was such, that I was as fearful of seeing them as of seeing the devil himself. I did not so much as go to look after my boat all this time, but began rather to think of making another; for I could not think of ever making any more attempts to bring the other boat round the island to me, lest I should meet with some of these creatures at sea; in which case, if I had happened to have fallen into their hands, I knew what would have been my lot.

Time, however, and the satisfaction I had that I was in no danger of being discovered by these people, began to wear off my uneasiness about them; and I began to live just in the same composed manner as before, only with this difference, that I used more caution, and kept my eyes more about me than I did before, lest I should happen to be seen by any of them; and particularly, I was more cautious of firing my gun, lest any of them, being on the island, should happen to hear it. It was, therefore, a very good providence to me that I had furnished myself with a tame breed of goats, and that I had no need to hunt any more about the woods, or shoot at them; and if I did catch any of them after this, it was by traps and snares, as I had done before; so that for two years after this I believe I never fired my gun once off, though I never went out without it; and what was more, as I had saved three pistols out of the ship, I always carried them out with me, or at least two of them, sticking them in my goatskin belt. I also furbished up one of the great cutlasses that I had out of the ship, and made me a belt to hang it on also; so that I was now a most formidable fellow to look at when I went abroad, if you add to the former description of myself the particular of two pistols, and a broadsword hanging at my side in a belt, but without a scabbard.

Things going on thus, as I have said, for some time, I seemed, excepting these cautions, to be reduced to my former calm, sedate way of living. All these things tended to show me more and more how far my condition was from being miserable, compared to some others; nay, to many other particulars of life which it might have pleased God to have made my lot. It put me upon reflecting how little repining there would be among mankind at any condition of life if people would rather compare their condition with those that were worse, in order to be thankful, than be always comparing them with those which are better, to assist their murmurings and complainings.

As in my present condition there were not really many things which I wanted, so indeed I thought that the frights I had been in about these savage wretches, and the concern I had been in for my own preservation, had taken off the edge of my invention, for my own conveniences; and I had dropped a good design, which I had once bent my thoughts upon, and that was to try if I could not make some of my barley into malt, and then try to brew myself some beer. This was really a whimsical thought, and I reproved myself often for the simplicity of it: for I presently saw there would be the want of several things necessary to the making my beer that it would be impossible for me to supply; as, first, casks to preserve it in, which was a thing that, as I have observed already, I could never compass: no, though I spent not only many days, but weeks, nay months, in attempting it, but to no purpose. In the next place, I had no hops to make it keep, no yeast to made it work, no copper or kettle to make it boil; and yet with all these things wanting, I verily believe, had not the frights and terrors I was in about the savages intervened, I had undertaken it, and perhaps brought it to pass too; for I seldom gave anything over without accomplishing it, when once I had it in my head to began it. But my invention now ran quite another way; for night and day I could think of nothing but how I might destroy some of the monsters in their cruel, bloody entertainment, and if possible save the victim they should bring hither to destroy. It would take up a larger volume than this whole work is intended to be to set down all the contrivances I hatched, or rather brooded upon, in my thoughts, for the destroying these creatures, or at least frightening them so as to prevent their coming hither any more: but all this was abortive; nothing could be possible to take effect, unless I was to be there to do it myself: and what could one man do among them, when perhaps there might be twenty or thirty of them together with their darts, or their bows and arrows, with which they could shoot as true to a mark as I could with my gun?

Sometimes I thought if digging a hole under the place where they made their fire, and putting in five or six pounds of gunpowder, which, when they kindled their fire, would consequently take fire, and blow up all that was near it: but as, in the first place, I should be unwilling to waste so much powder upon them, my store being now within the quantity of one barrel, so neither could I be sure of its going off at any certain time, when it might surprise them; and, at best, that it would do little more than just blow the fire about their ears and fright them, but not sufficient to make them forsake the place: so I laid it aside; and then proposed that I would place myself in ambush in some convenient place, with my three guns all double-loaded, and in the middle of their bloody ceremony let fly at them, when I should be sure to kill or wound perhaps two or three at every shot; and then falling in upon them with my three pistols and my sword, I made no doubt but that, if there were twenty, I should kill them all. This fancy pleased my thoughts for some weeks, and I was so full of it that I often dreamed of it, and, sometimes, that I was just going to let fly at them in my sleep. I went so far with it in my imagination that I employed myself several days to find out proper places to put myself in ambuscade, as I said, to watch for them, and I went frequently to the place itself, which was now grown more familiar to me; but while my mind was thus filled with thoughts of revenge and a bloody putting twenty or thirty of them to the sword, as I may call it, the horror I had at the place, and at the signals of the barbarous wretches devouring one another, abetted my malice. Well, at length I found a place in the side of the hill where I was satisfied I might securely wait till I saw any of their boats coming; and might then, even before they would be ready to come on shore, convey myself unseen into some thickets of trees, in one of which there was a hollow large enough to conceal me entirely; and there I might sit and observe all their bloody doings, and take my full aim at their heads, when they were so close together as that it would be next to impossible that I should miss my shot, or that I could fail wounding three or four of them at the first shot. In this place, then, I resolved to fulfil my design; and accordingly I prepared two muskets and my ordinary fowling-piece. The two muskets I loaded with a brace of slugs each, and four or five smaller bullets, about the size of pistol bullets; and the fowling-piece I loaded with near a handful of swan-shot of the largest size; I also loaded my pistols with about four bullets each; and, in this posture, well provided with ammunition for a second and third charge, I prepared myself for my expedition.

After I had thus laid the scheme of my design, and in my imagination put it in practice, I continually made my tour every morning to the top of the hill, which was from my castle, as I called it, about three miles or more, to see if I could observe any boats upon the sea, coming near the island, or standing over towards it; but I began to tire of this hard duty, after I had for two or three months constantly kept my watch, but came always back without any discovery; there having not, in all that time, been the least appearance, not only on or near the shore, but on the whole ocean, so far as my eye or glass could reach every way.

As long as I kept my daily tour to the hill, to look out, so long also I kept up the vigour of my design, and my spirits seemed to be all the while in a suitable frame for so outrageous an execution as the killing twenty or thirty naked savages, for an offence which I had not at all entered into any discussion of in my thoughts, any farther than my passions were at first fired by the horror I conceived at the unnatural custom of the people of that country, who, it seems, had been suffered by Providence, in His wise disposition of the world, to have no other guide than that of their own abominable and vitiated passions; and consequently were left, and perhaps had been so for some ages, to act such horrid things, and receive such dreadful customs, as nothing but nature, entirely abandoned by Heaven, and actuated by some hellish degeneracy, could have run them into. But now, when, as I have said, I began to be weary of the fruitless excursion which I had made so long and so far every morning in vain, so my opinion of the action itself began to alter; and I began, with cooler and calmer thoughts, to consider what I was going to engage in; what authority or call I had to pretend to be judge and executioner upon these men as criminals, whom Heaven had thought fit for so many ages to suffer unpunished to go on, and to be as it were the executioners of His judgments one upon another; how far these people were offenders against me, and what right I had to engage in the quarrel of that blood which they shed promiscuously upon one another. I debated this very often with myself thus: "How do I know what God Himself judges in this particular case? It is certain these people do not commit this as a crime; it is not against their own consciences reproving, or their light reproaching them; they do not know it to be an offence, and then commit it in defiance of divine justice, as we do in almost all the sins we commit. They think it no more a crime to kill a captive taken in war than we do to kill an ox; or to eat human flesh than we do to eat mutton."

When I considered this a little, it followed necessarily that I was certainly in the wrong; that these people were not murderers, in the sense that I had before condemned them in my thoughts, any more than those Christians were murderers who often put to death the prisoners taken in battle; or more frequently, upon many occasions, put whole troops of men to the sword, without giving quarter, though they threw down their arms and submitted. In the next place, it occurred to me that although the usage they gave one another was thus brutish and inhuman, yet it was really nothing to me: these people had done me no injury: that if they attempted, or I saw it necessary, for my immediate preservation, to fall upon them, something might be said for it: but that I was yet out of their power, and they really had no knowledge of me, and consequently no design upon me; and therefore it could not be just for me to fall upon them; that this would justify the conduct of the Spaniards in all their barbarities practised in America, where they destroyed millions of these people; who, however they were idolaters and barbarians, and had several bloody and barbarous rites in their customs, such as sacrificing human bodies to their idols, were yet, as to the Spaniards, very innocent people; and that the rooting them out of the country is spoken of with the utmost abhorrence and detestation by even the Spaniards themselves at this time, and by all other Christian nations of Europe, as a mere butchery, a bloody and unnatural piece of cruelty, unjustifiable either to God or man; and for which the very name of a Spaniard is reckoned to be frightful and terrible, to all people of humanity or of Christian compassion; as if the kingdom of Spain were particularly eminent for the produce of a race of men who were without principles of tenderness, or the common bowels of pity to the miserable, which is reckoned to be a mark of generous temper in the mind.

These considerations really put me to a pause, and to a kind of a full stop; and I began by little and little to be off my design, and to conclude I had taken wrong measures in my resolution to attack the savages; and that it was not my business to meddle with them, unless they first attacked me; and this it was my business, if possible, to prevent: but that, if I were discovered and attacked by them, I knew my duty. On the other hand, I argued with myself that this really was the way not to deliver myself, but entirely to ruin and destroy myself; for unless I was sure to kill every one that not only should be on shore at that time, but that should ever come on shore afterwards, if but one of them escaped to tell their country-people what had happened, they would come over again by thousands to revenge the death of their fellows, and I should only bring upon myself a certain destruction, which, at present, I had no manner of occasion for. Upon the whole, I concluded that I ought, neither in principle nor in policy, one way or other, to concern myself in this affair: that my business was, by all possible means to conceal myself from them, and not to leave the least sign for them to guess by that there were any living creatures upon the island – I mean of human shape. Religion joined in with this prudential resolution; and I was convinced now, many ways, that I was perfectly out of my duty when I was laying all my bloody schemes for the destruction of innocent creatures – I mean innocent as to me. As to the crimes they were guilty of towards one another, I had nothing to do with them; they were national, and I ought to leave them to the justice of God, who is the Governor of nations, and knows how, by national punishments, to make a just retribution for national offences, and to bring public judgments upon those who offend in a public manner, by such ways as best please Him. This appeared so clear to me now, that nothing was a greater satisfaction to me than that I had not been suffered to do a thing which I now saw so much reason to believe would have been no less a sin than that of wilful murder if I had committed it; and I gave most humble thanks on my knees to God, that He had thus delivered me from blood-guiltiness; beseeching Him to grant me the protection of His providence, that I might not fall into the hands of the barbarians, or that I might not lay my hands upon them, unless I had a more clear call from Heaven to do it, in defence of my own life.

In this disposition I continued for near a year after this; and so far was I from desiring an occasion for falling upon these wretches, that in all that time I never once went up the hill to see whether there were any of them in sight, or to know whether any of them had been on shore there or not, that I might not be tempted to renew any of my contrivances against them, or be provoked by any advantage that might present itself to fall upon them; only this I did: I went and removed my boat, which I had on the other side of the island, and carried it down to the east end of the whole island, where I ran it into a little cove, which I found under some high rocks, and where I knew, by reason of the currents, the savages durst not, at least would not, come with their boats upon any account whatever. With my boat I carried away everything that I had left there belonging to her, though not necessary for the bare going thither – *viz.* a mast and sail which I had made for her, and a thing like an anchor, but which, indeed, could not be called either anchor or grapnel; however, it was the best I could make of its kind: all these I removed, that there might not be the least shadow for discovery, or appearance of any boat, or of any human habitation upon the island. Besides this, I kept myself, as I said, more retired than ever, and seldom went from my cell except upon my constant employment, to milk my she-goats, and manage my little flock in the wood, which, as it was quite on the other part of the island, was out of danger; for certain, it is that these savage people, who sometimes haunted this island, never came with any thoughts of finding anything here, and consequently never wandered off from the coast, and I doubt not but they might have been several times on shore after my apprehensions of them had made me cautious, as well as before. Indeed, I looked back with some horror upon the thoughts of what my condition would have been if I had chopped upon them and been discovered before that; when, naked and unarmed, except with one gun, and that loaded often only with small shot, I walked everywhere, peeping and peering about the island, to see what I could get; what a surprise should I have been in if, when I discovered the print of a man's foot, I had, instead of that, seen fifteen or twenty savages, and found them pursuing me, and by the swiftness of their running no possibility of my escaping them! The thoughts of this sometimes sank my very soul within me, and distressed my mind so much that I could not soon recover it, to think what I should have done, and how I should not only have been unable to resist them, but even should not have had presence of mind enough to do what I might have done; much less what now, after so much consideration and preparation, I might be able to do. Indeed, after serious thinking of these things, I would be melancholy, and sometimes it would last a great while; but I resolved it all at last into thankfulness to that Providence which had delivered me from so many unseen dangers, and had kept me from those mischiefs which I could have no way been the agent in delivering myself from, because I had not the least notion of any such thing depending, or the least supposition of its being possible. This renewed a contemplation which often had come into my thoughts in former times, when first I began to see the merciful dispositions of Heaven, in the dangers we run through in this life; how wonderfully we are delivered when we know nothing of it; how, when we are in a quandary as we call it, a doubt or hesitation whether to go this way or that way, a secret hint shall direct us this way, when we intended to go that way: nay, when sense, our own inclination, and perhaps business has called us to go the other way, yet a strange impression upon the mind, from we know not what springs, and by we know not what power, shall overrule us to go this way; and it shall afterwards appear that had we gone that way, which we should have gone, and even to our imagination ought to have gone, we should have been ruined and lost. Upon these and many like reflections I afterwards made it a certain rule with me, that whenever I found those secret hints or pressings of mind to doing or not doing anything that presented, or going this way or that way, I never failed to obey the secret dictate; though I knew no other reason for it than such a pressure or such a hint hung upon my mind. I could give many examples of the success of this conduct in the course of my life, but more especially in the latter part of my inhabiting this unhappy island; besides many occasions which it is very likely I might have taken notice of, if I had seen with the same eyes then that I see with now. But it is never too late to be wise; and I cannot but advise all considering men, whose lives are attended with such extraordinary incidents as mine, or even though not so extraordinary, not to slight such secret intimations of Providence, let them come from what invisible intelligence they will. That I shall not discuss, and perhaps cannot account for; but certainly they are a proof of the converse of spirits, and a secret communication between those embodied and those unembodied, and such a proof as can never be withstood; of which I shall have occasion to give some remarkable instances in the remainder of my solitary residence in this dismal place.

I believe the reader of this will not think it strange if I confess that these anxieties, these constant dangers I lived in, and the concern that was now upon me, put an end to all invention, and to all the contrivances that I had laid for my future accommodations and conveniences. I had the care of my safety more now upon my hands than that of my food. I cared not to drive a nail, or chop a stick of wood now, for fear the noise I might make should be heard: much less would I fire a gun for the same reason: and above all I was intolerably uneasy at making any fire, lest the smoke, which is visible at a great distance in the day, should betray me. For this reason, I removed that part of my business which required fire, such as burning of pots and pipes, &c. into my new apartment in the woods; where, after I had been some time, I found, to my unspeakable consolation, a mere natural cave in the earth, which went in a vast way, and where, I daresay, no savage, had he been at the mouth of it, would be so hardy as to venture in; nor, indeed, would any man else, but one who, like me, wanted nothing so much as a safe retreat.

The mouth of this hollow was at the bottom of a great rock, where, by mere accident (I would say, if I did not see abundant reason to ascribe all such things now to Providence), I was cutting down some thick branches of trees to make charcoal; and before I go on I must observe the reason of my making this charcoal, which was this – I was afraid of making a smoke about my habitation, as I said before; and yet I could not live there without baking my bread, cooking my meat, &c. so I contrived to burn some wood here, as I had seen done in England, under turf, till it became chark or dry coal: and then putting the fire out, I preserved the coal to carry home, and perform the other services for which fire was wanting, without danger of smoke. But this is by-the-bye. While I was cutting down some wood here, I perceived that, behind a very thick branch of low brushwood or underwood, there was a kind of hollow place: I was curious to look in it; and getting with difficulty into the mouth of it, I found it was pretty large, that is to say, sufficient for me to stand upright in it, and perhaps another with me: but I must confess to you that I made more haste out than I did in, when looking farther into the place, and which was perfectly dark, I saw two broad shining eyes of some creature, whether devil or man I knew not, which twinkled like two stars; the dim light from the cave's mouth shining directly in, and making the reflection. However, after some pause I recovered myself, and began to call myself a thousand fools, and to think that he that was afraid to see the devil was not fit to live twenty years in an island all alone; and that I might well think there was nothing in this cave that was more frightful than myself. Upon this, plucking up my courage, I took up a firebrand, and in I rushed again, with the stick flaming in my hand: I had not gone three steps in before I was almost as frightened as before; for I heard a very loud sigh, like that of a man in some pain, and it was followed by a broken noise, as of words half expressed, and then a deep sigh again. I stepped back, and was indeed struck with such a surprise that it put me into a cold sweat, and if I had had a hat on my head, I will not answer for it that my hair might not have lifted it off. But still plucking up my spirits as well as I could, and encouraging myself a little with considering that the power and presence of God was everywhere, and was able to protect me, I stepped forward again, and by the light of the firebrand, holding it up a little over my head, I saw lying on the ground a monstrous, frightful old he-goat, just making his will, as we say, and gasping for life, and, dying, indeed, of mere old age. I stirred him a little to see if I could get him out, and he essayed to get up, but was not able to raise himself; and I thought with myself he might even lie there for if he had frightened me, so he would certainly fright any of the savages, if any of them should be so hardy as to come in there while he had any life in him.

I was now recovered from my surprise, and began to look round me, when I found the cave was but very small – that is to say, it might be about twelve feet over, but in no manner of shape, neither round nor square, no hands having ever been employed in making it but those of mere Nature. I observed also that there was a place at the farther side of it that went in further, but was so low that it required me to creep upon my hands and knees to go into it, and whither it went I knew not; so, having no candle, I gave it over for that time, but resolved to go again the next day provided with candles and a tinder-box, which I had made of the lock of one of the muskets, with some wildfire in the pan.

Accordingly, the next day I came provided with six large candles of my own making (for I made very good candles now of goat's tallow, but was hard set for candle-wick, using sometimes rags or rope-yarn, and sometimes the dried rind of a weed like nettles); and going into this low place I was obliged to creep upon all-fours as I have said, almost ten yards – which, by the way, I thought was a venture bold enough, considering that I knew not how far it might go, nor what was beyond it. When I had got through the strait, I found the roof rose higher up, I believe near twenty feet; but never was such a glorious sight seen in the island, I daresay, as it was to look round the sides and roof of this vault or cave – the wall reflected a hundred thousand lights to me from my two candles. What it was in the rock – whether diamonds or any other precious stones, or gold which I rather supposed it to be – I knew not. The place I was in was a most delightful cavity, or grotto, though perfectly dark; the floor was dry and level, and had a sort of a small loose gravel upon it, so that there was no nauseous or venomous creature to be seen, neither was there any damp or wet on the sides or roof. The only difficulty in it was the entrance – which, however, as it was a place of security, and such a retreat as I wanted; I thought was a convenience; so that I was really rejoiced at the discovery, and resolved, without any delay, to bring some of those things which I was most anxious about to this place: particularly, I resolved to bring hither my magazine of powder, and all my spare arms – *viz.* two fowling-pieces – for I had three in all – and three muskets – for of them I had eight in all; so I kept in my castle only five, which stood ready mounted like pieces of cannon on my outmost fence, and were ready also to take out upon any expedition. Upon this occasion of removing my ammunition I happened to open the barrel of powder which I took up out of the sea, and which had been wet, and I found that the water had penetrated about three or four inches into the powder on every side, which caking and growing hard, had preserved the inside like a kernel in the shell, so that I had near sixty pounds of very good powder in the centre of the cask. This was a very agreeable discovery to me at that time; so I carried all away thither, never keeping above two or three pounds of powder with me in my castle, for fear of a surprise of any kind; I also carried thither all the lead I had left for bullets.

I fancied myself now like one of the ancient giants who were said to live in caves and holes in the rocks, where none could come at them; for I persuaded myself, while I was here, that if five hundred savages were to hunt me, they could never find me out – or if they did, they would not venture to attack me here. The old goat whom I found expiring died in the mouth of the cave the next day after I made this discovery; and I found it much easier to dig a great hole there, and throw him in and cover him with earth, than to drag him out; so I interred him there, to prevent offence to my nose.

CHAPTER THIRTEEN

Wreck of a Spanish Ship

I WAS NOW IN THE 23rd year of my residence in this island, and was so naturalized to the place and the manner of living, that, could I but have enjoyed the certainty that no savages would come to the place to disturb me, I could have been content to have capitulated for spending the rest of my time there, even to the last moment, till I had laid me down and died, like the old goat in the cave. I had also arrived to some little diversions and amusements, which made the time pass a great deal more pleasantly with me than it did before – first, I had taught my Poll, as I noted before, to speak; and he did it so familiarly, and talked so articulately and plain, that it was very pleasant to me; and he lived with me no less than six-and-twenty years. How long he might have lived afterwards I know not, though I know they have a notion in the Brazils that they live a hundred years. My dog was a pleasant and loving companion to me for no less than sixteen years of my time, and then died of mere old age. As for my cats, they multiplied, as I have observed, to that degree that I was obliged to shoot several of them at first, to keep them from devouring me and all I had; but at length, when the two old ones I brought with me were gone, and after some time continually driving them from me, and letting them have no provision with me, they all ran wild into the woods, except two or three favourites, which I kept tame, and whose young, when they had any, I always drowned; and these were part of my family. Besides these I always kept two or three household kids about me, whom I taught to feed out of my hand; and I had two more parrots, which talked pretty well, and would all call "Robin Crusoe," but none like my first; nor, indeed, did I take the pains with any of them that I had done with him. I had also several tame sea-fowls, whose name I knew not, that I caught upon the shore, and cut their wings; and the little stakes which I had planted before my castle-wall being now grown up to a good thick grove, these fowls all lived among these low trees, and bred there, which was very agreeable to me; so that, as I said above, I began to he very well contented with the life I led, if I could have been secured from the dread of the savages. But it was otherwise directed; and it may not be amiss for all people who shall meet with my story to make this just observation from it: How frequently, in the course of our lives, the evil which in itself we seek most to shun, and which, when we are fallen into, is the most dreadful to us, is oftentimes the very means or door of our deliverance, by which alone we can be raised again from the affliction we are fallen into. I could give many examples of this in the course of my unaccountable life; but in nothing was it more particularly remarkable than in the circumstances of my last years of solitary residence in this island.

It was now the month of December, as I said above, in my 23rd year; and this, being the southern solstice (for winter I cannot call it), was the particular time of my harvest, and required me to be pretty much abroad in the fields, when, going out early in the morning, even before it was thorough daylight, I was surprised with seeing a light of some fire upon the shore, at a distance from me of about two miles, toward that part of the island where I had observed some savages had been, as before, and not on the other side; but, to my great affliction, it was on my side of the island.

I was indeed terribly surprised at the sight, and stopped short within my grove, not daring to go out, lest I might be surprised; and yet I had no more peace within, from the apprehensions I had that if these savages, in rambling over the island, should find my corn standing or cut, or any of my works or improvements, they would immediately conclude that there were people in the place, and would then never rest till they had found me out. In this extremity I went back directly to my castle, pulled up the ladder after me, and made all things without look as wild and natural as I could.

Then I prepared myself within, putting myself in a posture of defence. I loaded all my cannon, as I called them – that is to say, my muskets, which were mounted upon my new fortification – and all my pistols, and resolved to defend myself to the last gasp – not forgetting seriously to commend myself to the Divine protection, and earnestly to pray to God to deliver me out of the hands of the barbarians. I continued in this posture about two hours, and began to be impatient for intelligence abroad, for I had no spies to send out. After sitting a while longer, and musing what I should do in this case, I was not able to bear sitting in ignorance longer; so setting up my ladder to the side of the hill, where there was a flat place, as I observed before, and then pulling the ladder after me, I set it up again and mounted the top of the hill, and pulling out my perspective glass, which I had taken on purpose, I laid me down flat on my belly on the ground, and began to look for the place. I presently found there were no less than nine naked savages sitting round a small fire they had made, not to warm them, for they had no need of that, the weather being extremely hot, but, as I supposed, to dress some of their barbarous diet of human flesh which they had brought with them, whether alive or dead I could not tell.

They had two canoes with them, which they had hauled up upon the shore; and as it was then ebb of tide, they seemed to me to wait for the return of the flood to go away again. It is not easy to imagine what confusion this sight put me into, especially seeing them come on my side of the island, and so near to me; but when I considered their coming must be always with the current of the ebb, I began afterwards to be more sedate in my mind, being satisfied that I might go abroad with safety all the time of the flood of tide, if they were not on shore before; and having made this observation, I went abroad about my harvest work with the more composure.

As I expected, so it proved; for as soon as the tide made to the westward I saw them all take boat and row (or paddle as we call it) away. I should have observed, that for an hour or more before they went off they were dancing, and I could easily discern their postures and gestures by my glass. I could not perceive, by my nicest observation, but that they were stark naked, and had not the least covering upon them; but whether they were men or women I could not distinguish.

As soon as I saw them shipped and gone, I took two guns upon my shoulders, and two pistols in my girdle, and my great sword by my side without a scabbard, and with all the speed I was able to make went away to the hill where I had discovered the first appearance of all; and as soon as I get thither, which was not in less than two hours (for I could not go quickly, being so loaded with arms as I was), I perceived there had been three canoes more of the savages at that place; and looking out farther, I saw they were all at sea together, making over for the main. This was a dreadful sight to me, especially as, going down to the shore, I could see the marks of horror which the dismal work they had been about had left behind it – *viz.* the blood, the bones, and part of the flesh of human bodies eaten and devoured by those wretches with merriment and sport. I was so filled with indignation at the sight, that I now began to premeditate the destruction of the next that I saw there, let them be whom or how many soever. It seemed evident to me that the visits which they made thus to this island were not very frequent, for it was above fifteen months before any more of them came on shore there again – that is to say, I neither saw them nor any footsteps or signals of them in all that time; for as to the rainy seasons, then they are sure not to come abroad, at least not so far. Yet all this while I lived uncomfortably, by reason of the constant apprehensions of their coming upon me by surprise: from whence I observe, that the expectation of evil is more bitter than the suffering, especially if there is no room to shake off that expectation or those apprehensions.

During all this time I was in a murdering humour, and spent most of my hours, which should have been better employed, in contriving how to circumvent and fall upon them the very next time I should see them – especially if they should be divided, as they were the last time, into two parties; nor did I consider at all that if I killed one party – suppose ten or a dozen – I was still the next day, or week, or month, to kill another, and so another, even *ad infinitum*, till I should be, at length, no less a murderer than they were in being man-eaters – and perhaps much more so. I spent my days now in great perplexity and anxiety of mind, expecting that I should one day or other fall, into the hands of these merciless creatures; and if I did at any time venture abroad, it was not without looking around me with the greatest care and caution imaginable. And now I found, to my great comfort, how happy it was that I had provided a tame flock or herd of goats, for I durst not upon any account fire my gun, especially near that side of the island where they usually came, lest I should alarm the savages; and if they had fled from me now, I was sure to have them come again with perhaps two or three hundred canoes with them in a few days, and then I knew what to expect. However, I wore out a year and three months more before I ever saw any more of the savages, and then I found them again, as I shall soon observe. It is true they might have been there once or twice; but either they made no stay, or at least I did not see them; but in the month of May, as near as I could calculate, and in my four-and-twentieth year, I had a very strange encounter with them; of which in its place.

The perturbation of my mind during this fifteen or sixteen months' interval was very great; I slept unquietly, dreamed always frightful dreams, and often started out of my sleep in the night. In the day great troubles overwhelmed my mind; and in the night I dreamed often of killing the savages and of the reasons why I might justify doing it.

But to waive all this for a while. It was in the middle of May, on the 16th day, I think, as well as my poor wooden calendar would reckon, for

I marked all upon the post still; I say, it was on the 16th of May that it blew a very great storm of wind all day, with a great deal of lightning and thunder, and; a very foul night it was after it. I knew not what was the particular occasion of it, but as I was reading in the Bible, and taken up with very serious thoughts about my present condition, I was surprised with the noise of a gun, as I thought, fired at sea. This was, to be sure, a surprise quite of a different nature from any I had met with before; for the notions this put into my thoughts were quite of another kind. I started up in the greatest haste imaginable; and, in a trice, clapped my ladder to the middle place of the rock, and pulled it after me; and mounting it the second time, got to the top of the hill the very moment that a flash of fire bid me listen for a second gun, which, accordingly, in about half a minute I heard; and by the sound, knew that it was from that part of the sea where I was driven down the current in my boat. I immediately considered that this must be some ship in distress, and that they had some comrade, or some other ship in company, and fired these for signals of distress, and to obtain help. I had the presence of mind at that minute to think, that though I could not help them, it might be that they might help me; so I brought together all the dry wood I could get at hand, and making a good handsome pile, I set it on fire upon the hill. The wood was dry, and blazed freely; and, though the wind blew very hard, yet it burned fairly out; so that I was certain, if there was any such thing as a ship, they must needs see it. And no doubt they did; for as soon as ever my fire blazed up, I heard another gun, and after that several others, all from the same quarter. I plied my fire all night long, till daybreak: and when it was broad day, and the air cleared up, I saw something at a great distance at sea, full east of the island, whether a sail or a hull I could not distinguish – no, not with my glass: the distance was so great, and the weather still something hazy also; at least, it was so out at sea.

I looked frequently at it all that day, and soon perceived that it did not move; so I presently concluded that it was a ship at anchor; and being eager, you may be sure, to be satisfied, I took my gun in my hand, and ran towards the south side of the island to the rocks where I had formerly been carried away by the current; and getting up there, the weather by this time being perfectly clear, I could plainly see, to my great sorrow, the wreck of a ship, cast away in the night upon those concealed rocks which I found when I was out in my boat; and which rocks, as they checked the violence of the stream, and made a kind of counter-stream, or eddy, were the occasion of my recovering from the most desperate, hopeless condition that ever I had been in, in all my life. Thus, what is one man's safety is another man's destruction; for it seems these men, whoever they were, being out of their knowledge, and the rocks being wholly under water, had been driven upon them in the night, the wind blowing hard at E.N.E. Had they seen the island, as I must necessarily suppose they did not, they must, as I thought, have endeavoured to have saved themselves on shore by the help of their boat; but their firing off guns for help, especially when they saw, as I imagined, my fire, filled me with many thoughts. First, I imagined that upon seeing my light they might have put themselves into their boat, and endeavoured to make the shore: but that the sea running very high, they might have been cast away. Other times I imagined that they might have lost their boat before, as might be the case many ways; particularly by the breaking of the sea upon their ship, which many times obliged men to stave, or take in pieces, their boat, and sometimes to throw it overboard with their own hands. Other times I imagined they had some other ship or ships in company, who, upon the signals of distress they made, had taken them up, and carried them off. Other times I fancied they were all gone off to sea in their boat, and being hurried away by the current that I had been formerly in, were carried out into the great ocean, where there was nothing but misery and perishing: and that, perhaps, they might by this time think of starving, and of being in a condition to eat one another.

As all these were but conjectures at best, so, in the condition I was in, I could do no more than look on upon the misery of the poor men, and pity them; which had still this good effect upon my side, that it gave me more and more cause to give thanks to God, who had so happily and comfortably provided for me in my desolate condition; and that of two ships' companies, who were now cast away upon this part of the world, not one life should be spared but mine. I learned here again to observe, that it is very rare that the providence of God casts us into any condition so low, or any misery so great, but we may see something or other to be thankful for, and may see others in worse circumstances than our own. Such certainly was the case of these men, of whom I could not so much as see room to suppose any were saved; nothing could make it rational so much as to wish or expect that they did not all perish there, except the possibility only of their being taken up by another ship in company; and this was but mere possibility indeed, for I saw not the least sign or appearance of any such thing. I cannot explain, by any possible energy of words, what a strange longing I felt in my soul upon this sight, breaking out sometimes thus: "Oh that there had been but one or two, nay, or but one soul saved out of this ship, to have escaped to me, that I might but have had one companion, one fellow-creature, to have spoken to me and to have conversed with!" In all the time of my solitary life I never felt so earnest, so strong a desire after the society of my fellow-creatures, or so deep a regret at the want of it.

There are some secret springs in the affections which, when they are set a-going by some object in view, or, though not in view, yet rendered present to the mind by the power of imagination, that motion carries out the soul, by its impetuosity, to such violent, eager embracings of the object, that the absence of it is insupportable. Such were these earnest wishings that but one man had been saved. I believe I repeated the words, "Oh that it had been but one!" a thousand times; and my desires were so moved by it, that when I spoke the words my hands would clinch together, and my fingers would press the palms of my hands, so that if I had had any soft thing in my hand I should have crushed it involuntarily; and the teeth in my head would strike together, and set against one another so strong, that for some time I could not part them again. Let the naturalists explain these things, and the reason and manner of them. All I can do is to describe the fact, which was even surprising to me when I found it, though I knew not from whence it proceeded; it was doubtless the effect of ardent wishes, and of strong ideas formed in my mind, realizing the comfort which the conversation of one of my fellow-Christians would have been to me. But it was not to be; either their fate or mine, or both, forbade it; for, till the last year of my being on this island, I never knew whether any were saved out of that ship or no; and had only the affliction, some days after, to see the corpse of a drowned boy come on shore at the end of the island which was next the shipwreck. He had no clothes on but a seaman's waistcoat, a pair of open-kneed linen drawers, and a blue linen shirt; but nothing to direct me so much as to guess what nation he was of. He had nothing in his pockets but two pieces of eight and a tobacco pipe – the last was to me of ten times more value than the first.

It was now calm, and I had a great mind to venture out in my boat to this wreck, not doubting but I might find something on board that might be useful to me. But that did not altogether press me so much as the possibility that there might be yet some living creature on board, whose life I might not only save, but might, by saving that life, comfort my own to the last degree; and this thought clung so to my heart that I could not be quiet night or day, but I must venture out in my boat on board this wreck; and committing the rest to God's providence, I thought the impression was so strong upon my mind that it could not be resisted – that it must come from some invisible direction, and that I should be wanting to myself if I did not go.

Under the power of this impression, I hastened back to my castle, prepared everything for my voyage, took a quantity of bread, a great pot of fresh water, a compass to steer by, a bottle of rum (for I had still a great deal of that left), and a basket of raisins; and thus, loading myself with everything necessary. I went down to my boat, got the water out of her, got her afloat, loaded all my cargo in her, and then went home again for more. My second cargo was a great bag of rice, the umbrella to set up over my head for a shade, another large pot of water, and about two dozen of small loaves, or barley cakes, more than before, with a bottle of goat's milk and a cheese; all which with great labour and sweat I carried to my boat; and praying to God to direct my voyage, I put out, and rowing or paddling the canoe along the shore, came at last to the utmost point of the island on the north-east side. And now I was to launch out into the ocean, and either to venture or not to venture. I looked on the rapid currents which ran constantly on both sides of the island at a distance, and which were very terrible to me from the remembrance of the hazard I had been in before, and my heart began to fail me; for I foresaw that if I was driven into either of those currents, I should be carried a great way out to sea, and perhaps out of my reach or sight of the island again; and that then, as my boat was but small, if any little gale of wind should rise, I should be inevitably lost.

These thoughts so oppressed my mind that I began to give over my enterprise; and having hauled my boat into a little creek on the shore, I stepped out, and sat down upon a rising bit of ground, very pensive and anxious, between fear and desire, about my voyage; when, as I was musing, I could perceive that the tide was turned, and the flood come on; upon which my going was impracticable for so many hours. Upon this, presently it occurred to me that I should go up to the highest piece of ground I could find, and observe, if I could, how the sets of the tide or currents lay when the flood came in, that I might judge whether, if I was driven one way out, I might not expect to be driven another way home, with the same rapidity of the currents. This thought was no sooner in my head than I cast my eye upon a little hill which sufficiently overlooked the sea both ways, and from whence I had a clear view of the currents or sets of the tide, and which way I was to guide myself in my return. Here I found, that as the current of ebb set out close by the south point of the island, so the current of the flood set in close by the shore of the north side; and that I had nothing to do but to keep to the north side of the island in my return, and I should do well enough.

Encouraged by this observation, I resolved the next morning to set out with the first of the tide; and reposing myself for the night in my canoe, under the watch-coat I mentioned, I launched out. I first made a little out to sea, full north, till I began to feel the benefit of the current, which set eastward, and which carried me at a great rate; and yet did not so hurry me as the current on the south side had done before, so as to take from me all government of the boat; but having a strong steerage with my paddle, I went at a great rate directly for the wreck, and in less than two hours I came up to it. It was a dismal sight to look at; the ship, which by its building was Spanish, stuck fast, jammed in between two rocks. All the stern and quarter of her were beaten to pieces by the sea; and as her forecastle, which stuck in the rocks, had run on with great violence, her mainmast and foremast were brought by the board – that is to say, broken short off; but her bowsprit was sound, and the head and bow appeared firm. When I came close to her, a dog appeared upon her, who, seeing me coming, yelped and cried; and as soon as I called him, jumped into the sea to come to me. I took him into the boat, but found him almost dead with hunger and thirst. I gave him a cake of my bread, and he devoured it like a ravenous wolf that had been starving a fortnight in the snow; I then gave the poor creature some fresh water, with which, if I would have let him, he would have burst himself. After this I went on board; but the first sight I met with was two men drowned in the cook-room, or forecastle of the ship, with their arms fast about one another. I concluded, as is indeed probable, that when the ship struck, it being in a storm, the sea broke so high and so continually over her, that the men were not able to bear it, and were strangled with the constant rushing in of the water, as much as if they had been under water. Besides the dog, there was nothing left in the ship that had life; nor any goods, that I could see, but what were spoiled by the water. There were some casks of liquor, whether wine or brandy I knew not, which lay lower in the hold, and which, the water being ebbed out, I could see; but they were too big to meddle with. I saw several chests, which I believe belonged to some of the seamen; and I got two of them into the boat, without examining what was in them. Had the stern of the ship been fixed, and the forepart broken off, I am persuaded I might have made a good voyage; for by what I found in those two chests I had room to suppose the ship had a great deal of wealth on board; and, if I may guess from the course she steered, she must have been bound from Buenos Ayres, or the Rio de la Plata, in the south part of America, beyond the Brazils to the Havana, in the Gulf of Mexico, and so perhaps to Spain. She had, no doubt, a great treasure in her, but of no use, at that time, to anybody; and what became of the crew I then knew not.

I found, besides these chests, a little cask full of liquor, of about twenty gallons, which I got into my boat with much difficulty. There were several muskets in the cabin, and a great powder-horn, with about four pounds of powder in it; as for the muskets, I had no occasion for them, so I left them, but took the powder-horn. I took a fire-shovel and tongs, which I wanted extremely, as also two little brass kettles, a copper pot to make chocolate, and a gridiron; and with this cargo, and the dog, I came away, the tide beginning to make home again – and the same evening, about an hour within night, I reached the island again, weary and fatigued to the last degree. I reposed that night in the boat and in the morning I resolved to harbour what I had got in my new cave, and not carry it home to my castle. After refreshing myself, I got all my cargo on shore, and began to examine the particulars. The cask of liquor I found to be a kind of rum, but not such as we had at the Brazils; and, in a word, not at all good; but when I came to open the chests, I found several things of great use to me – for example, I found in one a fine case of bottles, of an extraordinary kind, and filled with cordial waters, fine and very good; the bottles held about three pints each, and were tipped with silver. I found two pots of very good succades, or sweetmeats, so fastened also on the top that the salt-water had not hurt them; and two more of the same, which the water had spoiled. I found some very good shirts, which were very welcome to me; and about a dozen and a half of white linen handkerchiefs and coloured neckcloths; the former were also very welcome, being exceedingly refreshing to wipe my face in a hot day. Besides this, when I came to the till in the chest, I found there three great bags of pieces of eight, which held about 1,100 pieces in all; and in one of them, wrapped up in a paper, 6 doubloons of gold, and some small bars or wedges of gold; I suppose they might all weigh near a pound. In the other chest were some clothes, but of little value; but, by the circumstances, it must have belonged to the gunner's Mate; though there was no powder in it, except two pounds of fine glazed powder, in three flasks, kept, I suppose, for charging their fowling-pieces on occasion. Upon the whole, I got very little by this voyage that was of any use to me; for, as to the money, I had no manner of occasion for it; it was to me as the dirt under my feet, and I would have given it all for three or four pair of English shoes and stockings, which were things I greatly wanted, but had had none on my feet for many years. I had, indeed, got two pair of shoes now, which I took off the feet of two drowned men whom I saw in the wreck, and I found two pair more in one of the chests, which were very welcome to me; but they were not like our English shoes, either for ease or service, being rather what we call pumps than shoes. I found in this seaman's chest about 50 pieces of eight, in Royals, but no gold: I supposed this belonged to a poorer man than the other, which seemed to belong to some officer. Well, however, I lugged this money home to my cave, and laid it up, as I had done that before which I had brought from our own ship; but it was a great pity, as I said, that the other part of this ship had not come to my share: for I am satisfied I might have loaded my canoe several times over with money; and, thought I, if I ever escape to England, it might lie here safe enough till I come again and fetch it.

CHAPTER FOURTEEN

A Dream Realised

HAVING NOW BROUGHT ALL MY THINGS on shore and secured them, I went back to my boat, and rowed or paddled her along the shore to her old harbour, where I laid her up, and made the best of my way to my old habitation, where I found everything safe and quiet. I began now to repose myself, live after my old fashion, and take care of my family affairs; and for a while I lived easy enough, only that I was more vigilant than I used to be, looked out oftener, and did not go abroad so much; and if at any time I did stir with any freedom, it was always to the east part of the island, where I was pretty well satisfied the savages never came, and where I could go without so many precautions, and such a load of arms and ammunition as I always carried with me if I went the other way. I lived in this condition near two years more; but my unlucky head, that was always to let me know it was born to make my body miserable, was all these two years filled with projects and designs how, if it were possible, I might get away from this island: for sometimes I was for making another voyage to the wreck, though my reason told me that there was nothing left there worth the hazard of my voyage; sometimes for a ramble one way, sometimes another – and I believe verily, if I had had the boat that I went from Sallee in, I should have ventured to sea, bound anywhere, I knew not whither. I have been, in all my circumstances, a memento to those who are touched with the general plague of mankind, whence, for aught I know, one half of their miseries flow: I mean that of not being satisfied with the station wherein God and Nature hath placed them – for, not to look back upon my primitive condition, and the excellent advice of my father, the opposition to which was, as I may call it, my *Original Sin*, my subsequent mistakes of the same kind had been the means of my coming into this miserable condition; for had that Providence which so happily seated me at the Brazils as a planter blessed me with confined desires, and I could have been contented to have gone on gradually, I might have been by this time – I mean in the time of my being in this island – one of the most considerable planters in the Brazils – nay, I am persuaded, that by the improvements I had made in that little time I lived there, and the increase I should probably have made if I had remained, I might have been worth a 100,000 Moidores – and what business had I to leave a settled fortune, a well-stocked plantation, improving and increasing, to turn supercargo to Guinea to fetch negroes, when patience and time would have so increased our stock at home, that we could have bought them at our own door from those whose business it was to fetch them? and though it had cost us something more, yet the difference of that price was by no means worth saving at so great a hazard. But as this is usually the fate of young heads, so reflection upon the folly of it is as commonly the exercise of more years, or of the dear-bought experience of time – so it was with me now; and yet so deep had the mistake taken root in my temper, that I could not satisfy myself in my station, but was continually poring upon the means and possibility of my escape from this place; and that I may, with greater pleasure to the reader, bring on the remaining part of my story, it may not be improper to give some account of my first conceptions on the subject of this foolish scheme for my escape, and how, and upon what foundation, I acted.

I am now to be supposed retired into my castle, after my late voyage to the wreck, my frigate laid up and secured under water, as usual, and my condition restored to what it was before: I had more wealth, indeed, than I had before, but was not at all the richer; for I had no more use for it than the Indians of Peru had before the Spaniards came there.

It was one of the nights in the rainy season in March, the four-and-twentieth year of my first setting foot in this island of solitude, I was lying in my bed or hammock, awake, very well in health, had no pain, no distemper, no uneasiness of body, nor any uneasiness of mind more than ordinary, but could by no means close my eyes, that is, so as to sleep; no, not a wink all night long, otherwise than as follows: It is impossible to set down the innumerable crowd of thoughts that whirled through that great thoroughfare of the brain, the memory, in this night's time. I ran over the whole history of my life in miniature, or by abridgment, as I may call it, to my coming to this island, and also of that part of my life since I came to this island. In my reflections upon the state of my case since I came on shore on this island, I was comparing the happy posture of my affairs in the first years of my habitation here, with the life of anxiety, fear, and care which I had lived in ever since I had seen the print of a foot in the sand. Not that I did not believe the savages had frequented the island even all the while, and might have been several hundreds of them at times on shore there; but I had never known it, and was incapable of any apprehensions about it; my satisfaction was perfect, though my danger was the same, and I was as happy in not knowing my danger as if I had never really been exposed to it. This furnished my thoughts with many very profitable reflections, and particularly this one: How infinitely good that Providence is, which has provided, in its government of mankind, such narrow bounds to his sight and knowledge of things; and though he walks in the midst of so many thousand dangers, the sight of which, if discovered to him, would distract his mind and sink his spirits, he is kept serene and calm, by having the events of things hid from his eyes, and knowing nothing of the dangers which surround him.

After these thoughts had for some time entertained me, I came to reflect seriously upon the real danger I had been in for so many years in this very island, and how I had walked about in the greatest security, and with all possible tranquillity, even when perhaps nothing but the brow of a hill, a great tree, or the casual approach of night, had been between me and the worst kind of destruction – *viz.* that of falling into the hands of cannibals and savages, who would have seized on me with the same view as I would on a goat or turtle; and have thought it no more crime to kill and devour me than I did of a pigeon or a curlew. I would unjustly slander myself if I should say I was not sincerely thankful to my great Preserver, to whose singular protection I acknowledged, with great humanity, all these unknown deliverances were due, and without which I must inevitably have fallen into their merciless hands.

When these thoughts were over, my head was for some time taken up in considering the nature of these wretched creatures, I mean the savages, and how it came to pass in the world that the wise Governor of all things should give up any of His creatures to such inhumanity – nay, to something so much below even brutality itself, as to devour its own kind: but as this ended in some (at that time) fruitless speculations, it occurred to me to inquire what part of the world these wretches lived in? how far off the coast was from whence they came? what they ventured over so far from home for? what kind of boats they had? and why I might not order myself and my business so that I might be able to go over thither, as they were to come to me?

I never so much as troubled myself to consider what I should do with myself when I went thither; what would become of me if I fell into the hands of these savages; or how I should escape them if they attacked me; no, nor so much as how it was possible for me to reach the coast, and not to be attacked by some or other of them, without any possibility of delivering myself: and if I should not fall into their hands, what I should do for provision, or whither I should bend my course: none of these thoughts, I say, so much as came in my way; but my mind was wholly bent upon the notion of my passing over in my boat to the mainland. I looked upon my present condition as the most miserable that could possibly be; that I was not able to throw myself into anything but death, that could be called worse; and if I reached the shore of the main I might perhaps meet with relief, or I might coast along, as I did on the African shore, till I came to some inhabited country, and where I might find some relief; and after all, perhaps I might fall in with some Christian ship that might take me in: and if the worst came to the worst, I could but die, which would put an end to all these miseries at once. Pray note, all this was the fruit of a disturbed mind, an impatient temper, made desperate, as it were, by the long continuance of my troubles, and the disappointments I had met in the wreck I had been on board of, and where I had been so near obtaining what I so earnestly longed for – somebody to speak to, and to learn some knowledge from them of the place where I was, and of the probable means of my deliverance. I was agitated wholly by these thoughts; all my calm of mind, in my resignation to Providence, and waiting the issue of the dispositions of Heaven, seemed to be suspended; and I had as it were no power to turn my thoughts to anything but to the project of a voyage to the main, which came upon me with such force, and such an impetuosity of desire, that it was not to be resisted.

When this had agitated my thoughts for two hours or more, with such violence that it set my very blood into a ferment, and my pulse beat as if I had been in a fever, merely with the extraordinary fervour of my mind about it, Nature – as if I had been fatigued and exhausted with the very thoughts of it – threw me into a sound sleep. One would have thought I should have dreamed of it, but I did not, nor of anything relating to it, but I dreamed that as I was going out in the morning as usual from my castle, I saw upon the shore two canoes and eleven savages coming to land, and that they brought with them another savage whom they were going to kill in order to eat him; when, on a sudden, the savage that they were going to kill jumped away, and ran for his life; and I thought in my sleep that he came running into my little thick grove before my fortification, to hide himself; and that I seeing him alone, and not perceiving that the others sought him that way, showed myself to him, and smiling upon him, encouraged him: that he kneeled down to me, seeming to pray me to assist him; upon which I showed him my ladder, made him go up, and carried him into my cave, and he became my servant; and that as soon as I had got this man, I said to myself, "Now I may certainly venture to the mainland, for this fellow will serve me as a pilot, and will tell me what to do, and whither to go for provisions, and whither not to go for fear of being devoured; what places to venture into, and what to shun." I waked with this thought; and was under such inexpressible impressions of joy at the prospect of my escape in my dream, that the disappointments which I felt upon coming to myself, and finding that it was no more than a dream, were equally extravagant the other way, and threw me into a very great dejection of spirits.

Upon this, however, I made this conclusion: that my only way to go about to attempt an escape was, to endeavour to get a savage into my possession: and, if possible, it should be one of their prisoners, whom they had condemned to be eaten, and should bring hither to kill. But these thoughts still were attended with this difficulty: that it was impossible to effect this without attacking a whole caravan of them, and killing them all; and this was not only a very desperate attempt, and might miscarry, but, on the other hand, I had greatly scrupled the lawfulness of it to myself; and my heart trembled at the thoughts of shedding so much blood, though it was for my deliverance. I need not repeat the arguments which occurred to me against this, they being the same mentioned before; but though I had other reasons to offer now – *viz.* that those men were enemies to my life, and would devour me if they could; that it was self-preservation, in the highest degree, to deliver myself from this death of a life, and was acting in my own defence as much as if they were actually assaulting me, and the like; I say though these things argued for it, yet the thoughts of shedding human blood for my deliverance were very terrible to me, and such as I could by no means reconcile myself to for a great while. However, at last, after many secret disputes with myself, and after great perplexities about it (for all these arguments, one way and another, struggled in my head a long time), the eager prevailing desire of deliverance at length mastered all the rest; and I resolved, if possible, to get one of these savages into my hands, cost what it would. My next thing was to contrive how to do it, and this, indeed, was very difficult to resolve on; but as I could pitch upon no probable means for it, so I resolved to put myself upon the watch, to see them when they came on shore, and leave the rest to the event; taking such measures as the opportunity should present, let what would be.

With these resolutions in my thoughts, I set myself upon the scout as often as possible, and indeed so often that I was heartily tired of it; for it was above a year and a half that I waited; and for great part of that time went out to the west end, and to the south-west corner of the island almost every day, to look for canoes, but none appeared. This was very discouraging, and began to trouble me much, though I cannot say that it did in this case (as it had done some time before) wear off the edge of my desire to the thing; but the longer it seemed to be delayed, the more eager I was for it: in a word, I was not at first so careful to shun the sight of these savages, and avoid being seen by them, as I was now eager to be upon them. Besides, I fancied myself able to manage one, nay, two or three savages, if I had them, so as to make them entirely slaves to me, to do whatever I should direct them, and to prevent their being able at any time to do me any hurt. It was a great while that I pleased myself with this affair; but nothing still presented itself; all my fancies and schemes came to nothing, for no savages came near me for a great while.

About a year and a half after I entertained these notions (and by long musing had, as it were, resolved them all into nothing, for want of an occasion to put them into execution), I was surprised one morning by seeing no less than five canoes all on shore together on my side the island, and the people who belonged to them all landed and out of my sight. The number of them broke all my measures; for seeing so many, and knowing that they always came four or six, or sometimes more in a boat, I could not tell what to think of it, or how to take my measures to attack twenty or thirty men single-handed; so lay still in my castle, perplexed and discomforted. However, I put myself into the same position for an attack that I had formerly provided, and was just ready for action, if anything had presented. Having waited a good while, listening to hear if they made any noise, at length, being very impatient, I set my guns at the foot of my ladder, and clambered up to the top of the hill, by my two stages, as usual; standing so, however, that my head did not appear above the hill, so that they could not perceive me by any means. Here I observed, by the help of my perspective glass, that they were no less than thirty in number; that they had a fire kindled, and that they had meat dressed. How they had cooked it I knew not, or what it was; but they were all dancing, in I know not how many barbarous gestures and figures, their own way, round the fire.

While I was thus looking on them, I perceived, by my perspective, two miserable wretches dragged from the boats, where, it seems, they were laid by, and were now brought out for the slaughter. I perceived one of them immediately fall; being knocked down, I suppose, with a club or wooden sword, for that was their way; and two or three others were at work immediately, cutting him open for their cookery, while the other victim was left standing by himself, till they should be ready for him. In that very moment this poor wretch, seeing himself a little at liberty and unbound, Nature inspired him with hopes of life, and he started away from them, and ran with incredible swiftness along the sands, directly towards me; I mean towards that part of the coast where my habitation was. I was dreadfully frightened, I must acknowledge, when I perceived him run my way; and especially when, as I thought, I saw him pursued by the whole body: and now I expected that part of my dream was coming to pass, and that he would certainly take shelter in my grove; but I could not depend, by any means, upon my dream, that the other savages would not pursue him thither and find him there. However, I kept my station, and my spirits began to recover when I found that there was not above three men that followed him; and still more was I encouraged, when I found that he outstripped them exceedingly in running, and gained ground on them; so that, if he could but hold out for half-an-hour, I saw easily he would fairly get away from them all.

There was between them and my castle the creek, which I mentioned often in the first part of my story, where I landed my cargoes out of the ship; and this I saw plainly he must necessarily swim over, or the poor wretch would be taken there; but when the savage escaping came thither, he made nothing of it, though the tide was then up; but plunging in, swam through in about thirty strokes, or thereabouts, landed, and ran with exceeding strength and swiftness. When the three persons came to the creek, I found that two of them could swim, but the third could not, and that, standing on the other side, he looked at the others, but went no farther, and soon after went softly back again; which, as it happened, was very well for him in the end. I observed that the two who swam were yet more than twice as strong swimming over the creek as the fellow was that fled from them. It came very warmly upon my thoughts, and indeed irresistibly, that now was the time to get me a servant, and, perhaps, a companion or assistant; and that I was plainly called by Providence to save this poor creature's life. I immediately ran down the ladders with all possible expedition, fetched my two guns, for they were both at the foot of the ladders, as I observed before, and getting up again with the same haste to the top of the hill, I crossed towards the sea; and having a very short cut, and all down hill, placed myself in the way between the pursuers and the pursued, hallowing aloud to him that fled, who, looking back, was at first perhaps as much frightened at me as at them; but I beckoned with my hand to him to come back; and, in the meantime, I slowly advanced towards the two that followed; then rushing at once upon the foremost, I knocked him down with the stock of my piece. I was loath to fire, because I would not have the rest hear; though, at that distance, it would not have been easily heard, and being out of sight of the smoke, too, they would not have known what to make of it. Having knocked this fellow down, the other who pursued him stopped, as if he had been frightened, and I advanced towards him: but as I came nearer, I perceived presently he had a bow and arrow, and was fitting it to shoot at me: so I was then obliged to shoot at him first, which I did, and killed him at the first shot. The poor savage who fled, but had stopped, though he saw both his enemies fallen and killed, as he thought, yet was so frightened with the fire and noise of my piece that he stood stock still, and neither came forward nor went backward, though he seemed rather inclined still to fly than to come on. I hallooed again to him, and made signs to come forward, which he easily understood, and came a little way; then stopped again, and then a little farther, and stopped again; and I could then perceive that he stood trembling, as if he had been taken prisoner, and had just been to be killed, as his two enemies were. I beckoned to him again to come to me, and gave him all the signs of encouragement that I could think of; and he came nearer and nearer, kneeling down every ten or twelve steps, in token of acknowledgment for saving his life. I smiled at him, and looked pleasantly, and beckoned to him to come still nearer; at length he came close to me; and then he kneeled down again, kissed the ground, and laid his head upon the ground, and taking me by the foot, set my foot upon his head; this, it seems, was in token of swearing to be my slave for ever. I took him up and made much of him, and encouraged him all I could. But there was more work to do yet; for I perceived the savage whom I had knocked down was not killed, but stunned with the blow, and began to come to himself: so I pointed to him, and showed him the savage, that he was not dead; upon this he spoke some words to me, and though I could not understand them, yet I thought they were pleasant to hear; for they were the first sound of a man's voice that I had heard, my own excepted, for above twenty-five years. But there was no time for such reflections now; the savage who was knocked down recovered himself so far as to sit up upon the ground, and I perceived that my savage began to be afraid; but when I saw that, I presented my other piece at the man, as if I would shoot him: upon this my savage, for so I call him now, made a motion to me to lend him my sword, which hung naked in a belt by my side, which I did. He no sooner had it, but he runs to his enemy, and at one blow cut off his head so cleverly, no executioner in Germany could have done it sooner or better; which I thought very strange for one who, I had reason to believe, never saw a sword in his life before, except their own wooden swords: however, it seems, as I learned afterwards, they make their wooden swords so sharp, so heavy, and the wood is so hard, that they will even cut off heads with them, ay, and arms, and that at one blow, too. When he had done this, he comes laughing to me in sign of triumph, and brought me the sword again, and with abundance of gestures which I did not understand, laid it down, with the head of the savage that he had killed, just before me. But that which astonished him most was to know how I killed the other Indian so far off; so, pointing to him, he made signs to me to let him go to him; and I bade him go, as well as I could. When he came to him, he stood like one amazed, looking at him, turning him first on one side, then on the other; looked at the wound the bullet had made, which it seems was just in his breast, where it had made a hole, and no great quantity of blood had followed; but he had bled inwardly, for he was quite dead. He took up his bow and arrows, and came back; so I turned to go away, and beckoned him to follow me, making signs to him that more might come after them. Upon this he made signs to me that he should bury them with sand, that they might not be seen by the rest, if they followed; and so I made signs to him again to do so. He fell to work; and in an instant he had scraped a hole in the sand with his hands big enough to bury the first in, and then dragged him into it, and covered him; and did so by the other also; I believe he had him buried them both in a quarter of an hour. Then, calling away, I carried him, not to my castle, but quite away to my cave, on the farther part of the island: so I did not let my dream come to pass in that part, that he came into my grove for shelter. Here I gave him bread and a bunch of raisins to eat, and a draught of water, which I found he was indeed in great distress for, from his running: and having refreshed him, I made signs for him to go and lie down to sleep, showing him a place where I had laid some rice-straw, and a blanket upon it, which I used to sleep upon myself sometimes; so the poor creature lay down, and went to sleep.

He was a comely, handsome fellow, perfectly well made, with straight, strong limbs, not too large; tall, and well-shaped; and, as I reckon, about twenty-six years of age. He had a very good countenance, not a fierce and surly aspect, but seemed to have something very manly in his face; and yet he had all the sweetness and softness of a European in his countenance too, especially when he smiled. His hair was long and black, not curled like wool; his forehead very high and large; and a great vivacity and sparkling sharpness in his eyes. The colour of his skin was not quite black, but very tawny; and yet not an ugly, yellow, nauseous tawny, as the Brazilians and Virginians, and other natives of America are, but of a bright kind of a dun olive-colour, that had in it something very agreeable, though not very easy to describe. His face was round and plump; his nose small, not flat, like the Negroes; a very good mouth, thin lips, and his fine teeth well set, and as white as ivory.

After he had slumbered, rather than slept, about half-an-hour, he awoke again, and came out of the cave to me: for I had been milking my goats which I had in the enclosure just by: when he espied me he came running to me, laying himself down again upon the ground, with all the possible signs of an humble, thankful disposition, making a great many antic gestures to show it. At last he lays his head flat upon the ground, close to my foot, and sets my other foot upon his head, as he had done before; and after this made all the signs to me of subjection, servitude, and submission imaginable, to let me know how he would serve me so long as he lived. I understood him in many things, and let him know I was very well pleased with him. In a little time I began to speak to him; and teach him to speak to me: and first, I let him know his name should be Friday, which was the day I saved his life: I called him so for the memory of the time. I likewise taught him to say Master; and then let him know that was to be my name: I likewise taught him to say *Yes* and *No* and to know the meaning of them. I gave him some milk in an earthen pot, and let him see me drink it before him, and sop my bread in it; and gave him a cake of bread to do the like, which he quickly complied with, and made signs that it was very good for him. I kept there with him all that night; but as soon as it was day I beckoned to him to come with me, and let him know I would give him some clothes; at which he seemed very glad, for he was stark naked. As we went by the place where he had buried the two men, he pointed exactly to the place, and showed me the marks that he had made to find them again, making signs to me that we should dig them up again and eat them. At this I appeared very angry, expressed my abhorrence of it, made as if I would vomit at the thoughts of it, and beckoned with my hand to him to come away, which he did immediately, with great submission. I then led him up to the top of the hill, to see if his enemies were gone; and pulling out my glass I looked, and saw plainly the place where they had been, but no appearance of them or their canoes; so that it was plain they were gone, and had left their two comrades behind them, without any search after them.

1903 illustration by Williams

But I was not content with this discovery; but having now more courage, and consequently more curiosity, I took my man Friday with me, giving him the sword in his hand, with the bow and arrows at his back, which I found he could use very dexterously, making him carry one gun for me, and I two for myself; and away we marched to the place where these creatures had been; for I had a mind now to get some further intelligence of them. When I came to the place my very blood ran chill in my veins, and my heart sunk within me, at the horror of the spectacle; indeed, it was a dreadful sight, at least it was so to me, though Friday made nothing of it. The place was covered with human bones, the ground dyed with their blood, and great pieces of flesh left here and there, half-eaten, mangled, and scorched; and, in short, all the tokens of the triumphant feast they had been making there, after a victory over their enemies. I saw three skulls, five hands, and the bones of three or four legs and feet, and abundance of other parts of the bodies; and Friday, by his signs, made me understand that they brought over four prisoners to feast upon; that three of them were eaten up, and that he, pointing to himself, was the fourth; that there had been a great battle between them and their next king, of whose subjects, it seems, he had been one, and that they had taken a great number of prisoners; all which were carried to several places by those who had taken them in the fight, in order to feast upon them, as was done here by these wretches upon those they brought hither.

I caused Friday to gather all the skulls, bones, flesh, and whatever remained, and lay them together in a heap, and make a great fire upon it, and burn them all to ashes. I found Friday had still a hankering stomach after some of the flesh, and was still a cannibal in his nature; but I showed so much abhorrence at the very thoughts of it, and at the least appearance of it, that he durst not discover it: for I had, by some means, let him know that I would kill him if he offered it.

When he had done this, we came back to our castle; and there I fell to work for my man Friday; and first of all, I gave him a pair of linen drawers, which I had out of the poor gunner's chest I mentioned, which I found in the wreck, and which, with a little alteration, fitted him very well; and then I made him a jerkin of goat's skin, as well as my skill would allow (for I was now grown a tolerably good tailor); and I gave him a cap which I made of hare's skin, very convenient, and fashionable enough; and thus he was cloathed, for the present, tolerably well, and was mighty well pleased to see himself almost as well cloathed as his Master. It is true he went awkwardly in these clothes at first: wearing the drawers was very awkward to him, and the sleeves of the waistcoat galled his shoulders and the inside of his arms; but a little easing them where he complained they hurt him, and using himself to them, he took to them at length very well.

The next day, after I came home to my hutch with him, I began to consider where I should lodge him: and that I might do well for him and yet be perfectly easy myself, I made a little tent for him in the vacant place between my two fortifications, in the inside of the last, and in the outside of the first. As there was a door or entrance there into my cave, I made a formal framed door-case, and a door to it, of boards, and set it up in the passage, a little within the entrance; and, causing the door to open in the inside, I barred it up in the night, taking in my ladders, too; so that Friday could no way come at me in the inside of my innermost wall, without making so much noise in getting over that it must needs awaken me; for my first wall had now a complete roof over it of long poles, covering all my tent, and leaning up to the side of the hill; which was again laid across with smaller sticks, instead of laths, and then thatched over a great thickness with the rice-straw, which was strong, like reeds; and at the hole or place which was left to go in or out by the ladder I had placed a kind of trap-door, which, if it had been attempted on the outside, would not have opened at all, but would have fallen down and made a great noise – as to weapons, I took them all into my side every night. But I needed none of all this precaution; for never man had a more faithful, loving, sincere servant than Friday was to me: without passions, sullenness, or designs, perfectly obliged and engaged; his very affections were tied to me, like those of a child to a father; and I daresay he would have sacrificed his life to save mine upon any occasion whatsoever – the many testimonies he gave me of this put it out of doubt, and soon convinced me that I needed to use no precautions for my safety on his account.

This frequently gave me occasion to observe, and that with wonder, that however it had pleased God in His providence, and in the government of the works of His hands, to take from so great a part of the world of His creatures the best uses to which their faculties and the powers of their souls are adapted, yet that He has bestowed upon them the same powers, the same reason, the same affections, the same sentiments of kindness and obligation, the same passions and resentments of wrongs, the same sense of gratitude, sincerity, fidelity, and all the capacities of doing good and receiving good that He has given to us; and that when He pleases to offer them occasions of exerting these, they are as ready, nay, more ready, to apply them to the right uses for which they were bestowed than we are. This made me very melancholy sometimes, in reflecting, as the several occasions presented, how mean a use we make of all these, even though we have these powers enlightened by the great lamp of instruction, the Spirit of God, and by the knowledge of His word added to our understanding; and why it has pleased God to hide the like saving knowledge from so many millions of souls, who, if I might judge by this poor savage, would make a much better use of it than we did. From hence I sometimes was led too far, to invade the sovereignty of Providence, and, as it were, arraign the justice of so arbitrary a disposition of things, that should hide that sight from some, and reveal it – to others, and yet expect a like duty from both; but I shut it up, and checked my thoughts with this conclusion: first, that we did not know by what light and law these should be condemned; but that as God was necessarily, and by the nature of His being, infinitely holy and just, so it could not be, but if these creatures were all sentenced to absence from Himself, it was on account of sinning against that light which, as the Scripture says, was a law to themselves, and by such rules as their consciences would acknowledge to be just, though the foundation was not discovered to us; and secondly, that still as we all are the clay in the hand of the potter, no vessel could say to him, "Why hast thou formed me thus?"

But to return to my new companion. I was greatly delighted with him, and made it my business to teach him everything that was proper to make him useful, handy, and helpful; but especially to make him speak, and understand me when I spoke; and he was the aptest scholar that ever was; and particularly was so merry, so constantly diligent, and so pleased when he could but understand me, or make me understand him, that it was very pleasant for me to talk to him. Now my life began to be so easy that I began to say to myself that could I but have been safe from more savages, I cared not if I was never to remove from the place where I lived.

CHAPTER FIFTEEN

Friday's Education

After I had been two or three days returned to my castle, I thought that, in order to bring Friday off from his horrid way of feeding, and from the relish of a cannibal's stomach, I ought to let him taste other flesh; so I took him out with me one morning to the woods. I went, indeed, intending to kill a kid out of my own flock; and bring it home and dress it; but as I was going I saw a she-goat lying down in the shade, and two young kids sitting by her. I catched hold of Friday. "Hold," said I, "stand still;" and made signs to him not to stir: immediately I presented my piece, shot, and killed one of the kids. The poor creature, who had at a distance, indeed, seen me kill the savage, his enemy, but did not know, nor could imagine how it was done, was sensibly surprised, trembled, and shook, and looked so amazed that I thought he would have sunk down. He did not see the kid I shot at, or perceive I had killed it, but ripped up his waistcoat to feel whether he was not wounded; and, as I found presently, thought I was resolved to kill him: for he came and kneeled down to me, and embracing my knees, said a great many things I did not understand; but I could easily see the meaning was to pray me not to kill him.

I soon found a way to convince him that I would do him no harm; and taking him up by the hand, laughed at him, and pointing to the kid which I had killed, beckoned to him to run and fetch it, which he did: and while he was wondering, and looking to see how the creature was killed, I loaded my gun again. By-and-by I saw a great fowl, like a hawk, sitting upon a tree within shot; so, to let Friday understand a little what I would do, I called him to me again, pointed at the fowl, which was indeed a parrot, though I thought it had been a hawk; I say, pointing to the parrot, and to my gun, and to the ground under the parrot, to let him see I would make it fall, I made him understand that I would shoot and kill that bird; accordingly, I fired, and bade him look, and immediately he saw the parrot fall. He stood like one frightened again, notwithstanding all I had said to him; and I found he was the more amazed, because he did not see me put anything into the gun, but thought that there must be some wonderful fund of death and destruction in that thing, able to kill man, beast, bird, or anything near or far off; and the astonishment this created in him was such as could not wear off for a long time; and I believe, if I would have let him, he would have worshipped me and my gun. As for the gun itself, he would not so much as touch it for several days after; but he would speak to it and talk to it, as if it had answered him, when he was by himself; which, as I afterwards learned of him, was to desire it not to kill him. Well, after his astonishment was a little over at this, I pointed to him to run and fetch the bird I had shot, which he did, but stayed some time; for the parrot, not being quite dead, had fluttered away a good distance from the place where she fell: however, he found her, took her up, and brought her to me; and as I had perceived his ignorance about the gun before, I took this advantage to charge the gun again, and not to let him see me do it, that I might be ready for any other mark that might present; but nothing more offered at that time: so I brought home the kid, and the same evening I took the skin off, and cut it out as well as I could; and having a pot fit for that purpose, I boiled or stewed some of the flesh, and made some very good broth. After I had begun to eat some I gave some to my man, who seemed very glad of it, and liked it very well; but that which was strangest to him was to see me eat salt with it. He made a sign to me that the salt was not good to eat; and putting a little into his own mouth, he seemed to nauseate it, and would spit and sputter at it, washing his mouth with fresh water after it: on the other hand, I took some meat into my mouth without salt, and I pretended to spit and sputter for want of salt, as much as he had done at the salt; but it would not do; he would never care for salt with meat or in his broth; at least, not for a great while, and then but a very little.

Having thus fed him with boiled meat and broth, I was resolved to feast him the next day by roasting a piece of the kid: this I did by hanging it before the fire on a string, as I had seen many people do in England, setting two poles up, one on each side of the fire, and one across the top, and tying the string to the cross stick, letting the meat turn continually. This Friday admired very much; but when he came to taste the flesh, he took so many ways to tell me how well he liked it, that I could not but understand him: and at last he told me, as well as he could, he would never eat man's flesh any more, which I was very glad to hear.

The next day I set him to work beating some corn out, and sifting it in the manner I used to do, as I observed before; and he soon understood how to do it as well as I, especially after he had seen what the meaning of it was, and that it was to make bread of; for after that I let him see me make my bread, and bake it too; and in a little time Friday was able to do all the work for me as well as I could do it myself.

I began now to consider, that having two mouths to feed instead of one, I must provide more ground for my harvest, and plant a larger quantity of corn than I used to do; so I marked out a larger piece of land, and began the fence in the same manner as before, in which Friday worked not only very willingly and very hard, but did it very cheerfully: and I told him what it was for; that it was for corn to make more bread, because he was now with me, and that I might have enough for him and myself too. He appeared very sensible of that part, and let me know that he thought I had much more labour upon me on his account than I had for myself; and that he would work the harder for me if I would tell him what to do.

This was the pleasantest year of all the life I led in this place. Friday began to talk pretty well, and understand the names of almost everything I had occasion to call for, and of every place I had to send him to, and talked a great deal to me; so that, in short, I began now to have some use for my tongue again, which, indeed, I had very little occasion for before. Besides the pleasure of talking to him, I had a singular satisfaction in the fellow himself: his simple, unfeigned honesty appeared to me more and more every day, and I began really to love the creature; and on his side I believe he loved me more than it was possible for him ever to love anything before.

I had a mind once to try if he had any inclination for his own country again; and having taught him English so well that he could answer me almost any question, I asked him whether the nation that he belonged to never conquered in battle? At which he smiled, and said – "Yes, yes, we always fight the better;" that is, he meant always get the better in fight; and so we began the following discourse:

Master. – You always fight the better; how came you to be taken prisoner, then, Friday?

Friday. – My nation beat much for all that.

Master. – How beat? If your nation beat them, how came you to be taken?

Friday. – They more many than my nation, in the place where me was; they take one, two, three, and me: my nation over-beat them in the yonder place, where me no was; there my nation take one, two, great thousand.

Master. – But why did not your side recover you from the hands of your enemies, then?

Friday. – They run, one, two, three, and me, and make go in the canoe; my nation have no canoe that time.

Master. – Well, Friday, and what does your nation do with the men they take? Do they carry them away and eat them, as these did?

Friday. – Yes, my nation eat mans too; eat all up.

Master. – Where do they carry them?

Friday. – Go to other place, where they think.

Master. – Do they come hither?

Friday. – Yes, yes, they come hither; come other else place.

Master. – Have you been here with them?

Friday. – Yes, I have been here (points to the NW. side of the island, which, it seems, was their side).

By this I understood that my man Friday had formerly been among the savages who used to come on shore on the farther part of the island, on the same man-eating occasions he was now brought for; and some time after, when I took the courage to carry him to that side, being the same I formerly mentioned, he presently knew the place, and told me he was there once, when they ate up twenty men, two women, and one child; he could not tell twenty in English, but he numbered them by laying so many stones in a row, and pointing to me to tell them over.

I have told this passage, because it introduces what follows: that after this discourse I had with him, I asked him how far it was from our island to the shore, and whether the canoes were not often lost. He told me there was no danger, no canoes ever lost: but that after a little way out to sea, there was a current and wind, always one way in the morning, the other in the afternoon. This I understood to be no more than the sets of the tide, as going out or coming in; but I afterwards understood it was occasioned by the great draft and reflux of the mighty river Orinoco, in the mouth or gulf of which river, as I found afterwards, our island lay; and that this land, which I perceived to be W. and N.W. was the great island Trinidad, on the north point of the mouth of the river. I asked Friday a thousand questions about the country, the inhabitants, the sea, the coast, and what nations were near; he told me all he knew with the greatest openness imaginable. I asked him the names of the several nations of his sort of people, but could get no other name than

Caribs; from whence I easily understood that these were the Caribbees, which our maps place on the part of America which reaches from the mouth of the river Orinoco to Guiana, and onwards to St. Martha. He told me that up a great way beyond the moon, that was beyond the setting of the moon, which must be west from their country, there dwelt white bearded men, like me, and pointed to my great whiskers, which I mentioned before; and that they had killed much mans, that was his word: by all which I understood he meant the Spaniards, whose cruelties in America had been spread over the whole country, and were remembered by all the nations from father to son.

I inquired if he could tell me how I might go from this island, and get among those white men. He told me, "Yes, yes, you may go in two canoe." I could not understand what he meant, or make him describe to me what he meant by two canoe, till at last, with great difficulty, I found he meant it must be in a large boat, as big as two canoes. This part of Friday's discourse I began to relish very well; and from this time I entertained some hopes that, one time or other, I might find an opportunity to make my escape from this place, and that this poor savage might be a means to help me.

During the long time that Friday had now been with me, and that he began to speak to me, and understand me, I was not wanting to lay a foundation of religious knowledge in his mind; particularly I asked him one time, who made him. The creature did not understand me at all, but thought I had asked who was his father – but I took it up by another handle, and asked him who made the sea, the ground we walked on, and the hills and woods. He told me, "It was one Benamuckee, that lived beyond all;" he could describe nothing of this great person, but that he was very old, "much older," he said, "than the sea or land, than the moon or the stars." I asked him then, if this old person had made all things, why did not all things worship him? He looked very grave, and, with a perfect look of innocence, said, "All things say O to him." I asked him if the people who die in his country went away anywhere? He said, "Yes; they all went to Benamuckee." Then I asked him whether those they eat up went thither too. He said, "Yes."

From these things, I began to instruct him in the knowledge of the true God; I told him that the great Maker of all things lived up there, pointing up towards heaven; that He governed the world by the same power and providence by which He made it; that He was omnipotent, and could do everything for us, give everything to us, take everything from us; and thus, by degrees, I opened his eyes. He listened with great attention, and received with pleasure the notion of Jesus Christ being sent to redeem us; and of the manner of making our prayers to God, and His being able to hear us, even in heaven. He told me one day, that if our God could hear us, up beyond the sun, he must needs be a greater God than their Benamuckee, who lived but a little way off, and yet could not hear till they went up to the great mountains where he dwelt to speak to them. I asked him if ever he went thither to speak to him. He said, "No; they never went that were young men; none went thither but the old men," whom he called their Oowokakee; that is, as I made him explain to me, their religious, or clergy; and that they went to say O (so he called saying prayers), and then came back and told them what Benamuckee said. By this I observed, that there is priestcraft even among the most blinded, ignorant pagans in the world; and the policy of making a secret of religion, in order to preserve the veneration of the people to the clergy, not only to be found in the Roman, but, perhaps, among all religions in the world, even among the most brutish and barbarous savages.

I endeavoured to clear up this fraud to my man Friday; and told him that the pretence of their old men going up to the mountains to say O to their god Benamuckee was a cheat; and their bringing word from thence what he said was much more so; that if they met with any answer, or spake with any one there, it must be with an evil spirit; and then I entered into a long discourse with him about the devil, the origin of him, his rebellion against God, his enmity to man, the reason of it, his setting himself up in the dark parts of the world to be worshipped instead of God, and as God, and the many stratagems he made use of to delude mankind to their ruin; how he had a secret access to our passions and to our affections, and to adapt his snares to our inclinations, so as to cause us even to be our own tempters, and run upon our destruction by our own choice.

I found it was not so easy to imprint right notions in his mind about the devil as it was about the being of a God. Nature assisted all my arguments to evidence to him even the necessity of a great First Cause, an overruling, governing Power, a secret directing Providence, and of the equity and justice of paying homage to Him that made us, and the like; but there appeared nothing of this kind in the notion of an evil spirit, of his origin, his being, his nature, and above all, of his inclination to do evil, and to draw us in to do so too; and the poor creature puzzled me once in such a manner, by a question merely natural and innocent, that I scarce knew what to say to him. I had been talking a great deal to him of the power of God, His omnipotence, His aversion to sin, His being a consuming fire to the workers of iniquity; how, as He had made us all, He could destroy us and all the world in a moment; and he listened with great seriousness to me all the while. After this I had been telling him how the devil was God's enemy in the hearts of men, and used all his malice and skill to defeat the good designs of Providence, and to ruin the kingdom of Christ in the world, and the like. "Well," says Friday, "but you say God is so strong, so great; is He not much strong, much might as the devil?" "Yes, yes," says I, "Friday; God is stronger than the devil – God is above the devil, and therefore we pray to God to tread him down under our feet, and enable us to resist his temptations and quench his fiery darts." "But," says he again, "if God much stronger, much might as the wicked devil, why God no kill the devil, so make him no more do wicked?" I was strangely surprised at this question; and, after all, though I was now an old man, yet I was but a young doctor, and ill qualified for a casuist or a solver of difficulties; and at first I could not tell what to say; so I pretended not to hear him, and asked him what he said; but he was too earnest for an answer to forget his question, so that he repeated it in the very same broken words as above. By this time I had recovered myself a little, and I said, "God will at last punish him severely; he is reserved for the judgment, and is to be cast into the bottomless pit, to dwell with everlasting fire." This did not satisfy Friday; but he returns upon me, repeating my words, "'*Reserve at last*!' me no understand – but why not kill the devil now; not kill great ago?" "You may as well ask me," said I, "why God does not kill you or me, when we do wicked things here that offend Him – we are preserved to repent and be pardoned." He mused some time on this. "Well, well," says he, mighty affectionately, "that well – so you, I, devil, all wicked, all preserve, repent, God pardon all." Here I was run down again by him to the last degree; and it was a testimony to me, how the mere notions of nature, though they will guide reasonable creatures to the knowledge of a God, and of a worship or homage due to the supreme being of God, as the consequence of our nature, yet nothing but divine revelation can form the knowledge of Jesus Christ, and of redemption purchased for us; of a mediator of the new covenant, and of an intercessor at the footstool of God's throne; I say, nothing but a revelation from Heaven can form these in the soul; and that, therefore, the gospel of our Lord and Saviour Jesus Christ, I mean the Word of God, and the Spirit of God, promised for the guide and sanctifier of His people, are the absolutely necessary instructors of the souls of men in the saving knowledge of God and the means of salvation.

I therefore diverted the present discourse between me and my man, rising up hastily, as upon some sudden occasion of going out; then sending him for something a good way off, I seriously prayed to God that He would enable me to instruct savingly this poor savage; assisting, by His Spirit, the heart of the poor ignorant creature to receive the light of the knowledge of God in Christ, reconciling him to Himself, and would guide me so to speak to him from the Word of God that his conscience might be convinced, his eyes opened, and his soul saved. When he came again to me, I entered into a long discourse with him upon the subject of the redemption of man by the Saviour of the world, and of the doctrine of the gospel preached from Heaven, *viz.* of repentance towards God, and faith in our blessed Lord Jesus. I then explained to him as well as I could why our blessed Redeemer took not on Him the nature of angels but the seed of Abraham; and how, for that reason, the fallen angels had no share in the redemption; that He came only to the lost sheep of the house of Israel, and the like.

I had, God knows, more sincerity than knowledge in all the methods I took for this poor creature's instruction, and must acknowledge, what I believe all that act upon the same principle will find, that in laying things open to him, I really informed and instructed myself in many things that either I did not know or had not fully considered before, but which occurred naturally to my mind upon searching into them, for the information of this poor savage; and I had more affection in my inquiry after things upon this occasion than ever I felt before: so that, whether this poor wild wretch was better for me or no, I had great reason to be thankful that ever he came to me; my grief sat lighter, upon me; my habitation grew comfortable to me beyond measure: and when I reflected that in this solitary life which I have been confined to, I had not only been moved to look up to heaven myself, and to seek the Hand that had brought me here, but was now to be made an instrument, under Providence, to save the life, and, for aught I knew, the soul of a poor savage, and bring him to the true knowledge of religion and of the Christian doctrine, that he might know Christ Jesus, in whom is life eternal; I say, when I reflected upon all these things, a secret joy ran through every part of my soul, and I frequently rejoiced that ever I was brought to this place, which I had so often thought the most dreadful of all afflictions that could possibly have befallen me.

I continued in this thankful frame all the remainder of my time; and the conversation which employed the hours between Friday and me was such as made the three years which we lived there together perfectly and completely happy, if any such thing as complete happiness can be formed in a sublunary state. This savage was now a good Christian, a much better than I; though I have reason to hope, and bless God for it, that we were equally penitent, and comforted, restored penitents. We had here the Word of God to read, and no farther off from His Spirit to instruct than if we had been in England. I always applied myself, in reading the Scripture, to let him know, as well as I could, the meaning of what I read; and he again, by his serious inquiries and questionings, made me, as I said before, a much better scholar in the Scripture knowledge than I should ever have been by my own mere private reading. Another thing I cannot refrain from observing here also, from experience in this retired part of my life, *viz.* how infinite and inexpressible a blessing it is that the knowledge of God, and of the doctrine of salvation by Christ Jesus, is so plainly laid down in the Word of God, so easy to be received and understood, that, as the bare reading the Scripture made me capable of understanding enough of my duty to carry me directly on to the great work of sincere repentance for my sins, and laying hold of a Saviour for life and salvation, to a stated reformation in practice, and obedience to all God's commands, and this without any teacher or instructor, I mean human; so the same plain instruction sufficiently served to the enlightening this savage creature, and bringing him to be such a Christian as I have known few equal to him in my life.

As to all the disputes, wrangling, strife, and contention which have happened in the world about religion, whether niceties in doctrines or schemes of church government, they were all perfectly useless to us, and, for aught I can yet see, they have been so to the rest of the world. We had the sure guide to heaven, *viz.* the Word of God; and we had, blessed be God, comfortable views of the Spirit of God teaching and instructing by His word, leading us into all truth, and making us both willing and obedient to the instruction of His word. And I cannot see the least use that the greatest knowledge of the disputed points of religion, which have made such confusion in the world, would have been to us, if we could have obtained it. But I must go on with the historical part of things, and take every part in its order.

After Friday and I became more intimately acquainted, and that he could understand almost all I said to him, and speak pretty fluently, though in broken English, to me, I acquainted him with my own history, or at least so much of it as related to my coming to this place: how I had lived there, and how long; I let him into the mystery, for such it was to him, of gunpowder and bullet, and taught him how to shoot. I gave him a knife, which he was wonderfully delighted with; and I made him a belt, with a frog hanging to it, such as in England we wear hangers in; and in the frog, instead of a hanger, I gave him a hatchet, which was not only as good a weapon in some cases, but much more useful upon other occasions.

I described to him the country of Europe, particularly England, which I came from; how we lived, how we worshipped God, how we behaved to one another, and how we traded in ships to all parts of the world. I gave him an account of the wreck which I had been on board of, and showed him, as near as I could, the place where she lay; but she was all beaten in pieces before, and gone. I showed him the ruins of our boat, which we lost when we escaped, and which I could not stir with my whole strength then; but was now fallen almost all to pieces. Upon seeing this boat, Friday stood, musing a great while, and said nothing. I asked him what it was he studied upon. At last says he, "Me see such boat like come to place at my nation." I did not understand him a good while; but at last, when I had examined further into it, I understood by him that a boat, such as that had been, came on shore upon the country where he lived: that is, as he explained it, was driven thither by stress of weather. I presently imagined that some European ship must have been cast away upon their coast, and the boat might get loose and drive ashore; but was so dull that I never once thought of men making their escape from a wreck thither, much less whence they might come: so I only inquired after a description of the boat.

Friday described the boat to me well enough; but brought me better to understand him when he added with some warmth, "We save the white mans from drown." Then I presently asked if there were any white mans, as he called them, in the boat. "Yes," he said; "the boat full of white mans." I asked him how many. He told upon his fingers seventeen. I asked him then what became of them. He told me, "They live, they dwell at my nation."

This put new thoughts into my head; for I presently imagined that these might be the men belonging to the ship that was cast away in the sight of my island, as I now called it; and who, after the ship was struck on the rock, and they saw her inevitably lost, had saved themselves in their boat, and were landed upon that wild shore among the savages. Upon this I inquired of him more critically what was become of them. He assured me they lived still there; that they had been there about four years; that the savages left them alone, and gave them victuals to live on. I asked him how it came to pass they did not kill them and eat them. He said, "No, they make brother with them;" that is, as I understood him, a truce; and then he added, "They no eat mans but when make the war fight;" that is to say, they never eat any men but such as come to fight with them and are taken in battle.

It was after this some considerable time, that being upon the top of the hill at the east side of the island, from whence, as I have said, I had, in a clear day, discovered the main or continent of America, Friday, the weather being very serene, looks very earnestly towards the mainland, and, in a kind of surprise, falls a jumping and dancing, and calls out to me, for I was at some distance from him. I asked him what was the matter. "Oh, joy!" says he; "Oh, glad! there see my country, there my nation!" I observed an extraordinary sense of pleasure appeared in his face, and his eyes sparkled, and his countenance discovered a strange eagerness, as if he had a mind to be in his own country again. This observation of mine put a great many thoughts into me, which made me at first not so easy about my new man Friday as I was before; and I made no doubt but that, if Friday could get back to his own nation again, he would not only forget all his religion but all his obligation to me, and would be forward enough to give his countrymen an account of me, and come back, perhaps with a hundred or two of them, and make a feast upon me, at which he might be as merry as he used to be with those of his enemies when they were taken in war. But I wronged the poor honest creature very much, for which I was very sorry afterwards. However, as my jealousy increased, and held some weeks, I was a little more circumspect, and not so familiar and kind to him as before: in which I was certainly wrong too; the honest, grateful creature having no thought about it but what consisted with the best principles, both as a religious Christian and as a grateful friend, as appeared afterwards to my full satisfaction.

While my jealousy of him lasted, you may be sure I was every day pumping him to see if he would discover any of the new thoughts which I suspected were in him; but I found everything he said was so honest and so innocent, that I could find nothing to nourish my suspicion; and in spite of all my uneasiness, he made me at last entirely his own again; nor did he in the least perceive that I was uneasy, and therefore I could not suspect him of deceit.

One day, walking up the same hill, but the weather being hazy at sea, so that we could not see the continent, I called to him, and said, "Friday, do not you wish yourself in your own country, your own nation?" "Yes," he said, "I be much O glad to be at my own nation." "What would you do there?" said I. "Would you turn wild again, eat men's flesh again, and be a savage as you were before?" He looked full of concern, and shaking his head, said, "No, no, Friday tell them to live good; tell them to pray God; tell them to eat corn-bread, cattle flesh, milk; no eat man again." "Why, then," said I to him, "they will kill you." He looked grave at that, and then said, "No, no, they no kill me, they willing love learn." He meant by this, they would be willing to learn. He added, they learned much of the bearded mans that came in the boat.

Then I asked him if he would go back to them. He smiled at that, and told me that he could not swim so far. I told him I would make a canoe for him. He told me he would go if I would go with him. "I go!" says I; "why, they will eat me if I come there." "No, no," says he, "me make they no eat you; me make they much love you." He meant, he would tell them how I had killed his enemies, and saved his life, and so he would make them love me. Then he told me, as well as he could, how kind they were to seventeen white men, or bearded men, as he called them who came on shore there in distress.

From this time, I confess, I had a mind to venture over, and see if I could possibly join with those bearded men, who I made no doubt were Spaniards and Portuguese; not doubting but, if I could, we might find some method to escape from thence, being upon the continent, and a good company together, better than I could from an island forty miles off the shore, alone and without help. So, after some days, I took Friday to work again by way of discourse, and told him I would give him a boat to go back to his own nation; and, accordingly, I carried him to my frigate, which lay on the other side of the island, and having cleared it of water (for I always kept it sunk in water), I brought it out, showed it him, and we both went into it. I found he was a most dexterous fellow at managing it, and would make it go almost as swift again as I could. So when he was in, I said to him, "Well, now, Friday, shall we go to your nation?" He looked very dull at my saying so; which it seems was because he thought the boat was too small to go so far. I then told him I had a bigger; so the next day I went to the place where the first boat lay which I had made, but which I could not get into the water. He said that was big enough; but then, as I had taken no care of it, and it had lain two or three and twenty years there, the sun had so split and dried it, that it was rotten. Friday told me such a boat would do very well, and would carry "much enough vittle, drink, bread;" this was his way of talking.

CHAPTER SIXTEEN

Rescue of Prisoners from Cannibals

UPON THE WHOLE, I was by this time so fixed upon my design of going over with him to the continent that I told him we would go and make one as big as that, and he should go home in it. He answered not one word, but looked very grave and sad. I asked him what was the matter with him. He asked me again, "Why you angry mad with Friday? – what me done?" I asked him what he meant. I told him I was not angry with him at all. "No angry!" says he, repeating the words several times; "why send Friday home away to my nation?" "Why," says I, "Friday, did not you say you wished you were there?" "Yes, yes," says he, "wish we both there; no wish Friday there, no Master there." In a word, he would not think of going there without me. "I go there, Friday?" says I; "what shall I do there?" He turned very quick upon me at this. "You do great deal much good," says he; "you teach wild mans be good, sober, tame mans; you tell them know God, pray God, and live new life." "Alas, Friday!" says I, "thou knowest not what thou sayest; I am but an ignorant man myself." "Yes, yes," says he, "you teachee me good, you teachee them good." "No, no, Friday," says I, "you shall go without me; leave me here to live by myself, as I did before." He looked confused again at that word; and running to one of the hatchets which he used to wear, he takes it up hastily, and gives it to me. "What must I do with this?" says I to him. "You take kill Friday," says he. "What must kill you for?" said I again. He returns very quick – "What you send Friday away for? Take kill Friday, no send Friday away." This he spoke so earnestly that I saw tears stand in his eyes. In a word, I so plainly discovered the utmost affection in him to me, and a firm resolution in him, that I told him then and often after, that I would never send him away from me if he was willing to stay with me.

Upon the whole, as I found by all his discourse a settled affection to me, and that nothing could part him from me, so I found all the foundation of his desire to go to his own country was laid in his ardent affection to the people, and his hopes of my doing them good; a thing which, as I had no notion of myself, so I had not the least thought or intention, or desire of undertaking it. But still I found a strong inclination to attempting my escape, founded on the supposition gathered from the discourse, that there were seventeen bearded men there; and therefore, without any more delay, I went to work with Friday to find out a great tree proper to fell, and make a large periagua, or canoe, to undertake the voyage. There were trees enough in the island to have built a little fleet, not of periaguas or canoes, but even of good, large vessels; but the main thing I looked at was, to get one so near the water that we might launch it when it was made, to avoid the mistake I committed at first. At last Friday pitched upon a tree; for I found he knew much better than I what kind of wood was fittest for it; nor can I tell to this day what wood to call the tree we cut down, except that it was very like the tree we call fustic, or between that and the Nicaragua wood, for it was much of the same colour and smell. Friday wished to burn the hollow or cavity of this tree out, to make it for a boat, but I showed him how to cut it with tools; which, after I had showed him how to use, he did very handily; and in about a month's hard labour we finished it and made it very handsome; especially when, with our axes, which I showed him how to handle, we cut and hewed the outside into the true shape of a boat. After this, however, it cost us near a fortnight's time to get her along, as it were inch by inch, upon great rollers into the water; but when she was in, she would have carried twenty men with great ease.

When she was in the water, though she was so big, it amazed me to see with what dexterity and how swift my man Friday could manage her, turn her, and paddle her along. So I asked him if he would, and if we might venture over in her. "Yes," he said, "we venture over in her very well, though great blow wind." However I had a further design that he knew nothing of, and that was, to make a mast and a sail, and to fit her with an anchor and cable. As to a mast, that was easy enough to get; so I pitched upon a straight young cedar-tree, which I found near the place, and which there were great plenty of in the island, and I set Friday to work to cut it down, and gave him directions how to shape and order it. But as to the sail, that was my particular care. I knew I had old sails, or rather pieces of old sails, enough; but as I had had them now six-and-twenty years by me, and had not been very careful to preserve them, not imagining that I should ever have this kind of use for them,

I did not doubt but they were all rotten; and, indeed, most of them were so. However, I found two pieces which appeared pretty good, and with these I went to work; and with a great deal of pains, and awkward stitching, you may be sure, for want of needles, I at length made a three-cornered ugly thing, like what we call in England a shoulder-of-mutton sail, to go with a boom at bottom, and a little short sprit at the top, such as usually our ships' long-boats sail with, and such as I best knew how to manage, as it was such a one as I had to the boat in which I made my escape from Barbary, as related in the first part of my story.

I was near two months performing this last work, *viz.* rigging and fitting my masts and sails; for I finished them very complete, making a small stay, and a sail, or foresail, to it, to assist if we should turn to windward; and, what was more than all, I fixed a rudder to the stern of her to steer with. I was but a bungling shipwright, yet as I knew the usefulness and even necessity of such a thing, I applied myself with so much pains to do it, that at last I brought it to pass; though, considering the many dull contrivances I had for it that failed, I think it cost me almost as much labour as making the boat.

After all this was done, I had my man Friday to teach as to what belonged to the navigation of my boat; though he knew very well how to paddle a canoe, he knew nothing of what belonged to a sail and a rudder; and was the most amazed when he saw me work the boat to and again in the sea by the rudder, and how the sail jibed, and filled this way or that way as the course we sailed changed; I say when he saw this he stood like one astonished and amazed. However, with a little use, I made all these things familiar to him, and he became an expert sailor, except that of the compass I could make him understand very little. On the other hand, as there was very little cloudy weather, and seldom or never any fogs in those parts, there was the less occasion for a compass, seeing the stars were always to be seen by night, and the shore by day, except in the rainy seasons, and then nobody cared to stir abroad either by land or sea.

I was now entered on the seven-and-twentieth year of my captivity in this place; though the three last years that I had this creature with me ought rather to be left out of the account, my habitation being quite of another kind than in all the rest of the time. I kept the anniversary of my landing here with the same thankfulness to God for His mercies as at first: and if I had such cause of acknowledgment at first, I had much more so now, having such additional testimonies of the care of Providence over me, and the great hopes I had of being effectually and speedily delivered; for I had an invincible impression upon my thoughts that my deliverance was at hand, and that I should not be another year in this place. I went on, however, with my husbandry; digging, planting, and fencing as usual. I gathered and cured my grapes, and did every necessary thing as before.

The rainy season was in the meantime upon me, when I kept more within doors than at other times. We had stowed our new vessel as secure as we could, bringing her up into the creek, where, as I said in the beginning, I landed my rafts from the ship; and hauling her up to the shore at high-water mark, I made my man Friday dig a little dock, just big enough to hold her, and just deep enough to give her water enough to float in; and then, when the tide was out, we made a strong dam across the end of it, to keep the water out; and so she lay, dry as to the tide from the sea: and to keep the rain off we laid a great many boughs of trees, so thick that she was as well thatched as a house; and thus we waited for the months of November and December, in which I designed to make my adventure.

When the settled season began to come in, as the thought of my design returned with the fair weather, I was preparing daily for the voyage. And the first thing I did was to lay by a certain quantity of provisions, being the stores for our voyage; and intended in a week or a fortnight's time to open the dock, and launch out our boat. I was busy one morning upon something of this kind, when I called to Friday, and bid him to go to the sea-shore and see if he could find a turtle or a tortoise, a thing which we generally got once a week, for the sake of the eggs as well as the flesh. Friday had not been long gone when he came running back, and flew over my outer wall or fence, like one that felt not the ground or the steps he set his foot on; and before I had time to speak to him he cries out to me, "O Master! O Master! O sorrow! O bad!" – "What's the matter, Friday?" says I. "O yonder there," says he, "one, two, three canoes; one, two, three!" By this way of speaking I concluded there were six; but on inquiry I found there were but three. "Well, Friday," says I, "do not be frightened." So I heartened him up as well as I could. However, I saw the poor fellow was most terribly scared, for nothing ran in his head but that they were come to look for him, and would cut him in pieces and eat him; and the poor fellow trembled so that I scarcely knew what to do with him. I comforted him as well as I could, and told him I was in as much danger as he, and that they would eat me as well as him. "But," says I, "Friday, we must resolve to fight them. Can you fight, Friday?" "Me shoot," says he, "but there come many great number." "No matter for that," said I again; "our guns will fright them that we do not kill." So I asked him whether, if I resolved to defend him, he would defend me, and stand by me, and do just as I bid him. He said, "Me die when you bid die, Master." So I went and fetched a good dram of rum and gave him; for I had been so good a husband of my rum that I had a great deal left. When we had drunk it, I made him take the two fowling-pieces, which we always carried, and loaded them with large swan-shot, as big as small pistol-bullets. Then I took four muskets, and loaded them with two slugs and five small bullets each; and my two pistols I loaded with a brace of bullets each. I hung my great sword, as usual, naked by my side, and gave Friday his hatchet. When I had thus prepared myself, I took my perspective glass, and went up to the side of the hill, to see what I could discover; and I found quickly by my glass that there were one-and-twenty savages, three prisoners, and three canoes; and that their whole business seemed to be the triumphant banquet upon these three human bodies: a barbarous feast, indeed! but nothing more than, as I had observed, was usual with them. I observed also that they had landed, not where they had done when Friday made his escape, but nearer to my creek, where the shore was low, and where a thick wood came almost close down to the sea. This, with the abhorrence of the inhuman errand these wretches came about, filled me with such indignation that I came down again to Friday, and told him I was resolved to go down to them and kill them all; and asked him if he would stand by me. He had now got over his fright, and his spirits being a little raised with the dram I had given him, he was very cheerful, and told me, as before, he would die when I bid die.

In this fit of fury I divided the arms which I had charged, as before, between us; I gave Friday one pistol to stick in his girdle, and three guns upon his shoulder, and I took one pistol and the other three guns myself; and in this posture we marched out. I took a small bottle of rum in my pocket, and gave Friday a large bag with more powder and bullets; and as to orders, I charged him to keep close behind me, and not to stir, or shoot, or do anything till I bid him, and in the meantime not to speak a word. In this posture I fetched a compass to my right hand of near a mile, as well to get over the creek as to get into the wood, so that I could come within shot of them before I should be discovered, which I had seen by my glass it was easy to do.

While I was making this march, my former thoughts returning, I began to abate my resolution: I do not mean that I entertained any fear of their number, for as they were naked, unarmed wretches, it is certain I was superior to them – nay, though I had been alone. But it occurred to my thoughts, what call, what occasion, much less what necessity I was in to go and dip my hands in blood, to attack people who had neither done or intended me any wrong? who, as to me, were innocent, and whose barbarous customs were their own disaster, being in them a token, indeed, of God's having left them, with the other nations of that part of the world, to such stupidity, and to such inhuman courses, but did not call me to take upon me to be a judge of their actions, much less an executioner of His justice – that whenever He thought fit He would take the cause into His own hands, and by national vengeance punish them as a people for national crimes, but that, in the meantime, it was none of my business – that it was true Friday might justify it, because he was a declared enemy and in a state of war with those very particular people, and it was lawful for him to attack them – but I could not say the same with regard to myself. These things were so warmly pressed upon my thoughts all the way as I went, that I resolved I would only go and place myself near them that I might observe their barbarous feast, and that I would act then as God should direct; but that unless something offered that was more a call to me than yet I knew of, I would not meddle with them.

With this resolution I entered the wood, and, with all possible wariness and silence, Friday following close at my heels, I marched till I came to the skirts of the wood on the side which was next to them, only that one corner of the wood lay between me and them. Here I called softly to Friday, and showing him a great tree which was just at the corner of the wood, I bade him go to the tree, and bring me word if he could see there plainly what they were doing. He did so, and came immediately back to me, and told me they might be plainly viewed there – that they were all about their fire, eating the flesh of one of their prisoners, and that another lay bound upon the sand a little from them, whom he said they would kill next; and this fired the very soul within me. He told me it was not one of their nation, but one of the bearded men he had told me of, that came to their country in the boat. I was filled with horror at the very naming of the white bearded man; and going to the tree, I saw plainly by my glass a white man, who lay upon the beach of the sea with his hands and his feet tied with flags, or things like rushes, and that he was an European, and had clothes on.

There was another tree and a little thicket beyond it, about fifty yards nearer to them than the place where I was, which, by going a little way about, I saw I might come at undiscovered, and that then I should be within half a shot of them; so I withheld my passion, though I was indeed enraged to the highest degree; and going back about twenty paces, I got behind some bushes, which held all the way till I came to the other tree, and then came to a little rising ground, which gave me a full view of them at the distance of about eighty yards.

I had now not a moment to lose, for nineteen of the dreadful wretches sat upon the ground, all close huddled together, and had just sent the other two to butcher the poor Christian, and bring him perhaps limb by limb to their fire, and they were stooping down to untie the bands at his feet. I turned to Friday. "Now, Friday," said I, "do as I bid thee." Friday said he would. "Then, Friday," says I, "do exactly as you see me do; fail in nothing." So I set down one of the muskets and the fowling-piece upon the ground, and Friday did the like by his, and with the other musket I took my aim at the savages, bidding him to do the like; then asking him if he was ready, he said, "Yes." "Then fire at them," said I; and at the same moment I fired also.

Friday took his aim so much better than I, that on the side that he shot he killed two of them, and wounded three more; and on my side I killed one, and wounded two. They were, you may be sure, in a dreadful consternation: and all of them that were not hurt jumped upon their feet, but did not immediately know which way to run, or which way to look, for they knew not from whence their destruction came. Friday kept his eyes close upon me, that, as I had bid him, he might observe what I did; so, as soon as the first shot was made, I threw down the piece, and took up the fowling-piece, and Friday did the like; he saw me cock and present; he did the same again. "Are you ready, Friday?" said I. "Yes," says he. "Let fly, then," says I, "in the name of God!" and with that I fired again among the amazed wretches, and so did Friday; and as our pieces were now loaded with what I call swan-shot, or small pistol-bullets, we found only two drop; but so many were wounded that they ran about yelling and screaming like mad creatures, all bloody, and most of them miserably wounded; whereof three more fell quickly after, though not quite dead.

"Now, Friday," says I, laying down the discharged pieces, and taking up the musket which was yet loaded, "follow me," which he did with a great deal of courage; upon which I rushed out of the wood and showed myself, and Friday close at my foot. As soon as I perceived they saw me, I shouted as loud as I could, and bade Friday do so too, and running as fast as I could, which, by the way, was not very fast, being loaded with arms as I was, I made directly towards the poor victim, who was, as I said, lying upon the beach or shore, between the place where they sat and the sea. The two butchers who were just going to work with him had left him at the surprise of our first fire, and fled in a terrible fright to the seaside, and had jumped into a canoe, and three more of the rest made the same way. I turned to Friday, and bade him step forwards and fire at them; he understood me immediately, and running about forty yards, to be nearer them, he shot at them; and I thought he had killed them all, for I saw them all fall of a heap into the boat, though I saw two of them up again quickly; however, he killed two of them, and wounded the third, so that he lay down in the bottom of the boat as if he had been dead.

While my man Friday fired at them, I pulled out my knife and cut the flags that bound the poor victim; and loosing his hands and feet, I lifted him up, and asked him in the Portuguese tongue what he was. He answered in Latin, Christianus; but was so weak and faint that he could scarce stand or speak. I took my bottle out of my pocket and gave it him, making signs that he should drink, which he did; and I gave him a piece of bread, which he ate. Then I asked him what countryman he was: and he said, Espagniole; and being a little recovered, let me know, by all the signs he could possibly make, how much he was in my debt for his deliverance. "Seignior," said I, with as much Spanish as I could make up, "we will talk afterwards, but we must fight now: if you have any strength left, take this pistol and sword, and lay about you." He took them very thankfully; and no sooner had he the arms in his hands, but, as if they had put new vigour into him, he flew upon his murderers like a fury, and had cut two of them in pieces in an instant; for the truth is, as the whole was a surprise to them, so the poor creatures were so much frightened with the noise of our pieces that they fell down for mere amazement and fear, and had no more power to attempt their own escape than their flesh had to resist our shot; and that was the case of those five that Friday shot at in the boat; for as three of them fell with the hurt they received, so the other two fell with the fright.

I kept my piece in my hand still without firing, being willing to keep my charge ready, because I had given the Spaniard my pistol and sword: so I called to Friday, and bade him run up to the tree from whence we first fired, and fetch the arms which lay there that had been discharged, which he did with great swiftness; and then giving him my musket, I sat down myself to load all the rest again, and bade them come to me when they wanted. While I was loading these pieces, there happened a fierce engagement between the Spaniard and one of the savages, who made at him with one of their great wooden swords, the weapon that was to have killed him before, if I had not prevented it. The Spaniard, who was as bold and brave as could be imagined, though weak, had fought the Indian a good while, and had cut two great wounds on his head; but the savage being a stout, lusty fellow, closing in with him, had thrown him down, being faint, and was wringing my sword out of his hand; when the Spaniard, though undermost, wisely quitting the sword, drew the pistol from his girdle, shot the savage through the body, and killed him upon the spot, before I, who was running to help him, could come near him.

Friday, being now left to his liberty, pursued the flying wretches, with no weapon in his hand but his hatchet: and with that he dispatched those three who as I said before, were wounded at first, and fallen, and all the rest he could come up with: and the Spaniard coming to me for a gun, I gave him one of the fowling-pieces, with which he pursued two of the savages, and wounded them both; but as he was not able to run, they both got from him into the wood, where Friday pursued them, and killed one of them, but the other was too nimble for him; and though he was wounded, yet had plunged himself into the sea, and swam with all his might off to those two who were left in the canoe; which three in the canoe, with one wounded, that we knew not whether he died or no, were all that escaped our hands of one-and-twenty. The account of the whole is as follows: Three killed at our first shot from the tree; two killed at the next shot; two killed by Friday in the boat; two killed by Friday of those at first wounded; one killed by Friday in the wood; three killed by the Spaniard; four killed, being found dropped here and there, of the wounds, or killed by Friday in his chase of them; four escaped in the boat, whereof one wounded, if not dead – twenty one in all.

Those that were in the canoe worked hard to get out of gun-shot, and though Friday made two or three shots at them, I did not find that he hit any of them. Friday would fain have had me take one of their canoes, and pursue them; and indeed I was very anxious about their escape, lest, carrying the news home to their people, they should come back perhaps with two or three hundred of the canoes and devour us by mere multitude; so I consented to pursue them by sea, and running to one of their canoes, I jumped in and bade Friday follow me: but when I was in the canoe I was surprised to find another poor creature lie there, bound hand and foot, as the Spaniard was, for the slaughter, and almost dead with fear, not knowing what was the matter; for he had not been able to look up over the side of the boat, he was tied so hard neck and heels, and had been tied so long that he had really but little life in him.

I immediately cut the twisted flags or rushes which they had bound him with, and would have helped him up; but he could not stand or speak, but groaned most piteously, believing, it seems, still, that he was only unbound in order to be killed. When Friday came to him I bade him speak to him, and tell him of his deliverance; and pulling out my bottle, made him give the poor wretch a dram, which, with the news of his being delivered, revived him, and he sat up in the boat. But when

Friday came to hear him speak, and look in his face, it would have moved any one to tears to have seen how Friday kissed him, embraced him, hugged him, cried, laughed, hallooed, jumped about, danced, sang; then cried again, wrung his hands, beat his own face and head; and then sang and jumped about again like a distracted creature. It was a good while before I could make him speak to me or tell me what was the matter; but when he came a little to himself he told me that it was his father.

It is not easy for me to express how it moved me to see what ecstasy and filial affection had worked in this poor savage at the sight of his father, and of his being delivered from death; nor indeed can I describe half the extravagances of his affection after this: for he went into the boat and out of the boat a great many times: when he went in to him he would sit down by him, open his breast, and hold his father's head close to his bosom for many minutes together, to nourish it; then he took his arms and ankles, which were numbed and stiff with the binding, and chafed and rubbed them with his hands; and I, perceiving what the case was, gave him some rum out of my bottle to rub them with, which did them a great deal of good.

This affair put an end to our pursuit of the canoe with the other savages, who were now almost out of sight; and it was happy for us that we did not, for it blew so hard within two hours after, and before they could be got a quarter of their way, and continued blowing so hard all night, and that from the north-west, which was against them, that I could not suppose their boat could live, or that they ever reached their own coast.

But to return to Friday; he was so busy about his father that I could not find in my heart to take him off for some time; but after I thought he could leave him a little, I called him to me, and he came jumping and laughing, and pleased to the highest extreme: then I asked him if he had given his father any bread. He shook his head, and said, "None; ugly dog eat all up self." I then gave him a cake of bread out of a little pouch I carried on purpose; I also gave him a dram for himself; but he would not taste it, but carried it to his father. I had in my pocket two or three bunches of raisins, so I gave him a handful of them for his father. He had no sooner given his father these raisins but I saw him come out of the boat, and run away as if he had been bewitched, for he was the swiftest fellow on his feet that ever I saw: I say, he ran at such a rate that he was out of sight, as it were, in an instant; and though I called, and hallooed out too after him, it was all one – away he went; and in a quarter of an hour I saw him come back again, though not so fast as he went; and as he came nearer I found his pace slacker, because he had something in his hand. When he came up to me I found he had been quite home for an earthen jug or pot, to bring his father some fresh water, and that he had got two more cakes or loaves of bread: the bread he gave me, but the water he carried to his father; however, as I was very thirsty too, I took a little of it. The water revived his father more than all the rum or spirits I had given him, for he was fainting with thirst.

When his father had drunk, I called to him to know if there was any water left. He said, "Yes"; and I bade him give it to the poor Spaniard, who was in as much want of it as his father; and I sent one of the cakes that Friday brought to the Spaniard too, who was indeed very weak, and was reposing himself upon a green place under the shade of a tree; and whose limbs were also very stiff, and very much swelled with the rude bandage he had been tied with. When I saw that upon Friday's coming to him with the water he sat up and drank, and took the bread and began to eat, I went to him and gave him a handful of raisins. He looked up in my face with all the tokens of gratitude and thankfulness that could appear in any countenance; but was so weak, notwithstanding he had so exerted himself in the fight, that he could not stand up upon his feet – he tried to do it two or three times, but was really not able, his ankles were so swelled and so painful to him; so I bade him sit still, and caused Friday to rub his ankles, and bathe them with rum, as he had done his father's.

I observed the poor affectionate creature, every two minutes, or perhaps less, all the while he was here, turn his head about to see if his father was in the same place and posture as he left him sitting; and at last he found he was not to be seen; at which he started up, and, without speaking a word, flew with that swiftness to him that one could scarce perceive his feet to touch the ground as he went; but when he came, he only found he had laid himself down to ease his limbs, so Friday came back to me presently; and then I spoke to the Spaniard to let Friday help him up if he could, and lead him to the boat, and then he should carry him to our dwelling, where I would take care of him. But Friday, a lusty, strong fellow, took the Spaniard upon his back, and carried him away to the boat, and set him down softly upon the side or gunnel of the canoe, with his feet in the inside of it; and then lifting him quite in, he set him close to his father; and presently stepping out again, launched the boat off, and paddled it along the shore faster than I could walk, though the wind blew pretty hard too; so he brought them both safe into our creek, and leaving them in the boat, ran away to fetch the other canoe. As he passed me I spoke to him, and asked him whither he went. He told me, "Go fetch more boat;" so away he went like the wind, for sure never man or horse ran like him; and he had the other canoe in the creek almost as soon as I got to it by land; so he wafted me over, and then went to help our new guests out of the boat, which he did; but they were neither of them able to walk; so that poor Friday knew not what to do.

To remedy this, I went to work in my thought, and calling to Friday to bid them sit down on the bank while he came to me, I soon made a kind of hand-barrow to lay them on, and Friday and I carried them both up together upon it between us.

But when we got them to the outside of our wall, or fortification, we were at a worse loss than before, for it was impossible to get them over, and I was resolved not to break it down; so I set to work again, and Friday and I, in about two hours' time, made a very handsome tent, covered with old sails, and above that with boughs of trees, being in the space without our outward fence and between that and the grove of young wood which I had planted; and here we made them two beds of such things as I had – *viz.* of good rice-straw, with blankets laid upon it to lie on, and another to cover them, on each bed.

My island was now peopled, and I thought myself very rich in subjects; and it was a merry reflection, which I frequently made, how like a king I looked. First of all, the whole country was my own property, so that I had an undoubted right of dominion. Secondly, my people were perfectly subjected – I was absolutely lord and lawgiver – they all owed their lives to me, and were ready to lay down their lives, if there had been occasion for it, for me. It was remarkable, too, I had but three subjects, and they were of three different religions – my man Friday was a Protestant, his father was a Pagan and a cannibal, and the Spaniard was a Papist. However, I allowed liberty of conscience throughout my dominions. But this is by the way.

As soon as I had secured my two weak, rescued prisoners, and given them shelter, and a place to rest them upon, I began to think of making some provision for them; and the first thing I did, I ordered Friday to take a yearling goat, betwixt a kid and a goat, out of my particular flock, to be killed; when I cut off the hinder-quarter, and chopping it into small pieces, I set Friday to work to boiling and stewing, and made them a very good dish, I assure you, of flesh and broth; and as I cooked it without doors, for I made no fire within my inner wall, so I carried it all into the new tent, and having set a table there for them, I sat down, and ate my own dinner also with them, and, as well as I could, cheered them and encouraged them. Friday was my interpreter, especially to his father, and, indeed, to the Spaniard too; for the Spaniard spoke the language of the savages pretty well.

After we had dined, or rather supped, I ordered Friday to take one of the canoes, and go and fetch our muskets and other firearms, which, for want of time, we had left upon the place of battle; and the next day I ordered him to go and bury the dead bodies of the savages, which lay open to the sun, and would presently be offensive. I also ordered him to bury the horrid remains of their barbarous feast, which I could not think of doing myself; nay, I could not bear to see them if I went that way; all which he punctually performed, and effaced the very appearance of the savages being there; so that when I went again, I could scarce know where it was, otherwise than by the corner of the wood pointing to the place.

I then began to enter into a little conversation with my two new subjects; and, first, I set Friday to inquire of his father what he thought of the escape of the savages in that canoe, and whether we might expect a return of them, with a power too great for us to resist. His first opinion was, that the savages in the boat never could live out the storm which blew that night they went off, but must of necessity be drowned, or driven south to those other shores, where they were as sure to be devoured as they were to be drowned if they were cast away; but, as to what they would do if they came safe on shore, he said he knew not; but it was his opinion that they were so dreadfully frightened with the manner of their being attacked, the noise, and the fire, that he believed they would tell the people they were all killed by thunder and lightning, not by the hand of man; and that the two which appeared – *viz.* Friday and I – were two heavenly spirits, or furies, come down to destroy them, and not men with weapons. This, he said, he knew; because he heard them all cry out so, in their language, one to another; for it was impossible for them to conceive that a man could dart fire, and speak thunder, and kill at a distance, without lifting up the hand, as was done now: and this old savage was in the right; for, as I understood since, by other hands, the savages never attempted to go over to the island afterwards, they were so terrified with the accounts given by those four men (for it seems they did escape the sea), that they believed whoever went to that enchanted island would be destroyed with fire from the gods. This, however, I knew not; and therefore was under continual apprehensions for a good while, and kept always upon my guard, with all my army: for, as there were now four of us, I would have ventured upon a hundred of them, fairly in the open field, at any time.

CHAPTER SEVENTEEN

Visit of Mutineers

In a little time, however, no more canoes appearing, the fear of their coming wore off; and I began to take my former thoughts of a voyage to the main into consideration; being likewise assured by Friday's father that I might depend upon good usage from their nation, on his account, if I would go. But my thoughts were a little suspended when I had a serious discourse with the Spaniard, and when I understood that there were sixteen more of his countrymen and Portuguese, who having been cast away and made their escape to that side, lived there at peace, indeed, with the savages, but were very sore put to it for necessaries, and, indeed, for life. I asked him all the particulars of their voyage, and found they were a Spanish ship, bound from the Rio de la Plata to the Havana, being directed to leave their loading there, which was chiefly hides and silver, and to bring back what European goods they could meet with there; that they had five Portuguese seamen on board, whom they took out of another wreck; that five of their own men were drowned when first the ship was lost, and that these escaped through infinite dangers and hazards, and arrived, almost starved, on the cannibal coast, where they expected to have been devoured every moment. He told me they had some arms with them, but they were perfectly useless, for that they had neither powder nor ball, the washing of the sea having spoiled all their powder but a little, which they used at their first landing to provide themselves with some food.

I asked him what he thought would become of them there, and if they had formed any design of making their escape. He said they had many consultations about it; but that having neither vessel nor tools to build one, nor provisions of any kind, their councils always ended in tears and despair. I asked him how he thought they would receive a proposal from me, which might tend towards an escape; and whether, if they were all here, it might not be done. I told him with freedom, I feared mostly their treachery and ill-usage of me, if I put my life in their hands; for that gratitude was no inherent virtue in the nature of man, nor did men always square their dealings by the obligations they had received so much as they did by the advantages they expected. I told him it would be very hard that I should be made the instrument of their deliverance, and that they should afterwards make me their prisoner in New Spain, where an Englishman was certain to be made a sacrifice, what necessity or what accident soever brought him thither; and that I had rather be delivered up to the savages, and be devoured alive, than fall into the merciless claws of the priests, and be carried into the Inquisition. I added that, otherwise, I was persuaded, if they were all here, we might, with so many hands, build a bark large enough to carry us all away, either to the Brazils southward, or to the islands or Spanish coast northward; but that if, in requital, they should, when I had put weapons into their hands, carry me by force among their own people, I might be ill-used for my kindness to them, and make my case worse than it was before.

He answered, with a great deal of candour and ingenuousness, that their condition was so miserable, and that they were so sensible of it, that he believed they would abhor the thought of using any man unkindly that should contribute to their deliverance; and that, if I pleased, he would go to them with the old man, and discourse with them about it, and return again and bring me their answer; that he would make conditions with them upon their solemn oath, that they should be absolutely under my direction as their commander and Captain; and they should swear upon the holy sacraments and gospel to be true to me, and go to such Christian country as I should agree to, and no other; and to be directed wholly and absolutely by my orders till they were landed safely in such country as I intended, and that he would bring a contract from them, under their hands, for that purpose. Then he told me he would first swear to me himself that he would never stir from me as long as he lived till I gave him orders; and that he would take my side to the last drop of his blood, if there should happen the least breach of faith among his countrymen. He told me they were all of them very civil, honest men, and they were under the greatest distress imaginable, having neither weapons nor clothes, nor any food, but at the mercy and discretion of the savages; out of all hopes of ever returning to their own country; and that he was sure, if I would undertake their relief, they would live and die by me.

Upon these assurances, I resolved to venture to relieve them, if possible, and to send the old savage and this Spaniard over to them to treat. But when we had got all things in readiness to go, the Spaniard himself started an objection, which had so much prudence in it on one hand, and so much sincerity on the other hand, that I could not but be very well satisfied in it; and, by his advice, put off the deliverance of his comrades for at least half a year. The case was thus: he had been with us now about a month, during which time I had let him see in what manner I had provided, with the assistance of Providence, for my support; and he saw evidently what stock of corn and rice I had laid up; which, though it was more than sufficient for myself, yet it was not sufficient, without good husbandry, for my family, now it was increased to four; but much less would it be sufficient if his countrymen, who were, as he said, sixteen, still alive, should come over; and least of all would it be sufficient to victual our vessel, if we should build one, for a voyage to any of the Christian colonies of America; so he told me he thought it would be more advisable to let him and the other two dig and cultivate some more land, as much as I could spare seed to sow, and that we should wait another harvest, that we might have a supply of corn for his countrymen, when they should come; for want might be a temptation to them to disagree, or not to think themselves delivered, otherwise than out of one difficulty into another. "You know," says he, "the children of Israel, though they rejoiced at first for their being delivered out of Egypt, yet rebelled even against God Himself, that delivered them, when they came to want bread in the wilderness."

His caution was so seasonable, and his advice so good, that I could not but be very well pleased with his proposal, as well as I was satisfied with his fidelity; so we fell to digging, all four of us, as well as the wooden tools we were furnished with permitted; and in about a month's time, by the end of which it was seed-time, we had got as much land cured and trimmed up as we sowed two-and-twenty bushels of barley on, and sixteen jars of rice, which was, in short, all the seed we had to spare: indeed, we left ourselves barely sufficient, for our own food for the six months that we had to expect our crop; that is to say reckoning from the time we set our seed aside for sowing; for it is not to be supposed it is six months in the ground in that country.

Having now society enough, and our numbers being sufficient to put us out of fear of the savages, if they had come, unless their number had been very great, we went freely all over the island, whenever we found occasion; and as we had our escape or deliverance upon our thoughts, it was impossible, at least for me, to have the means of it out of mine.

For this purpose I marked out several trees, which I thought fit for our work, and I set Friday and his father to cut them down; and then I caused the Spaniard, to whom I imparted my thoughts on that affair, to oversee and direct their work. I showed them with what indefatigable pains I had hewed a large tree into single planks, and I caused them to do the like, till they made about a dozen large planks, of good oak, near two feet broad, 35 feet long, and from two inches to four inches thick: what prodigious labour it took up any one may imagine.

At the same time I contrived to increase my little flock of tame goats as much as I could; and for this purpose I made Friday and the Spaniard go out one day, and myself with Friday the next day (for we took our turns), and by this means we got about twenty young kids to breed up with the rest; for whenever we shot the dam, we saved the kids, and added them to our flock. But above all, the season for curing the grapes coming on, I caused such a prodigious quantity to be hung up in the sun, that, I believe, had we been at Alicant, where the raisins of the sun are cured, we could have filled 60 or 80 barrels; and these, with our bread, formed a great part of our food – very good living too, I assure you, for they are exceedingly nourishing.

It was now harvest, and our crop in good order: it was not the most plentiful increase I had seen in the island, but, however, it was enough to answer our end; for from 22 bushels of barley we brought in and thrashed out above 220 bushels; and the like in proportion of the rice; which was store enough for our food to the next harvest, though all the sixteen Spaniards had been on shore with me; or, if we had been ready for a voyage, it would very plentifully have victualled our ship to have carried us to any part of the world; that is to say, any part of America. When we had thus housed and secured our magazine of corn, we fell to work to make more wicker-ware, *viz.* great baskets, in which we kept it; and the Spaniard was very handy and dexterous at this part, and often blamed me that I did not make some things for defence of this kind of work; but I saw no need of it.

And now, having a full supply of food for all the guests I expected, I gave the Spaniard leave to go over to the main, to see what he could do with those he had left behind him there. I gave him a strict charge not to bring any man who would not first swear in the presence of himself and the old savage that he would in no way injure, fight with, or attack the person he should find in the island, who was so kind as to send for them in order to their deliverance; but that they would stand by him and defend him against all such attempts, and wherever they went would be entirely under and subjected to his command; and that this should be put in writing, and signed in their hands. How they were to have done this, when I knew they had neither pen nor ink, was a question which we never asked. Under these instructions, the Spaniard and the old savage, the father of Friday, went away in one of the canoes which they might be said to have come in, or rather were brought in, when they came as prisoners to be devoured by the savages. I gave each of them a musket, with a firelock on it, and about eight charges of powder and ball, charging them to be very good husbands of both, and not to use either of them but upon urgent occasions.

This was a cheerful work, being the first measures used by me in view of my deliverance for now twenty-seven years and some days. I gave them provisions of bread and of dried grapes, sufficient for themselves for many days, and sufficient for all the Spaniards – for about eight days' time; and wishing them a good voyage, I saw them go, agreeing with them about a signal they should hang out at their return, by which I should know them again when they came back, at a distance, before they came on shore. They went away with a fair gale on the day that the moon was at full, by my account in the month of October; but as for an exact reckoning of days, after I had once lost it I could never recover it again; nor had I kept even the number of years so punctually as to be sure I was right; though, as it proved when I afterwards examined my account, I found I had kept a true reckoning of years.

It was no less than eight days I had waited for them, when a strange and unforeseen accident intervened, of which the like has not, perhaps, been heard of in history. I was fast asleep in my hutch one morning, when my man Friday came running in to me, and called aloud, "Master, Master, they are come, they are come!" I jumped up, and regardless of danger I went, as soon as I could get my clothes on, through my little grove, which, by the way, was by this time grown to be a very thick wood; I say, regardless of danger I went without my arms, which was not my custom to do; but I was surprised when, turning my eyes to the sea, I presently saw a boat at about a league and a half distance, standing in for the shore, with a shoulder-of-mutton sail, as they call it, and the wind blowing pretty fair to bring them in: also I observed, presently, that they did not come from that side which the shore lay on, but from the southernmost end of the island. Upon this I called Friday in, and bade him lie close, for these were not the people we looked for, and that we might not know yet whether they were friends or enemies. In the next place I went in to fetch my perspective glass to see what I could make of them; and having taken the ladder out, I climbed up to the top of the hill, as I used to do when I was apprehensive of anything, and to take my view the plainer without being discovered. I had scarce set my foot upon the hill when my eye plainly discovered a ship lying at anchor, at about two leagues and a half distance from me, S.S.E. but not above a league and a half from the shore. By my observation it appeared plainly to be an English ship, and the boat appeared to be an English long-boat.

I cannot express the confusion I was in, though the joy of seeing a ship, and one that I had reason to believe was manned by my own countrymen, and consequently friends, was such as I cannot describe; but yet I had some secret doubts hung about me – I cannot tell from whence they came – bidding me keep upon my guard. In the first place, it occurred to me to consider what business an English ship could have in that part of the world, since it was not the way to or from any part of the world where the English had any traffic; and I knew there had been no storms to drive them in there in distress; and that if they were really English it was most probable that they were here upon no good design; and that I had better continue as I was than fall into the hands of thieves and murderers.

Let no man despise the secret hints and notices of danger which sometimes are given him when he may think there is no possibility of its being real. That such hints and notices are given us I believe few that have made any observation of things can deny; that they are certain discoveries of an invisible world, and a converse of spirits, we cannot doubt; and if the tendency of them seems to be to warn us of danger, why should we not suppose they are from some friendly agent (whether supreme, or inferior and subordinate, is not the question), and that they are given for our good?

The present question abundantly confirms me in the justice of this reasoning; for had I not been made cautious by this secret admonition, come it from whence it will, I had been done inevitably, and in a far worse condition than before, as you will see presently. I had not kept myself long in this posture till I saw the boat draw near the shore, as if they looked for a creek to thrust in at, for the convenience of landing; however, as they did not come quite far enough, they did not see the little inlet where I formerly landed my rafts, but ran their boat on shore upon the beach, at about half a mile from me, which was very happy for me; for otherwise they would have landed just at my door, as I may say, and would soon have beaten me out of my castle, and perhaps have plundered me of all I had. When they were on shore I was fully satisfied they were Englishmen, at least most of them; one or two I thought were Dutch, but it did not prove so; there were in all eleven men, whereof three of them I found were unarmed and, as I thought, bound; and when the first four or five of them were jumped on shore, they took those three out of the boat as prisoners: one of the three I could perceive using the most passionate gestures of entreaty, affliction, and despair, even to a kind of extravagance; the other two, I could perceive, lifted up their hands sometimes, and appeared concerned indeed, but not to such a degree as the first. I was perfectly confounded at the sight, and knew not what the meaning of it should be. Friday called out to me in English, as well as he could, "O Master! you see English mans eat prisoner as well as savage mans." "Why, Friday," says I, "do you think they are going to eat them, then?" "Yes," says Friday, "they will eat them." "No no," says I, "Friday; I am afraid they will murder them, indeed; but you may be sure they will not eat them."

All this while I had no thought of what the matter really was, but stood trembling with the horror of the sight, expecting every moment when the three prisoners should be killed; nay, once I saw one of the villains lift up his arm with a great cutlass, as the seamen call it, or sword, to strike one of the poor men; and I expected to see him fall every moment; at which all the blood in my body seemed to run chill in my veins. I wished heartily now for the Spaniard, and the savage that had gone with him, or that I had any way to have come undiscovered within shot of them, that I might have secured the three men, for I saw no firearms they had among them; but it fell out to my mind another way. After I had observed the outrageous usage of the three men by the insolent seamen, I observed the fellows run scattering about the island, as if they wanted to see the country. I observed that the three other men had liberty to go also where they pleased; but they sat down all three upon the ground, very pensive, and looked like men in despair. This put me in mind of the first time when I came on shore, and began to look about me; how I gave myself over for lost; how wildly I looked round me; what dreadful apprehensions I had; and how I lodged in the tree all night for fear of being devoured by wild beasts. As I knew nothing that night of the supply I was to receive by the providential driving of the ship nearer the land by the storms and tide, by which I have since been so long nourished and supported; so these three poor desolate men knew nothing how certain of deliverance and supply they were, how near it was to them, and how effectually and really they were in a condition of safety, at the same time that they thought themselves lost and their case desperate. So little do we see before us in the world, and so much reason have we to depend cheerfully upon the great Maker of the world, that He does not leave His creatures so absolutely destitute, but that in the worst circumstances they have always something to be thankful for, and sometimes are nearer deliverance than they imagine; nay, are even brought to their deliverance by the means by which they seem to be brought to their destruction.

It was just at high-water when these people came on shore; and while they rambled about to see what kind of a place they were in, they had carelessly stayed till the tide was spent, and the water was ebbed considerably away, leaving their boat aground. They had left two men in the boat, who, as I found afterwards, having drunk a little too much brandy, fell asleep; however, one of them waking a little sooner than the other and finding the boat too fast aground for him to stir it, hallooed out for the rest, who were straggling about: upon which they all soon came to the boat: but it was past all their strength to launch her, the boat being very heavy, and the shore on that side being a soft oozy sand, almost like a quicksand. In this condition, like true seamen, who are, perhaps, the least of all mankind given to forethought, they gave it over, and away they strolled about the country again; and I heard one of them say aloud to another, calling them off from the boat, "Why, let her alone, Jack, can't you? she'll float next tide;" by which I was fully confirmed in the main inquiry of what countrymen they were. All this while I kept myself very close, not once daring to stir out of my castle any farther than to my place of observation near the top of the hill: and very glad I was to think how well it was fortified. I knew it was no less than ten hours before the boat could float again, and by that time it would be dark, and I might be at more liberty to see their motions, and to hear their discourse, if they had any. In the meantime I fitted myself up for a battle as before, though with more caution, knowing I had to do with another kind of enemy than I had at first. I ordered Friday also, whom I had made an excellent marksman with his gun, to load himself with arms. I took myself two fowling-pieces, and I gave him three muskets. My figure, indeed, was very fierce; I had my formidable goat-skin coat on, with the great cap I have mentioned, a naked sword by my side, two pistols in my belt, and a gun upon each shoulder.

It was my design, as I said above, not to have made any attempt till it was dark; but about two o'clock, being the heat of the day, I found that they were all gone straggling into the woods, and, as I thought, laid down to sleep. The three poor distressed men, too anxious for their condition to get any sleep, had, however, sat down under the shelter of a great tree, at about a quarter of a mile from me, and, as I thought, out of sight of any of the rest. Upon this I resolved to discover myself to them, and learn something of their condition; immediately I marched as above, my man Friday at a good distance behind me, as formidable for his arms as I, but not making quite so staring a spectre-like figure as I did. I came as near them undiscovered as I could, and then, before any of them saw me, I called aloud to them in Spanish, "What are ye, gentlemen?" They started up at the noise, but were ten times more confounded when they saw me, and the uncouth figure that I made. They made no answer at all, but I thought I perceived them just going to fly from me, when I spoke to them in English. "Gentlemen," said I, "do not be surprised at me; perhaps you may have a friend near when you did not expect it." "He must be sent directly from heaven then," said one of them very gravely to me, and pulling off his hat at the same time to me; "for our condition is past the help of man." "All help is from heaven, sir," said I, "but can you put a stranger in the way to help you? for you seem to be in some great distress. I saw you when you landed; and when you seemed to make application to the brutes that came with you, I saw one of them lift up his sword to kill you."

The poor man, with tears running down his face, and trembling, looking like one astonished, returned, "Am I talking to God or man? Is it a real man or an angel?" "Be in no fear about that, sir," said I; "if God had sent an angel to relieve you, he would have come better cloathed, and armed after another manner than you see me; pray lay aside your fears; I am a man, an Englishman, and disposed to assist you; you see I have one servant only; we have arms and ammunition; tell us freely, can we serve you? What is your case?" "Our case, sir," said he, "is too long to tell you while our murderers are so near us; but, in short, sir, I was commander of that ship – my men have mutinied against me; they have been hardly prevailed on not to murder me, and, at last, have set me on shore in this desolate place, with these two men with me – one my Mate, the other a passenger – where we expected to perish, believing the place to be uninhabited, and know not yet what to think of it." "Where are these brutes, your enemies?" said I; "do you know where they are gone? There they lie, sir," said he, pointing to a thicket of trees; "my heart trembles for fear they have seen us and heard you speak; if they have, they will certainly murder us all." "Have they any firearms?" said I. He answered, "They had only two pieces, one of which they left in the boat." "Well, then," said I, "leave the rest to me; I see they are all asleep; it is an easy thing to kill them all; but shall we rather take them prisoners?" He told me there were two desperate villains among them that it was scarce safe to show any mercy to; but if they were secured, he believed all the rest would return to their duty. I asked him which they were. He told me he could not at that distance distinguish them, but he would obey my orders in anything I would direct. "Well," says I, let us retreat out of their view or hearing, lest they awake, and we will resolve further." So they willingly went back with me, till the woods covered us from them.

"Look you, sir," said I, "if I venture upon your deliverance, are you willing to make two conditions with me?" He anticipated my proposals by telling me that both he and the ship, if recovered, should be wholly directed and commanded by me in everything; and if the ship was not recovered, he would live and die with me in what part of the world soever I would send him; and the two other men said the same. "Well," says I, "my conditions are but two; first, that while you stay in this island with me, you will not pretend to any authority here; and if I put arms in your hands, you will, upon all occasions, give them up to me, and do no prejudice to me or mine upon this island, and in the meantime be governed by my orders; secondly, that if the ship is or may be recovered, you will carry me and my man to England passage free."

He gave me all the assurances that the invention or faith of man could devise that he would comply with these most reasonable demands, and besides would owe his life to me, and acknowledge it upon all occasions as long as he lived. "Well, then," said I, "here are three muskets for you, with powder and ball; tell me next what you think is proper to be done." He showed all the testimonies of his gratitude that he was able, but offered to be wholly guided by me. I told him I thought it was very hard venturing anything; but the best method I could think of was to fire on them at once as they lay, and if any were not killed at the first volley, and offered to submit, we might save them, and so put it wholly upon God's providence to direct the shot. He said, very modestly, that he was loath to kill them if he could help it; but that those two were incorrigible villains, and had been the authors of all the mutiny in the ship, and if they escaped, we should be undone still, for they would go on board and bring the whole ship's company, and destroy us all. "Well, then," says I, "necessity legitimates my advice, for it is the only way to save our lives." However, seeing him still cautious of shedding blood, I told him they should go themselves, and manage as they found convenient.

In the middle of this discourse we heard some of them awake, and soon after we saw two of them on their feet. I asked him if either of them were the heads of the mutiny? He said, "No." "Well, then," said I, "you may let them escape; and Providence seems to have awakened them on purpose to save themselves. Now," says I, "if the rest escape you, it is your fault." Animated with this, he took the musket I had given him in his hand, and a pistol in his belt, and his two comrades with him, with each a piece in his hand; the two men who were with him going first made some noise, at which one of the seamen who was awake turned about, and seeing them coming, cried out to the rest; but was too late then, for the moment he cried out they fired – I mean the two men, the Captain wisely reserving his own piece. They had so well aimed their shot at the men they knew, that one of them was killed on the spot, and the other very much wounded; but not being dead, he started up on his feet, and called eagerly for help to the other; but the Captain stepping to him, told him it was too late to cry for help, he should call upon God to forgive his villainy, and with that word knocked him down with the stock of his musket, so that he never spoke more; there were three more in the company, and one of them was slightly wounded. By this time I was come; and when they saw their danger, and that it was in vain to resist, they begged for mercy. The Captain told them he would spare their lives if they would give him an assurance of their abhorrence of the treachery they had been guilty of, and would swear to be faithful to him in recovering the ship, and afterwards in carrying her back to Jamaica, from whence they came. They gave him all the protestations of their sincerity that could be desired; and he was willing to believe them, and spare their lives, which I was not against, only that I obliged him to keep them bound hand and foot while they were on the island.

While this was doing, I sent Friday with the Captain's Mate to the boat with orders to secure her, and bring away the oars and sails, which they did; and by-and-by three straggling men, that were (happily for them) parted from the rest, came back upon hearing the guns fired; and seeing the Captain, who was before their prisoner, now their conqueror, they submitted to be bound also; and so our victory was complete.

It now remained that the Captain and I should inquire into one another's circumstances. I began first, and told him my whole history, which he heard with an attention even to amazement – and particularly at the wonderful manner of my being furnished with provisions and ammunition; and, indeed, as my story is a whole collection of wonders, it affected him deeply. But when he reflected from thence upon himself, and how I seemed to have been preserved there on purpose to save his life, the tears ran down his face, and he could not speak a word more. After this communication was at an end, I carried him and his two men into my apartment, leading them in just where I came out, *viz.* at the top of the house, where I refreshed them with such provisions as I had, and showed them all the contrivances I had made during my long, long inhabiting that place.

All I showed them, all I said to them, was perfectly amazing; but above all, the Captain admired my fortification, and how perfectly I had concealed my retreat with a grove of trees, which having been now planted nearly twenty years, and the trees growing much faster than in England, was become a little wood, so thick that it was impassable in any part of it but at that one side where I had reserved my little winding passage into it. I told him this was my castle and my residence, but that I had a seat in the country, as most princes have, whither I could retreat upon occasion, and I would show him that too another time; but at present our business was to consider how to recover the ship. He agreed with me as to that, but told me he was perfectly at a loss what measures to take, for that there were still six-and-twenty hands on board, who, having entered into a cursed conspiracy, by which they had all forfeited their lives to the law, would be hardened in it now by desperation, and would carry it on, knowing that if they were subdued they would be brought to the gallows as soon as they came to England, or to any of the English colonies, and that, therefore, there would be no attacking them with so small a number as we were.

I mused for some time on what he had said, and found it was a very rational conclusion, and that therefore something was to be resolved on speedily, as well to draw the men on board into some snare for their surprise as to prevent their landing upon us, and destroying us. Upon this, it presently occurred to me that in a little while the ship's crew, wondering what was become of their comrades and of the boat, would certainly come on shore in their other boat to look for them, and that then, perhaps, they might come armed, and be too strong for us: this he allowed to be rational. Upon this, I told him the first thing we had to do was to stave the boat which lay upon the beach, so that they might not carry her of, and taking everything out of her, leave her so far useless as not to be fit to swim. Accordingly, we went on board, took the arms which were left on board out of her, and whatever else we found there – which was a bottle of brandy, and another of rum, a few biscuit-cakes, a horn of powder, and a great lump of sugar in a piece of canvas (the sugar was five or six pounds): all which was very welcome to me, especially the brandy and sugar, of which I had had none left for many years.

When we had carried all these things on shore (the oars, mast, sail, and rudder of the boat were carried away before), we knocked a great hole in her bottom, that if they had come strong enough to Master us, yet they could not carry off the boat. Indeed, it was not much in my thoughts that we could be able to recover the ship; but my view was, that if they went away without the boat, I did not much question to make her again fit to carry as to the Leeward Islands, and call upon our friends the Spaniards in my way, for I had them still in my thoughts.

CHAPTER EIGHTEEN

The Ship Recovered

While we were thus preparing our designs, and had first, by main strength, heaved the boat upon the beach, so high that the tide would not float her off at high-water mark, and besides, had broke a hole in her bottom too big to be quickly stopped, and were set down musing what we should do, we heard the ship fire a gun, and make a waft with her ensign as a signal for the boat to come on board – but no boat stirred; and they fired several times, making other signals for the boat. At last, when all their signals and firing proved fruitless, and they found the boat did not stir, we saw them, by the help of my glasses, hoist another boat out and row towards the shore; and we found, as they approached, that there were no less than ten men in her, and that they had firearms with them.

As the ship lay almost two leagues from the shore, we had a full view of them as they came, and a plain sight even of their faces; because the tide having set them a little to the east of the other boat, they rowed up under shore, to come to the same place where the other had landed, and where the boat lay; by this means, I say, we had a full view of them, and the Captain knew the persons and characters of all the men in the boat, of whom, he said, there were three very honest fellows, who, he was sure, were led into this conspiracy by the rest, being over-powered and frightened; but that as for the boatswain, who it seems was the chief officer among them, and all the rest, they were as outrageous as any of the ship's crew, and were no doubt made desperate in their new enterprise; and terribly apprehensive he was that they would be too powerful for us. I smiled at him, and told him that men in our circumstances were past the operation of fear; that seeing almost every condition that could be was better than that which we were supposed to be in, we ought to expect that the consequence, whether death or life, would be sure to be a deliverance. I asked him what he thought of the circumstances of my life, and whether a deliverance were not worth venturing for? "And where, sir," said I, "is your belief of my being preserved here on purpose to save your life, which elevated you a little while ago? For my part," said I, "there seems to be but one thing amiss in all the prospect of it." "What is that?" say she. "Why," said I, "it is, that as you say there are three or four honest fellows among them which should be spared, had they been all of the wicked part of the crew I should have thought God's providence had singled them out to deliver them into your hands; for depend upon it, every man that comes ashore is our own, and shall die or live as they behave to us." As I spoke this with a raised voice and cheerful countenance, I found it greatly encouraged him; so we set vigorously to our business.

We had, upon the first appearance of the boat's coming from the ship, considered of separating our prisoners; and we had, indeed, secured them effectually. Two of them, of whom the Captain was less assured than ordinary, I sent with Friday, and one of the three delivered men, to my cave, where they were remote enough, and out of danger of being heard or discovered, or of finding their way out of the woods if they could have delivered themselves. Here they left them bound, but gave them provisions; and promised them, if they continued there quietly, to give them their liberty in a day or two; but that if they attempted their escape they should be put to death without mercy. They promised faithfully to bear their confinement with patience, and were very thankful that they had such good usage as to have provisions and light left them; for Friday gave them candles (such as we made ourselves) for their comfort; and they did not know but that he stood sentinel over them at the entrance.

The other prisoners had better usage; two of them were kept pinioned, indeed, because the Captain was not able to trust them; but the other two were taken into my service, upon the Captain's recommendation, and upon their solemnly engaging to live and die with us; so with them and the three honest men we were seven men, well armed; and I made no doubt we should be able to deal well enough with the ten that were coming, considering that the Captain had said there were three or four honest men among them also. As soon as they got to the place where their other boat lay, they ran their boat into the beach and came all on shore, hauling the boat up after them, which I was glad to see, for I was afraid they would rather have left the boat at an anchor some distance from the shore, with some hands in her to guard her, and so we should not be able to seize the boat. Being on shore, the first thing they did, they ran all to their other boat; and it was easy to see they were under a great surprise to find her stripped, as above, of all that was in her, and a great hole in her bottom. After they had mused a while upon this, they set up two or three great shouts, hallooing with all their might, to try if they could make their companions hear; but all was to no purpose. Then they came all close in a ring, and fired a volley of their small arms, which indeed we heard, and the echoes made the woods ring. But it was all one; those in the cave, we were sure, could not hear; and those in our keeping, though they heard it well enough, yet durst give no answer to them. They were so astonished at the surprise of this, that, as they told us afterwards, they resolved to go all on board again to their ship, and let them know that the men were all murdered, and the long-boat staved; accordingly, they immediately launched their boat again, and got all of them on board.

The Captain was terribly amazed, and even confounded, at this, believing they would go on board the ship again and set sail, giving their comrades over for lost, and so he should still lose the ship, which he was in hopes we should have recovered; but he was quickly as much frightened the other way.

They had not been long put off with the boat, when we perceived them all coming on shore again; but with this new measure in their conduct, which it seems they consulted together upon, *viz.* to leave three men in the boat, and the rest to go on shore, and go up into the country to look for their fellows. This was a great disappointment to us, for now we were at a loss what to do, as our seizing those seven men on shore would be no advantage to us if we let the boat escape; because they would row away to the ship, and then the rest of them would be sure to weigh and set sail, and so our recovering the ship would be lost. However we had no remedy but to wait and see what the issue of things might present. The seven men came on shore, and the three who remained in the boat put her off to a good distance from the shore, and came to an anchor to wait for them; so that it was impossible for us to come at them in the boat. Those that came on shore kept close together, marching towards the top of the little hill under which my habitation lay; and we could see them plainly, though they could not perceive us. We should have been very glad if they would have come nearer us, so that we might have fired at them, or that they would have gone farther off, that we might come abroad. But when they were come to the brow of the hill where they could see a great way into the valleys and woods, which lay towards the north-east part, and where the island lay lowest, they shouted and hallooed till they were weary; and not caring, it seems, to venture far from the shore, nor far from one another, they sat down together under a tree to consider it. Had they thought fit to have gone to sleep there, as the other part of them had done, they had done the job for us; but they were too full of apprehensions of danger to venture to go to sleep, though they could not tell what the danger was they had to fear.

The Captain made a very just proposal to me upon this consultation of theirs, *viz.* that perhaps they would all fire a volley again, to endeavour to make their fellows hear, and that we should all sally upon them just at the juncture when their pieces were all discharged, and they would certainly yield, and we should have them without bloodshed. I liked this proposal, provided it was done while we were near enough to come up to them before they could load their pieces again. But this event did not happen; and we lay still a long time, very irresolute what course to take. At length I told them there would be nothing done, in my opinion, till night; and then, if they did not return to the boat, perhaps we might find a way to get between them and the shore, and so might use some stratagem with them in the boat to get them on shore. We waited a great while, though very impatient for their removing; and were very uneasy when, after long consultation, we saw them all start up and march down towards the sea; it seems they had such dreadful apprehensions of the danger of the place that they resolved to go on board the ship again, give their companions over for lost, and so go on with their intended voyage with the ship.

As soon as I perceived them go towards the shore, I imagined it to be as it really was that they had given over their search, and were going back again; and the Captain, as soon as I told him my thoughts, was ready to sink at the apprehensions of it; but I presently thought of a stratagem to fetch them back again, and which answered my end to a tittle. I ordered Friday and the Captain's Mate to go over the little creek westward, towards the place where the savages came on shore, when Friday was rescued, and so soon as they came to a little rising round, at about half a mile distant, I bid them halloo out, as loud as they could, and wait till they found the seamen heard them; that as soon as ever they heard the seamen answer them, they should return it again; and then, keeping out of sight, take a round, always answering when the others hallooed, to draw them as far into the island and among the woods as possible, and then wheel about again to me by such ways as I directed them.

They were just going into the boat when Friday and the Mate hallooed; and they presently heard them, and answering, ran along the shore westward, towards the voice they heard, when they were stopped by the creek, where the water being up, they could not get over, and called for the boat to come up and set them over; as, indeed, I expected. When they had set themselves over, I observed that the boat being gone a good way into the creek, and, as it were, in a harbour within the land, they took one of the three men out of her, to go along with them, and left only two in the boat, having fastened her to the stump of a little tree on the shore. This was what I wished for; and immediately leaving Friday and the Captain's Mate to their business, I took the rest with me; and, crossing the creek out of their sight, we surprised the two men before they were aware – one of them lying on the shore, and the other being in the boat. The fellow on shore was between sleeping and waking, and going to start up; the Captain, who was foremost, ran in upon him, and knocked him down; and then called out to him in the boat to yield, or he was a dead man. They needed very few arguments to persuade a single man to yield, when he saw five men upon him and his comrade knocked down: besides, this was, it seems, one of the three who were not so hearty in the mutiny as the rest of the crew, and therefore was easily persuaded not only to yield, but afterwards to join very sincerely with us. In the meantime, Friday and the Captain's Mate so well managed their business with the rest that they drew them, by hallooing and answering, from one hill to another, and from one wood to another, till they not only heartily tired them, but left them where they were, very sure they could not reach back to the boat before it was dark; and, indeed, they were heartily tired themselves also, by the time they came back to us.

We had nothing now to do but to watch for them in the dark, and to fall upon them, so as to make sure work with them. It was several hours after Friday came back to me before they came back to their boat; and we could hear the foremost of them, long before they came quite up, calling to those behind to come along; and could also hear them answer, and complain how lame and tired they were, and not able to come any faster: which was very welcome news to us. At length they came up to the boat: but it is impossible to express their confusion when they found the boat fast aground in the creek, the tide ebbed out, and their two men gone. We could hear them call one to another in a most lamentable manner, telling one another they were got into an enchanted island; that either there were inhabitants in it, and they should all be murdered, or else there were devils and spirits in it, and they should be all carried away and devoured. They hallooed again, and called their two comrades by their names a great many times; but no answer. After some time we could see them, by the little light there was, run about, wringing their hands like men in despair, and sometimes they would go and sit down in the boat to rest themselves: then come ashore again, and walk about again, and so the same thing over again. My men would fain have had me give them leave to fall upon them at once in the dark; but I was willing to take them at some advantage, so as to spare them, and kill as few of them as I could; and especially I was unwilling to hazard the killing of any of our men, knowing the others were very well armed. I resolved to wait, to see if they did not separate; and therefore, to make sure of them, I drew my ambuscade nearer, and ordered Friday and the Captain to creep upon their hands and feet, as close to the ground as they could, that they might not be discovered, and get as near them as they could possibly before they offered to fire.

They had not been long in that posture when the boatswain, who was the principal ringleader of the mutiny, and had now shown himself the most dejected and dispirited of all the rest, came walking towards them, with two more of the crew; the Captain was so eager at having this principal rogue so much in his power, that he could hardly have patience to let him come so near as to be sure of him, for they only heard his tongue before: but when they came nearer, the Captain and Friday, starting up on their feet, let fly at them. The boatswain was killed upon the spot: the next man was shot in the body, and fell just by him, though he did not die till an hour or two after; and the third ran for it. At the noise of the fire I immediately advanced with my whole army, which was now eight men, *viz.* myself, generalissimo; Friday, my Lieutenant-general; the Captain and his two men, and the three prisoners of war whom we had trusted with arms. We came upon them, indeed, in the dark, so that they could not see our number; and I made the man they had left in the boat, who was now one of us, to call them by name, to try if I could bring them to a parley, and so perhaps might reduce them to terms; which fell out just as we desired: for indeed it was easy to think, as their condition then was, they would be very willing to capitulate. So he calls out as loud as he could to one of them, "Tom Smith! Tom Smith!" Tom Smith answered immediately, "Is that Robinson?" for it seems he knew the voice. The other answered, "Ay, ay; for God's sake, Tom Smith, throw down your arms and yield, or you are all dead men this moment." "Who must we yield to? Where are they?" says Smith again. "Here they are," says he; "here's our Captain and fifty men with him, have been hunting you these two hours; the boatswain is killed; Will Fry is wounded, and I am a prisoner; and if you do not yield you are all lost." "Will they give us quarter, then?" says Tom Smith, "and we will yield." "I'll go and ask, if you promise to yield," said Robinson: so he asked the Captain, and the Captain himself then calls out, "You, Smith, you know my voice; if you lay down your arms immediately and submit, you shall have your lives, all but Will Atkins."

Upon this Will Atkins cried out, "For God's sake, Captain, give me quarter; what have I done? They have all been as bad as I:" which, by the way, was not true; for it seems this Will Atkins was the first man that laid hold of the Captain when they first mutinied, and used him barbarously in tying his hands and giving him injurious language. However, the Captain told him he must lay down his arms at discretion, and trust to the governor's mercy: by which he meant me, for they all called me governor. In a word, they all laid down their arms and begged their lives; and I sent the man that had parleyed with them, and two more, who bound them all; and then my great army of fifty men, which, with those three, were in all but eight, came up and seized upon them, and upon their boat; only that I kept myself and one more out of sight for reasons of state.

Our next work was to repair the boat, and think of seizing the ship: and as for the Captain, now he had leisure to parley with them, he expostulated with them upon the villainy of their practices with him, and upon the further wickedness of their design, and how certainly it must bring them to misery and distress in the end, and perhaps to the gallows. They all appeared very penitent, and begged hard for their lives. As for that, he told them they were not his prisoners, but the commander's of the island; that they thought they had set him on shore in a barren, uninhabited island; but it had pleased God so to direct them that it was inhabited, and that the governor was an Englishman; that he might hang them all there, if he pleased; but as he had given them all quarter, he supposed he would send them to England, to be dealt with there as justice required, except Atkins, whom he was commanded by the governor to advise to prepare for death, for that he would be hanged in the morning.

Though this was all but a fiction of his own, yet it had its desired effect; Atkins fell upon his knees to beg the Captain to intercede with the governor for his life; and all the rest begged of him, for God's sake, that they might not be sent to England.

It now occurred to me that the time of our deliverance was come, and that it would be a most easy thing to bring these fellows in to be hearty in getting possession of the ship; so I retired in the dark from them, that they might not see what kind of a governor they had, and called the Captain to me; when I called, at a good distance, one of the men was ordered to speak again, and say to the Captain, "Captain, the commander calls for you;" and presently the Captain replied, "Tell his Excellency I am just coming." This more perfectly amazed them, and they all believed that the commander was just by, with his 50 men. Upon the Captain coming to me, I told him my project for seizing the ship, which he liked wonderfully well, and resolved to put it in execution the next morning. But, in order to execute it with more art, and to be secure of success, I told him we must divide the prisoners, and that he should go and take Atkins, and two more of the worst of them, and send them pinioned to the cave where the others lay. This was committed to Friday and the two men who came on shore with the Captain. They conveyed them to the cave as to a prison: and it was, indeed, a dismal place, especially to men in their condition. The others I ordered to my bower, as I called it, of which I have given a full description: and as it was fenced in, and they pinioned, the place was secure enough, considering they were upon their behaviour.

To these in the morning I sent the Captain, who was to enter into a parley with them; in a word, to try them, and tell me whether he thought they might be trusted or not to go on board and surprise the ship. He talked to them of the injury done him, of the condition they were brought to, and that though the governor had given them quarter for their lives as to the present action, yet that if they were sent to England they would all be hanged in chains; but that if they would join in so just an attempt as to recover the ship, he would have the governor's engagement for their pardon.

Any one may guess how readily such a proposal would be accepted by men in their condition; they fell down on their knees to the Captain, and promised, with the deepest imprecations, that they would be faithful to him to the last drop, and that they should owe their lives to him, and would go with him all over the world; that they would own him as a father to them as long as they lived. "Well," says the Captain, "I must go and tell the governor what you say, and see what I can do to bring him to consent to it." So he brought me an account of the temper he found them in, and that he verily believed they would be faithful. However, that we might be very secure, I told him he should go back again and choose out those five, and tell them, that they might see he did not want men, that he would take out those five to be his assistants, and that the governor would keep the other two, and the three that were sent prisoners to the castle (my cave), as hostages for the fidelity of those five; and that if they proved unfaithful in the execution, the five hostages should be hanged in chains alive on the shore. This looked severe, and convinced them that the governor was in earnest; however, they had no way left them but to accept it; and it was now the business of the prisoners, as much as of the Captain, to persuade the other five to do their duty.

Our strength was now thus ordered for the expedition: first, the Captain, his Mate, and passenger; second, the two prisoners of the first gang, to whom, having their character from the Captain, I had given their liberty, and trusted them with arms; third, the other two that I had kept till now in my bower, pinioned, but on the Captain's motion had now released; fourth, these five released at last; so that there were twelve in all, besides five we kept prisoners in the cave for hostages.

I asked the Captain if he was willing to venture with these hands on board the ship; but as for me and my man Friday, I did not think it was proper for us to stir, having seven men left behind; and it was employment enough for us to keep them asunder, and supply them with victuals. As to the five in the cave, I resolved to keep them fast, but Friday went in twice a day to them, to supply them with necessaries; and I made the other two carry provisions to a certain distance, where Friday was to take them.

When I showed myself to the two hostages, it was with the Captain, who told them I was the person the governor had ordered to look after them; and that it was the governor's pleasure they should not stir anywhere but by my direction; that if they did, they would be fetched into the castle, and be laid in irons: so that as we never suffered them to see me as governor, I now appeared as another person, and spoke of the governor, the garrison, the castle, and the like, upon all occasions.

The Captain now had no difficulty before him, but to furnish his two boats, stop the breach of one, and man them. He made his passenger Captain of one, with four of the men; and himself, his Mate, and five more, went in the other; and they contrived their business very well, for they came up to the ship about midnight. As soon as they came within call of the ship, he made Robinson hail them, and tell them they had brought off the men and the boat, but that it was a long time before they had found them, and the like, holding them in a chat till they came to the ship's side; when the Captain and the Mate entering first with their arms, immediately knocked down the second Mate and carpenter with the butt-end of their muskets, being very faithfully seconded by their men; they secured all the rest that were upon the main and quarter decks, and began to fasten the hatches, to keep them down that were below; when the other boat and their men, entering at the fore chains, secured the forecastle of the ship, and the scuttle which went down into the cook-room, making three men they found there prisoners. When this was done, and all safe upon deck, the Captain ordered the Mate, with three men, to break into the round-house, where the new rebel Captain lay, who, having taken the alarm, had got up, and with two men and a boy had got firearms in their hands; and

1726 illustration by W. Mears & T. Woodward

when the Mate, with a crow, split open the door, the new Captain and his men fired boldly among them, and wounded the Mate with a musket ball, which broke his arm, and wounded two more of the men, but killed nobody. The Mate, calling for help, rushed, however, into the round-house, wounded as he was, and, with his pistol, shot the new Captain through the head, the bullet entering at his mouth, and came out again behind one of his ears, so that he never spoke a word more: upon which the rest yielded, and the ship was taken effectually, without any more lives lost.

As soon as the ship was thus secured, the Captain ordered seven guns to be fired, which was the signal agreed upon with me to give me notice of his success, which, you may be sure, I was very glad to hear, having sat watching upon the shore for it till near two o'clock in the morning. Having thus heard the signal plainly, I laid me down; and it having been a day of great fatigue to me, I slept very sound, till I was surprised with the noise of a gun; and presently starting up, I heard a man call me by the name of "Governor! Governor!" and presently I knew the Captain's voice; when, climbing up to the top of the hill, there he stood, and, pointing to the ship, he embraced me in his arms, "My dear friend and deliverer," says he, "there's your ship; for she is all yours, and so are we, and all that belong to her." I cast my eyes to the ship, and there she rode, within little more than half a mile of the shore; for they had weighed her anchor as soon as they were Masters of her, and, the weather being fair, had brought her to an anchor just against the mouth of the little creek; and the tide being up, the Captain had brought the pinnace in near the place where I had first landed my rafts, and so landed just at my door. I was at first ready to sink down with the surprise; for I saw my deliverance, indeed, visibly put into my hands, all things easy, and a large ship just ready to carry me away whither I pleased to go. At first, for some time, I was not able to answer him one word; but as he had taken me in his arms I held fast by him, or I should have fallen to the ground. He perceived the surprise, and immediately pulled a bottle out of his pocket and gave me a dram of cordial, which he had brought on purpose for me. After I had drunk it, I sat down upon the ground; and though it brought me to myself, yet it was a good while before I could speak a word to him. All this time the poor man was in as great an ecstasy as I, only not under any surprise as I was; and he said a thousand kind and tender things to me, to compose and bring me to myself; but such was the flood of joy in my breast, that it put all my spirits into confusion: at last it broke out into tears, and in a little while after I recovered my speech; I then took my turn, and embraced him as my deliverer, and we rejoiced together. I told him I looked upon him as a man sent by Heaven to deliver me, and that the whole transaction seemed to be a chain of wonders; that such things as these were the testimonies we had of a secret hand of Providence governing the world, and an evidence that the eye of an infinite Power could search into the remotest corner of the world, and send help to the miserable whenever He pleased. I forgot not to lift up my heart in thankfulness to Heaven; and what heart could forbear to bless Him, who had not only in a miraculous manner provided for me in such a wilderness, and in such a desolate condition, but from whom every deliverance must always be acknowledged to proceed.

When we had talked a while, the Captain told me he had brought me some little refreshment, such as the ship afforded, and such as the wretches that had been so long his Masters had not plundered him of. Upon this, he called aloud to the boat, and bade his men bring the things ashore that were for the governor; and, indeed, it was a present as if I had been one that was not to be carried away with them, but as if I had been to dwell upon the island still. First, he had brought me a case of bottles full of excellent cordial waters, six large bottles of Madeira wine (the bottles held two quarts each), two pounds of excellent good tobacco, twelve good pieces of the ship's beef, and six pieces of pork, with a bag of peas, and about a hundred-weight of biscuit; he also brought me a box of sugar, a box of flour, a bag full of lemons, and two bottles of lime-juice, and abundance of other things. But besides these, and what was a thousand times more useful to me, he brought me six new clean shirts, six very good neckclothes, two pair of gloves, one pair of shoes, a hat, and one pair of stockings, with a very good suit of clothes of his own, which had been worn but very little: in a word, he cloathed me from head to foot. It was a very kind and agreeable present, as any one may imagine, to one in my circumstances, but never was anything in the world of that kind so unpleasant, awkward, and uneasy as it was to me to wear such clothes at first.

After these ceremonies were past, and after all his good things were brought into my little apartment, we began to consult what was to be done with the prisoners we had; for it was worth considering whether we might venture to take them with us or no, especially two of them, whom he knew to be incorrigible and refractory to the last degree; and the Captain said he knew they were such rogues that there was no obliging them, and if he did carry them away, it must be in irons, as malefactors, to be delivered over to justice at the first English colony he could come to; and I found that the Captain himself was very anxious about it. Upon this, I told him that, if he desired it, I would undertake to bring the two men he spoke of to make it their own request that he should leave them upon the island. "I should be very glad of that," says the Captain, "with all my heart." "Well," says I, "I will send for them up and talk with them for you." So I caused Friday and the two hostages, for they were now discharged, their comrades having performed their promise; I say, I caused them to go to the cave, and bring up the five men, pinioned as they were, to the bower, and keep them there till I came. After some time, I came thither dressed in my new habit; and now I was called governor again. Being all met, and the Captain with me, I caused the men to be brought before me, and I told them I had got a full account of their villainous behaviour to the Captain, and how they had run away with the ship, and were preparing to commit further robberies, but that Providence had ensnared them in their own ways, and that they were fallen into the pit which they had dug for others. I let them know that by my direction the ship had been seized; that she lay now in the road; and they might see by-and-by that their new Captain had received the reward of his villainy, and that they would see him hanging at the yard-arm; that, as to them, I wanted to know what they had to say why I should not execute them as pirates taken in the fact, as by my commission they could not doubt but I had authority so to do.

One of them answered in the name of the rest, that they had nothing to say but this, that when they were taken the Captain promised them their lives, and they humbly implored my mercy. But I told them I knew not what mercy to show them; for as for myself, I had resolved to quit the island with all my men, and had taken passage with the Captain to go to England; and as for the Captain, he could not carry them to England other than as prisoners in irons, to be tried for mutiny and running away with the ship; the consequence of which, they must needs know, would be the gallows; so that I could not tell what was best for them, unless they had a mind to take their fate in the island. If they desired that, as I had liberty to leave the island, I had some inclination to give them their lives, if they thought they could shift on shore. They seemed very thankful for it, and said they would much rather venture to stay there than be carried to England to be hanged. So I left it on that issue.

However, the Captain seemed to make some difficulty of it, as if he durst not leave them there. Upon this I seemed a little angry with the Captain, and told him that they were my prisoners, not his; and that seeing I had offered them so much favour, I would be as good as my word; and that if he did not think fit to consent to it I would set them at liberty, as I found them: and if he did not like it he might take them again if he could catch them. Upon this they appeared very thankful, and I accordingly set them at liberty, and bade them retire into the woods, to the place whence they came, and I would leave them some firearms, some ammunition, and some directions how they should live very well if they thought fit. Upon this I prepared to go on board the ship; but told the Captain I would stay that night to prepare my things, and desired him to go on board in the meantime, and keep all right in the ship, and send the boat on shore next day for me; ordering him, at all events, to cause the new Captain, who was killed, to be hanged at the yard-arm, that these men might see him.

When the Captain was gone I sent for the men up to me to my apartment, and entered seriously into discourse with them on their circumstances. I told them I thought they had made a right choice; that if the Captain had carried them away they would certainly be hanged. I showed them the new Captain hanging at the yard-arm of the ship, and told them they had nothing less to expect.

When they had all declared their willingness to stay, I then told them I would let them into the story of my living there, and put them into the way of making it easy to them. Accordingly, I gave them the whole history of the place, and of my coming to it; showed them my fortifications, the way I made my bread, planted my corn, cured my grapes; and, in a word, all that was necessary to make them easy. I told them the story also of the seventeen Spaniards that were to be expected, for whom I left a letter, and made them promise to treat them in common with themselves. Here it may be noted that the Captain, who had ink on board, was greatly surprised that I never hit upon a way of making ink of charcoal and water, or of something else, as I had done things much more difficult.

I left them my firearms – *viz.* five muskets, three fowling-pieces, and three swords. I had above a barrel and a half of powder left; for after the first year or two I used but little, and wasted none. I gave them a description of the way I managed the goats, and directions to milk and fatten them, and to make both butter and cheese. In a word, I gave them every part of my own story; and told them I should prevail with the Captain to leave them two barrels of gunpowder more, and some garden-seeds, which I told them I would have been very glad of. Also, I gave them the bag of peas which the Captain had brought me to eat, and bade them be sure to sow and increase them.

CHAPTER NINETEEN

Return to England

HAVING DONE ALL THIS I left them the next day, and went on board the ship. We prepared immediately to sail, but did not weigh that night. The next morning early, two of the five men came swimming to the ship's side, and making the most lamentable complaint of the other three, begged to be taken into the ship for God's sake, for they should be murdered, and begged the Captain to take them on board, though he hanged them immediately. Upon this the Captain pretended to have no power without me; but after some difficulty, and after their solemn promises of amendment, they were taken on board, and were, some time after, soundly whipped and pickled; after which they proved very honest and quiet fellows.

Some time after this, the boat was ordered on shore, the tide being up, with the things promised to the men; to which the Captain, at my intercession, caused their chests and clothes to be added, which they took, and were very thankful for. I also encouraged them, by telling them that if it lay in my power to send any vessel to take them in, I would not forget them.

When I took leave of this island, I carried on board, for relics, the great goat-skin cap I had made, my umbrella, and one of my parrots; also, I forgot not to take the money I formerly mentioned, which had lain by me so long useless that it was grown rusty or tarnished, and could hardly pass for silver till it had been a little rubbed and handled, as also the money I found in the wreck of the Spanish ship. And thus I left the island, the 19th of December, as I found by the ship's account, in the year 1686, after I had been upon it eight-and-twenty years, two months, and nineteen days; being delivered from this second captivity the same day of the month that I first made my escape in the long-boat from among the Moors of Sallee. In this vessel, after a long voyage, I arrived in England the 11th of June, in the year 1687, having been thirty-five years absent.

When I came to England I was as perfect a stranger to all the world as if I had never been known there. My benefactor and faithful steward, whom I had left my money in trust with, was alive, but had had great misfortunes in the world; was become a widow the second time, and very low in the world. I made her very easy as to what she owed me, assuring her I would give her no trouble; but, on the contrary, in gratitude for her former care and faithfulness to me, I relieved her as my little stock would afford; which at that time would, indeed, allow me to do but little for her; but I assured her I would never forget her former kindness to me; nor did I forget her when I had sufficient to help her, as shall be observed in its proper place. I went down afterwards into Yorkshire; but my father was dead, and my mother and all the family extinct, except that I found two sisters, and two of the children of one of my brothers; and as I had been long ago given over for dead, there had been no provision made for me; so that, in a word, I found nothing to relieve or assist me; and that the little money I had would not do much for me as to settling in the world.

I met with one piece of gratitude indeed, which I did not expect; and this was, that the Master of the ship, whom I had so happily delivered, and by the same means saved the ship and cargo, having given a very handsome account to the owners of the manner how I had saved the lives of the men and the ship, they invited me to meet them and some other merchants concerned, and all together made me a very handsome compliment upon the subject, and a present of almost 200 pounds sterling.

But after making several reflections upon the circumstances of my life, and how little way this would go towards settling me in the world, I resolved to go to Lisbon, and see if I might not come at some information of the state of my plantation in the Brazils, and of what was become of my partner, who, I had reason to suppose, had some years past given me over for dead. With this view I took shipping for Lisbon, where I arrived in April following, my man Friday accompanying me very honestly in all these ramblings, and proving a most faithful servant upon all occasions. When I came to Lisbon, I found out, by inquiry, and to my particular satisfaction, my old friend, the Captain of the ship who first took me up at sea off the shore of Africa. He was now grown old, and had left off going to sea, having put his son, who was far from a young man, into his ship, and who still used the Brazil trade. The old man did not know me, and indeed I hardly knew him. But I soon brought him to my remembrance, and as soon brought myself to his remembrance, when I told him who I was.

After some passionate expressions of the old acquaintance between us, I inquired, you may he sure, after my plantation and my partner. The old man told me he had not been in the Brazils for about nine years; but that he could assure me that when he came away my partner was living, but the trustees whom I had joined with him to take cognizance of my part were both dead: that, however, he believed I would have a very good account of the improvement of the plantation; for that, upon the general belief of my being cast away and drowned, my trustees had given in the account of the produce of my part of the plantation to the procurator-fiscal, who had appropriated it, in case I never came to claim it, one-third to the king, and two-thirds to the monastery of St. Augustine, to be expended for the benefit of the poor, and for the conversion of the Indians to the Catholic faith: but that, if I appeared, or any one for me, to claim the inheritance, it would be restored; only that the improvement, or annual production, being distributed to charitable uses, could not be restored: but he assured me that the steward of the king's revenue from lands, and the Proviedore, or Steward of the monastery, had taken great care all along that the incumbent, that is to say my partner, gave every year a faithful account of the produce, of which they had duly received my moiety. I asked him if he knew to what height of improvement he had brought the plantation, and whether he thought it might be worth looking after; or whether, on my going thither, I should meet with any obstruction to my possessing my just right in the moiety. He told me he could not tell exactly to what degree the plantation was improved; but this he knew, that my partner was grown exceeding rich upon the enjoying his part of it; and that, to the best of his remembrance, he had heard that the king's third of my part, which was, it seems, granted away to some other monastery or religious house, amounted to above 200 Moidores a year: that as to my being restored to a quiet possession of it, there was no question to be made of that, my partner being alive to witness my title, and my name being also enrolled in the register of the country; also he told me that the survivors of my two trustees were very fair, honest people, and very wealthy; and he believed I would not only have their assistance for putting me in possession, but would find a very considerable sum of money in their hands for my account, being the produce of the farm while their fathers held the trust, and before it was given up, as above; which, as he remembered, was for about twelve years.

I showed myself a little concerned and uneasy at this account, and inquired of the old Captain how it came to pass that the trustees should thus dispose of my effects, when he knew that I had made my will, and had made him, the Portuguese Captain, my universal heir, &c.

He told me that was true; but that as there was no proof of my being dead, he could not act as executor until some certain account should come of my death; and, besides, he was not willing to intermeddle with a thing so remote: that it was true he had registered my will, and put in his claim; and could he have given any account of my being dead or alive, he would have acted by procuration, and taken possession of the Ingenio (so they call the sugar-house), and have given his son, who was now at the Brazils, orders to do it. "But," says the old man, "I have one piece of news to tell you, which perhaps may not be so acceptable to you as the rest; and that is, believing you were lost, and all the world believing so also, your partner and trustees did offer to account with me, in your name, for the first six or eight years' profits, which I received. There being at that time great disbursements for increasing the works, building an Ingenio, and buying slaves, it did not amount to near so much as afterwards it produced; however," says the old man, "I shall give you a true account of what I have received in all, and how I have disposed of it."

After a few days' further conference with this ancient friend, he brought me an account of the first six years' income of my plantation, signed by my partner and the merchant-trustees, being always delivered in goods, *viz.* tobacco in roll, and sugar in chests, besides rum, molasses, &c. which is the consequence of a sugar-work; and I found by this account, that every year the income considerably increased; but, as above, the disbursements being large, the sum at first was small: however, the old man let me see that he was debtor to me 470 Moidores of gold, besides 60 chests of sugar and 15 double rolls of tobacco, which were lost in his ship; he having been shipwrecked coming home to Lisbon, about eleven years after my having the place. The good man then began to complain of his misfortunes, and how he had been obliged to make use of my money to recover his losses, and buy him a share in a new ship. "However, my old friend," says he, "you shall not want a supply in your necessity; and as soon as my son returns you shall be fully satisfied." Upon this he pulls out an old pouch, and gives me 160 Portugal Moidores in gold; and giving the writings of his title to the ship, which his son was gone to the Brazils in, of which he was quarter-part owner, and his son another, he puts them both into my hands for security of the rest.

I was too much moved with the honesty and kindness of the poor man to be able to bear this; and remembering what he had done for me, how he had taken me up at sea, and how generously he had used me on all occasions, and particularly how sincere a friend he was now to me, I could hardly refrain weeping at what he had said to me; therefore I asked him if his circumstances admitted him to spare so much money at that time, and if it would not straiten him? He told me he could not say but it might straiten him a little; but, however, it was my money, and I might want it more than he.

Everything the good man said was full of affection, and I could hardly refrain from tears while he spoke; in short, I took 100 of the Moidores, and called for a pen and ink to give him a receipt for them: then I returned him the rest, and told him if ever I had possession of the plantation I would return the other to him also (as, indeed, I afterwards did); and that as to the bill of sale of his part in his son's ship, I would not take it by any means; but that if I wanted the money, I found he was honest enough to pay me; and if I did not, but came to receive what he gave me reason to expect, I would never have a penny more from him.

When this was past, the old man asked me if he should put me into a method to make my claim to my plantation. I told him I thought to go over to it myself. He said I might do so if I pleased, but that if I did not, there were ways enough to secure my right, and immediately to appropriate the profits to my use: and as there were ships in the river of Lisbon just ready to go away to Brazil, he made me enter my name in a public register, with his affidavit, affirming, upon oath, that I was alive, and that I was the same person who took up the land for the planting the said plantation at first. This being regularly attested by a notary, and a procuration affixed, he directed me to send it, with a letter of his writing, to a merchant of his acquaintance at the place; and then proposed my staying with him till an account came of the return.

Never was anything more honourable than the proceedings upon this procuration; for in less than seven months I received a large packet from the survivors of my trustees, the merchants, for whose account I went to sea, in which were the following, particular letters and papers enclosed:-

First, there was the account-current of the produce of my farm or plantation, from the year when their fathers had balanced with my old Portugal Captain, being for six years; the balance appeared to be 1,174 Moidores in my favour.

Secondly, there was the account of four years more, while they kept the effects in their hands, before the government claimed the administration, as being the effects of a person not to be found, which they called civil death; and the balance of this, the value of the plantation increasing, amounted to 38,892 Cruisadoes, being about 3,241 Moidores.

Thirdly, there was the Prior of St. Augustine's account, who had received the profits for above fourteen years; but not being able to account for what was disposed of by the hospital, very honestly declared he had 872 Moidores not distributed, which he acknowledged to my account: as to the king's part, that refunded nothing.

There was a letter of my partner's, congratulating me very affectionately upon my being alive, giving me an account how the estate was improved, and what it produced a year; with the particulars of the number of squares, or acres that it contained, how planted, how many slaves there were upon it: and making two-and-twenty crosses for blessings, told me he had said so many *ave marias* to thank the Blessed Virgin that I was alive; inviting me very passionately to come over and take possession of my own, and in the meantime to give him orders to whom he should deliver my effects if I did not come myself; concluding with a hearty tender of his friendship, and that of his family; and sent me as a present seven fine leopards' skins, which he had, it seems, received from Africa, by some other ship that he had sent thither, and which, it seems, had made a better voyage than I. He sent me also five chests of excellent sweetmeats, and 100 pieces of gold uncoined, not quite so large as Moidores. By the same fleet my two merchant-trustees shipped me 1,200 chests of sugar, 800 rolls of tobacco, and the rest of the whole account in gold.

I might well say now, indeed, that the latter end of Job was better than the beginning. It is impossible to express the flutterings of my very heart when I found all my wealth about me; for as the Brazil ships come all in fleets, the same ships which brought my letters brought my goods: and the effects were safe in the river before the letters came to my hand. In a word, I turned pale, and grew sick; and, had not the old man run and fetched me a cordial, I believe the sudden surprise of joy had overset nature, and I had died upon the spot: nay, after that I continued very ill, and was so some hours, till a physician being sent for, and something of the real cause of my illness being known, he ordered me to be let blood; after which I had relief, and grew well: but I verify believe, if I had not been eased by a vent given in that manner to the spirits, I should have died.

I was now Master, all on a sudden, of above 5,000 pounds sterling in money, and had an estate, as I might well call it, in the Brazils, of above 1,000 pounds a year, as sure as an estate of lands in England: and, in a word, I was in a condition which I scarce knew how to understand, or how to compose myself for the enjoyment of it. The first thing I did was to recompense my original benefactor, my good old Captain, who had been first charitable to me in my distress, kind to me in my beginning, and honest to me at the end. I showed him all that was sent to me; I told him that, next to the providence of Heaven, which disposed all things, it was owing to him; and that it now lay on me to reward him, which I would do a hundred-fold: so I first returned to him the 100 Moidores I had received of him; then I sent for a notary, and caused him to draw up a general release or discharge from the 470 Moidores, which he had acknowledged he owed me, in the fullest and firmest manner possible. After which I caused a procuration to be drawn, empowering him to be the receiver of the annual profits of my plantation: and appointing my partner to account with him, and make the returns, by the usual fleets, to him in my name; and by a clause in the end, made a grant of 100 Moidores a year to him during his life, out of the effects, and 50 Moidores a year to his son after him, for his life: and thus I requited my old man.

I had now to consider which way to steer my course next, and what to do with the estate that Providence had thus put into my hands; and, indeed, I had more care upon my head now than I had in my state of life in the island where I wanted nothing but what I had, and had nothing but what I wanted; whereas I had now a great charge upon me, and my business was how to secure it. I had not a cave now to hide my money in, or a place where it might lie without lock or key, till it grew mouldy and tarnished before anybody would meddle with it; on the contrary, I knew not where to put it, or whom to trust with it. My old Patron, the Captain, indeed, was honest, and that was the only refuge I had. In the next place, my interest in the Brazils seemed to summon me thither; but now I could not tell how to think of going thither till I had settled my affairs, and left my effects in some safe hands behind me. At first I thought of my old friend the widow, who I knew was honest, and would be just to me; but then she was in years, and but poor, and, for aught I knew, might be in debt: so that, in a word, I had no way but to go back to England myself and take my effects with me.

It was some months, however, before I resolved upon this; and, therefore, as I had rewarded the old Captain fully, and to his satisfaction, who had been my former benefactor, so I began to think of the poor widow, whose husband had been my first benefactor, and she, while it was in her power, my faithful steward and instructor. So, the first thing I did, I got a merchant in Lisbon to write to his correspondent in London, not only to pay a bill, but to go find her out, and carry her, in money, 100 pounds from me, and to talk with her, and comfort her in her poverty, by telling her she should, if I lived, have a further supply: at the same time I sent my two sisters in the country 100 pounds each, they being, though not in want, yet not in very good circumstances; one having been married and left a widow; and the other having a husband not so kind to her as he should be. But among all my relations or acquaintances I could not yet pitch upon one to whom I durst commit the gross of my stock, that I might go away to the Brazils, and leave things safe behind me; and this greatly perplexed me.

I had once a mind to have gone to the Brazils and have settled myself there, for I was, as it were, naturalized to the place; but I had some little scruple in my mind about religion, which insensibly drew me back. However, it was not religion that kept me from going there for the present; and as I had made no scruple of being openly of the religion of the country all the while I was among them, so neither did I yet; only that, now and then, having of late thought more of it than formerly, when I began to think of living and dying among them, I began to regret having professed myself a Papist, and thought it might not be the best religion to die with.

But, as I have said, this was not the main thing that kept me from going to the Brazils, but that really I did not know with whom to leave my effects behind me; so I resolved at last to go to England, where, if I arrived, I concluded that I should make some acquaintance, or find some relations, that would be faithful to me; and, accordingly, I prepared to go to England with all my wealth.

In order to prepare things for my going home, I first (the Brazil fleet being just going away) resolved to give answers suitable to the just and faithful account of things I had from thence; and, first, to the Prior of St. Augustine I wrote a letter full of thanks for his just dealings, and the offer of the 872 Moidores which were undisposed of, which I desired might be given, 500 to the monastery, and 372 to the poor, as the prior should direct; desiring the good padre's prayers for me, and the like. I wrote next a letter of thanks to my two trustees, with all the acknowledgment that so much justice and honesty called for: as for sending them any present, they were far above having any occasion of it. Lastly, I wrote to my partner, acknowledging his industry in the improving the plantation, and his integrity in increasing the stock of the works; giving him instructions for his future government of my part, according to the powers I had left with my old Patron, to whom I desired him to send whatever became due to me, till he should hear from me more particularly; assuring him that it was my intention not only to come to him, but to settle myself there for the remainder of my life. To this I added a very handsome present of some Italian silks for his wife and two daughters, for such the Captain's son informed me he had; with two pieces of fine English broadcloth, the best I could get in Lisbon, five pieces of black baize, and some Flanders lace of a good value.

Having thus settled my affairs, sold my cargo, and turned all my effects into good bills of exchange, my next difficulty was which way to go to England: I had been accustomed enough to the sea, and yet I had a strange aversion to go to England by the sea at that time, and yet I could give no reason for it, yet the difficulty increased upon me so much, that though I had once shipped my baggage in order to go, yet I altered my mind, and that not once but two or three times.

It is true I had been very unfortunate by sea, and this might be one of the reasons; but let no man slight the strong impulses of his own thoughts in cases of such moment: two of the ships which I had singled out to go in, I mean more particularly singled out than any other, having put my things on board one of them, and in the other having agreed with the Captain; I say two of these ships miscarried. One was taken by the Algerines, and the other was lost on the Start, near Torbay, and all the people drowned except three; so that in either of those vessels I had been made miserable.

Having been thus harassed in my thoughts, my old pilot, to whom I communicated everything, pressed me earnestly not to go by sea, but either to go by land to the Groyne, and cross over the Bay of Biscay to Rochelle, from whence it was but an easy and safe journey by land to Paris, and so to Calais and Dover; or to go up to Madrid, and so all the way by land through France. In a word, I was so prepossessed against my going by sea at all, except from Calais to Dover, that I resolved to travel all the way by land; which, as I was not in haste, and did not value the charge, was by much the pleasanter way: and to make it more so, my old Captain brought an English gentleman, the son of a merchant in Lisbon, who was willing to travel with me; after which we picked up two more English merchants also, and two young Portuguese gentlemen, the last going to Paris only; so that in all there were six of us and five servants; the two merchants and the two Portuguese, contenting themselves with one servant between two, to save the charge; and as for me, I got an English sailor to travel with me as a servant, besides my man Friday, who was too much a stranger to be capable of supplying the place of a servant on the road.

In this manner I set out from Lisbon; and our company being very well mounted and armed, we made a little troop, whereof they did me the honour to call me Captain, as well because I was the oldest man, as because I had two servants, and, indeed, was the origin of the whole journey.

As I have troubled you with none of my sea journals, so I shall trouble you now with none of my land journals; but some adventures that happened to us in this tedious and difficult journey I must not omit.

When we came to Madrid, we, being all of us strangers to Spain, were willing to stay some time to see the court of Spain, and what was worth observing; but it being the latter part of the summer, we hastened away, and set out from Madrid about the middle of October; but when we came to the edge of Navarre, we were alarmed, at several towns on the way, with an account that so much snow was falling on the French side of the mountains, that several travellers were obliged to come back to Pampeluna, after having attempted at an extreme hazard to pass on.

When we came to Pampeluna itself, we found it so indeed; and to me, that had been always used to a hot climate, and to countries where I could scarce bear any clothes on, the cold was insufferable; nor, indeed, was it more painful than surprising to come but ten days before out of Old Castile, where the weather was not only warm but very hot, and immediately to feel a wind from the Pyrenean Mountains so very keen, so severely cold, as to be intolerable and to endanger benumbing and perishing of our fingers and toes.

Poor Friday was really frightened when he saw the mountains all covered with snow, and felt cold weather, which he had never seen or felt before in his life. To mend the matter, when we came to Pampeluna it continued snowing with so much violence and so long, that the people said winter was come before its time; and the roads, which were difficult before, were now quite impassable; for, in a word, the snow lay in some places too thick for us to travel, and being not hard frozen, as is the case in the northern countries, there was no going without being in danger of being buried alive every step. We stayed no less than twenty days at Pampeluna; when (seeing the winter coming on, and no likelihood of its being better, for it was the severest winter all over Europe that had been known in the memory of man) I proposed that we should go away to Fontarabia, and there take shipping for Bordeaux, which was a very little voyage. But, while I was considering this, there came in four French gentlemen, who, having been stopped on the French side of the passes, as we were on the Spanish, had found out a guide, who, traversing the country near the head of Languedoc, had brought them over the mountains by such ways that they were not much incommoded with the snow; for where they met with snow in any quantity, they said it was frozen hard enough to bear them and their horses. We sent for this guide, who told us he would undertake to carry us the same way, with no hazard from the snow, provided we were armed sufficiently to protect ourselves from wild beasts; for, he said, in these great snows it was frequent for some wolves to show themselves at the foot of the mountains, being made ravenous for want of food, the ground being covered with snow. We told him we were well enough prepared for such creatures as they were, if he would insure us from a kind of two-legged wolves, which we were told we were in most danger from, especially on the French side of the mountains. He satisfied us that there was no danger of that kind in the way that we were to go; so we readily agreed to follow him, as did also twelve other gentlemen with their servants, some French, some Spanish, who, as I said, had attempted to go, and were obliged to come back again.

Accordingly, we set out from Pampeluna with our guide on the 15th of November; and indeed I was surprised when, instead of going forward, he came directly back with us on the same road that we came from Madrid, about twenty miles; when, having passed two rivers, and come into the plain country, we found ourselves in a warm climate again, where the country was pleasant, and no snow to be seen; but, on a sudden, turning to his left, he approached the mountains another way; and though it is true the hills and precipices looked dreadful, yet he made so many tours, such meanders, and led us by such winding ways, that we insensibly passed the height of the mountains without being much encumbered with the snow; and all on a sudden he showed us the pleasant and fruitful provinces of Languedoc and Gascony, all green and flourishing, though at a great distance, and we had some rough way to pass still.

We were a little uneasy, however, when we found it snowed one whole day and a night so fast that we could not travel; but he bid us be easy; we should soon be past it all: we found, indeed, that we began to descend every day, and to come more north than before; and so, depending upon our guide, we went on.

It was about two hours before night when, our guide being something before us, and not just in sight, out rushed three monstrous wolves, and after them a bear, from a hollow way adjoining to a thick wood; two of the wolves made at the guide, and had he been far before us, he would have been devoured before we could have helped him; one of them fastened upon his horse, and the other attacked the man with such violence, that he had not time, or presence of mind enough, to draw his pistol, but hallooed and cried out to us most lustily. My man Friday being next me, I bade him ride up and see what was the matter. As soon as Friday came in sight of the man, he hallooed out as loud as the other, "O Master! O Master!" but like a bold fellow, rode directly up to the poor man, and with his pistol shot the wolf in the head that attacked him.

It was happy for the poor man that it was my man Friday; for, having been used to such creatures in his country, he had no fear upon him, but went close up to him and shot him; whereas, any other of us would have fired at a farther distance, and have perhaps either missed the wolf or endangered shooting the man.

But it was enough to have terrified a bolder man than I; and, indeed, it alarmed all our company, when, with the noise of Friday's pistol, we heard on both sides the most dismal howling of wolves; and the noise, redoubled by the echo of the mountains, appeared to us as if there had been a prodigious number of them; and perhaps there was not such a few as that we had no cause of apprehension: however, as Friday had killed this wolf, the other that had fastened upon the horse left him immediately, and fled, without doing him any damage, having happily fastened upon his head, where the bosses of the bridle had stuck in his teeth. But the man was most hurt; for the raging creature had bit him twice, once in the arm, and the other time a little above his knee; and though he had made some defence, he was just tumbling down by the disorder of his horse, when Friday came up and shot the wolf.

It is easy to suppose that at the noise of Friday's pistol we all mended our pace, and rode up as fast as the way, which was very difficult, would give us leave, to see what was the matter. As soon as we came clear of the trees, which blinded us before, we saw clearly what had been the case, and how Friday had disengaged the poor guide, though we did not presently discern what kind of creature it was he had killed.

CHAPTER TWENTY

Fight Between Friday and a Bear

But never was a fight managed so hardily, and in such a surprising manner as that which followed between Friday and the bear, which gave us all, though at first we were surprised and afraid for him, the greatest diversion imaginable. As the bear is a heavy, clumsy creature, and does not gallop as the wolf does, who is swift and light, so he has two particular qualities, which generally are the rule of his actions; first, as to men, who are not his proper prey (he does not usually attempt them, except they first attack him, unless he be excessively hungry, which it is probable might now be the case, the ground being covered with snow), if you do not meddle with him, he will not meddle with you; but then you must take care to be very civil to him, and give him the road, for he is a very nice gentleman; he will not go a step out of his way for a prince; nay, if you are really afraid, your best way is to look another way and keep going on; for sometimes if you stop, and stand still, and look steadfastly at him, he takes it for an affront; but if you throw or toss anything at him, though it were but a bit of stick as big as your finger, he thinks himself abused, and sets all other business aside to pursue his revenge, and will have satisfaction in point of honour – that is his first quality: the next is, if he be once affronted, he will never leave you, night or day, till he has his revenge, but follows at a good round rate till he overtakes you.

My man Friday had delivered our guide, and when we came up to him he was helping him off his horse, for the man was both hurt and frightened, when on a sudden we espied the bear come out of the wood; and a monstrous one it was, the biggest by far that ever I saw. We were all a little surprised when we saw him; but when Friday saw him, it was easy to see joy and courage in the fellow's countenance. "O! O! O!" says Friday, three times, pointing to him; "O Master, you give me te leave, me shakee te hand with him; me makee you good laugh."

I was surprised to see the fellow so well pleased. "You fool," says I, "he will eat you up." – "Eatee me up! eatee me up!" says Friday, twice over again; "me eatee him up; me makee you good laugh; you all stay here, me show you good laugh." So down he sits, and gets off his boots in a moment, and puts on a pair of pumps (as we call the flat shoes they wear, and which he had in his pocket), gives my other servant his horse, and with his gun away he flew, swift like the wind.

The bear was walking softly on, and offered to meddle with nobody, till Friday coming pretty near, calls to him, as if the bear could understand him. "Hark ye, hark ye," says Friday, "me speakee with you." We followed at a distance, for now being down on the Gascony side of the mountains, we were entered a vast forest, where the country was plain and pretty open, though it had many trees in it scattered here and there. Friday, who had, as we say, the heels of the bear, came up with him quickly, and took up a great stone, and threw it at him, and hit him just on the head, but did him no more harm than if he had thrown it against a wall; but it answered Friday's end, for the rogue was so void of fear that he did it purely to make the bear follow him, and show us some laugh as he called it. As soon as the bear felt the blow, and saw him, he turns about and comes after him, taking very long strides, and shuffling on at a strange rate, so as would have put a horse to a middling gallop; away reins Friday, and takes his course as if he ran towards us for help; so we all resolved to fire at once upon the bear, and deliver my man; though I was angry at him for bringing the bear back upon us, when he was going about his own business another way; and especially I was angry that he had turned the bear upon us, and then ran away; and I called out, "You dog! is this your making us laugh? Come away, and take your horse, that we may shoot the creature." He heard me, and cried out, "No shoot, no shoot; stand still, and you get much laugh:" and as the nimble creature ran two feet for the bear's one, he turned on a sudden on one side of us, and seeing a great oak-tree fit for his purpose, he beckoned to us to follow; and doubling his pace, he got nimbly up the tree, laying his gun down upon the ground, at about five or six yards from the bottom of the tree. The bear soon came to the tree, and we followed at a distance: the first thing he did he stopped at the gun, smelt at it, but let it lie, and up he scrambles into the tree, climbing like a cat, though so monstrous heavy. I was amazed at the folly, as I thought it, of my man, and could not for my life see anything to laugh at, till seeing the bear get up the tree, we all rode near to him.

When we came to the tree, there was Friday got out to the small end of a large branch, and the bear got about half-way to him. As soon as the bear got out to that part where the limb of the tree was weaker, "Ha!" says he to us, "now you see me teachee the bear dance:" so he began jumping and shaking the bough, at which the bear began to totter, but stood still, and began to look behind him, to see how he should get back; then, indeed, we did laugh heartily. But Friday had not done with him by a great deal; when seeing him stand still, he called out to him again, as if he had supposed the bear could speak English, "What, you come no farther? pray you come farther;" so he left jumping and shaking the tree; and the bear, just as if he understood what he said, did come a little farther; then he began jumping again, and the bear stopped again. We thought now was a good time to knock him in the head, and called to Friday to stand still and we should shoot the bear: but he cried out earnestly, "Oh, pray! Oh, pray! no shoot, me shoot by and then:" he would have said by-and-by. However, to shorten the story, Friday danced so much, and the bear stood so ticklish, that we had laughing enough, but still could not imagine what the fellow would do: for first we thought he depended upon shaking the bear off; and we found the bear was too cunning for that too; for he would not go out far enough to be thrown down, but clung fast with his great broad claws and feet, so that we could not imagine what would be the end of it, and what the jest would be at last. But Friday put us out of doubt quickly: for seeing the bear cling fast to the bough, and that he would not be persuaded to come any farther, "Well, well," says Friday, "you no come farther, me go; you no come to me, me come to you;" and upon this he went out to the smaller end, where it would bend with his weight, and gently let himself down by it, sliding down the bough till he came near enough to jump down on his feet, and away he ran to his gun, took it up, and stood still. "Well," said I to him, "Friday, what will you do now? Why don't you shoot him?" "No shoot," says Friday, "no yet; me shoot now, me no kill; me stay, give you one more laugh:" and, indeed, so he did; for when the bear saw his enemy gone, he came back from the bough, where he stood, but did it very cautiously, looking behind him every step, and coming backward till he got into the body of the tree, then, with the same hinder end foremost, he came down the tree, grasping it with his claws, and moving one foot at a time, very leisurely. At this juncture, and just before he could set his hind foot on the ground, Friday stepped up close to him, clapped the muzzle of his piece into his ear, and shot him dead. Then the rogue turned about to see if we did not laugh; and when he saw we were pleased by our looks, he began to laugh very loud. "So we kill bear in my country," says Friday. "So you kill them?" says I; "why, you have no guns." – "No," says he, "no gun, but shoot great much long arrow." This was a good diversion to us; but we were still in a wild place, and our guide very much hurt, and what to do we hardly knew; the howling of wolves ran much in my head; and, indeed, except the noise I once heard on the shore of Africa, of which I have said something already, I never heard anything that filled me with so much horror.

These things, and the approach of night, called us off, or else, as Friday would have had us, we should certainly have taken the skin of this monstrous creature off, which was worth saving; but we had near three leagues to go, and our guide hastened us; so we left him, and went forward on our journey.

The ground was still covered with snow, though not so deep and dangerous as on the mountains; and the ravenous creatures, as we heard afterwards, were come down into the forest and plain country, pressed by hunger, to seek for food, and had done a great deal of mischief in the villages, where they surprised the country people, killed a great many of their sheep and horses, and some people too. We had one dangerous place to pass, and our guide told us if there were more wolves in the country we should find them there; and this was a small plain, surrounded with woods on every side, and a long, narrow defile, or lane, which we were to pass to get through the wood, and then we should come to the village where we were to lodge. It was within half-an-hour of sunset when we entered the wood, and a little after sunset when we came into the plain: we met with nothing in the first wood, except that in a little plain within the wood, which was not above two furlongs over, we saw five great wolves cross the road, full speed, one after another, as if they had been in chase of some prey, and had it in view; they took no notice of us, and were gone out of sight in a few moments. Upon this, our guide, who, by the way, was but a fainthearted fellow, bid us keep in a ready posture, for he believed there were more wolves a-coming. We kept our arms ready, and our eyes about us; but we saw no more wolves till we came through that wood, which was near half a league, and entered the plain. As soon as we came into the plain, we had occasion enough to look about us. The first object we met with was a dead horse; that is to say, a poor horse which the wolves had killed, and at least a dozen of them at work, we could not say eating him, but picking his bones rather; for they had eaten up all the flesh before. We did not think fit to disturb them at their feast, neither did they take much notice of us. Friday would have let fly at them, but I would not suffer him by any means; for I found we were like to have more business upon our hands than we were aware of. We had not gone half over the plain when we began to hear the wolves howl in the wood on our left in a frightful manner, and presently after we saw about a hundred coming on directly towards us, all in a body, and most of them in a line, as regularly as an army drawn up by experienced officers. I scarce knew in what manner to receive them, but found to draw ourselves in a close line was the only way; so we formed in a moment; but that we might not have too much interval, I ordered that only every other man should fire, and that the others, who had not fired, should stand ready to give them a second volley immediately, if they continued to advance upon us; and then that those that had fired at first should not pretend to load their fuzees again, but stand ready, every one with a pistol, for we were all armed with a fusee and a pair of pistols each man; so we were, by this method, able to fire six volleys, half of us at a time; however, at present we had no necessity; for upon firing the first volley, the enemy made a full stop, being terrified as well with the noise as with the fire. Four of them being shot in the head, dropped; several others were wounded, and went bleeding off, as we could see by the snow. I found they stopped, but did not immediately retreat; whereupon, remembering that I had been told that the fiercest creatures were terrified at the voice of a man, I caused all the company to halloo as loud as they could; and I found the notion not altogether mistaken; for upon our shout they began to retire and turn about. I then ordered a second volley to be fired in their rear, which put them to the gallop, and away they went to the woods. This gave us leisure to charge our pieces again; and that we might lose no time, we kept going; but we had but little more than loaded our fuzees, and put ourselves in readiness, when we heard a terrible noise in the same wood on our left, only that it was farther onward, the same way we were to go.

The night was coming on, and the light began to be dusky, which made it worse on our side; but the noise increasing, we could easily perceive that it was the howling and yelling of those hellish creatures; and on a sudden we perceived three troops of wolves, one on our left, one behind us, and one in our front, so that we seemed to be surrounded with them: however, as they did not fall upon us, we kept our way forward, as fast as we could make our horses go, which, the way being very rough, was only a good hard trot. In this manner, we came in view of the entrance of a wood, through which we were to pass, at the farther side of the plain; but we were greatly surprised, when coming nearer the lane or pass, we saw a confused number of wolves standing just at the entrance. On a sudden, at another opening of the wood, we heard the noise of a gun, and looking that way, out rushed a horse, with a saddle and a bridle on him, flying like the wind, and sixteen or seventeen wolves after him, full speed: the horse had the advantage of them; but as we supposed that he could not hold it at that rate, we doubted not but they would get up with him at last: no question but they did.

But here we had a most horrible sight; for riding up to the entrance where the horse came out, we found the carcasses of another horse and of two men, devoured by the ravenous creatures; and one of the men was no doubt the same whom we heard fire the gun, for there lay a gun just by him fired off; but as to the man, his head and the upper part of his body was eaten up. This filled us with horror, and we knew not what course to take; but the creatures resolved us soon, for they gathered about us presently, in hopes of prey; and I verily believe there were three hundred of them. It happened, very much to our advantage, that at the entrance into the wood, but a little way from it, there lay some large timber-trees, which had been cut down the summer before, and I suppose lay there for carriage. I drew my little troop in among those trees, and placing ourselves in a line behind one long tree, I advised them all to alight, and keeping that tree before us for a breastwork, to stand in a triangle, or three fronts, enclosing our horses in the centre. We did so, and it was well we did; for never was a more furious charge than the creatures made upon us in this place. They came on with a growling kind of noise, and mounted the piece of timber, which, as I said, was our breastwork, as if they were only rushing upon their prey; and this fury of theirs, it seems, was principally occasioned by their seeing our horses behind us. I ordered our men to fire as before, every other man; and they took their aim so sure that they killed several of the wolves at the first volley; but there was a necessity to keep a continual firing, for they came on like devils, those behind pushing on those before.

When we had fired a second volley of our fuzees, we thought they stopped a little, and I hoped they would have gone off, but it was but a moment, for others came forward again; so we fired two volleys of our pistols; and I believe in these four firings we had killed seventeen or eighteen of them, and lamed twice as many, yet they came on again. I was loath to spend our shot too hastily; so I called my servant, not my man Friday, for he was better employed, for, with the greatest dexterity imaginable, he had charged my fusee and his own while we were engaged – but, as I said, I called my other man, and giving him a horn of powder, I had him lay a train all along the piece of timber, and let it be a large train. He did so, and had but just time to get away, when the wolves came up to it, and some got upon it, when I, snapping an unchanged pistol close to the powder, set it on fire; those that were upon the timber were scorched with it, and six or seven of them fell; or rather jumped in among us with the force and fright of the fire; we dispatched these in an instant, and the rest were so frightened with the light, which the night – for it was now very near dark – made more terrible that they drew back a little; upon which I ordered our last pistols to be fired off in one volley, and after that we gave a shout; upon this the wolves turned tail, and we sallied immediately upon near twenty lame ones that we found struggling on the ground, and fell to cutting them with our swords, which answered our expectation, for the crying and howling they made was better understood by their fellows; so that they all fled and left us.

We had, first and last, killed about threescore of them, and had it been daylight we had killed many more. The field of battle being thus cleared, we made forward again, for we had still near a league to go. We heard the ravenous creatures howl and yell in the woods as we went several times, and sometimes we fancied we saw some of them; but the snow dazzling our eyes, we were not certain. In about an hour more we came to the town where we were to lodge, which we found in a terrible fright and all in arms; for, it seems, the night before the wolves and some bears had broken into the village, and put them in such terror that they were obliged to keep guard night and day, but especially in the night, to preserve their cattle, and indeed their people.

The next morning our guide was so ill, and his limbs swelled so much with the rankling of his two wounds, that he could go no farther; so we were obliged to take a new guide here, and go to Toulouse, where we found a warm climate, a fruitful, pleasant country, and no snow, no wolves, nor anything like them; but when we told our story at Toulouse, they told us it was nothing but what was ordinary in the great forest at the foot of the mountains, especially when the snow lay on the ground; but they inquired much what kind of guide we had got who would venture to bring us that way in such a severe season, and told us it was surprising we were not all devoured. When we told them how we placed ourselves and the horses in the middle, they blamed us exceedingly, and told us it was fifty to one but we had been all destroyed, for it was the sight of the horses which made the wolves so furious, seeing their prey, and that at other times they are really afraid of a gun; but being excessively hungry, and raging on that account, the eagerness to come at the horses had made them senseless of danger, and that if we had not by the continual fire, and at last by the stratagem of the train of powder, mastered them, it had been great odds but that we had been torn to pieces;

whereas, had we been content to have sat still on horseback, and fired as horsemen, they would not have taken the horses so much for their own, when men were on their backs, as otherwise; and withal, they told us that at last, if we had stood altogether, and left our horses, they would have been so eager to have devoured them, that we might have come off safe, especially having our firearms in our hands, being so many in number. For my part, I was never so sensible of danger in my life; for, seeing above three hundred devils come roaring and open-mouthed to devour us, and having nothing to shelter us or retreat to, I gave myself over for lost; and, as it was, I believe I shall never care to cross those mountains again: I think I would much rather go a thousand leagues by sea, though I was sure to meet with a storm once a-week.

I have nothing uncommon to take notice of in my passage through France – nothing but what other travellers have given an account of with much more advantage than I can. I travelled from Toulouse to Paris, and without any considerable stay came to Calais, and landed safe at Dover the 14th of January, after having had a severe cold season to travel in.

I was now come to the centre of my travels, and had in a little time all my new-discovered estate safe about me, the bills of exchange which I brought with me having been currently paid.

My principal guide and privy-counsellor was my good ancient widow, who, in gratitude for the money I had sent her, thought no pains too much nor care too great to employ for me; and I trusted her so entirely that I was perfectly easy as to the security of my effects; and, indeed, I was very happy from the beginning, and now to the end, in the unspotted integrity of this good gentlewoman.

And now, having resolved to dispose of my plantation in the Brazils, I wrote to my old friend at Lisbon, who, having offered it to the two merchants, the survivors of my trustees, who lived in the Brazils, they accepted the offer, and remitted 33,000 pieces of eight to a correspondent of theirs at Lisbon to pay for it.

In return, I signed the instrument of sale in the form which they sent from Lisbon, and sent it to my old man, who sent me the bills of exchange for 32,800 pieces of eight for the estate, reserving the payment of 100 Moidores a year to him (the old man) during his life, and 50 Moidores afterwards to his son for his life, which I had promised them, and which the plantation was to make good as a rent-charge. And thus I have given the first part of a life of fortune and adventure – a life of Providence's checquer-work, and of a variety which the world will seldom be able to show the like of; beginning foolishly, but closing much more happily than any part of it ever gave me leave so much as to hope for.

Any one would think that in this state of complicated good fortune I was past running any more hazards – and so, indeed, I had been, if other circumstances had concurred; but I was inured to a wandering life, had no family, nor many relations; nor, however rich, had I contracted fresh acquaintance; and though I had sold my estate in the Brazils, yet I could not keep that country out of my head, and had a great mind to be upon the wing again; especially I could not resist the strong inclination I had to see my island, and to know if the poor Spaniards were in being there. My true friend, the widow, earnestly dissuaded me from it, and so far prevailed with me, that for almost seven years she prevented my running abroad, during which time I took my two nephews, the children of one of my brothers, into my care; the eldest, having something of his own, I bred up as a gentleman, and gave him a settlement of some addition to his estate after my decease. The other I placed with the Captain of a ship; and after five years, finding him a sensible, bold, enterprising young fellow, I put him into a good ship, and sent him to sea; and this young fellow afterwards drew me in, as old as I was, to further adventures myself.

In the meantime, I in part settled myself here; for, first of all, I married, and that not either to my disadvantage or dissatisfaction, and had three children, two sons and one daughter; but my wife dying, and my nephew coming home with good success from a voyage to Spain, my inclination to go abroad, and his importunity, prevailed, and engaged me to go in his ship as a private trader to the East Indies; this was in the year 1694.

In this voyage I visited my new colony in the island, saw my successors the Spaniards, had the old story of their lives and of the villains I left there; how at first they insulted the poor Spaniards, how they afterwards agreed, disagreed, united, separated, and how at last the Spaniards were obliged to use violence with them; how they were subjected to the Spaniards, how honestly the Spaniards used them – a history, if it were entered into, as full of variety and wonderful accidents as my own part – particularly, also, as to their battles with the Caribbeans, who landed several times upon the island, and as to the improvement they made upon the island itself, and how five of them made an attempt upon the mainland, and brought away eleven men and five women prisoners, by which, at my coming, I found about twenty young children on the island.

Here I stayed about twenty days, left them supplies of all necessary things, and particularly of arms, powder, shot, clothes, tools, and two workmen, which I had brought from England with me, *viz.* a carpenter and a smith.

Besides this, I shared the lands into parts with them, reserved to myself the property of the whole, but gave them such parts respectively as they agreed on; and having settled all things with them, and engaged them not to leave the place, I left them there.

From thence I touched at the Brazils, from whence I sent a bark, which I bought there, with more people to the island; and in it, besides other supplies, I sent seven women, being such as I found proper for service, or for wives to such as would take them. As to the Englishmen, I promised to send them some women from England, with a good cargo of necessaries, if they would apply themselves to planting – which I afterwards could not perform. The fellows proved very honest and diligent after they were mastered and had their properties set apart for them. I sent them, also, from the Brazils, five cows, three of them being big with calf, some sheep, and some hogs, which when I came again were considerably increased.

But all these things, with an account how 300 Caribbees came and invaded them, and ruined their plantations, and how they fought with that whole number twice, and were at first defeated, and one of them killed; but at last, a storm destroying their enemies' canoes, they famished or destroyed almost all the rest, and renewed and recovered the possession of their plantation, and still lived upon the island.

All these things, with some very surprising incidents in some new adventures of my own, for ten years more, I shall give a farther account of in the Second Part of my Story.

GULLIVER'S TRAVELS

CONTENTS

THE PUBLISHER TO THE READER

THE AUTHOR of these Travels, Mr. Lemuel Gulliver, is my ancient and intimate friend; there is likewise some relation between us on the mother's side. About three years ago, Mr. Gulliver growing weary of the concourse of curious people coming to him at his house in Redriff, made a small purchase of land, with a convenient house, near Newark, in Nottinghamshire, his native country; where he now lives retired, yet in good esteem among his neighbours.

Although Mr. Gulliver was born in Nottinghamshire, where his father dwelt, yet I have heard him say his family came from Oxfordshire; to confirm which, I have observed in the churchyard at Banbury in that county, several tombs and monuments of the Gullivers.

Before he quitted Redriff, he left the custody of the following papers in my hands, with the liberty to dispose of them as I should think fit. I have carefully perused them three times. The style is very plain and simple; and the only fault I find is, that the author, after the manner of travellers, is a little too circumstantial. There is an air of truth apparent through the whole; and indeed the author was so distinguished for his veracity, that it became a sort of proverb among his neighbours at Redriff, when any one affirmed a thing, to say, it was as true as if Mr. Gulliver had spoken it.

By the advice of several worthy persons, to whom, with the author's permission, I communicated these papers, I now venture to send them into the world, hoping they may be, at least for some time, a better entertainment to our young noblemen, than the common scribbles of politics and party.

This volume would have been at least twice as large, if I had not made bold to strike out innumerable passages relating to the winds and tides, as well as to the variations and bearings in the several voyages, together with the minute descriptions of the management of the ship in storms, in the style of sailors; likewise the account of longitudes and latitudes; wherein I have reason to apprehend, that Mr. Gulliver may be a little dissatisfied. But I was resolved to fit the work as much as possible to the general capacity of readers. However, if my own ignorance in sea affairs shall have led me to commit some mistakes, I alone am answerable for them. And if any traveller hath a curiosity to see the whole work at large, as it came from the hands of the author, I will be ready to gratify him.

As for any further particulars relating to the author, the reader will receive satisfaction from the first pages of the book.

Richard Sympson.

A LETTER FROM CAPTAIN GULLIVER TO HIS COUSIN SYMPSON

Written in the Year 1727.

I HOPE YOU will be ready to own publicly, whenever you shall be called to it, that by your great and frequent urgency you prevailed on me to publish a very loose and uncorrect account of my travels, with directions to hire some young gentleman of either university to put them in order, and correct the style, as my cousin Dampier did, by my advice, in his book called "A Voyage round the world." But I do not remember I gave you power to consent that any thing should be omitted, and much less that any thing should be inserted; therefore, as to the latter, I do here renounce every thing of that kind; particularly a paragraph about her majesty Queen Anne, of most pious and glorious memory; although I did reverence and esteem her more than any of human species. But you, or your interpolator, ought to have considered, that it was not my inclination, so was it not decent to praise any animal of our composition before my master *Houyhnhnm*: And besides, the fact was altogether false; for to my knowledge, being in England during some part of her majesty's reign, she did govern by a chief minister; nay even by two successively, the first whereof was the lord of Godolphin, and the second the lord of Oxford; so that you have made me say the thing that was not. Likewise in the account of the academy of projectors, and several passages of my discourse to my master *Houyhnhnm*, you have either omitted some material circumstances, or minced or changed them in such a manner, that I do hardly know my own work. When I formerly hinted to you something of this in a letter, you were pleased to answer that you were afraid of giving offence; that people in power were very watchful over the press, and apt not only to interpret, but to punish every thing which looked like an *innuendo* (as I think you call it). But, pray how could that which I spoke so many years ago, and at about five thousand leagues distance, in another reign, be applied to any of the *Yahoos*, who now are said to govern the herd; especially at a time when I little thought, or feared, the unhappiness of living under them? Have not I the most reason to complain, when I see these very *Yahoos* carried by *Houyhnhnms* in a vehicle, as if they were brutes, and those the rational creatures? And indeed to avoid so monstrous and detestable a sight was one principal motive of my retirement hither.

Thus much I thought proper to tell you in relation to yourself, and to the trust I reposed in you.

I do, in the next place, complain of my own great want of judgment, in being prevailed upon by the entreaties and false reasoning of you and some others, very much against my own opinion, to suffer my travels to be published. Pray bring to your mind how often I desired you to consider, when you insisted on the motive of public good, that the *Yahoos* were a species of animals utterly incapable of amendment by precept or example: and so it has proved; for, instead of seeing a full stop put to all abuses and corruptions, at least in this little island, as I had reason to expect; behold, after above six months warning, I cannot learn that my book has produced one single effect according to my intentions. I desired you would let me know, by a letter, when party and faction were extinguished; judges learned and upright; pleaders honest and modest, with some tincture of common sense, and Smithfield blazing with pyramids of law books; the young nobility's education entirely changed; the physicians banished; the female *Yahoos* abounding in virtue, honour, truth, and good sense; courts and levees of great ministers thoroughly weeded and swept; wit, merit, and learning rewarded; all disgracers of the press in prose and verse condemned to eat nothing but their own cotton, and quench their thirst with their own ink. These, and a thousand other reformations, I firmly counted upon by your encouragement; as indeed they were plainly deducible from the precepts delivered in my book. And it must be owned, that seven months were a sufficient time to correct every vice and folly to which *Yahoos* are subject, if their natures had been capable of the least disposition to virtue or wisdom. Yet, so far have you been from answering my expectation in any of your letters; that on the contrary you are loading our carrier every week with libels, and keys, and reflections, and memoirs, and second parts; wherein I see myself accused of reflecting upon great state folk; of degrading human nature (for so they have still the confidence to style it), and of abusing the female sex. I find likewise that the writers of those bundles are not agreed among themselves; for some of them will not allow me to be the author of my own travels; and others make me author of books to which I am wholly a stranger.

I find likewise that your printer has been so careless as to confound the times, and mistake the dates, of my several voyages and returns; neither assigning the true year, nor the true month, nor day of the month: and I hear the original manuscript is all destroyed since the publication of my book; neither have I any copy left: however, I have sent you some corrections, which you may insert, if ever there should be a second edition: and yet I cannot stand to them; but shall leave that matter to my judicious and candid readers to adjust it as they please.

I hear some of our sea *Yahoos* find fault with my sea-language, as not proper in many parts, nor now in use. I cannot help it. In my first voyages, while I was young, I was instructed by the oldest mariners, and learned to speak as they did. But I have since found that the sea *Yahoos* are apt, like the land ones, to become new-fangled in their words, which the latter change every year; insomuch, as I remember upon each return to my own country their old dialect was so altered, that I could hardly understand the new. And I observe, when any *Yahoo* comes from London out of curiosity to visit me at my house, we neither of us are able to deliver our conceptions in a manner intelligible to the other.

If the censure of the *Yahoos* could any way affect me, I should have great reason to complain, that some of them are so bold as to think my book of travels a mere fiction out of mine own brain, and have gone so far as to drop hints, that the *Houyhnhnms* and *Yahoos* have no more existence than the inhabitants of Utopia.

Indeed I must confess, that as to the people of *Lilliput*, *Brobdingrag* (for so the word should have been spelt, and not erroneously *Brobdingnag*), and *Laputa*, I have never yet heard of any *Yahoo* so presumptuous as to dispute their being, or the facts I have related concerning them; because the truth immediately strikes every reader with conviction. And is there less probability in my account of the *Houyhnhnms* or *Yahoos*, when it is manifest as to the latter, there are so many thousands even in this country, who only differ from their brother brutes in *Houyhnhnmland*, because they use a sort of jabber, and do not go naked? I wrote for their amendment, and not their approbation. The united praise of the whole race would be of less consequence to me, than the neighing of those two degenerate *Houyhnhnms* I keep in my stable; because from these, degenerate as they are, I still improve in some virtues without any mixture of vice.

Do these miserable animals presume to think, that I am so degenerated as to defend my veracity? *Yahoo* as I am, it is well known through all *Houyhnhnmland*, that, by the instructions and example of my illustrious master, I was able in the compass of two years (although I confess with the utmost difficulty) to remove that infernal habit of lying, shuffling, deceiving, and equivocating, so deeply rooted in the very souls of all my species; especially the Europeans.

I have other complaints to make upon this vexatious occasion; but I forbear troubling myself or you any further. I must freely confess, that since my last return, some corruptions of my *Yahoo* nature have revived in me by conversing with a few of your species, and particularly those of my own family, by an unavoidable necessity; else I should never have attempted so absurd a project as that of reforming the *Yahoo* race in this kingdom: But I have now done with all such visionary schemes for ever.

April 2, 1727

PART ONE

A Voyage to Lilliput

CHAPTER ONE

The author gives some account of himself and family. His first inducements to travel. He is shipwrecked, and swims for his life. Gets safe on shore in the country of Lilliput; is made a prisoner, and carried up the country.

My father had a small estate in Nottinghamshire: I was the third of five sons. He sent me to Emanuel College in Cambridge at fourteen years old, where I resided three years, and applied myself close to my studies; but the charge of maintaining me, although I had a very scanty allowance, being too great for a narrow fortune, I was bound apprentice to Mr. James Bates, an eminent surgeon in London, with whom I continued four years. My father now and then sending me small sums of money, I laid them out in learning navigation, and other parts of the mathematics, useful to those who intend to travel, as I always believed it would be, some time or other, my fortune to do. When I left Mr. Bates, I went down to my father: where, by the assistance of him and my uncle John, and some other relations, I got forty pounds, and a promise of thirty pounds a year to maintain me at Leyden: there I studied physic two years and seven months, knowing it would be useful in long voyages.

Soon after my return from Leyden, I was recommended by my good master, Mr. Bates, to be surgeon to the Swallow, Captain Abraham Pannel, commander; with whom I continued three years and a half, making a voyage or two into the Levant, and some other parts. When I came back I resolved to settle in London; to which Mr. Bates, my master, encouraged me, and by him I was recommended to several patients. I took part of a small house in the Old Jewry; and being advised to alter my condition, I married Mrs. Mary Burton, second daughter to Mr. Edmund Burton, hosier, in Newgate-street, with whom I received four hundred pounds for a portion.

But my good master Bates dying in two years after, and I having few friends, my business began to fail; for my conscience would not suffer me to imitate the bad practice of too many among my brethren. Having therefore consulted with my wife, and some of my acquaintance, I determined to go again to sea. I was surgeon successively in two ships, and made several voyages, for six years, to the East and West Indies, by which I got some addition to my fortune. My hours of leisure I spent in reading the best authors, ancient and modern, being always provided with a good number of books; and when I was ashore, in observing the manners and dispositions of the people, as well as learning their language; wherein I had a great facility, by the strength of my memory.

The last of these voyages not proving very fortunate, I grew weary of the sea, and intended to stay at home with my wife and family. I removed from the Old Jewry to Fetter Lane, and from thence to Wapping, hoping to get business among the sailors; but it would not turn to account. After three years expectation that things would mend, I accepted an advantageous offer from Captain William Prichard, master of the Antelope, who was making a voyage to the South Sea. We set sail from Bristol, May 4, 1699, and our voyage was at first very prosperous.

It would not be proper, for some reasons, to trouble the reader with the particulars of our adventures in those seas; let it suffice to inform him, that in our passage from thence to the East Indies, we were driven by a violent storm to the north-west of Van Diemen's Land. By an observation, we found ourselves in the latitude of 30 degrees 2 minutes south. Twelve of our crew were dead by immoderate labour and ill food; the rest were in a very weak condition. On the 5th of November, which was the beginning of summer in those parts, the weather being very hazy, the seamen spied a rock within half a cable's length of the ship; but the wind was so strong, that we were driven directly upon it, and immediately split. Six of the crew, of whom I was one, having let down the boat into the sea, made a shift to get clear of the ship and the rock. We rowed, by my computation, about three leagues, till we were able to work no longer, being already spent with labour while we were in the ship. We therefore trusted ourselves to the mercy of the waves, and in about half an hour the boat was overset by a sudden flurry from the north. What became of my companions in the boat, as well as of those who escaped on the rock, or were left in the vessel, I cannot tell; but conclude they were all lost. For my own part, I swam as fortune directed me, and was pushed forward by wind and tide. I often let my legs drop, and could feel no bottom; but when I was almost gone, and able to struggle no longer, I found myself within my depth; and by this time the storm was much abated. The declivity was so small, that I walked near a mile before I got to the shore, which I conjectured was about eight o'clock in the evening. I then advanced forward near half a mile, but could not discover any sign of houses or inhabitants; at least I was in so weak a condition, that I did not observe them. I was extremely tired, and with that, and the heat of the weather, and about half a pint of brandy that I drank as I left the ship, I found myself much inclined to sleep. I lay down on the grass, which was very short and soft, where I slept sounder than ever I remembered to have done in my life, and, as I reckoned, about nine hours; for when I awaked, it was just day-light. I attempted to rise, but was not able to stir: for, as I happened to lie on my back, I found my arms and legs were strongly fastened on each side to the ground; and my hair, which was long and thick, tied down in the same manner. I likewise felt several slender ligatures across my body, from my arm-pits to my thighs. I could only look upwards; the sun began to grow hot, and the light offended my eyes. I heard a confused noise about me; but in the posture I lay, could see nothing except the sky. In a little time I felt something alive moving on my left leg, which advancing gently forward over my breast, came almost up to my chin; when, bending my eyes downwards as much as I could, I perceived it to be a human creature not six inches high, with a bow and arrow in his hands, and a quiver at his back. In the mean time, I felt at least forty more of the same kind (as I conjectured) following the first. I was in the utmost astonishment, and roared so loud, that they all ran back in a fright; and some of them, as I was afterwards told, were hurt with the falls they got by leaping from my sides upon the ground. However, they soon returned, and one of them, who ventured so far as to get a full sight of my face, lifting up his hands and eyes by way of admiration, cried out in a shrill but distinct voice, *Hekinah degul*: the others repeated the same words several times, but then I knew not what they meant. I lay all this while, as the reader may believe, in great uneasiness. At length, struggling to get loose, I had the fortune to break the strings, and wrench out the pegs that fastened my left arm to the ground; for, by lifting it up to my face, I discovered the methods they had taken to bind me, and at the same time with a violent pull, which gave me excessive pain, I a little loosened the strings that tied down my hair on the left side, so that I was just able to turn my head about two inches. But the creatures ran off a second time, before I could seize them; whereupon there was a great shout in a very shrill accent, and after it ceased I heard one of them cry aloud *Tolgo phonac*; when in an instant I felt above a hundred arrows discharged on my left hand, which, pricked me like so many needles; and besides, they shot another flight into the air, as we do bombs in Europe, whereof many, I suppose, fell on my body, (though I felt them not), and some on my face, which I immediately covered with my left hand. When this shower of arrows was over, I fell a groaning with grief and pain; and then striving again to get loose, they discharged another volley larger than the first, and some of them attempted with spears to stick me in the sides; but by good luck I had on a buff jerkin, which they could not pierce. I thought it the most prudent method to lie still, and my design was to continue so till night, when, my left hand being already loose, I could easily free myself: and as for the inhabitants, I had reason to believe I might be a match for the greatest army they could bring against me, if they were all of the same size with him that I saw. But fortune disposed otherwise of me. When the people observed I was quiet, they discharged no more arrows; but, by the noise I heard, I knew their numbers increased; and about four yards from me, over against my right ear, I heard a knocking for above an hour, like that of people at work; when turning my head that way, as well as the pegs and strings would permit me, I saw a stage erected about a foot and a half from the ground, capable of holding four of the inhabitants, with two or three ladders to mount it: from whence one of them, who seemed to be a person of quality, made me a long speech, whereof I understood not one syllable. But I should have mentioned, that before the principal person began his oration, he cried out three times, *Langro dehul san* (these words and the former were afterwards repeated and explained to me); whereupon, immediately, about fifty of the inhabitants came and cut the strings that fastened the left side of my head, which gave me the liberty of turning it to the right, and of observing the person and gesture of him that was to speak. He appeared to be of a middle age, and taller than any of the other three who attended him, whereof one was a page that held up his train, and seemed to be somewhat longer than my middle finger; the other two stood one on each side to support him. He acted every part of an orator, and I could observe many periods of threatenings, and others of promises, pity, and kindness. I answered in a few words, but in the most submissive manner, lifting up my left hand, and both my eyes to the sun, as calling him for a witness; and being almost famished with hunger, having not eaten a morsel for some hours before I left the ship, I found the demands of nature so strong upon me, that I could not forbear showing my impatience (perhaps against the strict rules of decency) by putting my finger frequently to my mouth, to signify that I wanted food. The *hurgo* (for so they call a great lord, as I afterwards learnt) understood me very well. He descended from the stage, and commanded that several ladders should be applied to my sides, on which above a hundred of the inhabitants mounted and walked towards my mouth, laden with baskets full of meat, which had been provided and sent thither by the king's orders, upon the first intelligence he received of me. I observed there was the flesh of several animals, but could not distinguish them by the taste. There were shoulders, legs, and loins, shaped like those of mutton, and very well dressed, but smaller than the wings of a lark. I ate them by two or three at a mouthful, and took three loaves at a time, about the bigness of musket bullets. They supplied me as fast as they could, showing a thousand marks of wonder and astonishment at my bulk and appetite. I then made another sign, that I wanted drink. They found by my eating that a small quantity would not suffice me; and being a most ingenious people, they slung up, with great dexterity, one of their largest hogsheads, then rolled it towards my hand, and beat out the top; I drank it off at a draught, which I might well do, for it did not hold half a pint, and tasted like a small wine of Burgundy, but much more delicious. They brought me a second hogshead, which I drank in the same manner, and made signs for more; but they had none to give me. When I had performed these wonders, they shouted for joy, and danced upon my breast, repeating several times as they did at first, *Hekinah degul.* They made me a sign that I should throw down the two hogsheads, but first warning the people below to stand out of the way, crying aloud, *Borach mevolah*; and when they saw the vessels in the air, there was a universal shout of *Hekinah degul.* I confess I was often tempted, while they were passing backwards and forwards on my body, to seize forty or fifty of the first that came in my reach, and dash them against the ground. But the remembrance of what I had felt, which probably might not be the worst they could do, and the promise of honour I made them – for so I interpreted my submissive behaviour – soon drove out these imaginations. Besides, I now considered myself as bound by the laws of hospitality, to a people who had treated me with so much expense and magnificence. However, in my thoughts I could not sufficiently wonder at the intrepidity of these diminutive mortals, who durst venture to mount and walk upon my body, while one of my hands was at liberty, without trembling at the very sight of so prodigious a creature as I must appear to them. After some time, when they observed that I made no more demands for meat, there appeared before me a person of high rank from his imperial majesty. His excellency, having mounted on the small of my right leg, advanced forwards up to my face, with about a dozen of his retinue; and producing his credentials under the signet royal, which he applied close to my eyes, spoke about ten minutes without any signs of anger, but with a kind of determinate resolution, often pointing forwards, which, as I afterwards found, was towards the capital city, about half a mile distant; whither it was agreed by his majesty in council that I must be conveyed. I answered in few words, but to no purpose, and made a sign with my hand that was loose, putting it to the other (but over his excellency's head for fear of hurting him or his train) and then to my own head and body, to signify that I desired my liberty. It appeared that he understood me well enough, for he shook his head by way of disapprobation, and held his hand in a posture to show that I must be carried as a prisoner. However, he made other signs to let me understand that I should have meat and drink enough, and very good treatment. Whereupon I once more thought of attempting to break my bonds; but again, when I felt the smart of their arrows upon my face and hands, which were all in blisters, and many of the darts still sticking in them, and observing likewise that the number of my enemies increased, I gave tokens to let them know that they might do with me what they pleased. Upon this, the *hurgo* and his train withdrew, with much civility and cheerful countenances. Soon after I heard a general shout, with frequent repetitions of the words *Peplom selan*; and I felt great numbers of people on my left side relaxing the cords to such a degree, that I was able to turn upon my right, and to ease myself with making water; which I very plentifully did, to the great astonishment of the people; who, conjecturing by my motion what I was going to do, immediately opened to the right and left on that side, to avoid the torrent, which fell with such noise and violence from me. But before this, they had daubed my face and both my hands with a sort of ointment, very pleasant to the smell, which, in a few minutes, removed all the smart of their arrows. These circumstances, added to the refreshment I had received by their victuals and drink, which were very nourishing, disposed me to sleep. I slept about eight hours, as I was afterwards assured; and it was no wonder, for the physicians, by the emperor's order, had mingled a sleepy potion in the hogsheads of wine.

It seems, that upon the first moment I was discovered sleeping on the ground, after my landing, the emperor had early notice of it by an express; and determined in council, that I should be tied in the manner I have related, (which was done in the night while I slept;) that plenty of meat and drink should be sent to me, and a machine prepared to carry me to the capital city.

This resolution perhaps may appear very bold and dangerous, and I am confident would not be imitated by any prince in Europe on the like occasion. However, in my opinion, it was extremely prudent, as well as generous: for, supposing these people had endeavoured to kill me with their spears and arrows, while I was asleep, I should certainly have awaked with the first sense of smart, which might so far have roused my rage and strength, as to have enabled me to break the strings wherewith I was tied; after which, as they were not able to make resistance, so they could expect no mercy.

These people are most excellent mathematicians, and arrived to a great perfection in mechanics, by the countenance and encouragement of the emperor, who is a renowned patron of learning. This prince has several machines fixed on wheels, for the carriage of trees and other great weights. He often builds his largest men of war, whereof some are nine feet long, in the woods where the timber grows, and has them carried on these engines three or four hundred yards to the sea. Five hundred carpenters and engineers were immediately set at work to prepare the greatest engine they had. It was a frame of wood raised three inches from the ground, about seven feet long, and four wide, moving upon twenty-two wheels. The shout I heard was upon the arrival of this engine, which, it seems, set out in four hours after my landing. It was brought parallel to me, as I lay. But the principal difficulty was to raise and place me in this vehicle. Eighty poles, each of one foot high, were erected for this purpose, and very strong cords, of the bigness of packthread, were fastened by hooks to many bandages, which the workmen had girt round my neck, my hands, my body, and my legs. Nine hundred of the strongest men were employed to draw up these cords, by many pulleys fastened on the poles; and thus, in less than three hours, I was raised and slung into the engine, and there tied fast. All this I was told; for, while the operation was performing, I lay in a profound sleep, by the force of that soporiferous medicine infused into my liquor. Fifteen hundred of the emperor's largest horses, each about four inches and a half high, were employed to draw me towards the metropolis, which, as I said, was half a mile distant.

About four hours after we began our journey, I awaked by a very ridiculous accident; for the carriage being stopped a while, to adjust something that was out of order, two or three of the young natives had the curiosity to see how I looked when I was asleep; they climbed up into the engine, and advancing very softly to my face, one of them, an officer in the guards, put the sharp end of his half-pike a good way up into my left nostril, which tickled my nose like a straw, and made me sneeze violently; whereupon they stole off unperceived, and it was three weeks before I knew the cause of my waking so suddenly. We made a long march the remaining part of the day, and, rested at night with five hundred guards on each side of me, half with torches, and half with bows and arrows, ready to shoot me if I should offer to stir. The next morning at sun-rise we continued our march, and arrived within two hundred yards of the city gates about noon. The emperor, and all his court, came out to meet us; but his great officers would by no means suffer his majesty to endanger his person by mounting on my body.

At the place where the carriage stopped there stood an ancient temple, esteemed to be the largest in the whole kingdom; which, having been polluted some years before by an unnatural murder, was, according to the zeal of those people, looked upon as profane, and therefore had been applied to common use, and all the ornaments and furniture carried away. In this edifice it was determined I should lodge. The great gate fronting to the north was about four feet high, and almost two feet wide, through which I could easily creep. On each side of the gate was a small window, not above six inches from the ground: into that on the left side, the king's smith conveyed fourscore and eleven chains, like those that hang to a lady's watch in Europe, and almost as large, which were locked to my left leg with six-and-thirty padlocks. Over against this temple, on the other side of the great highway, at twenty feet distance, there was a turret at least five feet high. Here the emperor ascended, with many principal lords of his court, to have an opportunity of viewing me, as I was told, for I could not see them. It was reckoned that above a hundred thousand inhabitants came out of the town upon the same errand; and, in spite of my guards, I believe there could not be fewer than ten thousand at several times, who mounted my body by the help of ladders. But a proclamation was soon issued, to forbid it upon pain of death. When the workmen found it was impossible for me to break loose, they cut all the strings that bound me; whereupon I rose up, with as melancholy a disposition as ever I had in my life. But the noise and astonishment of the people, at seeing me rise and walk, are not to be expressed. The chains that held my left leg were about two yards long, and gave me not only the liberty of walking backwards and forwards in a semicircle, but, being fixed within four inches of the gate, allowed me to creep in, and lie at my full length in the temple.

CHAPTER TWO

The emperor of Lilliput, attended by several of the nobility, comes to see the author in his confinement. The emperor's person and habit described. Learned men appointed to teach the author their language. He gains favour by his mild disposition. His pockets are searched, and his sword and pistols taken from him.

WHEN I FOUND myself on my feet, I looked about me, and must confess I never beheld a more entertaining prospect. The country around appeared like a continued garden, and the enclosed fields, which were generally forty feet square, resembled so many beds of flowers. These fields were intermingled with woods of half a stang,[1] and the tallest trees, as I could judge, appeared to be seven feet high. I viewed the town on my left hand, which looked like the painted scene of a city in a theatre.

I had been for some hours extremely pressed by the necessities of nature; which was no wonder, it being almost two days since I had last disburdened myself. I was under great difficulties between urgency and shame. The best expedient I could think of, was to creep into my house, which I accordingly did; and shutting the gate after me, I went as far as the length of my chain would suffer, and discharged my body of that uneasy load. But this was the only time I was ever guilty of so uncleanly an action; for which I cannot but hope the candid reader will give some allowance, after he has maturely and impartially considered my case, and the distress I was in. From this time my constant practice was, as soon as I rose, to perform that business in open air, at the full extent of my chain; and due care was taken every morning before company came, that the offensive matter should be carried off in wheel-barrows, by two servants appointed for that purpose. I would not have dwelt so long upon a circumstance that, perhaps, at first sight, may appear not very momentous, if I had not thought it necessary to justify my character, in point of cleanliness, to the world; which, I am told, some of my maligners have been pleased, upon this and other occasions, to call in question.

1 A stang is a pole or perch; sixteen feet and a half

When this adventure was at an end, I came back out of my house, having occasion for fresh air. The emperor was already descended from the tower, and advancing on horseback towards me, which had like to have cost him dear; for the beast, though very well trained, yet wholly unused to such a sight, which appeared as if a mountain moved before him, reared up on its hinder feet: but that prince, who is an excellent horseman, kept his seat, till his attendants ran in, and held the bridle, while his majesty had time to dismount. When he alighted, he surveyed me round with great admiration; but kept beyond the length of my chain. He ordered his cooks and butlers, who were already prepared, to give me victuals and drink, which they pushed forward in a sort of vehicles upon wheels, till I could reach them. I took these vehicles and soon emptied them all; twenty of them were filled with meat, and ten with liquor; each of the former afforded me two or three good mouthfuls; and I emptied the liquor of ten vessels, which was contained in earthen vials, into one vehicle, drinking it off at a draught; and so I did with the rest. The empress, and young princes of the blood of both sexes, attended by many ladies, sat at some distance in their chairs; but upon the accident that happened to the emperor's horse, they alighted, and came near his person, which I am now going to describe. He is taller by almost the breadth of my nail, than any of his court; which alone is enough to strike an awe into the beholders. His features are strong and masculine, with an Austrian lip and arched nose, his complexion olive, his countenance erect, his body and limbs well proportioned, all his motions graceful, and his deportment majestic. He was then past his prime, being twenty-eight years and three quarters old, of which he had reigned about seven in great felicity, and generally victorious. For the better convenience of beholding him, I lay on my side, so that my face was parallel to his, and he stood but three yards off: however, I have had him since many times in my hand, and therefore cannot be deceived in the description. His dress was very plain and simple, and the fashion of it between the Asiatic and the European; but he had on his head a light helmet of gold, adorned with jewels, and a plume on the crest. He held his sword drawn in his hand to defend himself, if I should happen to break loose; it was almost three inches long; the hilt and scabbard were gold enriched with diamonds. His voice was shrill, but very clear and articulate; and I could distinctly hear it when I stood up. The ladies and courtiers were all most magnificently clad; so that the spot they stood upon seemed to resemble a petticoat spread upon the ground, embroidered with figures of gold and silver. His imperial majesty spoke often to me, and I returned answers: but neither of us could understand a syllable. There were several of his priests and lawyers present (as I conjectured by their habits), who were commanded to address themselves to me; and I spoke to them in as many languages as I had the least smattering of, which were High and Low Dutch, Latin, French, Spanish, Italian, and Lingua Franca, but all to no purpose. After about two hours the court retired, and I was left with a strong guard, to prevent the impertinence, and probably the malice of the rabble, who were very impatient to crowd about me as near as they durst; and some of them had the impudence to shoot their arrows at me, as I sat on the ground by the door of my house, whereof one very narrowly missed my left eye. But the colonel ordered six of the ringleaders to be seized, and thought no punishment so proper as to deliver them bound into my hands; which some of his soldiers accordingly did, pushing them forward with the butt-ends of their pikes into my reach. I took them all in my right hand, put five of them into my coat-pocket; and as to the sixth, I made a countenance as if I would eat him alive. The poor man squalled terribly, and the colonel and his officers were in much pain, especially when they saw me take out my penknife: but I soon put them out of fear; for, looking mildly, and immediately cutting the strings he was bound with, I set him gently on the ground, and away he ran. I treated the rest in the same manner, taking them one by one out of my pocket; and I observed both the soldiers and people were highly delighted at this mark of my clemency, which was represented very much to my advantage at court.

Towards night I got with some difficulty into my house, where I lay on the ground, and continued to do so about a fortnight; during which time, the emperor gave orders to have a bed prepared for me. Six hundred beds of the common measure were brought in carriages, and worked up in my house; a hundred and fifty of their beds, sewn together, made up the breadth and length; and these were four double: which, however, kept me but very indifferently from the hardness of the floor, that was of smooth stone. By the same computation, they provided me with sheets, blankets, and coverlets, tolerable enough for one who had been so long inured to hardships.

As the news of my arrival spread through the kingdom, it brought prodigious numbers of rich, idle, and curious people to see me; so that the villages were almost emptied; and great neglect of tillage and household affairs must have ensued, if his imperial majesty had not provided, by several proclamations and orders of state, against this inconveniency. He directed that those who had already beheld me should return home, and not presume to come within fifty yards of my house, without license from the court; whereby the secretaries of state got considerable fees.

In the mean time the emperor held frequent councils, to debate what course should be taken with me; and I was afterwards assured by a particular friend, a person of great quality, who was as much in the secret as any, that the court was under many difficulties concerning me. They apprehended my breaking loose; that my diet would be very expensive, and might cause a famine. Sometimes they determined to starve me; or at least to shoot me in the face and hands with poisoned arrows, which would soon despatch me; but again they considered, that the stench of so large a carcass might produce a plague in the metropolis, and probably spread through the whole kingdom. In the midst of these consultations, several officers of the army went to the door of the great council-chamber, and two of them being admitted, gave an account of my behaviour to the six criminals above-mentioned; which made so favourable an impression in the breast of his majesty and the whole board, in my behalf, that an imperial commission was issued out, obliging all the villages, nine hundred yards round the city, to deliver in every morning six beeves, forty sheep, and other victuals for my sustenance; together with a proportionable quantity of bread, and wine, and other liquors; for the due payment of which, his majesty gave assignments upon his treasury: – for this prince lives chiefly upon his own demesnes; seldom, except upon great occasions, raising any subsidies upon his subjects, who are bound to attend him in his wars at their own expense. An establishment was also made of six hundred persons to be my domestics, who had board-wages allowed for their maintenance, and tents built for them very conveniently on each side of my door. It was likewise ordered, that three hundred tailors should make me a suit of clothes, after the fashion of the country; that six of his majesty's greatest scholars should be employed to instruct me in their language; and lastly, that the emperor's horses, and those of the nobility and troops of guards, should be frequently exercised in my sight, to accustom themselves to me. All these orders were duly put in execution; and in about three weeks I made a great progress in learning their language; during which time the emperor frequently honoured me with his visits, and was pleased to assist my masters in teaching me. We began already to converse together in some sort; and the first words I learnt, were to express my desire "that he would please give me my liberty;" which I every day repeated on my knees. His answer, as I could comprehend it, was, "that this must be a work of time, not to be thought on without the advice of his council, and that first I must *lumos kelmin pesso desmar lon emposo*;" that is, swear a peace with him and his kingdom. However, that I should be used with all kindness. And he advised me to "acquire, by my patience and discreet behaviour, the good opinion of himself and his subjects." He desired "I would not take it ill, if he gave orders to certain proper officers to search me; for probably I might carry about me several weapons, which must needs be dangerous things, if they answered the bulk of so prodigious a person." I said, "His majesty should be satisfied; for I was ready to strip myself, and turn up my pockets before him." This I delivered part in words, and part in signs. He replied, "that, by the laws of the kingdom, I must be searched by two of his officers; that he knew this could not be done without my consent and assistance; and he had so good an opinion of my generosity and justice, as to trust their persons in my hands; that whatever they took from me, should be returned when I left the country, or paid for at the rate which I would set upon them." I took up the two officers in my hands, put them first into my coat-pockets, and then into every other pocket about me, except my two fobs, and another secret pocket, which I had no mind should be searched, wherein I had some little necessaries that were of no consequence to any but myself. In one of my fobs there was a silver watch, and in the other a small quantity of gold in a purse. These gentlemen, having pen, ink, and paper, about them, made an exact inventory of every thing they saw; and when they had done, desired I would set them down, that they might deliver it to the emperor. This inventory I afterwards translated into English, and is, word for word, as follows:

"*Imprimis*: In the right coat-pocket of the great man-mountain" (for so I interpret the words *quinbus flestrin*,) "after the strictest search, we found only one great piece of coarse-cloth, large enough to be a foot-cloth for your majesty's chief room of state. In the left pocket we saw a huge silver chest, with a cover of the same metal, which we, the searchers, were not able to lift. We desired it should be opened, and one of us stepping into it, found himself up to the mid leg in a sort of dust, some part whereof flying up to our faces set us both a sneezing for several times together. In his right waistcoat-pocket we found a prodigious bundle of white thin substances, folded one over another, about the bigness of three men, tied with a strong cable, and marked with black figures; which we humbly conceive to be writings, every letter almost half as large as the palm of our hands. In the left there was a sort of engine, from the back of which were extended twenty long poles, resembling the pallisados before your majesty's court: wherewith we conjecture the man-mountain combs his head; for we did not always trouble him with questions, because we found it a great difficulty to make him understand us. In the large pocket, on the right side of his middle cover" (so I translate the word *ranfulo*, by which they meant my breeches,) "we saw a hollow pillar of iron, about the length of a man, fastened to a strong piece of timber larger than the pillar; and upon one side of the pillar, were huge pieces of iron sticking out, cut into strange figures, which we know not what to make of. In the left pocket, another engine of the same kind. In the smaller pocket on the right side, were several round flat pieces of white and red metal, of different bulk; some of the white, which seemed to be silver, were so large and heavy, that my comrade and I could hardly lift them. In the left pocket were two black pillars irregularly shaped: we could not, without difficulty, reach the top of them, as we stood at the bottom of his pocket. One of them was covered, and seemed all of a piece: but at the upper end of the other there appeared a white round substance, about twice the bigness of our heads. Within each of these was enclosed a prodigious plate of steel; which, by our orders, we obliged him to show us, because we apprehended they might be dangerous engines. He took them out of their cases, and told us, that in his own country his practice was to shave his beard with one of these, and cut his meat with the other. There were two pockets which we could not enter: these he called his fobs; they were two large slits cut into the top of his middle cover, but squeezed close by the pressure of his belly. Out of the right fob hung a great silver chain, with a wonderful kind of engine at the bottom. We directed him to draw out whatever was at the end of that chain; which appeared to be a globe, half silver, and half of some transparent metal; for, on the transparent side, we saw certain strange figures circularly drawn, and thought we could touch them, till we found our fingers stopped by the lucid substance. He put this engine into our ears, which made an incessant noise, like that of a water-mill: and we conjecture it is either some unknown animal, or the god that he worships; but we are more inclined to the latter opinion, because he assured us, (if we understood him right, for he expressed himself very imperfectly) that he seldom did any thing without consulting it. He called it his oracle, and said, it pointed out the time for every action of his life. From the left fob he took out a net almost large enough for a fisherman, but contrived to open and shut like a purse, and served him for the same use: we found therein several massy pieces of yellow metal, which, if they be real gold, must be of immense value.

"Having thus, in obedience to your majesty's commands, diligently searched all his pockets, we observed a girdle about his waist made of the hide of some prodigious animal, from which, on the left side, hung a sword of the length of five men; and on the right, a bag or pouch divided into two cells, each cell capable of holding three of your majesty's subjects. In one of these cells were several globes, or balls, of a most ponderous metal, about the bigness of our heads, and requiring a strong hand to lift them: the other cell contained a heap of certain black grains, but of no great bulk or weight, for we could hold above fifty of them in the palms of our hands.

"This is an exact inventory of what we found about the body of the man-mountain, who used us with great civility, and due respect to your majesty's commission. Signed and sealed on the fourth day of the eighty-ninth moon of your majesty's auspicious reign.

Clefrin Frelock, Marsi Frelock."

When this inventory was read over to the emperor, he directed me, although in very gentle terms, to deliver up the several particulars. He first called for my scimitar, which I took out, scabbard and all. In the mean time he ordered three thousand of his choicest troops (who then attended him) to surround me at a distance, with their bows and arrows just ready to discharge; but I did not observe it, for mine eyes were wholly fixed upon his majesty. He then desired me to draw my scimitar, which, although it had got some rust by the sea water, was, in most parts, exceeding bright. I did so, and immediately all the troops gave a shout between terror and surprise; for the sun shone clear, and the reflection dazzled their eyes, as I waved the scimitar to and fro in my hand. His majesty, who is a most magnanimous prince, was less daunted than I could expect: he ordered me to return it into the scabbard, and cast it on the ground as gently as I could, about six feet from the end of my chain. The next thing he demanded was one of the hollow iron pillars; by which he meant my pocket pistols. I drew it out, and at his desire, as well as I could, expressed to him the use of it; and charging it only with powder, which, by the closeness of my pouch, happened to escape wetting in the sea (an inconvenience against which all prudent mariners take special care to provide,) I first cautioned the emperor not to be afraid, and then I let it off in the air. The astonishment here was much greater than at the sight of my scimitar. Hundreds fell down as if they had been struck dead; and even the emperor, although he stood his ground, could not recover himself for some time. I delivered up both my pistols in the same manner as I had done my scimitar, and then my pouch of powder and bullets; begging him that the former might be kept from fire, for it would kindle with the smallest spark, and blow up his imperial palace into the air. I likewise delivered up my watch, which the emperor was very curious to see, and commanded two of his tallest yeomen of the guards to bear it on a pole upon their shoulders, as draymen in England do a barrel of ale. He was amazed at the continual noise it made, and the motion of the minute-hand, which he could easily discern; for their sight is much more acute than ours: he asked the opinions of his learned men about it, which were various and remote, as the reader may well imagine without my repeating; although indeed I could not very perfectly understand them. I then gave up my silver and copper money, my purse, with nine large pieces of gold, and some smaller ones; my knife and razor, my comb and silver snuff-box, my handkerchief and journal-book. My scimitar, pistols, and pouch, were conveyed in carriages to his majesty's stores; but the rest of my goods were returned me.

I had as I before observed, one private pocket, which escaped their search, wherein there was a pair of spectacles (which I sometimes use for the weakness of mine eyes,) a pocket perspective, and some other little conveniences; which, being of no consequence to the emperor, I did not think myself bound in honour to discover, and I apprehended they might be lost or spoiled if I ventured them out of my possession.

CHAPTER THREE

The author diverts the emperor, and his nobility of both sexes, in a very uncommon manner. The diversions of the court of Lilliput described. The author has his liberty granted him upon certain conditions.

My gentleness and good behaviour had gained so far on the emperor and his court, and indeed upon the army and people in general, that I began to conceive hopes of getting my liberty in a short time. I took all possible methods to cultivate this favourable disposition. The natives came, by degrees, to be less apprehensive of any danger from me. I would sometimes lie down, and let five or six of them dance on my hand; and at last the boys and girls would venture to come and play at hide-and-seek in my hair. I had now made a good progress in understanding and speaking the language. The emperor had a mind one day to entertain me with several of the country shows, wherein they exceed all nations I have known, both for dexterity and magnificence. I was diverted with none so much as that of the rope-dancers, performed upon a slender white thread, extended about two feet, and twelve inches from the ground. Upon which I shall desire liberty, with the reader's patience, to enlarge a little.

This diversion is only practised by those persons who are candidates for great employments, and high favour at court. They are trained in this art from their youth, and are not always of noble birth, or liberal education. When a great office is vacant, either by death or disgrace (which often happens,) five or six of those candidates petition the emperor to entertain his majesty and the court with a dance on the rope; and whoever jumps the highest, without falling, succeeds in the office. Very often the chief ministers themselves are commanded to show their skill, and to convince the emperor that they have not lost their faculty. Flimnap, the treasurer, is allowed to cut a caper on the straight rope, at least an inch higher than any other lord in the whole empire. I have seen him do the summerset several times together, upon a trencher fixed on a rope which is no thicker than a common packthread in

England. My friend Reldresal, principal secretary for private affairs, is, in my opinion, if I am not partial, the second after the treasurer; the rest of the great officers are much upon a par.

These diversions are often attended with fatal accidents, whereof great numbers are on record. I myself have seen two or three candidates break a limb. But the danger is much greater, when the ministers themselves are commanded to show their dexterity; for, by contending to excel themselves and their fellows, they strain so far that there is hardly one of them who has not received a fall, and some of them two or three. I was assured that, a year or two before my arrival, Flimnap would infallibly have broke his neck, if one of the king's cushions, that accidentally lay on the ground, had not weakened the force of his fall.

There is likewise another diversion, which is only shown before the emperor and empress, and first minister, upon particular occasions. The emperor lays on the table three fine silken threads of six inches long; one is blue, the other red, and the third green. These threads are proposed as prizes for those persons whom the emperor has a mind to distinguish by a peculiar mark of his favour. The ceremony is performed in his majesty's great chamber of state, where the candidates are to undergo a trial of dexterity very different from the former, and such as I have not observed the least resemblance of in any other country of the new or old world. The emperor holds a stick in his hands, both ends parallel to the horizon, while the candidates advancing, one by one, sometimes leap over the stick, sometimes creep under it, backward and forward, several times, according as the stick is advanced or depressed. Sometimes the emperor holds one end of the stick, and his first minister the other; sometimes the minister has it entirely to himself. Whoever performs his part with most agility, and holds out the longest in leaping and creeping, is rewarded with the blue-coloured silk; the red is given to the next, and the green to the third, which they all wear girt twice round about the middle; and you see few great persons about this court who are not adorned with one of these girdles.

The horses of the army, and those of the royal stables, having been daily led before me, were no longer shy, but would come up to my very feet without starting. The riders would leap them over my hand, as I held it on the ground; and one of the emperor's huntsmen, upon a large courser, took my foot, shoe and all; which was indeed a prodigious leap. I had the good fortune to divert the emperor one day after a very extraordinary manner. I desired he would order several sticks of two feet high, and the thickness of an ordinary cane, to be brought me; whereupon his majesty commanded the master of his woods to give directions accordingly; and the next morning six woodmen arrived with as many carriages, drawn by eight horses to each. I took nine of these sticks, and fixing them firmly in the ground in a quadrangular figure, two feet and a half square, I took four other sticks, and tied them parallel at each corner, about two feet from the ground; then I fastened my handkerchief to the nine sticks that stood erect; and extended it on all sides, till it was tight as the top of a drum; and the four parallel sticks, rising about five inches higher than the handkerchief, served as ledges on each side. When I had finished my work, I desired the emperor to let a troop of his best horses twenty-four in number, come and exercise upon this plain. His majesty approved of the proposal, and I took them up, one by one, in my hands, ready mounted and armed, with the proper officers to exercise them. As soon as they got into order they divided into two parties, performed mock skirmishes, discharged blunt arrows, drew their swords, fled and pursued, attacked and retired, and in short discovered the best military discipline I ever beheld. The parallel sticks secured them and their horses from falling over the stage; and the emperor was so much delighted, that he ordered this entertainment to be repeated several days, and once was pleased to be lifted up and give the word of command; and with great difficulty persuaded even the empress herself to let me hold her in her close chair within two yards of the stage, when she was able to take a full view of the whole performance. It was my good fortune, that no ill accident happened in these entertainments; only once a fiery horse, that belonged to one of the captains, pawing with his hoof, struck a hole in my handkerchief, and his foot slipping, he overthrew his rider and himself; but I immediately relieved them both, and covering the hole with one hand, I set down the troop with the other, in the same manner as I took them up. The horse that fell was strained in the left shoulder, but the rider got no hurt; and I repaired my handkerchief as well as I could: however, I would not trust to the strength of it any more, in such dangerous enterprises.

About two or three days before I was set at liberty, as I was entertaining the court with this kind of feat, there arrived an express to inform his majesty, that some of his subjects, riding near the place where I was first taken up, had seen a great black substance lying on the around, very oddly shaped, extending its edges round, as wide as his majesty's bedchamber, and rising up in the middle as high as a man; that it was no living creature, as they at first apprehended, for it lay on the grass without motion; and some of them had walked round it several times; that, by mounting upon each other's shoulders, they had got to the top, which was flat and even, and, stamping upon it, they found that it was hollow within; that they humbly conceived it might be something belonging to the man-mountain; and if his majesty pleased, they would undertake to bring it with only five horses. I presently knew what they meant, and was glad at heart to receive this intelligence. It seems, upon my first reaching the shore after our shipwreck, I was in such confusion, that before I came to the place where I went to sleep, my hat, which I had fastened with a string to my head while I was rowing, and had stuck on all the time I was swimming, fell off after I came to land; the string, as I conjecture, breaking by some accident, which I never observed, but thought my hat had been lost at sea. I entreated his imperial majesty to give orders it might be brought to me as soon as possible, describing to him the use and the nature of it: and the next day the waggoners arrived with it, but not in a very good condition; they had bored two holes in the brim, within an inch and half of the edge, and fastened two hooks in the holes; these hooks were tied by a long cord to the harness, and thus my hat was dragged along for above half an English mile; but, the ground in that country being extremely smooth and level, it received less damage than I expected.

Two days after this adventure, the emperor, having ordered that part of his army which quarters in and about his metropolis, to be in readiness, took a fancy of diverting himself in a very singular manner. He desired I would stand like a Colossus, with my legs as far asunder as I conveniently could. He then commanded his general (who was an old experienced leader, and a great patron of mine) to draw up the troops in close order, and march them under me; the foot by twenty-four abreast, and the horse by sixteen, with drums beating, colours flying, and pikes advanced. This body consisted of three thousand foot, and a thousand horse. His majesty gave orders, upon pain of death, that every soldier in his march should observe the strictest decency with regard to my person; which however could not prevent some of the younger officers from turning up their eyes as they passed under me: and, to confess the truth, my breeches were at that time in so ill a condition, that they afforded some opportunities for laughter and admiration.

I had sent so many memorials and petitions for my liberty, that his majesty at length mentioned the matter, first in the cabinet, and then in a full council; where it was opposed by none, except Skyresh Bolgolam, who was pleased, without any provocation, to be my mortal enemy. But it was carried against him by the whole board, and confirmed by the emperor. That minister was *galbet*, or admiral of the realm, very much in his master's confidence, and a person well versed in affairs, but of a morose and sour complexion. However, he was at length persuaded to comply; but prevailed that the articles and conditions upon which I should be set free, and to which I must swear, should be drawn up by himself. These articles were brought to me by Skyresh Bolgolam in person attended by two under-secretaries, and several persons of distinction. After they were read, I was demanded to swear to the performance of them; first in the manner of my own country, and afterwards in the method prescribed by their laws; which was, to hold my right foot in my left hand, and to place the middle finger of my right hand on the crown of my head, and my thumb on the tip of my right ear. But because the reader may be curious to have some idea of the style and manner of expression peculiar to that people, as well as to know the article upon which I recovered my liberty, I have made a translation of the whole instrument, word for word, as near as I was able, which I here offer to the public.

"Golbasto Momarem Evlame Gurdilo Shefin Mully Ully Gue, most mighty Emperor of Lilliput, delight and terror of the universe, whose dominions extend five thousand *blustrugs* (about twelve miles in circumference) to the extremities of the globe; monarch of all monarchs, taller than the sons of men; whose feet press down to the centre, and whose head strikes against the sun; at whose nod the princes of the earth shake their knees; pleasant as the spring, comfortable as the summer, fruitful as autumn, dreadful as winter: his most sublime majesty proposes to the man-mountain, lately arrived at our celestial dominions, the following articles, which, by a solemn oath, he shall be obliged to perform: –

"1st, The man-mountain shall not depart from our dominions, without our license under our great seal.

"2d, He shall not presume to come into our metropolis, without our express order; at which time, the inhabitants shall have two hours warning to keep within doors.

"3d, The said man-mountain shall confine his walks to our principal high roads, and not offer to walk, or lie down, in a meadow or field of corn.

"4th, As he walks the said roads, he shall take the utmost care not to trample upon the bodies of any of our loving subjects, their horses, or carriages, nor take any of our subjects into his hands without their own consent.

"5th, If an express requires extraordinary despatch, the man-mountain shall be obliged to carry, in his pocket, the messenger and horse a six days journey, once in every moon, and return the said messenger back (if so required) safe to our imperial presence.

"6th, He shall be our ally against our enemies in the island of Blefuscu, and do his utmost to destroy their fleet, which is now preparing to invade us.

"7th, That the said man-mountain shall, at his times of leisure, be aiding and assisting to our workmen, in helping to raise certain great stones, towards covering the wall of the principal park, and other our royal buildings.

"8th, That the said man-mountain shall, in two moons' time, deliver in an exact survey of the circumference of our dominions, by a computation of his own paces round the coast.

"Lastly, That, upon his solemn oath to observe all the above articles, the said man-mountain shall have a daily allowance of meat and drink sufficient for the support of 1724 of our subjects, with free access to our royal person, and other marks of our favour. Given at our palace at Belfaborac, the twelfth day of the ninety-first moon of our reign."

I swore and subscribed to these articles with great cheerfulness and content, although some of them were not so honourable as I could have wished; which proceeded wholly from the malice of Skyresh Bolgolam, the high-admiral: whereupon my chains were immediately unlocked, and I was at full liberty. The emperor himself, in person, did me the honour to be by at the whole ceremony. I made my acknowledgements by prostrating myself at his majesty's feet: but he commanded me to rise; and after many gracious expressions, which, to avoid the censure of vanity, I shall not repeat, he added, "that he hoped I should prove a useful servant, and well deserve all the favours he had already conferred upon me, or might do for the future."

The reader may please to observe, that, in the last article of the recovery of my liberty, the emperor stipulates to allow me a quantity of meat and drink sufficient for the support of 1724 Lilliputians. Some time after, asking a friend at court how they came to fix on that determinate number, he told me that his majesty's mathematicians, having taken the height of my body by the help of a quadrant, and finding it to exceed theirs in the proportion of twelve to one, they concluded from the similarity of their bodies, that mine must contain at least 1724 of theirs, and consequently would require as much food as was necessary to support that number of Lilliputians. By which the reader may conceive an idea of the ingenuity of that people, as well as the prudent and exact economy of so great a prince.

CHAPTER FOUR

Mildendo, the metropolis of Lilliput, described, together with the emperor's palace. A conversation between the author and a principal secretary, concerning the affairs of that empire. The author's offers to serve the emperor in his wars.

THE FIRST REQUEST I made, after I had obtained my liberty, was, that I might have license to see Mildendo, the metropolis; which the emperor easily granted me, but with a special charge to do no hurt either to the inhabitants or their houses. The people had notice, by proclamation, of my design to visit the town. The wall which encompassed it is two feet and a half high, and at least eleven inches broad, so that a coach and horses may be driven very safely round it; and it is flanked with strong towers at ten feet distance. I stepped over the great western gate, and passed very gently, and sidling, through the two principal streets, only in my short waistcoat, for fear of damaging the roofs and eaves of the houses with the skirts of my coat. I walked with the utmost circumspection, to avoid treading on any stragglers who might remain in the streets, although the orders were very strict, that all people should keep in their houses, at their own peril. The garret windows and tops of houses were so crowded with spectators, that I thought in all my travels I had not seen a more populous place. The city is an exact square, each side of the wall being five hundred feet long. The two great streets, which run across and divide it into four quarters, are five feet wide. The lanes and alleys, which I could not enter, but only view them as I passed, are from twelve to eighteen inches. The town is capable of holding five hundred thousand souls: the houses are from three to five stories: the shops and markets well provided.

The emperor's palace is in the centre of the city where the two great streets meet. It is enclosed by a wall of two feet high, and twenty feet distance from the buildings. I had his majesty's permission to step over this wall; and, the space being so wide between that and the palace, I could easily view it on every side. The outward court is a square of forty feet, and includes two other courts: in the inmost are the royal apartments, which I was very desirous to see, but found it extremely difficult; for the great gates, from one square into another, were but eighteen inches high, and seven inches wide. Now the buildings of the outer court were at least five feet high, and it was impossible for me to stride over them without infinite damage to the pile, though the walls were strongly built of hewn stone, and four inches thick. At the same time the emperor had a great desire that I should see the magnificence of his palace; but this I was not able to do till three days after, which I spent in cutting down with my knife some of the largest trees in the royal park, about a hundred yards distant from the city. Of these trees I made two stools, each about three feet high, and strong enough to bear my weight. The people having received notice a second time, I went again through the city to the palace with my two stools in my hands. When I came to the side of the outer court, I stood upon one stool, and took the other in my hand; this I lifted over the roof, and gently set it down on the space between the first and second court, which was eight feet wide. I then stept over the building very conveniently from one stool to the other, and drew up the first after me with a hooked stick. By this contrivance I got into the inmost court; and, lying down upon my side, I applied my face to the windows of the middle stories, which were left open on purpose, and discovered the most splendid apartments that can be imagined. There I saw the empress and the young princes, in their several lodgings, with their chief attendants about them. Her imperial majesty was pleased to smile very graciously upon me, and gave me out of the window her hand to kiss.

But I shall not anticipate the reader with further descriptions of this kind, because I reserve them for a greater work, which is now almost ready for the press; containing a general description of this empire, from its first erection, through along series of princes; with a particular account of their wars and politics, laws, learning, and religion; their plants and animals; their peculiar manners and customs, with other matters very curious and useful; my chief design at present being only to relate such events and transactions as happened to the public or to myself during a residence of about nine months in that empire.

One morning, about a fortnight after I had obtained my liberty, Reldresal, principal secretary (as they style him) for private affairs, came to my house attended only by one servant. He ordered his coach to wait at a distance, and desired I would give him an hours audience; which I readily consented to, on account of his quality and personal merits, as well as of the many good offices he had done me during my solicitations at court. I offered to lie down that he might the more conveniently reach my ear, but he chose rather to let me hold him in my hand during our conversation. He began with compliments on my liberty; said "he might pretend to some merit in it;" but, however, added, "that if it had not been for the present situation of things at court, perhaps I might not have obtained it so soon. For," said he, "as flourishing a condition as we may appear to be in to foreigners, we labour under two mighty evils: a violent faction at home, and the danger of an invasion, by a most potent enemy, from abroad. As to the first, you are to understand, that for about seventy moons past there have been two struggling parties in this empire, under the names of *Tramecksan* and *Slamecksan*, from the high and low heels of their shoes, by which they distinguish themselves. It is alleged, indeed, that the high heels are most agreeable to our ancient constitution; but, however this be, his majesty has determined to make use only of low heels in the administration of the government, and all offices in the gift of the crown, as you cannot but observe; and particularly that his majesty's imperial heels are lower at least by a *drurr* than any of his court (*drurr* is a measure about the fourteenth part of an inch). The animosities between these two parties run so high, that they will neither eat, nor drink, nor talk with each other. We compute the *Tramecksan*, or high heels, to exceed us in number; but the power is wholly on our side. We apprehend his imperial highness, the heir to the crown, to have some tendency towards the high heels; at least we can plainly discover that one of his heels is higher than the other, which gives him a hobble in his gait. Now, in the midst of these intestine disquiets, we are threatened with an invasion from the island of Blefuscu, which is the other great empire of the universe, almost as large and powerful as this of his majesty. For as to what we have heard you affirm, that there are other kingdoms and states in the world inhabited by human creatures as large as yourself, our philosophers are in much doubt, and would rather conjecture that you dropped from the moon, or one of the stars; because it is certain, that a hundred mortals of your bulk would in a short time destroy all the fruits and cattle of his majesty's dominions: besides, our histories of six thousand moons make no mention of any other regions than the two great empires of Lilliput and Blefuscu. Which two mighty powers have, as I was going to tell you, been engaged in a most obstinate war for six-and-thirty moons past. It began upon the following occasion. It is allowed on all hands, that the primitive way of breaking eggs, before we eat them, was upon the larger end; but his present majesty's grandfather, while he was a boy, going to eat an egg, and breaking it according to the ancient practice, happened to cut one of his fingers. Whereupon the emperor his father published an edict, commanding all his subjects, upon great penalties, to break the smaller end of their eggs. The people so highly resented this law, that our histories tell us, there have been six rebellions raised on that account; wherein one emperor lost his life, and another his crown. These civil commotions were constantly fomented by the monarchs of Blefuscu; and when they were quelled, the exiles always fled for refuge to that empire. It is computed that eleven thousand persons have at several times suffered death, rather than submit to break their eggs at the smaller end. Many hundred large volumes have been published upon this controversy: but the books of the Big-endians have been long forbidden, and the whole party rendered incapable by law of holding employments. During the course of these troubles, the emperors of Blefusca did frequently expostulate by their ambassadors, accusing us of making a schism in religion, by offending against a fundamental doctrine of our great prophet Lustrog, in the fifty-fourth chapter of the Blundecral (which is their Alcoran). This, however, is thought to be a mere strain upon the text; for the words are these: 'that all true believers break their eggs at the convenient end.' And which is the convenient end, seems, in my humble opinion to be left to every man's conscience, or at least in the power of the chief magistrate to determine. Now, the Big-endian exiles have found so much credit in the emperor of Blefuscu's court, and so much private assistance and encouragement from their party here at home, that a bloody war has been carried on between the two empires for six-and-thirty moons, with various success; during which time we have lost forty capital ships, and a much a greater number of smaller vessels, together with thirty thousand of our best seamen and soldiers; and the damage received by the enemy is reckoned to be somewhat greater than ours. However, they have now equipped a numerous fleet, and are just preparing to make a descent upon us; and his imperial majesty, placing great confidence in your valour and strength, has commanded me to lay this account of his affairs before you."

I desired the secretary to present my humble duty to the emperor; and to let him know, "that I thought it would not become me, who was a foreigner, to interfere with parties; but I was ready, with the hazard of my life, to defend his person and state against all invaders."

CHAPTER FIVE

The author, by an extraordinary stratagem, prevents an invasion. A high title of honour is conferred upon him. Ambassadors arrive from the emperor of Blefuscu, and sue for peace. The empress's apartment on fire by an accident; the author instrumental in saving the rest of the palace.

THE EMPIRE of Blefuscu is an island situated to the north-east of Lilliput, from which it is parted only by a channel of eight hundred yards wide. I had not yet seen it, and upon this notice of an intended invasion, I avoided appearing on that side of the coast, for fear of being discovered, by some of the enemy's ships, who had received no intelligence of me; all intercourse between the two empires having been strictly forbidden during the war, upon pain of death, and an embargo laid by our emperor upon all vessels whatsoever. I communicated to his majesty a project I had formed of seizing the enemy's whole fleet; which, as our scouts assured us, lay at anchor in the harbour, ready to sail with the first fair wind. I consulted the most experienced seamen upon the depth of the channel, which they had often plumbed; who told me, that in the middle, at high-water, it was seventy *glumgluffs* deep, which is about six feet of European measure; and the rest of it fifty *glumgluffs* at most. I walked towards the north-east coast, over against Blefuscu, where, lying down behind a hillock, I took out my small perspective glass, and viewed the enemy's fleet at anchor, consisting of about fifty men of war, and a great number of transports: I then came back to my house, and gave orders (for which I had a warrant) for a great quantity of the strongest cable and bars of iron. The cable was about as thick as packthread and the bars of the length and size of a knitting-needle. I trebled the cable to make it stronger, and for the same reason I twisted three of the iron bars together, bending the extremities into a hook. Having thus fixed fifty hooks to as many cables, I went back to the north-east coast, and putting off my coat, shoes, and stockings, walked into the sea, in my leathern jerkin, about half an hour before high water. I waded with what haste I could, and swam in the middle about thirty yards, till I felt ground. I arrived at the fleet in less than half an hour. The enemy was so frightened when they saw me, that they leaped out of their ships, and swam to shore, where there could not be fewer than thirty thousand souls. I then took my tackling, and, fastening a hook to the hole at the prow of each, I tied all the cords together at the end. While I was thus employed, the enemy discharged several thousand arrows, many of which stuck in my hands and face, and, beside the excessive smart, gave me much disturbance in my work. My greatest apprehension was for mine eyes, which I should have infallibly lost, if I had not suddenly thought of an expedient. I kept, among other little necessaries, a pair of spectacles in a private pocket, which, as I observed before, had escaped the emperor's searchers. These I took out and fastened as strongly as I could upon my nose, and thus armed, went on boldly with my work, in spite of the enemy's arrows, many of which struck against the glasses of my spectacles, but without any other effect, further than a little to discompose them. I had now fastened all the hooks, and, taking the knot in my hand, began to pull; but not a ship would stir, for they were all too fast held by their anchors, so that the boldest part of my enterprise remained. I therefore let go the cord, and leaving the looks fixed to the ships, I resolutely cut with my knife the cables that fastened the anchors, receiving about two hundred shots in my face and hands; then I took up the knotted end of the cables, to which my hooks were tied, and with great ease drew fifty of the enemy's largest men of war after me.

The Blefuscudians, who had not the least imagination of what I intended, were at first confounded with astonishment. They had seen me cut the cables, and thought my design was only to let the ships run adrift or fall foul on each other: but when they perceived the whole fleet moving in order, and saw me pulling at the end, they set up such a scream of grief and despair as it is almost impossible to describe or conceive. When I had got out of danger, I stopped awhile to pick out the arrows that stuck in my hands and face; and rubbed on some of the same ointment that was given me at my first arrival, as I have formerly mentioned. I then took off my spectacles, and waiting about an hour, till the tide was a little fallen, I waded through the middle with my cargo, and arrived safe at the royal port of Lilliput.

The emperor and his whole court stood on the shore, expecting the issue of this great adventure. They saw the ships move forward in a large half-moon, but could not discern me, who was up to my breast in water. When I advanced to the middle of the channel, they were yet more in pain, because I was under water to my neck. The emperor concluded me to be drowned, and that the enemy's fleet was approaching in a hostile manner: but he was soon eased of his fears; for the channel growing shallower every step I made, I came in a short time within hearing, and holding up the end of the cable, by which the fleet was fastened, I cried in a loud voice, "Long live the most puissant king of Lilliput!" This great prince received me at my landing with all possible encomiums, and created me a *nardac* upon the spot, which is the highest title of honour among them.

His majesty desired I would take some other opportunity of bringing all the rest of his enemy's ships into his ports. And so unmeasureable is the ambition of princes, that he seemed to think of nothing less than reducing the whole empire of Blefuscu into a province, and governing it, by a viceroy; of destroying the Big-endian exiles, and compelling that people to break the smaller end of their eggs, by which he would remain the sole monarch of the whole world. But I endeavoured to divert him from this design, by many arguments drawn from the topics of policy as well as justice; and I plainly protested, "that I would never be an instrument of bringing a free and brave people into slavery." And, when the matter was debated in council, the wisest part of the ministry were of my opinion.

This open bold declaration of mine was so opposite to the schemes and politics of his imperial majesty, that he could never forgive me. He mentioned it in a very artful manner at council, where I was told that some of the wisest appeared, at least by their silence, to be of my opinion; but others, who were my secret enemies, could not forbear some expressions which, by a side-wind, reflected on me. And from this time began an intrigue between his majesty and a junto of ministers, maliciously bent against me, which broke out in less than two months, and had like to have ended in my utter destruction. Of so little weight are the greatest services to princes, when put into the balance with a refusal to gratify their passions.

About three weeks after this exploit, there arrived a solemn embassy from Blefuscu, with humble offers of a peace, which was soon concluded, upon conditions very advantageous to our emperor, wherewith I shall not trouble the reader. There were six ambassadors, with a train of about five hundred persons, and their entry was very magnificent, suitable to the grandeur of their master, and the importance of their business. When their treaty was finished, wherein I did them several good offices by the credit I now had, or at least appeared to have, at court, their excellencies, who were privately told how much I had been their friend, made me a visit in form. They began with many compliments upon my valour and generosity, invited me to that kingdom in the emperor their master's name, and desired me to show them some proofs of my prodigious strength, of which they had heard so many wonders; wherein I readily obliged them, but shall not trouble the reader with the particulars.

When I had for some time entertained their excellencies, to their infinite satisfaction and surprise, I desired they would do me the honour to present my most humble respects to the emperor their master, the renown of whose virtues had so justly filled the whole world with admiration, and whose royal person I resolved to attend, before I returned to my own country. Accordingly, the next time I had the honour to see our emperor, I desired his general license to wait on the Blefuscudian monarch, which he was pleased to grant me, as I could perceive, in a very cold manner; but could not guess the reason, till I had a whisper from a certain person, "that Flimnap and Bolgolam had represented my intercourse with those ambassadors as a mark of disaffection;" from which I am sure my heart was wholly free. And this was the first time I began to conceive some imperfect idea of courts and ministers.

It is to be observed, that these ambassadors spoke to me, by an interpreter, the languages of both empires differing as much from each other as any two in Europe, and each nation priding itself upon the antiquity, beauty, and energy of their own tongue, with an avowed contempt for that of their neighbour; yet our emperor, standing upon the advantage he had got by the seizure of their fleet, obliged them to deliver their credentials, and make their speech, in the Lilliputian tongue. And it must be confessed, that from the great intercourse of trade and commerce between both realms, from the continual reception of exiles which is mutual among them, and from the custom, in each empire, to send their young nobility and richer gentry to the other, in order to polish themselves by seeing the world, and understanding men and manners; there are few persons of distinction, or merchants, or seamen, who dwell in the maritime parts, but what can hold conversation in both tongues; as I found some weeks after, when I went to pay my respects to the emperor of Blefuscu, which, in the midst of great misfortunes, through the malice of my enemies, proved a very happy adventure to me, as I shall relate in its proper place.

The reader may remember, that when I signed those articles upon which I recovered my liberty, there were some which I disliked, upon account of their being too servile; neither could anything but an extreme necessity have forced me to submit. But being now a *nardac* of the highest rank in that empire, such offices were looked upon as below my dignity, and the emperor (to do him justice), never once mentioned them to me. However, it was not long before I had an opportunity of doing his majesty, at least as I then thought, a most signal service. I was alarmed at midnight with the cries of many hundred people at my door; by which, being suddenly awaked, I was in some kind of terror. I heard the word *Burglum* repeated incessantly: several of the emperor's court, making their way through the crowd, entreated me to come immediately to the palace, where her imperial majesty's apartment was on fire, by the carelessness of a maid of honour, who fell asleep while she was reading a romance. I got up in an instant; and orders being given to clear the way before me, and it being likewise a moonshine night, I made a shift to get to the palace without trampling on any of the people. I found they had already applied ladders to the walls of the apartment, and were well provided with buckets, but the water was at some distance. These buckets were about the size of large thimbles, and the poor people supplied me with them as fast as they could: but the flame was so violent that they did little good. I might easily have stifled it with my coat, which I unfortunately left behind me for haste, and came away only in my leathern jerkin. The case seemed wholly desperate and deplorable; and this magnificent palace would have infallibly been burnt down to the ground, if, by a presence of mind unusual to me, I had not suddenly thought of an expedient. I had, the evening before, drunk plentifully of a most delicious wine called *glimigrim*, (the Blefuscudians call it *flunec*, but ours is esteemed the better sort,) which is very diuretic. By the luckiest chance in the world, I had not discharged myself of any part of it. The heat I had contracted by coming very near the flames, and by labouring to quench them, made the wine begin to operate by urine; which I voided in such a quantity, and applied so well to the proper places, that in three minutes the fire was wholly extinguished, and the rest of that noble pile, which had cost so many ages in erecting, preserved from destruction.

It was now day-light, and I returned to my house without waiting to congratulate with the emperor: because, although I had done a very eminent piece of service, yet I could not tell how his majesty might resent the manner by which I had performed it: for, by the fundamental laws of the realm, it is capital in any person, of what quality soever, to make water within the precincts of the palace. But I was a little comforted by a message from his majesty, "that he would give orders to the grand justiciary for passing my pardon in form:" which, however, I could not obtain; and I was privately assured, "that the empress, conceiving the greatest abhorrence of what I had done, removed to the most distant side of the court, firmly resolved that those buildings should never be repaired for her use: and, in the presence of her chief confidents could not forbear vowing revenge."

CHAPTER SIX

Of the inhabitants of Lilliput; their learning, laws, and customs; the manner of educating their children. The author's way of living in that country. His vindication of a great lady.

ALTHOUGH I INTEND to leave the description of this empire to a particular treatise, yet, in the mean time, I am content to gratify the curious reader with some general ideas. As the common size of the natives is somewhat under six inches high, so there is an exact proportion in all other animals, as well as plants and trees: for instance, the tallest horses and oxen are between four and five inches in height, the sheep an inch and half, more or less: their geese about the bigness of a sparrow, and so the several gradations downwards till you come to the smallest, which to my sight, were almost invisible; but nature has adapted the eyes of the Lilliputians to all objects proper for their view: they see with great exactness, but at no great distance. And, to show the sharpness of their sight towards objects that are near, I have been much pleased with observing a cook pulling a lark, which was not so large as a common fly; and a young girl threading an invisible needle with invisible silk. Their tallest trees are about seven feet high: I mean some of those in the great royal park, the tops whereof I could but just reach with my fist clenched. The other vegetables are in the same proportion; but this I leave to the reader's imagination.

I shall say but little at present of their learning, which, for many ages, has flourished in all its branches among them: but their manner of writing is very peculiar, being neither from the left to the right, like the Europeans, nor from the right to the left, like the Arabians, nor from up to down, like the Chinese, but aslant, from one corner of the paper to the other, like ladies in England.

They bury their dead with their heads directly downward, because they hold an opinion, that in eleven thousand moons they are all to rise again; in which period the earth (which they conceive to be flat) will turn upside down, and by this means they shall, at their resurrection, be found ready standing on their feet. The learned among them confess the absurdity of this doctrine; but the practice still continues, in compliance to the vulgar.

There are some laws and customs in this empire very peculiar; and if they were not so directly contrary to those of my own dear country, I should be tempted to say a little in their justification. It is only to be wished they were as well executed. The first I shall mention, relates to informers. All crimes against the state, are punished here with the utmost severity; but, if the person accused makes his innocence plainly to appear upon his trial, the accuser is immediately put to an ignominious death; and out of his goods or lands the innocent person is quadruply recompensed for the loss of his time, for the danger he underwent, for the hardship of his imprisonment, and for all the charges he has been at in making his defence; or, if that fund be deficient, it is largely supplied by the crown. The emperor also confers on him some public mark of his favour, and proclamation is made of his innocence through the whole city.

They look upon fraud as a greater crime than theft, and therefore seldom fail to punish it with death; for they allege, that care and vigilance, with a very common understanding, may preserve a man's goods from thieves, but honesty has no defence against superior cunning; and, since it is necessary that there should be a perpetual intercourse of buying and selling, and dealing upon credit, where fraud is permitted and connived at, or has no law to punish it, the honest dealer is always undone, and the knave gets the advantage. I remember, when I was once interceding with the emperor for a criminal who had wronged his master of a great sum of money, which he had received by order and ran away with; and happening to tell his majesty, by way of extenuation, that it was only a breach of trust, the emperor thought it monstrous in me to offer as a defence the greatest aggravation of the crime; and truly I had little to say in return, farther than the common answer, that different nations had different customs; for, I confess, I was heartily ashamed.[2]

Although we usually call reward and punishment the two hinges upon which all government turns, yet I could never observe this maxim to be put in practice by any nation except that of Lilliput. Whoever can there bring sufficient proof, that he has strictly observed the laws of his country for seventy-three moons, has a claim to certain privileges, according to his quality or condition of life, with a proportion-

2 An act of parliament has been since passed by which some breaches of trust have been made capital.

able sum of money out of a fund appropriated for that use: he likewise acquires the title of *snilpall*, or legal, which is added to his name, but does not descend to his posterity. And these people thought it a prodigious defect of policy among us, when I told them that our laws were enforced only by penalties, without any mention of reward. It is upon this account that the image of Justice, in their courts of judicature, is formed with six eyes, two before, as many behind, and on each side one, to signify circumspection; with a bag of gold open in her right hand, and a sword sheathed in her left, to show she is more disposed to reward than to punish.

In choosing persons for all employments, they have more regard to good morals than to great abilities; for, since government is necessary to mankind, they believe, that the common size of human understanding is fitted to some station or other; and that Providence never intended to make the management of public affairs a mystery to be comprehended only by a few persons of sublime genius, of which there seldom are three born in an age: but they suppose truth, justice, temperance, and the like, to be in every man's power; the practice of which virtues, assisted by experience and a good intention, would qualify any man for the service of his country, except where a course of study is required. But they thought the want of moral virtues was so far from being supplied by superior endowments of the mind, that employments could never be put into such dangerous hands as those of persons so qualified; and, at least, that the mistakes committed by ignorance, in a virtuous disposition, would never be of such fatal consequence to the public weal, as the practices of a man, whose inclinations led him to be corrupt, and who had great abilities to manage, to multiply, and defend his corruptions.

In like manner, the disbelief of a Divine Providence renders a man incapable of holding any public station; for, since kings avow themselves to be the deputies of Providence, the Lilliputians think nothing can be more absurd than for a prince to employ such men as disown the authority under which he acts.

In relating these and the following laws, I would only be understood to mean the original institutions, and not the most scandalous corruptions, into which these people are fallen by the degenerate nature of man. For, as to that infamous practice of acquiring great employments by dancing on the ropes, or badges of favour and distinction by leaping over sticks and creeping under them, the reader is to observe, that they were first introduced by the grandfather of the emperor now reigning, and grew to the present height by the gradual increase of party and faction.

Ingratitude is among them a capital crime, as we read it to have been in some other countries: for they reason thus; that whoever makes ill returns to his benefactor, must needs be a common enemy to the rest of mankind, from whom he has received no obligation, and therefore such a man is not fit to live.

Their notions relating to the duties of parents and children differ extremely from ours. For, since the conjunction of male and female is founded upon the great law of nature, in order to propagate and continue the species, the Lilliputians will needs have it, that men and women are joined together, like other animals, by the motives of concupiscence; and that their tenderness towards their young proceeds from the like natural principle: for which reason they will never allow that a child is under any obligation to his father for begetting him, or to his mother for bringing him into the world; which, considering the miseries of human life, was neither a benefit in itself, nor intended so by his parents, whose thoughts, in their love encounters, were otherwise employed. Upon these, and the like reasonings, their opinion is, that parents are the last of all others to be trusted with the education of their own children; and therefore they have in every town public nurseries, where all parents, except cottagers and labourers, are obliged to send their infants of both sexes to be reared and educated, when they come to the age of twenty moons, at which time they are supposed to have some rudiments of docility. These schools are of several kinds, suited to different qualities, and both sexes. They have certain professors well skilled in preparing children for such a condition of life as befits the rank of their parents, and their own capacities, as well as inclinations. I shall first say something of the male nurseries, and then of the female.

The nurseries for males of noble or eminent birth, are provided with grave and learned professors, and their several deputies. The clothes and food of the children are plain and simple. They are bred up in the principles of honour, justice, courage, modesty, clemency, religion, and love of their country; they are always employed in some business, except in the times of eating and sleeping, which are very short, and two hours for diversions consisting of bodily exercises. They are dressed by men till four years of age, and then are obliged to dress themselves, although their quality be ever so great; and the women attendant, who are aged proportionably to ours at fifty, perform only the most menial offices. They are never suffered to converse with servants, but go together in smaller or greater numbers to take their diversions, and always in the presence of a professor, or one of his deputies; whereby they avoid those early bad impressions of folly and vice, to which our children are subject. Their parents are suffered to see them only twice a year; the visit is to last but an hour; they are allowed to kiss the child at meeting and parting; but a professor, who always stands by on those occasions, will not suffer them to whisper, or use any fondling expressions, or bring any presents of toys, sweetmeats, and the like.

The pension from each family for the education and entertainment of a child, upon failure of due payment, is levied by the emperor's officers.

The nurseries for children of ordinary gentlemen, merchants, traders, and handicrafts, are managed proportionably after the same manner; only those designed for trades are put out apprentices at eleven years old, whereas those of persons of quality continue in their exercises till fifteen, which answers to twenty-one with us: but the confinement is gradually lessened for the last three years.

In the female nurseries, the young girls of quality are educated much like the males, only they are dressed by orderly servants of their own sex; but always in the presence of a professor or deputy, till they come to dress themselves, which is at five years old. And if it be found that these nurses ever presume to entertain the girls with frightful or foolish stories, or the common follies practised by chambermaids among us, they are publicly whipped thrice about the city, imprisoned for a year, and banished for life to the most desolate part of the country. Thus the young ladies are as much ashamed of being cowards and fools as the men, and despise all personal ornaments, beyond decency and cleanliness: neither did I perceive any difference in their education made by their difference of sex, only that the exercises of the females were not altogether so robust; and that some rules were given them relating to domestic life, and a smaller compass of learning was enjoined them: for their maxim is, that among peoples of quality, a wife should be always a reasonable and agreeable companion, because she cannot always be young. When the girls are twelve years old, which among them is the marriageable age, their parents or guardians take them home, with great expressions of gratitude to the professors, and seldom without tears of the young lady and her companions.

In the nurseries of females of the meaner sort, the children are instructed in all kinds of works proper for their sex, and their several degrees: those intended for apprentices are dismissed at seven years old, the rest are kept to eleven.

The meaner families who have children at these nurseries, are obliged, besides their annual pension, which is as low as possible, to return to the steward of the nursery a small monthly share of their gettings, to be a portion for the child; and therefore all parents are limited in their expenses by the law. For the Lilliputians think nothing can be more unjust, than for people, in subservience to their own appetites, to bring children into the world, and leave the burthen of supporting them on the public. As to persons of quality, they give security to appropriate a certain sum for each child, suitable to their condition; and these funds are always managed with good husbandry and the most exact justice.

The cottagers and labourers keep their children at home, their business being only to till and cultivate the earth, and therefore their education is of little consequence to the public: but the old and diseased among them, are supported by hospitals; for begging is a trade unknown in this empire.

And here it may, perhaps, divert the curious reader, to give some account of my domestics, and my manner of living in this country, during a residence of nine months, and thirteen days. Having a head mechanically turned, and being likewise forced by necessity, I had made for myself a table and chair convenient enough, out of the largest trees in the royal park. Two hundred sempstresses were employed to make me shirts, and linen for my bed and table, all of the strongest and coarsest kind they could get; which, however, they were forced to quilt together in several folds, for the thickest was some degrees finer than lawn. Their linen is usually three inches wide, and three feet make a piece. The sempstresses took my measure as I lay on the ground, one standing at my neck, and another at my mid-leg, with a strong cord extended, that each held by the end, while a third measured the length of the cord with a rule of an inch long. Then they measured my right thumb, and desired no more; for by a mathematical computation, that twice round the thumb is once round the wrist, and so on to the neck and the waist, and by the help of my old shirt, which I displayed on the ground before them for a pattern, they fitted me exactly. Three hundred tailors were employed in the same manner to make me clothes; but they had another contrivance for taking my measure. I kneeled down, and they raised a ladder from the ground to my neck; upon this ladder one of them mounted, and let fall a plumb-line from my collar to the floor, which just answered the length of my coat: but my waist and arms I measured myself. When my clothes were finished, which was done in my house (for the largest of theirs would not have been able to hold them), they looked like the patch-work made by the ladies in England, only that mine were all of a colour.

I had three hundred cooks to dress my victuals, in little convenient huts built about my house, where they and their families lived, and prepared me two dishes a-piece. I took up twenty waiters in my hand,

and placed them on the table: a hundred more attended below on the ground, some with dishes of meat, and some with barrels of wine and other liquors slung on their shoulders; all which the waiters above drew up, as I wanted, in a very ingenious manner, by certain cords, as we draw the bucket up a well in Europe. A dish of their meat was a good mouthful, and a barrel of their liquor a reasonable draught. Their mutton yields to ours, but their beef is excellent. I have had a sirloin so large, that I have been forced to make three bites of it; but this is rare. My servants were astonished to see me eat it, bones and all, as in our country we do the leg of a lark. Their geese and turkeys I usually ate at a mouthful, and I confess they far exceed ours. Of their smaller fowl I could take up twenty or thirty at the end of my knife.

One day his imperial majesty, being informed of my way of living, desired "that himself and his royal consort, with the young princes of the blood of both sexes, might have the happiness," as he was pleased to call it, "of dining with me." They came accordingly, and I placed them in chairs of state, upon my table, just over against me, with their guards about them. Flimnap, the lord high treasurer, attended there likewise with his white staff; and I observed he often looked on me with a sour countenance, which I would not seem to regard, but ate more than usual, in honour to my dear country, as well as to fill the court with admiration. I have some private reasons to believe, that this visit from his majesty gave Flimnap an opportunity of doing me ill offices to his master. That minister had always been my secret enemy, though he outwardly caressed me more than was usual to the moroseness of his nature. He represented to the emperor "the low condition of his treasury; that he was forced to take up money at a great discount; that exchequer bills would not circulate under nine per cent. below par; that I had cost his majesty above a million and a half of *sprugs*" (their greatest gold coin, about the bigness of a spangle) "and, upon the whole, that it would be advisable in the emperor to take the first fair occasion of dismissing me."

I am here obliged to vindicate the reputation of an excellent lady, who was an innocent sufferer upon my account. The treasurer took a fancy to be jealous of his wife, from the malice of some evil tongues, who informed him that her grace had taken a violent affection for my person; and the court scandal ran for some time, that she once came privately to my lodging. This I solemnly declare to be a most infamous falsehood, without any grounds, further than that her grace was pleased to treat me with all innocent marks of freedom and friendship. I own she came often to my house, but always publicly, nor ever without three more in the coach, who were usually her sister and young daughter, and some particular acquaintance; but this was common to many other ladies of the court. And I still appeal to my servants round, whether they at any time saw a coach at my door, without knowing what persons were in it. On those occasions, when a servant had given me notice, my custom was to go immediately to the door, and, after paying my respects, to take up the coach and two horses very carefully in my hands (for, if there were six horses, the postillion always unharnessed four,) and place them on a table, where I had fixed a movable rim quite round, of five inches high, to prevent accidents. And I have often had four coaches and horses at once on my table, full of company, while I sat in my chair, leaning my face towards them; and when I was engaged with one set, the coachmen would gently drive the others round my table. I have passed many an afternoon very agreeably in these conversations. But I defy the treasurer, or his two informers (I will name them, and let them make the best of it) Clustril and Drunlo, to prove that any person ever came to me *incognito*, except the secretary Reldresal, who was sent by express command of his imperial majesty, as I have before related. I should not have dwelt so long upon this particular, if it had not been a point wherein the reputation of a great lady is so nearly concerned, to say nothing of my own; though I then had the honour to be a *nardac*, which the treasurer himself is not; for all the world knows, that he is only a *glumglum*, a title inferior by one degree, as that of a marquis is to a duke in England; yet I allow he preceded me in right of his post. These false informations, which I afterwards came to the knowledge of by an accident not proper to mention, made the treasurer show his lady for some time an ill countenance, and me a worse; and although he was at last undeceived and reconciled to her, yet I lost all credit with him, and found my interest decline very fast with the emperor himself, who was, indeed, too much governed by that favourite.

CHAPTER SEVEN

The author, being informed of a design to accuse him of high-treason, makes his escape to Blefuscu. His reception there.

Before I proceed to give an account of my leaving this kingdom, it may be proper to inform the reader of a private intrigue which had been for two months forming against me.

I had been hitherto, all my life, a stranger to courts, for which I was unqualified by the meanness of my condition. I had indeed heard and read enough of the dispositions of great princes and ministers, but never expected to have found such terrible effects of them, in so remote a country, governed, as I thought, by very different maxims from those in Europe.

When I was just preparing to pay my attendance on the emperor of Blefuscu, a considerable person at court (to whom I had been very serviceable, at a time when he lay under the highest displeasure of his imperial majesty) came to my house very privately at night, in a close chair, and, without sending his name, desired admittance. The chairmen were dismissed; I put the chair, with his lordship in it, into my coat-pocket: and, giving orders to a trusty servant, to say I was indisposed and gone to sleep, I fastened the door of my house, placed the chair on the table, according to my usual custom, and sat down by it. After the common salutations were over, observing his lordship's countenance full of concern, and inquiring into the reason, he desired "I would hear him with patience, in a matter that highly concerned my honour and my life." His speech was to the following effect, for I took notes of it as soon as he left me: –

"You are to know," said he, "that several committees of council have been lately called, in the most private manner, on your account; and it is but two days since his majesty came to a full resolution.

"You are very sensible that Skyresh Bolgolam" (*galbet*, or high-admiral) "has been your mortal enemy, almost ever since your arrival. His original reasons I know not; but his hatred is increased since your great success against Blefuscu, by which his glory as admiral is much obscured. This lord, in conjunction with Flimnap the high-treasurer, whose enmity against you is notorious on account of his lady, Limtoc the general, Lalcon the chamberlain, and Balmuff the grand justiciary, have prepared articles of impeachment against you, for treason and other capital crimes."

This preface made me so impatient, being conscious of my own merits and innocence, that I was going to interrupt him; when he entreated me to be silent, and thus proceeded: –

"Out of gratitude for the favours you have done me, I procured information of the whole proceedings, and a copy of the articles; wherein I venture my head for your service.

"'*Articles of Impeachment against* QUINBUS FLESTRIN, (*the Man-Mountain.*)

Article I.

"'Whereas, by a statute made in the reign of his imperial majesty Calin Deffar Plune, it is enacted, that, whoever shall make water within the precincts of the royal palace, shall be liable to the pains and penalties of high-treason; notwithstanding, the said Quinbus Flestrin, in open breach of the said law, under colour of extinguishing the fire kindled in the apartment of his majesty's most dear imperial consort, did maliciously, traitorously, and devilishly, by discharge of his urine, put out the said fire kindled in the said apartment, lying and being within the precincts of the said royal palace, against the statute in that case provided, etc. against the duty, etc.

Article II.

"'That the said Quinbus Flestrin, having brought the imperial fleet of Blefuscu into the royal port, and being afterwards commanded by his imperial majesty to seize all the other ships of the said empire of Blefuscu, and reduce that empire to a province, to be governed by a viceroy from hence, and to destroy and put to death, not only all the Big-endian exiles, but likewise all the people of that empire who would not immediately forsake the Big-endian heresy, he, the said Flestrin, like a false traitor against his most auspicious, serene, imperial majesty, did petition to be excused from the said service, upon pretence of unwillingness to force the consciences, or destroy the liberties and lives of an innocent people.

Article III.

"'That, whereas certain ambassadors arrived from the Court of Blefuscu, to sue for peace in his majesty's court, he, the said Flestrin, did, like a false traitor, aid, abet, comfort, and divert, the said ambassadors, although he knew them to be servants to a prince who was lately an open enemy to his imperial majesty, and in an open war against his said majesty.

Article IV.

"'That the said Quinbus Flestrin, contrary to the duty of a faithful subject, is now preparing to make a voyage to the court and empire of

Blefuscu, for which he has received only verbal license from his imperial majesty; and, under colour of the said license, does falsely and traitorously intend to take the said voyage, and thereby to aid, comfort, and abet the emperor of Blefuscu, so lately an enemy, and in open war with his imperial majesty aforesaid.'

"There are some other articles; but these are the most important, of which I have read you an abstract.

"In the several debates upon this impeachment, it must be confessed that his majesty gave many marks of his great lenity; often urging the services you had done him, and endeavouring to extenuate your crimes. The treasurer and admiral insisted that you should be put to the most painful and ignominious death, by setting fire to your house at night, and the general was to attend with twenty thousand men, armed with poisoned arrows, to shoot you on the face and hands. Some of your servants were to have private orders to strew a poisonous juice on your shirts and sheets, which would soon make you tear your own flesh, and die in the utmost torture. The general came into the same opinion; so that for a long time there was a majority against you; but his majesty resolving, if possible, to spare your life, at last brought off the chamberlain.

"Upon this incident, Reldresal, principal secretary for private affairs, who always approved himself your true friend, was commanded by the emperor to deliver his opinion, which he accordingly did; and therein justified the good thoughts you have of him. He allowed your crimes to be great, but that still there was room for mercy, the most commendable virtue in a prince, and for which his majesty was so justly celebrated. He said, the friendship between you and him was so well known to the world, that perhaps the most honourable board might think him partial; however, in obedience to the command he had received, he would freely offer his sentiments. That if his majesty, in consideration of your services, and pursuant to his own merciful disposition, would please to spare your life, and only give orders to put out both your eyes, he humbly conceived, that by this expedient justice might in some measure be satisfied, and all the world would applaud the lenity of the emperor, as well as the fair and generous proceedings of those who have the honour to be his counsellors. That the loss of your eyes would be no impediment to your bodily strength, by which you might still be useful to his majesty; that blindness is an addition to courage, by concealing dangers from us; that the fear you had for your eyes, was the greatest difficulty in bringing over the enemy's fleet, and it would be sufficient for you to see by the eyes of the ministers, since the greatest princes do no more.

"This proposal was received with the utmost disapprobation by the whole board. Bolgolam, the admiral, could not preserve his temper, but, rising up in fury, said, he wondered how the secretary durst presume to give his opinion for preserving the life of a traitor; that the services you had performed were, by all true reasons of state, the great aggravation of your crimes; that you, who were able to extinguish the fire by discharge of urine in her majesty's apartment (which he mentioned with horror), might, at another time, raise an inundation by the same means, to drown the whole palace; and the same strength which enabled you to bring over the enemy's fleet, might serve, upon the first discontent, to carry it back; that he had good reasons to think you were a Big-endian in your heart; and, as treason begins in the heart, before it appears in overt-acts, so he accused you as a traitor on that account, and therefore insisted you should be put to death.

"The treasurer was of the same opinion: he showed to what straits his majesty's revenue was reduced, by the charge of maintaining you, which would soon grow insupportable; that the secretary's expedient of putting out your eyes, was so far from being a remedy against this evil, that it would probably increase it, as is manifest from the common practice of blinding some kind of fowls, after which they fed the faster, and grew sooner fat; that his sacred majesty and the council, who are your judges, were, in their own consciences, fully convinced of your guilt, which was a sufficient argument to condemn you to death, without the formal proofs required by the strict letter of the law.

"But his imperial majesty, fully determined against capital punishment, was graciously pleased to say, that since the council thought the loss of your eyes too easy a censure, some other way may be inflicted hereafter. And your friend the secretary, humbly desiring to be heard again, in answer to what the treasurer had objected, concerning the great charge his majesty was at in maintaining you, said, that his excellency, who had the sole disposal of the emperor's revenue, might easily provide against that evil, by gradually lessening your establishment; by which, for want of sufficient for you would grow weak and faint, and lose your appetite, and consequently, decay, and consume in a few months; neither would the stench of your carcass be then so dangerous, when it should become more than half diminished; and immediately upon your death five or six thousand of his majesty's subjects might, in two or three days, cut your flesh from your bones, take it away by cart-loads, and bury it in distant parts, to prevent infection, leaving the skeleton as a monument of admiration to posterity.

"Thus, by the great friendship of the secretary, the whole affair was compromised. It was strictly enjoined, that the project of starving you by degrees should be kept a secret; but the sentence of putting out your eyes was entered on the books; none dissenting, except Bolgolam the admiral, who, being a creature of the empress, was perpetually instigated by her majesty to insist upon your death, she having borne perpetual malice against you, on account of that infamous and illegal method you took to extinguish the fire in her apartment.

"In three days your friend the secretary will be directed to come to your house, and read before you the articles of impeachment; and then to signify the great lenity and favour of his majesty and council, whereby you are only condemned to the loss of your eyes, which his majesty does not question you will gratefully and humbly submit to; and twenty of his majesty's surgeons will attend, in order to see the operation well performed, by discharging very sharp-pointed arrows into the balls of your eyes, as you lie on the ground.

"I leave to your prudence what measures you will take; and to avoid suspicion, I must immediately return in as private a manner as I came."

His lordship did so; and I remained alone, under many doubts and perplexities of mind.

It was a custom introduced by this prince and his ministry (very different, as I have been assured, from the practice of former times,) that after the court had decreed any cruel execution, either to gratify the monarch's resentment, or the malice of a favourite, the emperor always made a speech to his whole council, expressing his great lenity and tenderness, as qualities known and confessed by all the world. This speech was immediately published throughout the kingdom; nor did any thing terrify the people so much as those encomiums on his majesty's mercy; because it was observed, that the more these praises were enlarged and insisted on, the more inhuman was the punishment, and the sufferer more innocent. Yet, as to myself, I must confess, having never been designed for a courtier, either by my birth or education, I was so ill a judge of things, that I could not discover the lenity and favour of this sentence, but conceived it (perhaps erroneously) rather to be rigorous than gentle. I sometimes thought of standing my trial, for, although I could not deny the facts alleged in the several articles, yet I hoped they would admit of some extenuation. But having in my life perused many state-trials, which I ever observed to terminate as the judges thought fit to direct, I durst not rely on so dangerous a decision, in so critical a juncture, and against such powerful enemies. Once I was strongly bent upon resistance, for, while I had liberty the whole strength of that empire could hardly subdue me, and I might easily with stones pelt the metropolis to pieces; but I soon rejected that project with horror, by remembering the oath I had made to the emperor, the favours

I received from him, and the high title of *nardac* he conferred upon me. Neither had I so soon learned the gratitude of courtiers, to persuade myself, that his majesty's present seventies acquitted me of all past obligations.

At last, I fixed upon a resolution, for which it is probable I may incur some censure, and not unjustly; for I confess I owe the preserving of mine eyes, and consequently my liberty, to my own great rashness and want of experience; because, if I had then known the nature of princes and ministers, which I have since observed in many other courts, and their methods of treating criminals less obnoxious than myself, I should, with great alacrity and readiness, have submitted to so easy a punishment. But hurried on by the precipitancy of youth, and having his imperial majesty's license to pay my attendance upon the emperor of Blefuscu, I took this opportunity, before the three days were elapsed, to send a letter to my friend the secretary, signifying my resolution of setting out that morning for Blefuscu, pursuant to the leave I had got; and, without waiting for an answer, I went to that side of the island where our fleet lay. I seized a large man of war, tied a cable to the prow, and, lifting up the anchors, I stripped myself, put my clothes (together with my coverlet, which I carried under my arm) into the vessel, and, drawing it after me, between wading and swimming arrived at the royal port of Blefuscu, where the people had long expected me: they lent me two guides to direct me to the capital city, which is of the same name. I held them in my hands, till I came within two hundred yards of the gate, and desired them "to signify my arrival to one of the secretaries, and let him know, I there waited his majesty's command." I had an answer in about an hour, "that his majesty, attended by the royal family, and great officers of the court, was coming out to receive me." I advanced a hundred yards. The emperor and his train alighted from their horses, the empress and ladies from their coaches, and I did not perceive they were in any fright or concern. I lay on the ground to kiss his majesty's and the empress's hands. I told his majesty, "that I was come according to my promise, and with the license of the emperor my master, to have the honour of seeing so mighty a monarch, and to offer him any service in my power, consistent with my duty to my own prince;" not mentioning a word of my disgrace, because I had hitherto no regular information of it, and might suppose myself wholly ignorant of any such design; neither could I reasonably conceive that the emperor would discover the secret, while I was out of his power; wherein, however, it soon appeared I was deceived.

I shall not trouble the reader with the particular account of my reception at this court, which was suitable to the generosity of so great a prince; nor of the difficulties I was in for want of a house and bed, being forced to lie on the ground, wrapped up in my coverlet.

CHAPTER EIGHT

The author, by a lucky accident, finds means to leave Blefuscu; and, after some difficulties, returns safe to his native country.

THREE DAYS after my arrival, walking out of curiosity to the north-east coast of the island, I observed, about half a league off in the sea, somewhat that looked like a boat overturned. I pulled off my shoes and stockings, and, wailing two or three hundred yards, I found the object to approach nearer by force of the tide; and then plainly saw it to be a real boat, which I supposed might by some tempest have been driven from a ship. Whereupon, I returned immediately towards the city, and desired his imperial majesty to lend me twenty of the tallest vessels he had left, after the loss of his fleet, and three thousand seamen, under the command of his vice-admiral. This fleet sailed round, while I went back the shortest way to the coast, where I first discovered the boat. I found the tide had driven it still nearer. The seamen were all provided with cordage, which I had beforehand twisted to a sufficient strength. When the ships came up, I stripped myself, and waded till I came within a hundred yards off the boat, after which I was forced to swim till I got up to it. The seamen threw me the end of the cord, which I fastened to a hole in the fore-part of the boat, and the other end to a man of war; but I found all my labour to little purpose; for, being out of my depth, I was not able to work. In this necessity I was forced to swim behind, and push the boat forward, as often as I could, with one of my hands; and the tide favouring me, I advanced so far that I could just hold up my chin and feel the ground. I rested two or three minutes, and then gave the boat another shove, and so on, till the sea was no higher than my arm-pits; and now, the most laborious part being over, I took out my other cables, which were stowed in one of the ships, and fastened them first to the boat, and then to nine of the vessels which attended me; the wind being favourable, the seamen towed, and I shoved, until we arrived within forty yards of the shore; and, waiting till the tide was out, I got dry to the boat, and by the assistance of two thousand men, with ropes and engines, I made a shift to turn it on its bottom, and found it was but little damaged.

I shall not trouble the reader with the difficulties I was under, by the help of certain paddles, which cost me ten days making, to get my boat to the royal port of Blefuscu, where a mighty concourse of people appeared upon my arrival, full of wonder at the sight of so prodigious a vessel. I told the emperor "that my good fortune had thrown this boat in my way, to carry me to some place whence I might return into my native country; and begged his majesty's orders for getting materials to fit it up, together with his license to depart;" which, after some kind expostulations, he was pleased to grant.

I did very much wonder, in all this time, not to have heard of any express relating to me from our emperor to the court of Blefuscu. But I was afterward given privately to understand, that his imperial majesty, never imagining I had the least notice of his designs, believed I was only gone to Blefuscu in performance of my promise, according to the license he had given me, which was well known at our court, and would return in a few days, when the ceremony was ended. But he was at last in pain at my long absence; and after consulting with the treasurer and the rest of that cabal, a person of quality was dispatched with the copy of the articles against me. This envoy had instructions to represent to the monarch of Blefuscu, "the great lenity of his master, who was content to punish me no farther than with the loss of mine eyes; that I had fled from justice; and if I did not return in two hours, I should be deprived of my title of *nardac*, and declared a traitor." The envoy further added, "that in order to maintain the peace and amity between both empires, his master expected that his brother of Blefuscu would give orders to have me sent back to Lilliput, bound hand and foot, to be punished as a traitor."

The emperor of Blefuscu, having taken three days to consult, returned an answer consisting of many civilities and excuses. He said, "that as for sending me bound, his brother knew it was impossible; that, although I had deprived him of his fleet, yet he owed great obligations to me for many good offices I had done him in making the peace. That, however, both their majesties would soon be made easy; for I had found a prodigious vessel on the shore, able to carry me on the sea, which he had given orders to fit up, with my own assistance and direction; and he hoped, in a few weeks, both empires would be freed from so insupportable an encumbrance."

With this answer the envoy returned to Lilliput; and the monarch of Blefuscu related to me all that had passed; offering me at the same time (but under the strictest confidence) his gracious protection, if I would continue in his service; wherein, although I believed him sincere, yet I resolved never more to put any confidence in princes or ministers, where I could possibly avoid it; and therefore, with all due acknowledgments for his favourable intentions, I humbly begged to be excused. I told him, "that since fortune, whether good or evil, had thrown a vessel in my way, I was resolved to venture myself on the ocean, rather than be an occasion of difference between two such mighty monarchs." Neither did I find the emperor at all displeased; and I discovered, by a certain accident, that he was very glad of my resolution, and so were most of his ministers.

These considerations moved me to hasten my departure somewhat sooner than I intended; to which the court, impatient to have me gone, very readily contributed. Five hundred workmen were employed to make two sails to my boat, according to my directions, by quilting thirteen folds of their strongest linen together. I was at the pains of making ropes and cables, by twisting ten, twenty, or thirty of the thickest and strongest of theirs. A great stone that I happened to find, after a long search, by the sea-shore, served me for an anchor. I had the tallow of three hundred cows, for greasing my boat, and other uses. I was at incredible pains in cutting down some of the largest timber-trees, for oars and masts, wherein I was, however, much assisted by his majesty's ship-carpenters, who helped me in smoothing them, after I had done the rough work.

In about a month, when all was prepared, I sent to receive his majesty's commands, and to take my leave. The emperor and royal family came out of the palace; I lay down on my face to kiss his hand, which he very graciously gave me: so did the empress and young princes of the blood. His majesty presented me with fifty purses of two hundred *sprugs* a-piece, together with his picture at full length, which I put immediately into one of my gloves, to keep it from being hurt. The ceremonies at my departure were too many to trouble the reader with at this time.

I stored the boat with the carcases of a hundred oxen, and three hundred sheep, with bread and drink proportionable, and as much meat ready dressed as four hundred cooks could provide. I took with me six cows and two bulls alive, with as many ewes and rams, intending to carry them into my own country, and propagate the breed. And to feed them on board, I had a good bundle of hay, and a bag of corn. I would gladly have taken a dozen of the natives, but this was a thing the emperor would by no means permit; and, besides a diligent search into my pockets, his majesty engaged my honour "not to carry away any of his subjects, although with their own consent and desire."

Having thus prepared all things as well as I was able, I set sail on the twenty-fourth day of September 1701, at six in the morning; and when I had gone about four-leagues to the northward, the wind being at south-east, at six in the evening I descried a small island, about half a league to the north-west. I advanced forward, and cast anchor on the lee-side of the island, which seemed to be uninhabited. I then took some refreshment, and went to my rest. I slept well, and as I conjectured at least six hours, for I found the day broke in two hours after I awaked. It was a clear night. I ate my breakfast before the sun was up; and heaving anchor, the wind being favourable, I steered the same course that I had done the day before, wherein I was directed by my pocket compass. My intention was to reach, if possible, one of those islands which I had reason to believe lay to the north-east of Van Diemen's Land. I discovered nothing all that day; but upon the next, about three in the afternoon, when I had by my computation made twenty-four leagues from Blefuscu, I descried a sail steering to the south-east; my course was due east. I hailed her, but could get no answer; yet I found I gained upon her, for the wind slackened. I made all the sail I could, and in half an hour she spied me, then hung out her ancient, and discharged a gun. It is not easy to express the joy I was in, upon the unexpected hope of once more seeing my beloved country, and the dear pledges I left in it. The ship slackened her sails, and I came up with her between five and six in the evening, September 26th; but my heart leaped within me to see her English colours. I put my cows and sheep into my coat-pockets, and got on board with all my little cargo of provisions. The vessel was an English merchantman, returning from Japan by the North and South seas; the captain, Mr. John Biddel, of Deptford, a very civil man, and an excellent sailor.

We were now in the latitude of 30 degrees south; there were about fifty men in the ship; and here I met an old comrade of mine, one Peter Williams, who gave me a good character to the captain. This gentleman treated me with kindness, and desired I would let him know what place I came from last, and whither I was bound; which I did in a few words, but he thought I was raving, and that the dangers I underwent had disturbed my head; whereupon I took my black cattle and sheep out of my pocket, which, after great astonishment, clearly convinced him of my veracity. I then showed him the gold given me by the emperor of Blefuscu, together with his majesty's picture at full length, and some other rarities of that country. I gave him two purses of two hundreds *sprugs* each, and promised, when we arrived in England, to make him a present of a cow and a sheep big with young.

I shall not trouble the reader with a particular account of this voyage, which was very prosperous for the most part. We arrived in the Downs on the 13th of April, 1702. I had only one misfortune, that the rats on board carried away one of my sheep; I found her bones in a hole, picked clean from the flesh. The rest of my cattle I got safe ashore, and set them a-grazing in a bowling-green at Greenwich, where the fineness of the grass made them feed very heartily, though I had always feared the contrary: neither could I possibly have preserved them in so long a voyage, if the captain had not allowed me some of his best biscuit, which, rubbed to powder, and mingled with water, was their constant food. The short time I continued in England, I made a considerable profit by showing my cattle to many persons of quality and others: and before I began my second voyage, I sold them for six hundred pounds. Since my last return I find the breed is considerably increased, especially the sheep, which I hope will prove much to the advantage of the woollen manufacture, by the fineness of the fleeces.

I stayed but two months with my wife and family, for my insatiable desire of seeing foreign countries, would suffer me to continue no longer. I left fifteen hundred pounds with my wife, and fixed her in a good house at Redriff. My remaining stock I carried with me, part in money and part in goods, in hopes to improve my fortunes. My eldest uncle John had left me an estate in land, near Epping, of about thirty pounds a-year; and I had a long lease of the Black Bull in Fetter-Lane, which yielded me as much more; so that I was not in any danger of leaving my family upon the parish. My son Johnny, named so after his uncle, was at the grammar-school, and a towardly child. My daughter Betty (who is now well married, and has children) was then at her needle-work. I took leave of my wife, and boy and girl, with tears on both sides, and went on board the Adventure, a merchant ship of three hundred tons, bound for Surat, captain John Nicholas, of Liverpool, commander. But my account of this voyage must be referred to the Second Part of my Travels.

PART TWO

A Voyage To Brobdingnag

CHAPTER ONE

A great storm described; the long boat sent to fetch water; the author goes with it to discover the country. He is left on shore, is seized by one of the natives, and carried to a farmer's house. His reception, with several accidents that happened there. A description of the inhabitants.

HAVING BEEN condemned, by nature and fortune, to active and restless life, in two months after my return, I again left my native country, and took shipping in the Downs, on the 20th day of June, 1702, in the Adventure, Captain John Nicholas, a Cornish man, commander, bound for Surat. We had a very prosperous gale, till we arrived at the Cape of Good Hope, where we landed for fresh water; but discovering a leak, we unshipped our goods and wintered there; for the captain falling sick of an ague, we could not leave the Cape till the end of March. We then set sail, and had a good voyage till we passed the Straits of Madagascar; but having got northward of that island, and to about five degrees south latitude, the winds, which in those seas are observed to blow a constant equal gale between the north and west, from the beginning of December to the beginning of May, on the 19th of April began to blow with much greater violence, and more westerly than usual, continuing so for twenty days together: during which time, we were driven a little to the east of the Molucca Islands, and about three degrees northward of the line, as our captain found by an observation he took the 2nd of May, at which time the wind ceased, and it was a perfect calm, whereat I was not a little rejoiced. But he, being a man well experienced in the navigation of those seas, bid us all prepare against a storm, which accordingly happened the day following: for the southern wind, called the southern monsoon, began to set in.

Finding it was likely to overblow, we took in our sprit-sail, and stood by to hand the fore-sail; but making foul weather, we looked the guns were all fast, and handed the mizen. The ship lay very broad off, so we thought it better spooning before the sea, than trying or hulling. We reefed the fore-sail and set him, and hauled aft the fore-sheet; the helm was hard a-weather. The ship wore bravely. We belayed the fore down-haul; but the sail was split, and we hauled down the yard, and got the sail into the ship, and unbound all the things clear of it. It was a very fierce storm; the sea broke strange and dangerous. We hauled off upon the laniard of the whip-staff, and helped the man at the helm. We would not get down our topmast, but let all stand, because she scudded before the sea very well, and we knew that the top-mast being aloft, the ship was the wholesomer, and made better way through the sea, seeing we had sea-room. When the storm was over, we set fore-sail and main-sail, and brought the ship to. Then we set the mizen, main-top-sail, and the fore-top-sail. Our course was east-north-east, the wind was at south-west. We got the starboard tacks aboard, we cast off our weather-braces and lifts; we set in the lee-braces, and hauled forward by the weather-bowlings, and hauled them tight, and belayed them, and hauled over the mizen tack to windward, and kept her full and by as near as she would lie.

During this storm, which was followed by a strong wind west-south-west, we were carried, by my computation, about five hundred leagues to the east, so that the oldest sailor on board could not tell in what part of the world we were. Our provisions held out well, our ship was staunch, and our crew all in good health; but we lay in the utmost distress for water. We thought it best to hold on the same course, rather than turn more northerly, which might have brought us to the north-west part of Great Tartary, and into the Frozen Sea.

On the 16th day of June, 1703, a boy on the top-mast discovered land. On the 17th, we came in full view of a great island, or continent (for we knew not whether;) on the south side whereof was a small neck of land jutting out into the sea, and a creek too shallow to hold a ship of above one hundred tons. We cast anchor within a league of this creek, and our captain sent a dozen of his men well armed in the long-boat, with vessels for water, if any could be found. I desired his leave to go with them, that I might see the country, and make what discoveries I could. When we came to land we saw no river or spring, nor any sign of inhabitants. Our men therefore wandered on the shore to find out some fresh water near the sea, and I walked alone about a mile on the other side, where I observed the country all barren and rocky. I now began to be weary, and seeing nothing to entertain my curiosity, I returned gently down towards the creek; and the sea being full in my view, I saw our men already got into the boat, and rowing for life to the ship. I was going to holla after them, although it had been to little purpose, when I observed a huge creature walking after them in the sea, as fast as he could: he waded not much deeper than his knees, and took prodigious strides: but our men had the start of him half a league, and, the sea thereabouts being full of sharp-pointed rocks, the monster was not able to overtake the boat. This I was afterwards told, for I durst not stay to see the issue of the adventure; but ran as fast as I could the way I first went, and then climbed up a steep hill, which gave me some prospect of the country. I found it fully cultivated; but that which first surprised me was the length of the grass, which, in those grounds that seemed to be kept for hay, was about twenty feet high.

I fell into a high road, for so I took it to be, though it served to the inhabitants only as a foot-path through a field of barley. Here I walked on for some time, but could see little on either side, it being now near harvest, and the corn rising at least forty feet. I was an hour walking to the end of this field, which was fenced in with a hedge of at least one hundred and twenty feet high, and the trees so lofty that I could make no computation of their altitude. There was a stile to pass from this field into the next. It had four steps, and a stone to cross over when you came to the uppermost. It was impossible for me to climb this stile, because every step was six-feet high, and the upper stone about twenty. I was endeavouring to find some gap in the hedge, when I discovered one of the inhabitants in the next field, advancing towards the stile, of the same size with him whom I saw in the sea pursuing our boat. He appeared as tall as an ordinary spire steeple, and took about ten yards at every stride, as near as I could guess. I was struck with the utmost fear and astonishment, and ran to hide myself in the corn, whence I saw him at the top of the stile looking back into the next field on the right hand, and heard him call in a voice many degrees louder than a speaking-trumpet: but the noise was so high in the air, that at first I certainly thought it was thunder. Whereupon seven monsters, like himself, came towards him with reaping-hooks in their hands, each hook about the largeness of six scythes. These people were not so well clad as the first, whose servants or labourers they seemed to be; for, upon some words he spoke, they went to reap the corn in the field where I lay. I kept from them at as great a distance as I could, but was forced to move with extreme difficulty, for the stalks of the corn were sometimes not above a foot distant, so that I could hardly squeeze my body betwixt them. However, I made a shift to go forward, till I came to a part of the field where the corn had been laid by the rain and wind. Here it was impossible for me to advance a step; for the stalks were so interwoven, that I could not creep through, and the beards of the fallen ears so strong and pointed, that they pierced through my clothes into my flesh. At the same time I heard the reapers not a hundred yards behind me. Being quite dispirited with toil, and wholly overcome by grief and dispair, I lay down between two ridges, and heartily wished I might there end my days. I bemoaned my desolate widow and fatherless children. I lamented my own folly and wilfulness, in attempting a second voyage, against the advice of all my friends and relations. In this terrible agitation of mind, I could not forbear thinking of Lilliput, whose inhabitants looked upon me as the greatest prodigy that ever appeared in the world; where I was able to draw an imperial fleet in my hand, and perform those other actions, which will be recorded for ever in the chronicles of that empire, while posterity shall hardly believe them, although attested by millions. I reflected what a mortification it must prove to me, to appear as inconsiderable in this nation, as one single Lilliputian would be among us. But this I conceived was to be the least of my misfortunes; for, as human creatures are observed to be more savage and cruel in proportion to their bulk, what could I expect but to be a morsel in the mouth of the first among these enormous barbarians that should happen to seize me? Undoubtedly philosophers are in the right, when they tell us that nothing is great or little otherwise than by comparison. It might have pleased fortune, to have let the Lilliputians find some nation, where the people were as diminutive with respect to them, as they were to me. And who knows but that even this prodigious race of mortals might be equally overmatched in some distant part of the world, whereof we have yet no discovery.

Scared and confounded as I was, I could not forbear going on with these reflections, when one of the reapers, approaching within ten yards of the ridge where I lay, made me apprehend that with the next step I should be squashed to death under his foot, or cut in two with his reaping-hook. And therefore, when he was again about to move, I screamed as loud as fear could make me: whereupon the huge creature trod short, and, looking round about under him for some time, at last espied me as I lay on the ground. He considered awhile, with the caution of one who endeavours to lay hold on a small dangerous animal in such a manner that it shall not be able either to scratch or bite him, as I myself have sometimes done with a weasel in England. At length he ventured to take me behind, by the middle, between his fore-finger and thumb, and brought me within three yards of his eyes, that he might behold my shape more perfectly. I guessed his meaning, and my good fortune gave me so much presence of mind, that I resolved not to struggle in the least as he held me in the air above sixty feet from the ground, although he grievously pinched my sides, for fear I should slip through his fingers. All I ventured was to raise mine eyes towards the sun, and place my hands together in a supplicating posture, and to speak some words in a humble melancholy tone, suitable to the condition I then was in: for I apprehended every moment that he would dash me against the ground, as we usually do any little hateful animal, which we have a mind to destroy. But my good star would have it, that he appeared pleased with my voice and gestures, and began to look upon me as a curiosity, much wondering to hear me pronounce articulate words, although he could not understand them. In the mean time I was not able to forbear groaning and shedding tears, and turning my head towards my sides; letting him know, as well as I could, how cruelly I was hurt by the pressure of his thumb and finger. He seemed to apprehend my meaning; for, lifting up the lappet of his coat, he put me gently into it, and immediately ran along with me to his master, who was a substantial farmer, and the same person I had first seen in the field.

The farmer having (as I suppose by their talk) received such an account of me as his servant could give him, took a piece of a small straw, about the size of a walking-staff, and therewith lifted up the lappets of my coat; which it seems he thought to be some kind of covering that nature had given me. He blew my hairs aside to take a better view of my face. He called his hinds about him, and asked them, as I afterwards learned, whether they had ever seen in the fields any little creature that resembled me. He then placed me softly on the ground upon all fours, but I got immediately up, and walked slowly backward and forward, to let those people see I had no intent to run away. They all sat down in a circle about me, the better to observe my motions. I pulled off my hat, and made a low bow towards the farmer. I fell on my knees, and lifted up my hands and eyes, and spoke several words as loud as I could: I took a purse of gold out of my pocket, and humbly presented it to him. He received it on the palm of his hand, then applied it close to his eye to see what it was, and afterwards turned it several times with the point of a pin (which he took out of his sleeve,) but could make nothing of it. Whereupon I made a sign that he should place his hand on the ground. I then took the purse, and, opening it, poured all the gold into his palm. There were six Spanish pieces of four pistoles each, beside twenty or thirty smaller coins. I saw him wet the tip of his little finger upon his tongue, and take up one of my largest pieces, and then another; but he seemed to be wholly ignorant what they were. He made me a sign to put them again into my purse, and the purse again into my pocket, which, after offering it to him several times, I thought it best to do.

The farmer, by this time, was convinced I must be a rational creature. He spoke often to me; but the sound of his voice pierced my ears like that of a water-mill, yet his words were articulate enough. I answered as loud as I could in several languages, and he often laid his ear within two yards of me: but all in vain, for we were wholly unintelligible to each other. He then sent his servants to their work, and taking his handkerchief out of his pocket, he doubled and spread it on his left hand, which he placed flat on the ground with the palm upward, making me a sign to step into it, as I could easily do, for it was not above a foot in thickness. I thought it my part to obey, and, for fear of falling, laid myself at full length upon the handkerchief, with the remainder of which he lapped me up to the head for further security, and in this manner carried me home to his house. There he called his wife, and showed me to her; but she screamed and ran back, as women in England do at the sight of a toad or a spider. However, when she had a while seen my behaviour, and how well I observed the signs her husband made, she was soon reconciled, and by degrees grew extremely tender of me.

It was about twelve at noon, and a servant brought in dinner. It was only one substantial dish of meat (fit for the plain condition of a husbandman,) in a dish of about four-and-twenty feet diameter. The company were, the farmer and his wife, three children, and an old grandmother. When they were sat down, the farmer placed me at some distance from him on the table, which was thirty feet high from the floor. I was in a terrible fright, and kept as far as I could from the edge, for fear of falling. The wife minced a bit of meat, then crumbled some bread on a trencher, and placed it before me. I made her a low bow, took out my knife and fork, and fell to eat, which gave them exceeding delight. The mistress sent her maid for a small dram cup, which held about two gallons, and filled it with drink; I took up the vessel with much difficulty in both hands, and in a most respectful manner drank to her ladyship's health, expressing the words as loud as I could in English, which made the company laugh so heartily, that I was almost deafened with the noise. This liquor tasted like a small cider, and was not unpleasant. Then the master made me a sign to come to his trencher side; but as I walked on the table, being in great surprise all the time, as the indulgent reader will easily conceive and excuse, I happened to stumble against a crust, and fell flat on my face, but received no hurt. I got up immediately, and observing the good people to be in much concern, I took my hat (which I held under my arm out of good manners,) and waving it over my head, made three huzzas, to show I had got no mischief by my fall. But advancing forward towards my master (as I shall henceforth call him,) his youngest son, who sat next to him, an arch boy of about ten years old, took me up by the legs, and held me so high in the air, that I trembled every limb: but his father snatched me from him, and at the same time gave him such a box on the left ear, as would have felled an European troop of horse to the earth, ordering him to be taken from the table. But being afraid the boy might owe me a spite, and well remembering how mischievous all children among us naturally are to sparrows, rabbits, young kittens, and puppy dogs, I fell on my knees, and pointing to the boy, made my master to understand, as well as I could, that I desired his son might be pardoned. The father complied, and the lad took his seat again, whereupon I went to him, and kissed his hand, which my master took, and made him stroke me gently with it.

In the midst of dinner, my mistress's favourite cat leaped into her lap. I heard a noise behind me like that of a dozen stocking-weavers at work; and turning my head, I found it proceeded from the purring of that animal, who seemed to be three times larger than an ox, as I computed by the view of her head, and one of her paws, while her mistress was feeding and stroking her. The fierceness of this creature's countenance altogether discomposed me; though I stood at the farther end of the table, above fifty feet off; and although my mistress held her fast, for fear she might give a spring, and seize me in her talons. But it happened there was no danger, for the cat took not the least notice of me when my master placed me within three yards of her. And as I have been always told, and found true by experience in my travels, that flying or discovering fear before a fierce animal, is a certain way to make it pursue or attack you, so I resolved, in this dangerous juncture, to show no manner of concern. I walked with intrepidity five or six times before the very head of the cat, and came within half a yard of her; whereupon she drew herself back, as if she were more afraid of me: I had less apprehension concerning the dogs, whereof three or four came into the room, as it is usual in farmers' houses; one of which was a mastiff, equal in bulk to four elephants, and another a greyhound, somewhat taller than the mastiff, but not so large.

When dinner was almost done, the nurse came in with a child of a year old in her arms, who immediately spied me, and began a squall that you might have heard from London-Bridge to Chelsea, after the usual oratory of infants, to get me for a plaything. The mother, out of pure indulgence, took me up, and put me towards the child, who presently seized me by the middle, and got my head into his mouth, where I roared so loud that the urchin was frighted, and let me drop, and I should infallibly have broke my neck, if the mother had not held her apron under me. The nurse, to quiet her babe, made use of a rattle which was a kind of hollow vessel filled with great stones, and fastened by a cable to the child's waist: but all in vain; so that she was forced to apply the last remedy by giving it suck. I must confess no object ever disgusted me so much as the sight of her monstrous breast, which I cannot tell what to compare with, so as to give the curious reader an idea of its bulk, shape, and colour. It stood prominent six feet, and could not be less than sixteen in circumference. The nipple was about half the bigness of my head, and the hue both of that and the dug, so varied with spots, pimples, and freckles, that nothing could appear more nauseous: for I had a near sight of her, she sitting down, the more conveniently to give suck, and I standing on the table. This made me reflect upon the fair skins of our English ladies, who appear so beautiful to us, only because they are of our own size, and their defects not to be seen but through a magnifying glass; where we find by experiment that the smoothest and whitest skins look rough, and coarse, and ill-coloured.

I remember when I was at Lilliput, the complexion of those diminutive people appeared to me the fairest in the world; and talking upon this subject with a person of learning there, who was an intimate friend of mine, he said that my face appeared much fairer and smoother when he looked on me from the ground, than it did upon a nearer view, when I took him up in my hand, and brought him close, which he confessed was at first a very shocking sight. He said, "he could discover great holes in my skin; that the stumps of my beard were ten times stronger than the bristles of a boar, and my complexion made up of several colours altogether disagreeable:" although I must beg leave to say for myself, that I am as fair as most of my sex and country, and very little sunburnt by all my travels. On the other side, discoursing of the ladies in that emperor's court, he used to tell me, "one had freckles; another too wide a mouth; a third too large a nose;" nothing of which I was able to distinguish. I confess this reflection was obvious enough; which, however, I could not forbear, lest the reader might think those vast creatures were actually deformed: for I must do them the justice to say, they are a comely race of people, and particularly the features of my master's countenance, although he was but a farmer, when I beheld him from the height of sixty feet, appeared very well proportioned.

When dinner was done, my master went out to his labourers, and, as I could discover by his voice and gesture, gave his wife strict charge to take care of me. I was very much tired, and disposed to sleep, which my mistress perceiving, she put me on her own bed, and covered me with a clean white handkerchief, but larger and coarser than the mainsail of a man-of-war.

I slept about two hours, and dreamt I was at home with my wife and children, which aggravated my sorrows when I awaked, and found myself alone in a vast room, between two and three hundred feet wide, and above two hundred high, lying in a bed twenty yards wide. My mistress was gone about her household affairs, and had locked me in. The bed was eight yards from the floor. Some natural necessities required me to get down; I durst not presume to call; and if I had, it would have been in vain, with such a voice as mine, at so great a distance from the room where I lay to the kitchen where the family kept. While I was under these circumstances, two rats crept up the curtains, and ran smelling backwards and forwards on the bed. One of them came up almost to my face, whereupon I rose in a fright, and drew out my hanger to defend myself. These horrible animals had the boldness to attack me on both sides, and one of them held his fore-feet at my collar; but I had the good fortune to rip up his belly before he could do me any mischief. He fell down at my feet; and the other, seeing the fate of his comrade, made his escape, but not without one good wound on the back, which I gave him as he fled, and made the blood run trickling from him. After this exploit, I walked gently to and fro on the bed, to recover my breath and loss of spirits. These creatures were of the size of a large mastiff, but infinitely more nimble and fierce; so that if I had taken off my belt before I went to sleep, I must have infallibly been torn to pieces and devoured. I measured the tail of the dead rat, and found it to be two yards long, wanting an inch; but it went against my stomach to drag the carcass off the bed, where it lay still bleeding; I observed it had yet some life, but with a strong slash across the neck, I thoroughly despatched it.

Soon after my mistress came into the room, who seeing me all bloody, ran and took me up in her hand. I pointed to the dead rat, smiling, and making other signs to show I was not hurt; whereat she was extremely rejoiced, calling the maid to take up the dead rat with a pair of tongs, and throw it out of the window. Then she set me on a table, where I showed her my hanger all bloody, and wiping it on the lappet of my coat, returned it to the scabbard. I was pressed to do more than one thing which another could not do for me, and therefore endeavoured to make my mistress understand, that I desired to be set down on the floor; which after she had done, my bashfulness would not suffer me to express myself farther, than by pointing to the door, and bowing several times. The good woman, with much difficulty, at last perceived what I would be at, and taking me up again in her hand, walked into the garden, where she set me down. I went on one side about two hundred yards, and beckoning to her not to look or to follow me, I hid myself between two leaves of sorrel, and there discharged the necessities of nature.

I hope the gentle reader will excuse me for dwelling on these and the like particulars, which, however insignificant they may appear to groveling vulgar minds, yet will certainly help a philosopher to enlarge his thoughts and imagination, and apply them to the benefit of public as well as private life, which was my sole design in presenting this and other accounts of my travels to the world; wherein I have been chiefly studious of truth, without affecting any ornaments of learning or of style. But the whole scene of this voyage made so strong an impression on my mind, and is so deeply fixed in my memory, that, in committing it to paper I did not omit one material circumstance: however, upon a strict review, I blotted out several passages. Of less moment which were in my first copy, for fear of being censured as tedious and trifling, whereof travellers are often, perhaps not without justice, accused.

CHAPTER TWO

A description of the farmer's daughter. The author carried to a market-town, and then to the metropolis. The particulars of his journey.

My mistress had a daughter of nine years old, a child of towardly parts for her age, very dexterous at her needle, and skilful in dressing her baby. Her mother and she contrived to fit up the baby's cradle for me against night: the cradle was put into a small drawer of a cabinet, and the drawer placed upon a hanging shelf for fear of the rats. This was my bed all the time I staid with those people, though made more convenient by degrees, as I began to learn their language and make my wants known. This young girl was so handy, that after I had once or twice pulled off my clothes before her, she was able to dress and undress me, though I never gave her that trouble when she would let me do either myself. She made me seven shirts, and some other linen, of as fine cloth as could be got, which indeed was coarser than sackcloth; and these she constantly washed for me with her own hands. She was likewise my school-mistress, to teach me the language: when I pointed to any thing, she told me the name of it in her own tongue, so that in a few days I was able to call for whatever I had a mind to. She was very good-natured, and not above forty feet high, being little for her age. She gave me the name of *Grildrig*, which the family took up, and afterwards the whole kingdom. The word imports what the Latins call *nanunculus*, the Italians *homunceletino*, and the English *mannikin*. To her I chiefly owe my preservation in that country: we never parted while I was there; I called her my *Glumdalclitch*, or little nurse; and should be guilty of great ingratitude, if I omitted this honourable mention of her care and affection towards me, which I heartily wish it lay in my power to requite as she deserves, instead of being the innocent, but unhappy instrument of her disgrace, as I have too much reason to fear.

It now began to be known and talked of in the neighbourhood, that my master had found a strange animal in the field, about the bigness of a *splacnuck*, but exactly shaped in every part like a human creature; which it likewise imitated in all its actions; seemed to speak in a little language of its own, had already learned several words of theirs, went erect upon two legs, was tame and gentle, would come when it was called, do whatever it was bid, had the finest limbs in the world, and a complexion fairer than a nobleman's daughter of three years old. Another farmer, who lived hard by, and was a particular friend of my master, came on a visit on purpose to inquire into the truth of this story. I was immediately produced, and placed upon a table, where I walked as I was commanded, drew my hanger, put it up again, made my reverence to my master's guest, asked him in his own language how he did, and told him *he was welcome*, just as my little nurse had instructed me. This man, who was old and dim-sighted, put on his spectacles to behold me better; at which I could not forbear laughing very heartily, for his eyes appeared like the full moon shining into a chamber at two windows. Our people, who discovered the cause of my mirth, bore me company in laughing, at which the old fellow was fool enough to be angry and out of countenance. He had the character of a great miser; and, to my misfortune, he well deserved it, by the cursed advice he gave my master, to show me as a sight upon a market-day in the next town, which was half an hour's riding, about two-and-twenty miles from our house. I guessed there was some mischief when I observed my master and his friend whispering together, sometimes pointing at me; and my fears made me fancy that I overheard and understood some of their words. But the next morning Glumdalclitch, my little nurse, told me the whole matter, which she had cunningly picked out from her mother. The poor girl laid me on her bosom, and fell a weeping with shame and grief. She apprehended some mischief would happen to me from rude vulgar folks, who might squeeze me to death, or break one of my limbs by taking me in their hands. She had also observed how modest I was in my nature, how nicely I regarded my honour, and what an indignity I should conceive it, to be exposed for money as a public spectacle, to the meanest of the people. She said, her papa and mamma had promised that Grildrig should be hers; but now she found they meant to serve her as they did last year, when they pretended to give her a lamb, and yet, as soon as it was fat, sold it to a butcher. For my own part, I may truly affirm, that I was less concerned than my nurse. I had a strong hope, which never left me, that I should one day recover my liberty: and as to the ignominy of being carried about for a monster, I considered myself to be a perfect stranger in the country, and that such a misfortune could never be charged upon me as a reproach, if ever I should return to England, since the king of Great Britain himself, in my condition, must have undergone the same distress.

My master, pursuant to the advice of his friend, carried me in a box the next market-day to the neighbouring town, and took along with him his little daughter, my nurse, upon a pillion behind him. The box was close on every side, with a little door for me to go in and out, and a few gimlet holes to let in air. The girl had been so careful as to put the quilt of her baby's bed into it, for me to lie down on. However, I was terribly shaken and discomposed in this journey, though it was but of half an hour: for the horse went about forty feet at every step and trotted so high, that the agitation was equal to the rising and falling of a ship in a great storm, but much more frequent. Our journey was somewhat farther than from London to St. Alban's. My master alighted at an inn which he used to frequent; and after consulting awhile with the inn-keeper, and making some necessary preparations, he hired the *grultrud*, or crier, to give notice through the town of a strange creature to be seen at the sign of the Green Eagle, not so big as a *splacnuck* (an animal in that country very finely shaped, about six feet long,) and in every part of the body resembling a human creature, could speak several words, and perform a hundred diverting tricks.

I was placed upon a table in the largest room of the inn, which might be near three hundred feet square. My little nurse stood on a low stool close to the table, to take care of me, and direct what I should do. My master, to avoid a crowd, would suffer only thirty people at a time to see me. I walked about on the table as the girl commanded; she asked me questions, as far as she knew my understanding of the language reached, and I answered them as loud as I could. I turned about several times to the company, paid my humble respects, said *they were welcome*, and used some other speeches I had been taught. I took up a thimble filled with liquor, which Glumdalclitch had given me for a cup, and drank their health, I drew out my hanger, and flourished with it after the manner of fencers in England. My nurse gave me a part of a straw, which I exercised as a pike, having learnt the art in my youth. I was that day shown to twelve sets of company, and as often forced to act over again the same fopperies, till I was half dead with weariness and vexation; for those who had seen me made such wonderful reports, that the people were ready to break down the doors to come in. My master, for his own interest, would not suffer any one to touch me except my nurse; and to prevent danger, benches were set round the table at such a distance as to put me out of every body's reach. However, an unlucky school-boy aimed a hazel nut directly at my head, which very narrowly missed me; otherwise it came with so much violence, that it would have infallibly knocked out my brains, for it was almost as large as a small pumpkin, but I had the satisfaction to see the young rogue well beaten, and turned out of the room.

My master gave public notice that he would show me again the next market-day; and in the meantime he prepared a convenient vehicle for me, which he had reason enough to do; for I was so tired with my first journey, and with entertaining company for eight hours together, that I could hardly stand upon my legs, or speak a word. It was at least three days before I recovered my strength; and that I might have no rest at home, all the neighbouring gentlemen from a hundred miles round, hearing of my fame, came to see me at my master's own house. There could not be fewer than thirty persons with their wives and children (for the country is very populous;) and my master demanded the rate of a full room whenever he showed me at home, although it were only to a single family; so that for some time I had but little ease every day of the week (except Wednesday, which is their Sabbath,) although I were not carried to the town.

My master, finding how profitable I was likely to be, resolved to carry me to the most considerable cities of the kingdom. Having therefore provided himself with all things necessary for a long journey, and settled his affairs at home, he took leave of his wife, and upon the 17th of August, 1703, about two months after my arrival, we set out for the metropolis, situate near the middle of that empire, and about three thousand miles distance from our house. My master made his daughter Glumdalclitch ride behind him. She carried me on her lap, in a box tied about her waist. The girl had lined it on all sides with the softest cloth she could get, well quilted underneath, furnished it with her baby's bed, provided me with linen and other necessaries, and made everything as convenient as she could. We had no other company but a boy of the house, who rode after us with the luggage.

My master's design was to show me in all the towns by the way, and to step out of the road for fifty or a hundred miles, to any village, or person of quality's house, where he might expect custom. We made easy journeys, of not above seven or eight score miles a-day; for Glumdalclitch, on purpose to spare me, complained she was tired with the trotting of the horse. She often took me out of my box, at my own desire, to give me air, and show me the country, but always held me fast by a leading-string. We passed over five or six rivers, many degrees broader and deeper than the Nile or the Ganges: and there was hardly a rivulet so small as the Thames at London-bridge. We were ten weeks in our journey, and I was shown in eighteen large towns, besides many villages, and private families.

On the 26th day of October we arrived at the metropolis, called in their language *Lorbrulgrud*, or Pride of the Universe. My master took a lodging in the principal street of the city, not far from the royal palace, and put out bills in the usual form, containing an exact description of my person and parts. He hired a large room between three and four hundred feet wide. He provided a table sixty feet in diameter, upon which I was to act my part, and pallisadoed it round three feet from the edge, and as many high, to prevent my falling over. I was shown ten times a-day, to the wonder and satisfaction of all people. I could now speak the language tolerably well, and perfectly understood every word, that was spoken to me. Besides, I had learnt their alphabet, and could make a shift to explain a sentence here and there; for Glumdalclitch had been my instructor while we were at home, and at leisure hours during our journey. She carried a little book in her pocket, not much larger than a Sanson's Atlas; it was a common treatise for the use of young girls, giving a short account of their religion: out of this she taught me my letters, and interpreted the words.

CHAPTER THREE

The author sent for to court. The queen buys him of his master the farmer, and presents him to the king. He disputes with his majesty's great scholars. An apartment at court provided for the author. He is in high favour with the queen. He stands up for the honour of his own country. His quarrels with the queen's dwarf.

THE FREQUENT labours I underwent every day, made, in a few weeks, a very considerable change in my health: the more my master got by me, the more insatiable he grew. I had quite lost my stomach, and was almost reduced to a skeleton. The farmer observed it, and concluding I must soon die, resolved to make as good a hand of me as he could. While he was thus reasoning and resolving with himself, a *sardral*, or gentleman-usher, came from court, commanding my master to carry me immediately thither for the diversion of the queen and her ladies. Some of the latter had already been to see me, and reported strange things of my beauty, behaviour, and good sense. Her majesty, and those who attended her, were beyond measure delighted with my demeanour. I fell on my knees, and begged the honour of kissing her imperial foot; but this gracious princess held out her little finger towards me, after I was set on the table, which I embraced in both my arms, and put the tip of it with the utmost respect to my lip. She made me some general questions about my country and my travels, which I answered as distinctly, and in as few words as I could. She asked, "whether I could be content to live at court?" I bowed down to the board of the table, and humbly answered "that I was my master's slave: but, if I were at my own disposal, I should be proud to devote my life to her majesty's service." She then asked my master, "whether he was willing to sell me at a good price?" He, who apprehended I could not live a month, was ready enough to part with me, and demanded a thousand pieces of gold, which were ordered him on the spot, each piece being about the bigness of eight hundred moidores; but allowing for the proportion of all things between that country and Europe, and the high price of gold among them, was hardly so great a sum as a thousand guineas would be in England. I then said to the queen, "since I was now her majesty's most humble creature and vassal, I must beg the favour, that Glumdalclitch, who had always tended me with so much care and kindness, and understood to do it so well, might be admitted into her service, and continue to be my nurse and instructor."

Her majesty agreed to my petition, and easily got the farmer's consent, who was glad enough to have his daughter preferred at court, and the poor girl herself was not able to hide her joy. My late master withdrew, bidding me farewell, and saying he had left me in a good service; to which I replied not a word, only making him a slight bow.

The queen observed my coldness; and, when the farmer was gone out of the apartment, asked me the reason. I made bold to tell her majesty, "that I owed no other obligation to my late master, than his not dashing out the brains of a poor harmless creature, found by chance in his fields: which obligation was amply recompensed, by the gain he had made in showing me through half the kingdom, and the price he had now sold me for. That the life I had since led was laborious enough to kill an animal of ten times my strength. That my health was much impaired, by the continual drudgery of entertaining the rabble every hour of the day; and that, if my master had not thought my life in danger, her majesty would not have got so cheap a bargain. But as I was out of all fear of being ill-treated under the protection of so great and good an empress, the ornament of nature, the darling of the world, the delight of her subjects, the phoenix of the creation, so I hoped my late master's apprehensions would appear to be groundless; for I already found my spirits revive, by the influence of her most august presence."

This was the sum of my speech, delivered with great improprieties and hesitation. The latter part was altogether framed in the style peculiar to that people, whereof I learned some phrases from Glumdalclitch, while she was carrying me to court.

The queen, giving great allowance for my defectiveness in speaking, was, however, surprised at so much wit and good sense in so diminutive an animal. She took me in her own hand, and carried me to the king, who was then retired to his cabinet. His majesty, a prince of much gravity and austere countenance, not well observing my shape at first view, asked the queen after a cold manner "how long it was since she grew fond of a *splacnuck*?" for such it seems he took me to be, as I lay upon my breast in her majesty's right hand. But this princess, who has an infinite deal of wit and humour, set me gently on my feet upon the scrutoire, and commanded me to give his majesty an account of myself, which I did in a very few words: and Glumdalclitch who attended at the cabinet door, and could not endure I should be out of her sight, being admitted, confirmed all that had passed from my arrival at her father's house.

The king, although he be as learned a person as any in his dominions, had been educated in the study of philosophy, and particularly mathematics; yet when he observed my shape exactly, and saw me walk erect, before I began to speak, conceived I might be a piece of clock-work (which is in that country arrived to a very great perfection) contrived by some ingenious artist. But when he heard my voice, and found what I delivered to be regular and rational, he could not conceal his astonishment. He was by no means satisfied with the relation I gave him of the manner I came into his kingdom, but thought it a story concerted between Glumdalclitch and her father, who had taught me a set of words to make me sell at a better price. Upon this imagination, he put several other questions to me, and still received rational answers: no otherwise defective than by a foreign accent, and an imperfect knowledge in the language, with some rustic phrases which I had learned at the farmer's house, and did not suit the polite style of a court.

His majesty sent for three great scholars, who were then in their weekly waiting, according to the custom in that country. These gentlemen, after they had a while examined my shape with much nicety, were of different opinions concerning me. They all agreed that I could not be produced according to the regular laws of nature, because I was not framed with a capacity of preserving my life, either by swiftness, or climbing of trees, or digging holes in the earth. They observed by my teeth, which they viewed with great exactness, that I was a carnivorous animal; yet most quadrupeds being an overmatch for me, and field mice, with some others, too nimble, they could not imagine how I should be able to support myself, unless I fed upon snails and other insects, which they offered, by many learned arguments, to evince that I could not possibly do. One of these virtuosi seemed to think that I might be an embryo, or abortive birth. But this opinion was rejected by the other two, who observed my limbs to be perfect and finished; and that I had lived several years, as it was manifest from my beard, the stumps whereof they plainly discovered through a magnifying glass. They would not allow me to be a dwarf, because my littleness was beyond all degrees of comparison; for the queen's favourite dwarf, the smallest ever known in that kingdom, was near thirty feet high. After much debate, they concluded unanimously, that I was only *relplum scalcath*, which is interpreted literally *lusus naturæ*; a determination exactly agreeable to the modern philosophy of Europe, whose professors, disdaining the old evasion of occult causes, whereby the followers of Aristotle endeavoured in vain to disguise their ignorance, have invented this wonderful solution of all difficulties, to the unspeakable advancement of human knowledge.

After this decisive conclusion, I entreated to be heard a word or two. I applied myself to the king, and assured his majesty, "that I came from a country which abounded with several millions of both sexes, and of my own stature; where the animals, trees, and houses, were all in proportion, and where, by consequence, I might be as able to defend myself, and to find sustenance, as any of his majesty's subjects could do here; which I took for a full answer to those gentlemen's arguments." To this they only replied with a smile of contempt, saying, "that the farmer had instructed me very well in my lesson." The king, who had a much better understanding, dismissing his learned men, sent for the farmer, who by good fortune was not yet gone out of town. Having therefore first examined him privately, and then confronted him with me and the young girl, his majesty began to think that what we told him might possibly be true. He desired the queen to order that a particular care should be taken of me; and was of opinion that Glumdalclitch should still continue in her office of tending me, because he observed we had a great affection for each other. A convenient apartment was provided for her at court: she had a sort of governess appointed to take care of her education, a maid to dress her, and two other servants for menial offices; but the care of me was wholly appropriated to herself. The queen commanded her own cabinet-maker to contrive a box, that might serve me for a bedchamber, after the model that Glumdalclitch and I should agree upon. This man was a most ingenious artist, and according to my direction, in three weeks finished for me a wooden chamber of sixteen feet square, and twelve high, with sash-windows, a door, and two closets, like a London bed-chamber. The board, that made the ceiling, was to be lifted up and down by two hinges, to put in a bed ready furnished by her majesty's upholsterer, which Glumdalclitch took out every day to air, made it with her own hands, and letting it down at night, locked up the roof over me. A nice workman, who was famous for little curiosities, undertook to make me two chairs, with backs and frames, of a substance not unlike ivory, and two tables, with a cabinet to put my things in. The room was quilted on all sides, as well as the floor and the ceiling, to prevent any accident from the carelessness of those who carried me, and to break the force of a jolt, when I went in a coach. I desired a lock for my door, to prevent rats and mice from coming in. The smith, after several attempts, made the smallest that ever was seen among them, for

I have known a larger at the gate of a gentleman's house in England. I made a shift to keep the key in a pocket of my own, fearing Glumdalclitch might lose it. The queen likewise ordered the thinnest silks that could be gotten, to make me clothes, not much thicker than an English blanket, very cumbersome till I was accustomed to them. They were after the fashion of the kingdom, partly resembling the Persian, and partly the Chinese, and are a very grave and decent habit.

The queen became so fond of my company, that she could not dine without me. I had a table placed upon the same at which her majesty ate, just at her left elbow, and a chair to sit on. Glumdalclitch stood on a stool on the floor near my table, to assist and take care of me. I had an entire set of silver dishes and plates, and other necessaries, which, in proportion to those of the queen, were not much bigger than what I have seen in a London toy-shop for the furniture of a baby-house: these my little nurse kept in her pocket in a silver box, and gave me at meals as I wanted them, always cleaning them herself. No person dined with the queen but the two princesses royal, the eldest sixteen years old, and the younger at that time thirteen and a month. Her majesty used to put a bit of meat upon one of my dishes, out of which I carved for myself, and her diversion was to see me eat in miniature: for the queen (who had indeed but a weak stomach) took up, at one mouthful, as much as a dozen English farmers could eat at a meal, which to me was for some time a very nauseous sight. She would craunch the wing of a lark, bones and all, between her teeth, although it were nine times as large as that of a full-grown turkey; and put a bit of bread into her mouth as big as two twelve-penny loaves. She drank out of a golden cup, above a hogshead at a draught. Her knives were twice as long as a scythe, set straight upon the handle. The spoons, forks, and other instruments, were all in the same proportion. I remember when Glumdalclitch carried me, out of curiosity, to see some of the tables at court, where ten or a dozen of those enormous knives and forks were lifted up together, I thought I had never till then beheld so terrible a sight.

It is the custom, that every Wednesday (which, as I have observed, is their Sabbath) the king and queen, with the royal issue of both sexes, dine together in the apartment of his majesty, to whom I was now become a great favourite; and at these times, my little chair and table were placed at his left hand, before one of the salt-cellars. This prince took a pleasure in conversing with me, inquiring into the manners, religion, laws, government, and learning of Europe; wherein I gave him the best account I was able. His apprehension was so clear, and his judgment so exact, that he made very wise reflections and observations upon all I said. But I confess, that, after I had been a little too copious in talking of my own beloved country, of our trade and wars by sea and land, of our schisms in religion, and parties in the state; the prejudices of his education prevailed so far, that he could not forbear taking me up in his right hand, and stroking me gently with the other, after a hearty fit of laughing, asked me, "whether I was a whig or tory?" Then turning to his first minister, who waited behind him with a white staff, near as tall as the mainmast of the Royal Sovereign, he observed "how contemptible a thing was human grandeur, which could be mimicked by such diminutive insects as I: and yet," says he, "I dare engage these creatures have their titles and distinctions of honour; they contrive little nests and burrows, that they call houses and cities; they make a figure in dress and equipage; they love, they fight, they dispute, they cheat, they betray!" And thus he continued on, while my colour came and went several times, with indignation, to hear our noble country, the mistress of arts and arms, the scourge of France, the arbitress of Europe, the seat of virtue, piety, honour, and truth, the pride and envy of the world, so contemptuously treated.

But as I was not in a condition to resent injuries, so upon mature thoughts I began to doubt whether I was injured or no. For, after having been accustomed several months to the sight and converse of this people, and observed every object upon which I cast mine eyes to be of proportionable magnitude, the horror I had at first conceived from their bulk and aspect was so far worn off, that if I had then beheld a company of English lords and ladies in their finery and birth-day clothes, acting their several parts in the most courtly manner of strutting, and bowing, and prating, to say the truth, I should have been strongly tempted to laugh as much at them as the king and his grandees did at me. Neither, indeed, could I forbear smiling at myself, when the queen used to place me upon her hand towards a looking-glass, by which both our persons appeared before me in full view together; and there could be nothing more ridiculous than the comparison; so that I really began to imagine myself dwindled many degrees below my usual size.

Nothing angered and mortified me so much as the queen's dwarf; who being of the lowest stature that was ever in that country (for I verily think he was not full thirty feet high), became so insolent at seeing a creature so much beneath him, that he would always affect to swagger and look big as he passed by me in the queen's antechamber, while I was standing on some table talking with the lords or ladies of the court, and he seldom failed of a smart word or two upon my littleness; against which I could only revenge myself by calling him brother, challenging him to wrestle, and such repartees as are usually in the mouths of court pages. One day, at dinner, this malicious little cub was so nettled with something I had said to him, that, raising himself upon the frame of her majesty's chair, he took me up by the middle, as I was sitting down, not thinking any harm, and let me drop into a large silver bowl of cream, and then ran away as fast as he could. I fell over head and ears, and, if I had not been a good swimmer, it might have gone very hard with me; for Glumdalclitch in that instant happened to be at the other end of the room, and the queen was in such a fright, that she wanted presence of mind to assist me. But my little nurse ran to my relief, and took me out, after I had swallowed above a quart of cream. I was put to bed: however, I received no other damage than the loss of a suit of clothes, which was utterly spoiled. The dwarf was soundly whipt, and as a farther punishment, forced to drink up the bowl of cream into which he had thrown me: neither was he ever restored to favour; for soon after the queen bestowed him on a lady of high quality, so that I saw him no more, to my very great satisfaction; for I could not tell to what extremities such a malicious urchin might have carried his resentment.

He had before served me a scurvy trick, which set the queen a-laughing, although at the same time she was heartily vexed, and would have immediately cashiered him, if I had not been so generous as to intercede. Her majesty had taken a marrow-bone upon her plate, and, after knocking out the marrow, placed the bone again in the dish erect, as it stood before; the dwarf, watching his opportunity, while Glumdalclitch was gone to the side-board, mounted the stool that she stood on to take care of me at meals, took me up in both hands, and squeezing my legs together, wedged them into the marrow bone above my waist, where I stuck for some time, and made a very ridiculous figure. I believe it was near a minute before any one knew what was become of me; for I thought it below me to cry out. But, as princes seldom get their meat hot, my legs were not scalded, only my stockings and breeches in a sad condition. The dwarf, at my entreaty, had no other punishment than a sound whipping.

I was frequently rallied by the queen upon account of my fearfulness; and she used to ask me whether the people of my country were as great cowards as myself? The occasion was this: the kingdom is much pestered with flies in summer; and these odious insects, each of them as big as a Dunstable lark, hardly gave me any rest while I sat at dinner, with their continual humming and buzzing about mine ears. They would sometimes alight upon my victuals, and leave their loathsome excrement, or spawn behind, which to me was very visible, though not to the natives of that country, whose large optics were not so acute as mine, in viewing smaller objects. Sometimes they would fix upon my nose, or forehead, where they stung me to the quick, smelling very offensively; and I could easily trace that viscous matter, which, our naturalists tell us, enables those creatures to walk with their feet upwards upon a ceiling. I had much ado to defend myself against these detestable animals, and could not forbear starting when they came on my face. It was the common practice of the dwarf, to catch a number of these insects in his hand, as schoolboys do among us, and let them out suddenly under my nose, on purpose to frighten me, and divert the queen. My remedy was to cut them in pieces with my knife, as they flew in the air, wherein my dexterity was much admired.

I remember, one morning, when Glumdalclitch had set me in a box upon a window, as she usually did in fair days to give me air (for I durst not venture to let the box be hung on a nail out of the window, as we do with cages in England), after I had lifted up one of my sashes, and sat down at my table to eat a piece of sweet cake for my breakfast, above twenty wasps, allured by the smell, came flying into the room, humming louder than the drones of as many bagpipes. Some of them seized my cake, and carried it piecemeal away; others flew about my head and face, confounding me with the noise, and putting me in the utmost terror of their stings. However, I had the courage to rise and draw my hanger, and attack them in the air. I dispatched four of them, but the rest got away, and I presently shut my window. These insects were as large as partridges: I took out their stings, found them an inch and a half long, and as sharp as needles. I carefully preserved them all; and having since shown them, with some other curiosities, in several parts of Europe, upon my return to England I gave three of them to Gresham College, and kept the fourth for myself.

CHAPTER FOUR

The country described. A proposal for correcting modern maps. The king's palace; and some account of the metropolis. The author's way of travelling. The chief temple described.

I NOW INTEND to give the reader a short description of this country, as far as I travelled in it, which was not above two thousand miles round Lorbrulgrud, the metropolis. For the queen, whom I always attended, never went farther when she accompanied the king in his progresses, and there staid till his majesty returned from viewing his frontiers. The whole extent of this prince's dominions reaches about six thousand miles in length, and from three to five in breadth: whence I cannot but conclude, that our geographers of Europe are in a great error, by supposing nothing but sea between Japan and California; for it was ever my opinion, that there must be a balance of earth to counterpoise the great continent of Tartary; and therefore they ought to correct their maps and charts, by joining this vast tract of land to the north-west parts of America, wherein I shall be ready to lend them my assistance.

The kingdom is a peninsula, terminated to the north-east by a ridge of mountains thirty miles high, which are altogether impassable, by reason of the volcanoes upon the tops: neither do the most learned know what sort of mortals inhabit beyond those mountains, or whether they be inhabited at all. On the three other sides, it is bounded by the ocean. There is not one seaport in the whole kingdom: and those parts of the coasts into which the rivers issue, are so full of pointed rocks, and the sea generally so rough, that there is no venturing with the smallest of their boats; so that these people are wholly excluded from any commerce with the rest of the world. But the large rivers are full of vessels, and abound with excellent fish; for they seldom get any from the sea, because the sea fish are of the same size with those in Europe, and consequently not worth catching; whereby it is manifest, that nature, in the production of plants and animals of so extraordinary a bulk, is wholly confined to this continent, of which I leave the reasons to be determined by philosophers. However, now and then they take a whale that happens to be dashed against the rocks, which the common people feed on heartily. These whales I have known so large, that a man could hardly carry one upon his shoulders; and sometimes, for curiosity, they are brought in hampers to Lorbrulgrud; I saw one of them in a dish at the king's table, which passed for a rarity, but I did not observe he was fond of it; for I think, indeed, the bigness disgusted him, although I have seen one somewhat larger in Greenland.

The country is well inhabited, for it contains fifty-one cities, near a hundred walled towns, and a great number of villages. To satisfy my curious reader, it may be sufficient to describe Lorbrulgrud. This city stands upon almost two equal parts, on each side the river that passes through. It contains above eighty thousand houses, and about six hundred thousand inhabitants. It is in length three *glomglungs* (which make about fifty-four English miles,) and two and a half in breadth; as I measured it myself in the royal map made by the king's order, which was laid on the ground on purpose for me, and extended a hundred feet: I paced the diameter and circumference several times barefoot, and, computing by the scale, measured it pretty exactly.

The king's palace is no regular edifice, but a heap of buildings, about seven miles round: the chief rooms are generally two hundred and forty feet high, and broad and long in proportion. A coach was allowed to Glumdalclitch and me, wherein her governess frequently took her out to see the town, or go among the shops; and I was always of the party, carried in my box; although the girl, at my own desire, would often take me out, and hold me in her hand, that I might more conveniently view the houses and the people, as we passed along the streets. I reckoned our coach to be about a square of Westminster-hall, but not altogether so high: however, I cannot be very exact. One day the governess ordered our coachman to stop at several shops, where the beggars, watching their opportunity, crowded to the sides of the coach, and gave me the most horrible spectacle that ever a European eye beheld. There was a woman with a cancer in her breast, swelled to a monstrous size, full of holes, in two or three of which I could have easily crept, and covered my whole body. There was a fellow with a wen in his neck, larger than five wool-packs; and another, with a couple of wooden legs, each about twenty feet high. But the most hateful sight of all, was the lice crawling on their clothes. I could see distinctly the limbs of these vermin with my naked eye, much better than those of a European louse through a microscope, and their snouts with which they rooted like swine. They were the first I had ever beheld, and I should have been curious enough to dissect one of them, if I had had proper instruments, which I unluckily left behind me in the ship, although, indeed, the sight was so nauseous, that it perfectly turned my stomach.

Besides the large box in which I was usually carried, the queen ordered a smaller one to be made for me, of about twelve feet square, and ten high, for the convenience of travelling; because the other was somewhat too large for Glumdalclitch's lap, and cumbersome in the coach; it was made by the same artist, whom I directed in the whole contrivance. This travelling-closet was an exact square, with a window in the middle of three of the squares, and each window was latticed with iron wire on the outside, to prevent accidents in long journeys. On the fourth side, which had no window, two strong staples were fixed, through which the person that carried me, when I had a mind to be on horseback, put a leathern belt, and buckled it about his waist. This was always the office of some grave trusty servant, in whom I could confide, whether I attended the king and queen in their progresses, or were disposed to see the gardens, or pay a visit to some great lady or minister of state in the court, when Glumdalclitch happened to be out of order; for I soon began to be known and esteemed among the greatest officers, I suppose more upon account of their majesties' favour, than any merit of my own. In journeys, when I was weary of the coach, a servant on horseback would buckle on my box, and place it upon a cushion before him; and there I had a full prospect of the country on three sides, from my three windows. I had, in this closet, a field-bed and a hammock, hung from the ceiling, two chairs and a table, neatly screwed to the floor, to prevent being tossed about by the agitation of the horse or the coach. And having been long used to sea-voyages, those motions, although sometimes very violent, did not much discompose me.

Whenever I had a mind to see the town, it was always in my travelling-closet; which Glumdalclitch held in her lap in a kind of open sedan, after the fashion of the country, borne by four men, and attended by two others in the queen's livery. The people, who had often heard of me, were very curious to crowd about the sedan, and the girl was complaisant enough to make the bearers stop, and to take me in her hand, that I might be more conveniently seen.

I was very desirous to see the chief temple, and particularly the tower belonging to it, which is reckoned the highest in the kingdom. Accordingly one day my nurse carried me thither, but I may truly say I came back disappointed; for the height is not above three thousand feet, reckoning from the ground to the highest pinnacle top; which, allowing for the difference between the size of those people and us in Europe, is no great matter for admiration, nor at all equal in proportion (if I rightly remember) to Salisbury steeple. But, not to detract from a nation, to which, during my life, I shall acknowledge myself extremely obliged, it must be allowed, that whatever this famous tower wants in height, is amply made up in beauty and strength: for the walls are near a hundred feet thick, built of hewn stone, whereof each is about forty feet square, and adorned on all sides with statues of gods and emperors, cut in marble, larger than the life, placed in their several niches. I measured a little finger which had fallen down from one of these statues, and lay unperceived among some rubbish, and found it exactly four feet and an inch in length. Glumdalclitch wrapped it up in her handkerchief, and carried it home in her pocket, to keep among other trinkets, of which the girl was very fond, as children at her age usually are.

The king's kitchen is indeed a noble building, vaulted at top, and about six hundred feet high. The great oven is not so wide, by ten paces, as the cupola at St. Paul's: for I measured the latter on purpose, after my return. But if I should describe the kitchen grate, the prodigious pots and kettles, the joints of meat turning on the spits, with many other particulars, perhaps I should be hardly believed; at least a severe critic would be apt to think I enlarged a little, as travellers are often suspected to do. To avoid which censure I fear I have run too much into the other extreme; and that if this treatise should happen to be translated into the language of Brobdingnag (which is the general name of that kingdom,) and transmitted thither, the king and his people would have reason to complain that I had done them an injury, by a false and diminutive representation.

His majesty seldom keeps above six hundred horses in his stables: they are generally from fifty-four to sixty feet high. But, when he goes abroad on solemn days, he is attended, for state, by a military guard of five hundred horse, which, indeed, I thought was the most splendid sight that could be ever beheld, till I saw part of his army in battalia, whereof I shall find another occasion to speak.

CHAPTER FIVE

Several adventurers that happened to the author. The execution of a criminal. The author shows his skill in navigation.

I SHOULD HAVE lived happy enough in that country, if my littleness had not exposed me to several ridiculous and troublesome accidents; some of which I shall venture to relate. Glumdalclitch often carried me into the gardens of the court in my smaller box, and would sometimes take me out of it, and hold me in her hand, or set me down to walk. I remember, before the dwarf left the queen, he followed us one day into those gardens, and my nurse having set me down, he and I being close together, near some dwarf apple trees, I must needs show my wit, by a silly allusion between him and the trees, which happens to hold in their language as it does in ours. Whereupon, the malicious rogue, watching his opportunity, when I was walking under one of them, shook it directly over my head, by which a dozen apples, each of them near as large as a Bristol barrel, came tumbling about my ears; one of them hit me on the back as I chanced to stoop, and knocked me down flat on my face; but I received no other hurt, and the dwarf was pardoned at my desire, because I had given the provocation.

Another day, Glumdalclitch left me on a smooth grass-plot to divert myself, while she walked at some distance with her governess. In the meantime, there suddenly fell such a violent shower of hail, that I was immediately by the force of it, struck to the ground: and when I was down, the hailstones gave me such cruel bangs all over the body, as if I had been pelted with tennis-balls; however, I made a shift to creep on all fours, and shelter myself, by lying flat on my face, on the lee-side of a border of lemon-thyme, but so bruised from head to foot, that I could not go abroad in ten days. Neither is this at all to be wondered at, because nature, in that country, observing the same proportion through all her operations, a hailstone is near eighteen hundred times as large as one in Europe; which I can assert upon experience, having been so curious as to weigh and measure them.

But a more dangerous accident happened to me in the same garden, when my little nurse, believing she had put me in a secure place (which I often entreated her to do, that I might enjoy my own thoughts,) and having left my box at home, to avoid the trouble of carrying it, went to another part of the garden with her governess and some ladies of her acquaintance. While she was absent, and out of hearing, a small white spaniel that belonged to one of the chief gardeners, having got by accident into the garden, happened to range near the place where I lay: the dog, following the scent, came directly up, and taking me in his mouth, ran straight to his master wagging his tail, and set me gently on the ground. By good fortune he had been so well taught, that I was carried between his teeth without the least hurt, or even tearing my clothes. But the poor gardener, who knew me well, and had a great kindness for me, was in a terrible fright: he gently took me up in both his hands, and asked me how I did? but I was so amazed and out of breath, that I could not speak a word. In a few minutes I came to myself, and he carried me safe to my little nurse, who, by this time, had returned to the place where she left me, and was in cruel agonies when I did not appear, nor answer when she called. She severely reprimanded the gardener on account of his dog. But the thing was hushed up, and never known at court, for the girl was afraid of the queen's anger; and truly, as to myself, I thought it would not be for my reputation, that such a story should go about.

This accident absolutely determined Glumdalclitch never to trust me abroad for the future out of her sight. I had been long afraid of this resolution, and therefore concealed from her some little unlucky adventures, that happened in those times when I was left by myself. Once a kite, hovering over the garden, made a stoop at me, and if I had not resolutely drawn my hanger, and run under a thick espalier, he would have certainly carried me away in his talons. Another time, walking to the top of a fresh mole-hill, I fell to my neck in the hole, through which that animal had cast up the earth, and coined some lie, not worth remembering, to excuse myself for spoiling my clothes. I likewise broke my right shin against the shell of a snail, which I happened to stumble over, as I was walking alone and thinking on poor England.

I cannot tell whether I were more pleased or mortified to observe, in those solitary walks, that the smaller birds did not appear to be at all afraid of me, but would hop about within a yard's distance, looking for worms and other food, with as much indifference and security as if no creature at all were near them. I remember, a thrush had the confidence to snatch out of my hand, with his bill, a of cake that Glumdalclitch had just given me for my breakfast. When I attempted to catch any of these birds, they would boldly turn against me, endeavouring to peck my fingers, which I durst not venture within their reach; and then they would hop back unconcerned, to hunt for worms or snails, as they did before. But one day, I took a thick cudgel, and threw it with all my strength so luckily, at a linnet, that I knocked him down, and seizing him by the neck with both my hands, ran with him in triumph to my nurse. However, the bird, who had only been stunned, recovering himself gave me so many boxes with his wings, on both sides of my head and body, though I held him at arm's-length, and was out of the reach of his claws, that I was twenty times thinking to let him go. But I was soon relieved by one of our servants, who wrung off the bird's neck, and I had him next day for dinner, by the queen's command. This linnet, as near as I can remember, seemed to be somewhat larger than an English swan.

The maids of honour often invited Glumdalclitch to their apartments, and desired she would bring me along with her, on purpose to have the pleasure of seeing and touching me. They would often strip me naked from top to toe, and lay me at full length in their bosoms; wherewith I was much disgusted because, to say the truth, a very offensive smell came from their skins; which I do not mention, or intend, to the disadvantage of those excellent ladies, for whom I have all manner of respect; but I conceive that my sense was more acute in proportion to my littleness, and that those illustrious persons were no more disagreeable to their lovers, or to each other, than people of the same quality are with us in England. And, after all, I found their natural smell was much more supportable, than when they used perfumes, under which I immediately swooned away. I cannot forget, that an intimate friend of mine in Lilliput, took the freedom in a warm day, when I had used a good deal of exercise, to complain of a strong smell about me, although I am as little faulty that way, as most of my sex: but I suppose his faculty of smelling was as nice with regard to me, as mine was to that of this people. Upon this point, I cannot forbear doing justice to the queen my mistress, and Glumdalclitch my nurse, whose persons were as sweet as those of any lady in England.

That which gave me most uneasiness among these maids of honour (when my nurse carried me to visit then) was, to see them use me without any manner of ceremony, like a creature who had no sort of consequence: for they would strip themselves to the skin, and put on their smocks in my presence, while I was placed on their toilet, directly before their naked bodies, which I am sure to me was very far from being a tempting sight, or from giving me any other emotions than those of horror and disgust: their skins appeared so coarse and uneven, so variously coloured, when I saw them near, with a mole here and there as broad as a trencher, and hairs hanging from it thicker than pack-threads, to say nothing farther concerning the rest of their persons. Neither did they at all scruple, while I was by, to discharge what they had drank, to the quantity of at least two hogsheads, in a vessel that held above three tuns. The handsomest among these maids of honour, a pleasant, frolicsome girl of sixteen, would sometimes set me astride upon one of her nipples, with many other tricks, wherein the reader will excuse me for not being over particular. But I was so much displeased, that I entreated Glumdalclitch to contrive some excuse for not seeing that young lady any more.

One day, a young gentleman, who was nephew to my nurse's governess, came and pressed them both to see an execution. It was of a man, who had murdered one of that gentleman's intimate acquaintance. Glumdalclitch was prevailed on to be of the company, very much against her inclination, for she was naturally tender-hearted: and, as for myself, although I abhorred such kind of spectacles, yet my curiosity tempted me to see something that I thought must be extraordinary. The malefactor was fixed in a chair upon a scaffold erected for that purpose, and his head cut off at one blow, with a sword of about forty feet long. The veins and arteries spouted up such a prodigious quantity of blood, and so high in the air, that the great *jet d'eau* at Versailles was not equal to it for the time it lasted: and the head, when it fell on the scaffold floor, gave such a bounce as made me start, although I was at least half an English mile distant.

The queen, who often used to hear me talk of my sea-voyages, and took all occasions to divert me when I was melancholy, asked me whether I understood how to handle a sail or an oar, and whether a little exercise of rowing might not be convenient for my health? I answered, that I understood both very well: for although my proper employment had been to be surgeon or doctor to the ship, yet often, upon a pinch, I was forced to work like a common mariner. But I could not see how this could be done in their country, where the smallest wherry was equal to a first-rate man of war among us; and such a boat as I could manage would never live in any of their rivers. Her majesty said, if I would contrive a boat, her own joiner should make it, and she would provide a place for me to sail in. The fellow was an ingenious workman, and by my instructions, in ten days, finished a pleasure-boat with all its tackling, able conveniently to hold eight Europeans. When it was finished, the queen was so delighted, that she ran with it in her lap to the king, who ordered it to be put into a cistern full of water, with me in it, by way of trial, where I could not manage my two sculls, or little oars, for want of room. But the queen had before contrived another project. She ordered the joiner to make a wooden trough of three hundred feet long, fifty broad, and eight deep; which, being well pitched, to prevent leaking, was placed on the floor, along the wall, in an outer room of the palace. It had a cock near the bottom to let out the water, when it began to grow stale; and two servants could easily fill it in half an hour. Here I often used to row for my own diversion, as well as that of the queen and her ladies, who thought themselves well entertained with my skill and agility. Sometimes I would put up my sail, and then my business was only to steer, while the ladies gave me a gale with their fans; and, when they were weary, some of their pages would blow my sail forward with their breath, while I showed my art by steering starboard or larboard as I pleased. When I had done, Glumdalclitch always carried back my boat into her closet, and hung it on a nail to dry.

In this exercise I once met an accident, which had like to have cost me my life; for, one of the pages having put my boat into the trough, the governess who attended Glumdalclitch very officiously lifted me up, to place me in the boat: but I happened to slip through her fingers, and should infallibly have fallen down forty feet upon the floor, if, by the luckiest chance in the world, I had not been stopped by a corking-pin that stuck in the good gentlewoman's stomacher; the head of the pin passing between my shirt and the waistband of my breeches, and thus I was held by the middle in the air, till Glumdalclitch ran to my relief.

Another time, one of the servants, whose office it was to fill my trough every third day with fresh water, was so careless as to let a huge frog (not perceiving it) slip out of his pail. The frog lay concealed till I was put into my boat, but then, seeing a resting-place, climbed up, and made it lean so much on one side, that I was forced to balance it with all my weight on the other, to prevent overturning. When the frog was got in, it hopped at once half the length of the boat, and then over my head, backward and forward, daubing my face and clothes with its odious slime. The largeness of its features made it appear the most deformed animal that can be conceived. However, I desired Glumdalclitch to let me deal with it alone. I banged it a good while with one of my sculls, and at last forced it to leap out of the boat.

But the greatest danger I ever underwent in that kingdom, was from a monkey, who belonged to one of the clerks of the kitchen. Glumdalclitch had locked me up in her closet, while she went somewhere upon business, or a visit. The weather being very warm, the closet-window was left open, as well as the windows and the door of my bigger box, in which I usually lived, because of its largeness and conveniency. As I sat quietly meditating at my table, I heard something bounce in at the closet-window, and skip about from one side to the other: whereat, although I was much alarmed, yet I ventured to look out, but not stirring from my seat; and then I saw this frolicsome animal frisking and leaping up and down, till at last he came to my box, which he seemed to view with great pleasure and curiosity, peeping in at the door and every window. I retreated to the farther corner of my room; or box; but the monkey looking in at every side, put me in such a fright, that I wanted presence of mind to conceal myself under the bed, as I might easily have done. After some time spent in peeping, grinning, and chattering, he at last espied me; and reaching one of his paws in at the door, as a cat does when she plays with a mouse, although I often shifted place to avoid him, he at length seized the lappet of my coat (which being made of that country silk, was very thick and strong), and dragged me out. He took me up in his right fore-foot and held me as a nurse does a child she is going to suckle, just as I have seen the same sort of creature do with a kitten in Europe; and when I offered to struggle he squeezed me so hard, that I thought it more prudent to submit. I have good reason to believe, that he took me for a young one of his own species, by his often stroking my face very gently with his other paw. In these diversions he was interrupted by a noise at the closet door, as if somebody were opening it: whereupon he suddenly leaped up to the window at which he had come in, and thence upon the leads and gutters, walking upon three legs, and holding me in the fourth, till he clambered up to a roof that was next to ours. I heard Glumdalclitch give a shriek at the moment he was carrying me out. The poor girl was almost distracted: that quarter of the palace was all in an uproar; the servants ran for ladders; the monkey was seen by hundreds in the court, sitting upon the ridge of a building, holding me like a baby in one of his forepaws, and feeding me with the other, by cramming into my mouth some victuals he had squeezed out of the bag on one side of his chaps, and patting me when I would not eat; whereat many of the rabble below could not forbear laughing; neither do I think they justly ought to be blamed, for, without question, the sight was ridiculous enough to every body but myself. Some of the people threw up stones, hoping to drive the monkey down; but this was strictly forbidden, or else, very probably, my brains had been dashed out.

The ladders were now applied, and mounted by several men; which the monkey observing, and finding himself almost encompassed, not being able to make speed enough with his three legs, let me drop on a ridge tile, and made his escape. Here I sat for some time, five hundred yards from the ground, expecting every moment to be blown down by the wind, or to fall by my own giddiness, and come tumbling over and over from the ridge to the eaves; but an honest lad, one of my nurse's footmen, climbed up, and putting me into his breeches pocket, brought me down safe.

I was almost choked with the filthy stuff the monkey had crammed down my throat: but my dear little nurse picked it out of my mouth with a small needle, and then I fell a-vomiting, which gave me great relief. Yet I was so weak and bruised in the sides with the squeezes given me by this odious animal, that I was forced to keep my bed a fortnight. The king, queen, and all the court, sent every day to inquire after my health; and her majesty made me several visits during my sickness. The monkey was killed, and an order made, that no such animal should be kept about the palace.

When I attended the king after my recovery, to return him thanks for his favours, he was pleased to rally me a good deal upon this adventure. He asked me, "what my thoughts and speculations were, while I lay in the monkey's paw; how I liked the victuals he gave me; his manner of feeding; and whether the fresh air on the roof had sharpened my stomach." He desired to know, "what I would have done upon such an occasion in my own country." I told his majesty, "that in Europe we had no monkeys, except such as were brought for curiosity from other places, and so small, that I could deal with a dozen of them together, if they presumed to attack me. And as for that monstrous animal with whom I was so lately engaged (it was indeed as large as an elephant), if my fears had suffered me to think so far as to make use of my hanger," (looking fiercely, and clapping my hand on the hilt, as I spoke) "when he poked his paw into my chamber, perhaps I should have given him such a wound, as would have made him glad to withdraw it with more haste than he put it in." This I delivered in a firm tone, like a person who was jealous lest his courage should be called in question. However, my speech produced nothing else beside a laud laughter, which all the respect due to his majesty from those about him could not make them contain. This made me reflect, how vain an attempt it is for a man to endeavour to do himself honour among those who are out of all degree of equality or comparison with him. And yet I have seen the moral of my own behaviour very frequent in England since my return; where a little contemptible varlet, without the least title to birth, person, wit, or common sense, shall presume to look with importance, and put himself upon a foot with the greatest persons of the kingdom.

I was every day furnishing the court with some ridiculous story: and Glumdalclitch, although she loved me to excess, yet was arch enough to inform the queen, whenever I committed any folly that she thought would be diverting to her majesty. The girl, who had been out of order, was carried by her governess to take the air about an hour's distance, or thirty miles from town. They alighted out of the coach near a small foot-path in a field, and Glumdalclitch setting down my travelling box, I went out of it to walk. There was a cow-dung in the path, and I must need try my activity by attempting to leap over it. I took a run, but unfortunately jumped short, and found myself just in the middle up to my knees. I waded through with some difficulty, and one of the foot-men wiped me as clean as he could with his handkerchief, for I was filthily bemired; and my nurse confined me to my box, till we returned home; where the queen was soon informed of what had passed, and the footmen spread it about the court: so that all the mirth for some days was at my expense.

CHAPTER SIX

Several contrivances of the author to please the king and queen. He shows his skill in music. The king inquires into the state of England, which the author relates to him. The king's observations thereon.

I USED TO attend the king's levee once or twice a week, and had often seen him under the barber's hand, which indeed was at first very terrible to behold; for the razor was almost twice as long as an ordinary scythe. His majesty, according to the custom of the country, was only shaved twice a-week. I once prevailed on the barber to give me some of the suds or lather, out of which I picked forty or fifty of the strongest stumps of hair. I then took a piece of fine wood, and cut it like the back of a comb, making several holes in it at equal distances with as small a needle as I could get from Glumdalclitch. I fixed in the stumps so artificially, scraping and sloping them with my knife toward the points, that I made a very tolerable comb; which was a seasonable supply, my own being so much broken in the teeth, that it was almost useless: neither did I know any artist in that country so nice and exact, as would undertake to make me another.

And this puts me in mind of an amusement, wherein I spent many of my leisure hours. I desired the queen's woman to save for me the combings of her majesty's hair, whereof in time I got a good quantity; and consulting with my friend the cabinet-maker, who had received general orders to do little jobs for me, I directed him to make two chair-frames, no larger than those I had in my box, and to bore little holes with a fine awl, round those parts where I designed the backs and seats; through these holes I wove the strongest hairs I could pick out, just after the manner of cane chairs in England. When they were finished, I made a present of them to her majesty; who kept them in her cabinet, and used to show them for curiosities, as indeed they were the wonder of every one that beheld them. The queen would have me sit upon one of these chairs, but I absolutely refused to obey her, protesting I would rather die than place a dishonourable part of my body on those precious hairs, that once adorned her majesty's head. Of these hairs (as I had always a mechanical genius) I likewise made a neat little purse, about five feet long, with her majesty's name deciphered in gold letters, which I gave to Glumdalclitch, by the queen's consent. To say the truth, it was more for show than use, being not of strength to bear the weight of the larger coins, and therefore she kept nothing in it but some little toys that girls are fond of.

The king, who delighted in music, had frequent concerts at court, to which I was sometimes carried, and set in my box on a table to hear them: but the noise was so great that I could hardly distinguish the tunes. I am confident that all the drums and trumpets of a royal army, beating and sounding together just at your ears, could not equal it. My practice was to have my box removed from the place where the performers sat, as far as I could, then to shut the doors and windows of it, and draw the window curtains; after which I found their music not disagreeable.

I had learned in my youth to play a little upon the spinet. Glumdalclitch kept one in her chamber, and a master attended twice a-week to teach her: I called it a spinet, because it somewhat resembled that instrument, and was played upon in the same manner. A fancy came into my head, that I would entertain the king and queen with an English tune upon this instrument. But this appeared extremely difficult: for the spinet was near sixty feet long, each key being almost a foot wide, so that with my arms extended I could not reach to above five keys, and to press them down required a good smart stroke with my fist, which would be too great a labour, and to no purpose. The method I contrived was this: I prepared two round sticks, about the bigness of common cudgels; they were thicker at one end than the other, and I covered the thicker ends with pieces of a mouse's skin, that by rapping on them I might neither damage the tops of the keys nor interrupt the sound. Before the spinet a bench was placed, about four feet below the keys, and I was put upon the bench. I ran sideling upon it, that way and this, as fast as I could, banging the proper keys with my two sticks, and made a shift to play a jig, to the great satisfaction of both their majesties; but it was the most violent exercise I ever underwent; and yet I could not strike above sixteen keys, nor consequently play the bass and treble together, as other artists do; which was a great disadvantage to my performance.

The king, who, as I before observed, was a prince of excellent understanding, would frequently order that I should be brought in my box, and set upon the table in his closet: he would then command me to bring one of my chairs out of the box, and sit down within three yards distance upon the top of the cabinet, which brought me almost to a level with his face. In this manner I had several conversations with him. I one day took the freedom to tell his majesty, "that the contempt he discovered towards Europe, and the rest of the world, did not seem answerable to those excellent qualities of mind that he was master of; that reason did not extend itself with the bulk of the body; on the contrary, we observed in our country, that the tallest persons were usually the least provided with it; that among other animals, bees and ants had the reputation of more industry, art, and sagacity, than many of the larger kinds; and that, as inconsiderable as he took me to be, I hoped I might live to do his majesty some signal service." The king heard me with attention, and began to conceive a much better opinion of me than he had ever before. He desired "I would give him as exact an account of the government of England as I possibly could; because, as fond as princes commonly are of their own customs (for so he conjectured of other monarchs, by my former discourses), he should be glad to hear of any thing that might deserve imitation."

Imagine with thyself, courteous reader, how often I then wished for the tongue of Demosthenes or Cicero, that might have enabled me to celebrate the praise of my own dear native country in a style equal to its merits and felicity.

I began my discourse by informing his majesty, that our dominions consisted of two islands, which composed three mighty kingdoms, under one sovereign, beside our plantations in America. I dwelt long upon the fertility of our soil, and the temperature of our climate. I then spoke at large upon the constitution of an English parliament; partly made up of an illustrious body called the House of Peers; persons of the noblest blood, and of the most ancient and ample patrimonies. I described that extraordinary care always taken of their education in arts and arms, to qualify them for being counsellors both to the king and kingdom; to have a share in the legislature; to be members of the highest court of judicature, whence there can be no appeal; and to be champions always ready for the defence of their prince and country, by their valour, conduct, and fidelity. That these were the ornament and bulwark of the kingdom, worthy followers of their most renowned ancestors, whose honour had been the reward of their virtue, from which their posterity were never once known to degenerate. To these were joined several holy persons, as part of that assembly, under the title of bishops, whose peculiar business is to take care of religion, and of those who instruct the people therein.

These were searched and sought out through the whole nation, by the prince and his wisest counsellors, among such of the priesthood as were most deservedly distinguished by the sanctity of their lives, and the depth of their erudition; who were indeed the spiritual fathers of the clergy and the people.

That the other part of the parliament consisted of an assembly called the House of Commons, who were all principal gentlemen, freely picked and culled out by the people themselves, for their great abilities and love of their country, to represent the wisdom of the whole nation. And that these two bodies made up the most august assembly in Europe; to whom, in conjunction with the prince, the whole legislature is committed.

I then descended to the courts of justice; over which the judges, those venerable sages and interpreters of the law, presided, for determining the disputed rights and properties of men, as well as for the punishment of vice and protection of innocence. I mentioned the prudent management of our treasury; the valour and achievements of our forces, by sea and land. I computed the number of our people, by reckoning how many millions there might be of each religious sect, or political party among us. I did not omit even our sports and pastimes, or any other particular which I thought might redound to the honour of my country. And I finished all with a brief historical account of affairs and events in England for about a hundred years past.

This conversation was not ended under five audiences, each of several hours; and the king heard the whole with great attention, frequently taking notes of what I spoke, as well as memorandums of what questions he intended to ask me.

When I had put an end to these long discources, his majesty, in a sixth audience, consulting his notes, proposed many doubts, queries, and objections, upon every article. He asked, "What methods were used to cultivate the minds and bodies of our young nobility, and in what kind of business they commonly spent the first and teachable parts of their lives? What course was taken to supply that assembly, when any noble family became extinct? What qualifications were necessary in those who are to be created new lords: whether the humour of the prince, a sum of money to a court lady, or a design of strengthening a party opposite to the public interest, ever happened to be the motive in those advancements? What share of knowledge these lords had in the laws of their country, and how they came by it, so as to enable them to decide the properties of their fellow-subjects in the last resort? Whether they were always so free from avarice, partialities, or want, that a bribe, or some other sinister view, could have no place among them? Whether those holy lords I spoke of were always promoted to that rank upon account of their knowledge in religious matters, and the sanctity of their lives; had never been compliers with the times, while they were common priests; or slavish prostitute chaplains to some nobleman, whose opinions they continued servilely to follow, after they were admitted into that assembly?"

He then desired to know, "What arts were practised in electing those whom I called commoners: whether a stranger, with a strong purse, might not influence the vulgar voters to choose him before their own landlord, or the most considerable gentleman in the neighbourhood? How it came to pass, that people were so violently bent upon getting into this assembly, which I allowed to be a great trouble and expense, often to the ruin of their families, without any salary or pension? because this appeared such an exalted strain of virtue and public spirit, that his majesty seemed to doubt it might possibly not be always sincere." And he desired to know, "Whether such zealous gentlemen could have any views of refunding themselves for the charges and trouble they were at by sacrificing the public good to the designs of a weak and vicious prince, in conjunction with a corrupted ministry?" He multiplied his questions, and sifted me thoroughly upon every part of this head, proposing numberless inquiries and objections, which I think it not prudent or convenient to repeat.

Upon what I said in relation to our courts of justice, his majesty desired to be satisfied in several points: and this I was the better able to do, having been formerly almost ruined by a long suit in chancery, which was decreed for me with costs. He asked, "What time was usually spent in determining between right and wrong, and what degree of expense? Whether advocates and orators had liberty to plead in causes manifestly known to be unjust, vexatious, or oppressive? Whether party, in religion or politics, were observed to be of any weight in the scale of justice? Whether those pleading orators were persons educated in the general knowledge of equity, or only in provincial, national, and other local customs? Whether they or their judges had any part in penning those laws, which they assumed the liberty of interpreting, and glossing upon at their pleasure? Whether they had ever, at different times, pleaded for and against the same cause, and cited precedents to prove contrary opinions? Whether they were a rich or a poor corporation? Whether they received any pecuniary reward for pleading, or delivering their opinions? And particularly, whether they were ever admitted as members in the lower senate?"

He fell next upon the management of our treasury; and said, "he thought my memory had failed me, because I computed our taxes at about five or six millions a-year, and when I came to mention the issues, he found they sometimes amounted to more than double; for the notes he had taken were very particular in this point, because he hoped, as he told me, that the knowledge of our conduct might be useful to him, and he could not be deceived in his calculations. But, if what I told him were true, he was still at a loss how a kingdom could run out of its estate, like a private person." He asked me, "who were our creditors; and where we found money to pay them?" He wondered to hear me talk of such chargeable and expensive wars; "that certainly we must be a quarrelsome people, or live among very bad neighbours, and that our generals must needs be richer than our kings." He asked, what business we had out of our own islands, unless upon the score of trade, or treaty, or to defend the coasts with our fleet?" Above all, he was amazed to hear me talk of a mercenary standing army, in the midst of peace, and among a free people. He said, "if we were governed by our own consent, in the persons of our representatives, he could not imagine of whom we were afraid, or against whom we were to fight; and would hear my opinion, whether a private man's house might not be better defended by himself, his children, and family, than by half-a-dozen rascals, picked up at a venture in the streets for small wages, who might get a hundred times more by cutting their throats?"

He laughed at my "odd kind of arithmetic," as he was pleased to call it, "in reckoning the numbers of our people, by a computation drawn from the several sects among us, in religion and politics." He said, "he knew no reason why those, who entertain opinions prejudicial to the public, should be obliged to change, or should not be obliged to conceal them. And as it was tyranny in any government to require the first, so it was weakness not to enforce the second: for a man may be allowed to keep poisons in his closet, but not to vend them about for cordials."

He observed, "that among the diversions of our nobility and gentry, I had mentioned gaming: he desired to know at what age this entertainment was usually taken up, and when it was laid down; how much of their time it employed; whether it ever went so high as to affect their fortunes; whether mean, vicious people, by their dexterity in that art, might not arrive at great riches, and sometimes keep our very nobles in dependence, as well as habituate them to vile companions, wholly take them from the improvement of their minds, and force them, by the losses they received, to learn and practise that infamous dexterity upon others?"

He was perfectly astonished with the historical account gave him of our affairs during the last century; protesting "it was only a heap of conspiracies, rebellions, murders, massacres, revolutions, banishments, the very worst effects that avarice, faction, hypocrisy, perfidiousness, cruelty, rage, madness, hatred, envy, lust, malice, and ambition, could produce."

His majesty, in another audience, was at the pains to recapitulate the sum of all I had spoken; compared the questions he made with the answers I had given; then taking me into his hands, and stroking me gently, delivered himself in these words, which I shall never forget, nor the manner he spoke them in: "My little friend Grildrig, you have made a most admirable panegyric upon your country; you have clearly proved, that ignorance, idleness, and vice, are the proper ingredients for qualifying a legislator; that laws are best explained, interpreted, and applied, by those whose interest and abilities lie in perverting, confounding, and eluding them. I observe among you some lines of an institution, which, in its original, might have been tolerable, but these half erased, and the rest wholly blurred and blotted by corruptions. It does not appear, from all you have said, how any one perfection is required toward the procurement of any one station among you; much less, that men are ennobled on account of their virtue; that priests are advanced for their piety or learning; soldiers, for their conduct or valour; judges, for their integrity; senators, for the love of their country; or counsellors for their wisdom. As for yourself," continued the king, "who have spent the greatest part of your life in travelling, I am well disposed to hope you may hitherto have escaped many vices of your country. But by what I have gathered from your own relation, and the answers I have with much pains wrung and extorted from you, I cannot but conclude the bulk of your natives to be the most pernicious race of little odious vermin that nature ever suffered to crawl upon the surface of the earth."

CHAPTER SEVEN

The author's love of his country. He makes a proposal of much advantage to the king, which is rejected. The king's great ignorance in politics. The learning of that country very imperfect and confined. The laws, and military affairs, and parties in the state.

NOTHING BUT an extreme love of truth could have hindered me from concealing this part of my story. It was in vain to discover my resentments, which were always turned into ridicule; and I was forced to rest with patience, while my noble and beloved country was so injuriously treated. I am as heartily sorry as any of my readers can possibly be, that such an occasion was given: but this prince happened to be so curious and inquisitive upon every particular, that it could not consist either with gratitude or good manners, to refuse giving him what satisfaction I was able. Yet thus much I may be allowed to say in my own vindication, that I artfully eluded many of his questions, and gave to every point a more favourable turn, by many degrees, than the strictness of truth would allow. For I have always borne that laudable partiality to my own country, which Dionysius Halicarnassensis, with so much justice, recommends to an historian: I would hide the frailties and deformities of my political mother, and place her virtues and beauties in the most advantageous light. This was my sincere endeavour in those many discourses I had with that monarch, although it unfortunately failed of success.

But great allowances should be given to a king, who lives wholly secluded from the rest of the world, and must therefore be altogether unacquainted with the manners and customs that most prevail in other nations: the want of which knowledge will ever produce many prejudices, and a certain narrowness of thinking, from which we, and the politer countries of Europe, are wholly exempted. And it would be hard indeed, if so remote a prince's notions of virtue and vice were to be offered as a standard for all mankind.

To confirm what I have now said, and further to show the miserable effects of a confined education, I shall here insert a passage, which will hardly obtain belief. In hopes to ingratiate myself further into his majesty's favour, I told him of "an invention, discovered between three and four hundred years ago, to make a certain powder, into a heap of which, the smallest spark of fire falling, would kindle the whole in a moment, although it were as big as a mountain, and make it all fly up in the air together, with a noise and agitation greater than thunder. That a proper quantity of this powder rammed into a hollow tube of brass or iron, according to its bigness, would drive a ball of iron or lead, with such violence and speed, as nothing was able to sustain its force. That the largest balls thus discharged, would not only destroy whole ranks of an army at once, but batter the strongest walls to the ground, sink down ships, with a thousand men in each, to the bottom of the sea, and when linked together by a chain, would cut through masts and rigging, divide hundreds of bodies in the middle, and lay all waste before them. That we often put this powder into large hollow balls of iron, and discharged them by an engine into some city we were besieging, which would rip up the pavements, tear the houses to pieces, burst and throw splinters on every side, dashing out the brains of all who came near. That I knew the ingredients very well, which were cheap and common; I understood the manner of compounding them, and could direct his workmen how to make those tubes, of a size proportionable to all other things in his majesty's kingdom, and the largest need not be above a hundred feet long; twenty or thirty of which tubes, charged with the proper quantity of powder and balls, would batter down the walls of the strongest town in his dominions in a few hours, or destroy the whole metropolis, if ever it should pretend to dispute his absolute commands." This I humbly offered to his majesty, as a small tribute of acknowledgment, in turn for so many marks that I had received, of his royal favour and protection.

The king was struck with horror at the description I had given of those terrible engines, and the proposal I had made. "He was amazed, how so impotent and grovelling an insect as I" (these were his expressions) "could entertain such inhuman ideas, and in so familiar a manner, as to appear wholly unmoved at all the scenes of blood and desolation which I had painted as the common effects of those destructive machines; whereof," he said, "some evil genius, enemy to mankind, must have been the first contriver. As for himself, he protested, that although few things delighted him so much as new discoveries in art or in nature, yet he would rather lose half his kingdom, than be privy to such a secret; which he commanded me, as I valued any life, never to mention any more."

A strange effect of narrow principles and views! that a prince possessed of every quality which procures veneration, love, and esteem; of strong parts, great wisdom, and profound learning, endowed with admirable talents, and almost adored by his subjects, should, from a nice, unnecessary scruple, whereof in Europe we can have no conception, let slip an opportunity put into his hands that would have made him absolute master of the lives, the liberties, and the fortunes of his people! Neither do I say this, with the least intention to detract from the many virtues of that excellent king, whose character, I am sensible, will, on this account, be very much lessened in the opinion of an English reader: but I take this defect among them to have risen from their ignorance, by not having hitherto reduced politics into a science, as the more acute wits of Europe have done. For, I remember very well, in a discourse one day with the king, when I happened to say, "there were several thousand books among us written upon the art of government," it gave him (directly contrary to my intention) a very mean opinion of our understandings. He professed both to abominate and despise all mystery, refinement, and intrigue, either in a prince or a minister. He could not tell what I meant by secrets of state, where an enemy, or some rival nation, were not in the case. He confined the knowledge of governing within very narrow bounds, to common sense and reason, to justice and lenity, to the speedy determination of civil and criminal causes; with some other obvious topics, which are not worth considering. And he gave it for his opinion, "that whoever could make two ears of corn, or two blades of grass, to grow upon a spot of ground where only one grew before, would deserve better of mankind, and do more essential service to his country, than the whole race of politicians put together."

The learning of this people is very defective, consisting only in morality, history, poetry, and mathematics, wherein they must be allowed to excel. But the last of these is wholly applied to what may be useful in life, to the improvement of agriculture, and all mechanical arts; so that among us, it would be little esteemed. And as to ideas, entities, abstractions, and transcendentals, I could never drive the least conception into their heads.

No law in that country must exceed in words the number of letters in their alphabet, which consists only of two and twenty. But indeed few of them extend even to that length. They are expressed in the most plain and simple terms, wherein those people are not mercurial enough to discover above one interpretation: and to write a comment upon any law, is a capital crime. As to the decision of civil causes, or proceedings against criminals, their precedents are so few, that they have little reason to boast of any extraordinary skill in either.

They have had the art of printing, as well as the Chinese, time out of mind: but their libraries are not very large; for that of the king, which is reckoned the largest, does not amount to above a thousand volumes, placed in a gallery of twelve hundred feet long, whence I had liberty to borrow what books I pleased. The queen's joiner had contrived in one of Glumdalclitch's rooms, a kind of wooden machine five-and-twenty feet high, formed like a standing ladder; the steps were each fifty feet long. It was indeed a moveable pair of stairs, the lowest end placed at ten feet distance from the wall of the chamber. The book I had a mind to read, was put up leaning against the wall: I first mounted to the upper step of the ladder, and turning my face towards the book, began at the top of the page, and so walking to the right and left about eight or ten paces, according to the length of the lines, till I had gotten a little below the level of mine eyes, and then descending gradually till I came to the bottom: after which I mounted again, and began the other page in the same manner, and so turned over the leaf, which I could easily do with both my hands, for it was as thick and stiff as a pasteboard, and in the largest folios not above eighteen or twenty feet long.

Their style is clear, masculine, and smooth, but not florid; for they avoid nothing more than multiplying unnecessary words, or using various expressions. I have perused many of their books, especially those in history and morality. Among the rest, I was much diverted with a little old treatise, which always lay in Glumdalclitch's bed chamber, and belonged to her governess, a grave elderly gentlewoman, who dealt in writings of morality and devotion. The book treats of the weakness of human kind, and is in little esteem, except among the women and the vulgar. However, I was curious to see what an author of that country could say upon such a subject. This writer went through all the usual topics of European moralists, showing "how diminutive, contemptible, and helpless an animal was man in his own nature; how unable to defend himself from inclemencies of the air, or the fury of wild beasts: how much he was excelled by one creature in strength, by another in speed, by a third in foresight, by a fourth in industry." He added, "that nature was degenerated in these latter declining ages of the world, and could now produce only small abortive births, in comparison of those in ancient times." He said "it was very reasonable to think, not only that the species of men were originally much larger, but also that there must have been giants in former ages; which, as it is asserted by history and tradition, so it has been confirmed by huge bones and skulls, casually dug up in several parts of the kingdom, far exceeding the common dwindled race of men in our days." He argued, "that the very laws of nature absolutely required we should have been made, in the beginning of a size more large and robust; not so liable to destruction from every little accident, of a tile falling from a house, or a stone cast from the hand of a boy, or being drowned in a little brook."

From this way of reasoning, the author drew several moral applications, useful in the conduct of life, but needless here to repeat. For my own part, I could not avoid reflecting how universally this talent was spread, of drawing lectures in morality, or indeed rather matter of discontent and repining, from the quarrels we raise with nature. And I believe, upon a strict inquiry, those quarrels might be shown as ill-grounded among us as they are among that people.

As to their military affairs, they boast that the king's army consists of a hundred and seventy-six thousand foot, and thirty-two thousand horse: if that may be called an army, which is made up of tradesmen in the several cities, and farmers in the country, whose commanders are only the nobility and gentry, without pay or reward. They are indeed perfect enough in their exercises, and under very good discipline, wherein I saw no great merit; for how should it be otherwise, where every farmer is under the command of his own landlord, and every citizen under that of the principal men in his own city, chosen after the manner of Venice, by ballot?

I have often seen the militia of Lorbrulgrud drawn out to exercise, in a great field near the city of twenty miles square. They were in all not above twenty-five thousand foot, and six thousand horse; but it was impossible for me to compute their number, considering the space of ground they took up. A cavalier, mounted on a large steed, might be about ninety feet high. I have seen this whole body of horse, upon a word of command, draw their swords at once, and brandish them in the air. Imagination can figure nothing so grand, so surprising, and so astonishing! it looked as if ten thousand flashes of lightning were darting at the same time from every quarter of the sky.

I was curious to know how this prince, to whose dominions there is no access from any other country, came to think of armies, or to teach his people the practice of military discipline. But I was soon informed, both by conversation and reading their histories; for, in the course of many ages, they have been troubled with the same disease to which the whole race of mankind is subject; the nobility often contending for power, the people for liberty, and the king for absolute dominion. All which, however happily tempered by the laws of that kingdom, have been sometimes violated by each of the three parties, and have more than once occasioned civil wars; the last whereof was happily put an end to by this prince's grand-father, in a general composition; and the militia, then settled with common consent, has been ever since kept in the strictest duty.

CHAPTER EIGHT

The king and queen make a progress to the frontiers. The author attends them. The manner in which he leaves the country very particularly related. He returns to England.

I HAD ALWAYS a strong impulse that I should some time recover my liberty, though it was impossible to conjecture by what means, or to form any project with the least hope of succeeding. The ship in which I sailed, was the first ever known to be driven within sight of that coast, and the king had given strict orders, that if at any time another appeared, it should be taken ashore, and with all its crew and passengers brought in a tumbril to Lorbrulgrud. He was strongly bent to get me a woman of my own size, by whom I might propagate the breed: but I think I should rather have died than undergone the disgrace of leaving a posterity to be kept in cages, like tame canary-birds, and perhaps, in time, sold about the kingdom, to persons of quality, for curiosities. I was indeed treated with much kindness: I was the favourite of a great king and queen, and the delight of the whole court; but it was upon such a foot as ill became the dignity of humankind. I could never forget those domestic pledges I had left behind me. I wanted to be among people, with whom I could converse upon even terms, and walk about the streets and fields without being afraid of being trod to death like a frog or a young puppy. But my deliverance came sooner than I expected, and in a manner not very common; the whole story and circumstances of which I shall faithfully relate.

I had now been two years in this country; and about the beginning of the third, Glumdalclitch and I attended the king and queen, in a progress to the south coast of the kingdom. I was carried, as usual, in my travelling-box, which as I have already described, was a very convenient closet, of twelve feet wide. And I had ordered a hammock to be fixed, by silken ropes from the four corners at the top, to break the jolts, when a servant carried me before him on horseback, as I sometimes desired; and would often sleep in my hammock, while we were upon the road. On the roof of my closet, not directly over the middle of the hammock, I ordered the joiner to cut out a hole of a foot square, to give me air in hot weather, as I slept; which hole I shut at pleasure with a board that drew backward and forward through a groove.

When we came to our journey's end, the king thought proper to pass a few days at a palace he has near Flanflasnic, a city within eighteen English miles of the seaside. Glumdalclitch and I were much fatigued: I had gotten a small cold, but the poor girl was so ill as to be confined to her chamber. I longed to see the ocean, which must be the only scene of my escape, if ever it should happen. I pretended to be worse than I really was, and desired leave to take the fresh air of the sea, with a page, whom I was very fond of, and who had sometimes been trusted with me. I shall never forget with what unwillingness Glumdalclitch consented, nor the strict charge she gave the page to be careful of me, bursting at the same time into a flood of tears, as if she had some forboding of what was to happen. The boy took me out in my box, about half an hours walk from the palace, towards the rocks on the sea-shore. I ordered him to set me down, and lifting up one of my sashes, cast many a wistful melancholy look towards the sea. I found myself not very well, and told the page that I had a mind to take a nap in my hammock, which I hoped would do me good. I got in, and the boy shut the window close down, to keep out the cold. I soon fell asleep, and all I can conjecture is, while I slept, the page, thinking no danger could happen, went among the rocks to look for birds' eggs, having before observed him from my window searching about, and picking up one or two in the clefts. Be that as it will, I found myself suddenly awaked with a violent pull upon the ring, which was fastened at the top of my box for the conveniency of carriage. I felt my box raised very high in the air, and then borne forward with prodigious speed. The first jolt had like to have shaken me out of my hammock, but afterward the motion was easy enough. I called out several times, as loud as I could raise my voice, but all to no purpose. I looked towards my windows, and could see nothing but the clouds and sky. I heard a noise just over my head, like the clapping of wings, and then began to perceive the woful condition I was in; that some eagle had got the ring of my box in his beak, with an intent to let it fall on a rock, like a tortoise in a shell, and then pick out my body, and devour it: for the sagacity and smell of this bird enables him to discover his quarry at a great distance, though better concealed than I could be within a two-inch board.

In a little time, I observed the noise and flutter of wings to increase very fast, and my box was tossed up and down, like a sign in a windy day. I heard several bangs or buffets, as I thought given to the eagle (for such I am certain it must have been that held the ring of my box in his beak), and then, all on a sudden, felt myself falling perpendicularly down, for above a minute, but with such incredible swiftness, that I almost lost my breath. My fall was stopped by a terrible squash, that sounded louder to my ears than the cataract of Niagara; after which, I was quite in the dark for another minute, and then my box began to rise so high, that I could see light from the tops of the windows. I now perceived I was fallen into the sea. My box, by the weight of my body, the goods that were in, and the broad plates of iron fixed for strength at the four corners of the top and bottom, floated about five feet deep in water. I did then, and do now suppose, that the eagle which flew away with my box was pursued by two or three others, and forced to let me drop, while he defended himself against the rest, who hoped to share in the prey. The plates of iron fastened at the bottom of the box (for those were the strongest) preserved the balance while it fell, and hindered it from being broken on the surface of the water. Every joint of it was well grooved; and the door did not move on hinges, but up and down like a sash, which kept my closet so tight that very little water came in. I got with much difficulty out of my hammock, having first ventured to draw back the slip-board on the roof already mentioned, contrived on purpose to let in air, for want of which I found myself almost stifled.

How often did I then wish myself with my dear Glumdalclitch, from whom one single hour had so far divided me! And I may say with truth, that in the midst of my own misfortunes I could not forbear lamenting my poor nurse, the grief she would suffer for my loss, the displeasure of the queen, and the ruin of her fortune. Perhaps many travellers have not been under greater difficulties and distress than I was at this juncture, expecting every moment to see my box dashed to pieces, or at least overset by the first violent blast, or rising wave. A breach in one single pane of glass would have been immediate death: nor could any thing have preserved the windows, but the strong lattice wires placed on the outside, against accidents in travelling. I saw the water ooze in at several crannies, although the leaks were not considerable, and I endeavoured to stop them as well as I could. I was not able to lift up the roof of my closet, which otherwise I certainly should have done, and sat on the top of it; where I might at least preserve myself some hours longer, than by being shut up (as I may call it) in the hold. Or if I escaped these dangers for a day or two, what could I expect but a miserable death of cold and hunger? I was four hours under these circumstances, expecting, and indeed wishing, every moment to be my last.

I have already told the reader that there were two strong staples fixed upon that side of my box which had no window, and into which the servant, who used to carry me on horseback, would put a leathern belt, and buckle it about his waist. Being in this disconsolate state, I heard, or at least thought I heard, some kind of grating noise on that side of my box where the staples were fixed; and soon after I began to fancy that the box was pulled or towed along the sea; for I now and then felt a sort of tugging, which made the waves rise near the tops of my windows, leaving me almost in the dark. This gave me some faint hopes of relief, although I was not able to imagine how it could be brought about. I ventured to unscrew one of my chairs, which were always fastened to the floor; and having made a hard shift to screw it down again, directly under the slipping-board that I had lately opened, I mounted on the chair, and putting my mouth as near as I could to the hole, I called for help in a loud voice, and in all the languages I understood. I then fastened my handkerchief to a stick I usually carried, and thrusting it up the hole, waved it several times in the air, that if any boat or ship were near, the seamen might conjecture some unhappy mortal to be shut up in the box.

I found no effect from all I could do, but plainly perceived my closet to be moved along; and in the space of an hour, or better, that side of the box where the staples were, and had no windows, struck against something that was hard. I apprehended it to be a rock, and found myself tossed more than ever. I plainly heard a noise upon the cover of my closet, like that of a cable, and the grating of it as it passed through the ring. I then found myself hoisted up, by degrees, at least three feet higher than I was before. Whereupon I again thrust up my stick and handkerchief, calling for help till I was almost hoarse. In return to which, I heard a great shout repeated three times, giving me such transports of joy as are not to be conceived but by those who feel them. I now heard a trampling over my head, and somebody calling through the hole with a loud voice, in the English tongue, "If there be any body below, let them speak." I answered, "I was an Englishman, drawn by ill fortune into the greatest calamity that ever any creature underwent, and begged, by all that was moving, to be delivered out of the dungeon I was in." The voice replied, "I was safe, for my box was fastened to their ship; and the carpenter should immediately come and saw a hole in the cover, large enough to pull me out." I answered, "that was needless, and would take up too much time; for there was no more to be done, but let one of the crew put his finger into the ring, and take the box out of the sea into the ship, and so into the captain's cabin." Some of them, upon hearing me talk so wildly, thought I was mad: others laughed; for indeed it never came into my head, that I was now got among people of my own stature and strength. The carpenter came, and in a few minutes sawed a passage about four feet square, then let down a small ladder, upon which I mounted, and thence was taken into the ship in a very weak condition.

The sailors were all in amazement, and asked me a thousand questions, which I had no inclination to answer. I was equally confounded at the sight of so many pigmies, for such I took them to be, after having so long accustomed mine eyes to the monstrous objects I had left. But the captain, Mr. Thomas Wilcocks, an honest worthy Shropshire man, observing I was ready to faint, took me into his cabin, gave me a cordial to comfort me, and made me turn in upon his own bed, advising me to take a little rest, of which I had great need. Before I went to sleep, I gave him to understand that I had some valuable furniture in my box, too good to be lost: a fine hammock, a handsome field-bed, two chairs, a table, and a cabinet; that my closet was hung on all sides, or rather quilted, with silk and cotton; that if he would let one of the crew bring my closet into his cabin, I would open it there before him, and show him my goods. The captain, hearing me utter these absurdities, concluded I was raving; however (I suppose to pacify me) he promised to give order as I desired, and going upon deck, sent some of his men down into my closet, whence (as I afterwards found) they drew up all my goods, and stripped off the quilting; but the chairs, cabinet, and bedstead, being screwed to the floor, were much damaged by the ignorance of the seamen, who tore them up by force. Then they knocked off some of the boards for the use of the ship, and when they had got all they had a mind for, let the hull drop into the sea, which by reason of many breaches made in the bottom and sides, sunk to rights. And, indeed, I was glad not to have been a spectator of the havoc they made, because I am confident it would have sensibly touched me, by bringing former passages into my mind, which I would rather have forgot.

I slept some hours, but perpetually disturbed with dreams of the place I had left, and the dangers I had escaped. However, upon waking, I found myself much recovered. It was now about eight o'clock at night, and the captain ordered supper immediately, thinking I had already fasted too long. He entertained me with great kindness, observing me not to look wildly, or talk inconsistently: and, when we were left alone, desired I would give him a relation of my travels, and by what accident I came to be set adrift, in that monstrous wooden chest. He said "that about twelve o'clock at noon, as he was looking through his glass, he spied it at a distance, and thought it was a sail, which he had a mind to make, being not much out of his course, in hopes of buying some biscuit, his own beginning to fall short. That upon coming nearer, and finding his error, he sent out his long-boat to discover what it was; that his men came back in a fright, swearing they had seen a swimming house. That he laughed at their folly, and went himself in the boat, ordering his men to take a strong cable along with them. That the weather being calm, he rowed round me several times, observed my windows and wire lattices that defended them. That he discovered two staples upon one side, which was all of boards, without any passage for light. He then commanded his men to row up to that side, and fastening a cable to one of the staples, ordered them to tow my chest, as they called it, toward the ship. When it was there, he gave directions to fasten another cable to the ring fixed in the cover, and to raise up my chest with pulleys, which all the sailors were not able to do above two or three feet." He said, "they saw my stick and handkerchief thrust out of the hole, and concluded that some unhappy man must be shut up in the cavity." I asked, "whether he or the crew had seen any prodigious birds in the air, about the time he first discovered me." To which he answered, "that discoursing this matter with the sailors while I was asleep, one of them said, he had observed three eagles flying towards the north, but remarked nothing of their being larger than the usual size:" which I suppose must be imputed to the great height they were at; and he could not guess the reason of my question. I then asked the captain, "how far he reckoned we might be from land?" He said, "by the best computation he could make, we were at least a hundred leagues." I assured him, "that he must be mistaken by almost half, for I had not left the country whence I came above two hours before I dropped into the sea." Whereupon he began again to think that my brain was disturbed, of which he gave me a hint, and advised me to go to bed in a cabin he had provided. I assured him, "I was well refreshed with his good entertainment and company, and as much in my senses as ever I was in my life." He then grew serious, and desired to ask me freely, "whether I were not troubled in my mind by the consciousness of some enormous crime, for which I was punished, at the command of some prince, by exposing me in that chest; as great criminals, in other countries, have been forced to sea in a leaky vessel, without provisions: for although he should be sorry to have taken so ill a man into his ship, yet he would engage his word to set me safe ashore, in the first port where we arrived." He added, "that his suspicions were much increased by some very absurd speeches I had delivered at first to his sailors, and afterwards to himself, in relation to my closet or chest, as well as by my odd looks and behaviour while I was at supper."

I begged his patience to hear me tell my story, which I faithfully did, from the last time I left England, to the moment he first discovered me. And, as truth always forces its way into rational minds, so this honest worthy gentleman, who had some tincture of learning, and very good sense, was immediately convinced of my candour and veracity. But further to confirm all I had said, I entreated him to give order that my cabinet should be brought, of which I had the key in my pocket; for he had already informed me how the seamen disposed of my closet. I opened it in his own presence, and showed him the small collection of rarities I made in the country from which I had been so strangely delivered. There was the comb I had contrived out of the stumps of the king's beard, and another of the same materials, but fixed into a paring of her majesty's thumb-nail, which served for the back. There was a collection of needles and pins, from a foot to half a yard long; four wasp stings, like joiner's tacks; some combings of the queen's hair; a gold ring, which one day she made me a present of, in a most obliging manner, taking it from her little finger, and throwing it over my head like a collar. I desired the captain would please to accept this ring in return for his civilities; which he absolutely refused. I showed him a corn that I had cut off with my own hand, from a maid of honour's toe; it was about the bigness of Kentish pippin, and grown so hard, that when I returned England, I got it hollowed into a cup, and set in silver. Lastly, I desired him to see the breeches I had then on, which were made of a mouse's skin.

I could force nothing on him but a footman's tooth, which I observed him to examine with great curiosity, and found he had a fancy for it. He received it with abundance of thanks, more than such a trifle could deserve. It was drawn by an unskilful surgeon, in a mistake, from one of Glumdalclitch's men, who was afflicted with the tooth-ache, but it was as sound as any in his head. I got it cleaned, and put it into my cabinet. It was about a foot long, and four inches in diameter.

The captain was very well satisfied with this plain relation I had given him, and said, "he hoped, when we returned to England, I would oblige the world by putting it on paper, and making it public." My answer was, "that we were overstocked with books of travels: that nothing could now pass which was not extraordinary; wherein I doubted some authors less consulted truth, than their own vanity, or interest, or the diversion of ignorant readers; that my story could contain little beside common events, without those ornamental descriptions of strange plants, trees, birds, and other animals; or of the barbarous customs and idolatry of savage people, with which most writers abound. However, I thanked him for his good opinion, and promised to take the matter into my thoughts."

He said "he wondered at one thing very much, which was, to hear me speak so loud;" asking me "whether the king or queen of that country were thick of hearing?" I told him, "it was what I had been used to for above two years past, and that I admired as much at the voices of him and his men, who seemed to me only to whisper, and yet I could hear them well enough. But, when I spoke in that country, it was like a man talking in the streets, to another looking out from the top of a steeple, unless when I was placed on a table, or held in any person's hand." I told him, "I had likewise observed another thing, that, when I first got into the ship, and the sailors stood all about me, I thought they were the most little contemptible creatures I had ever beheld." For indeed, while I was in that prince's country, I could never endure to look in a glass, after mine eyes had been accustomed to such prodigious objects, because the comparison gave me so despicable a conceit of myself. The captain said, "that while we were at supper, he observed me to look at every thing with a sort of wonder, and that I often seemed hardly able to contain my laughter, which he knew not well how to take, but imputed it to some disorder in my brain." I answered, "it was very true; and I wondered how I could forbear, when I saw his dishes of the size of a silver three-pence, a leg of pork hardly a mouthful, a cup not so big as a nut-shell;" and so I went on, describing the rest of his household-stuff and provisions, after the same manner. For, although he queen had ordered a little equipage of all things necessary for me, while I was in her service, yet my ideas were wholly taken up with what I saw on every side of me, and I winked at my own littleness, as people do at their own faults. The captain understood my raillery very well, and merrily replied with the old English proverb, "that he doubted mine eyes were bigger than my belly, for he did not observe my stomach so good, although I had fasted all day;" and, continuing in his mirth, protested "he would have gladly given a hundred pounds, to have seen my closet in the eagle's bill, and afterwards in its fall from so great a height into the sea; which would certainly have been a most astonishing object, worthy to have the description of it transmitted to future ages:" and the comparison of Phaëton was so obvious, that he could not forbear applying it, although I did not much admire the conceit.

The captain having been at Tonquin, was, in his return to England, driven north-eastward to the latitude of 44 degrees, and longitude of 143. But meeting a trade-wind two days after I came on board him, we sailed southward a long time, and coasting New Holland, kept our course west-south-west, and then south-south-west, till we doubled the Cape of Good Hope. Our voyage was very prosperous, but I shall not trouble the reader with a journal of it. The captain called in at one or two ports, and sent in his long-boat for provisions and fresh water; but I never went out of the ship till we came into the Downs, which was on the third day of June, 1706, about nine months after my escape. I offered to leave my goods in security for payment of my freight: but the captain protested he would not receive one farthing. We took a kind leave of each other, and I made him promise he would come to see me at my house in Redriff. I hired a horse and guide for five shillings, which I borrowed of the captain.

As I was on the road, observing the littleness of the houses, the trees, the cattle, and the people, I began to think myself in Lilliput. I was afraid of trampling on every traveller I met, and often called aloud to have them stand out of the way, so that I had like to have gotten one or two broken heads for my impertinence.

When I came to my own house, for which I was forced to inquire, one of the servants opening the door, I bent down to go in, (like a goose under a gate,) for fear of striking my head. My wife run out to embrace me, but I stooped lower than her knees, thinking she could otherwise never be able to reach my mouth. My daughter kneeled to ask my blessing, but I could not see her till she arose, having been so long used to stand with my head and eyes erect to above sixty feet; and then I went to take her up with one hand by the waist. I looked down upon the servants, and one or two friends who were in the house, as if they had been pigmies and I a giant. I told my wife, "she had been too thrifty, for I found she had starved herself and her daughter to nothing." In short, I behaved myself so unaccountably, that they were all of the captain's opinion when he first saw me, and concluded I had lost my wits. This I mention as an instance of the great power of habit and prejudice.

In a little time, I and my family and friends came to a right understanding: but my wife protested "I should never go to sea any more;" although my evil destiny so ordered, that she had not power to hinder me, as the reader may know hereafter. In the mean time, I here conclude the second part of my unfortunate voyages.

PART THREE

A Voyage to Laputa, Balnibarbi, Luggnagg, Glubbdubdrib, and Japan

CHAPTER ONE

The author sets out on his third voyage. Is taken by pirates. The malice of a Dutchman. His arrival at an island. He is received into Laputa.

I HAD NOT BEEN at home above ten days, when Captain William Robinson, a Cornish man, commander of the Hopewell, a stout ship of three hundred tons, came to my house. I had formerly been surgeon of another ship where he was master, and a fourth part owner, in a voyage to the Levant. He had always treated me more like a brother, than an inferior officer; and, hearing of my arrival, made me a visit, as I apprehended only out of friendship, for nothing passed more than what is usual after long absences. But repeating his visits often, expressing his joy to find I me in good health, asking, "whether I were now settled for life?" adding, "that he intended a voyage to the East Indies in two months," at last he plainly invited me, though with some apologies, to be surgeon of the ship; "that I should have another surgeon under me, beside our two mates; that my salary should be double to the usual pay; and that having experienced my knowledge in sea-affairs to be at least equal to his, he would enter into any engagement to follow my advice, as much as if I had shared in the command."

He said so many other obliging things, and I knew him to be so honest a man, that I could not reject this proposal; the thirst I had of seeing the world, notwithstanding my past misfortunes, continuing as violent as ever. The only difficulty that remained, was to persuade my wife, whose consent however I at last obtained, by the prospect of advantage she proposed to her children.

We set out the 5th day of August, 1706, and arrived at Fort St. George the 11th of April, 1707. We staid there three weeks to refresh our crew, many of whom were sick. From thence we went to Tonquin, where the captain resolved to continue some time, because many of the goods he intended to buy were not ready, nor could he expect to be dispatched in several months. Therefore, in hopes to defray some of the charges he must be at, he bought a sloop, loaded it with several sorts of goods, wherewith the Tonquinese usually trade to the neighbouring islands, and putting fourteen men on board, whereof three were of the country, he appointed me master of the sloop, and gave me power to traffic, while he transacted his affairs at Tonquin.

We had not sailed above three days, when a great storm arising, we were driven five days to the north-north-east, and then to the east: after which we had fair weather, but still with a pretty strong gale from the west. Upon the tenth day we were chased by two pirates, who soon overtook us; for my sloop was so deep laden, that she sailed very slow, neither were we in a condition to defend ourselves.

We were boarded about the same time by both the pirates, who entered furiously at the head of their men; but finding us all prostrate upon our faces (for so I gave order), they pinioned us with strong ropes, and setting guard upon us, went to search the sloop.

I observed among them a Dutchman, who seemed to be of some authority, though he was not commander of either ship. He knew us by our countenances to be Englishmen, and jabbering to us in his own language, swore we should be tied back to back and thrown into the sea. I spoken Dutch tolerably well; I told him who we were, and begged him, in consideration of our being Christians and Protestants, of neighbouring countries in strict alliance, that he would move the captains to take some pity on us. This inflamed his rage; he repeated his threatenings, and turning to his companions, spoke with great vehemence in the Japanese language, as I suppose, often using the word *Christianos*.

The largest of the two pirate ships was commanded by a Japanese captain, who spoke a little Dutch, but very imperfectly. He came up to me, and after several questions, which I answered in great humility, he said, "we should not die." I made the captain a very low bow, and then, turning to the Dutchman, said, "I was sorry to find more mercy in a heathen, than in a brother christian." But I had soon reason to repent those foolish words: for that malicious reprobate, having often endeavoured in vain to persuade both the captains that I might be thrown into the sea (which they would not yield to, after the promise made me that I should not die), however, prevailed so far, as to have a punishment inflicted on me, worse, in all human appearance, than death itself. My men were sent by an equal division into both the pirate ships, and my sloop new manned. As to myself, it was determined that I should be set adrift in a small canoe, with paddles and a sail, and four days' provisions; which last, the Japanese captain was so kind to double out of his own stores, and would permit no man to search me. I got down into the canoe, while the Dutchman, standing upon the deck, loaded me with all the curses and injurious terms his language could afford.

About an hour before we saw the pirates I had taken an observation, and found we were in the latitude of 46 N. and longitude of 183. When I was at some distance from the pirates, I discovered, by my pocket-glass, several islands to the south-east. I set up my sail, the wind being fair, with a design to reach the nearest of those islands, which I made a shift to do, in about three hours. It was all rocky: however I got many birds' eggs; and, striking fire, I kindled some heath and dry sea-weed, by which I roasted my eggs. I ate no other supper, being resolved to spare my provisions as much as I could. I passed the night under the shelter of a rock, strewing some heath under me, and slept pretty well.

The next day I sailed to another island, and thence to a third and fourth, sometimes using my sail, and sometimes my paddles. But, not to trouble the reader with a particular account of my distresses, let it suffice, that on the fifth day I arrived at the last island in my sight, which lay south-south-east to the former.

This island was at a greater distance than I expected, and I did not reach it in less than five hours. I encompassed it almost round, before I could find a convenient place to land in; which was a small creek, about three times the wideness of my canoe. I found the island to be all rocky, only a little intermingled with tufts of grass, and sweet-smelling herbs. I took out my small provisions and after having refreshed myself, I secured the remainder in a cave, whereof there were great numbers; I gathered plenty of eggs upon the rocks, and got a quantity of dry sea-weed, and parched grass, which I designed to kindle the next day, and roast my eggs as well as I could, for I had about me my flint, steel, match, and burning-glass. I lay all night in the cave where I had lodged my provisions. My bed was the same dry grass and sea-weed which I intended for fuel. I slept very little, for the disquiets of my mind prevailed over my weariness, and kept me awake. I considered how impossible it was to preserve my life in so desolate a place, and how miserable my end must be: yet found myself so listless and desponding, that I had not the heart to rise; and before I could get spirits enough to creep out of my cave, the day was far advanced. I walked awhile among the rocks: the sky was perfectly clear, and the sun so hot, that I was forced to turn my face from it: when all on a sudden it became obscure, as I thought, in a manner very different from what happens by the interposition of a cloud. I turned back, and perceived a vast opaque body between me and the sun moving forwards towards the island: it seemed to be about two miles high, and hid the sun six or seven minutes; but I did not observe the air to be much colder, or the sky more darkened, than if I had stood under the shade of a mountain. As it approached nearer over the place where I was, it appeared to be a firm substance, the bottom flat, smooth, and shining very bright, from the reflection of the sea below. I stood upon a height about two hundred yards from the shore, and saw this vast body descending almost to a parallel with me, at less than an English mile distance. I took out my pocket perspective, and could plainly discover numbers of people moving up and down the sides of it, which appeared to be sloping; but what those people where doing I was not able to distinguish.

The natural love of life gave me some inward motion of joy, and I was ready to entertain a hope that this adventure might, some way or other, help to deliver me from the desolate place and condition I was in. But at the same time the reader can hardly conceive my astonishment, to behold an island in the air, inhabited by men, who were able (as it should seem) to raise or sink, or put it into progressive motion, as they pleased. But not being at that time in a disposition to philosophise upon this phenomenon, I rather chose to observe what course the island would take, because it seemed for awhile to stand still. Yet soon after, it advanced nearer, and I could see the sides of it encompassed with several gradations of galleries, and stairs, at certain intervals, to descend from one to the other. In the lowest gallery, I beheld some people fishing with long angling rods, and others looking on. I waved my cap (for my hat was long since worn out) and my handkerchief toward the island; and upon its nearer approach, I called and shouted with the utmost strength of my voice; and then looking circumspectly, I beheld a crowd gather to that side which was most in my view. I found by their pointing towards me and to each other, that they plainly discovered me, although they made no return to my shouting. But I could see four or five men running in great haste, up the stairs, to the top of the island, who then disappeared. I happened rightly to conjecture, that these were sent for orders to some person in authority upon this occasion.

The number of people increased, and, in less than half all hour, the island was moved and raised in such a manner, that the lowest gallery appeared in a parallel of less then a hundred yards distance from the height where I stood. I then put myself in the most supplicating posture, and spoke in the humblest accent, but received no answer. Those who stood nearest over against me, seemed to be persons of distinction, as I supposed by their habit. They conferred earnestly with each other, looking often upon me. At length one of them called out in a clear, polite, smooth dialect, not unlike in sound to the Italian: and therefore I returned an answer in that language, hoping at least that the cadence might be more agreeable to his ears. Although neither of us understood the other, yet my meaning was easily known, for the people saw the distress I was in.

They made signs for me to come down from the rock, and go towards the shore, which I accordingly did; and the flying island being raised to a convenient height, the verge directly over me, a chain was let down from the lowest gallery, with a seat fastened to the bottom, to which I fixed myself, and was drawn up by pulleys.

CHAPTER TWO

The humours and dispositions of the Laputians described. An account of their learning. Of the king and his court. The author's reception there. The inhabitants subject to fear and disquietudes. An account of the women.

At my alighting, I was surrounded with a crowd of people, but those who stood nearest seemed to be of better quality. They beheld me with all the marks and circumstances of wonder; neither indeed was I much in their debt, having never till then seen a race of mortals so singular in their shapes, habits, and countenances. Their heads were all reclined, either to the right, or the left; one of their eyes turned inward, and the other directly up to the zenith. Their outward garments were adorned with the figures of suns, moons, and stars; interwoven with those of fiddles, flutes, harps, trumpets, guitars, harpsichords, and many other instruments of music, unknown to us in Europe. I observed, here and there, many in the habit of servants, with a blown bladder, fastened like a flail to the end of a stick, which they carried in their hands. In each bladder was a small quantity of dried peas, or little pebbles, as I was afterwards informed. With these bladders, they now and then flapped the mouths and ears of those who stood near them, of which practice I could not then conceive the meaning. It seems the minds of these people are so taken up with intense speculations, that they neither can speak, nor attend to the discourses of others, without being roused by some external taction upon the organs of speech and hearing; for which reason, those persons who are able to afford it always keep a flapper (the original is *climenole*) in their family, as one of their domestics; nor ever walk abroad, or make visits, without him. And the business of this officer is, when two, three, or more persons are in company, gently to strike with his bladder the mouth of him who is to speak, and the right ear of him or them to whom the speaker addresses himself. This flapper is likewise employed diligently to attend his master in his walks, and upon occasion to give him a soft flap on his eyes; because he is always so wrapped up in cogitation, that he is in manifest danger of falling down every precipice, and bouncing his head against every post; and in the streets, of justling others, or being justled himself into the kennel.

It was necessary to give the reader this information, without which he would be at the same loss with me to understand the proceedings of these people, as they conducted me up the stairs to the top of the island, and from thence to the royal palace. While we were ascending, they forgot several times what they were about, and left me to myself, till their memories were again roused by their flappers; for they appeared altogether unmoved by the sight of my foreign habit and countenance, and by the shouts of the vulgar, whose thoughts and minds were more disengaged.

At last we entered the palace, and proceeded into the chamber of presence, where I saw the king seated on his throne, attended on each side by persons of prime quality. Before the throne, was a large table filled with globes and spheres, and mathematical instruments of all kinds. His majesty took not the least notice of us, although our entrance was not without sufficient noise, by the concourse of all persons belonging to the court. But he was then deep in a problem; and we attended at least an hour, before he could solve it. There stood by him, on each side, a young page with flaps in their hands, and when they saw he was at leisure, one of them gently struck his mouth, and the other his right ear; at which he startled like one awaked on the sudden, and looking towards me and the company I was in, recollected the occasion of our coming, whereof he had been informed before. He spoke some words, whereupon immediately a young man with a flap came up to my side, and flapped me gently on the right ear; but I made signs, as well as I could, that I had no occasion for such an instrument; which, as I afterwards found, gave his majesty, and the whole court, a very mean opinion of my understanding. The king, as far as I could conjecture, asked me several questions, and I addressed myself to him in all the languages I had. When it was found I could neither understand nor be understood, I was conducted by his order to an apartment in his palace (this prince being distinguished above all his predecessors for his hospitality to strangers), where two servants were appointed to attend me. My dinner was brought, and four persons of quality, whom I remembered to have seen very near the king's person, did me the honour to dine with me. We had two courses, of three dishes each. In the first course, there was a shoulder of mutton cut into an equilateral triangle, a piece of beef into a rhomboides, and a pudding into a cycloid. The second course was two ducks trussed up in the form of fiddles; sausages and puddings resembling flutes and hautboys, and a breast of veal in the shape of a harp. The servants cut our bread into cones, cylinders, parallelograms, and several other mathematical figures.

While we were at dinner, I made bold to ask the names of several things in their language, and those noble persons, by the assistance of their flappers, delighted to give me answers, hoping to raise my admiration of their great abilities if I could be brought to converse with them. I was soon able to call for bread and drink, or whatever else I wanted.

After dinner my company withdrew, and a person was sent to me by the king's order, attended by a flapper. He brought with him pen, ink, and paper, and three or four books, giving me to understand by signs, that he was sent to teach me the language. We sat together four hours, in which time I wrote down a great number of words in columns, with the translations over against them; I likewise made a shift to learn several short sentences; for my tutor would order one of my servants to fetch something, to turn about, to make a bow, to sit, or to stand, or walk, and the like. Then I took down the sentence in writing. He showed me also, in one of his books, the figures of the sun, moon, and stars, the zodiac, the tropics, and polar circles, together with the denominations of many plains and solids. He gave me the names and descriptions of all the musical instruments, and the general terms of art in playing on each of them. After he had left me, I placed all my words, with their interpretations, in alphabetical order. And thus, in a few days, by the help of a very faithful memory, I got some insight into their language. The word, which I interpret the flying or floating island, is in the original *Laputa*, whereof I could never learn the true etymology. *Lap*, in the old obsolete language, signifies high; and *untuh*, a governor; from which they say, by corruption, was derived *Laputa*, from *Lapuntuh*. But I do not approve of this derivation, which seems to be a little strained. I ventured to offer to the learned among them a conjecture of my own, that Laputa was *quasi lap outed*; *lap*, signifying properly, the dancing of the sunbeams in the sea, and *outed*, a wing; which, however, I shall not obtrude, but submit to the judicious reader.

Those to whom the king had entrusted me, observing how ill I was clad, ordered a tailor to come next morning, and take measure for a suit of clothes. This operator did his office after a different manner from those of his trade in Europe. He first took my altitude by a quadrant, and then, with a rule and compasses, described the dimensions and outlines of my whole body, all which he entered upon paper; and in six days brought my clothes very ill made, and quite out of shape, by happening to mistake a figure in the calculation. But my comfort was, that I observed such accidents very frequent, and little regarded.

During my confinement for want of clothes, and by an indisposition that held me some days longer, I much enlarged my dictionary; and when I went next to court, was able to understand many things the king spoke, and to return him some kind of answers. His majesty had given orders, that the island should move north-east and by east, to the vertical point over Lagado, the metropolis of the whole kingdom below, upon the firm earth. It was about ninety leagues distant, and our voyage lasted four days and a half. I was not in the least sensible of the progressive motion made in the air by the island. On the second morning, about eleven o'clock, the king himself in person, attended by his nobility, courtiers, and officers, having prepared all their musical instruments, played on them for three hours without intermission, so that I was quite stunned with the noise; neither could I possibly guess the meaning, till my tutor informed me. He said that, the people of their island had their ears adapted to hear "the music of the spheres, which always played at certain periods, and the court was now prepared to bear their part, in whatever instrument they most excelled."

In our journey towards Lagado, the capital city, his majesty ordered that the island should stop over certain towns and villages, from whence he might receive the petitions of his subjects. And to this purpose, several packthreads were let down, with small weights at the bottom. On these packthreads the people strung their petitions, which mounted up directly, like the scraps of paper fastened by school boys at the end of the string that holds their kite. Sometimes we received wine and victuals from below, which were drawn up by pulleys.

The knowledge I had in mathematics, gave me great assistance in acquiring their phraseology, which depended much upon that science, and music; and in the latter I was not unskilled. Their ideas are perpetually conversant in lines and figures. If they would, for example, praise the beauty of a woman, or any other animal, they describe it by rhombs, circles, parallelograms, ellipses, and other geometrical terms, or by words of art drawn from music, needless here to repeat. I observed in the king's kitchen all sorts of mathematical and musical instruments, after the figures of which they cut up the joints that were served to his majesty's table.

Their houses are very ill built, the walls bevil, without one right angle in any apartment; and this defect arises from the contempt they bear to practical geometry, which they despise as vulgar and mechanic; those instructions they give being too refined for the intellects of their workmen, which occasions perpetual mistakes. And although they are dexterous enough upon a piece of paper, in the management of the rule, the pencil, and the divider, yet in the common actions and behaviour of life, I have not seen a more clumsy, awkward, and unhandy people, nor so slow and perplexed in their conceptions upon all other subjects, except those of mathematics and music. They are very bad reasoners, and vehemently given to opposition, unless when they happen to be of the right opinion, which is seldom their case. Imagination, fancy, and invention, they are wholly strangers to, nor have any words in their language, by which those ideas can be expressed; the whole compass of their thoughts and mind being shut up within the two forementioned sciences.

Most of them, and especially those who deal in the astronomical part, have great faith in judicial astrology, although they are ashamed to own it publicly. But what I chiefly admired, and thought altogether unaccountable, was the strong disposition I observed in them towards news and politics, perpetually inquiring into public affairs, giving their judgments in matters of state, and passionately disputing every inch of a party opinion. I have indeed observed the same disposition among most of the mathematicians I have known in Europe, although I could never discover the least analogy between the two sciences; unless those people suppose, that because the smallest circle has as many degrees as the largest, therefore the regulation and management of the world require no more abilities than the handling and turning of a globe; but I rather take this quality to spring from a very common infirmity of human nature, inclining us to be most curious and conceited in matters where we have least concern, and for which we are least adapted by study or nature.

These people are under continual disquietudes, never enjoying a minutes peace of mind; and their disturbances proceed from causes which very little affect the rest of mortals. Their apprehensions arise from several changes they dread in the celestial bodies: for instance, that the earth, by the continual approaches of the sun towards it, must, in course of time, be absorbed, or swallowed up; that the face of the sun, will, by degrees, be encrusted with its own effluvia, and give no more light to the world; that the earth very narrowly escaped a brush from the tail of the last comet, which would have infallibly reduced it to ashes; and that the next, which they have calculated for one-and-thirty years hence, will probably destroy us. For if, in its perihelion, it should approach within a certain degree of the sun (as by their calculations they have reason to dread) it will receive a degree of heat ten thousand times more intense than that of red hot glowing iron, and in its absence from the sun, carry a blazing tail ten hundred thousand and fourteen miles long, through which, if the earth should pass at the distance of one hundred thousand miles from the nucleus, or main body of the comet, it must in its passage be set on fire, and reduced to ashes: that the sun, daily spending its rays without any nutriment to supply them, will at last be wholly consumed and annihilated; which must be attended with the destruction of this earth, and of all the planets that receive their light from it.

They are so perpetually alarmed with the apprehensions of these, and the like impending dangers, that they can neither sleep quietly in their beds, nor have any relish for the common pleasures and amusements of life. When they meet an acquaintance in the morning, the first question is about the sun's health, how he looked at his setting and rising, and what hopes they have to avoid the stroke of the approaching comet. This conversation they are apt to run into with the same temper that boys discover in delighting to hear terrible stories of spirits and hobgoblins, which they greedily listen to, and dare not go to bed for fear.

The women of the island have abundance of vivacity: they, contemn their husbands, and are exceedingly fond of strangers, whereof there is always a considerable number from the continent below, attending at court, either upon affairs of the several towns and corporations, or their own particular occasions, but are much despised, because they want the same endowments. Among these the ladies choose their gallants: but the vexation is, that they act with too much ease and security; for the husband is always so rapt in speculation, that the mistress and lover may proceed to the greatest familiarities before his face, if he be but provided with paper and implements, and without his flapper at his side.

The wives and daughters lament their confinement to the island, although I think it the most delicious spot of ground in the world; and although they live here in the greatest plenty and magnificence, and are allowed to do whatever they please, they long to see the world, and take the diversions of the metropolis, which they are not allowed to do without a particular license from the king; and this is not easy to be obtained, because the people of quality have found, by frequent experience, how hard it is to persuade their women to return from below. I was told that a great court lady, who had several children, – is married to the prime minister, the richest subject in the kingdom, a very graceful person, extremely fond of her, and lives in the finest palace of the island, – went down to Lagado on the pretence of health, there hid herself for several months, till the king sent a warrant to search for her; and she was found in an obscure eating-house all in rags, having pawned her clothes to maintain an old deformed footman, who beat her every day, and in whose company she was taken, much against her will. And although her husband received her with all possible kindness, and without the least reproach, she soon after contrived to steal down again, with all her jewels, to the same gallant, and has not been heard of since.

This may perhaps pass with the reader rather for an European or English story, than for one of a country so remote. But he may please to consider, that the caprices of womankind are not limited by any climate or nation, and that they are much more uniform, than can be easily imagined.

In about a month's time, I had made a tolerable proficiency in their language, and was able to answer most of the king's questions, when I had the honour to attend him. His majesty discovered not the least curiosity to inquire into the laws, government, history, religion, or manners of the countries where I had been; but confined his questions to the state of mathematics, and received the account I gave him with great contempt and indifference, though often roused by his flapper on each side.

CHAPTER THREE

A phenomenon solved by modern philosophy and astronomy. The Laputians' great improvements in the latter. The king's method of suppressing insurrections.

I DESIRED LEAVE of this prince to see the curiosities of the island, which he was graciously pleased to grant, and ordered my tutor to attend me. I chiefly wanted to know, to what cause, in art or in nature, it owed its several motions, whereof I will now give a philosophical account to the reader.

The flying or floating island is exactly circular, its diameter 7837 yards, or about four miles and a half, and consequently contains ten thousand acres. It is three hundred yards thick. The bottom, or under surface, which appears to those who view it below, is one even regular plate of adamant, shooting up to the height of about two hundred yards. Above it lie the several minerals in their usual order, and over all is a coat of rich mould, ten or twelve feet deep. The declivity of the upper surface, from the circumference to the centre, is the natural cause why all the dews and rains, which fall upon the island, are conveyed in small rivulets toward the middle, where they are emptied into four large basins, each of about half a mile in circuit, and two hundred yards distant from the centre. From these basins the water is continually exhaled by the sun in the daytime, which effectually prevents their overflowing. Besides, as it is in the power of the monarch to raise the island above the region of clouds and vapours, he can prevent the falling of dews and rain whenever he pleases. For the highest clouds cannot rise above two miles, as naturalists agree, at least they were never known to do so in that country.

At the centre of the island there is a chasm about fifty yards in diameter, whence the astronomers descend into a large dome, which is therefore called *flandona gagnole*, or the astronomer's cave, situated at the depth of a hundred yards beneath the upper surface of the adamant. In this cave are twenty lamps continually burning, which, from the reflection of the adamant, cast a strong light into every part. The place is stored with great variety of sextants, quadrants, telescopes, astrolabes, and other astronomical instruments. But the greatest curiosity, upon which the fate of the island depends, is a loadstone of a prodigious size, in shape resembling a weaver's shuttle. It is in length six yards, and in the thickest part at least three yards over. This magnet is sustained by a very strong axle of adamant passing through its middle, upon which it plays, and is poised so exactly that the weakest hand can turn it. It is hooped round with a hollow cylinder of adamant, four feet yards in diameter, placed horizontally, and supported by eight adamantine feet, each six yards high. In the middle of the concave side, there is a groove twelve inches deep, in which the extremities of the axle are lodged, and turned round as there is occasion.

The stone cannot be removed from its place by any force, because the hoop and its feet are one continued piece with that body of adamant which constitutes the bottom of the island.

By means of this loadstone, the island is made to rise and fall, and move from one place to another. For, with respect to that part of the earth over which the monarch presides, the stone is endued at one of its sides with an attractive power, and at the other with a repulsive. Upon placing the magnet erect, with its attracting end towards the earth, the island descends; but when the repelling extremity points downwards, the island mounts directly upwards. When the position of the stone is oblique, the motion of the island is so too: for in this magnet, the forces always act in lines parallel to its direction.

By this oblique motion, the island is conveyed to different parts of the monarch's dominions. To explain the manner of its progress, let *A B* represent a line drawn across the dominions of Balnibarbi, let the line *c d* represent the loadstone, of which let *d* be the repelling end, and *c* the attracting end, the island being over *C*: let the stone be placed in position *c d*, with its repelling end downwards; then the island will be driven upwards obliquely towards *D*. When it is arrived at *D*, let the stone be turned upon its axle, till its attracting end points towards *E*, and then the island will be carried obliquely towards *E*; where, if the stone be again turned upon its axle till it stands in the position *E F*, with its repelling point downwards, the island will rise obliquely towards *F*, where, by directing the attracting end towards *G*, the island may be carried to *G*, and from *G* to *H*, by turning the stone, so as to make its repelling extremity to point directly downward. And thus, by changing the situation of the stone, as often as there is occasion, the island is made to rise and fall by turns in an oblique direction, and by those alternate risings and fallings (the obliquity being not considerable) is conveyed from one part of the dominions to the other.

But it must be observed, that this island cannot move beyond the extent of the dominions below, nor can it rise above the height of four miles. For which the astronomers (who have written large systems concerning the stone) assign the following reason: that the magnetic virtue does not extend beyond the distance of four miles, and that the mineral, which acts upon the stone in the bowels of the earth, and in the sea about six leagues distant from the shore, is not diffused through the whole globe, but terminated with the limits of the king's dominions; and it was easy, from the great advantage of such a superior situation, for a prince to bring under his obedience whatever country lay within the attraction of that magnet.

When the stone is put parallel to the plane of the horizon, the island stands still; for in that case the extremities of it, being at equal distance from the earth, act with equal force, the one in drawing downwards, the other in pushing upwards, and consequently no motion can ensue.

This loadstone is under the care of certain astronomers, who, from time to time, give it such positions as the monarch directs. They spend the greatest part of their lives in observing the celestial bodies, which they do by the assistance of glasses, far excelling ours in goodness. For, although their largest telescopes do not exceed three feet, they magnify much more than those of a hundred with us, and show the stars with greater clearness. This advantage has enabled them to extend their discoveries much further than our astronomers in Europe; for they have made a catalogue of ten thousand fixed stars, whereas the largest of ours do not contain above one third part of that number. They have likewise discovered two lesser stars, or satellites, which revolve about Mars; whereof the innermost is distant from the centre of the primary planet exactly three of his diameters, and the outermost, five; the former revolves in the space of ten hours, and the latter in twenty-one and a half; so that the squares of their periodical times are very near in the same proportion with the cubes of their distance from the centre of Mars; which evidently shows them to be governed by the same law of gravitation that influences the other heavenly bodies.

They have observed ninety-three different comets, and settled their periods with great exactness. If this be true (and they affirm it with great confidence) it is much to be wished, that their observations were made public, whereby the theory of comets, which at present is very lame and defective, might be brought to the same perfection with other arts of astronomy.

The king would be the most absolute prince in the universe, if he could but prevail on a ministry to join with him; but these having their estates below on the continent, and considering that the office of a favourite has a very uncertain tenure, would never consent to the enslaving of their country.

If any town should engage in rebellion or mutiny, fall into violent factions, or refuse to pay the usual tribute, the king has two methods of reducing them to obedience. The first and the mildest course is, by keeping the island hovering over such a town, and the lands about it, whereby he can deprive them of the benefit of the sun and the rain, and consequently afflict the inhabitants with dearth and diseases: and if the crime deserve it, they are at the same time pelted from above with great stones, against which they have no defence but by creeping into cellars or caves, while the roofs of their houses are beaten to pieces. But if they still continue obstinate, or offer to raise insurrections, he proceeds to the last remedy, by letting the island drop directly upon their heads, which makes a universal destruction both of houses and men. However, this is an extremity to which the prince is seldom driven, neither indeed is he willing to put it in execution; nor dare his ministers advise him to an action, which, as it would render them odious to the people, so it would be a great damage to their own estates, which all lie below; for the island is the king's demesne.

But there is still indeed a more weighty reason, why the kings of this country have been always averse from executing so terrible an action, unless upon the utmost necessity. For, if the town intended to be destroyed should have in it any tall rocks, as it generally falls out in the larger cities, a situation probably chosen at first with a view to prevent such a catastrophe; or if it abound in high spires, or pillars of stone, a sudden fall might endanger the bottom or under surface of the island, which, although it consist, as I have said, of one entire adamant, two hundred yards thick, might happen to crack by too great a shock, or burst by approaching too near the fires from the houses below, as the backs, both of iron and stone, will often do in our chimneys. Of all this the people are well apprised, and understand how far to carry their obstinacy, where their liberty or property is concerned. And the king, when he is highest provoked, and most determined to press a city to rubbish, orders the island to descend with great gentleness, out of a pretence of tenderness to his people, but, indeed, for fear of breaking the adamantine bottom; in which case, it is the opinion of all their philosophers, that the loadstone could no longer hold it up, and the whole mass would fall to the ground.

By a fundamental law of this realm, neither the king, nor either of his two eldest sons, are permitted to leave the island; nor the queen, till she is past child-bearing.

CHAPTER FOUR

The author leaves Laputa; is conveyed to Balnibarbi; arrives at the metropolis. A description of the metropolis, and the country adjoining. The author hospitably received by a great lord. His conversation with that lord.

ALTHOUGH I CANNOT say that I was ill treated in this island, yet I must confess I thought myself too much neglected, not without some degree of contempt; for neither prince nor people appeared to be curious in any part of knowledge, except mathematics and music, wherein I was far their inferior, and upon that account very little regarded.

On the other side, after having seen all the curiosities of the island, I was very desirous to leave it, being heartily weary of those people. They were indeed excellent in two sciences for which I have great esteem, and wherein I am not unversed; but, at the same time, so abstracted and involved in speculation, that I never met with such disagreeable companions. I conversed only with women, tradesmen, flappers, and court-pages, during two months of my abode there; by which, at last, I rendered myself extremely contemptible; yet these were the only people from whom I could ever receive a reasonable answer.

I had obtained, by hard study, a good degree of knowledge in their language: I was weary of being confined to an island where I received so little countenance, and resolved to leave it with the first opportunity.

There was a great lord at court, nearly related to the king, and for that reason alone used with respect. He was universally reckoned the most ignorant and stupid person among them. He had performed many eminent services for the crown, had great natural and acquired parts, adorned with integrity and honour; but so ill an ear for music, that his detractors reported, "he had been often known to beat time in the wrong place;" neither could his tutors, without extreme difficulty, teach him to demonstrate the most easy proposition in the mathematics. He was pleased to show me many marks of favour, often did me the honour of a visit, desired to be informed in the affairs of Europe, the laws and customs, the manners and learning of the several countries where I had travelled. He listened to me with great attention, and made very wise observations on all I spoke. He had two flappers attending him for state, but never made use of them, except at court and in visits of ceremony, and would always command them to withdraw, when we were alone together.

I entreated this illustrious person, to intercede in my behalf with his majesty, for leave to depart; which he accordingly did, as he was pleased to tell me, with regret: for indeed he had made me several offers very advantageous, which, however, I refused, with expressions of the highest acknowledgment.

On the 16th of February I took leave of his majesty and the court. The king made me a present to the value of about two hundred pounds English, and my protector, his kinsman, as much more, together with a letter of recommendation to a friend of his in Lagado, the metropolis. The island being then hovering over a mountain about two miles from it, I was let down from the lowest gallery, in the same manner as I had been taken up.

The continent, as far as it is subject to the monarch of the flying island, passes under the general name of *Balnibarbi*; and the metropolis, as I said before, is called *Lagado*. I felt some little satisfaction in finding myself on firm ground. I walked to the city without any concern, being clad like one of the natives, and sufficiently instructed to converse with them. I soon found out the person's house to whom I was recommended, presented my letter from his friend the grandee in the island, and was received with much kindness. This great lord, whose name was Munodi, ordered me an apartment in his own house, where I continued during my stay, and was entertained in a most hospitable manner.

The next morning after my arrival, he took me in his chariot to see the town, which is about half the bigness of London; but the houses very strangely built, and most of them out of repair. The people in the streets walked fast, looked wild, their eyes fixed, and were generally in rags. We passed through one of the town gates, and went about three miles into the country, where I saw many labourers working with several sorts of tools in the ground, but was not able to conjecture what they were about: neither did observe any expectation either of corn or grass, although the soil appeared to be excellent. I could not forbear admiring at these odd appearances, both in town and country; and I made bold to desire my conductor, that he would be pleased to explain to me, what could be meant by so many busy heads, hands, and faces, both in the streets and the fields, because I did not discover any good effects they produced; but, on the contrary, I never knew a soil so unhappily cultivated, houses so ill contrived and so ruinous, or a people whose countenances and habit expressed so much misery and want.

This lord Munodi was a person of the first rank, and had been some years governor of Lagado; but, by a cabal of ministers, was discharged for insufficiency. However, the king treated him with tenderness, as a well-meaning man, but of a low contemptible understanding.

When I gave that free censure of the country and its inhabitants, he made no further answer than by telling me, "that I had not been long enough among them to form a judgment; and that the different nations of the world had different customs;" with other common topics to the same purpose. But, when we returned to his palace, he asked me "how I liked the building, what absurdities I observed, and what quarrel I had with the dress or looks of his domestics?" This he might safely do; because every thing about him was magnificent, regular, and polite. I answered, "that his excellency's prudence, quality, and fortune, had exempted him from those defects, which folly and beggary had produced in others." He said, "if I would go with him to his country-house, about twenty miles distant, where his estate lay, there would be more leisure for this kind of conversation." I told his excellency "that I was entirely at his disposal;" and accordingly we set out next morning.

During our journey he made me observe the several methods used by farmers in managing their lands, which to me were wholly unaccountable; for, except in some very few places, I could not discover one ear of corn or blade of grass. But, in three hours travelling, the scene was wholly altered; we came into a most beautiful country; farmers' houses, at small distances, neatly built; the fields enclosed, containing vineyards, corn-grounds, and meadows. Neither do I remember to have seen a more delightful prospect. His excellency observed my countenance to clear up; he told me, with a sigh, "that there his estate began, and would continue the same, till we should come to his house: that his countrymen ridiculed and despised him, for managing his affairs no better, and for setting so ill an example to the kingdom; which, however, was followed by very few, such as were old, and wilful, and weak like himself."

We came at length to the house, which was indeed a noble structure, built according to the best rules of ancient architecture. The fountains, gardens, walks, avenues, and groves, were all disposed with exact judgment and taste. I gave due praises to every thing I saw, whereof his excellency took not the least notice till after supper; when, there being no third companion, he told me with a very melancholy air "that he doubted he must throw down his houses in town and country, to rebuild them after the present mode; destroy all his plantations, and cast others into such a form as modern usage required, and give the same directions to all his tenants, unless he would submit to incur the censure of pride, singularity, affectation, ignorance, caprice, and perhaps increase his majesty's displeasure; that the admiration I appeared to be under would cease or diminish, when he had informed me of some particulars which, probably, I never heard of at court, the people there being too much taken up in their own speculations, to have regard to what passed here below."

The sum of his discourse was to this effect: "That about forty years ago, certain persons went up to Laputa, either upon business or diversion, and, after five months continuance, came back with a very little smattering in mathematics, but full of volatile spirits acquired in that airy region: that these persons, upon their return, began to dislike the management of every thing below, and fell into schemes of putting all arts, sciences, languages, and mechanics, upon a new foot. To this end, they procured a royal patent for erecting an academy of projectors in Lagado; and the humour prevailed so strongly among the people, that there is not a town of any consequence in the kingdom without such an academy. In these colleges the professors contrive new rules and methods of agriculture and building, and new instruments, and tools for all trades and manufactures; whereby, as they undertake, one man shall do the work of ten; a palace may be built in a week, of materials so durable as to last for ever without repairing. All the fruits of the earth shall come to maturity at whatever season we think fit to choose, and increase a hundred fold more than they do at present; with innumerable other happy proposals. The only inconvenience is, that none of these projects are yet brought to perfection; and in the mean time, the whole country lies miserably waste, the houses in ruins, and the people without food or clothes. By all which, instead of being discouraged, they are fifty times more violently bent upon prosecuting their schemes, driven equally on by hope and despair: that as for himself, being not of an enterprising spirit, he was content to go on in the old forms, to live in the houses his ancestors had built, and act as they did, in every part of life, without innovation: that some few other persons of quality and gentry had done the same, but were looked on with an eye of contempt and ill-will, as enemies to art, ignorant, and ill common-wealth's men, preferring their own ease and sloth before the general improvement of their country."

His lordship added, "That he would not, by any further particulars, prevent the pleasure I should certainly take in viewing the grand academy, whither he was resolved I should go." He only desired me to observe a ruined building, upon the side of a mountain about three miles distant, of which he gave me this account: "That he had a very convenient mill within half a mile of his house, turned by a current from a large river, and sufficient for his own family, as well as a great number of his tenants; that about seven years ago, a club of those projectors came to him with proposals to destroy this mill, and build another on the side of that mountain, on the long ridge whereof a long canal must be cut, for a repository of water, to be conveyed up by pipes and engines to supply the mill, because the wind and air upon a height agitated the water, and thereby made it fitter for motion, and because the water, descending down a declivity, would turn the mill with half the current of a river whose course is more upon a level." He said, "that being then not very well with the court, and pressed by many of his friends, he complied with the proposal; and after employing a hundred men for two years, the work miscarried, the projectors went off, laying the blame entirely upon him, railing at him ever since, and putting others upon the same experiment, with equal assurance of success, as well as equal disappointment."

In a few days we came back to town; and his excellency, considering the bad character he had in the academy, would not go with me himself, but recommended me to a friend of his, to bear me company thither. My lord was pleased to represent me as a great admirer of projects, and a person of much curiosity and easy belief; which, indeed, was not without truth; for I had myself been a sort of projector in my younger days.

CHAPTER FIVE

The author permitted to see the grand academy of Lagado. The academy largely described. The arts wherein the professors employ themselves.

THIS ACADEMY is not an entire single building, but a continuation of several houses on both sides of a street, which growing waste, was purchased and applied to that use.

I was received very kindly by the warden, and went for many days to the academy. Every room has in it one or more projectors; and I believe I could not be in fewer than five hundred rooms.

The first man I saw was of a meagre aspect, with sooty hands and face, his hair and beard long, ragged, and singed in several places. His clothes, shirt, and skin, were all of the same colour. He has been eight years upon a project for extracting sunbeams out of cucumbers, which were to be put in phials hermetically sealed, and let out to warm the air in raw inclement summers. He told me, he did not doubt, that, in eight years more, he should be able to supply the governor's gardens with sunshine, at a reasonable rate: but he complained that his stock was low, and entreated me "to give him something as an encouragement to ingenuity, especially since this had been a very dear season for cucumbers." I made him a small present, for my lord had furnished me with money on purpose, because he knew their practice of begging from all who go to see them.

I went into another chamber, but was ready to hasten back, being almost overcome with a horrible stink. My conductor pressed me forward, conjuring me in a whisper "to give no offence, which would be highly resented;" and therefore I durst not so much as stop my nose. The projector of this cell was the most ancient student of the academy; his face and beard were of a pale yellow; his hands and clothes daubed over with filth. When I was presented to him, he gave me a close embrace, a compliment I could well have excused. His employment, from his first coming into the academy, was an operation to reduce human excrement to its original food, by separating the several parts, removing the tincture which it receives from the gall, making the odour exhale, and scumming off the saliva. He had a weekly allowance, from the society, of a vessel filled with human ordure, about the bigness of a Bristol barrel.

I saw another at work to calcine ice into gunpowder; who likewise showed me a treatise he had written concerning the malleability of fire, which he intended to publish.

There was a most ingenious architect, who had contrived a new method for building houses, by beginning at the roof, and working downward to the foundation; which he justified to me, by the like practice of those two prudent insects, the bee and the spider.

There was a man born blind, who had several apprentices in his own condition: their employment was to mix colours for painters, which their master taught them to distinguish by feeling and smelling. It was indeed my misfortune to find them at that time not very perfect in their lessons, and the professor himself happened to be generally mistaken. This artist is much encouraged and esteemed by the whole fraternity.

In another apartment I was highly pleased with a projector who had found a device of ploughing the ground with hogs, to save the charges of ploughs, cattle, and labour. The method is this: in an acre of ground you bury, at six inches distance and eight deep, a quantity of acorns, dates, chestnuts, and other mast or vegetables, whereof these animals are fondest; then you drive six hundred or more of them into the field, where, in a few days, they will root up the whole ground in search of their food, and make it fit for sowing, at the same time manuring it with their dung: it is true, upon experiment, they found the charge and trouble very great, and they had little or no crop. However it is not doubted, that this invention may be capable of great improvement.

I went into another room, where the walls and ceiling were all hung round with cobwebs, except a narrow passage for the artist to go in and out. At my entrance, he called aloud to me, "not to disturb his webs." He lamented "the fatal mistake the world had been so long in, of using silkworms, while we had such plenty of domestic insects who infinitely excelled the former, because they understood how to weave, as well as spin." And he proposed further, "that by employing spiders, the charge of dyeing silks should be wholly saved;" whereof I was fully convinced, when he showed me a vast number of flies most beautifully coloured, wherewith he fed his spiders, assuring us "that the webs would take a tincture from them; and as he had them of all hues, he hoped to fit everybody's fancy, as soon as he could find proper food for the flies, of certain gums, oils, and other glutinous matter, to give a strength and consistence to the threads."

There was an astronomer, who had undertaken to place a sun-dial upon the great weathercock on the town-house, by adjusting the annual and diurnal motions of the earth and sun, so as to answer and coincide with all accidental turnings of the wind.

I was complaining of a small fit of the colic, upon which my conductor led me into a room where a great physician resided, who was famous for curing that disease, by contrary operations from the same instrument. He had a large pair of bellows, with a long slender muzzle of ivory: this he conveyed eight inches up the anus, and drawing in the wind, he affirmed he could make the guts as lank as a dried bladder. But when the disease was more stubborn and violent, he let in the muzzle while the bellows were full of wind, which he discharged into the body of the patient; then withdrew the instrument to replenish it, clapping his thumb strongly against the orifice of then fundament; and this being repeated three or four times, the adventitious wind would rush out, bringing the noxious along with it, (like water put into a pump), and the patient recovered. I saw him try both experiments upon a dog, but could not discern any effect from the former. After the latter the animal was ready to burst, and made so violent a discharge as was very offensive to me and my companion. The dog died on the spot, and we left the doctor endeavouring to recover him, by the same operation.

I visited many other apartments, but shall not trouble my reader with all the curiosities I observed, being studious of brevity.

I had hitherto seen only one side of the academy, the other being appropriated to the advancers of speculative learning, of whom I shall say something, when I have mentioned one illustrious person more, who is called among them "the universal artist." He told us "he had been thirty years employing his thoughts for the improvement of human life." He had two large rooms full of wonderful curiosities, and fifty men at work. Some were condensing air into a dry tangible substance, by extracting the nitre, and letting the aqueous or fluid particles percolate; others softening marble, for pillows and pin-cushions; others petrifying the hoofs of a living horse, to preserve them from foundering. The artist himself was at that time busy upon two great designs; the first, to sow land with chaff, wherein he affirmed the true seminal virtue to be contained, as he demonstrated by several experiments, which I was not skilful enough to comprehend. The other was, by a certain composition of gums, minerals, and vegetables, outwardly applied, to prevent the growth of wool upon two young lambs; and he hoped, in a reasonable time to propagate the breed of naked sheep, all over the kingdom.

We crossed a walk to the other part of the academy, where, as I have already said, the projectors in speculative learning resided.

The first professor I saw, was in a very large room, with forty pupils about him. After salutation, observing me to look earnestly upon a frame, which took up the greatest part of both the length and breadth of the room, he said, "Perhaps I might wonder to see him employed in a project for improving speculative knowledge, by practical and mechanical operations. But the world would soon be sensible of its usefulness; and he flattered himself, that a more noble, exalted thought never sprang in any other man's head. Every one knew how laborious the usual method is of attaining to arts and sciences; whereas, by his contrivance, the most ignorant person, at a reasonable charge, and with a little bodily labour, might write books in philosophy, poetry, politics, laws, mathematics, and theology, without the least assistance from genius or study." He then led me to the frame, about the sides, whereof all his pupils stood in ranks. It was twenty feet square, placed in the middle of the room. The superfices was composed of several bits of wood, about the bigness of a die, but some larger than others. They were all linked together by slender wires. These bits of wood were covered, on every square, with paper pasted on them; and on these papers were written all the words of their language, in their several moods, tenses, and declensions; but without any order. The professor then desired me "to observe; for he was going to set his engine at work." The pupils, at his command, took each of them hold of an iron handle, whereof there were forty fixed round the edges of the frame; and giving them a sudden turn, the whole disposition of the words was entirely changed. He then commanded six-and-thirty of the lads, to read the several lines softly, as they appeared upon the frame; and where they found three or four words together that might make part of a sentence, they dictated to the four remaining boys, who were scribes. This work was repeated three or four times, and at every turn, the engine was so contrived, that the words shifted into new places, as the square bits of wood moved upside down.

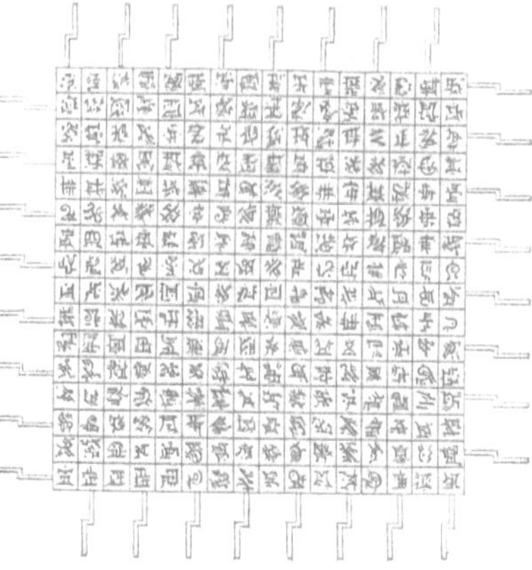

Six hours a day the young students were employed in this labour; and the professor showed me several volumes in large folio, already collected, of broken sentences, which he intended to piece together, and out of those rich materials, to give the world a complete body of all arts and sciences; which, however, might be still improved, and much expedited, if the public would raise a fund for making and employing five hundred such frames in Lagado, and oblige the managers to contribute in common their several collections.

He assured me "that this invention had employed all his thoughts from his youth; that he had emptied the whole vocabulary into his frame, and made the strictest computation of the general proportion there is in books between the numbers of particles, nouns, and verbs, and other parts of speech."

I made my humblest acknowledgment to this illustrious person, for his great communicativeness; and promised, "if ever I had the good fortune to return to my native country, that I would do him justice, as the sole inventor of this wonderful machine;" the form and contrivance of which I desired leave to delineate on paper, as in the figure here annexed. I told him, "although it were the custom of our learned in Europe to steal inventions from each other, who had thereby at least this advantage, that it became a controversy which was the right owner; yet I would take such caution, that he should have the honour entire, without a rival."

We next went to the school of languages, where three professors sat in consultation upon improving that of their own country.

The first project was, to shorten discourse, by cutting polysyllables into one, and leaving out verbs and participles, because, in reality, all things imaginable are but norms.

The other project was, a scheme for entirely abolishing all words whatsoever; and this was urged as a great advantage in point of health, as well as brevity. For it is plain, that every word we speak is, in some degree, a diminution of our lunge by corrosion, and, consequently, contributes to the shortening of our lives. An expedient was therefore offered, "that since words are only names for things, it would be more convenient for all men to carry about them such things as were necessary to express a particular business they are to discourse on." And this invention would certainly have taken place, to the great ease as well as health of the subject, if the women, in conjunction with the vulgar and illiterate, had not threatened to raise a rebellion unless they might be allowed the liberty to speak with their tongues, after the manner of their forefathers; such constant irreconcilable enemies to science are the common people. However, many of the most learned and wise adhere to the new scheme of expressing themselves by things; which has only this inconvenience attending it, that if a man's business be very great, and of various kinds, he must be obliged, in proportion, to carry a greater bundle of things upon his back, unless he can afford one or two strong servants to attend him. I have often beheld two of those sages almost sinking under the weight of their packs, like pedlars among us, who, when they met in the street, would lay down their loads, open their sacks, and hold conversation for an hour together; then put up their implements, help each other to resume their burdens, and take their leave.

But for short conversations, a man may carry implements in his pockets, and under his arms, enough to supply him; and in his house, he cannot be at a loss. Therefore the room where company meet who practise this art, is full of all things, ready at hand, requisite to furnish matter for this kind of artificial converse.

Another great advantage proposed by this invention was, that it would serve as a universal language, to be understood in all civilised nations, whose goods and utensils are generally of the same kind, or nearly resembling, so that their uses might easily be comprehended. And thus ambassadors would be qualified to treat with foreign princes, or ministers of state, to whose tongues they were utter strangers.

I was at the mathematical school, where the master taught his pupils after a method scarce imaginable to us in Europe. The proposition, and demonstration, were fairly written on a thin wafer, with ink composed of a cephalic tincture. This, the student was to swallow upon a fasting stomach, and for three days following, eat nothing but bread and water. As the wafer digested, the tincture mounted to his brain, bearing the proposition along with it. But the success has not hitherto been answerable, partly by some error in the *quantum* or composition, and partly by the perverseness of lads, to whom this bolus is so nauseous, that they generally steal aside, and discharge it upwards, before it can operate; neither have they been yet persuaded to use so long an abstinence, as the prescription requires.

CHAPTER SIX

A further account of the academy. The author proposes some improvements, which are honourably received.

In the school of political projectors, I was but ill entertained; the professors appearing, in my judgment, wholly out of their senses, which is a scene that never fails to make me melancholy. These unhappy people were proposing schemes for persuading monarchs to choose favourites upon the score of their wisdom, capacity, and virtue; of teaching ministers to consult the public good; of rewarding merit, great abilities, eminent services; of instructing princes to know their true interest, by placing it on the same foundation with that of their people; of choosing for employments persons qualified to exercise them, with many other wild, impossible chimeras, that never entered before into the heart of man to conceive; and confirmed in me the old observation, "that there is nothing so extravagant and irrational, which some philosophers have not maintained for truth."

But, however, I shall so far do justice to this part of the Academy, as to acknowledge that all of them were not so visionary. There was a most ingenious doctor, who seemed to be perfectly versed in the whole nature and system of government. This illustrious person had very usefully employed his studies, in finding out effectual remedies for all diseases and corruptions to which the several kinds of public administration are subject, by the vices or infirmities of those who govern, as well as by the licentiousness of those who are to obey. For instance: whereas all writers and reasoners have agreed, that there is a strict universal resemblance between the natural and the political body; can there be any thing more evident, than that the health of both must be preserved, and the diseases cured, by the same prescriptions? It is allowed, that senates and great councils are often troubled with redundant, ebullient, and other peccant humours; with many diseases of the head, and more of the heart; with strong convulsions, with grievous contractions of the nerves and sinews in both hands, but especially the right; with spleen, flatus, vertigos, and deliriums; with scrofulous tumours, full of fetid purulent matter; with sour frothy ructations: with canine appetites, and crudeness of digestion, besides many others, needless to mention. This doctor therefore proposed, "that upon the meeting of the senate, certain physicians should attend it the three first days of their sitting, and at the close of each day's debate feel the pulses of every senator; after which, having maturely considered and consulted upon the nature of the several maladies, and the methods of cure, they should on the fourth day return to the senate house, attended by their apothecaries stored with proper medicines; and before the members sat, administer to each of them lenitives, aperitives, abstersives, corrosives, restringents, palliatives, laxatives, cephalalgics, icterics, apophlegmatics, acoustics, as their several cases required; and, according as these medicines should operate, repeat, alter, or omit them, at the next meeting."

This project could not be of any great expense to the public; and might in my poor opinion, be of much use for the despatch of business, in those countries where senates have any share in the legislative power; beget unanimity, shorten debates, open a few mouths which are now closed, and close many more which are now open; curb the petulancy of the young, and correct the positiveness of the old; rouse the stupid, and damp the pert.

Again: because it is a general complaint, that the favourites of princes are troubled with short and weak memories; the same doctor proposed, "that whoever attended a first minister, after having told his business, with the utmost brevity and in the plainest words, should, at his departure, give the said minister a tweak by the nose, or a kick in the belly, or tread on his corns, or lug him thrice by both ears, or run a pin into his breech; or pinch his arm black and blue, to prevent forgetfulness; and at every levee day, repeat the same operation, till the business were done, or absolutely refused."

He likewise directed, "that every senator in the great council of a nation, after he had delivered his opinion, and argued in the defence of it, should be obliged to give his vote directly contrary; because if that were done, the result would infallibly terminate in the good of the public."

When parties in a state are violent, he offered a wonderful contrivance to reconcile them. The method is this: You take a hundred leaders of each party; you dispose them into couples of such whose heads are nearest of a size; then let two nice operators saw off the occiput of each couple at the same time, in such a manner that the brain may be equally divided. Let the occiputs, thus cut off, be interchanged, applying each to the head of his opposite party-man. It seems indeed to be a work that requires some exactness, but the professor assured us, "that if it were dexterously performed, the cure would be infallible." For he argued thus: "that the two half brains being left to debate the matter between themselves within the space of one skull, would soon come to a good understanding, and produce that moderation, as well as regularity of thinking, so much to be wished for in the heads of those, who imagine they come into the world only to watch and govern its motion: and as to the difference of brains, in quantity or quality, among those who are directors in faction, the doctor assured us, from his own knowledge, that "it was a perfect trifle."

I heard a very warm debate between two professors, about the most commodious and effectual ways and means of raising money, without grieving the subject. The first affirmed, "the justest method would be, to lay a certain tax upon vices and folly; and the sum fixed upon every man to be rated, after the fairest manner, by a jury of his neighbours." The second was of an opinion directly contrary; "to tax those qualities of body and mind, for which men chiefly value themselves; the rate to be more or less, according to the degrees of excelling; the decision whereof should be left entirely to their own breast." The highest tax was upon men who are the greatest favourites of the other sex, and the assessments, according to the number and nature of the favours they have received; for which, they are allowed to be their own vouchers. Wit, valour, and politeness, were likewise proposed to be largely taxed, and collected in the same manner, by every person's giving his own word for the quantum of what he possessed. But as to honour, justice, wisdom, and learning, they should not be taxed at all; because they are qualifications of so singular a kind, that no man will either allow them in his neighbour or value them in himself.

The women were proposed to be taxed according to their beauty and skill in dressing, wherein they had the same privilege with the men, to be determined by their own judgment. But constancy, chastity, good sense, and good nature, were not rated, because they would not bear the charge of collecting.

To keep senators in the interest of the crown, it was proposed that the members should raffle for employment; every man first taking an oath, and giving security, that he would vote for the court, whether he won or not; after which, the losers had, in their turn, the liberty of raffling upon the next vacancy. Thus, hope and expectation would be kept alive; none would complain of broken promises, but impute their disappointments wholly to fortune, whose shoulders are broader and stronger than those of a ministry.

Another professor showed me a large paper of instructions for discovering plots and conspiracies against the government. He advised great statesmen to examine into the diet of all suspected persons; their times of eating; upon which side they lay in bed; with which hand they wipe their posteriors; take a strict view of their excrements, and, from the colour, the odour, the taste, the consistence, the crudeness or maturity of digestion, form a judgment of their thoughts and designs; because men are never so serious, thoughtful, and intent, as when they are at stool, which he found by frequent experiment; for, in such conjunctures, when he used, merely as a trial, to consider which was the best way of murdering the king, his ordure would have a tincture of green; but quite different, when he thought only of raising an insurrection, or burning the metropolis.

The whole discourse was written with great acuteness, containing many observations, both curious and useful for politicians; but, as I conceived, not altogether complete. This I ventured to tell the author, and offered, if he pleased, to supply him with some additions. He received my proposition with more compliance than is usual among writers, especially those of the projecting species, professing "he would be glad to receive further information."

I told him, "that in the kingdom of Tribnia,[3] by the natives called Langdon,[4] where I had sojourned some time in my travels, the bulk of the people consist in a manner wholly of discoverers, witnesses, informers, accusers, prosecutors, evidences, swearers, together with their several subservient and subaltern instruments, all under the colours, the conduct, and the pay of ministers of state, and their deputies. The plots, in that kingdom, are usually the workmanship of those persons who desire to raise their own characters of profound politicians; to restore new vigour to a crazy administration; to stifle or divert general discontents; to fill their coffers with forfeitures; and raise, or sink the opinion of public credit, as either shall best answer their private advantage. It is first agreed and settled among them, what suspected persons shall be accused of a plot; then, effectual care is taken to secure all their letters and papers, and put the owners in chains. These papers are delivered to a set of artists, very dexterous in finding out the mysterious meanings of words, syllables, and letters: for instance, they can discover a close stool, to signify a privy council; a flock of geese, a senate; a lame dog, an invader; the plague, a standing army; a buzzard, a prime minis-

3 Britannia. – *Sir W. Scott.*

4 London. – *Sir W. Scott.*

ter; the gout, a high priest; a gibbet, a secretary of state; a chamber pot, a committee of grandees; a sieve, a court lady; a broom, a revolution; a mouse-trap, an employment; a bottomless pit, a treasury; a sink, a court; a cap and bells, a favourite; a broken reed, a court of justice; an empty tun, a general; a running sore, the administration.[5]

"When this method fails, they have two others more effectual, which the learned among them call acrostics and anagrams. First, they can decipher all initial letters into political meanings. Thus *N*, shall signify a plot; *B*, a regiment of horse; *L*, a fleet at sea; or, secondly, by transposing the letters of the alphabet in any suspected paper, they can lay open the deepest designs of a discontented party. So, for example, if I should say, in a letter to a friend, 'Our brother Tom has just got the piles,' a skilful decipherer would discover, that the same letters which compose that sentence, may be analysed into the following words, 'Resist ---, a plot is brought home – The tour.' And this is the anagrammatic method."

The professor made me great acknowledgments for communicating these observations, and promised to make honourable mention of me in his treatise.

I saw nothing in this country that could invite me to a longer continuance, and began to think of returning home to England.

5 This is the revised text adopted by Dr. Hawksworth (1766). The above paragraph in the original editions (1726) takes another form, commencing: – "I told him that should I happen to live in a kingdom where lots were in vogue," &c. The names Tribnia and Langdon an not mentioned, and the "close stool" and its signification do not occur.

CHAPTER SEVEN

The author leaves Lagado: arrives at Maldonada. No ship ready. He takes a short voyage to Glubbdubdrib. His reception by the governor.

The continent, of which this kingdom is apart, extends itself, as I have reason to believe, eastward, to that unknown tract of America westward of California; and north, to the Pacific Ocean, which is not above a hundred and fifty miles from Lagado; where there is a good port, and much commerce with the great island of Luggnagg, situated to the north-west about 29 degrees north latitude, and 140 longitude. This island of Luggnagg stands south-eastward of Japan, about a hundred leagues distant. There is a strict alliance between the Japanese emperor and the king of Luggnagg; which affords frequent opportunities of sailing from one island to the other. I determined therefore to direct my course this way, in order to my return to Europe. I hired two mules, with a guide, to show me the way, and carry my small baggage. I took leave of my noble protector, who had shown me so much favour, and made me a generous present at my departure.

My journey was without any accident or adventure worth relating. When I arrived at the port of Maldonada (for so it is called) there was no ship in the harbour bound for Luggnagg, nor likely to be in some time. The town is about as large as Portsmouth. I soon fell into some acquaintance, and was very hospitably received. A gentleman of distinction said to me, "that since the ships bound for Luggnagg could not be ready in less than a month, it might be no disagreeable amusement for me to take a trip to the little island of Glubbdubdrib, about five leagues off to the south-west." He offered himself and a friend to accompany me, and that I should be provided with a small convenient bark for the voyage.

Glubbdubdrib, as nearly as I can interpret the word, signifies the island of sorcerers or magicians. It is about one third as large as the Isle of Wight, and extremely fruitful: it is governed by the head of a certain tribe, who are all magicians. This tribe marries only among each other, and the eldest in succession is prince or governor. He has a noble palace, and a park of about three thousand acres, surrounded by a wall of hewn stone twenty feet high. In this park are several small enclosures for cattle, corn, and gardening.

The governor and his family are served and attended by domestics of a kind somewhat unusual. By his skill in necromancy he has a power of calling whom he pleases from the dead, and commanding their service for twenty-four hours, but no longer; nor can he call the same persons up again in less than three months, except upon very extraordinary occasions.

When we arrived at the island, which was about eleven in the morning, one of the gentlemen who accompanied me went to the governor, and desired admittance for a stranger, who came on purpose to have the honour of attending on his highness. This was immediately granted, and we all three entered the gate of the palace between two rows of guards, armed and dressed after a very antic manner, and with something in their countenances that made my flesh creep with a horror I cannot express. We passed through several apartments, between servants of the same sort, ranked on each side as before, till we came to the chamber of presence; where, after three profound obeisances, and a few general questions, we were permitted to sit on three stools, near the lowest step of his highness's throne. He understood the language of Balnibarbi, although it was different from that of this island. He desired me to give him some account of my travels; and, to let me see that I should be treated without ceremony, he dismissed all his attendants with a turn of his finger; at which, to my great astonishment, they vanished in an instant, like visions in a dream when we awake on a sudden. I could not recover myself in some time, till the governor assured me, "that I should receive no hurt:" and observing my two companions to be under no concern, who had been often entertained in the same manner, I began to take courage, and related to his highness a short history of my several adventures; yet not without some hesitation, and frequently looking behind me to the place where I had seen those domestic spectres. I had the honour to dine with the governor, where a new set of ghosts served up the meat, and waited at table. I now observed myself to be less terrified than I had been in the morning. I stayed till sunset, but humbly desired his highness to excuse me for not accepting his invitation of lodging in the palace. My two friends and I lay at a private house in the town adjoining, which is the capital of this little island; and the next morning we returned to pay our duty to the governor, as he was pleased to command us.

After this manner we continued in the island for ten days, most part of every day with the governor, and at night in our lodging. I soon grew so familiarized to the sight of spirits, that after the third or fourth time they gave me no emotion at all: or, if I had any apprehensions left, my curiosity prevailed over them. For his highness the governor ordered me "to call up whatever persons I would choose to name, and in whatever numbers, among all the dead from the beginning of the world to the present time, and command them to answer any questions I should think fit to ask; with this condition, that my questions must be confined within the compass of the times they lived in. And one thing I might depend upon, that they would certainly tell me the truth, for lying was a talent of no use in the lower world."

I made my humble acknowledgments to his highness for so great a favour. We were in a chamber, from whence there was a fair prospect into the park. And because my first inclination was to be entertained with scenes of pomp and magnificence, I desired to see Alexander the Great at the head of his army, just after the battle of Arbela: which, upon a motion of the governor's finger, immediately appeared in a large field, under the window where we stood. Alexander was called up into the room: it was with great difficulty that I understood his Greek, and had but little of my own. He assured me upon his honour "that he was not poisoned, but died of a bad fever by excessive drinking."

Next, I saw Hannibal passing the Alps, who told me "he had not a drop of vinegar in his camp."

I saw Cæsar and Pompey at the head of their troops, just ready to engage. I saw the former, in his last great triumph. I desired that the senate of Rome might appear before me, in one large chamber, and an assembly of somewhat a later age in counterview, in another. The first seemed to be an assembly of heroes and demigods; the other, a knot of pedlars, pick-pockets, highwayman, and bullies.

The governor, at my request, gave the sign for Cæsar and Brutus to advance towards us. I was struck with a profound veneration at the sight of Brutus, and could easily discover the most consummate virtue, the greatest intrepidity and firmness of mind, the truest love of his country, and general benevolence for mankind, in every lineament of his countenance. I observed, with much pleasure, that these two persons were in good intelligence with each other; and Cæsar freely confessed to me, "that the greatest actions of his own life were not equal, by many degrees, to the glory of taking it away." I had the honour to have much conversation with Brutus; and was told, "that his ancestor Junius, Socrates, Epaminondas, Cato the younger, Sir Thomas More, and himself were perpetually together:" a sextumvirate, to which all the ages of the world cannot add a seventh.

It would be tedious to trouble the reader with relating what vast numbers of illustrious persons were called up to gratify that insatiable desire I had to see the world in every period of antiquity placed before me. I chiefly fed mine eyes with beholding the destroyers of tyrants and usurpers, and the restorers of liberty to oppressed and injured nations. But it is impossible to express the satisfaction I received in my own mind, after such a manner as to make it a suitable entertainment to the reader.

CHAPTER EIGHT

A further account of Glubbdubdrib. Ancient and modern history corrected.

Having a desire to see those ancients who were most renowned for wit and learning, I set apart one day on purpose. I proposed that Homer and Aristotle might appear at the head of all their commentators; but these were so numerous, that some hundreds were forced to attend in the court, and outward rooms of the palace. I knew, and could distinguish those two heroes, at first sight, not only from the crowd, but from each other. Homer was the taller and comelier person of the two, walked very erect for one of his age, and his eyes were the most quick and piercing I ever beheld. Aristotle stooped much, and made use of a staff. His visage was meagre, his hair lank and thin, and his voice hollow. I soon discovered that both of them were perfect strangers to the rest of the company, and had never seen or heard of them before; and I had a whisper from a ghost who shall be nameless, "that these commentators always kept in the most distant quarters from their principals, in the lower world, through a consciousness of shame and guilt, because they had so horribly misrepresented the meaning of those authors to posterity." I introduced Didymus and Eustathius to Homer, and prevailed on him to treat them better than perhaps they deserved, for he soon found they wanted a genius to enter into the spirit of a poet. But Aristotle was out of all patience with the account I gave him of Scotus and Ramus, as I presented them to him; and he asked them, "whether the rest of the tribe were as great dunces as themselves?"

I then desired the governor to call up Descartes and Gassendi, with whom I prevailed to explain their systems to Aristotle. This great philosopher freely acknowledged his own mistakes in natural philosophy, because he proceeded in many things upon conjecture, as all men must do; and he found that Gassendi, who had made the doctrine of Epicurus as palatable as he could, and the vortices of Descartes, were equally to be exploded. He predicted the same fate to *attraction*, whereof the present learned are such zealous asserters. He said, "that new systems of nature were but new fashions, which would vary in every age; and even those, who pretend to demonstrate them from mathematical principles, would flourish but a short period of time, and be out of vogue when that was determined."

I spent five days in conversing with many others of the ancient learned. I saw most of the first Roman emperors. I prevailed on the governor to call up Heliogabalus's cooks to dress us a dinner, but they could not show us much of their skill, for want of materials. A helot of Agesilaus made us a dish of Spartan broth, but I was not able to get down a second spoonful.

The two gentlemen, who conducted me to the island, were pressed by their private affairs to return in three days, which I employed in seeing some of the modern dead, who had made the greatest figure, for two or three hundred years past, in our own and other countries of Europe; and having been always a great admirer of old illustrious families, I desired the governor would call up a dozen or two of kings, with their ancestors in order for eight or nine generations. But my disappointment was grievous and unexpected. For, instead of a long train with royal diadems, I saw in one family two fiddlers, three spruce courtiers, and an Italian prelate. In another, a barber, an abbot, and two cardinals. I have too great a veneration for crowned heads, to dwell any longer on so nice a subject. But as to counts, marquises, dukes, earls, and the like, I was not so scrupulous. And I confess, it was not without some pleasure, that I found myself able to trace the particular features, by which certain families are distinguished, up to their originals. I could plainly discover whence one family derives a long chin; why a second has abounded with knaves for two generations, and fools for two more; why a third happened to be crack-brained, and a fourth to be sharpers; whence it came, what Polydore Virgil says of a certain great house, *Nec vir fortis, nec foemina casta*; how cruelty, falsehood, and cowardice, grew to be characteristics by which certain families are distinguished as much as by their coats of arms; who first brought the pox into a noble house, which has lineally descended scrofulous tumours to their posterity. Neither could I wonder at all this, when I saw such an interruption of lineages, by pages, lackeys, valets, coachmen, gamesters, fiddlers, players, captains, and pickpockets.

I was chiefly disgusted with modern history. For having strictly examined all the persons of greatest name in the courts of princes, for a hundred years past, I found how the world had been misled by prostitute writers, to ascribe the greatest exploits in war, to cowards; the wisest counsel, to fools; sincerity, to flatterers; Roman virtue, to betrayers of their country;

piety, to atheists; chastity, to sodomites; truth, to informers: how many innocent and excellent persons had been condemned to death or banishment by the practising of great ministers upon the corruption of judges, and the malice of factions: how many villains had been exalted to the highest places of trust, power, dignity, and profit: how great a share in the motions and events of courts, councils, and senates might be challenged by bawds, whores, pimps, parasites, and buffoons. How low an opinion I had of human wisdom and integrity, when I was truly informed of the springs and motives of great enterprises and revolutions in the world, and of the contemptible accidents to which they owed their success.

Here I discovered the roguery and ignorance of those who pretend to write anecdotes, or secret history; who send so many kings to their graves with a cup of poison; will repeat the discourse between a prince and chief minister, where no witness was by; unlock the thoughts and cabinets of ambassadors and secretaries of state; and have the perpetual misfortune to be mistaken. Here I discovered the true causes of many great events that have surprised the world; how a whore can govern the back-stairs, the back-stairs a council, and the council a senate. A general confessed, in my presence, "that he got a victory purely by the force of cowardice and ill conduct;" and an admiral, "that, for want of proper intelligence, he beat the enemy, to whom he intended to betray the fleet." Three kings protested to me, "that in their whole reigns they never did once prefer any person of merit, unless by mistake, or treachery of some minister in whom they confided; neither would they do it if they were to live again:" and they showed, with great strength of reason, "that the royal throne could not be supported without corruption, because that positive, confident, restiff temper, which virtue infused into a man, was a perpetual clog to public business."

I had the curiosity to inquire in a particular manner, by what methods great numbers had procured to themselves high titles of honour, and prodigious estates; and I confined my inquiry to a very modern period: however, without grating upon present times, because I would be sure to give no offence even to foreigners (for I hope the reader need not be told, that I do not in the least intend my own country, in what I say upon this occasion,) a great number of persons concerned were called up; and, upon a very slight examination, discovered such a scene of infamy, that I cannot reflect upon it without some seriousness. Perjury, oppression, subornation, fraud, pandarism, and the like infirmities, were among the most excusable arts they had to mention; and for these I gave, as it was reasonable, great allowance. But when some confessed they owed their greatness and wealth to sodomy, or incest;

others, to the prostituting of their own wives and daughters; others, to the betraying of their country or their prince; some, to poisoning; more to the perverting of justice, in order to destroy the innocent, I hope I may be pardoned, if these discoveries inclined me a little to abate of that profound veneration, which I am naturally apt to pay to persons of high rank, who ought to be treated with the utmost respect due to their sublime dignity, by us their inferiors.

I had often read of some great services done to princes and states, and desired to see the persons by whom those services were performed. Upon inquiry I was told, "that their names were to be found on no record, except a few of them, whom history has represented as the vilest of rogues and traitors." As to the rest, I had never once heard of them. They all appeared with dejected looks, and in the meanest habit; most of them telling me, "they died in poverty and disgrace, and the rest on a scaffold or a gibbet."

Among others, there was one person, whose case appeared a little singular. He had a youth about eighteen years old standing by his side. He told me, "he had for many years been commander of a ship; and in the sea fight at Actium had the good fortune to break through the enemy's great line of battle, sink three of their capital ships, and take a fourth, which was the sole cause of Antony's flight, and of the victory that ensued; that the youth standing by him, his only son, was killed in the action." He added, "that upon the confidence of some merit, the war being at an end, he went to Rome, and solicited at the court of Augustus to be preferred to a greater ship, whose commander had been killed; but, without any regard to his pretensions, it was given to a boy who had never seen the sea, the son of Libertina, who waited on one of the emperor's mistresses. Returning back to his own vessel, he was charged with neglect of duty, and the ship given to a favourite page of Publicola, the vice-admiral; whereupon he retired to a poor farm at a great distance from Rome, and there ended his life." I was so curious to know the truth of this story, that I desired Agrippa might be called, who was admiral in that fight. He appeared, and confirmed the whole account: but with much more advantage to the captain, whose modesty had extenuated or concealed a great part of his merit.

I was surprised to find corruption grown so high and so quick in that empire, by the force of luxury so lately introduced; which made me less wonder at many parallel cases in other countries, where vices of all kinds have reigned so much longer, and where the whole praise, as well as pillage, has been engrossed by the chief commander, who perhaps had the least title to either.

As every person called up made exactly the same appearance he had done in the world, it gave me melancholy reflections to observe how much the race of human kind was degenerated among us within these hundred years past; how the pox, under all its consequences and denominations had altered every lineament of an English countenance; shortened the size of bodies, unbraced the nerves, relaxed the sinews and muscles, introduced a sallow complexion, and rendered the flesh loose and rancid.

I descended so low, as to desire some English yeoman of the old stamp might be summoned to appear; once so famous for the simplicity of their manners, diet, and dress; for justice in their dealings; for their true spirit of liberty; for their valour, and love of their country. Neither could I be wholly unmoved, after comparing the living with the dead, when I considered how all these pure native virtues were prostituted for a piece of money by their grand-children; who, in selling their votes and managing at elections, have acquired every vice and corruption that can possibly be learned in a court.

CHAPTER NINE

The author returns to Maldonada. Sails to the kingdom of Luggnagg. The author confined. He is sent for to court. The manner of his admittance. The king's great lenity to his subjects.

THE DAY OF our departure being come, I took leave of his highness, the Governor of Glubbdubdrib, and returned with my two companions to Maldonada, where, after a fortnight's waiting, a ship was ready to sail for Luggnagg. The two gentlemen, and some others, were so generous and kind as to furnish me with provisions, and see me on board. I was a month in this voyage. We had one violent storm, and were under a necessity of steering westward to get into the trade wind, which holds for above sixty leagues. On the 21st of April, 1708, we sailed into the river of Clumegnig, which is a seaport town, at the south-east point of Luggnagg. We cast anchor within a league of the town, and made a signal for a pilot. Two of them came on board in less than half an hour, by whom we were guided between certain shoals and rocks, which are very dangerous in the passage, to a large basin, where a fleet may ride in safety within a cable's length of the town-wall.

Some of our sailors, whether out of treachery or inadvertence, had informed the pilots "that I was a stranger, and great traveller;" whereof these gave notice to a custom-house officer, by whom I was examined very strictly upon my landing. This officer spoke to me in the language of Balnibarbi, which, by the force of much commerce, is generally understood in that town, especially by seamen and those employed in the customs. I gave him a short account of some particulars, and made my story as plausible and consistent as I could; but I thought it necessary to disguise my country, and call myself a Hollander; because my intentions were for Japan, and I knew the Dutch were the only Europeans permitted to enter into that kingdom. I therefore told the officer, "that having been shipwrecked on the coast of Balnibarbi, and cast on a rock, I was received up into Laputa, or the flying island (of which he had often heard), and was now endeavouring to get to Japan, whence I might find a convenience of returning to my own country." The officer said, "I must be confined till he could receive orders from court, for which he would write immediately, and hoped to receive an answer in a fortnight." I was carried to a convenient lodging with a sentry placed at the door; however, I had the liberty of a large garden, and was treated with humanity enough, being maintained all the time at the king's charge. I was invited by several persons, chiefly out of curiosity, because it was reported that I came from countries very remote, of which they had never heard.

I hired a young man, who came in the same ship, to be an interpreter; he was a native of Luggnagg, but had lived some years at Maldonada, and was a perfect master of both languages. By his assistance, I was able to hold a conversation with those who came to visit me; but this consisted only of their questions, and my answers.

The despatch came from court about the time we expected. It contained a warrant for conducting me and my retinue to *Traldragdubh*, or *Trildrogdrib* (for it is pronounced both ways as near as I can remember), by a party of ten horse. All my retinue was that poor lad for an interpreter, whom I persuaded into my service, and, at my humble request, we had each of us a mule to ride on. A messenger was despatched half a day's journey before us, to give the king notice of my approach, and to desire, "that his majesty would please to appoint a day and hour, when it would by his gracious pleasure that I might have the honour to lick the dust before his footstool." This is the court style, and I found it to be more than matter of form: for, upon my admittance two days after my arrival, I was commanded to crawl upon my belly, and lick the floor as I advanced; but, on account of my being a stranger, care was taken to have it made so clean, that the dust was not offensive. However, this was a peculiar grace, not allowed to any but persons of the highest rank, when they desire an admittance. Nay, sometimes the floor is strewed with dust on purpose, when the person to be admitted happens to have powerful enemies at court; and I have seen a great lord with his mouth so crammed, that when he had crept to the proper distance from the throne; he was not able to speak a word. Neither is there any remedy; because it is capital for those, who receive an audience to spit or wipe their mouths in his majesty's presence. There is indeed another custom, which I cannot altogether approve of: when the king has a mind to put any of his nobles to death in a gentle indulgent manner, he commands the floor to be strewed with a certain brown powder of a deadly composition, which being licked up, infallibly kills him in twenty-four hours. But in justice to this prince's great clemency, and the care he has of his subjects' lives (wherein it were much to be wished that the Monarchs of Europe would imitate him), it must be mentioned for his honour, that strict orders are given to have the infected parts of the floor well washed after every such execution, which, if his domestics neglect, they are in danger of incurring his royal displeasure. I myself heard him give directions, that one of his pages should be whipped, whose turn it was to give notice about washing the floor after an execution, but maliciously had omitted it; by which neglect a young lord of great hopes, coming to an audience, was unfortunately poisoned, although the king at that time had no design against his life. But this good prince was so gracious as to forgive the poor page his whipping, upon promise that he would do so no more, without special orders.

To return from this digression. When I had crept within four yards of the throne, I raised myself gently upon my knees, and then striking my forehead seven times against the ground, I pronounced the following words, as they had been taught me the night before, *Inckpling gloffthrobb squut serummblhiop mlashnalt zwin tnodbalkuffh slhiophad gurdlubh asht*. This is the compliment, established by the laws of the land, for all persons admitted to the king's presence. It may be rendered into English thus: "May your celestial majesty outlive the sun, eleven moons and a half!" To this the king returned some answer, which, although I could not understand, yet I replied as I had been directed: *Fluft drin yalerick dwuldom prastrad mirpush*, which properly signifies, "My tongue is in the mouth of my friend;" and by this expression was meant, that I desired leave to bring my interpreter; whereupon the young man already mentioned was accordingly introduced, by whose intervention I answered as many questions as his majesty could put in above an hour. I spoke in the Balnibarbian tongue, and my interpreter delivered my meaning in that of Luggnagg.

The king was much delighted with my company, and ordered his *bliffmarklub*, or high-chamberlain, to appoint a lodging in the court for me and my interpreter; with a daily allowance for my table, and a large purse of gold for my common expenses.

I staid three months in this country, out of perfect obedience to his majesty; who was pleased highly to favour me, and made me very honourable offers. But I thought it more consistent with prudence and justice to pass the remainder of my days with my wife and family.

CHAPTER TEN

The Luggnaggians commended. A particular description of the Struldbrugs, with many conversations between the author and some eminent persons upon that subject.

THE LUGGNAGGIANS are a polite and generous people; and although they are not without some share of that pride which is peculiar to all Eastern countries, yet they show themselves courteous to strangers, especially such who are countenanced by the court. I had many acquaintance, and among persons of the best fashion; and being always attended by my interpreter, the conversation we had was not disagreeable.

One day, in much good company, I was asked by a person of quality, "whether I had seen any of their *struldbrugs*, or immortals?" I said, "I had not;" and desired he would explain to me "what he meant by such an appellation, applied to a mortal creature." He told me "that sometimes, though very rarely, a child happened to be born in a family, with a red circular spot in the forehead, directly over the left eyebrow, which was an infallible mark that it should never die." The spot, as he described it, "was about the compass of a silver threepence, but in the course of time grew larger, and changed its colour; for at twelve years old it became green, so continued till five and twenty, then turned to a deep blue: at five and forty it grew coal black, and as large as an English shilling; but never admitted any further alteration." He said, "these births were so rare, that he did not believe there could be above eleven hundred struldbrugs, of both sexes, in the whole kingdom; of which he computed about fifty in the metropolis, and, among the rest, a young girl born; about three years ago: that these productions were not peculiar to any family, but a mere effect of chance; and the children of the *struldbrugs* themselves were equally mortal with the rest of the people."

I freely own myself to have been struck with inexpressible delight, upon hearing this account: and the person who gave it me happening to understand the Balnibarbian language, which I spoke very well, I could not forbear breaking out into expressions, perhaps a little too extravagant. I cried out, as in a rapture, "Happy nation, where every child hath at least a chance for being immortal! Happy people, who enjoy so many living examples of ancient virtue, and have masters ready to instruct them in the wisdom of all former ages! but happiest, beyond all comparison, are those excellent *struldbrugs*, who, being born exempt from that universal calamity of human nature, have their minds free and disengaged, without the weight and depression of spirits caused by the continual apprehensions of death!" I discovered my admiration that I had not observed any of these illustrious persons at court; the black spot on the forehead being so remarkable a distinction, that I could not have easily overlooked it: and it was impossible that his majesty, a most judicious prince, should not provide himself with a good number of such wise and able counsellors. Yet perhaps the virtue of those reverend sages was too strict for the corrupt and libertine manners of a court: and we often find by experience, that young men are too opinionated and volatile to be guided by the sober dictates of their seniors. However, since the king was pleased to allow me access to his royal person, I was resolved, upon the very first occasion, to deliver my opinion to him on this matter freely and at large, by the help of my interpreter; and whether he would please to take my advice or not, yet in one thing I was determined, that his majesty having frequently offered me an establishment in this country, I would, with great thankfulness, accept the favour, and pass my life here in the conversation of those superior beings the *struldbrugs*, if they would please to admit me."

The gentleman to whom I addressed my discourse, because (as I have already observed) he spoke the language of Balnibarbi, said to me, with a sort of a smile which usually arises from pity to the ignorant, "that he was glad of any occasion to keep me among them, and desired my permission to explain to the company what I had spoke." He did so, and they talked together for some time in their own language, whereof I understood not a syllable, neither could I observe by their countenances, what impression my discourse had made on them. After a short silence, the same person told me, "that his friends and mine (so he thought fit to express himself) were very much pleased with the judicious remarks I had made on the great happiness and advantages of immortal life, and they were desirous to know, in a particular manner, what scheme of living I should have formed to myself, if it had fallen to my lot to have been born a *struldbrug*."

I answered, "it was easy to be eloquent on so copious and delightful a subject, especially to me, who had been often apt to amuse myself with visions of what I should do, if I were a king, a general, or a great lord: and upon this very case, I had frequently run over the whole system how I should employ myself, and pass the time, if I were sure to live for ever.

"That, if it had been my good fortune to come into the world a *struldbrug*, as soon as I could discover my own happiness, by understanding the difference between life and death, I would first resolve, by all arts and methods, whatsoever, to procure myself riches. In the pursuit of which, by thrift and management, I might reasonably expect, in about two hundred years, to be the wealthiest man in the kingdom. In the second place, I would, from my earliest youth, apply myself to the study of arts and sciences, by which I should arrive in time to excel all others in learning. Lastly, I would carefully record every action and event of consequence, that happened in the public, impartially draw the characters of the several successions of princes and great ministers of state, with my own observations on every point. I would exactly set down the several changes in customs, language, fashions of dress, diet, and diversions. By all which acquirements, I should be a living treasure of knowledge and wisdom, and certainly become the oracle of the nation.

"I would never marry after threescore, but live in a hospitable manner, yet still on the saving side. I would entertain myself in forming and directing the minds of hopeful young men, by convincing them, from my own remembrance, experience, and observation, fortified by numerous examples, of the usefulness of virtue in public and private life. But my choice and constant companions should be a set of my own immortal brotherhood; among whom, I would elect a dozen from the most ancient, down to my own contemporaries. Where any of these wanted fortunes, I would provide them with convenient lodges round my own estate, and have some of them always at my table; only mingling a few of the most valuable among you mortals, whom length of time would harden me to lose with little or no reluctance, and treat your posterity after the same manner; just as a man diverts himself with the annual succession of pinks and tulips in his garden, without regretting the loss of those which withered the preceding year.

"These *struldbrugs* and I would mutually communicate our observations and memorials, through the course of time; remark the several gradations by which corruption steals into the world, and oppose it in every step, by giving perpetual warning and instruction to mankind; which, added to the strong influence of our own example, would probably prevent that continual degeneracy of human nature so justly complained of in all ages.

"Add to this, the pleasure of seeing the various revolutions of states and empires; the changes in the lower and upper world; ancient cities in ruins, and obscure villages become the seats of kings; famous rivers lessening into shallow brooks; the ocean leaving one coast dry, and overwhelming another; the discovery of many countries yet unknown; barbarity overrunning the politest nations, and the most barbarous become civilized. I should then see the discovery of the longitude, the perpetual motion, the universal medicine, and many other great inventions, brought to the utmost perfection.

"What wonderful discoveries should we make in astronomy, by outliving and confirming our own predictions; by observing the progress and return of comets, with the changes of motion in the sun, moon, and stars!"

I enlarged upon many other topics, which the natural desire of endless life, and sublunary happiness, could easily furnish me with. When I had ended, and the sum of my discourse had been interpreted, as before, to the rest of the company, there was a good deal of talk among them in the language of the country, not without some laughter at my expense. At last, the same gentleman who had been my interpreter, said, "he was desired by the rest to set me right in a few mistakes, which I had fallen into through the common imbecility of human nature, and upon that allowance was less answerable for them. That this breed of *struldbrugs* was peculiar to their country, for there were no such people either in Balnibarbi or Japan, where he had the honour to be ambassador from his majesty, and found the natives in both those kingdoms very hard to believe that the fact was possible: and it appeared from my astonishment when he first mentioned the matter to me, that I received it as a thing wholly new, and scarcely to be credited. That in the two kingdoms above mentioned, where, during his residence, he had conversed very much, he observed long life to be the universal desire and wish of mankind. That whoever had one foot in the grave was sure to hold back the other as strongly as he could. That the oldest had still hopes of living one day longer, and looked on death as the greatest evil, from which nature always prompted him to retreat. Only in this island of Luggnagg the appetite for living was not so eager, from the continual example of the *struldbrugs* before their eyes.

"That the system of living contrived by me, was unreasonable and unjust; because it supposed a perpetuity of youth, health, and vigour, which no man could be so foolish to hope, however extravagant he may be in his wishes. That the question therefore was not, whether a man would choose to be always in the prime of youth, attended with prosperity and health; but how he would pass a perpetual life under all the usual disadvantages which old age brings along with it. For although few men will avow their desires of being immortal, upon such hard conditions, yet in the two kingdoms before mentioned, of Balnibarbi and Japan, he observed that every man desired to put off death some time longer, let it approach ever so late: and he rarely heard of any man who died willingly, except he were incited by the extremity of grief or torture. And he appealed to me, whether in those countries I had travelled, as well as my own, I had not observed the same general disposition."

After this preface, he gave me a particular account of the *struldbrugs* among them. He said, "they commonly acted like mortals till about thirty years old; after which, by degrees, they grew melancholy and dejected, increasing in both till they came to fourscore. This he learned from their own confession: for otherwise, there not being above two or three of that species born in an age, they were too few to form a general observation by. When they came to fourscore years, which is reckoned the extremity of living in this country, they had not only all the follies and infirmities of other old men, but many more which arose from the dreadful prospect of never dying. They were not only opinionative, peevish, covetous, morose, vain, talkative, but incapable of friendship, and dead to all natural affection, which never descended below their grandchildren. Envy and impotent desires are their prevailing passions. But those objects against which their envy seems principally directed, are the vices of the younger sort and the deaths of the old. By reflecting on the former, they find themselves cut off from all possibility of pleasure; and whenever they see a funeral, they lament and repine that others have gone to a harbour of rest to which they themselves never can hope to arrive. They have no remembrance of anything but what they learned and observed in their youth and middle-age, and even that is very imperfect; and for the truth or particulars of any fact, it is safer to depend on common tradition, than upon their best recollections. The least miserable among them appear to be those who turn to dotage, and entirely lose their memories; these meet with more pity and assistance, because they want many bad qualities which abound in others.

"If a *struldbrug* happen to marry one of his own kind, the marriage is dissolved of course, by the courtesy of the kingdom, as soon as the younger of the two comes to be fourscore; for the law thinks it a reasonable indulgence, that those who are condemned, without any fault of their own, to a perpetual continuance in the world, should not have their misery doubled by the load of a wife.

"As soon as they have completed the term of eighty years, they are looked on as dead in law; their heirs immediately succeed to their estates; only a small pittance is reserved for their support; and the poor ones are maintained at the public charge. After that period, they are held incapable of any employment of trust or profit; they cannot purchase lands, or take leases; neither are they allowed to be witnesses in any cause, either civil or criminal, not even for the decision of meers and bounds.

"At ninety, they lose their teeth and hair; they have at that age no distinction of taste, but eat and drink whatever they can get, without relish or appetite. The diseases they were subject to still continue, without increasing or diminishing. In talking, they forget the common appellation of things, and the names of persons, even of those who are their nearest friends and relations. For the same reason, they never can amuse themselves with reading, because their memory will not serve to carry them from the beginning of a sentence to the end; and by this defect, they are deprived of the only entertainment whereof they might otherwise be capable.

"The language of this country being always upon the flux, the *struldbrugs* of one age do not understand those of another; neither are they able, after two hundred years, to hold any conversation (farther than by a few general words) with their neighbours the mortals; and thus they lie under the disadvantage of living like foreigners in their own country."

This was the account given me of the *struldbrugs*, as near as I can remember. I afterwards saw five or six of different ages, the youngest not above two hundred years old, who were brought to me at several times by some of my friends; but although they were told, "that I was a great traveller, and had seen all the world," they had not the least curiosity to ask me a question; only desired "I would give them *slumskudask*," or a token of remembrance; which is a modest way of begging, to avoid the law, that strictly forbids it, because they are provided for by the public, although indeed with a very scanty allowance.

They are despised and hated by all sorts of people. When one of them is born, it is reckoned ominous, and their birth is recorded very particularly so that you may know their age by consulting the register, which, however, has not been kept above a thousand years past, or at least has been destroyed by time or public disturbances. But the usual way of computing how old they are, is by asking them what kings or great persons they can remember, and then consulting history; for infallibly the last prince in their mind did not begin his reign after they were fourscore years old.

They were the most mortifying sight I ever beheld; and the women more horrible than the men. Besides the usual deformities in extreme old age, they acquired an additional ghastliness, in proportion to their number of years, which is not to be described; and among half a dozen, I soon distinguished which was the eldest, although there was not above a century or two between them.

The reader will easily believe, that from what I had hear and seen, my keen appetite for perpetuity of life was much abated. I grew heartily ashamed of the pleasing visions I had formed; and thought no tyrant could invent a death into which I would not run with pleasure, from such a life. The king heard of all that had passed between me and my friends upon this occasion, and rallied me very pleasantly; wishing I could send a couple of *struldbrugs* to my own country, to arm our people against the fear of death; but this, it seems, is forbidden by the fundamental laws of the kingdom, or else I should have been well content with the trouble and expense of transporting them.

I could not but agree, that the laws of this kingdom relative to the *struldbrugs* were founded upon the strongest reasons, and such as any other country would be under the necessity of enacting, in the like circumstances. Otherwise, as avarice is the necessary consequence of old age, those immortals would in time become proprietors of the whole nation, and engross the civil power, which, for want of abilities to manage, must end in the ruin of the public.

CHAPTER ELEVEN

The author leaves Luggnagg, and sails to Japan. From thence he returns in a Dutch ship to Amsterdam, and from Amsterdam to England.

I THOUGHT this account of the *struldbrugs* might be some entertainment to the reader, because it seems to be a little out of the common way; at least I do not remember to have met the like in any book of travels that has come to my hands: and if I am deceived, my excuse must be, that it is necessary for travellers who describe the same country, very often to agree in dwelling on the same particulars, without deserving the censure of having borrowed or transcribed from those who wrote before them.

There is indeed a perpetual commerce between this kingdom and the great empire of Japan; and it is very probable, that the Japanese authors may have given some account of the *struldbrugs*; but my stay in Japan was so short, and I was so entirely a stranger to the language, that I was not qualified to make any inquiries. But I hope the Dutch, upon this notice, will be curious and able enough to supply my defects.

His majesty having often pressed me to accept some employment in his court, and finding me absolutely determined to return to my native country, was pleased to give me his license to depart; and honoured me with a letter of recommendation, under his own hand, to the Emperor of Japan. He likewise presented me with four hundred and forty-four large pieces of gold (this nation delighting in even numbers), and a red diamond, which I sold in England for eleven hundred pounds.

On the 6th of May, 1709, I took a solemn leave of his majesty, and all my friends. This prince was so gracious as to order a guard to conduct me to Glanguenstald, which is a royal port to the south-west part of the island. In six days I found a vessel ready to carry me to Japan, and spent fifteen days in the voyage. We landed at a small port-town called Xamoschi, situated on the south-east part of Japan; the town lies on the western point, where there is a narrow strait leading northward into along arm of the sea, upon the north-west part of which, Yedo, the metropolis, stands. At landing, I showed the custom-house officers my letter from the king of Luggnagg to his imperial majesty. They knew the seal perfectly well; it was as broad as the palm of my hand. The impression was, *A king lifting up a lame beggar from the earth.* The magistrates of the town, hearing of my letter, received me as a public minister. They provided me with carriages and servants, and bore my charges to Yedo; where I was admitted to an audience, and delivered my letter, which was opened with great ceremony, and explained to the Emperor by an interpreter, who then gave me notice, by his majesty's order, "that I should signify my request, and, whatever it were, it should be granted, for the sake of his royal brother of Luggnagg." This interpreter was a person employed to transact affairs with the Hollanders. He soon conjectured, by my countenance, that I was a European, and therefore repeated his majesty's commands in Low Dutch, which he spoke perfectly well. I answered, as I had before determined, "that I was a Dutch merchant, shipwrecked in a very remote country, whence I had travelled by sea and land to Luggnagg, and then took shipping for Japan; where I knew my countrymen often traded, and with some of these I hoped to get an opportunity of returning into Europe: I therefore most humbly entreated his royal favour, to give order that I should be conducted in safety to Nangasac." To this I added another petition, "that for the sake of my patron the king of Luggnagg, his majesty would condescend to excuse my performing the ceremony imposed on my countrymen, of trampling upon the crucifix: because I had been thrown into his kingdom by my misfortunes, without any intention of trading." When this latter petition was interpreted to the Emperor, he seemed a little surprised; and said, "he believed I was the first of my countrymen who ever made any scruple in this point; and that he began to doubt, whether I was a real Hollander, or not; but rather suspected I must be a Christian. However, for the reasons I had offered, but chiefly to gratify the king of Luggnagg by an uncommon mark of his favour, he would comply with the singularity of my humour; but the affair must be managed with dexterity, and his officers should be commanded to let me pass, as it were by forgetfulness. For he assured me, that if the secret should be discovered by my countrymen the Dutch, they would cut my throat in the voyage." I returned my thanks, by the interpreter, for so unusual a favour; and some troops being at that time on their march to Nangasac, the commanding officer had orders to convey me safe thither, with particular instructions about the business of the crucifix.

On the 9th day of June, 1709, I arrived at Nangasac, after a very long and troublesome journey. I soon fell into the company of some Dutch sailors belonging to the Amboyna, of Amsterdam, a stout ship of 450 tons. I had lived long in Holland, pursuing my studies at Leyden, and I spoke Dutch well. The seamen soon knew whence I came last: they were curious to inquire into my voyages and course of life. I made up a story as short and probable as I could, but concealed the greatest part. I knew many persons in Holland. I was able to invent names for my parents, whom I pretended to be obscure people in the province of Gelderland. I would have given the captain (one Theodorus Vangrult) what he pleased to ask for my voyage to Holland; but understanding I was a surgeon, he was contented to take half the usual rate, on condition that I would serve him in the way of my calling. Before we took shipping, I was often asked by some of the crew, whether I had performed the ceremony above mentioned? I evaded the question by general answers; "that I had satisfied the Emperor and court in all particulars." However, a malicious rogue of a skipper went to an officer, and pointing to me, told him, "I had not yet trampled on the crucifix;" but the other, who had received instructions to let me pass, gave the rascal twenty strokes on the shoulders with a bamboo; after which I was no more troubled with such questions.

Nothing happened worth mentioning in this voyage. We sailed with a fair wind to the Cape of Good Hope, where we staid only to take in fresh water. On the 10th of April, 1710, we arrived safe at Amsterdam, having lost only three men by sickness in the voyage, and a fourth, who fell from the foremast into the sea, not far from the coast of Guinea. From Amsterdam I soon after set sail for England, in a small vessel belonging to that city.

On the 16th of April we put in at the Downs. I landed next morning, and saw once more my native country, after an absence of five years and six months complete. I went straight to Redriff, where I arrived the same day at two in the afternoon, and found my wife and family in good health.

PART FOUR

A Voyage to the Country of the Houyhnhnms

CHAPTER ONE

The author sets out as captain of a ship. His men conspire against him, confine him a long time to his cabin, and set him on shore in an unknown land. He travels up into the country. The Yahoos, a strange sort of animal, described. The author meets two Houyhnhnms.

I CONTINUED at home with my wife and children about five months, in a very happy condition, if I could have learned the lesson of knowing when I was well. I left my poor wife big with child, and accepted an advantageous offer made me to be captain of the Adventurer, a stout merchantman of 350 tons: for I understood navigation well, and being grown weary of a surgeon's employment at sea, which, however, I could exercise upon occasion, I took a skilful young man of that calling, one Robert Purefoy, into my ship. We set sail from Portsmouth upon the 7th day of September, 1710; on the 14th we met with Captain Pocock, of Bristol, at Teneriffe, who was going to the bay of Campechy to cut logwood. On the 16th, he was parted from us by a storm; I heard since my return, that his ship foundered, and none escaped but one cabin boy. He was an honest man, and a good sailor, but a little too positive in his own opinions, which was the cause of his destruction, as it has been with several others; for if he had followed my advice, he might have been safe at home with his family at this time, as well as myself.

I had several men who died in my ship of calentures, so that I was forced to get recruits out of Barbadoes and the Leeward Islands, where I touched, by the direction of the merchants who employed me; which I had soon too much cause to repent: for I found afterwards, that most of them had been buccaneers. I had fifty hands onboard; and my orders were, that I should trade with the Indians in the South-Sea, and make what discoveries I could. These rogues, whom I had picked up, debauched my other men, and they all formed a conspiracy to seize the ship, and secure me; which they did one morning, rushing into my cabin, and binding me hand and foot, threatening to throw me overboard, if I offered to stir. I told them, "I was their prisoner, and would submit." This they made me swear to do, and then they unbound me, only fastening one of my legs with a chain, near my bed, and placed a sentry at my door with his piece charged, who was commanded to shoot me dead if I attempted my liberty. They sent me own victuals and drink, and took the government of the ship to themselves. Their design was to turn pirates and, plunder the Spaniards, which they could not do till they got more men. But first they resolved to sell the goods the ship, and then go to Madagascar for recruits, several among them having died since my confinement. They sailed many weeks, and traded with the Indians; but I knew not what course they took, being kept a close prisoner in my cabin, and expecting nothing less than to be murdered, as they often threatened me.

Upon the 9th day of May, 1711, one James Welch came down to my cabin, and said, "he had orders from the captain to set me ashore." I expostulated with him, but in vain; neither would he so much as tell me who their new captain was. They forced me into the long-boat, letting me put on my best suit of clothes, which were as good as new, and take a small bundle of linen, but no arms, except my hanger; and they were so civil as not to search my pockets, into which I conveyed what money I had, with some other little necessaries. They rowed about a league, and then set me down on a strand. I desired them to tell me what country it was. They all swore, "they knew no more than myself;" but said, "that the captain" (as they called him) "was resolved, after they had sold the lading, to get rid of me in the first place where they could discover land." They pushed off immediately, advising me to make haste for fear of being overtaken by the tide, and so bade me farewell.

In this desolate condition I advanced forward, and soon got upon firm ground, where I sat down on a bank to rest myself, and consider what I had best do. When I was a little refreshed, I went up into the country, resolving to deliver myself to the first savages I should meet, and purchase my life from them by some bracelets, glass rings, and other toys, which sailors usually provide themselves with in those voyages, and whereof I had some about me. The land was divided by long rows of trees, not regularly planted, but naturally growing; there was great plenty of grass, and several fields of oats. I walked very circumspectly, for fear of being surprised, or suddenly shot with an arrow from behind, or on either side. I fell into a beaten road, where I saw many tracts of human feet, and some of cows, but most of horses. At last I beheld several animals in a field, and one or two of the same kind sitting in trees. Their shape was very singular and deformed, which a little discomposed me, so that I lay down behind a thicket to observe them better. Some of them coming forward near the place where I lay, gave me an opportunity of distinctly marking their form. Their heads and breasts were covered with a thick hair, some frizzled, and others lank; they had beards like goats, and a long ridge of hair down their backs, and the fore parts of their legs and feet; but the rest of their bodies was bare, so that I might see their skins, which were of a brown buff colour. They had no tails, nor any hair at all on their buttocks, except about the anus, which, I presume, nature had placed there to defend them as they sat on the ground, for this posture they used, as well as lying down, and often stood on their hind feet. They climbed high trees as nimbly as a squirrel, for they had strong extended claws before and behind, terminating in sharp points, and hooked. They would often spring, and bound, and leap, with prodigious agility. The females were not so large as the males; they had long lank hair on their heads, but none on their faces, nor any thing more than a sort of down on the rest of their bodies, except about the anus and pudenda. The dugs hung between their fore feet, and often reached almost to the ground as they walked. The hair of both sexes was of several colours, brown, red, black, and yellow. Upon the whole, I never beheld, in all my travels, so disagreeable an animal, or one against which I naturally conceived so strong an antipathy. So that, thinking I had seen enough, full of contempt and aversion, I got up, and pursued the beaten road, hoping it might direct me to the cabin of some Indian. I had not got far, when I met one of these creatures full in my way, and coming up directly to me. The ugly monster, when he saw me, distorted several ways, every feature of his visage, and stared, as at an object he had never seen before; then approaching nearer, lifted up his fore-paw, whether out of curiosity or mischief I could not tell; but I drew my hanger, and gave him a good blow with the flat side of it, for I durst not strike with the edge, fearing the inhabitants might be provoked against me, if they should come to know that I had killed or maimed any of their cattle. When the beast felt the smart, he drew back, and roared so loud, that a herd of at least forty came flocking about me from the next field, howling and making odious faces; but I ran to the body of a tree, and leaning my back against it, kept them off by waving my hanger. Several of this cursed brood, getting hold of the branches behind, leaped up into the tree, whence they began to discharge their excrements on my head; however, I escaped pretty well by sticking close to the stem of the tree, but was almost stifled with the filth, which fell about me on every side.

In the midst of this distress, I observed them all to run away on a sudden as fast as they could; at which I ventured to leave the tree and pursue the road, wondering what it was that could put them into this fright. But looking on my left hand, I saw a horse walking softly in the field; which my persecutors having sooner discovered, was the cause of their flight. The horse started a little, when he came near me, but soon recovering himself, looked full in my face with manifest tokens of wonder; he viewed my hands and feet, walking round me several times. I would have pursued my journey, but he placed himself directly in the way, yet looking with a very mild aspect, never offering the least violence. We stood gazing at each other for some time; at last I took the boldness to reach my hand towards his neck with a design to stroke it, using the common style and whistle of jockeys, when they are going to handle a strange horse. But this animal seemed to receive my civilities with disdain, shook his head, and bent his brows, softly raising up his right fore-foot to remove my hand. Then he neighed three or four times, but in so different a cadence, that I almost began to think he was speaking to himself, in some language of his own.

While he and I were thus employed, another horse came up; who applying himself to the first in a very formal manner, they gently struck each other's right hoof before, neighing several times by turns, and varying the sound, which seemed to be almost articulate. They went some paces off, as if it were to confer together, walking side by side, backward and forward, like persons deliberating upon some affair of weight, but often turning their eyes towards me, as it were to watch that I might not escape. I was amazed to see such actions and behaviour in brute beasts; and concluded with myself, that if the inhabitants of this country were endued with a proportionable degree of reason, they must needs be the wisest people upon earth. This thought gave me so much comfort, that I resolved to go forward, until I could discover some house or village, or meet with any of the natives, leaving the two horses to discourse together as they pleased. But the first, who was a dapple gray, observing me to steal off, neighed after me in so expressive a tone, that I fancied myself to understand what he meant; whereupon I turned back, and came near to him to expect his farther commands: but concealing my fear as much as I could, for I began to be in some pain how this adventure might terminate; and the reader will easily believe I did not much like my present situation.

The two horses came up close to me, looking with great earnestness upon my face and hands. The gray steed rubbed my hat all round with his right fore-hoof, and discomposed it so much that I was forced to adjust it better by taking it off and settling it again; whereat, both he and his companion (who was a brown bay) appeared to be much surprised: the latter felt the lappet of my coat, and finding it to hang loose about me, they both looked with new signs of wonder. He stroked my right hand, seeming to admire the softness and colour; but he squeezed it so hard between his hoof and his pastern, that I was forced to roar; after which they both touched me with all possible tenderness. They were under great perplexity about my shoes and stockings, which they felt very often, neighing to each other, and using various gestures, not unlike those of a philosopher, when he would attempt to solve some new and difficult phenomenon.

Upon the whole, the behaviour of these animals was so orderly and rational, so acute and judicious, that I at last concluded they must needs be magicians, who had thus metamorphosed themselves upon some design, and seeing a stranger in the way, resolved to divert themselves with him; or, perhaps, were really amazed at the sight of a man so very different in habit, feature, and complexion, from those who might probably live in so remote a climate. Upon the strength of this reasoning, I ventured to address them in the following manner: "Gentlemen, if you be conjurers, as I have good cause to believe, you can understand my language; therefore I make bold to let your worships know that I am a poor distressed Englishman, driven by his misfortunes upon your coast; and I entreat one of you to let me ride upon his back, as if he were a real horse, to some house or village where I can be relieved. In return of which favour, I will make you a present of this knife and bracelet," taking them out of my pocket. The two creatures stood silent while I spoke, seeming to listen with great attention, and when I had ended, they neighed frequently towards each other, as if they were engaged in serious conversation. I plainly observed that their language expressed the passions very well, and the words might, with little pains, be resolved into an alphabet more easily than the Chinese.

I could frequently distinguish the word *Yahoo*, which was repeated by each of them several times: and although it was impossible for me to conjecture what it meant, yet while the two horses were busy in conversation, I endeavoured to practise this word upon my tongue; and as soon as they were silent, I boldly pronounced *Yahoo* in a loud voice, imitating at the same time, as near as I could, the neighing of a horse; at which they were both visibly surprised; and the gray repeated the same word twice, as if he meant to teach me the right accent; wherein I spoke after him as well as I could, and found myself perceivably to improve every time, though very far from any degree of perfection. Then the bay tried me with a second word, much harder to be pronounced; but reducing it to the English orthography, may be spelt thus, *Houyhnhnm*. I did not succeed in this so well as in the former; but after two or three farther trials, I had better fortune; and they both appeared amazed at my capacity.

After some further discourse, which I then conjectured might relate to me, the two friends took their leaves, with the same compliment of striking each other's hoof; and the gray made me signs that I should walk before him; wherein I thought it prudent to comply, till I could find a better director. When I offered to slacken my pace, he would cry *hhuun hhuun*: I guessed his meaning, and gave him to understand, as well as I could, "that I was weary, and not able to walk faster;" upon which he would stand awhile to let me rest.

CHAPTER TWO

The author conducted by a Houyhnhnm to his house. The house described. The author's reception. The food of the Houyhnhnms. The author in distress for want of meat. Is at last relieved. His manner of feeding in this country.

Having travelled about three miles, we came to a long kind of building, made of timber stuck in the ground, and wattled across; the roof was low and covered with straw. I now began to be a little comforted; and took out some toys, which travellers usually carry for presents to the savage Indians of America, and other parts, in hopes the people of the house would be thereby encouraged to receive me kindly. The horse made me a sign to go in first; it was a large room with a smooth clay floor, and a rack and manger, extending the whole length on one side. There were three nags and two mares, not eating, but some of them sitting down upon their hams, which I very much wondered at; but wondered more to see the rest employed in domestic business; these seemed but ordinary cattle. However, this confirmed my first opinion, that a people who could so far civilise brute animals, must needs excel in wisdom all the nations of the world. The gray came in just after, and thereby prevented any ill treatment which the others might have given me. He neighed to them several times in a style of authority, and received answers.

Beyond this room there were three others, reaching the length of the house, to which you passed through three doors, opposite to each other, in the manner of a vista. We went through the second room towards the third. Here the gray walked in first, beckoning me to attend: I waited in the second room, and got ready my presents for the master and mistress of the house; they were two knives, three bracelets of false pearls, a small looking-glass, and a bead necklace. The horse neighed three or four times, and I waited to hear some answers in a human voice, but I heard no other returns than in the same dialect, only one or two a little shriller than his. I began to think that this house must belong to some person of great note among them, because there appeared so much ceremony before I could gain admittance. But, that a man of quality should be served all by horses, was beyond my comprehension. I feared my brain was disturbed by my sufferings and misfortunes. I roused myself, and looked about me in the room where I was left alone: this was furnished like the first, only after a more elegant manner. I rubbed my eyes often, but the same objects still occurred. I pinched my arms and sides to awake myself, hoping I might be in a dream. I then absolutely concluded, that all these appearances could be nothing else but necromancy and magic. But I had no time to pursue these reflections; for the gray horse came to the door, and made me a sign to follow him into the third room where I saw a very comely mare, together with a colt and foal, sitting on their haunches upon mats of straw, not unartfully made, and perfectly neat and clean.

The mare soon after my entrance rose from her mat, and coming up close, after having nicely observed my hands and face, gave me a most contemptuous look; and turning to the horse, I heard the word *Yahoo* often repeated betwixt them; the meaning of which word I could not then comprehend, although it was the first I had learned to pronounce. But I was soon better informed, to my everlasting mortification; for the horse, beckoning to me with his head, and repeating the *hhuun, hhuun*, as he did upon the road, which I understood was to attend him, led me out into a kind of court, where was another building, at some distance from the house. Here we entered, and I saw three of those detestable creatures, which I first met after my landing, feeding upon roots, and the flesh of some animals, which I afterwards found to be that of asses and dogs, and now and then a cow, dead by accident or disease. They were all tied by the neck with strong withes fastened to a beam; they held their food between the claws of their fore feet, and tore it with their teeth.

The master horse ordered a sorrel nag, one of his servants, to untie the largest of these animals, and take him into the yard. The beast and I were brought close together, and by our countenances diligently compared both by master and servant, who thereupon repeated several times the word *Yahoo*. My horror and astonishment are not to be described, when I observed in this abominable animal, a perfect human figure: the face of it indeed was flat and broad, the nose depressed, the lips large, and the mouth wide; but these differences are common to all savage nations, where the lineaments of the countenance are distorted, by the natives suffering their infants to lie grovelling on the earth, or by carrying them on their backs, nuzzling with their face against the mothers' shoulders. The fore-feet of the *Yahoo* differed from my hands in nothing else but the length of the nails, the coarseness and brownness of the palms, and the hairiness on the backs. There was the same resemblance between our feet, with the same differences; which I knew very well, though the horses did not, because of my shoes and stockings; the same in every part of our bodies except as to hairiness and colour, which I have already described.

The great difficulty that seemed to stick with the two horses, was to see the rest of my body so very different from that of a *Yahoo*, for which I was obliged to my clothes, whereof they had no conception. The sorrel nag offered me a root, which he held (after their manner, as we shall describe in its proper place) between his hoof and pastern; I took it in my hand, and, having smelt it, returned it to him again as civilly as I could. He brought out of the *Yahoos*' kennel a piece of ass's flesh; but it smelt so offensively that I turned from it with loathing: he then threw it to the *Yahoo*, by whom it was greedily devoured. He afterwards showed me a wisp of hay, and a fetlock full of oats; but I shook my head, to signify that neither of these were food for me. And indeed I now apprehended that I must absolutely starve, if I did not get to some of my own species; for as to those filthy *Yahoos*, although there were few greater lovers of mankind at that time than myself, yet I confess I never saw any sensitive being so detestable on all accounts; and the more I came near them the more hateful they grew, while I stayed in that country. This the master horse observed by my behaviour, and therefore sent the *Yahoo* back to his kennel. He then put his fore-hoof to his mouth, at which I was much surprised, although he did it with ease, and with a motion that appeared perfectly natural, and made other signs, to know what I would eat; but I could not return him such an answer as he was able to apprehend; and if he had understood me, I did not see how it was possible to contrive any way for finding myself nourishment. While we were thus engaged, I observed a cow passing by, whereupon I pointed to her, and expressed a desire to go and milk her. This had its effect; for he led me back into the house, and ordered a mare-servant to open a room, where a good store of milk lay in earthen and wooden vessels, after a very orderly and cleanly manner. She gave me a large bowlful, of which I drank very heartily, and found myself well refreshed.

About noon, I saw coming towards the house a kind of vehicle drawn like a sledge by four *Yahoos*. There was in it an old steed, who seemed to be of quality; he alighted with his hind-feet forward, having by accident got a hurt in his left fore-foot. He came to dine with our horse, who received him with great civility. They dined in the best room, and had oats boiled in milk for the second course, which the old horse ate warm, but the rest cold. Their mangers were placed circular in the middle of the room, and divided into several partitions, round which they sat on their haunches, upon bosses of straw. In the middle was a large rack, with angles answering to every partition of the manger; so that each horse and mare ate their own hay, and their own mash of oats and milk, with much decency and regularity. The behaviour of the young colt and foal appeared very modest, and that of the master and mistress extremely cheerful and complaisant to their guest. The gray ordered me to stand by him; and much discourse passed between him and his friend concerning me, as I found by the stranger's often looking on me, and the frequent repetition of the word *Yahoo*.

I happened to wear my gloves, which the master gray observing, seemed perplexed, discovering signs of wonder what I had done to my fore-feet. He put his hoof three or four times to them, as if he would signify, that I should reduce them to their former shape, which I presently did, pulling off both my gloves, and putting them into my pocket. This occasioned farther talk; and I saw the company was pleased with my behaviour, whereof I soon found the good effects. I was ordered to speak the few words I understood; and while they were at dinner, the master taught me the names for oats, milk, fire, water, and some others, which I could readily pronounce after him, having from my youth a great facility in learning languages.

When dinner was done, the master horse took me aside, and by signs and words made me understand the concern he was in that I had nothing to eat. Oats in their tongue are called *hlunnh*. This word I pronounced two or three times; for although I had refused them at first, yet, upon second thoughts, I considered that I could contrive to make of them a kind of bread, which might be sufficient, with milk, to keep me alive, till I could make my escape to some other country, and to creatures of my own species. The horse immediately ordered a white mare servant of his family to bring me a good quantity of oats in a sort of wooden tray. These I heated before the fire, as well as I could, and rubbed them till the husks came off, which I made a shift to winnow from the grain. I ground and beat them between two stones; then took water, and made them into a paste or cake, which I toasted at the fire and eat warm with milk. It was at first a very insipid diet, though common enough in many parts of Europe, but grew tolerable by time; and having been often reduced to hard fare in my life, this was not the first experiment I had made how easily nature is satisfied. And I cannot but observe, that I never had one hours sickness while I stayed in this island. It is true, I sometimes made a shift to catch a rabbit, or bird, by springs made of *Yahoo's* hairs; and I often gathered wholesome herbs, which I boiled, and ate as salads with my bread; and now and then, for a rarity, I made a little butter, and drank the whey. I was at first at a great loss for salt, but custom soon reconciled me to the want of it; and I am confident that the frequent use of salt among us is an effect of luxury, and was first introduced only as a provocative to drink, except where it is necessary for preserving flesh in long voyages, or in places remote from great markets; for we observe no animal to be fond of it but man, and as to myself, when I left this country, it was a great while before I could endure the taste of it in anything that I ate.

This is enough to say upon the subject of my diet, wherewith other travellers fill their books, as if the readers were personally concerned whether we fare well or ill. However, it was necessary to mention this matter, lest the world should think it impossible that I could find sustenance for three years in such a country, and among such inhabitants.

When it grew towards evening, the master horse ordered a place for me to lodge in; it was but six yards from the house and separated from the stable of the *Yahoos*. Here I got some straw, and covering myself with my own clothes, slept very sound. But I was in a short time better accommodated, as the reader shall know hereafter, when I come to treat more particularly about my way of living.

CHAPTER THREE

The author studies to learn the language. The Houyhnhnm, his master, assists in teaching him. The language described. Several Houyhnhnms of quality come out of curiosity to see the author. He gives his master a short account of his voyage.

My principal endeavour was to learn the language, which my master (for so I shall henceforth call him), and his children, and every servant of his house, were desirous to teach me; for they looked upon it as a prodigy, that a brute animal should discover such marks of a rational creature. I pointed to every thing, and inquired the name of it, which I wrote down in my journal-book when I was alone, and corrected my bad accent by desiring those of the family to pronounce it often. In this employment, a sorrel nag, one of the under-servants, was very ready to assist me.

In speaking, they pronounced through the nose and throat, and their language approaches nearest to the High-Dutch, or German, of any I know in Europe; but is much more graceful and significant. The emperor Charles V. made almost the same observation, when he said "that if he were to speak to his horse, it should be in High-Dutch."

The curiosity and impatience of my master were so great, that he spent many hours of his leisure to instruct me. He was convinced (as he afterwards told me) that I must be a *Yahoo*; but my teachableness, civility, and cleanliness, astonished him; which were qualities altogether opposite to those animals. He was most perplexed about my clothes, reasoning sometimes with himself, whether they were a part of my body: for I never pulled them off till the family were asleep, and got them on before they waked in the morning. My master was eager to learn "whence I came; how I acquired those appearances of reason, which I discovered in all my actions; and to know my story from my own mouth, which he hoped he should soon do by the great proficiency I made in learning and pronouncing their words and sentences." To help my memory, I formed all I learned into the English alphabet, and writ the words down, with the translations. This last, after some time,

I ventured to do in my master's presence. It cost me much trouble to explain to him what I was doing; for the inhabitants have not the least idea of books or literature.

In about ten weeks time, I was able to understand most of his questions; and in three months, could give him some tolerable answers. He was extremely curious to know "from what part of the country I came, and how I was taught to imitate a rational creature; because the *Yahoos* (whom he saw I exactly resembled in my head, hands, and face, that were only visible), with some appearance of cunning, and the strongest disposition to mischief, were observed to be the most unteachable of all brutes." I answered, "that I came over the sea, from a far place, with many others of my own kind, in a great hollow vessel made of the bodies of trees: that my companions forced me to land on this coast, and then left me to shift for myself." It was with some difficulty, and by the help of many signs, that I brought him to understand me. He replied, "that I must needs be mistaken, or that I said the thing which was not;" for they have no word in their language to express lying or falsehood. "He knew it was impossible that there could be a country beyond the sea, or that a parcel of brutes could move a wooden vessel whither they pleased upon water. He was sure no *Houyhnhnm* alive could make such a vessel, nor would trust *Yahoos* to manage it."

The word *Houyhnhnm*, in their tongue, signifies a *horse*, and, in its etymology, the *perfection of nature*. I told my master, "that I was at a loss for expression, but would improve as fast as I could; and hoped, in a short time, I should be able to tell him wonders." He was pleased to direct his own mare, his colt, and foal, and the servants of the family, to take all opportunities of instructing me; and every day, for two or three hours, he was at the same pains himself. Several horses and mares of quality in the neighbourhood came often to our house, upon the report spread of "a wonderful *Yahoo*, that could speak like a *Houyhnhnm*, and seemed, in his words and actions, to discover some glimmerings of reason." These delighted to converse with me: they put many questions, and received such answers as I was able to return. By all these advantages I made so great a progress, that, in five months from my arrival I understood whatever was spoken, and could express myself tolerably well.

The *Houyhnhnms*, who came to visit my master out of a design of seeing and talking with me, could hardly believe me to be a right *Yahoo*, because my body had a different covering from others of my kind. They were astonished to observe me without the usual hair or skin, except on my head, face, and hands; but I discovered that secret to my master upon an accident which happened about a fortnight before.

I have already told the reader, that every night, when the family were gone to bed, it was my custom to strip, and cover myself with my clothes. It happened, one morning early, that my master sent for me by the sorrel nag, who was his valet. When he came I was fast asleep, my clothes fallen off on one side, and my shirt above my waist. I awaked at the noise he made, and observed him to deliver his message in some disorder; after which he went to my master, and in a great fright gave him a very confused account of what he had seen. This I presently discovered, for, going as soon as I was dressed to pay my attendance upon his honour, he asked me "the meaning of what his servant had reported, that I was not the same thing when I slept, as I appeared to be at other times; that his vale assured him, some part of me was white, some yellow, at least not so white, and some brown."

I had hitherto concealed the secret of my dress, in order to distinguish myself, as much as possible, from that cursed race of *Yahoos*; but now I found it in vain to do so any longer. Besides, I considered that my clothes and shoes would soon wear out, which already were in a declining condition, and must be supplied by some contrivance from the hides of *Yahoos*, or other brutes; whereby the whole secret would be known. I therefore told my master, "that in the country whence I came, those of my kind always covered their bodies with the hairs of certain animals prepared by art, as well for decency as to avoid the inclemencies of air, both hot and cold; of which, as to my own person, I would give him immediate conviction, if he pleased to command me: only desiring his excuse, if I did not expose those parts that nature taught us to conceal." He said, "my discourse was all very strange, but especially the last part; for he could not understand, why nature should teach us to conceal what nature had given; that neither himself nor family were ashamed of any parts of their bodies; but, however, I might do as I pleased." Whereupon I first unbuttoned my coat, and pulled it off. I did the same with my waistcoat. I drew off my shoes, stockings, and breeches. I let my shirt down to my waist, and drew up the bottom; fastening it like a girdle about my middle, to hide my nakedness.

My master observed the whole performance with great signs of curiosity and admiration. He took up all my clothes in his pastern, one piece after another, and examined them diligently; he then stroked my body very gently, and looked round me several times; after which, he said, it was plain I must be a perfect *Yahoo*; but that I differed very much from the rest of my species in the softness, whiteness, and smoothness of my skin; my want of hair in several parts of my body; the shape and shortness of my claws behind and before; and my affectation of walking continually on my two hinder feet. He desired to see no more; and gave me leave to put on my clothes again, for I was shuddering with cold.

I expressed my uneasiness at his giving me so often the appellation of *Yahoo*, an odious animal, for which I had so utter a hatred and contempt: I begged he would forbear applying that word to me, and make the same order in his family and among his friends whom he suffered to see me. I requested likewise, "that the secret of my having a false covering to my body, might be known to none but himself, at least as long as my present clothing should last; for as to what the sorrel nag, his valet, had observed, his honour might command him to conceal it."

All this my master very graciously consented to; and thus the secret was kept till my clothes began to wear out, which I was forced to supply by several contrivances that shall hereafter be mentioned. In the meantime, he desired "I would go on with my utmost diligence to learn their language, because he was more astonished at my capacity for speech and reason, than at the figure of my body, whether it were covered or not;" adding, "that he waited with some impatience to hear the wonders which I promised to tell him."

Thenceforward he doubled the pains he had been at to instruct me: he brought me into all company, and made them treat me with civility; "because," as he told them, privately, "this would put me into good humour, and make me more diverting."

Every day, when I waited on him, beside the trouble he was at in teaching, he would ask me several questions concerning myself, which I answered as well as I could, and by these means he had already received some general ideas, though very imperfect. It would be tedious to relate the several steps by which I advanced to a more regular conversation; but the first account I gave of myself in any order and length was to this purpose:

"That I came from a very far country, as I already had attempted to tell him, with about fifty more of my own species; that we travelled upon the seas in a great hollow vessel made of wood, and larger than his honour's house. I described the ship to him in the best terms I could, and explained, by the help of my handkerchief displayed, how it was driven forward by the wind. That upon a quarrel among us, I was set on shore on this coast, where I walked forward, without knowing whither, till he delivered me from the persecution of those execrable *Yahoos*." He asked me, "who made the ship, and how it was possible that the *Houyhnhnms* of my country would leave it to the management of brutes?" My answer was, "that I durst proceed no further in my relation, unless he would give me his word and honour that he would not be offended, and then I would tell him the wonders I had so often promised." He agreed; and I went on by assuring him, that the ship was made by creatures like myself; who, in all the countries I had travelled, as well as in my own, were the only governing rational animals; and that upon my arrival hither, I was as much astonished to see the *Houyhnhnms* act like rational beings, as he, or his friends, could be, in finding some marks of reason in a creature he was pleased to call a *Yahoo*; to which I owned my resemblance in every part, but could not account for their degenerate and brutal nature. I said farther, "that if good fortune ever restored me to my native country, to relate my travels hither, as I resolved to do, everybody would believe, that I said the thing that was not, that I invented the story out of my own head; and (with all possible respect to himself, his family, and friends, and under his promise of not being offended) our countrymen would hardly think it probable that a *Houyhnhnm* should be the presiding creature of a nation, and a *Yahoo* the brute."

CHAPTER FOUR

The Houyhnhnm's notion of truth and falsehood. The author's discourse disapproved by his master. The author gives a more particular account of himself, and the accidents of his voyage.

My master heard me with great appearances of uneasiness in his countenance; because doubting, or not believing, are so little known in this country, that the inhabitants cannot tell how to behave themselves under such circumstances. And I remember, in frequent discourses with my master concerning the nature of manhood in other parts of the world, having occasion to talk of lying and false representation, it was with much difficulty that he comprehended what I meant, although he had otherwise a most acute judgment. For he argued thus: "that the use of speech was to make us understand one another, and to receive information of facts; now, if any one said the thing which was not, these ends were defeated, because I cannot properly be said to understand him; and I am so far from receiving information, that he leaves me worse than in ignorance; for I am led to believe a thing black, when it is white, and short, when it is long." And these were all the notions he had concerning that faculty of lying, so perfectly well understood, and so universally practised, among human creatures.

To return from this digression. When I asserted that the *Yahoos* were the only governing animals in my country, which my master said was altogether past his conception, he desired to know, "whether we had *Houyhnhnms* among us, and what was their employment?" I told him, "we had great numbers; that in summer they grazed in the fields, and in winter were kept in houses with hay and oats, where *Yahoo* servants were employed to rub their skins smooth, comb their manes, pick their feet, serve them with food, and make their beds." "I understand you well," said my master: "it is now very plain, from all you have spoken, that whatever share of reason the *Yahoos* pretend to, the *Houyhnhnms* are your masters; I heartily wish our *Yahoos* would be so tractable." I begged "his honour would please to excuse me from proceeding any further, because I was very certain that the account he expected from me would be highly displeasing." But he insisted in commanding me to let him know the best and the worst. I told him "he should be obeyed." I owned "that the *Houyhnhnms* among us, whom we called horses, were the most generous and comely animals we had; that they excelled in strength and swiftness; and when they belonged to persons of quality, were employed in travelling, racing, or drawing chariots; they were treated with much kindness and care, till they fell into diseases, or became foundered in the feet; but then they were sold, and used to all kind of drudgery till they died; after which their skins were stripped, and sold for what they were worth, and their bodies left to be devoured by dogs and birds of prey. But the common race of horses had not so good fortune, being kept by farmers and carriers, and other mean people, who put them to greater labour, and fed them worse." I described, as well as I could, our way of riding; the shape and use of a bridle, a saddle, a spur, and a whip; of harness and wheels. I added, "that we fastened plates of a certain hard substance, called iron, at the bottom of their feet, to preserve their hoofs from being broken by the stony ways, on which we often travelled."

My master, after some expressions of great indignation, wondered "how we dared to venture upon a *Houyhnhnm's* back; for he was sure, that the weakest servant in his house would be able to shake off the strongest *Yahoo*; or by lying down and rolling on his back, squeeze the brute to death." I answered "that our horses were trained up, from three or four years old, to the several uses we intended them for; that if any of them proved intolerably vicious, they were employed for carriages; that they were severely beaten, while they were young, for any mischievous tricks; that the males, designed for the common use of riding or draught, were generally castrated about two years after their birth, to take down their spirits, and make them more tame and gentle; that they were indeed sensible of rewards and punishments; but his honour would please to consider, that they had not the least tincture of reason, any more than the *Yahoos* in this country."

It put me to the pains of many circumlocutions, to give my master a right idea of what I spoke; for their language does not abound in variety of words, because their wants and passions are fewer than among us. But it is impossible to express his noble resentment at our savage treatment of the *Houyhnhnm* race; particularly after I had explained the manner and use of castrating horses among us, to hinder them from propagating their kind, and to render them more servile. He said, "if it were possible there could be any country where *Yahoos* alone were endued with reason, they certainly must be the governing animal; because reason in time will always prevail against brutal strength. But, considering the frame of our bodies, and especially of mine, he thought no creature of equal bulk was so ill-contrived for employing that reason in the common offices of life;" whereupon he desired to know "whether those among whom I lived resembled me, or the *Yahoos* of his country?" I assured him, "that I was as well shaped as most of my age; but the younger, and the females, were much more soft and tender, and the skins of the latter generally as white as milk." He said, "I differed indeed from other *Yahoos*, being much more cleanly, and not altogether so deformed; but, in point of real advantage, he thought I differed for the worse: that my nails were of no use either to my fore or hinder feet; as to my fore feet, he could not properly call them by that name, for he never observed me to walk upon them; that they were too soft to bear the ground; that I generally went with them uncovered; neither was the covering I sometimes wore on them of the same shape, or so strong as that on my feet behind: that I could not walk with any security, for if either of my hinder feet slipped, I must inevitably fail." He then began to find fault with other parts of my body: "the flatness of my face, the prominence of my nose, mine eyes placed directly in front, so that I could not look on either side without turning my head: that I was not able to feed myself, without lifting one of my fore-feet to my mouth: and therefore nature had placed those joints to answer that necessity. He knew not what could be the use of those several clefts and divisions in my feet behind; that these were too soft to bear the hardness and sharpness of stones, without a covering made from the skin of some other brute; that my whole body wanted a fence against heat and cold, which I was forced to put on and off every day, with tediousness and trouble: and lastly, that he observed every animal in this country naturally to abhor the *Yahoos*, whom the weaker avoided, and the stronger drove from them. So that, supposing us to have the gift of reason, he could not see how it were possible to cure that natural antipathy, which every creature discovered against us; nor consequently how we could tame and render them serviceable. However, he would," as he said, "debate the matter no farther, because he was more desirous to know my own story, the country where I was born, and the several actions and events of my life, before I came hither."

I assured him, "how extremely desirous I was that he should be satisfied on every point; but I doubted much, whether it would be possible for me to explain myself on several subjects, whereof his honour could have no conception; because I saw nothing in his country to which I could resemble them; that, however, I would do my best, and strive to express myself by similitudes, humbly desiring his assistance when I wanted proper words;" which he was pleased to promise me.

I said, "my birth was of honest parents, in an island called England; which was remote from his country, as many days' journey as the strongest of his honour's servants could travel in the annual course of the sun; that I was bred a surgeon, whose trade it is to cure wounds and hurts in the body, gotten by accident or violence; that my country was governed by a female man, whom we called queen; that I left it to get riches, whereby I might maintain myself and family, when I should return; that, in my last voyage, I was commander of the ship, and had about fifty *Yahoos* under me, many of which died at sea, and I was forced to supply them by others picked out from several nations; that our ship was twice in danger of being sunk, the first time by a great storm, and the second by striking against a rock." Here my master interposed, by asking me, "how I could persuade strangers, out of different countries, to venture with me, after the losses I had sustained, and the hazards I had run?" I said, "they were fellows of desperate fortunes, forced to fly from the places of their birth on account of their poverty or their crimes. Some were undone by lawsuits; others spent all they had in drinking, whoring, and gaming; others fled for treason; many for murder, theft, poisoning, robbery, perjury, forgery, coining false money, for committing rapes, or sodomy; for flying from their colours, or deserting to the enemy; and most of them had broken prison; none of these durst return to their native countries, for fear of being hanged, or of starving in a jail; and therefore they were under the necessity of seeking a livelihood in other places."

During this discourse, my master was pleased to interrupt me several times. I had made use of many circumlocutions in describing to him the nature of the several crimes for which most of our crew had been forced to fly their country. This labour took up several days' conversation, before he was able to comprehend me. He was wholly at a loss to know what could be the use or necessity of practising those vices. To clear up which, I endeavoured to give some ideas of the desire of power and riches; of the terrible effects of lust, intemperance, malice, and envy. All this I was forced to define and describe by putting cases and making suppositions. After which, like one whose imagination was struck with something never seen or heard of before, he would lift up his eyes with amazement and indignation. Power, government, war, law, punishment, and a thousand other things, had no terms wherein that language could express them, which made the difficulty almost insuperable, to give my master any conception of what I meant. But being of an excellent understanding, much improved by contemplation and converse, he at last arrived at a competent knowledge of what human nature, in our parts of the world, is capable to perform, and desired I would give him some particular account of that land which we call Europe, but especially of my own country.

CHAPTER FIVE

The author at his master's command, informs him of the state of England. The causes of war among the princes of Europe. The author begins to explain the English constitution.

THE READER may please to observe, that the following extract of many conversations I had with my master, contains a summary of the most material points which were discoursed at several times for above two years; his honour often desiring fuller satisfaction, as I farther improved in the *Houyhnhnm* tongue. I laid before him, as well as I could, the whole state of Europe; I discoursed of trade and manufactures, of arts and sciences; and the answers I gave to all the questions he made, as they arose upon several subjects, were a fund of conversation not to be exhausted. But I shall here only set down the substance of what passed between us concerning my own country, reducing it in order as well as I can, without any regard to time or other circumstances, while I strictly adhere to truth. My only concern is, that I shall hardly be able to do justice to my master's arguments and expressions, which must needs suffer by my want of capacity, as well as by a translation into our barbarous English.

In obedience, therefore, to his honour's commands, I related to him the Revolution under the Prince of Orange; the long war with France, entered into by the said prince, and renewed by his successor, the present queen, wherein the greatest powers of Christendom were engaged, and which still continued: I computed, at his request, "that about a million of *Yahoos* might have been killed in the whole progress of it; and perhaps a hundred or more cities taken, and five times as many ships burnt or sunk."

He asked me, "what were the usual causes or motives that made one country go to war with another?" I answered "they were innumerable; but I should only mention a few of the chief. Sometimes the ambition of princes, who never think they have land or people enough to govern; sometimes the corruption of ministers, who engage their master in a war, in order to stifle or divert the clamour of the subjects against their evil administration. Difference in opinions has cost many millions of lives: for instance, whether flesh be bread, or bread be flesh; whether the juice of a certain berry be blood or wine; whether whistling be a vice or a virtue; whether it be better to kiss a post, or throw it into the fire; what is the best colour for a coat, whether black, white, red, or gray; and whether it should be long or short, narrow or wide, dirty or clean; with many more. Neither are any wars so furious and bloody, or of so long a continuance, as those occasioned by difference in opinion, especially if it be in things indifferent.

"Sometimes the quarrel between two princes is to decide which of them shall dispossess a third of his dominions, where neither of them pretend to any right. Sometimes one prince quarrels with another for fear the other should quarrel with him. Sometimes a war is entered upon, because the enemy is too strong; and sometimes, because he is too weak. Sometimes our neighbours want the things which we have, or have the things which we want, and we both fight, till they take ours, or give us theirs. It is a very justifiable cause of a war, to invade a country after the people have been wasted by famine, destroyed by pestilence, or embroiled by factions among themselves. It is justifiable to enter into war against our nearest ally, when one of his towns lies convenient for us, or a territory of land, that would render our dominions round and complete. If a prince sends forces into a nation, where the people are poor and ignorant, he may lawfully put half of them to death, and make slaves of the rest, in order to civilize and reduce them from their barbarous way of living. It is a very kingly, honourable, and frequent practice, when one prince desires the assistance of another, to secure him against an invasion, that the assistant, when he has driven out the invader, should seize on the dominions himself, and kill, imprison, or banish, the prince he came to relieve. Alliance by blood, or marriage, is a frequent cause of war between princes; and the nearer the kindred is, the greater their disposition to quarrel; poor nations are hungry, and rich nations are proud; and pride and hunger will ever be at variance. For these reasons, the trade of a soldier is held the most honourable of all others; because a soldier is a *Yahoo* hired to kill, in cold blood, as many of his own species, who have never offended him, as possibly he can.

"There is likewise a kind of beggarly princes in Europe, not able to make war by themselves, who hire out their troops to richer nations, for so much a day to each man; of which they keep three-fourths to themselves, and it is the best part of their maintenance: such are those in many northern parts of Europe."

"What you have told me," said my master, "upon the subject of war, does indeed discover most admirably the effects of that reason you pretend to: however, it is happy that the shame is greater than the danger; and that nature has left you utterly incapable of doing much mischief. For, your mouths lying flat with your faces, you can hardly bite each other to any purpose, unless by consent. Then as to the claws upon your feet before and behind, they are so short and tender, that one of our *Yahoos* would drive a dozen of yours before him. And therefore, in recounting the numbers of those who have been killed in battle, I cannot but think you have said the thing which is not."

I could not forbear shaking my head, and smiling a little at his ignorance. And being no stranger to the art of war, I gave him a description of cannons, culverins, muskets, carabines, pistols, bullets, powder, swords, bayonets, battles, sieges, retreats, attacks, undermines, countermines, bombardments, sea fights, ships sunk with a thousand men, twenty thousand killed on each side, dying groans, limbs flying in the air, smoke, noise, confusion, trampling to death under horses' feet, flight, pursuit, victory; fields strewed with carcases, left for food to dogs and wolves and birds of prey; plundering, stripping, ravishing, burning, and destroying. And to set forth the valour of my own dear countrymen, I assured him, "that I had seen them blow up a hundred enemies at once in a siege, and as many in a ship, and beheld the dead bodies drop down in pieces from the clouds, to the great diversion of the spectators."

I was going on to more particulars, when my master commanded me silence. He said, "whoever understood the nature of *Yahoos*, might easily believe it possible for so vile an animal to be capable of every action I had named, if their strength and cunning equalled their malice. But as my discourse had increased his abhorrence of the whole species, so he found it gave him a disturbance in his mind to which he was wholly a stranger before. He thought his ears, being used to such abominable words, might, by degrees, admit them with less detestation: that although he hated the *Yahoos* of this country, yet he no more blamed them for their odious qualities, than he did a *gnnayh* (a bird of prey) for its cruelty, or a sharp stone for cutting his hoof. But when a creature pretending to reason could be capable of such enormities, he dreaded lest the corruption of that faculty might be worse than brutality itself. He seemed therefore confident, that, instead of reason we were only possessed of some quality fitted to increase our natural vices; as the reflection from a troubled stream returns the image of an ill shapen body, not only larger but more distorted."

He added, "that he had heard too much upon the subject of war, both in this and some former discourses. There was another point, which a little perplexed him at present. I had informed him, that some of our crew left their country on account of being ruined by law; that I had already explained the meaning of the word; but he was at a loss how it should come to pass, that the law, which was intended for every man's preservation, should be any man's ruin. Therefore he desired to be further satisfied what I meant by law, and the dispensers thereof, according to the present practice in my own country; because he thought nature and reason were sufficient guides for a reasonable animal, as we pretended to be, in showing us what he ought to do, and what to avoid."

I assured his honour, "that the law was a science in which I had not much conversed, further than by employing advocates, in vain, upon some injustices that had been done me: however, I would give him all the satisfaction I was able."

I said, "there was a society of men among us, bred up from their youth in the art of proving, by words multiplied for the purpose, that white is black, and black is white, according as they are paid. To this society all the rest of the people are slaves. For example, if my neighbour has a mind to my cow, he has a lawyer to prove that he ought to have my cow from me. I must then hire another to defend my right, it being against all rules of law that any man should be allowed to speak for himself. Now, in this case, I, who am the right owner, lie under two great disadvantages: first, my lawyer, being practised almost from his cradle in defending falsehood, is quite out of his element when he would be an advocate for justice, which is an unnatural office he always attempts with great awkwardness, if not with ill-will. The second disadvantage is, that my lawyer must proceed with great caution, or else he will be reprimanded by the judges, and abhorred by his brethren, as one that would lessen the practice of the law. And therefore I have but two methods to preserve my cow. The first is, to gain over my adversary's lawyer with a double fee, who will then betray his client by insinuating that he hath justice on his side. The second way is for my lawyer to make my cause appear as unjust as he can, by allowing the cow to belong to my adversary: and this, if it be skilfully done, will certainly bespeak the favour of the bench. Now your honour is to know, that these judges are persons appointed to decide all controversies of property, as well as for the trial of criminals, and picked out from the most dexterous lawyers, who are grown old or lazy; and having been biassed all their lives against truth and equity, lie under such a fatal necessity of favouring fraud, perjury, and oppression, that I have known some of them refuse a large bribe from the side where justice lay, rather than injure the faculty, by doing any thing unbecoming their nature or their office.

"It is a maxim among these lawyers that whatever has been done before, may legally be done again: and therefore they take special care to record all the decisions formerly made against common justice, and the general reason of mankind. These, under the name of precedents, they produce as authorities to justify the most iniquitous opinions; and the judges never fail of directing accordingly.

"In pleading, they studiously avoid entering into the merits of the cause; but are loud, violent, and tedious, in dwelling upon all circumstances which are not to the purpose. For instance, in the case already mentioned; they never desire to know what claim or title my adversary has to my cow; but whether the said cow were red or black; her horns long or short; whether the field I graze her in be round or square; whether she was milked at home or abroad; what diseases she is subject to, and the like; after which they consult precedents, adjourn the cause from time to time, and in ten, twenty, or thirty years, come to an issue.

"It is likewise to be observed, that this society has a peculiar cant and jargon of their own, that no other mortal can understand, and wherein all their laws are written, which they take special care to multiply; whereby they have wholly confounded the very essence of truth and falsehood, of right and wrong; so that it will take thirty years to decide, whether the field left me by my ancestors for six generations belongs to me, or to a stranger three hundred miles off.

"In the trial of persons accused for crimes against the state, the method is much more short and commendable: the judge first sends to sound the disposition of those in power, after which he can easily hang or save a criminal, strictly preserving all due forms of law."

Here my master interposing, said, "it was a pity, that creatures endowed with such prodigious abilities of mind, as these lawyers, by the description I gave of them, must certainly be, were not rather encouraged to be instructors of others in wisdom and knowledge." In answer to which I assured his honour, "that in all points out of their own trade, they were usually the most ignorant and stupid generation among us, the most despicable in common conversation, avowed enemies to all knowledge and learning, and equally disposed to pervert the general reason of mankind in every other subject of discourse as in that of their own profession."

CHAPTER SIX

A continuation of the state of England under Queen Anne. The character of a first minister of state in European courts.

My master was yet wholly at a loss to understand what motives could incite this race of lawyers to perplex, disquiet, and weary themselves, and engage in a confederacy of injustice, merely for the sake of injuring their fellow-animals; neither could he comprehend what I meant in saying, they did it for hire. Whereupon I was at much pains to describe to him the use of money, the materials it was made of, and the value of the metals; "that when a *Yahoo* had got a great store of this precious substance, he was able to purchase whatever he had a mind to; the finest clothing, the noblest houses, great tracts of land, the most costly meats and drinks, and have his choice of the most beautiful females. Therefore since money alone was able to perform all these feats, our *Yahoos* thought they could never have enough of it to spend, or to save, as they found themselves inclined, from their natural bent either to profusion or avarice; that the rich man enjoyed the fruit of the poor man's labour, and the latter were a thousand to one in proportion to the former; that the bulk of our people were forced to live miserably, by labouring every day for small wages, to make a few live plentifully."

I enlarged myself much on these, and many other particulars to the same purpose; but his honour was still to seek; for he went upon a supposition, that all animals had a title to their share in the productions of the earth, and especially those who presided over the rest. Therefore he desired I would let him know, "what these costly meats were, and how any of us happened to want them?" Whereupon I enumerated as many sorts as came into my head, with the various methods of dressing them, which could not be done without sending vessels by sea to every part of the world, as well for liquors to drink as for sauces and innumerable other conveniences. I assured him "that this whole globe of earth must be at least three times gone round before one of our better female *Yahoos* could get her breakfast, or a cup to put it in." He said "that must needs be a miserable country which cannot furnish food for its own inhabitants. But what he chiefly wondered at was, how such vast tracts of ground as I described should be wholly without fresh water, and the people put to the necessity of sending over the sea for drink." I replied "that England (the dear place of my nativity) was computed to produce three times the quantity of food more than its inhabitants are able to consume, as well as liquors extracted from grain, or pressed out of the fruit of certain trees, which made excellent drink, and the same proportion in every other convenience of life. But, in order to feed the luxury and intemperance of the males, and the vanity of the females, we sent away the greatest part of our necessary things to other countries, whence, in return, we brought the materials of diseases, folly, and vice, to spend among ourselves. Hence it follows of necessity, that vast numbers of our people are compelled to seek their livelihood by begging, robbing, stealing, cheating, pimping, flattering, suborning, forswearing, forging, gaming, lying, fawning, hectoring, voting, scribbling, star-gazing, poisoning, whoring, canting, libelling, freethinking, and the like occupations:" every one of which terms I was at much pains to make him understand.

"That wine was not imported among us from foreign countries to supply the want of water or other drinks, but because it was a sort of liquid which made us merry by putting us out of our senses, diverted all melancholy thoughts, begat wild extravagant imaginations in the brain, raised our hopes and banished our fears, suspended every office of reason for a time, and deprived us of the use of our limbs, till we fell into a profound sleep; although it must be confessed, that we always awaked sick and dispirited; and that the use of this liquor filled us with diseases which made our lives uncomfortable and short.

"But beside all this, the bulk of our people supported themselves by furnishing the necessities or conveniences of life to the rich and to each other. For instance, when I am at home, and dressed as I ought to be, I carry on my body the workmanship of a hundred tradesmen; the building and furniture of my house employ as many more, and five times the number to adorn my wife."

I was going on to tell him of another sort of people, who get their livelihood by attending the sick, having, upon some occasions, informed his honour that many of my crew had died of diseases. But here it was with the utmost difficulty that I brought him to apprehend what I meant. "He could easily conceive, that a *Houyhnhnm*, grew weak and heavy a few days before his death, or by some accident might hurt a limb; but that nature, who works all things to perfection, should suffer any pains to breed in our bodies, he thought impossible, and desired to know the reason of so unaccountable an evil."

I told him "we fed on a thousand things which operated contrary to each other; that we ate when we were not hungry, and drank without the provocation of thirst; that we sat whole nights drinking strong liquors, without eating a bit, which disposed us to sloth, inflamed our bodies, and precipitated or prevented digestion; that prostitute female *Yahoos* acquired a certain malady, which bred rottenness in the bones of those who fell into their embraces; that this, and many other diseases, were propagated from father to son; so that great numbers came into the world with complicated maladies upon them; that it would be endless to give him a catalogue of all diseases incident to human bodies, for they would not be fewer than five or six hundred, spread over every limb and joint – in short, every part, external and intestine, having diseases appropriated to itself. To remedy which, there was a sort of people bred up among us in the profession, or pretence, of curing the sick. And because I had some skill in the faculty, I would, in gratitude to his honour, let him know the whole mystery and method by which they proceed.

"Their fundamental is, that all diseases arise from repletion; whence they conclude, that a great evacuation of the body is necessary, either through the natural passage or upwards at the mouth. Their next business is from herbs, minerals, gums, oils, shells, salts, juices, sea-weed, excrements, barks of trees, serpents, toads, frogs, spiders, dead men's flesh and bones, birds, beasts, and fishes, to form a composition, for smell and taste, the most abominable, nauseous, and detestable, they can possibly contrive, which the stomach immediately rejects with loathing, and this they call a vomit; or else, from the same store-house, with some other poisonous additions, they command us to take in at the orifice above or below (just as the physician then happens to be disposed) a medicine equally annoying and disgustful to the bowels; which, relaxing the belly, drives down all before it; and this they call a purge, or a clyster. For nature (as the physicians allege) having intended the superior anterior orifice only for the intromission of solids and liquids, and the inferior posterior for ejection, these artists ingeniously considering that in all diseases nature is forced out of her seat, therefore, to replace her in it, the body must be treated in a manner directly contrary, by interchanging the use of each orifice; forcing solids and liquids in at the anus, and making evacuations at the mouth.

"But, besides real diseases, we are subject to many that are only imaginary, for which the physicians have invented imaginary cures; these have their several names, and so have the drugs that are proper for them; and with these our female *Yahoos* are always infested.

"One great excellency in this tribe, is their skill at prognostics, wherein they seldom fail; their predictions in real diseases, when they rise to any degree of malignity, generally portending death, which is always in their power, when recovery is not: and therefore, upon any unexpected signs of amendment, after they have pronounced their sentence, rather than be accused as false prophets, they know how to approve their sagacity to the world, by a seasonable dose.

"They are likewise of special use to husbands and wives who are grown weary of their mates; to eldest sons, to great ministers of state, and often to princes."

I had formerly, upon occasion, discoursed with my master upon the nature of government in general, and particularly of our own excellent constitution, deservedly the wonder and envy of the whole world. But having here accidentally mentioned a minister of state, he commanded me, some time after, to inform him, "what species of *Yahoo* I particularly meant by that appellation."

I told him, "that a first or chief minister of state, who was the person I intended to describe, was the creature wholly exempt from joy and grief, love and hatred, pity and anger; at least, makes use of no other passions, but a violent desire of wealth, power, and titles; that he applies his words to all uses, except to the indication of his mind; that he never tells a truth but with an intent that you should take it for a lie; nor a lie, but with a design that you should take it for a truth; that those he speaks worst of behind their backs are in the surest way of preferment; and whenever he begins to praise you to others, or to yourself, you are from that day forlorn. The worst mark you can receive is a promise, especially when it is confirmed with an oath; after which, every wise man retires, and gives over all hopes.

"There are three methods, by which a man may rise to be chief minister. The first is, by knowing how, with prudence, to dispose of a wife, a daughter, or a sister; the second, by betraying or undermining his predecessor; and the third is, by a furious zeal, in public assemblies, against the corruption's of the court. But a wise prince would rather choose to employ those who practise the last of these methods; because such zealots prove always the most obsequious and subservient to the will and passions of their master. That these ministers, having all employments at their disposal, preserve themselves in power, by bribing the majority of a senate or great council; and at last, by an expedient, called an act of indemnity" (whereof I described the nature to him), "they secure themselves from after-reckonings, and retire from the public laden with the spoils of the nation.

"The palace of a chief minister is a seminary to breed up others in his own trade: the pages, lackeys, and porters, by imitating their master, become ministers of state in their several districts, and learn to excel in the three principal ingredients, of insolence, lying, and bribery. Accordingly, they have a subaltern court paid to them by persons of the best rank; and sometimes by the force of dexterity and impudence, arrive, through several gradations, to be successors to their lord.

"He is usually governed by a decayed wench, or favourite footman, who are the tunnels through which all graces are conveyed, and may properly be called, in the last resort, the governors of the kingdom."

One day, in discourse, my master, having heard me mention the nobility of my country, was pleased to make me a compliment which I could not pretend to deserve: "that he was sure I must have been born of some noble family, because I far exceeded in shape, colour, and cleanliness, all the *Yahoos* of his nation, although I seemed to fail in strength and agility, which must be imputed to my different way of living from those other brutes; and besides I was not only endowed with the faculty of speech, but likewise with some rudiments of reason, to a degree that, with all his acquaintance, I passed for a prodigy."

He made me observe, "that among the *Houyhnhnms*, the white, the sorrel, and the iron-gray, were not so exactly shaped as the bay, the dapple-gray, and the black; nor born with equal talents of mind, or a capacity to improve them; and therefore continued always in the condition of servants, without ever aspiring to match out of their own race, which in that country would be reckoned monstrous and unnatural."

I made his honour my most humble acknowledgments for the good opinion he was pleased to conceive of me, but assured him at the same time, "that my birth was of the lower sort, having been born of plain honest parents, who were just able to give me a tolerable education; that nobility, among us, was altogether a different thing from the idea he had of it; that our young noblemen are bred from their childhood in idleness and luxury; that, as soon as years will permit, they consume their vigour, and contract odious diseases among lewd females; and when their fortunes are almost ruined, they marry some woman of mean birth, disagreeable person, and unsound constitution (merely for the sake of money), whom they hate and despise. That the productions of such marriages are generally scrofulous, rickety, or deformed children; by which means the family seldom continues above three generations, unless the wife takes care to provide a healthy father, among her neighbours or domestics, in order to improve and continue the breed. That a weak diseased body, a meagre countenance, and sallow complexion, are the true marks of noble blood; and a healthy robust appearance is so disgraceful in a man of quality, that the world concludes his real father to have been a groom or a coachman. The imperfections of his mind run parallel with those of his body, being a composition of spleen, dullness, ignorance, caprice, sensuality, and pride.

"Without the consent of this illustrious body, no law can be enacted, repealed, or altered: and these nobles have likewise the decision of all our possessions, without appeal."[6]

6 This paragraph is not in the original editions.

CHAPTER SEVEN

The author's great love of his native country. His master's observations upon the constitution and administration of England, as described by the author, with parallel cases and comparisons. His master's observations upon human nature.

THE READER may be disposed to wonder how I could prevail on myself to give so free a representation of my own species, among a race of mortals who are already too apt to conceive the vilest opinion of humankind, from that entire congruity between me and their *Yahoos*. But I must freely confess, that the many virtues of those excellent quadrupeds, placed in opposite view to human corruptions, had so far opened my eyes and enlarged my understanding, that I began to view the actions and passions of man in a very different light, and to think the honour of my own kind not worth managing; which, besides, it was impossible for me to do, before a person of so acute a judgment as my master, who daily convinced me of a thousand faults in myself, whereof I had not the least perception before, and which, with us, would never be numbered even among human infirmities. I had likewise learned, from his example, an utter detestation of all falsehood or disguise; and truth appeared so amiable to me, that I determined upon sacrificing every thing to it.

Let me deal so candidly with the reader as to confess that there was yet a much stronger motive for the freedom I took in my representation of things. I had not yet been a year in this country before I contracted such a love and veneration for the inhabitants, that I entered on a firm resolution never to return to humankind, but to pass the rest of my life among these admirable *Houyhnhnms*, in the contemplation and practice of every virtue, where I could have no example or incitement to vice. But it was decreed by fortune, my perpetual enemy, that so great a felicity should not fall to my share. However, it is now some comfort to reflect, that in what I said of my countrymen, I extenuated their faults as much as I durst before so strict an examiner; and upon every article gave as favourable a turn as the matter would bear. For, indeed, who is there alive that will not be swayed by his bias and partiality to the place of his birth?

I have related the substance of several conversations I had with my master during the greatest part of the time I had the honour to be in his service; but have, indeed, for brevity sake, omitted much more than is here set down.

When I had answered all his questions, and his curiosity seemed to be fully satisfied, he sent for me one morning early, and commanded me to sit down at some distance (an honour which he had never before conferred upon me). He said, "he had been very seriously considering my whole story, as far as it related both to myself and my country; that he looked upon us as a sort of animals, to whose share, by what accident he could not conjecture, some small pittance of reason had fallen, whereof we made no other use, than by its assistance, to aggravate our natural corruptions, and to acquire new ones, which nature had not given us; that we disarmed ourselves of the few abilities she had bestowed; had been very successful in multiplying our original wants, and seemed to spend our whole lives in vain endeavours to supply them by our own inventions; that, as to myself, it was manifest I had neither the strength nor agility of a common *Yahoo*; that I walked infirmly on my hinder feet; had found out a contrivance to make my claws of no use or defence, and to remove the hair from my chin, which was intended as a shelter from the sun and the weather: lastly, that I could neither run with speed, nor climb trees like my brethren," as he called them, "the *Yahoos* in his country.

"That our institutions of government and law were plainly owing to our gross defects in reason, and by consequence in virtue; because reason alone is sufficient to govern a rational creature; which was, therefore, a character we had no pretence to challenge, even from the account I had given of my own people; although he manifestly perceived, that, in order to favour them, I had concealed many particulars, and often said the thing which was not.

"He was the more confirmed in this opinion, because, he observed, that as I agreed in every feature of my body with other *Yahoos*, except where it was to my real disadvantage in point of strength, speed, and activity, the shortness of my claws, and some other particulars where nature had no part; so from the representation I had given him of our lives, our manners, and our actions, he found as near a resemblance in the disposition of our minds." He said, "the *Yahoos* were known to hate one another, more than they did any different species of animals; and the reason usually assigned was, the odiousness of their own shapes, which all could see in the rest, but not in themselves. He had therefore begun to think it not unwise in us to cover our bodies, and by that invention conceal many of our deformities from each other, which would else be hardly supportable. But he now found he had been mistaken, and that the dissensions of those brutes in his country were owing to the same cause with ours, as I had described them. For if," said he, "you throw among five *Yahoos* as much food as would be sufficient for fifty, they will, instead of eating peaceably, fall together by the ears, each single one impatient to have all to itself; and therefore a servant was usually employed to stand by while they were feeding abroad, and those kept at home were tied at a distance from each other: that if a cow died of age or accident, before a *Houyhnhnm* could secure it for his own *Yahoos*, those in the neighbourhood would come in herds to seize it, and then would ensue such a battle as I had described, with terrible wounds made by their claws on both sides, although they seldom were able to kill one another, for want of such convenient instruments of death as we had invented. At other times, the like battles have been fought between the *Yahoos* of several neighbourhoods, without any visible cause; those of one district watching all opportunities to surprise the next, before they are prepared. But if they find their project has miscarried, they return home, and, for want of enemies, engage in what I call a civil war among themselves.

"That in some fields of his country there are certain shining stones of several colours, whereof the *Yahoos* are violently fond: and when part of these stones is fixed in the earth, as it sometimes happens, they will dig with their claws for whole days to get them out; then carry them away, and hide them by heaps in their kennels; but still looking round with great caution, for fear their comrades should find out their treasure." My master said, "he could never discover the reason of this unnatural appetite, or how these stones could be of any use to a *Yahoo*; but now he believed it might proceed from the same principle of avarice which I had ascribed to mankind. That he had once, by way of experiment, privately removed a heap of these stones from the place where one of his *Yahoos* had buried it; whereupon the sordid animal, missing his treasure, by his loud lamenting brought the whole herd to the place, there miserably howled, then fell to biting and tearing the rest, began to pine away, would neither eat, nor sleep, nor work, till he ordered a servant privately to convey the stones into the same hole, and hide them as before; which, when his *Yahoo* had found, he presently recovered his spirits and good humour, but took good care to remove them to a better hiding place, and has ever since been a very serviceable brute."

My master further assured me, which I also observed myself, "that in the fields where the shining stones abound, the fiercest and most frequent battles are fought, occasioned by perpetual inroads of the neighbouring *Yahoos*."

He said, "it was common, when two *Yahoos* discovered such a stone in a field, and were contending which of them should be the proprietor, a third would take the advantage, and carry it away from them both;" which my master would needs contend to have some kind of resemblance with our suits at law; wherein I thought it for our credit not to undeceive him; since the decision he mentioned was much more equitable than many decrees among us; because the plaintiff and defendant there lost nothing beside the stone they contended for: whereas our courts of equity would never have dismissed the cause, while either of them had any thing left.

My master, continuing his discourse, said, "there was nothing that rendered the *Yahoos* more odious, than their undistinguishing appetite to devour every thing that came in their way, whether herbs, roots, berries, the corrupted flesh of animals, or all mingled together: and it was peculiar in their temper, that they were fonder of what they could get by rapine or stealth, at a greater distance, than much better food provided for them at home. If their prey held out, they would eat till they were ready to burst; after which, nature had pointed out to them a certain root that gave them a general evacuation.

"There was also another kind of root, very juicy, but somewhat rare and difficult to be found, which the *Yahoos* sought for with much eagerness, and would suck it with great delight; it produced in them the same effects that wine has upon us. It would make them sometimes hug, and sometimes tear one another; they would howl, and grin, and chatter, and reel, and tumble, and then fall asleep in the mud."

I did indeed observe that the *Yahoos* were the only animals in this country subject to any diseases; which, however, were much fewer than horses have among us, and contracted, not by any ill-treatment they meet with, but by the nastiness and greediness of that sordid brute. Neither has their language any more than a general appellation for those maladies, which is borrowed from the name of the beast, and called *hnea-yahoo*, or *Yahoo's evil*; and the cure prescribed is a mixture of their own dung and urine, forcibly put down the *Yahoo's* throat. This I have since often known to have been taken with success, and do here freely recommend it to my countrymen for the public good, as an admirable specific against all diseases produced by repletion.

"As to learning, government, arts, manufactures, and the like," my master confessed, "he could find little or no resemblance between the *Yahoos* of that country and those in ours; for he only meant to observe what parity there was in our natures. He had heard, indeed, some curious *Houyhnhnms* observe, that in most herds there was a sort of ruling *Yahoo* (as among us there is generally some leading or principal stag in a park), who was always more deformed in body, and mischievous in disposition, than any of the rest; that this leader had usually a favourite as like himself as he could get, whose employment was to lick his master's feet and posteriors, and drive the female *Yahoos* to his kennel; for which he was now and then rewarded with a piece of ass's flesh. This favourite is hated by the whole herd, and therefore, to protect himself, keeps always near the person of his leader. He usually continues in office till a worse can be found; but the very moment he is discarded, his successor, at the head of all the *Yahoos* in that district, young and old, male and female, come in a body, and discharge their excrements upon him from head to foot. But how far this might be applicable to our courts, and favourites, and ministers of state, my master said I could best determine."

I durst make no return to this malicious insinuation, which debased human understanding below the sagacity of a common hound, who has judgment enough to distinguish and follow the cry of the ablest dog in the pack, without being ever mistaken.

My master told me, "there were some qualities remarkable in the *Yahoos*, which he had not observed me to mention, or at least very slightly, in the accounts I had given of humankind." He said, "those animals, like other brutes, had their females in common; but in this they differed, that the she *Yahoo* would admit the males while she was pregnant; and that the hes would quarrel and fight with the females, as fiercely as with each other; both which practices were such degrees of infamous brutality, as no other sensitive creature ever arrived at.

"Another thing he wondered at in the *Yahoos*, was their strange disposition to nastiness and dirt; whereas there appears to be a natural love of cleanliness in all other animals." As to the two former accusations, I was glad to let them pass without any reply, because I had not a word to offer upon them in defence of my species, which otherwise I certainly had done from my own inclinations. But I could have easily vindicated humankind from the imputation of singularity upon the last article, if there had been any swine in that country (as unluckily for me there were not), which, although it may be a sweeter quadruped than a *Yahoo*, cannot, I humbly conceive, in justice, pretend to more cleanliness; and so his honour himself must have owned, if he had seen their filthy way of feeding, and their custom of wallowing and sleeping in the mud.

My master likewise mentioned another quality which his servants had discovered in several Yahoos, and to him was wholly unaccountable. He said, "a fancy would sometimes take a *Yahoo* to retire into a corner, to lie down, and howl, and groan, and spurn away all that came near him, although he were young and fat, wanted neither food nor water, nor did the servant imagine what could possibly ail him. And the only remedy they found was, to set him to hard work, after which he would infallibly come to himself." To this I was silent out of partiality to my own kind; yet here I could plainly discover the true seeds of spleen, which only seizes on the lazy, the luxurious, and the rich; who, if they were forced to undergo the same regimen, I would undertake for the cure.

His honour had further observed, "that a female *Yahoo* would often stand behind a bank or a bush, to gaze on the young males passing by, and then appear, and hide, using many antic gestures and grimaces, at which time it was observed that she had a most offensive smell; and when any of the males advanced, would slowly retire, looking often back, and with a counterfeit show of fear, run off into some convenient place, where she knew the male would follow her.

"At other times, if a female stranger came among them, three or four of her own sex would get about her, and stare, and chatter, and grin, and smell her all over; and then turn off with gestures, that seemed to express contempt and disdain."

Perhaps my master might refine a little in these speculations, which he had drawn from what he observed himself, or had been told him by others; however, I could not reflect without some amazement, and much sorrow, that the rudiments of lewdness, coquetry, censure, and scandal, should have place by instinct in womankind.

I expected every moment that my master would accuse the *Yahoos* of those unnatural appetites in both sexes, so common among us. But nature, it seems, has not been so expert a school-mistress; and these politer pleasures are entirely the productions of art and reason on our side of the globe.

CHAPTER EIGHT

The author relates several particulars of the Yahoos. The great virtues of the Houyhnhnms. The education and exercise of their youth. Their general assembly.

As I ought to have understood human nature much better than I supposed it possible for my master to do, so it was easy to apply the character he gave of the *Yahoos* to myself and my countrymen; and I believed I could yet make further discoveries, from my own observation. I therefore often begged his honour to let me go among the herds of *Yahoos* in the neighbourhood; to which he always very graciously consented, being perfectly convinced that the hatred I bore these brutes would never suffer me to be corrupted by them; and his honour ordered one of his servants, a strong sorrel nag, very honest and good-natured, to be my guard; without whose protection I durst not undertake such adventures. For I have already told the reader how much I was pestered by these odious animals, upon my first arrival; and I afterwards failed very narrowly, three or four times, of falling into their clutches, when I happened to stray at any distance without my hanger. And I have reason to believe they had some imagination that I was of their own species, which I often assisted myself by stripping up my sleeves, and showing my naked arms and breasts in their sight, when my protector was with me. At which times they would approach as near as they durst, and imitate my actions after the manner of monkeys, but ever with great signs of hatred; as a tame jackdaw with cap and stockings is always persecuted by the wild ones, when he happens to be got among them.

They are prodigiously nimble from their infancy. However, I once caught a young male of three years old, and endeavoured, by all marks of tenderness, to make it quiet; but the little imp fell a squalling, and scratching, and biting with such violence, that I was forced to let it go; and it was high time, for a whole troop of old ones came about us at the noise, but finding the cub was safe (for away it ran), and my sorrel nag being by, they durst not venture near us. I observed the young animal's flesh to smell very rank, and the stink was somewhat between a weasel and a fox, but much more disagreeable. I forgot another circumstance (and perhaps I might have the reader's pardon if it were wholly omitted), that while I held the odious vermin in my hands, it voided its filthy excrements of a yellow liquid substance all over my clothes; but by good fortune there was a small brook hard by, where I washed myself as clean as I could; although I durst not come into my master's presence until I were sufficiently aired.

By what I could discover, the *Yahoos* appear to be the most unteachable of all animals: their capacity never reaching higher than to draw or carry burdens. Yet I am of opinion, this defect arises chiefly from a perverse, restive disposition; for they are cunning, malicious, treacherous, and revengeful. They are strong and hardy, but of a cowardly spirit, and, by consequence, insolent, abject, and cruel. It is observed, that the red haired of both sexes are more libidinous and mischievous than the rest, whom yet they much exceed in strength and activity.

The *Houyhnhnms* keep the *Yahoos* for present use in huts not far from the house; but the rest are sent abroad to certain fields, where they dig up roots, eat several kinds of herbs, and search about for carrion, or sometimes catch weasels and *luhimuhs* (a sort of wild rat), which they greedily devour. Nature has taught them to dig deep holes with their nails on the side of a rising ground, wherein they lie by themselves; only the kennels of the females are larger, sufficient to hold two or three cubs.

They swim from their infancy like frogs, and are able to continue long under water, where they often take fish, which the females carry home to their young. And, upon this occasion, I hope the reader will pardon my relating an odd adventure.

Being one day abroad with my protector the sorrel nag, and the weather exceeding hot, I entreated him to let me bathe in a river that was near. He consented, and I immediately stripped myself stark naked, and went down softly into the stream. It happened that a young female *Yahoo*, standing behind a bank, saw the whole proceeding, and inflamed by desire, as the nag and I conjectured, came running with all speed, and leaped into the water, within five yards of the place where I bathed. I was never in my life so terribly frightened. The nag was grazing at some distance, not suspecting any harm. She embraced me after a most fulsome manner. I roared as loud as I could, and the nag came galloping towards me, whereupon she quitted her grasp, with the utmost reluctancy, and leaped upon the opposite bank, where she stood gazing and howling all the time I was putting on my clothes.

This was a matter of diversion to my master and his family, as well as of mortification to myself. For now I could no longer deny that I was a real *Yahoo* in every limb and feature, since the females had a natural propensity to me, as one of their own species. Neither was the hair of this brute of a red colour (which might have been some excuse for an appetite a little irregular), but black as a sloe, and her countenance did not make an appearance altogether so hideous as the rest of her kind; for I think she could not be above eleven years old.

Having lived three years in this country, the reader, I suppose, will expect that I should, like other travellers, give him some account of the manners and customs of its inhabitants, which it was indeed my principal study to learn.

As these noble *Houyhnhnms* are endowed by nature with a general disposition to all virtues, and have no conceptions or ideas of what is evil in a rational creature, so their grand maxim is, to cultivate reason, and to be wholly governed by it. Neither is reason among them a point problematical, as with us, where men can argue with plausibility on both sides of the question, but strikes you with immediate conviction; as it must needs do, where it is not mingled, obscured, or discoloured, by passion and interest. I remember it was with extreme difficulty that I could bring my master to understand the meaning of the word opinion, or how a point could be disputable; because reason taught us to affirm or deny only where we are certain; and beyond our knowledge we cannot do either. So that controversies, wranglings, disputes, and positiveness, in false or dubious propositions, are evils unknown among the *Houyhnhnms*. In the like manner, when I used to explain to him our several systems of natural philosophy, he would laugh, "that a creature pretending to reason, should value itself upon the knowledge of other people's conjectures, and in things where that knowledge, if it were certain, could be of no use." Wherein he agreed entirely with the sentiments of Socrates, as Plato delivers them; which I mention as the highest honour I can do that prince of philosophers. I have often since reflected, what destruction such doctrine would make in the libraries of Europe; and how many paths of fame would be then shut up in the learned world.

Friendship and benevolence are the two principal virtues among the *Houyhnhnms*; and these not confined to particular objects, but universal to the whole race; for a stranger from the remotest part is equally treated with the nearest neighbour, and wherever he goes, looks upon himself as at home. They preserve decency and civility in the highest degrees, but are altogether ignorant of ceremony. They have no fondness for their colts or foals, but the care they take in educating them proceeds entirely from the dictates of reason. And I observed my master to show the same affection to his neighbour's issue, that he had for his own. They will have it that nature teaches them to love the whole species, and it is reason only that makes a distinction of persons, where there is a superior degree of virtue.

When the matron *Houyhnhnms* have produced one of each sex, they no longer accompany with their consorts, except they lose one of their issue by some casualty, which very seldom happens; but in such a case they meet again; or when the like accident befalls a person whose wife is past bearing, some other couple bestow on him one of their own colts, and then go together again until the mother is pregnant. This caution is necessary, to prevent the country from being overburdened with numbers. But the race of inferior *Houyhnhnms*, bred up to be servants, is not so strictly limited upon this article: these are allowed to produce three of each sex, to be domestics in the noble families.

In their marriages, they are exactly careful to choose such colours as will not make any disagreeable mixture in the breed. Strength is chiefly valued in the male, and comeliness in the female; not upon the account of love, but to preserve the race from degenerating; for where a female happens to excel in strength, a consort is chosen, with regard to comeliness.

Courtship, love, presents, jointures, settlements have no place in their thoughts, or terms whereby to express them in their language. The young couple meet, and are joined, merely because it is the determination of their parents and friends; it is what they see done every day, and they look upon it as one of the necessary actions of a reasonable being. But the violation of marriage, or any other unchastity, was never heard of; and the married pair pass their lives with the same friendship and mutual benevolence, that they bear to all others of the same species who come in their way, without jealousy, fondness, quarrelling, or discontent.

In educating the youth of both sexes, their method is admirable, and highly deserves our imitation. These are not suffered to taste a grain of oats, except upon certain days, till eighteen years old; nor milk, but very rarely; and in summer they graze two hours in the morning, and as many in the evening, which their parents likewise observe; but the servants are not allowed above half that time, and a great part of their grass is brought home, which they eat at the most convenient hours, when they can be best spared from work.

Temperance, industry, exercise, and cleanliness, are the lessons equally enjoined to the young ones of both sexes: and my master thought it monstrous in us, to give the females a different kind of education from the males, except in some articles of domestic management; whereby, as he truly observed, one half of our natives were good for nothing but bringing children into the world; and to trust the care of our children to such useless animals, he said, was yet a greater instance of brutality.

But the *Houyhnhnms* train up their youth to strength, speed, and hardiness, by exercising them in running races up and down steep hills, and over hard stony grounds; and when they are all in a sweat, they are ordered to leap over head and ears into a pond or river. Four times a year the youth of a certain district meet to show their proficiency in running and leaping, and other feats of strength and agility; where the victor is rewarded with a song in his or her praise. On this festival, the servants drive a herd of *Yahoos* into the field, laden with hay, and oats, and milk, for a repast to the *Houyhnhnms*; after which, these brutes are immediately driven back again, for fear of being noisome to the assembly.

Every fourth year, at the vernal equinox, there is a representative council of the whole nation, which meets in a plain about twenty miles from our house, and continues about five or six days. Here they inquire into the state and condition of the several districts; whether they abound or be deficient in hay or oats, or cows, or *Yahoos*; and wherever there is any want (which is but seldom) it is immediately supplied by unanimous consent and contribution. Here likewise the regulation of children is settled: as for instance, if a *Houyhnhnm* has two males, he changes one of them with another that has two females; and when a child has been lost by any casualty, where the mother is past breeding, it is determined what family in the district shall breed another to supply the loss.

CHAPTER NINE

A grand debate at the general assembly of the Houyhnhnms, and how it was determined. The learning of the Houyhnhnms. Their buildings. Their manner of burials. The defectiveness of their language.

One of these grand assemblies was held in my time, about three months before my departure, whither my master went as the representative of our district. In this council was resumed their old debate, and indeed the only debate that ever happened in their country; whereof my master, after his return, give me a very particular account.

The question to be debated was, "whether the *Yahoos* should be exterminated from the face of the earth?" One of the members for the affirmative offered several arguments of great strength and weight, alleging, "that as the *Yahoos* were the most filthy, noisome, and deformed animals which nature ever produced, so they were the most restive and indocible, mischievous and malicious; they would privately suck the teats of the *Houyhnhnms'* cows, kill and devour their cats, trample down their oats and grass, if they were not continually watched, and commit a thousand other extravagancies." He took notice of a general tradition, "that *Yahoos* had not been always in their country; but that many ages ago, two of these brutes appeared together upon a mountain; whether produced by the heat of the sun upon corrupted mud and slime, or from the ooze and froth of the sea, was never known; that these *Yahoos* engendered, and their brood, in a short time, grew so numerous as to overrun and infest the whole nation; that the *Houyhnhnms*, to get rid of this evil, made a general hunting, and at last enclosed the whole herd; and destroying the elder, every *Houyhnhnm* kept two young ones in a kennel, and brought them to such a degree of tameness, as an animal, so savage by nature, can be capable of acquiring, using them for draught and carriage; that there seemed to be much truth in this tradition, and that those creatures could not be *yinhniamshy* (or *aborigines* of the land), because of the violent hatred the *Houyhnhnms*, as well as all other animals, bore them, which, although their evil disposition sufficiently deserved, could never have arrived at so high a degree if they had been *aborigines*, or else they would have long since been rooted out; that the inhabitants, taking a fancy to use the service of the *Yahoos*, had, very imprudently, neglected to cultivate the breed of asses, which are a comely animal, easily kept, more tame and orderly, without any offensive smell, strong enough for labour, although they yield to the other in agility of body, and if their braying be no agreeable sound, it is far preferable to the horrible howlings of the *Yahoos*."

Several others declared their sentiments to the same purpose, when my master proposed an expedient to the assembly, whereof he had indeed borrowed the hint from me. "He approved of the tradition mentioned by the honourable member who spoke before, and affirmed, that the two *Yahoos* said to be seen first among them, had been driven thither over the sea; that coming to land, and being forsaken by their companions, they retired to the mountains, and degenerating by degrees, became in process of time much more savage than those of their own species in the country whence these two originals came. The reason of this assertion was, that he had now in his possession a certain wonderful *Yahoo* (meaning myself) which most of them had heard of, and many of them had seen. He then related to them how he first found me; that my body was all covered with an artificial composure of the skins and hairs of other animals; that I spoke in a language of my own, and had thoroughly learned theirs; that I had related to him the accidents which brought me thither; that when he saw me without my covering, I was an exact *Yahoo* in every part, only of a whiter colour, less hairy, and with shorter claws. He added, how I had endeavoured to persuade him, that in my own and other countries, the *Yahoos* acted as the governing, rational animal, and held the *Houyhnhnms* in servitude; that he observed in me all the qualities of a *Yahoo*, only a little more civilized by some tincture of reason, which, however, was in a degree as far inferior to the *Houyhnhnm* race, as the *Yahoos* of their country were to me; that, among other things, I mentioned a custom we had of castrating *Houyhnhnms* when they were young, in order to render them tame; that the operation was easy and safe; that it was no shame to learn wisdom from brutes, as industry is taught by the ant, and building by the swallow (for so I translate the word *lyhannh*, although it be a much larger fowl); that this invention might be practised upon the younger *Yahoos* here, which besides rendering them tractable and fitter for use, would in an age put an end to the whole species, without destroying life; that in the mean time the *Houyhnhnms* should be exhorted to cultivate the breed of asses, which, as they are in all respects more valuable brutes, so they have this advantage, to be fit for service at five years old, which the others are not till twelve."

This was all my master thought fit to tell me, at that time, of what passed in the grand council. But he was pleased to conceal one particular, which related personally to myself, whereof I soon felt the unhappy effect, as the reader will know in its proper place, and whence I date all the succeeding misfortunes of my life.

The *Houyhnhnms* have no letters, and consequently their knowledge is all traditional. But there happening few events of any moment among a people so well united, naturally disposed to every virtue, wholly governed by reason, and cut off from all commerce with other nations, the historical part is easily preserved without burdening their memories. I have already observed that they are subject to no diseases, and therefore can have no need of physicians. However, they have excellent medicines, composed of herbs, to cure accidental bruises and cuts in the pastern or frog of the foot, by sharp stones, as well as other maims and hurts in the several parts of the body.

They calculate the year by the revolution of the sun and moon, but use no subdivisions into weeks. They are well enough acquainted with the motions of those two luminaries, and understand the nature of eclipses; and this is the utmost progress of their astronomy.

In poetry, they must be allowed to excel all other mortals; wherein the justness of their similes, and the minuteness as well as exactness of their descriptions, are indeed inimitable. Their verses abound very much in both of these, and usually contain either some exalted notions of friendship and benevolence or the praises of those who were victors in races and other bodily exercises. Their buildings, although very rude and simple, are not inconvenient, but well contrived to defend them from all injuries of cold and heat. They have a kind of tree, which at forty years old loosens in the root, and falls with the first storm: it grows very straight, and being pointed like stakes with a sharp stone (for the *Houyhnhnms* know not the use of iron), they stick them erect in the ground, about ten inches asunder, and then weave in oat straw, or sometimes wattles, between them. The roof is made after the same manner, and so are the doors.

The *Houyhnhnms* use the hollow part, between the pastern and the hoof of their fore-foot, as we do our hands, and this with greater dexterity than I could at first imagine. I have seen a white mare of our family thread a needle (which I lent her on purpose) with that joint. They milk their cows, reap their oats, and do all the work which requires hands, in the same manner. They have a kind of hard flints, which, by grinding against other stones, they form into instruments, that serve instead of wedges, axes, and hammers. With tools made of these flints, they likewise cut their hay, and reap their oats, which there grow naturally in several fields; the *Yahoos* draw home the sheaves in carriages, and the servants tread them in certain covered huts to get out the grain, which is kept in stores. They make a rude kind of earthen and wooden vessels, and bake the former in the sun.

If they can avoid casualties, they die only of old age, and are buried in the obscurest places that can be found, their friends and relations expressing neither joy nor grief at their departure; nor does the dying person discover the least regret that he is leaving the world, any more than if he were upon returning home from a visit to one of his neighbours. I remember my master having once made an appointment with a friend and his family to come to his house, upon some affair of importance: on the day fixed, the mistress and her two children came very late; she made two excuses, first for her husband, who, as she said, happened that very morning to *shnuwnh*. The word is strongly expressive in their language, but not easily rendered into English; it signifies, "to retire to his first mother." Her excuse for not coming sooner, was, that her husband dying late in the morning, she was a good while consulting her servants about a convenient place where his body should be laid; and I observed, she behaved herself at our house as cheerfully as the rest. She died about three months after.

They live generally to seventy, or seventy-five years, very seldom to fourscore. Some weeks before their death, they feel a gradual decay; but without pain. During this time they are much visited by their friends, because they cannot go abroad with their usual ease and satisfaction. However, about ten days before their death, which they seldom fail in computing, they return the visits that have been made them by those who are nearest in the neighbourhood, being carried in a convenient sledge drawn by *Yahoos*; which vehicle they use, not only upon this occasion, but when they grow old, upon long journeys, or when they are lamed by any accident: and therefore when the dying *Houyhnhnms* return those visits, they take a solemn leave of their friends, as if they were going to some remote part of the country, where they designed to pass the rest of their lives.

I know not whether it may be worth observing, that the *Houyhnhnms* have no word in their language to express any thing that is evil, except what they borrow from the deformities or ill qualities of the *Yahoos*. Thus they denote the folly of a servant, an omission of a child, a stone that cuts their feet, a continuance of foul or unseasonable weather, and the like, by adding to each the epithet of *Yahoo*. For instance, *hhnm Yahoo*; *whnaholm Yahoo*, *ynlhmndwihlma Yahoo*, and an ill-contrived house *ynholmhnmrohlnw Yahoo*.

I could, with great pleasure, enlarge further upon the manners and virtues of this excellent people; but intending in a short time to publish a volume by itself, expressly upon that subject, I refer the reader thither; and, in the mean time, proceed to relate my own sad catastrophe.

CHAPTER TEN

The author's economy, and happy life, among the Houyhnhnms. His great improvement in virtue by conversing with them. Their conversations. The author has notice given him by his master, that he must depart from the country. He falls into a swoon for grief; but submits. He contrives and finishes a canoe by the help of a fellow-servant, and puts to sea at a venture.

I HAD SETTLED my little economy to my own heart's content. My master had ordered a room to be made for me, after their manner, about six yards from the house: the sides and floors of which I plastered with clay, and covered with rush-mats of my own contriving. I had beaten hemp, which there grows wild, and made of it a sort of ticking; this I filled with the feathers of several birds I had taken with springes made of *Yahoos'* hairs, and were excellent food. I had worked two chairs with my knife, the sorrel nag helping me in the grosser and more laborious part. When my clothes were worn to rags, I made myself others with the skins of rabbits, and of a certain beautiful animal, about the same size, called *nnuhnoh*, the skin of which is covered with a fine down. Of these I also made very tolerable stockings. I soled my shoes with wood, which I cut from a tree, and fitted to the upper-leather; and when this was worn out, I supplied it with the skins of *Yahoos* dried in the sun. I often got honey out of hollow trees, which I mingled with water, or ate with my bread. No man could more verify the truth of these two maxims, "That nature is very easily satisfied;" and, "That necessity is the mother of invention." I enjoyed perfect health of body, and tranquillity of mind; I did not feel the treachery or inconstancy of a friend, nor the injuries of a secret or open enemy. I had no occasion of bribing, flattering, or pimping, to procure the favour of any great man, or of his minion; I wanted no fence against fraud or oppression: here was neither physician to destroy my body, nor lawyer to ruin my fortune; no informer to watch my words and actions, or forge accusations against me for hire: here were no gibers, censurers, backbiters, pickpockets, highwaymen, housebreakers, attorneys, bawds, buffoons, gamesters, politicians, wits, splenetics, tedious talkers, controvertists, ravishers, murderers, robbers, virtuosos; no leaders, or followers, of party and faction; no encouragers to vice, by seducement or examples; no dungeon, axes, gibbets, whipping-posts, or pillories; no cheating shopkeepers or mechanics; no pride, vanity, or affectation; no fops, bullies, drunkards, strolling whores, or poxes; no ranting, lewd, expensive wives; no stupid, proud pedants; no importunate, overbearing, quarrelsome, noisy, roaring, empty, conceited, swearing companions; no scoundrels raised from the dust upon the merit of their vices, or nobility thrown into it on account of their virtues; no lords, fiddlers, judges, or dancing-masters.

I had the favour of being admitted to several *Houyhnhnms*, who came to visit or dine with my master; where his honour graciously suffered me to wait in the room, and listen to their discourse. Both he and his company would often descend to ask me questions, and receive my answers. I had also sometimes the honour of attending my master in his visits to others. I never presumed to speak, except in answer to a question; and then I did it with inward regret, because it was a loss of so much time for improving myself; but I was infinitely delighted with the station of an humble auditor in such conversations, where nothing passed but what was useful, expressed in the fewest and most significant words; where, as I have already said, the greatest decency was observed, without the least degree of ceremony; where no person spoke without being pleased himself, and pleasing his companions; where there was no interruption, tediousness, heat, or difference of sentiments. They have a notion, that when people are met together, a short silence does much improve conversation: this I found to be true; for during those little intermissions of talk, new ideas would arise in their minds, which very much enlivened the discourse. Their subjects are, generally on friendship and benevolence, on order and economy; sometimes upon the visible operations of nature, or ancient traditions; upon the bounds and limits of virtue; upon the unerring rules of reason, or upon some determinations to be taken at the next great assembly: and often upon the various excellences of poetry. I may add, without vanity, that my presence often gave them sufficient matter for discourse, because it afforded my master an occasion of letting his friends into the history of me and my country, upon which they were all pleased to descant, in a manner not very advantageous to humankind: and for that reason I shall not repeat what they said; only I may be allowed to observe, that his honour, to my great admiration, appeared to understand the nature of *Yahoos* much better than myself. He went through all our vices and follies, and discovered many, which I had never mentioned to him, by only supposing what qualities a *Yahoo* of their country, with a small proportion of reason, might be capable of exerting; and concluded, with too much probability, "how vile, as well as miserable, such a creature must be."

I freely confess, that all the little knowledge I have of any value, was acquired by the lectures I received from my master, and from hearing the discourses of him and his friends; to which I should be prouder to listen, than to dictate to the greatest and wisest assembly in Europe. I admired the strength, comeliness, and speed of the inhabitants; and such a constellation of virtues, in such amiable persons, produced in me the highest veneration. At first, indeed, I did not feel that natural awe, which the *Yahoos* and all other animals bear toward them; but it grew upon me by decrees, much sooner than I imagined, and was mingled with a respectful love and gratitude, that they would condescend to distinguish me from the rest of my species.

When I thought of my family, my friends, my countrymen, or the human race in general, I considered them, as they really were, *Yahoos* in shape and disposition, perhaps a little more civilized, and qualified with the gift of speech; but making no other use of reason, than to improve and multiply those vices whereof their brethren in this country had only the share that nature allotted them. When I happened to behold the reflection of my own form in a lake or fountain, I turned away my face in horror and detestation of myself, and could better endure the sight of a common *Yahoo* than of my own person. By conversing with the *Houyhnhnms*, and looking upon them with delight, I fell to imitate their gait and gesture, which is now grown into a habit; and my friends often tell me, in a blunt way, "that I trot like a horse;" which, however, I take for a great compliment. Neither shall I disown, that in speaking I am apt to fall into the voice and manner of the *Houyhnhnms*, and hear myself ridiculed on that account, without the least mortification.

In the midst of all this happiness, and when I looked upon myself to be fully settled for life, my master sent for me one morning a little earlier than his usual hour. I observed by his countenance that he was in some perplexity, and at a loss how to begin what he had to speak. After a short silence, he told me, "he did not know how I would take what he was going to say: that in the last general assembly, when the affair of the *Yahoos* was entered upon, the representatives had taken offence at his keeping a *Yahoo* (meaning myself) in his family, more like a *Houyhnhnm* than a brute animal; that he was known frequently to converse with me, as if he could receive some advantage or pleasure in my company; that such a practice was not agreeable to reason or nature, or a thing ever heard of before among them; the assembly did therefore exhort him either to employ me like the rest of my species, or command me to swim back to the place whence I came: that the first of these expedients was utterly rejected by all the *Houyhnhnms* who had ever seen me at his house or their own; for they alleged, that because I had some rudiments of reason, added to the natural pravity of those animals, it was to be feared I might be able to seduce them into the woody and mountainous parts of the country, and bring them in troops by night to destroy the *Houyhnhnms'* cattle, as being naturally of the ravenous kind, and averse from labour."

My master added, "that he was daily pressed by the *Houyhnhnms* of the neighbourhood to have the assembly's exhortation executed, which he could not put off much longer. He doubted it would be impossible for me to swim to another country; and therefore wished I would contrive some sort of vehicle, resembling those I had described to him, that might carry me on the sea; in which work I should have the assistance of his own servants, as well as those of his neighbours." He concluded, "that for his own part, he could have been content to keep me in his service as long as I lived; because he found I had cured myself of some bad habits and dispositions, by endeavouring, as far as my inferior nature was capable, to imitate the *Houyhnhnms*."

I should here observe to the reader, that a decree of the general assembly in this country is expressed by the word *hnhloayn*, which signifies an exhortation, as near as I can render it; for they have no conception how a rational creature can be compelled, but only advised, or exhorted; because no person can disobey reason, without giving up his claim to be a rational creature.

I was struck with the utmost grief and despair at my master's discourse; and being unable to support the agonies I was under, I fell into a swoon at his feet. When I came to myself, he told me "that he concluded I had been dead;" for these people are subject to no such imbecilities of nature. I answered in a faint voice, "that death would have been too great a happiness; that although I could not blame the assembly's exhortation, or the urgency of his friends; yet, in my weak and corrupt judgment, I thought it might consist with reason to have been less rigorous; that I could not swim a league, and probably the nearest land to theirs might be distant above a hundred: that many materials, necessary for making a small vessel to carry me off, were wholly wanting in this country; which, however, I would attempt, in obedience and gratitude to his honour, although I concluded the thing to be impossible, and therefore looked on myself as already devoted to destruction; that the certain prospect of an unnatural death was the least of my evils; for, supposing I should escape with life by some strange adventure, how could I think with temper of passing my days among *Yahoos*, and relapsing into my old corruptions, for want of examples to lead and keep me within the paths of virtue? that I knew too well upon what solid reasons all the determinations of the wise *Houyhnhnms* were founded, not to be shaken by arguments of mine, a miserable *Yahoo*; and therefore, after presenting him with my humble thanks for the offer of his servants' assistance in making a vessel, and desiring a reasonable time for so difficult a work, I told him I would endeavour to preserve a wretched being; and if ever I returned to England, was not without hopes of being useful to my own species, by celebrating the praises of the renowned *Houyhnhnms*, and proposing their virtues to the imitation of mankind."

My master, in a few words, made me a very gracious reply; allowed me the space of two months to finish my boat; and ordered the sorrel nag, my fellow-servant (for so, at this distance, I may presume to call him), to follow my instruction; because I told my master, "that his help would be sufficient, and I knew he had a tenderness for me."

In his company, my first business was to go to that part of the coast where my rebellious crew had ordered me to be set on shore. I got upon a height, and looking on every side into the sea; fancied I saw a small island toward the north-east. I took out my pocket glass, and could then clearly distinguish it above five leagues off, as I computed; but it appeared to the sorrel nag to be only a blue cloud: for as he had no conception of any country beside his own, so he could not be as expert in distinguishing remote objects at sea, as we who so much converse in that element.

After I had discovered this island, I considered no further; but resolved it should if possible, be the first place of my banishment, leaving the consequence to fortune.

I returned home, and consulting with the sorrel nag, we went into a copse at some distance, where I with my knife, and he with a sharp flint, fastened very artificially after their manner, to a wooden handle, cut down several oak wattles, about the thickness of a walking-staff, and some larger pieces. But I shall not trouble the reader with a particular description of my own mechanics; let it suffice to say, that in six weeks time with the help of the sorrel nag, who performed the parts that required most labour, I finished a sort of Indian canoe, but much larger, covering it with the skins of *Yahoos*, well stitched together with hempen threads of my own making. My sail was likewise composed of the skins of the same animal; but I made use of the youngest I could get, the older being too tough and thick; and I likewise provided myself with four paddles. I laid in a stock of boiled flesh, of rabbits and fowls, and took with me two vessels, one filled with milk and the other with water.

I tried my canoe in a large pond, near my master's house, and then corrected in it what was amiss; stopping all the chinks with *Yahoos'* tallow, till I found it staunch, and able to bear me and my freight; and, when it was as complete as I could possibly make it, I had it drawn on a carriage very gently by *Yahoos* to the sea-side, under the conduct of the sorrel nag and another servant.

When all was ready, and the day came for my departure, I took leave of my master and lady and the whole family, my eyes flowing with tears, and my heart quite sunk with grief. But his honour, out of curiosity, and, perhaps, (if I may speak without vanity,) partly out of kindness, was determined to see me in my canoe, and got several of his neighbouring friends to accompany him. I was forced to wait above an hour for the tide; and then observing the wind very fortunately bearing toward the island to which I intended to steer my course, I took a second leave of my master: but as I was going to prostrate myself to kiss his hoof, he did me the honour to raise it gently to my mouth. I am not ignorant how much I have been censured for mentioning this last particular. Detractors are pleased to think it improbable, that so illustrious a person should descend to give so great a mark of distinction to a creature so inferior as I. Neither have I forgotten how apt some travellers are to boast of extraordinary favours they have received. But, if these censurers were better acquainted with the noble and courteous disposition of the *Houyhnhnms*, they would soon change their opinion.

I paid my respects to the rest of the *Houyhnhnms* in his honour's company; then getting into my canoe, I pushed off from shore.

CHAPTER ELEVEN

The author's dangerous voyage. He arrives at New Holland, hoping to settle there. Is wounded with an arrow by one of the natives. Is seized and carried by force into a Portuguese ship. The great civilities of the captain. The author arrives at England.

I BEGAN THIS desperate voyage on February 15, 1714–15, at nine o'clock in the morning. The wind was very favourable; however, I made use at first only of my paddles; but considering I should soon be weary, and that the wind might chop about, I ventured to set up my little sail; and thus, with the help of the tide, I went at the rate of a league and a half an hour, as near as I could guess. My master and his friends continued on the shore till I was almost out of sight; and I often heard the sorrel nag (who always loved me) crying out, "*Hnuy illa nyha, majah Yahoo*;" "Take care of thyself, gentle *Yahoo*."

My design was, if possible, to discover some small island uninhabited, yet sufficient, by my labour, to furnish me with the necessaries of life, which I would have thought a greater happiness, than to be first minister in the politest court of Europe; so horrible was the idea I conceived of returning to live in the society, and under the government of *Yahoos*. For in such a solitude as I desired, I could at least enjoy my own thoughts, and reflect with delight on the virtues of those inimitable *Houyhnhnms*, without an opportunity of degenerating into the vices and corruptions of my own species.

The reader may remember what I related, when my crew conspired against me, and confined me to my cabin; how I continued there several weeks without knowing what course we took; and when I was put ashore in the long-boat, how the sailors told me, with oaths, whether true or false, "that they knew not in what part of the world we were." However, I did then believe us to be about 10 degrees southward of the Cape of Good Hope, or about 45 degrees southern latitude, as I gathered from some general words I overheard among them, being I supposed to the south-east in their intended voyage to Madagascar. And although this were little better than conjecture, yet I resolved to steer my course eastward, hoping to reach the south-west coast of New Holland, and perhaps some such island as I desired lying westward of it. The wind was full west, and by six in the evening I computed I had gone eastward at least eighteen leagues; when I spied a very small island about half a league off, which I soon reached. It was nothing but a rock, with one creek naturally arched by the force of tempests. Here I put in my canoe, and climbing a part of the rock, I could plainly discover land to the east, extending from south to north. I lay all night in my canoe; and repeating my voyage early in the morning, I arrived in seven hours to the south-east point of New Holland. This confirmed me in the opinion I have long entertained, that the maps and charts place this country at least three degrees more to the east than it really is; which thought I communicated many years ago to my worthy friend, Mr. Herman Moll, and gave him my reasons for it, although he has rather chosen to follow other authors.

I saw no inhabitants in the place where I landed, and being unarmed, I was afraid of venturing far into the country. I found some shellfish on the shore, and ate them raw, not daring to kindle a fire, for fear of being discovered by the natives. I continued three days feeding on oysters and limpets, to save my own provisions; and I fortunately found a brook of excellent water, which gave me great relief.

On the fourth day, venturing out early a little too far, I saw twenty or thirty natives upon a height not above five hundred yards from me. They were stark naked, men, women, and children, round a fire, as I could discover by the smoke. One of them spied me, and gave notice to the rest; five of them advanced toward me, leaving the women and children at the fire. I made what haste I could to the shore, and, getting into my canoe, shoved off: the savages, observing me retreat, ran after me: and before I could get far enough into the sea, discharged an arrow which wounded me deeply on the inside of my left knee: I shall carry the mark to my grave. I apprehended the arrow might be poisoned, and paddling out of the reach of their darts (being a calm day), I made a shift to suck the wound, and dress it as well as I could.

I was at a loss what to do, for I durst not return to the same landing-place, but stood to the north, and was forced to paddle, for the wind, though very gentle, was against me, blowing north-west. As I was looking about for a secure landing-place, I saw a sail to the north-north-east, which appearing every minute more visible, I was in some doubt whether I should wait for them or not; but at last my detestation of the *Yahoo* race prevailed: and turning my canoe, I sailed and paddled together to the south, and got into the same creek whence I set out in the morning, choosing rather to trust myself among these barbarians, than live with European *Yahoos*. I drew up my canoe as close as I could to the shore, and hid myself behind a stone by the little brook, which, as I have already said, was excellent water.

The ship came within half a league of this creek, and sent her long boat with vessels to take in fresh water (for the place, it seems, was very well known); but I did not observe it, till the boat was almost on shore; and it was too late to seek another hiding-place. The seamen at their landing observed my canoe, and rummaging it all over, easily conjectured that the owner could not be far off. Four of them, well armed, searched every cranny and lurking-hole, till at last they found me flat on my face behind the stone. They gazed awhile in admiration at my strange uncouth dress; my coat made of skins, my wooden-soled shoes, and my furred stockings; whence, however, they concluded, I was not a native of the place, who all go naked. One of the seamen, in Portuguese, bid me rise, and asked who I was. I understood that language very well, and getting upon my feet, said, "I was a poor *Yahoo* banished from the *Houyhnhnms*, and desired they would please to let me depart." They admired to hear me answer them in their own tongue, and saw by my complexion I must be a European; but were at a loss to know what I meant by *Yahoos* and *Houyhnhnms*; and at the same time fell a-laughing at my strange tone in speaking, which resembled the neighing of a horse. I trembled all the while betwixt fear and hatred. I again desired leave to depart, and was gently moving to my canoe; but they laid hold of me, desiring to know, "what country I was of? whence I came?" with many other questions. I told them "I was born in England, whence I came about five years ago, and then their country and ours were at peace. I therefore hoped they would not treat me as an enemy, since I meant them no harm, but was a poor *Yahoo* seeking some desolate place where to pass the remainder of his unfortunate life."

When they began to talk, I thought I never heard or saw any thing more unnatural; for it appeared to me as monstrous as if a dog or a cow should speak in England, or a *Yahoo* in *Houyhnhnmland*. The honest Portuguese were equally amazed at my strange dress, and the odd manner of delivering my words, which, however, they understood very well. They spoke to me with great humanity, and said, "they were sure the captain would carry me *gratis* to Lisbon, whence I might return to my own country; that two of the seamen would go back to the ship, inform the captain of what they had seen, and receive his orders; in the mean time, unless I would give my solemn oath not to fly, they would secure me by force. I thought it best to comply with their proposal. They were very curious to know my story, but I gave them very little satisfaction, and they all conjectured that my misfortunes had impaired my reason. In two hours the boat, which went laden with vessels of water, returned, with the captain's command to fetch me on board. I fell on my knees to preserve my liberty; but all was in vain; and the men, having tied me with cords, heaved me into the boat, whence I was taken into the ship, and thence into the captain's cabin.

His name was Pedro de Mendez; he was a very courteous and generous person. He entreated me to give some account of myself, and desired to know what I would eat or drink; said, "I should be used as well as himself;" and spoke so many obliging things, that I wondered to find such civilities from a *Yahoo*. However, I remained silent and sullen; I was ready to faint at the very smell of him and his men. At last I desired something to eat out of my own canoe; but he ordered me a chicken, and some excellent wine, and then directed that I should be put to bed in a very clean cabin. I would not undress myself, but lay on the bed-clothes, and in half an hour stole out, when I thought the crew was at dinner, and getting to the side of the ship, was going to leap into the sea, and swim for my life, rather than continue among *Yahoos*. But one of the seamen prevented me, and having informed the captain, I was chained to my cabin.

After dinner, Don Pedro came to me, and desired to know my reason for so desperate an attempt; assured me, "he only meant to do me all the service he was able;" and spoke so very movingly, that at last I descended to treat him like an animal which had some little portion of reason. I gave him a very short relation of my voyage; of the conspiracy against me by my own men; of the country where they set me on shore, and of my five years residence there. All which he looked upon as if it were a dream or a vision; whereat I took great offence; for I had quite forgot the faculty of lying, so peculiar to *Yahoos*, in all countries where they preside, and, consequently, their disposition of suspecting truth in others of their own species. I asked him, "whether it were the custom in his country to say the thing which was not?" I assured him, "I had almost forgot what he meant by falsehood, and if I had lived a thousand years in *Houyhnhnmland*, I should never have heard a lie from the meanest servant; that I was altogether indifferent whether he believed me or not; but, however, in return for his favours, I would give so much allowance to the corruption of his nature, as to answer any objection he would please to make, and then he might easily discover the truth."

The captain, a wise man, after many endeavours to catch me tripping in some part of my story, at last began to have a better opinion of my veracity. But he added, "that since I professed so inviolable an attachment to truth, I must give him my word and honour to bear him company in this voyage, without attempting any thing against my life; or else he would continue me a prisoner till we arrived at Lisbon." I gave him the promise he required; but at the same time protested, "that I would suffer the greatest hardships, rather than return to live among *Yahoos*."

Our voyage passed without any considerable accident. In gratitude to the captain, I sometimes sat with him, at his earnest request, and strove to conceal my antipathy against human kind, although it often broke out; which he suffered to pass without observation. But the greatest part of the day I confined myself to my cabin, to avoid seeing any of the crew. The captain had often entreated me to strip myself of my savage dress, and offered to lend me the best suit of clothes he had. This I would not be prevailed on to accept, abhorring to cover myself with any thing that had been on the back of a *Yahoo*. I only desired he would lend me two clean shirts, which, having been washed since he wore them, I believed would not so much defile me. These I changed every second day, and washed them myself.

We arrived at Lisbon, Nov. 5, 1715. At our landing, the captain forced me to cover myself with his cloak, to prevent the rabble from crowding about me. I was conveyed to his own house; and at my earnest request he led me up to the highest room backwards. I conjured him "to conceal from all persons what I had told him of the *Houyhnhnms*; because the least hint of such a story would not only draw numbers of people to see me, but probably put me in danger of being imprisoned, or burnt by the Inquisition." The captain persuaded me to accept a suit of clothes newly made; but I would not suffer the tailor to take my measure; however, Don Pedro being almost of my size, they fitted me well enough. He accoutred me with other necessaries, all new, which I aired for twenty-four hours before I would use them.

The captain had no wife, nor above three servants, none of which were suffered to attend at meals; and his whole deportment was so obliging, added to very good human understanding, that I really began to tolerate his company. He gained so far upon me, that I ventured to look out of the back window. By degrees I was brought into another room, whence I peeped into the street, but drew my head back in a fright. In a week's time he seduced me down to the door. I found my terror gradually lessened, but my hatred and contempt seemed to increase. I was at last bold enough to walk the street in his company, but kept my nose well stopped with rue, or sometimes with tobacco.

In ten days, Don Pedro, to whom I had given some account of my domestic affairs, put it upon me, as a matter of honour and conscience, "that I ought to return to my native country, and live at home with my wife and children." He told me, "there was an English ship in the port just ready to sail, and he would furnish me with all things necessary."

It would be tedious to repeat his arguments, and my contradictions. He said, "it was altogether impossible to find such a solitary island as I desired to live in; but I might command in my own house, and pass my time in a manner as recluse as I pleased."

I complied at last, finding I could not do better. I left Lisbon the 24th day of November, in an English merchantman, but who was the master I never inquired. Don Pedro accompanied me to the ship, and lent me twenty pounds. He took kind leave of me, and embraced me at parting, which I bore as well as I could. During this last voyage I had no commerce with the master or any of his men; but, pretending I was sick, kept close in my cabin. On the fifth of December, 1715, we cast anchor in the Downs, about nine in the morning, and at three in the afternoon I got safe to my house at Rotherhith.[7]

My wife and family received me with great surprise and joy, because they concluded me certainly dead; but I must freely confess the sight of them filled me only with hatred, disgust, and contempt; and the more, by reflecting on the near alliance I had to them. For although, since my unfortunate exile from the *Houyhnhnm* country, I had compelled myself to tolerate the sight of *Yahoos*, and to converse with Don Pedro de Mendez, yet my memory and imagination were perpetually filled with the virtues and ideas of those exalted *Houyhnhnms*. And when I began to consider that, by copulating with one of the *Yahoo* species I had become a parent of more, it struck me with the utmost shame, confusion, and horror.

As soon as I entered the house, my wife took me in her arms, and kissed me; at which, having not been used to the touch of that odious animal for so many years, I fell into a swoon for almost an hour. At the time I am writing, it is five years since my last return to England. During the first year, I could not endure my wife or children in my presence; the very smell of them was intolerable; much less could I suffer them to eat in the same room. To this hour they dare not presume to touch my bread, or drink out of the same cup, neither was I ever able to let one of them take me by the hand. The first money I laid out was to buy two young stone-horses, which I keep in a good stable; and next to them, the groom is my greatest favourite, for I feel my spirits revived by the smell he contracts in the stable. My horses understand me tolerably well; I converse with them at least four hours every day. They are strangers to bridle or saddle; they live in great amity with me and friendship to each other.

7 The original editions and Hawksworth's have Rotherhith here, though earlier in the work, Redriff is said to have been Gulliver's home in England.

CHAPTER TWELVE

The author's veracity. His design in publishing this work. His censure of those travellers who swerve from the truth. The author clears himself from any sinister ends in writing. An objection answered. The method of planting colonies. His native country commended. The right of the crown to those countries described by the author is justified. The difficulty of conquering them. The author takes his last leave of the reader; proposes his manner of living for the future; gives good advice, and concludes.

THUS, gentle reader, I have given thee a faithful history of my travels for sixteen years and above seven months: wherein I have not been so studious of ornament as of truth. I could, perhaps, like others, have astonished thee with strange improbable tales; but I rather chose to relate plain matter of fact, in the simplest manner and style; because my principal design was to inform, and not to amuse thee.

It is easy for us who travel into remote countries, which are seldom visited by Englishmen or other Europeans, to form descriptions of wonderful animals both at sea and land. Whereas a traveller's chief aim should be to make men wiser and better, and to improve their minds by the bad, as well as good, example of what they deliver concerning foreign places.

I could heartily wish a law was enacted, that every traveller, before he were permitted to publish his voyages, should be obliged to make oath before the Lord High Chancellor, that all he intended to print was absolutely true to the best of his knowledge; for then the world would no longer be deceived, as it usually is, while some writers, to make their works pass the better upon the public, impose the grossest falsities on the unwary reader. I have perused several books of travels with great delight in my younger days; but having since gone over most parts of the globe, and been able to contradict many fabulous accounts from my own observation, it has given me a great disgust against this part of reading, and some indignation to see the credulity of mankind so impudently abused. Therefore, since my acquaintance were pleased to think my poor endeavours might not be unacceptable to my country, I imposed on myself, as a maxim never to be swerved from, that I would strictly adhere to truth; neither indeed can I be ever under the least temptation to vary from it, while I retain in my mind the lectures and example of my noble master and the other illustrious *Houyhnhnms* of whom I had so long the honour to be an humble hearer.

– Nec si miserum Fortuna Sinonem
Finxit, vanum etiam, mendacemque improba finget.

I know very well, how little reputation is to be got by writings which require neither genius nor learning, nor indeed any other talent, except a good memory, or an exact journal. I know likewise, that writers of travels, like dictionary-makers, are sunk into oblivion by the weight and bulk of those who come last, and therefore lie uppermost. And it is highly probable, that such travellers, who shall hereafter visit the countries described in this work of mine, may, by detecting my errors (if there be any), and adding many new discoveries of their own, justle me out of vogue, and stand in my place, making the world forget that ever I was an author. This indeed would be too great a mortification, if I wrote for fame: but as my sole intention was the public good, I cannot be altogether disappointed. For who can read of the virtues I have mentioned in the glorious *Houyhnhnms*, without being ashamed of his own vices, when he considers himself as the reasoning, governing animal of his country? I shall say nothing of those remote nations where *Yahoos* preside; among which the least corrupted are the *Brobdingnagians*; whose wise maxims in morality and government it would be our happiness to observe. But I forbear descanting further, and rather leave the judicious reader to his own remarks and application.

I am not a little pleased that this work of mine can possibly meet with no censurers: for what objections can be made against a writer, who relates only plain facts, that happened in such distant countries, where we have not the least interest, with respect either to trade or negotiations? I have carefully avoided every fault with which common writers of travels are often too justly charged. Besides, I meddle not the least with any party, but write without passion, prejudice, or ill-will against any man, or number of men, whatsoever. I write for the noblest end, to inform and instruct mankind; over whom I may, without breach of modesty, pretend to some superiority, from the advantages I received by conversing so long among the most accomplished *Houyhnhnms*. I write without any view to profit or praise. I never suffer a word to pass that may look like reflection, or possibly give the least offence, even to those who are most ready to take it. So that I hope I may with justice pronounce myself an author perfectly blameless; against whom the tribes of Answerers, Considerers, Observers, Reflectors, Detectors, Remarkers, will never be able to find matter for exercising their talents.

I confess, it was whispered to me, "that I was bound in duty, as a subject of England, to have given in a memorial to a secretary of state at my first coming over; because, whatever lands are discovered by a subject belong to the crown." But I doubt whether our conquests in the countries I treat of would be as easy as those of Ferdinando Cortez over the naked Americans. The *Lilliputians*, I think, are hardly worth the charge of a fleet and army to reduce them; and I question whether it might be prudent or safe to attempt the *Brobdingnagians*; or whether an English army would be much at their ease with the Flying Island over their heads. The *Houyhnhnms* indeed appear not to be so well prepared for war, a science to which they are perfect strangers, and especially against missive weapons. However, supposing myself to be a minister of state, I could never give my advice for invading them. Their prudence, unanimity, unacquaintedness with fear, and their love of their country, would amply supply all defects in the military art. Imagine twenty thousand of them breaking into the midst of an European army, confounding the ranks, overturning the carriages, battering the warriors' faces into mummy by terrible yerks from their hinder hoofs; for they would well deserve the character given to Augustus, *Recalcitrat undique tutus*. But, instead of proposals for conquering that magnanimous nation, I rather wish they were in a capacity, or disposition, to send a sufficient number of their inhabitants for civilizing Europe, by teaching us the first principles of honour, justice, truth, temperance, public spirit, fortitude, chastity, friendship, benevolence, and fidelity. The names of all which virtues are still retained among us in most languages, and are to be met with in modern, as well as ancient authors; which I am able to assert from my own small reading.

But I had another reason, which made me less forward to enlarge his majesty's dominions by my discoveries. To say the truth, I had conceived a few scruples with relation to the distributive justice of princes upon those occasions. For instance, a crew of pirates are driven by a storm they know not whither; at length a boy discovers land from the topmast; they go on shore to rob and plunder, they see a harmless people, are entertained with kindness; they give the country a new name; they take formal possession of it for their king; they set up a rotten plank, or a stone, for a memorial; they murder two or three dozen of the natives, bring away a couple more, by force, for a sample; return home, and get their pardon. Here commences a new dominion acquired with a title by divine right. Ships are sent with the first opportunity; the natives driven out or destroyed; their princes tortured to discover their gold; a free license given to all acts of inhumanity and lust, the earth reeking with the blood of its inhabitants: and this execrable crew of butchers, employed in so pious an expedition, is a modern colony, sent to convert and civilize an idolatrous and barbarous people!

But this description, I confess, does by no means affect the British nation, who may be an example to the whole world for their wisdom, care, and justice in planting colonies; their liberal endowments for the advancement of religion and learning; their choice of devout and able pastors to propagate Christianity; their caution in stocking their provinces with people of sober lives and conversations from this the mother kingdom; their strict regard to the distribution of justice, in supplying the civil administration through all their colonies with officers of the greatest abilities, utter strangers to corruption; and, to crown all, by sending the most vigilant and virtuous governors, who have no other views than the happiness of the people over whom they preside, and the honour of the king their master.

But as those countries which I have described do not appear to have any desire of being conquered and enslaved, murdered or driven out by colonies, nor abound either in gold, silver, sugar, or tobacco, I did humbly conceive, they were by no means proper objects of our zeal, our valour, or our interest. However, if those whom it more concerns think fit to be of another opinion, I am ready to depose, when I shall be lawfully called, that no European did ever visit those countries before me. I mean, if the inhabitants ought to be believed, unless a dispute may arise concerning the two *Yahoos*, said to have been seen many years ago upon a mountain in *Houyhnhnmland*.

But, as to the formality of taking possession in my sovereign's name, it never came once into my thoughts; and if it had, yet, as my affairs then stood, I should perhaps, in point of prudence and self-preservation, have put it off to a better opportunity.

Having thus answered the only objection that can ever be raised against me as a traveller, I here take a final leave of all my courteous readers, and return to enjoy my own speculations in my little garden at Redriff; to apply those excellent lessons of virtue which I learned among the *Houyhnhnms*; to instruct the *Yahoos* of my own family, is far as I shall find them docible animals; to behold my figure often in a glass, and thus, if possible, habituate myself by time to tolerate the sight of a human creature; to lament the brutality to *Houyhnhnms* in my own country, but always treat their persons with respect, for the sake of my noble master, his family, his friends, and the whole *Houyhnhnm* race, whom these of ours have the honour to resemble in all their lineaments, however their intellectuals came to degenerate.

I began last week to permit my wife to sit at dinner with me, at the farthest end of a long table; and to answer (but with the utmost brevity) the few questions I asked her. Yet, the smell of a *Yahoo* continuing very offensive, I always keep my nose well stopped with rue, lavender, or tobacco leaves. And, although it be hard for a man late in life to remove old habits, I am not altogether out of hopes, in some time, to suffer a neighbour *Yahoo* in my company, without the apprehensions I am yet under of his teeth or his claws.

My reconcilement to the *Yahoo* kind in general might not be so difficult, if they would be content with those vices and follies only which nature has entitled them to. I am not in the least provoked at the sight of a lawyer, a pickpocket, a colonel, a fool, a lord, a gamester, a politician, a whoremonger, a physician, an evidence, a suborner, an attorney, a traitor, or the like; this is all according to the due course of things: but when I behold a lump of deformity and diseases, both in body and mind, smitten with pride, it immediately breaks all the measures of my patience; neither shall I be ever able to comprehend how such an animal, and such a vice, could tally together. The wise and virtuous *Houyhnhnms*, who abound in all excellences that can adorn a rational creature, have no name for this vice in their language, which has no terms to express any thing that is evil, except those whereby they describe the detestable qualities of their *Yahoos*, among which they were not able to distinguish this of pride, for want of thoroughly understanding human nature, as it shows itself in other countries where that animal presides. But I, who had more experience, could plainly observe some rudiments of it among the wild *Yahoos*.

But the *Houyhnhnms*, who live under the government of reason, are no more proud of the good qualities they possess, than I should be for not wanting a leg or an arm; which no man in his wits would boast of, although he must be miserable without them. I dwell the longer upon this subject from the desire I have to make the society of an English *Yahoo* by any means not insupportable; and therefore I here entreat those who have any tincture of this absurd vice, that they will not presume to come in my sight.

TREASURE ISLAND

To S.L.O., an American gentleman in accordance with whose classic taste the following narrative has been designed, it is now, in return for numerous delightful hours, and with the kindest wishes, dedicated by his affectionate friend, the author.

TO THE HESITATING PURCHASER

If sailor tales to sailor tunes,
Storm and adventure, heat and cold,
If schooners, islands, and maroons,
And buccaneers, and buried gold,
And all the old romance, retold
Exactly in the ancient way,
Can please, as me they pleased of old,
The wiser youngsters of today:
– So be it, and fall on! If not,
If studious youth no longer crave,
His ancient appetites forgot,
Kingston, or Ballantyne the brave,
Or Cooper of the wood and wave:
So be it, also! And may I
And all my pirates share the grave
Where these and their creations lie!

CONTENTS

PART ONE

The Old Buccaneer

"IF YOU DO NOT PUT THAT KNIFE THIS INSTANT IN

CHAPTER ONE

The Old Sea-dog at the "Admiral Benbow"

Squire Trelawney, Dr. Livesey, and the rest of these gentlemen having asked me to write down the whole particulars about Treasure Island, from the beginning to the end, keeping nothing back but the bearings of the island, and that only because there is still treasure not yet lifted, I take up my pen in the year of grace 17__ and go back to the time when my father kept the Admiral Benbow inn and the brown old seaman with the sabre cut first took up his lodging under our roof.

I remember him as if it were yesterday, as he came plodding to the inn door, his sea-chest following behind him in a hand-barrow – a tall, strong, heavy, nut-brown man, his tarry pigtail falling over the shoulder of his soiled blue coat, his hands ragged and scarred, with black, broken nails, and the sabre cut across one cheek, a dirty, livid white. I remember him looking round the cover and whistling to himself as he did so, and then breaking out in that old sea-song that he sang so often afterwards:

> *"Fifteen men on the dead man's chest –*
> *Yo-ho-ho, and a bottle of rum!"*

in the high, old tottering voice that seemed to have been tuned and broken at the capstan bars. Then he rapped on the door with a bit of stick like a handspike that he carried, and when my father appeared, called roughly for a glass of rum. This, when it was brought to him, he drank slowly, like a connoisseur, lingering on the taste and still looking about him at the cliffs and up at our signboard.

"This is a handy cove," says he at length; "and a pleasant sittyated grog-shop. Much company, mate?"

My father told him no, very little company, the more was the pity.

"Well, then," said he, "this is the berth for me. Here you, matey," he cried to the man who trundled the barrow; "bring up alongside and help up my chest. I'll stay here a bit," he continued. "I'm a plain man; rum and bacon and eggs is what I want, and that head up there for to watch ships off. What you mought call me? You mought call me captain. Oh, I see what you're at – there"; and he threw down three or four gold pieces on the threshold. "You can tell me when I've worked through that," says he, looking as fierce as a commander.

And indeed bad as his clothes were and coarsely as he spoke, he had none of the appearance of a man who sailed before the mast, but seemed like a mate or skipper accustomed to be obeyed or to strike. The man who came with the barrow told us the mail had set him down the morning before at the Royal George, that he had inquired what inns there were along the coast, and hearing ours well spoken of, I suppose, and described as lonely, had chosen it from the others for his place of residence. And that was all we could learn of our guest.

He was a very silent man by custom. All day he hung round the cove or upon the cliffs with a brass telescope; all evening he sat in a corner of the parlour next the fire and drank rum and water very strong. Mostly he would not speak when spoken to, only look up sudden and fierce and blow through his nose like a fog-horn; and we and the people who came about our house soon learned to let him be. Every day when he came back from his stroll he would ask if any seafaring men had gone by along the road. At first we thought it was the want of company of his own kind that made him ask this question, but at last we began to see he was desirous to avoid them. When a seaman did put up at the Admiral Benbow (as now and then some did, making by the coast road for Bristol) he would look in at him through the curtained door before he entered the parlour; and he was always sure to be as silent as a mouse when any such was present. For me, at least, there was no secret about the matter, for I was, in a way, a sharer in his alarms. He had taken me aside one day and promised me a silver fourpenny on the first of every month if I would only keep my "weather-eye open for a seafaring man with one leg" and let him know the moment he appeared. Often enough when the first of the month came round and I applied to him for my wage, he would only blow through his nose at me and stare me down, but before the week was out he was sure to think better of it, bring me my four-penny piece, and repeat his orders to look out for "the seafaring man with one leg."

How that personage haunted my dreams, I need scarcely tell you. On stormy nights, when the wind shook the four corners of the house and the surf roared along the cove and up the cliffs, I would see him in a thousand forms, and with a thousand diabolical expressions. Now the leg would be cut off at the knee, now at the hip; now he was a monstrous kind of a creature who had never had but the one leg, and that in the middle of his body. To see him leap and run and pursue me over hedge and ditch was the worst of nightmares. And altogether I paid pretty dear for my monthly fourpenny piece, in the shape of these abominable fancies.

But though I was so terrified by the idea of the seafaring man with one leg, I was far less afraid of the captain himself than anybody else who knew him. There were nights when he took a deal more rum and water than his head would carry; and then he would sometimes sit and sing his wicked, old, wild sea-songs, minding nobody; but sometimes he would call for glasses round and force all the trembling company to listen to his stories or bear a chorus to his singing. Often I have heard the house shaking with "Yo-ho-ho, and a bottle of rum," all the neighbours joining in for dear life, with the fear of death upon them, and each singing louder than the other to avoid remark. For in these fits he was the most overriding companion ever known; he would slap his hand on the table for silence all round; he would fly up in a passion of anger at a question, or sometimes because none was put, and so he judged the company was not following his story. Nor would he allow anyone to leave the inn till he had drunk himself sleepy and reeled off to bed.

His stories were what frightened people worst of all. Dreadful stories they were – about hanging, and walking the plank, and storms at sea, and the Dry Tortugas, and wild deeds and places on the Spanish Main. By his own account he must have lived his life among some of the wickedest men that God ever allowed upon the sea, and the language in which he told these stories shocked our plain country people almost as much as the crimes that he described. My father was always saying the inn would be ruined, for people would soon cease coming there to be tyrannized over and put down, and sent shivering to their beds; but I really believe his presence did us good. People were frightened at the time, but on looking back they rather liked it; it was a fine excitement in a quiet country life, and there was even a party of the younger men who pretended to admire him, calling him a "true sea-dog" and a "real old salt" and such like names, and saying there was the sort of man that made England terrible at sea.

In one way, indeed, he bade fair to ruin us, for he kept on staying week after week, and at last month after month, so that all the money had been long exhausted, and still my father never plucked up the heart to insist on having more. If ever he mentioned it, the captain blew through his nose so loudly that you might say he roared, and stared my poor father out of the room. I have seen him wringing his hands after such a rebuff, and I am sure the annoyance and the terror he lived in must have greatly hastened his early and unhappy death.

All the time he lived with us the captain made no change whatever in his dress but to buy some stockings from a hawker. One of the cocks of his hat having fallen down, he let it hang from that day forth, though it was a great annoyance when it blew. I remember the appearance of his coat, which he patched himself upstairs in his room, and which, before the end, was nothing but patches. He never wrote or received a letter, and he never spoke with any but the neighbours, and with these, for the most part, only when drunk on rum. The great sea-chest none of us had ever seen open.

He was only once crossed, and that was towards the end, when my poor father was far gone in a decline that took him off. Dr. Livesey came late one afternoon to see the patient, took a bit of dinner from my mother, and went into the parlour to smoke a pipe until his horse should come down from the hamlet, for we had no stabling at the old Benbow. I followed him in, and I remember observing the contrast the neat, bright doctor, with his powder as white as snow and his bright, black eyes and pleasant manners, made with the coltish country folk, and above all, with that filthy, heavy, bleared scarecrow of a pirate of ours, sitting, far gone in rum, with his arms on the table. Suddenly he – the captain, that is – began to pipe up his eternal song:

"Fifteen men on the dead man's chest –
Yo-ho-ho, and a bottle of rum!
Drink and the devil had done for the rest –
Yo-ho-ho, and a bottle of rum!"

At first I had supposed "the dead man's chest" to be that identical big box of his upstairs in the front room, and the thought had been mingled in my nightmares with that of the one-legged seafaring man. But by this time we had all long ceased to pay any particular notice to the song; it was new, that night, to nobody but Dr. Livesey, and on him I observed it did not produce an agreeable effect, for he looked up for a moment quite angrily before he went on with his talk to old Taylor, the gardener, on a new cure for the rheumatics. In the meantime, the captain gradually brightened up at his own music, and at last flapped his hand upon the table before him in a way we all knew to mean silence. The voices stopped at once, all but Dr. Livesey's; he went on as before speaking clear and kind and drawing briskly at his pipe between every word or two. The captain glared at him for a while, flapped his hand again, glared still harder, and at last broke out with a villainous, low oath, "Silence, there, between decks!"

"Were you addressing me, sir?" says the doctor; and when the ruffian had told him, with another oath, that this was so, "I have only one thing to say to you, sir," replies the doctor, "that if you keep on drinking rum, the world will soon be quit of a very dirty scoundrel!"

The old fellow's fury was awful. He sprang to his feet, drew and opened a sailor's clasp-knife, and balancing it open on the palm of his hand, threatened to pin the doctor to the wall.

The doctor never so much as moved. He spoke to him as before, over his shoulder and in the same tone of voice, rather high, so that all the room might hear, but perfectly calm and steady: "If you do not put that knife this instant in your pocket, I promise, upon my honour, you shall hang at the next assizes."

Then followed a battle of looks between them, but the captain soon knuckled under, put up his weapon, and resumed his seat, grumbling like a beaten dog.

"And now, sir," continued the doctor, "since I now know there's such a fellow in my district, you may count I'll have an eye upon you day and night. I'm not a doctor only; I'm a magistrate; and if I catch a breath of complaint against you, if it's only for a piece of incivility like tonight's, I'll take effectual means to have you hunted down and routed out of this. Let that suffice."

Soon after, Dr. Livesey's horse came to the door and he rode away, but the captain held his peace that evening, and for many evenings to come.

CHAPTER TWO

Black Dog Appears and Disappears

It was not very long after this that there occurred the first of the mysterious events that rid us at last of the captain, though not, as you will see, of his affairs. It was a bitter cold winter, with long, hard frosts and heavy gales; and it was plain from the first that my poor father was little likely to see the spring. He sank daily, and my mother and I had all the inn upon our hands, and were kept busy enough without paying much regard to our unpleasant guest.

It was one January morning, very early – a pinching, frosty morning – the cove all grey with hoar-frost, the ripple lapping softly on the stones, the sun still low and only touching the hilltops and shining far to seaward. The captain had risen earlier than usual and set out down the beach, his cutlass swinging under the broad skirts of the old blue coat, his brass telescope under his arm, his hat tilted back upon his head. I remember his breath hanging like smoke in his wake as he strode off, and the last sound I heard of him as he turned the big rock was a loud snort of indignation, as though his mind was still running upon Dr. Livesey.

Well, mother was upstairs with father and I was laying the breakfast-table against the captain's return when the parlour door opened and a man stepped in on whom I had never set my eyes before. He was a pale, tallowy creature, wanting two fingers of the left hand, and though he wore a cutlass, he did not look much like a fighter. I had always my eye open for seafaring men, with one leg or two, and I remember this one puzzled me. He was not sailorly, and yet he had a smack of the sea about him too.

I asked him what was for his service, and he said he would take rum; but as I was going out of the room to fetch it, he sat down upon a table and motioned me to draw near. I paused where I was, with my napkin in my hand.

"Come here, sonny," says he. "Come nearer here."

I took a step nearer.

"Is this here table for my mate Bill?" he asked with a kind of leer.

I told him I did not know his mate Bill, and this was for a person who stayed in our house whom we called the captain.

"Well," said he, "my mate Bill would be called the captain, as like as not. He has a cut on one cheek and a mighty pleasant way with him, particularly in drink, has my mate Bill. We'll put it, for argument like, that your captain has a cut on one cheek – and we'll put it, if you like, that that cheek's the right one. Ah, well! I told you. Now, is my mate Bill in this here house?"

I told him he was out walking.

"Which way, sonny? Which way is he gone?"

And when I had pointed out the rock and told him how the captain was likely to return, and how soon, and answered a few other questions, "Ah," said he, "this'll be as good as drink to my mate Bill."

The expression of his face as he said these words was not at all pleasant, and I had my own reasons for thinking that the stranger was mistaken, even supposing he meant what he said. But it was no affair of mine, I thought; and besides, it was difficult to know what to do. The stranger kept hanging about just inside the inn door, peering round the corner like a cat waiting for a mouse. Once I stepped out myself into the road, but he immediately called me back, and as I did not obey quick enough for his fancy, a most horrible change came over his tallowy face, and he ordered me in with an oath that made me jump. As soon as I was back again he returned to his former manner, half fawning, half sneering, patted me on the shoulder, told me I was a good boy and he had taken quite a fancy to me. "I have a son of my own," said he, "as like you as two blocks, and he's all the pride of my 'art. But the great thing for boys is discipline, sonny – discipline. Now, if you had sailed along of Bill, you wouldn't have stood there to be spoke to twice – not you. That was never Bill's way, nor the way of sich as sailed with him. And here, sure enough, is my mate Bill, with a spy-glass under his arm, bless his old 'art, to be sure. You and me'll just go back into the parlour, sonny, and get behind the door, and we'll give Bill a little surprise – bless his 'art, I say again."

So saying, the stranger backed along with me into the parlour and put me behind him in the corner so that we were both hidden by the open door. I was very uneasy and alarmed, as you may fancy, and it rather added to my fears to observe that the stranger was certainly frightened himself. He cleared the hilt of his cutlass and loosened the blade in the sheath; and all the time we were waiting there he kept swallowing as if he felt what we used to call a lump in the throat.

At last in strode the captain, slammed the door behind him, without looking to the right or left, and marched straight across the room to where his breakfast awaited him.

"Bill," said the stranger in a voice that I thought he had tried to make bold and big.

The captain spun round on his heel and fronted us; all the brown had gone out of his face, and even his nose was blue; he had the look of a man who sees a ghost, or the evil one, or something worse, if anything can be; and upon my word, I felt sorry to see him all in a moment turn so old and sick.

"Come, Bill, you know me; you know an old shipmate, Bill, surely," said the stranger.

The captain made a sort of gasp.

"Black Dog!" said he.

"And who else?" returned the other, getting more at his ease. "Black Dog as ever was, come for to see his old shipmate Billy, at the Admiral Benbow inn. Ah, Bill, Bill, we have seen a sight of times, us two, since I lost them two talons," holding up his mutilated hand.

"Now, look here," said the captain; "you've run me down; here I am; well, then, speak up; what is it?"

"That's you, Bill," returned Black Dog, "you're in the right of it, Billy. I'll have a glass of rum from this dear child here, as I've took such a liking to; and we'll sit down, if you please, and talk square, like old shipmates."

When I returned with the rum, they were already seated on either side of the captain's breakfast-table – Black Dog next to the door and sitting sideways so as to have one eye on his old shipmate and one, as I thought, on his retreat.

He bade me go and leave the door wide open. "None of your key-holes for me, sonny," he said; and I left them together and retired into the bar.

For a long time, though I certainly did my best to listen, I could hear nothing but a low gattling; but at last the voices began to grow higher, and I could pick up a word or two, mostly oaths, from the captain.

"No, no, no, no; and an end of it!" he cried once. And again, "If it comes to swinging, swing all, say I."

Then all of a sudden there was a tremendous explosion of oaths and other noises – the chair and table went over in a lump, a clash of steel followed, and then a cry of pain, and the next instant I saw

Black Dog in full flight, and the captain hotly pursuing, both with drawn cutlasses, and the former streaming blood from the left shoulder. Just at the door the captain aimed at the fugitive one last tremendous cut, which would certainly have split him to the chine had it not been intercepted by our big signboard of Admiral Benbow. You may see the notch on the lower side of the frame to this day.

That blow was the last of the battle. Once out upon the road, Black Dog, in spite of his wound, showed a wonderful clean pair of heels and disappeared over the edge of the hill in half a minute. The captain, for his part, stood staring at the signboard like a bewildered man. Then he passed his hand over his eyes several times and at last turned back into the house.

"Jim," says he, "rum"; and as he spoke, he reeled a little, and caught himself with one hand against the wall.

"Are you hurt?" cried I.

"Rum," he repeated. "I must get away from here. Rum! Rum!"

I ran to fetch it, but I was quite unsteadied by all that had fallen out, and I broke one glass and fouled the tap, and while I was still getting in my own way, I heard a loud fall in the parlour, and running in, beheld the captain lying full length upon the floor. At the same instant my mother, alarmed by the cries and fighting, came running downstairs to help me. Between us we raised his head. He was breathing very loud and hard, but his eyes were closed and his face a horrible colour.

"Dear, deary me," cried my mother, "what a disgrace upon the house! And your poor father sick!"

In the meantime, we had no idea what to do to help the captain, nor any other thought but that he had got his death-hurt in the scuffle with the stranger. I got the rum, to be sure, and tried to put it down his throat, but his teeth were tightly shut and his jaws as strong as iron. It was a happy relief for us when the door opened and Doctor Livesey came in, on his visit to my father.

"Oh, doctor," we cried, "what shall we do? Where is he wounded?"

"Wounded? A fiddle-stick's end!" said the doctor. "No more wounded than you or I. The man has had a stroke, as I warned him. Now, Mrs. Hawkins, just you run upstairs to your husband and tell him, if possible, nothing about it. For my part, I must do my best to save this fellow's trebly worthless life; Jim, you get me a basin."

When I got back with the basin, the doctor had already ripped up the captain's sleeve and exposed his great sinewy arm. It was tattooed in several places. "Here's luck," "A fair wind," and "Billy Bones his fancy," were very neatly and clearly executed on the forearm; and up near the shoulder there was a sketch of a gallows and a man hanging from it – done, as I thought, with great spirit.

"Prophetic," said the doctor, touching this picture with his finger. "And now, Master Billy Bones, if that be your name, we'll have a look at the colour of your blood. Jim," he said, "are you afraid of blood?"

"No, sir," said I.

"Well, then," said he, "you hold the basin"; and with that he took his lancet and opened a vein.

A great deal of blood was taken before the captain opened his eyes and looked mistily about him. First he recognized the doctor with an unmistakable frown; then his glance fell upon me, and he looked relieved. But suddenly his colour changed, and he tried to raise himself, crying, "Where's Black Dog?"

"There is no Black Dog here," said the doctor, "except what you have on your own back. You have been drinking rum; you have had a stroke, precisely as I told you; and I have just, very much against my own will, dragged you headforemost out of the grave. Now, Mr. Bones – "

"That's not my name," he interrupted.

"Much I care," returned the doctor. "It's the name of a buccaneer of my acquaintance; and I call you by it for the sake of shortness, and what I have to say to you is this; one glass of rum won't kill you, but if you take one you'll take another and another, and I stake my wig if you don't break off short, you'll die – do you understand that? – die, and go to your own place, like the man in the Bible. Come, now, make an effort. I'll help you to your bed for once."

Between us, with much trouble, we managed to hoist him upstairs, and laid him on his bed, where his head fell back on the pillow as if he were almost fainting.

"Now, mind you," said the doctor, "I clear my conscience – the name of rum for you is death."

And with that he went off to see my father, taking me with him by the arm.

"This is nothing," he said as soon as he had closed the door. "I have drawn blood enough to keep him quiet awhile; he should lie for a week where he is – that is the best thing for him and you; but another stroke would settle him."

CHAPTER THREE

The Black Spot

About noon I stopped at the captain's door with some cooling drinks and medicines. He was lying very much as we had left him, only a little higher, and he seemed both weak and excited.

"Jim," he said, "you're the only one here that's worth anything, and you know I've been always good to you. Never a month but I've given you a silver fourpenny for yourself. And now you see, mate, I'm pretty low, and deserted by all; and Jim, you'll bring me one noggin of rum, now, won't you, matey?"

"The doctor – " I began.

But he broke in cursing the doctor, in a feeble voice but heartily. "Doctors is all swabs," he said; "and that doctor there, why, what do he know about seafaring men? I been in places hot as pitch, and mates dropping round with Yellow Jack, and the blessed land a-heaving like the sea with earthquakes – what to the doctor know of lands like that? – and I lived on rum, I tell you. It's been meat and drink, and man and wife, to me; and if I'm not to have my rum now I'm a poor old hulk on a lee shore, my blood'll be on you, Jim, and that doctor swab"; and he ran on again for a while with curses. "Look, Jim, how my fingers fidges," he continued in the pleading tone. "I can't keep 'em still, not I. I haven't had a drop this blessed day. That doctor's a fool, I tell you. If I don't have a drain o' rum, Jim, I'll have the horrors; I seen some on 'em already. I seen old Flint in the corner there, behind you; as plain as print, I seen him; and if I get the horrors, I'm a man that has lived rough, and I'll raise Cain. Your doctor hisself said one glass wouldn't hurt me. I'll give you a golden guinea for a noggin, Jim."

He was growing more and more excited, and this alarmed me for my father, who was very low that day and needed quiet; besides, I was reassured by the doctor's words, now quoted to me, and rather offended by the offer of a bribe.

"I want none of your money," said I, "but what you owe my father. I'll get you one glass, and no more."

When I brought it to him, he seized it greedily and drank it out.

"Aye, aye," said he, "that's some better, sure enough. And now, matey, did that doctor say how long I was to lie here in this old berth?"

"A week at least," said I.

"Thunder!" he cried. "A week! I can't do that; they'd have the black spot on me by then. The lubbers is going about to get the wind of me this blessed moment; lubbers as couldn't keep what they got, and want to nail what is another's. Is that seamanly behaviour, now, I want to know? But I'm a saving soul. I never wasted good money of mine, nor lost it neither; and I'll trick 'em again. I'm not afraid on 'em. I'll shake out another reef, matey, and daddle 'em again."

As he was thus speaking, he had risen from bed with great difficulty, holding to my shoulder with a grip that almost made me cry out, and moving his legs like so much dead weight. His words, spirited as they were in meaning, contrasted sadly with the weakness of the voice in which they were uttered. He paused when he had got into a sitting position on the edge.

"That doctor's done me," he murmured. "My ears is singing. Lay me back."

Before I could do much to help him he had fallen back again to his former place, where he lay for a while silent.

"Jim," he said at length, "you saw that seafaring man today?"

"Black Dog?" I asked.

"Ah! Black Dog," says he. "*He's* a bad un; but there's worse that put him on. Now, if I can't get away nohow, and they tip me the black spot, mind you, it's my old sea-chest they're after; you get on a horse – you can, can't you? Well, then, you get on a horse, and go to – well, yes, I will! – to that eternal doctor swab, and tell him to pipe all hands – magistrates and sich – and he'll lay 'em aboard at the Admiral Benbow – all old Flint's crew, man and boy, all on 'em that's left. I was first mate, I was, old Flint's first mate, and I'm the on'y one as knows the place. He gave it me at Savannah, when he lay a-dying, like as if I was to now, you see. But you won't peach unless they get the black spot on me, or unless you see that Black Dog again or a seafaring man with one leg, Jim – him above all."

"But what is the black spot, captain?" I asked.

"That's a summons, mate. I'll tell you if they get that. But you keep your weather-eye open, Jim, and I'll share with you equals, upon my honour."

He wandered a little longer, his voice growing weaker; but soon after I had given him his medicine, which he took like a child, with the remark, "If ever a seaman wanted drugs, it's me," he fell at last into a heavy, swoon-like sleep, in which I left him. What I should have done had all gone well I do not know. Probably I should have told the whole story to the doctor, for I was in mortal fear lest the captain should repent of his confessions and make an end of me. But as things fell out, my poor father died quite suddenly that evening, which put all other matters on one side. Our natural distress, the visits of the neighbours, the arranging of the funeral, and all the work of the inn to be carried on in the meanwhile kept me so busy that I had scarcely time to think of the captain, far less to be afraid of him.

He got downstairs next morning, to be sure, and had his meals as usual, though he ate little and had more, I am afraid, than his usual supply of rum, for he helped himself out of the bar, scowling and blowing through his nose, and no one dared to cross him. On the night before the funeral he was as drunk as ever; and it was shocking, in that house of mourning, to hear him singing away at his ugly old sea-song; but weak as he was, we were all in the fear of death for him, and the doctor was suddenly taken up with a case many miles away and was never near the house after my father's death. I have said the captain was weak, and indeed he seemed rather to grow weaker than regain his strength. He clambered up and down stairs, and went from the parlour to the bar and back again, and sometimes put his nose out of doors to smell the sea, holding on to the walls as he went for support and breathing hard and fast like a man on a steep mountain. He never particularly addressed me, and it is my belief he had as good as forgotten his confidences; but his temper was more flighty, and allowing for his bodily weakness, more violent than ever. He had an alarming way now when he was drunk of drawing his cutlass and laying it bare before him on the table. But with all that, he minded people less and seemed shut up in his own thoughts and rather wandering. Once, for instance, to our extreme wonder, he piped up to a different air, a kind of country love-song that he must have learned in his youth before he had begun to follow the sea.

So things passed until, the day after the funeral, and about three o'clock of a bitter, foggy, frosty afternoon, I was standing at the door for a moment, full of sad thoughts about my father, when I saw someone drawing slowly near along the road. He was plainly blind, for he tapped before him with a stick and wore a great green shade over his eyes and nose; and he was hunched, as if with age or weakness, and wore a huge old tattered sea-cloak with a hood that made him appear positively deformed. I never saw in my life a more dreadful-looking figure. He stopped a little from the inn, and raising his voice in an odd sing-song, addressed the air in front of him, "Will any kind friend inform a poor blind man, who has lost the precious sight of his eyes in the gracious defence of his native country, England – and God bless King George! – where or in what part of this country he may now be?"

"You are at the Admiral Benbow, Black Hill Cove, my good man," said I.

"I hear a voice," said he, "a young voice. Will you give me your hand, my kind young friend, and lead me in?"

I held out my hand, and the horrible, soft-spoken, eyeless creature gripped it in a moment like a vise. I was so much startled that I struggled to withdraw, but the blind man pulled me close up to him with a single action of his arm.

"Now, boy," he said, "take me in to the captain."

"Sir," said I, "upon my word I dare not."

"Oh," he sneered, "that's it! Take me in straight or I'll break your arm."

And he gave it, as he spoke, a wrench that made me cry out.

"Sir," said I, "it is for yourself I mean. The captain is not what he used to be. He sits with a drawn cutlass. Another gentleman – "

"Come, now, march," interrupted he; and I never heard a voice so cruel, and cold, and ugly as that blind man's. It cowed me more than the pain, and I began to obey him at once, walking straight in at the

door and towards the parlour, where our sick old buccaneer was sitting, dazed with rum. The blind man clung close to me, holding me in one iron fist and leaning almost more of his weight on me than I could carry. "Lead me straight up to him, and when I'm in view, cry out, 'Here's a friend for you, Bill.' If you don't, I'll do this," and with that he gave me a twitch that I thought would have made me faint. Between this and that, I was so utterly terrified of the blind beggar that I forgot my terror of the captain, and as I opened the parlour door, cried out the words he had ordered in a trembling voice.

The poor captain raised his eyes, and at one look the rum went out of him and left him staring sober. The expression of his face was not so much of terror as of mortal sickness. He made a movement to rise, but I do not believe he had enough force left in his body.

"Now, Bill, sit where you are," said the beggar. "If I can't see, I can hear a finger stirring. Business is business. Hold out your left hand. Boy, take his left hand by the wrist and bring it near to my right."

We both obeyed him to the letter, and I saw him pass something from the hollow of the hand that held his stick into the palm of the captain's, which closed upon it instantly.

"And now that's done," said the blind man; and at the words he suddenly left hold of me, and with incredible accuracy and nimbleness, skipped out of the parlour and into the road, where, as I still stood motionless, I could hear his stick go tap-tap-tapping into the distance.

It was some time before either I or the captain seemed to gather our senses, but at length, and about at the same moment, I released his wrist, which I was still holding, and he drew in his hand and looked sharply into the palm.

"Ten o'clock!" he cried. "Six hours. We'll do them yet," and he sprang to his feet.

Even as he did so, he reeled, put his hand to his throat, stood swaying for a moment, and then, with a peculiar sound, fell from his whole height face foremost to the floor.

I ran to him at once, calling to my mother. But haste was all in vain. The captain had been struck dead by thundering apoplexy. It is a curious thing to understand, for I had certainly never liked the man, though of late I had begun to pity him, but as soon as I saw that he was dead, I burst into a flood of tears. It was the second death I had known, and the sorrow of the first was still fresh in my heart.

CHAPTER FOUR

The Sea-chest

I Lost no time, of course, in telling my mother all that I knew, and perhaps should have told her long before, and we saw ourselves at once in a difficult and dangerous position. Some of the man's money – if he had any – was certainly due to us, but it was not likely that our captain's shipmates, above all the two specimens seen by me, Black Dog and the blind beggar, would be inclined to give up their booty in payment of the dead man's debts. The captain's order to mount at once and ride for Doctor Livesey would have left my mother alone and unprotected, which was not to be thought of. Indeed, it seemed impossible for either of us to remain much longer in the house; the fall of coals in the kitchen grate, the very ticking of the clock, filled us with alarms. The neighbourhood, to our ears, seemed haunted by approaching footsteps; and what between the dead body of the captain on the parlour floor and the thought of that detestable blind beggar hovering near at hand and ready to return, there were moments when, as the saying goes, I jumped in my skin for terror. Something must speedily be resolved upon, and it occurred to us at last to go forth together and seek help in the neighbouring hamlet. No sooner said than done. Bare-headed as we were, we ran out at once in the gathering evening and the frosty fog.

The hamlet lay not many hundred yards away, though out of view, on the other side of the next cove; and what greatly encouraged me, it was in an opposite direction from that whence the blind man had made his appearance and whither he had presumably returned. We were not many minutes on the road, though we sometimes stopped to lay hold of each other and hearken. But there was no unusual sound – nothing but the low wash of the ripple and the croaking of the inmates of the wood.

It was already candle-light when we reached the hamlet, and I shall never forget how much I was cheered to see the yellow shine in doors and windows; but that, as it proved, was the best of the help we were likely to get in that quarter. For – you would have thought men would have been ashamed of themselves – no soul would consent to return with us to the Admiral Benbow. The more we told of our troubles, the more – man, woman, and child – they clung to the shelter of their houses. The name of Captain Flint, though it was strange to me, was well enough known to some there and carried a great weight of terror. Some of the men who had been to field-work on the far side of the Admiral Benbow remembered, besides, to have seen several strangers on the road, and taking them to be smugglers, to have bolted away; and one at least had seen a little lugger in what we called Kitt's Hole. For that matter, anyone who was a comrade of the captain's was enough to frighten them to death. And the short and the long of the matter was, that while we could get several who were willing enough to ride to Dr. Livesey's, which lay in another direction, not one would help us to defend the inn.

They say cowardice is infectious; but then argument is, on the other hand, a great emboldener; and so when each had said his say, my mother made them a speech. She would not, she declared, lose money that belonged to her fatherless boy; "If none of the rest of you dare," she said, "Jim and I dare. Back we will go, the way we came, and small thanks to you big, hulking, chicken-hearted men. We'll have that chest open, if we die for it. And I'll thank you for that bag, Mrs. Crossley, to bring back our lawful money in."

Of course I said I would go with my mother, and of course they all cried out at our foolhardiness, but even then not a man would go along with us. All they would do was to give me a loaded pistol lest we were attacked, and to promise to have horses ready saddled in case we were pursued on our return, while one lad was to ride forward to the doctor's in search of armed assistance.

My heart was beating finely when we two set forth in the cold night upon this dangerous venture. A full moon was beginning to rise and peered redly through the upper edges of the fog, and this increased our haste, for it was plain, before we came forth again, that all would be as bright as day, and our departure exposed to the eyes of any watchers. We slipped along the hedges, noiseless and swift, nor did we see or hear anything to increase our terrors, till, to our relief, the door of the Admiral Benbow had closed behind us.

I slipped the bolt at once, and we stood and panted for a moment in the dark, alone in the house with the dead captain's body. Then my mother got a candle in the bar, and holding each other's hands, we advanced into the parlour. He lay as we had left him, on his back, with his eyes open and one arm stretched out.

"Draw down the blind, Jim," whispered my mother; "they might come and watch outside. And now," said she when I had done so, "we have to get the key off *that*; and who's to touch it, I should like to know!" and she gave a kind of sob as she said the words.

I went down on my knees at once. On the floor close to his hand there was a little round of paper, blackened on the one side. I could not doubt that this was the *black spot*; and taking it up, I found written on the other side, in a very good, clear hand, this short message: "You have till ten tonight."

"He had till ten, Mother," said I; and just as I said it, our old clock began striking. This sudden noise startled us shockingly; but the news was good, for it was only six.

"Now, Jim," she said, "that key."

I felt in his pockets, one after another. A few small coins, a thimble, and some thread and big needles, a piece of pigtail tobacco bitten away at the end, his gully with the crooked handle, a pocket compass, and a tinder box were all that they contained, and I began to despair.

"Perhaps it's round his neck," suggested my mother.

Overcoming a strong repugnance, I tore open his shirt at the neck, and there, sure enough, hanging to a bit of tarry string, which I cut with his own gully, we found the key. At this triumph we were filled with hope and hurried upstairs without delay to the little room where he had slept so long and where his box had stood since the day of his arrival.

It was like any other seaman's chest on the outside, the initial "B" burned on the top of it with a hot iron, and the corners somewhat smashed and broken as by long, rough usage.

"Give me the key," said my mother; and though the lock was very stiff, she had turned it and thrown back the lid in a twinkling.

A strong smell of tobacco and tar rose from the interior, but nothing was to be seen on the top except a suit of very good clothes, carefully brushed and folded. They had never been worn, my mother said. Under that, the miscellany began – a quadrant, a tin canikin, several sticks of tobacco, two brace of very handsome pistols, a piece of bar silver, an old Spanish watch and some other trinkets of little value and mostly of foreign make, a pair of compasses mounted with brass, and five or six curious West Indian shells. I have often wondered since why he should have carried about these shells with him in his wandering, guilty, and hunted life.

In the meantime, we had found nothing of any value but the silver and the trinkets, and neither of these were in our way. Underneath there was an old boat-cloak, whitened with sea-salt on many a harbour-bar. My mother pulled it up with impatience, and there lay before us, the last things in the chest, a bundle tied up in oilcloth, and looking like papers, and a canvas bag that gave forth, at a touch, the jingle of gold.

"I'll show these rogues that I'm an honest woman," said my mother. "I'll have my dues, and not a farthing over. Hold Mrs. Crossley's bag." And she began to count over the amount of the captain's score from the sailor's bag into the one that I was holding.

It was a long, difficult business, for the coins were of all countries and sizes – doubloons, and louis d'ors, and guineas, and pieces of eight, and I know not what besides, all shaken together at random. The guineas, too, were about the scarcest, and it was with these only that my mother knew how to make her count.

When we were about half-way through, I suddenly put my hand upon her arm, for I had heard in the silent frosty air a sound that brought my heart into my mouth – the tap-tapping of the blind man's stick upon the

frozen road. It drew nearer and nearer, while we sat holding our breath. Then it struck sharp on the inn door, and then we could hear the handle being turned and the bolt rattling as the wretched being tried to enter; and then there was a long time of silence both within and without. At last the tapping recommenced, and, to our indescribable joy and gratitude, died slowly away again until it ceased to be heard.

"Mother," said I, "take the whole and let's be going," for I was sure the bolted door must have seemed suspicious and would bring the whole hornet's nest about our ears, though how thankful I was that I had bolted it, none could tell who had never met that terrible blind man.

But my mother, frightened as she was, would not consent to take a fraction more than was due to her and was obstinately unwilling to be content with less. It was not yet seven, she said, by a long way; she knew her rights and she would have them; and she was still arguing with me when a little low whistle sounded a good way off upon the hill. That was enough, and more than enough, for both of us.

"I'll take what I have," she said, jumping to her feet.

"And I'll take this to square the count," said I, picking up the oilskin packet.

Next moment we were both groping downstairs, leaving the candle by the empty chest; and the next we had opened the door and were in full retreat. We had not started a moment too soon. The fog was rapidly dispersing; already the moon shone quite clear on the high ground on either side; and it was only in the exact bottom of the dell and round the tavern door that a thin veil still hung unbroken to conceal the first steps of our escape. Far less than half-way to the hamlet, very little beyond the bottom of the hill, we must come forth into the moonlight. Nor was this all, for the sound of several footsteps running came already to our ears, and as we looked back in their direction, a light tossing to and fro and still rapidly advancing showed that one of the newcomers carried a lantern.

"My dear," said my mother suddenly, "take the money and run on. I am going to faint."

This was certainly the end for both of us, I thought. How I cursed the cowardice of the neighbours; how I blamed my poor mother for her honesty and her greed, for her past foolhardiness and present weakness! We were just at the little bridge, by good fortune; and I helped her, tottering as she was, to the edge of the bank, where, sure enough, she gave a sigh and fell on my shoulder. I do not know how I found the strength to do it at all, and I am afraid it was roughly done, but I managed to drag her down the bank and a little way under the arch. Farther I could not move her, for the bridge was too low to let me do more than crawl below it. So there we had to stay – my mother almost entirely exposed and both of us within earshot of the inn.

CHAPTER FIVE

The Last of the Blind Man

My curiosity, in a sense, was stronger than my fear, for I could not remain where I was, but crept back to the bank again, whence, sheltering my head behind a bush of broom, I might command the road before our door. I was scarcely in position ere my enemies began to arrive, seven or eight of them, running hard, their feet beating out of time along the road and the man with the lantern some paces in front. Three men ran together, hand in hand; and I made out, even through the mist, that the middle man of this trio was the blind beggar. The next moment his voice showed me that I was right.

"Down with the door!" he cried.

"Aye, aye, sir!" answered two or three; and a rush was made upon the Admiral Benbow, the lantern-bearer following; and then I could see them pause, and hear speeches passed in a lower key, as if they were surprised to find the door open. But the pause was brief, for the blind man again issued his commands. His voice sounded louder and higher, as if he were afire with eagerness and rage.

"In, in, in!" he shouted, and cursed them for their delay.

Four or five of them obeyed at once, two remaining on the road with the formidable beggar. There was a pause, then a cry of surprise, and then a voice shouting from the house, "Bill's dead."

But the blind man swore at them again for their delay.

"Search him, some of you shirking lubbers, and the rest of you aloft and get the chest," he cried.

I could hear their feet rattling up our old stairs, so that the house must have shook with it. Promptly afterwards, fresh sounds of astonishment arose; the window of the captain's room was thrown open with a slam and a jingle of broken glass, and a man leaned out into the moonlight, head and shoulders, and addressed the blind beggar on the road below him.

"Pew," he cried, "they've been before us. Someone's turned the chest out alow and aloft."

"Is it there?" roared Pew.

"The money's there."

The blind man cursed the money.

"Flint's fist, I mean," he cried.

"We don't see it here nohow," returned the man.

"Here, you below there, is it on Bill?" cried the blind man again.

At that another fellow, probably him who had remained below to search the captain's body, came to the door of the inn. "Bill's been overhauled a'ready," said he; "nothin' left."

"It's these people of the inn – it's that boy. I wish I had put his eyes out!" cried the blind man, Pew. "There were no time ago – they had the door bolted when I tried it. Scatter, lads, and find 'em."

"Sure enough, they left their glim here," said the fellow from the window.

"Scatter and find 'em! Rout the house out!" reiterated Pew, striking with his stick upon the road.

Then there followed a great to-do through all our old inn, heavy feet pounding to and fro, furniture thrown over, doors kicked in, until the very rocks re-echoed and the men came out again, one after another, on the road and declared that we were nowhere to be found. And just the same whistle that had alarmed my mother and myself over the dead captain's money was once more clearly audible through the night, but this time twice repeated. I had thought it to be the blind man's trumpet, so to speak, summoning his crew to the assault, but I now found that it was a signal from the hillside towards the hamlet, and from its effect upon the buccaneers, a signal to warn them of approaching danger.

"There's Dirk again," said one. "Twice! We'll have to budge, mates."

"Budge, you skulk!" cried Pew. "Dirk was a fool and a coward from the first – you wouldn't mind him. They must be close by; they can't be far; you have your hands on it. Scatter and look for them, dogs! Oh, shiver my soul," he cried, "if I had eyes!"

This appeal seemed to produce some effect, for two of the fellows began to look here and there among the lumber, but half-heartedly, I thought, and with half an eye to their own danger all the time, while the rest stood irresolute on the road.

"You have your hands on thousands, you fools, and you hang a leg! You'd be as rich as kings if you could find it, and you know it's here, and you stand there skulking. There wasn't one of you dared face Bill, and I did it – a blind man! And I'm to lose my chance for you! I'm to be a poor, crawling beggar, sponging for rum, when I might be rolling in a coach! If you had the pluck of a weevil in a biscuit you would catch them still."

"Hang it, Pew, we've got the doubloons!" grumbled one.

"They might have hid the blessed thing," said another. "Take the Georges, Pew, and don't stand here squalling."

Squalling was the word for it; Pew's anger rose so high at these objections till at last, his passion completely taking the upper hand, he struck at them right and left in his blindness and his stick sounded heavily on more than one.

These, in their turn, cursed back at the blind miscreant, threatened him in horrid terms, and tried in vain to catch the stick and wrest it from his grasp.

This quarrel was the saving of us, for while it was still raging, another sound came from the top of the hill on the side of the hamlet – the tramp of horses galloping. Almost at the same time a pistol-shot, flash and report, came from the hedge side. And that was plainly the last signal of danger, for the buccaneers turned at once and ran, separating in every direction, one seaward along the cove, one slant across the hill, and so on, so that in half a minute not a sign of them remained but

Pew. Him they had deserted, whether in sheer panic or out of revenge for his ill words and blows I know not; but there he remained behind, tapping up and down the road in a frenzy, and groping and calling for his comrades. Finally he took a wrong turn and ran a few steps past me, towards the hamlet, crying, "Johnny, Black Dog, Dirk," and other names, "you won't leave old Pew, mates – not old Pew!"

Just then the noise of horses topped the rise, and four or five riders came in sight in the moonlight and swept at full gallop down the slope.

At this Pew saw his error, turned with a scream, and ran straight for the ditch, into which he rolled. But he was on his feet again in a second and made another dash, now utterly bewildered, right under the nearest of the coming horses.

The rider tried to save him, but in vain. Down went Pew with a cry that rang high into the night; and the four hoofs trampled and spurned him and passed by. He fell on his side, then gently collapsed upon his face and moved no more.

I leaped to my feet and hailed the riders. They were pulling up, at any rate, horrified at the accident; and I soon saw what they were. One, tailing out behind the rest, was a lad that had gone from the hamlet to Dr. Livesey's; the rest were revenue officers, whom he had met by the way, and with whom he had had the intelligence to return at once. Some news of the lugger in Kitt's Hole had found its way to Supervisor Dance and set him forth that night in our direction, and to that circumstance my mother and I owed our preservation from death.

Pew was dead, stone dead. As for my mother, when we had carried her up to the hamlet, a little cold water and salts and that soon brought her back again, and she was none the worse for her terror, though she still continued to deplore the balance of the money. In the meantime the supervisor rode on, as fast as he could, to Kitt's Hole; but his men had to dismount and grope down the dingle, leading, and sometimes supporting, their horses, and in continual fear of ambushes; so it was no great matter for surprise that when they got down to the Hole the lugger was already under way, though still close in. He hailed her. A voice replied, telling him to keep out of the moonlight or he would get some lead in him, and at the same time a bullet whistled close by his arm. Soon after, the lugger doubled the point and disappeared. Mr. Dance stood there, as he said, "like a fish out of water," and all he could do was to dispatch a man to B – – to warn the cutter. "And that," said he, "is just about as good as nothing. They've got off clean, and there's an end. Only," he added, "I'm glad I trod on Master Pew's corns," for by this time he had heard my story.

I went back with him to the Admiral Benbow, and you cannot imagine a house in such a state of smash; the very clock had been thrown down by these fellows in their furious hunt after my mother and myself; and though nothing had actually been taken away except the captain's money-bag and a little silver from the till, I could see at once that we were ruined. Mr. Dance could make nothing of the scene.

"They got the money, you say? Well, then, Hawkins, what in fortune were they after? More money, I suppose?"

"No, sir; not money, I think," replied I. "In fact, sir, I believe I have the thing in my breast pocket; and to tell you the truth, I should like to get it put in safety."

"To be sure, boy; quite right," said he. "I'll take it, if you like."

"I thought perhaps Dr. Livesey – " I began.

"Perfectly right," he interrupted very cheerily, "perfectly right – a gentleman and a magistrate. And, now I come to think of it, I might as well ride round there myself and report to him or squire. Master Pew's dead, when all's done; not that I regret it, but he's dead, you see, and people will make it out against an officer of his Majesty's revenue, if make it out they can. Now, I'll tell you, Hawkins, if you like, I'll take you along."

I thanked him heartily for the offer, and we walked back to the hamlet where the horses were. By the time I had told mother of my purpose they were all in the saddle.

"Dogger," said Mr. Dance, "you have a good horse; take up this lad behind you."

As soon as I was mounted, holding on to Dogger's belt, the supervisor gave the word, and the party struck out at a bouncing trot on the road to Dr. Livesey's house.

CHAPTER SIX

The Captain's Papers

WE RODE HARD all the way till we drew up before Dr. Livesey's door. The house was all dark to the front.

Mr. Dance told me to jump down and knock, and Dogger gave me a stirrup to descend by. The door was opened almost at once by the maid.

"Is Dr. Livesey in?" I asked.

No, she said, he had come home in the afternoon but had gone up to the hall to dine and pass the evening with the squire.

"So there we go, boys," said Mr. Dance.

This time, as the distance was short, I did not mount, but ran with Dogger's stirrup-leather to the lodge gates and up the long, leafless, moonlit avenue to where the white line of the hall buildings looked on either hand on great old gardens. Here Mr. Dance dismounted, and taking me along with him, was admitted at a word into the house.

The servant led us down a matted passage and showed us at the end into a great library, all lined with bookcases and busts upon the top of them, where the squire and Dr. Livesey sat, pipe in hand, on either side of a bright fire.

I had never seen the squire so near at hand. He was a tall man, over six feet high, and broad in proportion, and he had a bluff, rough-and-ready face, all roughened and reddened and lined in his long travels. His eyebrows were very black, and moved readily, and this gave him a look of some temper, not bad, you would say, but quick and high.

"Come in, Mr. Dance," says he, very stately and condescending.

"Good evening, Dance," says the doctor with a nod. "And good evening to you, friend Jim. What good wind brings you here?"

The supervisor stood up straight and stiff and told his story like a lesson; and you should have seen how the two gentlemen leaned forward and looked at each other, and forgot to smoke in their surprise and interest. When they heard how my mother went back to the inn, Dr. Livesey fairly slapped his thigh, and the squire cried "Bravo!" and broke his long pipe against the grate. Long before it was done, Mr. Trelawney (that, you will remember, was the squire's name) had got up from his seat and was striding about the room, and the doctor, as if to hear the better, had taken off his powdered wig and sat there looking very strange indeed with his own close-cropped black poll.

At last Mr. Dance finished the story.

"Mr. Dance," said the squire, "you are a very noble fellow. And as for riding down that black, atrocious miscreant, I regard it as an act of virtue, sir, like stamping on a cockroach. This lad Hawkins is a trump, I perceive. Hawkins, will you ring that bell? Mr. Dance must have some ale."

"And so, Jim," said the doctor, "you have the thing that they were after, have you?"

"Here it is, sir," said I, and gave him the oilskin packet.

The doctor looked it all over, as if his fingers were itching to open it; but instead of doing that, he put it quietly in the pocket of his coat.

"Squire," said he, "when Dance has had his ale he must, of course, be off on his Majesty's service; but I mean to keep Jim Hawkins here to sleep at my house, and with your permission, I propose we should have up the cold pie and let him sup."

"As you will, Livesey," said the squire; "Hawkins has earned better than cold pie."

So a big pigeon pie was brought in and put on a sidetable, and I made a hearty supper, for I was as hungry as a hawk, while Mr. Dance was further complimented and at last dismissed.

"And now, squire," said the doctor.

"And now, Livesey," said the squire in the same breath.

"One at a time, one at a time," laughed Dr. Livesey. "You have heard of this Flint, I suppose?"

"Heard of him!" cried the squire. "Heard of him, you say! He was the bloodthirstiest buccaneer that sailed. Blackbeard was a child to Flint. The Spaniards were so prodigiously afraid of him that, I tell you, sir, I was sometimes proud he was an Englishman. I've seen his top-sails with these eyes, off Trinidad, and the cowardly son of a rum-puncheon that I sailed with put back – put back, sir, into Port of Spain."

"Well, I've heard of him myself, in England," said the doctor. "But the point is, had he money?"

"Money!" cried the squire. "Have you heard the story? What were these villains after but money? What do they care for but money? For what would they risk their rascal carcasses but money?"

"That we shall soon know," replied the doctor. "But you are so confoundedly hot-headed and exclamatory that I cannot get a word in. What I want to know is this: Supposing that I have here in my pocket some clue to where Flint buried his treasure, will that treasure amount to much?"

"Amount, sir!" cried the squire. "It will amount to this: If we have the clue you talk about, I fit out a ship in Bristol dock, and take you and Hawkins here along, and I'll have that treasure if I search a year."

"Very well," said the doctor. "Now, then, if Jim is agreeable, we'll open the packet"; and he laid it before him on the table.

The bundle was sewn together, and the doctor had to get out his instrument case and cut the stitches with his medical scissors. It contained two things – a book and a sealed paper.

"First of all we'll try the book," observed the doctor.

The squire and I were both peering over his shoulder as he opened it, for Dr. Livesey had kindly motioned me to come round from the side-table, where I had been eating, to enjoy the sport of the search. On the first page there were only some scraps of writing, such as a man with a pen in his hand might make for idleness or practice. One was the same as the tattoo mark, "Billy Bones his fancy"; then there was "Mr. W. Bones, mate," "No more rum," "Off Palm Key he got itt," and some other snatches, mostly single words and unintelligible. I could not help wondering who it was that had "got itt," and what "itt" was that he got. A knife in his back as like as not.

"Not much instruction there," said Dr. Livesey as he passed on.

The next ten or twelve pages were filled with a curious series of entries. There was a date at one end of the line and at the other a sum of money, as in common account-books, but instead of explanatory writing, only a varying number of crosses between the two. On the 12th of June, 1745, for instance, a sum of seventy pounds had plainly become due to someone, and there was nothing but six crosses to explain the cause. In a few cases, to be sure, the name of a place would be added, as "Offe Caraccas," or a mere entry of latitude and longitude, as "620 17' 20", 190 2' 40"."

The record lasted over nearly twenty years, the amount of the separate entries growing larger as time went on, and at the end a grand total had been made out after five or six wrong additions, and these words appended, "Bones, his pile."

"I can't make head or tail of this," said Dr. Livesey.

"The thing is as clear as noonday," cried the squire. "This is the black-hearted hound's account-book. These crosses stand for the names of ships or towns that they sank or plundered. The sums are the scoundrel's share, and where he feared an ambiguity, you see he added something clearer.

'Offe Caraccas,' now; you see, here was some unhappy vessel boarded off that coast. God help the poor souls that manned her – coral long ago."

"Right!" said the doctor. "See what it is to be a traveller. Right! And the amounts increase, you see, as he rose in rank."

There was little else in the volume but a few bearings of places noted in the blank leaves towards the end and a table for reducing French, English, and Spanish moneys to a common value.

"Thrifty man!" cried the doctor. "He wasn't the one to be cheated."

"And now," said the squire, "for the other."

The paper had been sealed in several places with a thimble by way of seal; the very thimble, perhaps, that I had found in the captain's pocket. The doctor opened the seals with great care, and there fell out the map of an island, with latitude and longitude, soundings, names of hills and bays and inlets, and every particular that would be needed to bring a

ship to a safe anchorage upon its shores. It was about nine miles long and five across, shaped, you might say, like a fat dragon standing up, and had two fine land-locked harbours, and a hill in the centre part marked "The Spy-glass." There were several additions of a later date, but above all, three crosses of red ink – two on the north part of the island, one in the southwest – and beside this last, in the same red ink, and in a small, neat hand, very different from the captain's tottery characters, these words: "Bulk of treasure here."

Over on the back the same hand had written this further information:

Tall tree, Spy-glass shoulder, bearing a point to the N. of N.N.E.

Skeleton Island E.S.E. and by E.

Ten feet.

The bar silver is in the north cache; you can find it by the trend of the east hummock, ten fathoms south of the black crag with the face on it.

The arms are easy found, in the sand-hill, N. point of north inlet cape, bearing E. and a quarter N.

J.F.

That was all; but brief as it was, and to me incomprehensible, it filled the squire and Dr. Livesey with delight.

"Livesey," said the squire, "you will give up this wretched practice at once. Tomorrow I start for Bristol. In three weeks' time – three weeks! – two weeks – ten days – we'll have the best ship, sir, and the choicest crew in England. Hawkins shall come as cabin-boy. You'll make a famous cabin-boy, Hawkins. You, Livesey, are ship's doctor; I am admiral. We'll take Redruth, Joyce, and Hunter. We'll have favourable winds, a quick passage, and not the least difficulty in finding the spot, and money to eat, to roll in, to play duck and drake with ever after."

"Trelawney," said the doctor, "I'll go with you; and I'll go bail for it, so will Jim, and be a credit to the undertaking. There's only one man I'm afraid of."

"And who's that?" cried the squire. "Name the dog, sir!"

"You," replied the doctor; "for you cannot hold your tongue. We are not the only men who know of this paper. These fellows who attacked the inn tonight – bold, desperate blades, for sure – and the rest who stayed aboard that lugger, and more, I dare say, not far off, are, one and all, through thick and thin, bound that they'll get that money. We must none of us go alone till we get to sea. Jim and I shall stick together in the meanwhile; you'll take Joyce and Hunter when you ride to Bristol, and from first to last, not one of us must breathe a word of what we've found."

"Livesey," returned the squire, "you are always in the right of it. I'll be as silent as the grave."

PART TWO

The Sea-cook

CHAPTER SEVEN

I Go to Bristol

IT WAS LONGER than the squire imagined ere we were ready for the sea, and none of our first plans – not even Dr. Livesey's, of keeping me beside him – could be carried out as we intended. The doctor had to go to London for a physician to take charge of his practice; the squire was hard at work at Bristol; and I lived on at the hall under the charge of old Redruth, the gamekeeper, almost a prisoner, but full of sea-dreams and the most charming anticipations of strange islands and adventures. I brooded by the hour together over the map, all the details of which I well remembered. Sitting by the fire in the housekeeper's room, I approached that island in my fancy from every possible direction; I explored every acre of its surface; I climbed a thousand times to that tall hill they call the Spy-glass, and from the top enjoyed the most wonderful and changing prospects. Sometimes the isle was thick with savages, with whom we fought, sometimes full of dangerous animals that hunted us, but in all my fancies nothing occurred to me so strange and tragic as our actual adventures.

So the weeks passed on, till one fine day there came a letter addressed to Dr. Livesey, with this addition, "To be opened, in the case of his absence, by Tom Redruth or young Hawkins." Obeying this order, we found, or rather I found – for the gamekeeper was a poor hand at reading anything but print – the following important news:

Old Anchor Inn, Bristol, March 1, 17 –

Dear Livesey – As I do not know whether you are at the hall or still in London, I send this in double to both places.

The ship is bought and fitted. She lies at anchor, ready for sea. You never imagined a sweeter schooner – a child might sail her – two hundred tons; name, *Hispaniola.*

I got her through my old friend, Blandly, who has proved himself throughout the most surprising trump. The admirable fellow literally slaved in my interest, and so, I may say, did everyone in Bristol, as soon as they got wind of the port we sailed for – treasure, I mean.

"Redruth," said I, interrupting the letter, "Dr. Livesey will not like that. The squire has been talking, after all."

"Well, who's a better right?" growled the gamekeeper. "A pretty rum go if squire ain't to talk for Dr. Livesey, I should think."

At that I gave up all attempts at commentary and read straight on:

Blandly himself found the *Hispaniola*, and by the most admirable management got her for the merest trifle. There is a class of men in Bristol monstrously prejudiced against Blandly. They go the length of declaring that this honest creature would do anything for money, that the *Hispaniola* belonged to him, and that he sold it me absurdly high – the most transparent calumnies. None of them dare, however, to deny the merits of the ship.

So far there was not a hitch. The workpeople, to be sure – riggers and what not – were most annoyingly slow; but time cured that. It was the crew that troubled me.

I wished a round score of men – in case of natives, buccaneers, or the odious French – and I had the worry of the deuce itself to find so much as half a dozen, till the most remarkable stroke of fortune brought me the very man that I required.

I was standing on the dock, when, by the merest accident, I fell in talk with him. I found he was an old sailor, kept a public-house, knew all the seafaring men in Bristol, had lost his health ashore, and wanted a good berth as cook to get to sea again. He had hobbled down there that morning, he said, to get a smell of the salt.

I was monstrously touched – so would you have been – and, out of pure pity, I engaged him on the spot to be ship's cook. Long John Silver, he is called, and has lost a leg; but that I regarded as a recommendation, since he lost it in his country's service, under the immortal Hawke. He has no pension, Livesey. Imagine the abominable age we live in!

Well, sir, I thought I had only found a cook, but it was a crew I had discovered. Between Silver and myself we got together in a few days a company of the toughest old salts imaginable – not pretty to look at, but fellows, by their faces, of the most indomitable spirit. I declare we could fight a frigate.

Long John even got rid of two out of the six or seven I had already engaged. He showed me in a moment that they were just the sort of fresh-water swabs we had to fear in an adventure of importance.

I am in the most magnificent health and spirits, eating like a bull, sleeping like a tree, yet I shall not enjoy a moment till I hear my old tarpaulins tramping round the capstan. Seaward, ho! Hang the treasure! It's the glory of the sea that has turned my head. So now, Livesey, come post; do not lose an hour, if you respect me.

Let young Hawkins go at once to see his mother, with Redruth for a guard; and then both come full speed to Bristol.

John Trelawney

Postscript – I did not tell you that Blandly, who, by the way, is to send a consort after us if we don't turn up by the end of August, had found an admirable fellow for sailing master – a stiff man, which I regret, but in all other respects a treasure. Long John Silver unearthed a very competent man for a mate, a man named Arrow. I have a boatswain who pipes, Livesey; so things shall go man-o'-war fashion on board the good ship *Hispaniola.*

I forgot to tell you that Silver is a man of substance; I know of my own knowledge that he has a banker's account, which has never been overdrawn. He leaves his wife to manage the inn; and as she is a woman of colour, a pair of old bachelors like you and I may be excused for guessing that it is the wife, quite as much as the health, that sends him back to roving.

J. T.

P.P.S. – Hawkins may stay one night with his mother.

J. T.

You can fancy the excitement into which that letter put me. I was half beside myself with glee; and if ever I despised a man, it was old Tom Redruth, who could do nothing but grumble and lament. Any of the under-gamekeepers would gladly have changed places with him; but such was not the squire's pleasure, and the squire's pleasure was like law among them all. Nobody but old Redruth would have dared so much as even to grumble.

The next morning he and I set out on foot for the Admiral Benbow, and there I found my mother in good health and spirits. The captain, who had so long been a cause of so much discomfort, was gone where the wicked cease from troubling. The squire had had everything repaired, and the public rooms and the sign repainted, and had added some furniture – above all a beautiful armchair for mother in the bar. He had found her a boy as an apprentice also so that she should not want help while I was gone.

It was on seeing that boy that I understood, for the first time, my situation. I had thought up to that moment of the adventures before me, not at all of the home that I was leaving; and now, at sight of this clumsy stranger, who was to stay here in my place beside my mother, I had my first attack of tears. I am afraid I led that boy a dog's life, for as he was new to the work, I had a hundred opportunities of setting him right and putting him down, and I was not slow to profit by them.

The night passed, and the next day, after dinner, Redruth and I were afoot again and on the road. I said good-bye to Mother and the cove where I had lived since I was born, and the dear old Admiral Benbow – since he was repainted, no longer quite so dear. One of my last thoughts was of the captain, who had so often strode along the beach with his cocked hat, his sabre-cut cheek, and his old brass telescope. Next moment we had turned the corner and my home was out of sight.

The mail picked us up about dusk at the Royal George on the heath. I was wedged in between Redruth and a stout old gentleman, and in spite of the swift motion and the cold night air, I must have dozed a great deal from the very first, and then slept like a log up hill and down dale through stage after stage, for when I was awakened at last it was by a punch in the ribs, and I opened my eyes to find that we were standing still before a large building in a city street and that the day had already broken a long time.

"Where are we?" I asked.

"Bristol," said Tom. "Get down."

Mr. Trelawney had taken up his residence at an inn far down the docks to superintend the work upon the schooner. Thither we had now to walk, and our way, to my great delight, lay along the quays and beside the great multitude of ships of all sizes and rigs and nations. In one, sailors were singing at their work, in another there were men aloft, high over my head, hanging to threads that seemed no thicker than a spider's. Though I had lived by the shore all my life, I seemed never to have been near the sea till then. The smell of tar and salt was something new. I saw the most wonderful figureheads, that had all been far over the ocean. I saw, besides, many old sailors, with rings in their ears, and whiskers curled in ringlets, and tarry pigtails, and their swaggering, clumsy sea-walk; and if I had seen as many kings or archbishops I could not have been more delighted.

And I was going to sea myself, to sea in a schooner, with a piping boatswain and pig-tailed singing seamen, to sea, bound for an unknown island, and to seek for buried treasure!

While I was still in this delightful dream, we came suddenly in front of a large inn and met Squire Trelawney, all dressed out like a sea-officer, in stout blue cloth, coming out of the door with a smile on his face and a capital imitation of a sailor's walk.

"Here you are," he cried, "and the doctor came last night from London. Bravo! The ship's company complete!"

"Oh, sir," cried I, "when do we sail?"

"Sail!" says he. "We sail tomorrow!"

CHAPTER EIGHT

At the Sign of the Spy-glass

WHEN I HAD DONE breakfasting the squire gave me a note addressed to John Silver, at the sign of the Spy-glass, and told me I should easily find the place by following the line of the docks and keeping a bright lookout for a little tavern with a large brass telescope for sign. I set off, overjoyed at this opportunity to see some more of the ships and seamen, and picked my way among a great crowd of people and carts and bales, for the dock was now at its busiest, until I found the tavern in question.

It was a bright enough little place of entertainment. The sign was newly painted; the windows had neat red curtains; the floor was cleanly sanded. There was a street on each side and an open door on both, which made the large, low room pretty clear to see in, in spite of clouds of tobacco smoke.

The customers were mostly seafaring men, and they talked so loudly that I hung at the door, almost afraid to enter.

As I was waiting, a man came out of a side room, and at a glance I was sure he must be Long John. His left leg was cut off close by the hip, and under the left shoulder he carried a crutch, which he managed with wonderful dexterity, hopping about upon it like a bird. He was very tall and strong, with a face as big as a ham – plain and pale, but intelligent and smiling. Indeed, he seemed in the most cheerful spirits, whistling as he moved about among the tables, with a merry word or a slap on the shoulder for the more favoured of his guests.

Now, to tell you the truth, from the very first mention of Long John in Squire Trelawney's letter I had taken a fear in my mind that he might prove to be the very one-legged sailor whom I had watched for so long at the old Benbow. But one look at the man before me was enough. I had seen the captain, and Black Dog, and the blind man, Pew, and I thought I knew what a buccaneer was like – a very different creature, according to me, from this clean and pleasant-tempered landlord.

I plucked up courage at once, crossed the threshold, and walked right up to the man where he stood, propped on his crutch, talking to a customer.

"Mr. Silver, sir?" I asked, holding out the note.

"Yes, my lad," said he; "such is my name, to be sure. And who may you be?" And then as he saw the squire's letter, he seemed to me to give something almost like a start.

"Oh!" said he, quite loud, and offering his hand. "I see. You are our new cabin-boy; pleased I am to see you."

And he took my hand in his large firm grasp.

Just then one of the customers at the far side rose suddenly and made for the door. It was close by him, and he was out in the street in a moment. But his hurry had attracted my notice, and I recognized him at glance. It was the tallow-faced man, wanting two fingers, who had come first to the Admiral Benbow.

"Oh," I cried, "stop him! It's Black Dog!"

"I don't care two coppers who he is," cried Silver. "But he hasn't paid his score. Harry, run and catch him."

One of the others who was nearest the door leaped up and started in pursuit.

"If he were Admiral Hawke he shall pay his score," cried Silver; and then, relinquishing my hand, "Who did you say he was?" he asked. "Black what?"

"Dog, sir," said I. "Has Mr. Trelawney not told you of the buccaneers? He was one of them."

"So?" cried Silver. "In my house! Ben, run and help Harry. One of those swabs, was he? Was that you drinking with him, Morgan? Step up here."

The man whom he called Morgan – an old, grey-haired, mahogany-faced sailor – came forward pretty sheepishly, rolling his quid.

"Now, Morgan," said Long John very sternly, "you never clapped your eyes on that Black – Black Dog before, did you, now?"

"Not I, sir," said Morgan with a salute.

"You didn't know his name, did you?"

"No, sir."

"By the powers, Tom Morgan, it's as good for you!" exclaimed the landlord. "If you had been mixed up with the like of that, you would never have put another foot in my house, you may lay to that. And what was he saying to you?"

"I don't rightly know, sir," answered Morgan.

"Do you call that a head on your shoulders, or a blessed dead-eye?" cried Long John. "Don't rightly know, don't you! Perhaps you don't happen to rightly know who you was speaking to, perhaps? Come, now, what was he jawing – v'yages, cap'ns, ships? Pipe up! What was it?"

"We was a-talkin' of keel-hauling," answered Morgan.

"Keel-hauling, was you? And a mighty suitable thing, too, and you may lay to that. Get back to your place for a lubber, Tom."

And then, as Morgan rolled back to his seat, Silver added to me in a confidential whisper that was very flattering, as I thought, "He's quite an honest man, Tom Morgan, on'y stupid. And now," he ran on again, aloud, "let's see – Black Dog? No, I don't know the name, not I. Yet I kind of think I've – yes, I've seen the swab. He used to come here with a blind beggar, he used."

"That he did, you may be sure," said I. "I knew that blind man too. His name was Pew."

"It was!" cried Silver, now quite excited. "Pew! That were his name for certain. Ah, he looked a shark, he did! If we run down this Black Dog, now, there'll be news for Cap'n Trelawney! Ben's a good runner; few seamen run better than Ben. He should run him down, hand over hand, by the powers! He talked o' keel-hauling, did he? *I'll* keel-haul him!"

All the time he was jerking out these phrases he was stumping up and down the tavern on his crutch, slapping tables with his hand, and giving such a show of excitement as would have convinced an Old Bailey judge or a Bow Street runner. My suspicions had been thoroughly reawakened on finding Black Dog at the Spy-glass, and I watched the cook narrowly. But he was too deep, and too ready, and too clever for me, and by the time the two men had come back out of breath and confessed that they had lost the track in a crowd, and been scolded like thieves, I would have gone bail for the innocence of Long John Silver.

"See here, now, Hawkins," said he, "here's a blessed hard thing on a man like me, now, ain't it? There's Cap'n Trelawney – what's he to think? Here I have this confounded son of a Dutchman sitting in my own house drinking of my own rum! Here you comes and tells me of it plain; and here I let him give us all the slip before my blessed dead-lights! Now, Hawkins, you do me justice with the cap'n. You're a lad, you are, but you're as smart as paint. I see that when you first come in. Now, here it is: What could I do, with this old timber I hobble on? When I was an A B master mariner I'd have come up alongside of him, hand over hand, and broached him to in a brace of old shakes, I would; but now – "

And then, all of a sudden, he stopped, and his jaw dropped as though he had remembered something.

"The score!" he burst out. "Three goes o' rum! Why, shiver my timbers, if I hadn't forgotten my score!"

And falling on a bench, he laughed until the tears ran down his cheeks. I could not help joining, and we laughed together, peal after peal, until the tavern rang again.

"Why, what a precious old sea-calf I am!" he said at last, wiping his cheeks. "You and me should get on well, Hawkins, for I'll take my davy I should be rated ship's boy. But come now, stand by to go about. This won't do. Dooty is dooty, messmates. I'll put on my old cockerel hat, and step along of you to Cap'n Trelawney, and report this here affair. For mind you, it's serious, young Hawkins; and neither you nor me's come out of it with what I should make so bold as to call credit. Nor you neither, says you; not smart – none of the pair of us smart. But dash my buttons! That was a good un about my score."

And he began to laugh again, and that so heartily, that though I did not see the joke as he did, I was again obliged to join him in his mirth.

On our little walk along the quays, he made himself the most interesting companion, telling me about the different ships that we passed by, their rig, tonnage, and nationality, explaining the work that was going forward – how one was discharging, another taking in cargo, and a third making ready for sea – and every now and then telling me some little anecdote of ships or seamen or repeating a nautical phrase till I had learned it perfectly. I began to see that here was one of the best of possible shipmates.

When we got to the inn, the squire and Dr. Livesey were seated together, finishing a quart of ale with a toast in it, before they should go aboard the schooner on a visit of inspection.

Long John told the story from first to last, with a great deal of spirit and the most perfect truth. "That was how it were, now, weren't it, Hawkins?" he would say, now and again, and I could always bear him entirely out.

The two gentlemen regretted that Black Dog had got away, but we all agreed there was nothing to be done, and after he had been complimented, Long John took up his crutch and departed.

"All hands aboard by four this afternoon," shouted the squire after him.

"Aye, aye, sir," cried the cook, in the passage.

"Well, squire," said Dr. Livesey, "I don't put much faith in your discoveries, as a general thing; but I will say this, John Silver suits me."

"The man's a perfect trump," declared the squire.

"And now," added the doctor, "Jim may come on board with us, may he not?"

"To be sure he may," says squire. "Take your hat, Hawkins, and we'll see the ship."

CHAPTER NINE

Powder and Arms

THE *Hispaniola* lay some way out, and we went under the figureheads and round the sterns of many other ships, and their cables sometimes grated underneath our keel, and sometimes swung above us. At last, however, we got alongside, and were met and saluted as we stepped aboard by the mate, Mr. Arrow, a brown old sailor with earrings in his ears and a squint. He and the squire were very thick and friendly, but I soon observed that things were not the same between Mr. Trelawney and the captain.

This last was a sharp-looking man who seemed angry with everything on board and was soon to tell us why, for we had hardly got down into the cabin when a sailor followed us.

"Captain Smollett, sir, axing to speak with you," said he.

"I am always at the captain's orders. Show him in," said the squire.

The captain, who was close behind his messenger, entered at once and shut the door behind him.

"Well, Captain Smollett, what have you to say? All well, I hope; all shipshape and seaworthy?"

"Well, sir," said the captain, "better speak plain, I believe, even at the risk of offence. I don't like this cruise; I don't like the men; and I don't like my officer. That's short and sweet."

"Perhaps, sir, you don't like the ship?" inquired the squire, very angry, as I could see.

"I can't speak as to that, sir, not having seen her tried," said the captain. "She seems a clever craft; more I can't say."

"Possibly, sir, you may not like your employer, either?" says the squire.

But here Dr. Livesey cut in.

"Stay a bit," said he, "stay a bit. No use of such questions as that but to produce ill feeling. The captain has said too much or he has said too little, and I'm bound to say that I require an explanation of his words. You don't, you say, like this cruise. Now, why?"

"I was engaged, sir, on what we call sealed orders, to sail this ship for that gentleman where he should bid me," said the captain. "So far so good. But now I find that every man before the mast knows more than I do. I don't call that fair, now, do you?"

"No," said Dr. Livesey, "I don't."

"Next," said the captain, "I learn we are going after treasure – hear it from my own hands, mind you. Now, treasure is ticklish work; I don't like treasure voyages on any account, and I don't like them, above all, when they are secret and when (begging your pardon, Mr. Trelawney) the secret has been told to the parrot."

"Silver's parrot?" asked the squire.

"It's a way of speaking," said the captain. "Blabbed, I mean. It's my belief neither of you gentlemen know what you are about, but I'll tell you my way of it – life or death, and a close run."

"That is all clear, and, I dare say, true enough," replied Dr. Livesey. "We take the risk, but we are not so ignorant as you believe us. Next, you say you don't like the crew. Are they not good seamen?"

"I don't like them, sir," returned Captain Smollett. "And I think I should have had the choosing of my own hands, if you go to that."

"Perhaps you should," replied the doctor. "My friend should, perhaps, have taken you along with him; but the slight, if there be one, was unintentional. And you don't like Mr. Arrow?"

"I don't, sir. I believe he's a good seaman, but he's too free with the crew to be a good officer. A mate should keep himself to himself – shouldn't drink with the men before the mast!"

"Do you mean he drinks?" cried the squire.

"No, sir," replied the captain, "only that he's too familiar."

"Well, now, and the short and long of it, captain?" asked the doctor. "Tell us what you want."

"Well, gentlemen, are you determined to go on this cruise?"

"Like iron," answered the squire.

"Very good," said the captain. "Then, as you've heard me very patiently, saying things that I could not prove, hear me a few words more. They are putting the powder and the arms in the fore hold. Now, you have a good place under the cabin; why not put them there? – first point. Then, you are bringing four of your own people with you, and they tell me some of them are to be berthed forward. Why not give them the berths here beside the cabin? – second point."

"Any more?" asked Mr. Trelawney.

"One more," said the captain. "There's been too much blabbing already."

"Far too much," agreed the doctor.

"I'll tell you what I've heard myself," continued Captain Smollett: "that you have a map of an island, that there's crosses on the map to show where treasure is, and that the island lies – " And then he named the latitude and longitude exactly.

"I never told that," cried the squire, "to a soul!"

"The hands know it, sir," returned the captain.

"Livesey, that must have been you or Hawkins," cried the squire.

"It doesn't much matter who it was," replied the doctor. And I could see that neither he nor the captain paid much regard to Mr. Trelawney's protestations. Neither did I, to be sure, he was so loose a talker; yet in this case I believe he was really right and that nobody had told the situation of the island.

"Well, gentlemen," continued the captain, "I don't know who has this map; but I make it a point, it shall be kept secret even from me and Mr. Arrow. Otherwise I would ask you to let me resign."

"I see," said the doctor. "You wish us to keep this matter dark and to make a garrison of the stern part of the ship, manned with my friend's own people, and provided with all the arms and powder on board. In other words, you fear a mutiny."

"Sir," said Captain Smollett, "with no intention to take offence, I deny your right to put words into my mouth. No captain, sir, would be justified in going to sea at all if he had ground enough to say that. As for Mr. Arrow, I believe him thoroughly honest; some of the men are the same; all may be for what I know. But I am responsible for the ship's safety and the life of every man Jack aboard of her. I see things going, as I think, not quite right. And I ask you to take certain precautions or let me resign my berth. And that's all."

"Captain Smollett," began the doctor with a smile, "did ever you hear the fable of the mountain and the mouse? You'll excuse me, I dare say, but you remind me of that fable. When you came in here, I'll stake my wig, you meant more than this."

"Doctor," said the captain, "you are smart. When I came in here I meant to get discharged. I had no thought that Mr. Trelawney would hear a word."

"No more I would," cried the squire. "Had Livesey not been here I should have seen you to the deuce. As it is, I have heard you. I will do as you desire, but I think the worse of you."

"That's as you please, sir," said the captain. "You'll find I do my duty."

And with that he took his leave.

"Trelawney," said the doctor, "contrary to all my notions, I believed you have managed to get two honest men on board with you – that man and John Silver."

"Silver, if you like," cried the squire; "but as for that intolerable humbug, I declare I think his conduct unmanly, unsailorly, and downright un-English."

"Well," says the doctor, "we shall see."

When we came on deck, the men had begun already to take out the arms and powder, yo-ho-ing at their work, while the captain and Mr. Arrow stood by superintending.

The new arrangement was quite to my liking. The whole schooner had been overhauled; six berths had been made astern out of what had been the after-part of the main hold; and this set of cabins was only joined to the galley and forecastle by a sparred passage on the port side. It had been originally meant that the captain, Mr. Arrow, Hunter, Joyce, the doctor, and the squire were to occupy these six berths. Now Redruth and I were to get two of them and Mr. Arrow and the captain were to sleep on deck in the companion, which had been enlarged on each side till you might almost have called it a round-house. Very low it was still, of course; but there was room to swing two hammocks, and even the mate seemed pleased with the arrangement. Even he, perhaps, had been doubtful as to the crew, but that is only guess, for as you shall hear, we had not long the benefit of his opinion.

We were all hard at work, changing the powder and the berths, when the last man or two, and Long John along with them, came off in a shore-boat.

The cook came up the side like a monkey for cleverness, and as soon as he saw what was doing, "So ho, mates!" says he. "What's this?"

"We're a-changing of the powder, Jack," answers one.

"Why, by the powers," cried Long John, "if we do, we'll miss the morning tide!"

"My orders!" said the captain shortly. "You may go below, my man. Hands will want supper."

"Aye, aye, sir," answered the cook, and touching his forelock, he disappeared at once in the direction of his galley.

"That's a good man, captain," said the doctor.

"Very likely, sir," replied Captain Smollett. "Easy with that, men – easy," he ran on, to the fellows who were shifting the powder; and then suddenly observing me examining the swivel we carried amidships, a long brass nine, "Here you, ship's boy," he cried, "out o' that! Off with you to the cook and get some work."

And then as I was hurrying off I heard him say, quite loudly, to the doctor, "I'll have no favourites on my ship."

I assure you I was quite of the squire's way of thinking, and hated the captain deeply.

CHAPTER TEN

The Voyage

ALL THAT NIGHT we were in a great bustle getting things stowed in their place, and boatfuls of the squire's friends, Mr. Blandly and the like, coming off to wish him a good voyage and a safe return. We never had a night at the Admiral Benbow when I had half the work; and I was dog-tired when, a little before dawn, the boatswain sounded his pipe and the crew began to man the capstan-bars. I might have been twice as weary, yet I would not have left the deck, all was so new and interesting to me – the brief commands, the shrill note of the whistle, the men bustling to their places in the glimmer of the ship's lanterns.

"Now, Barbecue, tip us a stave," cried one voice.

"The old one," cried another.

"Aye, aye, mates," said Long John, who was standing by, with his crutch under his arm, and at once broke out in the air and words I knew so well:

"Fifteen men on the dead man's chest – "

And then the whole crew bore chorus: –

"Yo-ho-ho, and a bottle of rum!"

And at the third "Ho!" drove the bars before them with a will.

Even at that exciting moment it carried me back to the old Admiral Benbow in a second, and I seemed to hear the voice of the captain piping in the chorus. But soon the anchor was short up; soon it was hanging dripping at the bows; soon the sails began to draw, and the land and shipping to flit by on either side; and before I could lie down to snatch an hour of slumber the *Hispaniola* had begun her voyage to the Isle of Treasure.

I am not going to relate that voyage in detail. It was fairly prosperous. The ship proved to be a good ship, the crew were capable seamen, and the captain thoroughly understood his business. But before we came the length of Treasure Island, two or three things had happened which require to be known.

Mr. Arrow, first of all, turned out even worse than the captain had feared. He had no command among the men, and people did what they pleased with him. But that was by no means the worst of it, for after a day or two at sea he began to appear on deck with hazy eye, red cheeks, stuttering tongue, and other marks of drunkenness. Time after time he was ordered below in disgrace. Sometimes he fell and cut himself; sometimes he lay all day long in his little bunk at one side of the companion; sometimes for a day or two he would be almost sober and attend to his work at least passably.

In the meantime, we could never make out where he got the drink. That was the ship's mystery. Watch him as we pleased, we could do nothing to solve it; and when we asked him to his face, he would only laugh if he were drunk, and if he were sober deny solemnly that he ever tasted anything but water.

He was not only useless as an officer and a bad influence amongst the men, but it was plain that at this rate he must soon kill himself outright, so nobody was much surprised, nor very sorry, when one dark night, with a head sea, he disappeared entirely and was seen no more.

"Overboard!" said the captain. "Well, gentlemen, that saves the trouble of putting him in irons."

But there we were, without a mate; and it was necessary, of course, to advance one of the men. The boatswain, Job Anderson, was the likeliest man aboard, and though he kept his old title, he served in a way as mate. Mr. Trelawney had followed the sea, and his knowledge made him very useful, for he often took a watch himself in easy weather. And the coxswain, Israel Hands, was a careful, wily, old, experienced seaman who could be trusted at a pinch with almost anything.

He was a great confidant of Long John Silver, and so the mention of his name leads me on to speak of our ship's cook, Barbecue, as the men called him.

Aboard ship he carried his crutch by a lanyard round his neck, to have both hands as free as possible. It was something to see him wedge the foot of the crutch against a bulkhead, and propped against it, yielding to every movement of the ship, get on with his cooking like someone safe ashore. Still more strange was it to see him in the heaviest of weather cross the deck. He had a line or two rigged up to help him across the widest spaces – Long John's earrings, they were called; and he would hand himself from one place to another, now using the crutch, now trailing it alongside by the lanyard, as quickly as another man could walk. Yet some of the men who had sailed with him before expressed their pity to see him so reduced.

"He's no common man, Barbecue," said the coxswain to me. "He had good schooling in his young days and can speak like a book when so minded; and brave – a lion's nothing alongside of Long John! I seen him grapple four and knock their heads together – him unarmed."

All the crew respected and even obeyed him. He had a way of talking to each and doing everybody some particular service. To me he was unweariedly kind, and always glad to see me in the galley, which he kept as clean as a new pin, the dishes hanging up burnished and his parrot in a cage in one corner.

"Come away, Hawkins," he would say; "come and have a yarn with John. Nobody more welcome than yourself, my son. Sit you down and hear the news. Here's Cap'n Flint – I calls my parrot Cap'n Flint, after the famous buccaneer – here's Cap'n Flint predicting success to our v'yage. Wasn't you, cap'n?"

And the parrot would say, with great rapidity, "Pieces of eight! Pieces of eight! Pieces of eight!" till you wondered that it was not out of breath, or till John threw his handkerchief over the cage.

"Now, that bird," he would say, "is, maybe, two hundred years old, Hawkins – they live forever mostly; and if anybody's seen more wickedness, it must be the devil himself. She's sailed with England, the great Cap'n England, the pirate. She's been at Madagascar, and at Malabar, and Surinam, and Providence, and Portobello. She was at the fishing up of the wrecked plate ships. It's there she learned 'Pieces of eight,' and little wonder; three hundred and fifty thousand of 'em, Hawkins! She was at the boarding of the viceroy of the Indies out of Goa, she was; and to look at her you would think she was a babby. But you smelt powder – didn't you, cap'n?"

"Stand by to go about," the parrot would scream.

"Ah, she's a handsome craft, she is," the cook would say, and give her sugar from his pocket, and then the bird would peck at the bars and swear straight on, passing belief for wickedness. "There," John would add, "you can't touch pitch and not be mucked, lad. Here's this poor old innocent bird o' mine swearing blue fire, and none the wiser, you may lay to that. She would swear the same, in a manner of speaking, before chaplain." And John would touch his forelock with a solemn way he had that made me think he was the best of men.

In the meantime, the squire and Captain Smollett were still on pretty distant terms with one another. The squire made no bones about the matter; he despised the captain. The captain, on his part, never spoke but when he was spoken to, and then sharp and short and dry, and not a word wasted. He owned, when driven into a corner, that he seemed to have been wrong about the crew, that some of them were as brisk as he wanted to see and all had behaved fairly well. As for the ship, he had taken a downright fancy to her. "She'll lie a point nearer the wind than a man has a right to expect of his own married wife, sir. But," he would add, "all I say is, we're not home again, and I don't like the cruise."

The squire, at this, would turn away and march up and down the deck, chin in air.

"A trifle more of that man," he would say, "and I shall explode."

We had some heavy weather, which only proved the qualities of the *Hispaniola*. Every man on board seemed well content, and they must have been hard to please if they had been otherwise, for it is my belief there was never a ship's company so spoiled since Noah put to sea. Double grog was going on the least excuse; there was duff on odd days, as, for instance, if the squire heard it was any man's birthday, and always a barrel of apples standing broached in the waist for anyone to help himself that had a fancy.

"Never knew good come of it yet," the captain said to Dr. Livesey. "Spoil forecastle hands, make devils. That's my belief."

But good did come of the apple barrel, as you shall hear, for if it had not been for that, we should have had no note of warning and might all have perished by the hand of treachery.

This was how it came about.

We had run up the trades to get the wind of the island we were after – I am not allowed to be more plain – and now we were running down for it with a bright lookout day and night. It was about the last day of our outward voyage by the largest computation; some time that night, or at latest before noon of the morrow, we should sight the Treasure Island. We were heading S.S.W. and had a steady breeze abeam and a quiet sea. The *Hispaniola* rolled steadily, dipping her bowsprit now and then with a whiff of spray. All was drawing alow and aloft; everyone was in the bravest spirits because we were now so near an end of the first part of our adventure.

Now, just after sundown, when all my work was over and I was on my way to my berth, it occurred to me that I should like an apple. I ran on deck. The watch was all forward looking out for the island. The man at the helm was watching the luff of the sail and whistling away gently to himself, and that was the only sound excepting the swish of the sea against the bows and around the sides of the ship.

In I got bodily into the apple barrel, and found there was scarce an apple left; but sitting down there in the dark, what with the sound of the waters and the rocking movement of the ship, I had either fallen asleep or was on the point of doing so when a heavy man sat down with rather a clash close by. The barrel shook as he leaned his shoulders against it, and I was just about to jump up when the man began to speak. It was Silver's voice, and before I had heard a dozen words, I would not have shown myself for all the world, but lay there, trembling and listening, in the extreme of fear and curiosity, for from these dozen words I understood that the lives of all the honest men aboard depended upon me alone.

CHAPTER ELEVEN

What I Heard in the Apple Barrel

No, not I," said Silver. "Flint was cap'n; I was quartermaster, along of my timber leg. The same broadside I lost my leg, old Pew lost his deadlights. It was a master surgeon, him that ampytated me – out of college and all – Latin by the bucket, and what not; but he was hanged like a dog, and sun-dried like the rest, at Corso Castle. That was Roberts' men, that was, and comed of changing names to their ships – *Royal Fortune* and so on. Now, what a ship was christened, so let her stay, I says. So it was with the *Cassandra*, as brought us all safe home from Malabar, after England took the viceroy of the Indies; so it was with the old *Walrus*, Flint's old ship, as I've seen amuck with the red blood and fit to sink with gold."

"Ah!" cried another voice, that of the youngest hand on board, and evidently full of admiration. "He was the flower of the flock, was Flint!"

"Davis was a man too, by all accounts," said Silver. "I never sailed along of him; first with England, then with Flint, that's my story; and now here on my own account, in a manner of speaking. I laid by nine hundred safe, from England, and two thousand after Flint. That ain't bad for a man before the mast – all safe in bank. 'Tain't earning now, it's saving does it, you may lay to that. Where's all England's men now? I dunno. Where's Flint's? Why, most on 'em aboard here, and glad to get the duff – been begging before that, some on 'em. Old Pew, as had lost his sight, and might have thought shame, spends twelve hundred pound in a year, like a lord in Parliament. Where is he now? Well, he's dead now and under hatches; but for two year before that, shiver my timbers, the man was starving! He begged, and he stole, and he cut throats, and starved at that, by the powers!"

"Well, it ain't much use, after all," said the young seaman.

"'Tain't much use for fools, you may lay to it – that, nor nothing," cried Silver. "But now, you look here: you're young, you are, but you're as smart as paint. I see that when I set my eyes on you, and I'll talk to you like a man."

You may imagine how I felt when I heard this abominable old rogue addressing another in the very same words of flattery as he had used to myself. I think, if I had been able, that I would have killed him through the barrel. Meantime, he ran on, little supposing he was overheard.

"Here it is about gentlemen of fortune. They lives rough, and they risk swinging, but they eat and drink like fighting-cocks, and when a cruise is done, why, it's hundreds of pounds instead of hundreds of farthings in their pockets. Now, the most goes for rum and a good fling, and to sea again in their shirts. But that's not the course I lay. I puts it all away, some here, some there, and none too much anywheres, by reason of suspicion. I'm fifty, mark you; once back from this cruise, I set up gentleman in earnest. Time enough too, says you. Ah, but I've lived easy in the meantime, never denied myself o' nothing heart desires, and slep' soft and ate dainty all my days but when at sea. And how did I begin? Before the mast, like you!"

"Well," said the other, "but all the other money's gone now, ain't it? You daren't show face in Bristol after this."

"Why, where might you suppose it was?" asked Silver derisively.

"At Bristol, in banks and places," answered his companion.

"It were," said the cook; "it were when we weighed anchor. But my old missis has it all by now. And the Spy-glass is sold, lease and goodwill and rigging; and the old girl's off to meet me. I would tell you where, for I trust you, but it'd make jealousy among the mates."

"And can you trust your missis?" asked the other.

"Gentlemen of fortune," returned the cook, "usually trusts little among themselves, and right they are, you may lay to it. But I have a way with me, I have. When a mate brings a slip on his cable – one as knows me, I mean – it won't be in the same world with old John. There was some that was feared of Pew, and some that was feared of Flint; but Flint his own self was feared of me. Feared he was, and proud. They was the roughest crew afloat, was Flint's; the devil himself would have been feared to go to sea with them. Well now, I tell you, I'm not a boasting man, and you seen yourself how easy I keep company, but when I was quartermaster, *lambs* wasn't the word for Flint's old buccaneers. Ah, you may be sure of yourself in old John's ship."

"Well, I tell you now," replied the lad, "I didn't half a quarter like the job till I had this talk with you, John; but there's my hand on it now."

"And a brave lad you were, and smart too," answered Silver, shaking hands so heartily that all the barrel shook, "and a finer figurehead for a gentleman of fortune I never clapped my eyes on."

By this time I had begun to understand the meaning of their terms. By a "gentleman of fortune" they plainly meant neither more nor less than a common pirate, and the little scene that I had overheard was the last act in the corruption of one of the honest hands – perhaps of the last one left aboard. But on this point I was soon to be relieved, for Silver giving a little whistle, a third man strolled up and sat down by the party.

"Dick's square," said Silver.

"Oh, I know'd Dick was square," returned the voice of the coxswain, Israel Hands. "He's no fool, is Dick." And he turned his quid and spat. "But look here," he went on, "here's what I want to know, Barbecue: how long are we a-going to stand off and on like a blessed bumboat? I've had a'most enough o' Cap'n Smollett; he's hazed me long enough, by thunder! I want to go into that cabin, I do. I want their pickles and wines, and that."

"Israel," said Silver, "your head ain't much account, nor ever was. But you're able to hear, I reckon; leastways, your ears is big enough. Now, here's what I say: you'll berth forward, and you'll live hard, and you'll speak soft, and you'll keep sober till I give the word; and you may lay to that, my son."

"Well, I don't say no, do I?" growled the coxswain. "What I say is, when? That's what I say."

"When! By the powers!" cried Silver. "Well now, if you want to know, I'll tell you when. The last moment I can manage, and that's when. Here's a first-rate seaman, Cap'n Smollett, sails the blessed ship for us. Here's this squire and doctor with a map and such – I don't know where it is, do I? No more do you, says you. Well then, I mean this squire and doctor shall find the stuff, and help us to get it aboard, by the powers. Then we'll see. If I was sure of you all, sons of double Dutchmen, I'd have Cap'n Smollett navigate us half-way back again before I struck."

"Why, we're all seamen aboard here, I should think," said the lad Dick.

"We're all forecastle hands, you mean," snapped Silver. "We can steer a course, but who's to set one? That's what all you gentlemen split on, first and last. If I had my way, I'd have Cap'n Smollett work us back into the trades at least; then we'd have no blessed miscalculations and a spoonful of water a day. But I know the sort you are. I'll finish with 'em at the island, as soon's the blunt's on board, and a pity it is. But you're never happy till you're drunk. Split my sides, I've a sick heart to sail with the likes of you!"

"Easy all, Long John," cried Israel. "Who's a-crossin' of you?"

"Why, how many tall ships, think ye, now, have I seen laid aboard? And how many brisk lads drying in the sun at Execution Dock?" cried

Silver. "And all for this same hurry and hurry and hurry. You hear me? I seen a thing or two at sea, I have. If you would on'y lay your course, and a p'int to windward, you would ride in carriages, you would. But not you! I know you. You'll have your mouthful of rum tomorrow, and go hang."

"Everybody knowed you was a kind of a chapling, John; but there's others as could hand and steer as well as you," said Israel. "They liked a bit o' fun, they did. They wasn't so high and dry, nohow, but took their fling, like jolly companions every one."

"So?" says Silver. "Well, and where are they now? Pew was that sort, and he died a beggar-man. Flint was, and he died of rum at Savannah. Ah, they was a sweet crew, they was! On'y, where are they?"

"But," asked Dick, "when we do lay 'em athwart, what are we to do with 'em, anyhow?"

"There's the man for me!" cried the cook admiringly. "That's what I call business. Well, what would you think? Put 'em ashore like maroons? That would have been England's way. Or cut 'em down like that much pork? That would have been Flint's, or Billy Bones's."

"Billy was the man for that," said Israel. "'Dead men don't bite,' says he. Well, he's dead now hisself; he knows the long and short on it now; and if ever a rough hand come to port, it was Billy."

"Right you are," said Silver; "rough and ready. But mark you here, I'm an easy man – I'm quite the gentleman, says you; but this time it's serious. Dooty is dooty, mates. I give my vote – death. When I'm in Parlyment and riding in my coach, I don't want none of these sea-lawyers in the cabin a-coming home, unlooked for, like the devil at prayers. Wait is what I say; but when the time comes, why, let her rip!"

"John," cries the coxswain, "you're a man!"

"You'll say so, Israel when you see," said Silver. "Only one thing I claim – I claim Trelawney. I'll wring his calf's head off his body with these hands, Dick!" he added, breaking off. "You just jump up, like a sweet lad, and get me an apple, to wet my pipe like."

You may fancy the terror I was in! I should have leaped out and run for it if I had found the strength, but my limbs and heart alike misgave me. I heard Dick begin to rise, and then someone seemingly stopped him, and the voice of Hands exclaimed, "Oh, stow that! Don't you get sucking of that bilge, John. Let's have a go of the rum."

"Dick," said Silver, "I trust you. I've a gauge on the keg, mind. There's the key; you fill a pannikin and bring it up."

Terrified as I was, I could not help thinking to myself that this must have been how Mr. Arrow got the strong waters that destroyed him.

Dick was gone but a little while, and during his absence Israel spoke straight on in the cook's ear. It was but a word or two that I could catch, and yet I gathered some important news, for besides other scraps that tended to the same purpose, this whole clause was audible: "Not another man of them'll jine." Hence there were still faithful men on board.

When Dick returned, one after another of the trio took the pannikin and drank – one "To luck," another with a "Here's to old Flint," and Silver himself saying, in a kind of song, "Here's to ourselves, and hold your luff, plenty of prizes and plenty of duff."

Just then a sort of brightness fell upon me in the barrel, and looking up, I found the moon had risen and was silvering the mizzen-top and shining white on the luff of the fore-sail; and almost at the same time the voice of the lookout shouted, "Land ho!"

CHAPTER TWELVE

Council of War

There was a great rush of feet across the deck. I could hear people tumbling up from the cabin and the forecastle, and slipping in an instant outside my barrel, I dived behind the fore-sail, made a double towards the stern, and came out upon the open deck in time to join Hunter and Dr. Livesey in the rush for the weather bow.

There all hands were already congregated. A belt of fog had lifted almost simultaneously with the appearance of the moon. Away to the south-west of us we saw two low hills, about a couple of miles apart, and rising behind one of them a third and higher hill, whose peak was still buried in the fog. All three seemed sharp and conical in figure.

So much I saw, almost in a dream, for I had not yet recovered from my horrid fear of a minute or two before. And then I heard the voice of Captain Smollett issuing orders. The *Hispaniola* was laid a couple of points nearer the wind and now sailed a course that would just clear the island on the east.

"And now, men," said the captain, when all was sheeted home, "has any one of you ever seen that land ahead?"

"I have, sir," said Silver. "I've watered there with a trader I was cook in."

"The anchorage is on the south, behind an islet, I fancy?" asked the captain.

"Yes, sir; Skeleton Island they calls it. It were a main place for pirates once, and a hand we had on board knowed all their names for it. That hill to the nor'ard they calls the Fore-mast Hill; there are three hills in a row running south'ard – fore, main, and mizzen, sir. But the main – that's the big un, with the cloud on it – they usually calls the Spy-glass, by reason of a lookout they kept when they was in the anchorage cleaning, for it's there they cleaned their ships, sir, asking your pardon."

"I have a chart here," says Captain Smollett. "See if that's the place."

Long John's eyes burned in his head as he took the chart, but by the fresh look of the paper I knew he was doomed to disappointment. This was not the map we found in Billy Bones's chest, but an accurate copy, complete in all things – names and heights and soundings – with the single exception of the red crosses and the written notes. Sharp as must have been his annoyance, Silver had the strength of mind to hide it.

"Yes, sir," said he, "this is the spot, to be sure, and very prettily drawed out. Who might have done that, I wonder? The pirates were too ignorant, I reckon. Aye, here it is: 'Capt. Kidd's Anchorage' – just the name my shipmate called it. There's a strong current runs along the south, and then away nor'ard up the west coast. Right you was, sir," says he, "to haul your wind and keep the weather of the island. Leastways, if such was your intention as to enter and careen, and there ain't no better place for that in these waters."

"Thank you, my man," says Captain Smollett. "I'll ask you later on to give us a help. You may go."

I was surprised at the coolness with which John avowed his knowledge of the island, and I own I was half-frightened when I saw him drawing nearer to myself. He did not know, to be sure, that I had overheard his council from the apple barrel, and yet I had by this time taken such a horror of his cruelty, duplicity, and power that I could scarce conceal a shudder when he laid his hand upon my arm.

"Ah," says he, "this here is a sweet spot, this island – a sweet spot for a lad to get ashore on. You'll bathe, and you'll climb trees, and you'll hunt goats, you will; and you'll get aloft on them hills like a goat yourself. Why, it makes me young again. I was going to forget my timber leg, I was. It's a pleasant thing to be young and have ten toes, and you may lay to that. When you want to go a bit of exploring, you just ask old John, and he'll put up a snack for you to take along."

And clapping me in the friendliest way upon the shoulder, he hobbled off forward and went below.

Captain Smollett, the squire, and Dr. Livesey were talking together on the quarter-deck, and anxious as I was to tell them my story, I durst not interrupt them openly. While I was still casting about in my thoughts to find some probable excuse, Dr. Livesey called me to his side. He had left his pipe below, and being a slave to tobacco, had meant that I should fetch it; but as soon as I was near enough to speak and not to be overheard, I broke immediately, "Doctor, let me speak. Get the captain and squire down to the cabin, and then make some pretence to send for me. I have terrible news."

The doctor changed countenance a little, but next moment he was master of himself.

"Thank you, Jim," said he quite loudly, "that was all I wanted to know," as if he had asked me a question.

And with that he turned on his heel and rejoined the other two. They spoke together for a little, and though none of them started, or raised his voice, or so much as whistled, it was plain enough that Dr. Livesey had communicated my request, for the next thing that I heard was the captain giving an order to Job Anderson, and all hands were piped on deck.

"My lads," said Captain Smollett, "I've a word to say to you. This land that we have sighted is the place we have been sailing for. Mr. Trelawney, being a very open-handed gentleman, as we all know, has just asked me a word or two, and as I was able to tell him that every man on board had done his duty, alow and aloft, as I never ask to see it done better, why, he and I and the doctor are going below to the cabin to drink *your* health and luck, and you'll have grog served out for you to drink *our* health and luck. I'll tell you what I think of this: I think it handsome. And if you think as I do, you'll give a good sea-cheer for the gentleman that does it."

The cheer followed – that was a matter of course; but it rang out so full and hearty that I confess I could hardly believe these same men were plotting for our blood.

"One more cheer for Cap'n Smollett," cried Long John when the first had subsided.

And this also was given with a will.

On the top of that the three gentlemen went below, and not long after, word was sent forward that Jim Hawkins was wanted in the cabin.

I found them all three seated round the table, a bottle of Spanish wine and some raisins before them, and the doctor smoking away, with his wig on his lap, and that, I knew, was a sign that he was agitated. The stern window was open, for it was a warm night, and you could see the moon shining behind on the ship's wake.

"Now, Hawkins," said the squire, "you have something to say. Speak up."

I did as I was bid, and as short as I could make it, told the whole details of Silver's conversation. Nobody interrupted me till I was done, nor did any one of the three of them make so much as a movement, but they kept their eyes upon my face from first to last.

"Jim," said Dr. Livesey, "take a seat."

And they made me sit down at table beside them, poured me out a glass of wine, filled my hands with raisins, and all three, one after the other, and each with a bow, drank my good health, and their service to me, for my luck and courage.

"Now, captain," said the squire, "you were right, and I was wrong. I own myself an ass, and I await your orders."

"No more an ass than I, sir," returned the captain. "I never heard of a crew that meant to mutiny but what showed signs before, for any man that had an eye in his head to see the mischief and take steps according. But this crew," he added, "beats me."

"Captain," said the doctor, "with your permission, that's Silver. A very remarkable man."

"He'd look remarkably well from a yard-arm, sir," returned the captain. "But this is talk; this don't lead to anything. I see three or four points, and with Mr. Trelawney's permission, I'll name them."

"You, sir, are the captain. It is for you to speak," says Mr. Trelawney grandly.

"First point," began Mr. Smollett. "We must go on, because we can't turn back. If I gave the word to go about, they would rise at once. Second point, we have time before us – at least until this treasure's found. Third point, there are faithful hands. Now, sir, it's got to come to blows sooner or later, and what I propose is to take time by the forelock, as the saying is, and come to blows some fine day when they least expect it. We can count, I take it, on your own home servants, Mr. Trelawney?"

"As upon myself," declared the squire.

"Three," reckoned the captain; "ourselves make seven, counting Hawkins here. Now, about the honest hands?"

"Most likely Trelawney's own men," said the doctor; "those he had picked up for himself before he lit on Silver."

"Nay," replied the squire. "Hands was one of mine."

"I did think I could have trusted Hands," added the captain.

"And to think that they're all Englishmen!" broke out the squire. "Sir, I could find it in my heart to blow the ship up."

"Well, gentlemen," said the captain, "the best that I can say is not much. We must lay to, if you please, and keep a bright lookout. It's trying on a man, I know. It would be pleasanter to come to blows. But there's no help for it till we know our men. Lay to, and whistle for a wind, that's my view."

"Jim here," said the doctor, "can help us more than anyone. The men are not shy with him, and Jim is a noticing lad."

"Hawkins, I put prodigious faith in you," added the squire.

I began to feel pretty desperate at this, for I felt altogether helpless; and yet, by an odd train of circumstances, it was indeed through me that safety came. In the meantime, talk as we pleased, there were only seven out of the twenty-six on whom we knew we could rely; and out of these seven one was a boy, so that the grown men on our side were six to their nineteen.

PART THREE

My Shore Adventure

CHAPTER THIRTEEN

How My Shore Adventure Began

The appearance of the island when I came on deck next morning was altogether changed. Although the breeze had now utterly ceased, we had made a great deal of way during the night and were now lying becalmed about half a mile to the south-east of the low eastern coast. Grey-coloured woods covered a large part of the surface. This even tint was indeed broken up by streaks of yellow sand-break in the lower lands, and by many tall trees of the pine family, out-topping the others – some singly, some in clumps; but the general colouring was uniform and sad. The hills ran up clear above the vegetation in spires of naked rock. All were strangely shaped, and the Spy-glass, which was by three or four hundred feet the tallest on the island, was likewise the strangest in configuration, running up sheer from almost every side and then suddenly cut off at the top like a pedestal to put a statue on.

The *Hispaniola* was rolling scuppers under in the ocean swell. The booms were tearing at the blocks, the rudder was banging to and fro, and the whole ship creaking, groaning, and jumping like a manufactory. I had to cling tight to the backstay, and the world turned giddily before my eyes, for though I was a good enough sailor when there was way on, this standing still and being rolled about like a bottle was a thing I never learned to stand without a qualm or so, above all in the morning, on an empty stomach.

Perhaps it was this – perhaps it was the look of the island, with its grey, melancholy woods, and wild stone spires, and the surf that we could both see and hear foaming and thundering on the steep beach – at least, although the sun shone bright and hot, and the shore birds were fishing and crying all around us, and you would have thought anyone would have been glad to get to land after being so long at sea, my heart sank, as the saying is, into my boots; and from the first look onward, I hated the very thought of Treasure Island.

We had a dreary morning's work before us, for there was no sign of any wind, and the boats had to be got out and manned, and the ship warped three or four miles round the corner of the island and up the narrow passage to the haven behind Skeleton Island. I volunteered for one of the boats, where I had, of course, no business. The heat was sweltering, and the men grumbled fiercely over their work. Anderson was in command of my boat, and instead of keeping the crew in order, he grumbled as loud as the worst.

"Well," he said with an oath, "it's not forever."

I thought this was a very bad sign, for up to that day the men had gone briskly and willingly about their business; but the very sight of the island had relaxed the cords of discipline.

All the way in, Long John stood by the steersman and conned the ship. He knew the passage like the palm of his hand, and though the man in the chains got everywhere more water than was down in the chart, John never hesitated once.

"There's a strong scour with the ebb," he said, "and this here passage has been dug out, in a manner of speaking, with a spade."

We brought up just where the anchor was in the chart, about a third of a mile from each shore, the mainland on one side and Skeleton Island on the other. The bottom was clean sand. The plunge of our anchor sent up clouds of birds wheeling and crying over the woods, but in less than a minute they were down again and all was once more silent.

The place was entirely land-locked, buried in woods, the trees coming right down to high-water mark, the shores mostly flat, and the hilltops standing round at a distance in a sort of amphitheatre, one here, one there. Two little rivers, or rather two swamps, emptied out into this pond, as you might call it; and the foliage round that part of the shore had a kind of poisonous brightness. From the ship we could see nothing of the house or stockade, for they were quite buried among trees; and if it had not been for the chart on the companion, we might have been the first that had ever anchored there since the island arose out of the seas.

There was not a breath of air moving, nor a sound but that of the surf booming half a mile away along the beaches and against the rocks outside. A peculiar stagnant smell hung over the anchorage – a smell of sodden leaves and rotting tree trunks. I observed the doctor sniffing and sniffing, like someone tasting a bad egg.

"I don't know about treasure," he said, "but I'll stake my wig there's fever here."

If the conduct of the men had been alarming in the boat, it became truly threatening when they had come aboard. They lay about the deck growling together in talk. The slightest order was received with a black look and grudgingly and carelessly obeyed. Even the honest hands must have caught the infection, for there was not one man aboard to mend another. Mutiny, it was plain, hung over us like a thunder-cloud.

And it was not only we of the cabin party who perceived the danger. Long John was hard at work going from group to group, spending himself in good advice, and as for example no man could have shown a better. He fairly outstripped himself in willingness and civility; he was all smiles to everyone. If an order were given, John would be on his crutch in an instant, with the cheeriest "Aye, aye, sir!" in the world; and when there was nothing else to do, he kept up one song after another, as if to conceal the discontent of the rest.

Of all the gloomy features of that gloomy afternoon, this obvious anxiety on the part of Long John appeared the worst.

We held a council in the cabin.

"Sir," said the captain, "if I risk another order, the whole ship'll come about our ears by the run. You see, sir, here it is. I get a rough answer, do I not? Well, if I speak back, pikes will be going in two shakes; if I don't, Silver will see there's something under that, and the game's up. Now, we've only one man to rely on."

"And who is that?" asked the squire.

"Silver, sir," returned the captain; "he's as anxious as you and I to smother things up. This is a tiff; he'd soon talk 'em out of it if he had the chance, and what I propose to do is to give him the chance. Let's allow the men an afternoon ashore. If they all go, why we'll fight the ship. If they none of them go, well then, we hold the cabin, and God defend the right. If some go, you mark my words, sir, Silver'll bring 'em aboard again as mild as lambs."

It was so decided; loaded pistols were served out to all the sure men; Hunter, Joyce, and Redruth were taken into our confidence and received the news with less surprise and a better spirit than we had looked for, and then the captain went on deck and addressed the crew.

"My lads," said he, "we've had a hot day and are all tired and out of sorts. A turn ashore'll hurt nobody – the boats are still in the water; you can take the gigs, and as many as please may go ashore for the afternoon. I'll fire a gun half an hour before sundown."

I believe the silly fellows must have thought they would break their shins over treasure as soon as they were landed, for they all came out of their sulks in a moment and gave a cheer that started the echo in a faraway hill and sent the birds once more flying and squalling round the anchorage.

The captain was too bright to be in the way. He whipped out of sight in a moment, leaving Silver to arrange the party, and I fancy it was as well he did so. Had he been on deck, he could no longer so much as have pretended not to understand the situation. It was as plain as day. Silver was the captain, and a mighty rebellious crew he had of it. The honest hands – and I was soon to see it proved that there were such on board – must have been very stupid fellows. Or rather, I suppose the truth was this, that all hands were disaffected by the example of the ringleaders – only some more, some less; and a few, being good fellows in the main, could neither be led nor driven any further. It is one thing to be idle and skulk and quite another to take a ship and murder a number of innocent men.

At last, however, the party was made up. Six fellows were to stay on board, and the remaining thirteen, including Silver, began to embark.

Then it was that there came into my head the first of the mad notions that contributed so much to save our lives. If six men were left by Silver, it was plain our party could not take and fight the ship; and since only six were left, it was equally plain that the cabin party had no present

need of my assistance. It occurred to me at once to go ashore. In a jiffy I had slipped over the side and curled up in the fore-sheets of the nearest boat, and almost at the same moment she shoved off.

No one took notice of me, only the bow oar saying, "Is that you, Jim? Keep your head down." But Silver, from the other boat, looked sharply over and called out to know if that were me; and from that moment I began to regret what I had done.

The crews raced for the beach, but the boat I was in, having some start and being at once the lighter and the better manned, shot far ahead of her consort, and the bow had struck among the shore-side trees and I had caught a branch and swung myself out and plunged into the nearest thicket while Silver and the rest were still a hundred yards behind.

"Jim, Jim!" I heard him shouting.

But you may suppose I paid no heed; jumping, ducking, and breaking through, I ran straight before my nose till I could run no longer.

CHAPTER FOURTEEN

The First Blow

I WAS SO PLEASED at having given the slip to Long John that I began to enjoy myself and look around me with some interest on the strange land that I was in.

I had crossed a marshy tract full of willows, bulrushes, and odd, outlandish, swampy trees; and I had now come out upon the skirts of an open piece of undulating, sandy country, about a mile long, dotted with a few pines and a great number of contorted trees, not unlike the oak in growth, but pale in the foliage, like willows. On the far side of the open stood one of the hills, with two quaint, craggy peaks shining vividly in the sun.

I now felt for the first time the joy of exploration. The isle was uninhabited; my shipmates I had left behind, and nothing lived in front of me but dumb brutes and fowls. I turned hither and thither among the trees. Here and there were flowering plants, unknown to me; here and there I saw snakes, and one raised his head from a ledge of rock and hissed at me with a noise not unlike the spinning of a top. Little did I suppose that he was a deadly enemy and that the noise was the famous rattle.

Then I came to a long thicket of these oaklike trees – live, or evergreen, oaks, I heard afterwards they should be called – which grew low along the sand like brambles, the boughs curiously twisted, the foliage compact, like thatch. The thicket stretched down from the top of one of the sandy knolls, spreading and growing taller as it went, until it reached the margin of the broad, reedy fen, through which the nearest of the little rivers soaked its way into the anchorage. The marsh was steaming in the strong sun, and the outline of the Spy-glass trembled through the haze.

All at once there began to go a sort of bustle among the bulrushes; a wild duck flew up with a quack, another followed, and soon over the whole surface of the marsh a great cloud of birds hung screaming and circling in the air. I judged at once that some of my shipmates must be drawing near along the borders of the fen. Nor was I deceived, for soon I heard the very distant and low tones of a human voice, which, as I continued to give ear, grew steadily louder and nearer.

This put me in a great fear, and I crawled under cover of the nearest live-oak and squatted there, hearkening, as silent as a mouse.

Another voice answered, and then the first voice, which I now recognized to be Silver's, once more took up the story and ran on for a long while in a stream, only now and again interrupted by the other. By the sound they must have been talking earnestly, and almost fiercely; but no distinct word came to my hearing.

At last the speakers seemed to have paused and perhaps to have sat down, for not only did they cease to draw any nearer, but the birds themselves began to grow more quiet and to settle again to their places in the swamp.

And now I began to feel that I was neglecting my business, that since I had been so foolhardy as to come ashore with these desperadoes, the least I could do was to overhear them at their councils, and that my plain and obvious duty was to draw as close as I could manage, under the favourable ambush of the crouching trees.

I could tell the direction of the speakers pretty exactly, not only by the sound of their voices but by the behaviour of the few birds that still hung in alarm above the heads of the intruders.

Crawling on all fours, I made steadily but slowly towards them, till at last, raising my head to an aperture among the leaves, I could see clear down into a little green dell beside the marsh, and closely set about with trees, where Long John Silver and another of the crew stood face to face in conversation.

The sun beat full upon them. Silver had thrown his hat beside him on the ground, and his great, smooth, blond face, all shining with heat, was lifted to the other man's in a kind of appeal.

"Mate," he was saying, "it's because I thinks gold dust of you – gold dust, and you may lay to that! If I hadn't took to you like pitch, do you think I'd have been here a-warning of you? All's up – you can't make nor mend; it's to save your neck that I'm a-speaking, and if one of the wild uns knew it, where'd I be, Tom – now, tell me, where'd I be?"

"Silver," said the other man – and I observed he was not only red in the face, but spoke as hoarse as a crow, and his voice shook too, like a taut rope – "Silver," says he, "you're old, and you're honest, or has the name for it; and you've money too, which lots of poor sailors hasn't; and you're brave, or I'm mistook. And will you tell me you'll let yourself be led away with that kind of a mess of swabs? Not you! As sure as God sees me, I'd sooner lose my hand. If I turn agin my dooty – "

And then all of a sudden he was interrupted by a noise. I had found one of the honest hands – well, here, at that same moment, came news of another. Far away out in the marsh there arose, all of a sudden, a sound like the cry of anger, then another on the back of it; and then one horrid, long-drawn scream. The rocks of the Spy-glass re-echoed it a score of times; the whole troop of marsh-birds rose again, darkening heaven, with a simultaneous whirr; and long after that death yell was still ringing in my brain, silence had re-established its empire, and only the rustle of the redescending birds and the boom of the distant surges disturbed the languor of the afternoon.

Tom had leaped at the sound, like a horse at the spur, but Silver had not winked an eye. He stood where he was, resting lightly on his crutch, watching his companion like a snake about to spring.

"John!" said the sailor, stretching out his hand.

"Hands off!" cried Silver, leaping back a yard, as it seemed to me, with the speed and security of a trained gymnast.

"Hands off, if you like, John Silver," said the other. "It's a black conscience that can make you feared of me. But in heaven's name, tell me, what was that?"

"That?" returned Silver, smiling away, but warier than ever, his eye a mere pin-point in his big face, but gleaming like a crumb of glass. "That? Oh, I reckon that'll be Alan."

And at this point Tom flashed out like a hero.

"Alan!" he cried. "Then rest his soul for a true seaman! And as for you, John Silver, long you've been a mate of mine, but you're mate of mine no more. If I die like a dog, I'll die in my dooty. You've killed Alan, have you? Kill me too, if you can. But I defies you."

And with that, this brave fellow turned his back directly on the cook and set off walking for the beach. But he was not destined to go far. With a cry John seized the branch of a tree, whipped the crutch out of his armpit, and sent that uncouth missile hurtling through the air. It struck poor Tom, point foremost, and with stunning violence, right between the shoulders in the middle of his back. His hands flew up, he gave a sort of gasp, and fell.

Whether he were injured much or little, none could ever tell. Like enough, to judge from the sound, his back was broken on the spot. But he had no time given him to recover. Silver, agile as a monkey even

without leg or crutch, was on the top of him next moment and had twice buried his knife up to the hilt in that defenceless body. From my place of ambush, I could hear him pant aloud as he struck the blows.

I do not know what it rightly is to faint, but I do know that for the next little while the whole world swam away from before me in a whirling mist; Silver and the birds, and the tall Spy-glass hilltop, going round and round and topsy-turvy before my eyes, and all manner of bells ringing and distant voices shouting in my ear.

When I came again to myself the monster had pulled himself together, his crutch under his arm, his hat upon his head. Just before him Tom lay motionless upon the sward; but the murderer minded him not a whit, cleansing his blood-stained knife the while upon a wisp of grass. Everything else was unchanged, the sun still shining mercilessly on the steaming marsh and the tall pinnacle of the mountain, and I could scarce persuade myself that murder had been actually done and a human life cruelly cut short a moment since before my eyes.

But now John put his hand into his pocket, brought out a whistle, and blew upon it several modulated blasts that rang far across the heated air. I could not tell, of course, the meaning of the signal, but it instantly awoke my fears. More men would be coming. I might be discovered. They had already slain two of the honest people; after Tom and Alan, might not I come next?

Instantly I began to extricate myself and crawl back again, with what speed and silence I could manage, to the more open portion of the wood. As I did so, I could hear hails coming and going between the old buccaneer and his comrades, and this sound of danger lent me wings. As soon as I was clear of the thicket, I ran as I never ran before, scarce minding the direction of my flight, so long as it led me from the murderers; and as I ran, fear grew and grew upon me until it turned into a kind of frenzy.

Indeed, could anyone be more entirely lost than I? When the gun fired, how should I dare to go down to the boats among those fiends, still smoking from their crime? Would not the first of them who saw me wring my neck like a snipe's? Would not my absence itself be an evidence to them of my alarm, and therefore of my fatal knowledge? It was all over, I thought. Good-bye to the *Hispaniola*; good-bye to the squire, the doctor, and the captain! There was nothing left for me but death by starvation or death by the hands of the mutineers.

All this while, as I say, I was still running, and without taking any notice, I had drawn near to the foot of the little hill with the two peaks and had got into a part of the island where the live-oaks grew more widely apart and seemed more like forest trees in their bearing and dimensions. Mingled with these were a few scattered pines, some fifty, some nearer seventy, feet high. The air too smelt more freshly than down beside the marsh.

And here a fresh alarm brought me to a standstill with a thumping heart.

CHAPTER FIFTEEN

The Man of the Island

From the side of the hill, which was here steep and stony, a spout of gravel was dislodged and fell rattling and bounding through the trees. My eyes turned instinctively in that direction, and I saw a figure leap with great rapidity behind the trunk of a pine. What it was, whether bear or man or monkey, I could in no wise tell. It seemed dark and shaggy; more I knew not. But the terror of this new apparition brought me to a stand.

I was now, it seemed, cut off upon both sides; behind me the murderers, before me this lurking nondescript. And immediately I began to prefer the dangers that I knew to those I knew not. Silver himself appeared less terrible in contrast with this creature of the woods, and I turned on my heel, and looking sharply behind me over my shoulder, began to retrace my steps in the direction of the boats.

Instantly the figure reappeared, and making a wide circuit, began to head me off. I was tired, at any rate; but had I been as fresh as when I rose, I could see it was in vain for me to contend in speed with such an adversary. From trunk to trunk the creature flitted like a deer, running manlike on two legs, but unlike any man that I had ever seen, stooping almost double as it ran. Yet a man it was, I could no longer be in doubt about that.

I began to recall what I had heard of cannibals. I was within an ace of calling for help. But the mere fact that he was a man, however wild, had somewhat reassured me, and my fear of Silver began to revive in proportion. I stood still, therefore, and cast about for some method of escape; and as I was so thinking, the recollection of my pistol flashed into my mind. As soon as I remembered I was not defenceless, courage glowed again in my heart and I set my face resolutely for this man of the island and walked briskly towards him.

He was concealed by this time behind another tree trunk; but he must have been watching me closely, for as soon as I began to move in his direction he reappeared and took a step to meet me. Then he hesitated, drew back, came forward again, and at last, to my wonder and confusion, threw himself on his knees and held out his clasped hands in supplication.

At that I once more stopped.

"Who are you?" I asked.

"Ben Gunn," he answered, and his voice sounded hoarse and awkward, like a rusty lock. "I'm poor Ben Gunn, I am; and I haven't spoke with a Christian these three years."

I could now see that he was a white man like myself and that his features were even pleasing. His skin, wherever it was exposed, was burnt by the sun; even his lips were black, and his fair eyes looked quite startling in so dark a face. Of all the beggar-men that I had seen or fancied, he was the chief for raggedness. He was clothed with tatters of old ship's canvas and old sea-cloth, and this extraordinary patchwork was all held together by a system of the most various and incongruous fastenings, brass buttons, bits of stick, and loops of tarry gaskin. About his waist he wore an old brass-buckled leather belt, which was the one thing solid in his whole accoutrement.

"Three years!" I cried. "Were you shipwrecked?"

"Nay, mate," said he; "marooned."

I had heard the word, and I knew it stood for a horrible kind of punishment common enough among the buccaneers, in which the offender is put ashore with a little powder and shot and left behind on some desolate and distant island.

"Marooned three years agone," he continued, "and lived on goats since then, and berries, and oysters. Wherever a man is, says I, a man can do for himself. But, mate, my heart is sore for Christian diet. You mightn't happen to have a piece of cheese about you, now? No? Well, many's the long night I've dreamed of cheese – toasted, mostly – and woke up again, and here I were."

"If ever I can get aboard again," said I, "you shall have cheese by the stone."

All this time he had been feeling the stuff of my jacket, smoothing my hands, looking at my boots, and generally, in the intervals of his speech, showing a childish pleasure in the presence of a fellow creature. But at my last words he perked up into a kind of startled slyness.

"If ever you can get aboard again, says you?" he repeated. "Why, now, who's to hinder you?"

"Not you, I know," was my reply.

"And right you was," he cried. "Now you – what do you call yourself, mate?"

"Jim," I told him.

"Jim, Jim," says he, quite pleased apparently. "Well, now, Jim, I've lived that rough as you'd be ashamed to hear of. Now, for instance, you wouldn't think I had had a pious mother – to look at me?" he asked.

"Why, no, not in particular," I answered.

"Ah, well," said he, "but I had – remarkable pious. And I was a civil, pious boy, and could rattle off my catechism that fast, as you couldn't tell one word from another. And here's what it come to, Jim, and it begun with chuck-farthen on the blessed grave-stones! That's what it begun with, but it went further'n that; and so my mother told me, and predicked the whole, she did, the pious woman! But it were Providence that put me here. I've thought it all out in this here lonely island, and I'm back on piety. You don't catch me tasting rum so much, but just a thimbleful for luck, of course, the first chance I have. I'm bound I'll be good, and I see the way to. And, Jim" – looking all round him and lowering his voice to a whisper – "I'm rich."

I now felt sure that the poor fellow had gone crazy in his solitude, and I suppose I must have shown the feeling in my face, for he repeated the statement hotly: "Rich! Rich! I says. And I'll tell you what: I'll make a man of you, Jim. Ah, Jim, you'll bless your stars, you will, you was the first that found me!"

And at this there came suddenly a lowering shadow over his face, and he tightened his grasp upon my hand and raised a forefinger threateningly before my eyes.

"Now, Jim, you tell me true: that ain't Flint's ship?" he asked.

At this I had a happy inspiration. I began to believe that I had found an ally, and I answered him at once.

"It's not Flint's ship, and Flint is dead; but I'll tell you true, as you ask me – there are some of Flint's hands aboard; worse luck for the rest of us."

"Not a man – with one – leg?" he gasped.

"Silver?" I asked.

"Ah, Silver!" says he. "That were his name."

"He's the cook, and the ringleader too."

He was still holding me by the wrist, and at that he give it quite a wring.

"If you was sent by Long John," he said, "I'm as good as pork, and I know it. But where was you, do you suppose?"

I had made my mind up in a moment, and by way of answer told him the whole story of our voyage and the predicament in which we found ourselves. He heard me with the keenest interest, and when I had done he patted me on the head.

"You're a good lad, Jim," he said; "and you're all in a clove hitch, ain't you? Well, you just put your trust in Ben Gunn – Ben Gunn's the man to do it. Would you think it likely, now, that your squire would prove a liberal-minded one in case of help – him being in a clove hitch, as you remark?"

I told him the squire was the most liberal of men.

"Aye, but you see," returned Ben Gunn, "I didn't mean giving me a gate to keep, and a suit of livery clothes, and such; that's not my mark, Jim. What I mean is, would he be likely to come down to the toon of, say one thousand pounds out of money that's as good as a man's own already?"

"I am sure he would," said I. "As it was, all hands were to share."

"*And* a passage home?" he added with a look of great shrewdness.

"Why," I cried, "the squire's a gentleman. And besides, if we got rid of the others, we should want you to help work the vessel home."

"Ah," said he, "so you would." And he seemed very much relieved.

"Now, I'll tell you what," he went on. "So much I'll tell you, and no more. I were in Flint's ship when he buried the treasure; he and six along – six strong seamen. They was ashore nigh on a week, and us standing off and on in the old *Walrus*. One fine day up went the signal, and here come Flint by himself in a little boat, and his head done up in a blue scarf. The sun was getting up, and mortal white he looked about the cutwater. But, there he was, you mind, and the six all dead – dead and buried. How he done it, not a man aboard us could make out. It was battle, murder, and sudden death, leastways – him against six. Billy Bones was the mate; Long John, he was quartermaster; and they asked him where the treasure was. 'Ah,' says he, 'you can go ashore, if you like, and stay,' he says; 'but as for the ship, she'll beat up for more, by thunder!' That's what he said.

"Well, I was in another ship three years back, and we sighted this island. 'Boys,' said I, 'here's Flint's treasure; let's land and find it.' The cap'n was displeased at that, but my messmates were all of a mind and landed. Twelve days they looked for it, and every day they had the worse word for me, until one fine morning all hands went aboard. 'As for you, Benjamin Gunn,' says they, 'here's a musket,' they says, 'and a spade, and pick-axe. You can stay here and find Flint's money for yourself,' they says.

"Well, Jim, three years have I been here, and not a bite of Christian diet from that day to this. But now, you look here; look at me. Do I look like a man before the mast? No, says you. Nor I weren't, neither, I says."

And with that he winked and pinched me hard.

"Just you mention them words to your squire, Jim," he went on. "Nor he weren't, neither – that's the words. Three years he were the man of this island, light and dark, fair and rain; and sometimes he would maybe think upon a prayer (says you), and sometimes he would maybe think of his old mother, so be as she's alive (you'll say); but the most part of Gunn's time (this is what you'll say) – the most part of his time was took up with another matter. And then you'll give him a nip, like I do."

And he pinched me again in the most confidential manner.

"Then," he continued, "then you'll up, and you'll say this: Gunn is a good man (you'll say), and he puts a precious sight more confidence – a precious sight, mind that – in a gen'leman born than in these gen'leman of fortune, having been one hisself."

"Well," I said, "I don't understand one word that you've been saying. But that's neither here nor there; for how am I to get on board?"

"Ah," said he, "that's the hitch, for sure. Well, there's my boat, that I made with my two hands. I keep her under the white rock. If the worst come to the worst, we might try that after dark. Hi!" he broke out. "What's that?"

For just then, although the sun had still an hour or two to run, all the echoes of the island awoke and bellowed to the thunder of a cannon.

"They have begun to fight!" I cried. "Follow me."

And I began to run towards the anchorage, my terrors all forgotten, while close at my side the marooned man in his goatskins trotted easily and lightly.

"Left, left," says he; "keep to your left hand, mate Jim! Under the trees with you! Theer's where I killed my first goat. They don't come down here now; they're all mastheaded on them mountings for the fear of Benjamin Gunn. Ah! And there's the cetemery" – cemetery, he must have meant. "You see the mounds? I come here and prayed, nows and thens, when I thought maybe a Sunday would be about doo. It weren't quite a chapel, but it seemed more solemn like; and then, says you, Ben Gunn was short-handed – no chapling, nor so much as a Bible and a flag, you says."

So he kept talking as I ran, neither expecting nor receiving any answer.

The cannon-shot was followed after a considerable interval by a volley of small arms.

Another pause, and then, not a quarter of a mile in front of me, I beheld the Union Jack flutter in the air above a wood.

PART FOUR

The Stockade

CHAPTER SIXTEEN

Narrative Continued by the Doctor: How the Ship Was Abandoned

It was about half past one – three bells in the sea phrase – that the two boats went ashore from the *Hispaniola*. The captain, the squire, and I were talking matters over in the cabin. Had there been a breath of wind, we should have fallen on the six mutineers who were left aboard with us, slipped our cable, and away to sea. But the wind was wanting; and to complete our helplessness, down came Hunter with the news that Jim Hawkins had slipped into a boat and was gone ashore with the rest.

It never occurred to us to doubt Jim Hawkins, but we were alarmed for his safety. With the men in the temper they were in, it seemed an even chance if we should see the lad again. We ran on deck. The pitch was bubbling in the seams; the nasty stench of the place turned me sick; if ever a man smelt fever and dysentery, it was in that abominable anchorage. The six scoundrels were sitting grumbling under a sail in the forecastle; ashore we could see the gigs made fast and a man sitting in each, hard by where the river runs in. One of them was whistling "Lillibullero."

Waiting was a strain, and it was decided that Hunter and I should go ashore with the jolly-boat in quest of information.

The gigs had leaned to their right, but Hunter and I pulled straight in, in the direction of the stockade upon the chart. The two who were left guarding their boats seemed in a bustle at our appearance; "Lillibullero" stopped off, and I could see the pair discussing what they ought to do. Had they gone and told Silver, all might have turned out differently; but they had their orders, I suppose, and decided to sit quietly where they were and hark back again to "Lillibullero."

There was a slight bend in the coast, and I steered so as to put it between us; even before we landed we had thus lost sight of the gigs. I jumped out and came as near running as I durst, with a big silk handkerchief under my hat for coolness' sake and a brace of pistols ready primed for safety.

I had not gone a hundred yards when I reached the stockade.

This was how it was: a spring of clear water rose almost at the top of a knoll. Well, on the knoll, and enclosing the spring, they had clapped a stout loghouse fit to hold two score of people on a pinch and loopholed for musketry on either side. All round this they had cleared a wide space, and then the thing was completed by a paling six feet high, without door or opening, too strong to pull down without time and labour and too open to shelter the besiegers. The people in the log-house had them in every way; they stood quiet in shelter and shot the others like partridges. All they wanted was a good watch and food; for, short of a complete surprise, they might have held the place against a regiment.

What particularly took my fancy was the spring. For though we had a good enough place of it in the cabin of the *Hispaniola*, with plenty of arms and ammunition, and things to eat, and excellent wines, there had been one thing overlooked – we had no water. I was thinking this over when there came ringing over the island the cry of a man at the point of death. I was not new to violent death – I have served his Royal Highness the Duke of Cumberland, and got a wound myself at Fontenoy – but I know my pulse went dot and carry one. "Jim Hawkins is gone," was my first thought.

It is something to have been an old soldier, but more still to have been a doctor. There is no time to dilly-dally in our work. And so now I made up my mind instantly, and with no time lost returned to the shore and jumped on board the jolly-boat.

By good fortune Hunter pulled a good oar. We made the water fly, and the boat was soon alongside and I aboard the schooner.

I found them all shaken, as was natural. The squire was sitting down, as white as a sheet, thinking of the harm he had led us to, the good soul! And one of the six forecastle hands was little better.

"There's a man," says Captain Smollett, nodding towards him, "new to this work. He came nigh-hand fainting, doctor, when he heard the cry. Another touch of the rudder and that man would join us."

I told my plan to the captain, and between us we settled on the details of its accomplishment.

We put old Redruth in the gallery between the cabin and the forecastle, with three or four loaded muskets and a mattress for protection. Hunter brought the boat round under the stern-port, and Joyce and I set to work loading her with powder tins, muskets, bags of biscuits, kegs of pork, a cask of cognac, and my invaluable medicine chest.

In the meantime, the squire and the captain stayed on deck, and the latter hailed the coxswain, who was the principal man aboard.

"Mr. Hands," he said, "here are two of us with a brace of pistols each. If any one of you six make a signal of any description, that man's dead."

They were a good deal taken aback, and after a little consultation one and all tumbled down the fore companion, thinking no doubt to take us on the rear. But when they saw Redruth waiting for them in the sparred galley, they went about ship at once, and a head popped out again on deck.

"Down, dog!" cries the captain.

And the head popped back again; and we heard no more, for the time, of these six very faint-hearted seamen.

By this time, tumbling things in as they came, we had the jolly-boat loaded as much as we dared. Joyce and I got out through the stern-port, and we made for shore again as fast as oars could take us.

This second trip fairly aroused the watchers along shore. "Lillibullero" was dropped again; and just before we lost sight of them behind the little point, one of them whipped ashore and disappeared. I had half a mind to change my plan and destroy their boats, but I feared that Silver and the others might be close at hand, and all might very well be lost by trying for too much.

We had soon touched land in the same place as before and set to provision the block house. All three made the first journey, heavily laden, and tossed our stores over the palisade. Then, leaving Joyce to guard them – one man, to be sure, but with half a dozen muskets – Hunter and I returned to the jolly-boat and loaded ourselves once more. So we proceeded without pausing to take breath, till the whole cargo was bestowed, when the two servants took up their position in the block house, and I, with all my power, sculled back to the *Hispaniola*.

That we should have risked a second boat load seems more daring than it really was. They had the advantage of numbers, of course, but we had the advantage of arms. Not one of the men ashore had a musket, and before they could get within range for pistol shooting, we flattered ourselves we should be able to give a good account of a half-dozen at least.

The squire was waiting for me at the stern window, all his faintness gone from him. He caught the painter and made it fast, and we fell to loading the boat for our very lives. Pork, powder, and biscuit was the cargo, with only a musket and a cutlass apiece for the squire and me and Redruth and the captain. The rest of the arms and powder we dropped overboard in two fathoms and a half of water, so that we could see the bright steel shining far below us in the sun, on the clean, sandy bottom.

By this time the tide was beginning to ebb, and the ship was swinging round to her anchor. Voices were heard faintly halloaing in the direction of the two gigs; and though this reassured us for Joyce and Hunter, who were well to the eastward, it warned our party to be off.

Redruth retreated from his place in the gallery and dropped into the boat, which we then brought round to the ship's counter, to be handier for Captain Smollett.

"Now, men," said he, "do you hear me?"

There was no answer from the forecastle.

"It's to you, Abraham Gray – it's to you I am speaking."

Still no reply.

"Gray," resumed Mr. Smollett, a little louder, "I am leaving this ship, and I order you to follow your captain. I know you are a good man at bottom, and I dare say not one of the lot of you's as bad as he makes out. I have my watch here in my hand; I give you thirty seconds to join me in."

There was a pause.

"Come, my fine fellow," continued the captain; "don't hang so long in stays. I'm risking my life and the lives of these good gentlemen every second."

There was a sudden scuffle, a sound of blows, and out burst Abraham Gray with a knife cut on the side of the cheek, and came running to the captain like a dog to the whistle.

"I'm with you, sir," said he.

And the next moment he and the captain had dropped aboard of us, and we had shoved off and given way.

We were clear out of the ship, but not yet ashore in our stockade.

CHAPTER SEVENTEEN

Narrative Continued by the Doctor: The Jolly-boat's Last Trip

THIS FIFTH TRIP was quite different from any of the others. In the first place, the little gallipot of a boat that we were in was gravely overloaded. Five grown men, and three of them – Trelawney, Redruth, and the captain – over six feet high, was already more than she was meant to carry. Add to that the powder, pork, and bread-bags. The gunwale was lipping astern. Several times we shipped a little water, and my breeches and the tails of my coat were all soaking wet before we had gone a hundred yards.

The captain made us trim the boat, and we got her to lie a little more evenly. All the same, we were afraid to breathe.

In the second place, the ebb was now making – a strong rippling current running westward through the basin, and then south'ard and seaward down the straits by which we had entered in the morning. Even the ripples were a danger to our overloaded craft, but the worst of it was that we were swept out of our true course and away from our proper landing-place behind the point. If we let the current have its way we should come ashore beside the gigs, where the pirates might appear at any moment.

"I cannot keep her head for the stockade, sir," said I to the captain. I was steering, while he and Redruth, two fresh men, were at the oars. "The tide keeps washing her down. Could you pull a little stronger?"

"Not without swamping the boat," said he. "You must bear up, sir, if you please – bear up until you see you're gaining."

I tried and found by experiment that the tide kept sweeping us westward until I had laid her head due east, or just about right angles to the way we ought to go.

"We'll never get ashore at this rate," said I.

"If it's the only course that we can lie, sir, we must even lie it," returned the captain. "We must keep upstream. You see, sir," he went on, "if once we dropped to leeward of the landing-place, it's hard to say where we should get ashore, besides the chance of being boarded by the gigs; whereas, the way we go the current must slacken, and then we can dodge back along the shore."

"The current's less a'ready, sir," said the man Gray, who was sitting in the fore-sheets; "you can ease her off a bit."

"Thank you, my man," said I, quite as if nothing had happened, for we had all quietly made up our minds to treat him like one of ourselves.

Suddenly the captain spoke up again, and I thought his voice was a little changed.

"The gun!" said he.

"I have thought of that," said I, for I made sure he was thinking of a bombardment of the fort. "They could never get the gun ashore, and if they did, they could never haul it through the woods."

"Look astern, doctor," replied the captain.

We had entirely forgotten the long nine; and there, to our horror, were the five rogues busy about her, getting off her jacket, as they called the stout tarpaulin cover under which she sailed. Not only that, but it flashed into my mind at the same moment that the round-shot and the powder for the gun had been left behind, and a stroke with an axe would put it all into the possession of the evil ones abroad.

"Israel was Flint's gunner," said Gray hoarsely.

At any risk, we put the boat's head direct for the landing-place. By this time we had got so far out of the run of the current that we kept steerage way even at our necessarily gentle rate of rowing, and I could keep her steady for the goal. But the worst of it was that with the course I now held we turned our broadside instead of our stern to the *Hispaniola* and offered a target like a barn door.

I could hear as well as see that brandy-faced rascal Israel Hands plumping down a round-shot on the deck.

"Who's the best shot?" asked the captain.

"Mr. Trelawney, out and away," said I.

"Mr. Trelawney, will you please pick me off one of these men, sir? Hands, if possible," said the captain.

Trelawney was as cool as steel. He looked to the priming of his gun.

"Now," cried the captain, "easy with that gun, sir, or you'll swamp the boat. All hands stand by to trim her when he aims."

The squire raised his gun, the rowing ceased, and we leaned over to the other side to keep the balance, and all was so nicely contrived that we did not ship a drop.

They had the gun, by this time, slewed round upon the swivel, and Hands, who was at the muzzle with the rammer, was in consequence the most

exposed. However, we had no luck, for just as Trelawney fired, down he stooped, the ball whistled over him, and it was one of the other four who fell.

The cry he gave was echoed not only by his companions on board but by a great number of voices from the shore, and looking in that direction I saw the other pirates trooping out from among the trees and tumbling into their places in the boats.

"Here come the gigs, sir," said I.

"Give way, then," cried the captain. "We mustn't mind if we swamp her now. If we can't get ashore, all's up."

"Only one of the gigs is being manned, sir," I added; "the crew of the other most likely going round by shore to cut us off."

"They'll have a hot run, sir," returned the captain. "Jack ashore, you know. It's not them I mind; it's the round-shot. Carpet bowls! My lady's maid couldn't miss. Tell us, squire, when you see the match, and we'll hold water."

In the meanwhile we had been making headway at a good pace for a boat so overloaded, and we had shipped but little water in the process. We were now close in; thirty or forty strokes and we should beach her, for the ebb had already disclosed a narrow belt of sand below the clustering trees. The gig was no longer to be feared; the little point had already concealed it from our eyes. The ebb-tide, which had so cruelly delayed us, was now making reparation and delaying our assailants. The one source of danger was the gun.

"If I durst," said the captain, "I'd stop and pick off another man."

But it was plain that they meant nothing should delay their shot. They had never so much as looked at their fallen comrade, though he was not dead, and I could see him trying to crawl away.

"Ready!" cried the squire.

"Hold!" cried the captain, quick as an echo.

And he and Redruth backed with a great heave that sent her stern bodily under water. The report fell in at the same instant of time. This was the first that Jim heard, the sound of the squire's shot not having reached him. Where the ball passed, not one of us precisely knew, but I fancy it must have been over our heads and that the wind of it may have contributed to our disaster.

At any rate, the boat sank by the stern, quite gently, in three feet of water, leaving the captain and myself, facing each other, on our feet. The other three took complete headers, and came up again drenched and bubbling.

So far there was no great harm. No lives were lost, and we could wade ashore in safety. But there were all our stores at the bottom, and to make things worse, only two guns out of five remained in a state for service. Mine I had snatched from my knees and held over my head, by a sort of instinct. As for the captain, he had carried his over his shoulder by a bandoleer, and like a wise man, lock uppermost. The other three had gone down with the boat.

To add to our concern, we heard voices already drawing near us in the woods along shore, and we had not only the danger of being cut off from the stockade in our half-crippled state but the fear before us whether, if Hunter and Joyce were attacked by half a dozen, they would have the sense and conduct to stand firm. Hunter was steady, that we knew; Joyce was a doubtful case – a pleasant, polite man for a valet and to brush one's clothes, but not entirely fitted for a man of war.

With all this in our minds, we waded ashore as fast as we could, leaving behind us the poor jolly-boat and a good half of all our powder and provisions.

CHAPTER EIGHTEEN

Narrative Continued by the Doctor: End of the First Day's Fighting

We made our best speed across the strip of wood that now divided us from the stockade, and at every step we took the voices of the buccaneers rang nearer. Soon we could hear their footfalls as they ran and the cracking of the branches as they breasted across a bit of thicket.

I began to see we should have a brush for it in earnest and looked to my priming.

"Captain," said I, "Trelawney is the dead shot. Give him your gun; his own is useless."

They exchanged guns, and Trelawney, silent and cool as he had been since the beginning of the bustle, hung a moment on his heel to see that all was fit for service. At the same time, observing Gray to be unarmed, I handed him my cutlass. It did all our hearts good to see him spit in his hand, knit his brows, and make the blade sing through the air. It was plain from every line of his body that our new hand was worth his salt.

Forty paces farther we came to the edge of the wood and saw the stockade in front of us. We struck the enclosure about the middle of the south side, and almost at the same time, seven mutineers – Job Anderson, the boatswain, at their head – appeared in full cry at the southwestern corner.

They paused as if taken aback, and before they recovered, not only the squire and I, but Hunter and Joyce from the block house, had time to fire. The four shots came in rather a scattering volley, but they did the business: one of the enemy actually fell, and the rest, without hesitation, turned and plunged into the trees.

After reloading, we walked down the outside of the palisade to see to the fallen enemy. He was stone dead – shot through the heart.

We began to rejoice over our good success when just at that moment a pistol cracked in the bush, a ball whistled close past my ear, and poor Tom Redruth stumbled and fell his length on the ground. Both the squire and I returned the shot, but as we had nothing to aim at, it is probable we only wasted powder. Then we reloaded and turned our attention to poor Tom.

The captain and Gray were already examining him, and I saw with half an eye that all was over.

I believe the readiness of our return volley had scattered the mutineers once more, for we were suffered without further molestation to get the poor old gamekeeper hoisted over the stockade and carried, groaning and bleeding, into the log-house.

Poor old fellow, he had not uttered one word of surprise, complaint, fear, or even acquiescence from the very beginning of our troubles till now, when we had laid him down in the log-house to die. He had lain like a Trojan behind his mattress in the gallery; he had followed every order silently, doggedly, and well; he was the oldest of our party by a score of years; and now, sullen, old, serviceable servant, it was he that was to die.

The squire dropped down beside him on his knees and kissed his hand, crying like a child.

"Be I going, doctor?" he asked.

"Tom, my man," said I, "you're going home."

"I wish I had had a lick at them with the gun first," he replied.

"Tom," said the squire, "say you forgive me, won't you?"

"Would that be respectful like, from me to you, squire?" was the answer. "Howsoever, so be it, amen!"

After a little while of silence, he said he thought somebody might read a prayer. "It's the custom, sir," he added apologetically. And not long after, without another word, he passed away.

In the meantime the captain, whom I had observed to be wonderfully swollen about the chest and pockets, had turned out a great many various stores – the British colours, a Bible, a coil of stoutish rope, pen, ink, the log-book, and pounds of tobacco. He had found a longish firtree lying felled and trimmed in the enclosure, and with the help of Hunter he had set it up at the corner of the log-house where the trunks crossed and made an angle. Then, climbing on the roof, he had with his own hand bent and run up the colours.

This seemed mightily to relieve him. He re-entered the log-house and set about counting up the stores as if nothing else existed. But he had an eye on Tom's passage for all that, and as soon as all was over, came forward with another flag and reverently spread it on the body.

"Don't you take on, sir," he said, shaking the squire's hand. "All's well with him; no fear for a hand that's been shot down in his duty to captain and owner. It mayn't be good divinity, but it's a fact."

Then he pulled me aside.

"Dr. Livesey," he said, "in how many weeks do you and squire expect the consort?"

I told him it was a question not of weeks but of months, that if we were not back by the end of August Blandly was to send to find us, but neither sooner nor later. "You can calculate for yourself," I said.

"Why, yes," returned the captain, scratching his head; "and making a large allowance, sir, for all the gifts of Providence, I should say we were pretty close hauled."

"How do you mean?" I asked.

"It's a pity, sir, we lost that second load. That's what I mean," replied the captain. "As for powder and shot, we'll do. But the rations are short, very short – so short, Dr. Livesey, that we're perhaps as well without that extra mouth."

And he pointed to the dead body under the flag.

Just then, with a roar and a whistle, a round-shot passed high above the roof of the log-house and plumped far beyond us in the wood.

"Oho!" said the captain. "Blaze away! You've little enough powder already, my lads."

At the second trial, the aim was better, and the ball descended inside the stockade, scattering a cloud of sand but doing no further damage.

"Captain," said the squire, "the house is quite invisible from the ship. It must be the flag they are aiming at. Would it not be wiser to take it in?"

"Strike my colours!" cried the captain. "No, sir, not I"; and as soon as he had said the words, I think we all agreed with him. For it was not only a piece of stout, seamanly, good feeling; it was good policy besides and showed our enemies that we despised their cannonade.

All through the evening they kept thundering away. Ball after ball flew over or fell short or kicked up the sand in the enclosure, but they had to fire so high that the shot fell dead and buried itself in the soft sand. We had no ricochet to fear, and though one popped in through the roof of the log-house and out again through the floor, we soon got used to that sort of horse-play and minded it no more than cricket.

"There is one good thing about all this," observed the captain; "the wood in front of us is likely clear. The ebb has made a good while; our stores should be uncovered. Volunteers to go and bring in pork."

Gray and Hunter were the first to come forward. Well armed, they stole out of the stockade, but it proved a useless mission. The mutineers were bolder than we fancied or they put more trust in Israel's gunnery. For four or five of them were busy carrying off our stores and wading out with them to one of the gigs that lay close by, pulling an oar or so to hold her steady against the current. Silver was in the stern-sheets in command; and every man of them was now provided with a musket from some secret magazine of their own.

The captain sat down to his log, and here is the beginning of the entry:

Alexander Smollett, master; David Livesey, ship's doctor; Abraham Gray, carpenter's mate; John Trelawney, owner; John Hunter and Richard Joyce, owner's servants, landsmen – being all that is left faithful of the ship's company – with stores for ten days at short rations, came ashore this day and flew British colours on the log-house in Treasure Island. Thomas Redruth, owner's servant, landsman, shot by the mutineers; James Hawkins, cabin-boy –

And at the same time, I was wondering over poor Jim Hawkins' fate.

A hail on the land side.

"Somebody hailing us," said Hunter, who was on guard.

"Doctor! Squire! Captain! Hullo, Hunter, is that you?" came the cries.

And I ran to the door in time to see Jim Hawkins, safe and sound, come climbing over the stockade.

CHAPTER NINETEEN

Narrative Resumed by Jim Hawkins: The Garrison in the Stockade

As SOON AS Ben Gunn saw the colours he came to a halt, stopped me by the arm, and sat down.

"Now," said he, "there's your friends, sure enough."

"Far more likely it's the mutineers," I answered.

"That!" he cried. "Why, in a place like this, where nobody puts in but gen'lemen of fortune, Silver would fly the Jolly Roger, you don't make no doubt of that. No, that's your friends. There's been blows too, and I reckon your friends has had the best of it; and here they are ashore in the old stockade, as was made years and years ago by Flint. Ah, he was the man to have a headpiece, was Flint! Barring rum, his match were never seen. He were afraid of none, not he; on'y Silver – Silver was that genteel."

"Well," said I, "that may be so, and so be it; all the more reason that I should hurry on and join my friends."

"Nay, mate," returned Ben, "not you. You're a good boy, or I'm mistook; but you're on'y a boy, all told. Now, Ben Gunn is fly. Rum wouldn't bring me there, where you're going – not rum wouldn't, till I see your born gen'leman and gets it on his word of honour. And you won't forget my words; 'A precious sight (that's what you'll say), a precious sight more confidence' – and then nips him."

And he pinched me the third time with the same air of cleverness.

"And when Ben Gunn is wanted, you know where to find him, Jim. Just wheer you found him today. And him that comes is to have a white thing in his hand, and he's to come alone. Oh! And you'll say this: 'Ben Gunn,' says you, 'has reasons of his own.'"

"Well," said I, "I believe I understand. You have something to propose, and you wish to see the squire or the doctor, and you're to be found where I found you. Is that all?"

"And when? says you," he added. "Why, from about noon observation to about six bells."

"Good," said I, "and now may I go?"

"You won't forget?" he inquired anxiously. "Precious sight, and reasons of his own, says you. Reasons of his own; that's the mainstay; as between man and man. Well, then" – still holding me – "I reckon you can go, Jim. And, Jim, if you was to see Silver, you wouldn't go for to sell Ben Gunn? Wild horses wouldn't draw it from you? No, says you. And if them pirates camp ashore, Jim, what would you say but there'd be widders in the morning?"

Here he was interrupted by a loud report, and a cannonball came tearing through the trees and pitched in the sand not a hundred yards from where we two were talking. The next moment each of us had taken to his heels in a different direction.

For a good hour to come frequent reports shook the island, and balls kept crashing through the woods. I moved from hiding-place to hiding-place, always pursued, or so it seemed to me, by these terrifying missiles. But towards the end of the bombardment, though still I durst not venture in the direction of the stockade, where the balls fell oftenest, I had begun, in a manner, to pluck up my heart again, and after a long detour to the east, crept down among the shore-side trees.

The sun had just set, the sea breeze was rustling and tumbling in the woods and ruffling the grey surface of the anchorage; the tide, too, was far out, and great tracts of sand lay uncovered; the air, after the heat of the day, chilled me through my jacket.

The *Hispaniola* still lay where she had anchored; but, sure enough, there was the Jolly Roger – the black flag of piracy – flying from her peak. Even as I looked, there came another red flash and another report that sent the echoes clattering, and one more round-shot whistled through the air. It was the last of the cannonade.

I lay for some time watching the bustle which succeeded the attack. Men were demolishing something with axes on the beach near the stockade – the poor jolly-boat, I afterwards discovered. Away, near the mouth of the river, a great fire was glowing among the trees, and between that point and the ship one of the gigs kept coming and going, the men, whom I had seen so gloomy, shouting at the oars like children. But there was a sound in their voices which suggested rum.

At length I thought I might return towards the stockade. I was pretty far down on the low, sandy spit that encloses the anchorage to the east, and is joined at half-water to Skeleton Island; and now, as I rose to my feet, I saw, some distance further down the spit and rising from among low bushes, an isolated rock, pretty high, and peculiarly white in colour. It occurred to me that this might be the white rock of which Ben Gunn had spoken and that some day or other a boat might be wanted and I should know where to look for one.

Then I skirted among the woods until I had regained the rear, or shoreward side, of the stockade, and was soon warmly welcomed by the faithful party.

I had soon told my story and began to look about me. The log-house was made of unsquared trunks of pine – roof, walls, and floor. The latter stood in several places as much as a foot or a foot and a half above the surface of the sand. There was a porch at the door, and under this porch the little spring welled up into an artificial basin of a rather odd kind – no other than a great ship's kettle of iron, with the bottom knocked out, and sunk "to her bearings," as the captain said, among the sand.

Little had been left besides the framework of the house, but in one corner there was a stone slab laid down by way of hearth and an old rusty iron basket to contain the fire.

The slopes of the knoll and all the inside of the stockade had been cleared of timber to build the house, and we could see by the stumps what a fine and lofty grove had been destroyed. Most of the soil had been washed away or buried in drift after the removal of the trees; only where the streamlet ran down from the kettle a thick bed of moss and some ferns and little creeping bushes were still green among the sand. Very close around the stockade – too close for defence, they said – the wood still flourished high and dense, all of fir on the land side, but towards the sea with a large admixture of live-oaks.

The cold evening breeze, of which I have spoken, whistled through every chink of the rude building and sprinkled the floor with a continual rain of fine sand. There was sand in our eyes, sand in our teeth, sand in our suppers, sand dancing in the spring at the bottom of the kettle, for all the world like porridge beginning to boil. Our chimney was a square hole in the roof; it was but a little part of the smoke that found its way out, and the rest eddied about the house and kept us coughing and piping the eye.

Add to this that Gray, the new man, had his face tied up in a bandage for a cut he had got in breaking away from the mutineers and that poor old Tom Redruth, still unburied, lay along the wall, stiff and stark, under the Union Jack.

If we had been allowed to sit idle, we should all have fallen in the blues, but Captain Smollett was never the man for that. All hands were called up before him, and he divided us into watches. The doctor and Gray and I for one; the squire, Hunter, and Joyce upon the other. Tired though we all were, two were sent out for firewood; two more were set to dig a grave for Redruth; the doctor was named cook; I was put sentry at the door; and the captain himself went from one to another, keeping up our spirits and lending a hand wherever it was wanted.

From time to time the doctor came to the door for a little air and to rest his eyes, which were almost smoked out of his head, and whenever he did so, he had a word for me.

"That man Smollett," he said once, "is a better man than I am. And when I say that it means a deal, Jim."

Another time he came and was silent for a while. Then he put his head on one side, and looked at me.

"Is this Ben Gunn a man?" he asked.

"I do not know, sir," said I. "I am not very sure whether he's sane."

"If there's any doubt about the matter, he is," returned the doctor. "A man who has been three years biting his nails on a desert island, Jim, can't expect to appear as sane as you or me. It doesn't lie in human nature. Was it cheese you said he had a fancy for?"

"Yes, sir, cheese," I answered.

"Well, Jim," says he, "just see the good that comes of being dainty in your food. You've seen my snuff-box, haven't you? And you never saw me take snuff, the reason being that in my snuff-box I carry a piece of Parmesan cheese – a cheese made in Italy, very nutritious. Well, that's for Ben Gunn!"

Before supper was eaten we buried old Tom in the sand and stood round him for a while bare-headed in the breeze. A good deal of firewood had been got in, but not enough for the captain's fancy, and he shook his head over it and told us we "must get back to this tomorrow rather livelier." Then, when we had eaten our pork and each had a good stiff glass of brandy grog, the three chiefs got together in a corner to discuss our prospects.

It appears they were at their wits' end what to do, the stores being so low that we must have been starved into surrender long before help came. But our best hope, it was decided, was to kill off the buccaneers until they either hauled down their flag or ran away with the *Hispaniola*. From nineteen they were already reduced to fifteen, two others were wounded, and one at least – the man shot beside the gun – severely wounded, if he were not dead. Every time we had a crack at them, we were to take it, saving our own lives, with the extremest care. And besides that, we had two able allies – rum and the climate.

As for the first, though we were about half a mile away, we could hear them roaring and singing late into the night; and as for the second, the doctor staked his wig that, camped where they were in the marsh and unprovided with remedies, the half of them would be on their backs before a week.

"So," he added, "if we are not all shot down first they'll be glad to be packing in the schooner. It's always a ship, and they can get to buccaneering again, I suppose."

"First ship that ever I lost," said Captain Smollett.

I was dead tired, as you may fancy; and when I got to sleep, which was not till after a great deal of tossing, I slept like a log of wood.

The rest had long been up and had already breakfasted and increased the pile of firewood by about half as much again when I was wakened by a bustle and the sound of voices.

"Flag of truce!" I heard someone say; and then, immediately after, with a cry of surprise, "Silver himself!"

And at that, up I jumped, and rubbing my eyes, ran to a loophole in the wall.

CHAPTER TWENTY

Silver's Embassy

Sure enough, there were two men just outside the stockade, one of them waving a white cloth, the other, no less a person than Silver himself, standing placidly by.

It was still quite early, and the coldest morning that I think I ever was abroad in – a chill that pierced into the marrow. The sky was bright and cloudless overhead, and the tops of the trees shone rosily in the sun. But where Silver stood with his lieutenant, all was still in shadow, and they waded knee-deep in a low white vapour that had crawled during the night out of the morass. The chill and the vapour taken together told a poor tale of the island. It was plainly a damp, feverish, unhealthy spot.

"Keep indoors, men," said the captain. "Ten to one this is a trick."

Then he hailed the buccaneer.

"Who goes? Stand, or we fire."

"Flag of truce," cried Silver.

The captain was in the porch, keeping himself carefully out of the way of a treacherous shot, should any be intended. He turned and spoke to us, "Doctor's watch on the lookout. Dr. Livesey take the north side, if you please; Jim, the east; Gray, west. The watch below, all hands to load muskets. Lively, men, and careful."

And then he turned again to the mutineers.

"And what do you want with your flag of truce?" he cried.

This time it was the other man who replied.

"Cap'n Silver, sir, to come on board and make terms," he shouted.

"Cap'n Silver! Don't know him. Who's he?" cried the captain. And we could hear him adding to himself, "Cap'n, is it? My heart, and here's promotion!"

Long John answered for himself. "Me, sir. These poor lads have chosen me cap'n, after your desertion, sir" – laying a particular emphasis upon the word "desertion." "We're willing to submit, if we can come to terms, and no bones about it. All I ask is your word, Cap'n Smollett, to let me safe and sound out of this here stockade, and one minute to get out o' shot before a gun is fired."

"My man," said Captain Smollett, "I have not the slightest desire to talk to you. If you wish to talk to me, you can come, that's all. If there's any treachery, it'll be on your side, and the Lord help you."

"That's enough, cap'n," shouted Long John cheerily. "A word from you's enough. I know a gentleman, and you may lay to that."

We could see the man who carried the flag of truce attempting to hold Silver back. Nor was that wonderful, seeing how cavalier had been the captain's answer. But Silver laughed at him aloud and slapped him on the back as if the idea of alarm had been absurd. Then he advanced to the stockade, threw over his crutch, got a leg up, and with great vigour and skill succeeded in surmounting the fence and dropping safely to the other side.

I will confess that I was far too much taken up with what was going on to be of the slightest use as sentry; indeed, I had already deserted my eastern loophole and crept up behind the captain, who had now seated himself on the threshold, with his elbows on his knees, his head in his hands, and his eyes fixed on the water as it bubbled out of the old iron kettle in the sand. He was whistling "Come, Lasses and Lads."

Silver had terrible hard work getting up the knoll. What with the steepness of the incline, the thick tree stumps, and the soft sand, he and his crutch were as helpless as a ship in stays. But he stuck to it like a man in silence, and at last arrived before the captain, whom he saluted in the handsomest style. He was tricked out in his best; an immense blue coat, thick with brass buttons, hung as low as to his knees, and a fine laced hat was set on the back of his head.

"Here you are, my man," said the captain, raising his head. "You had better sit down."

"You ain't a-going to let me inside, cap'n?" complained Long John. "It's a main cold morning, to be sure, sir, to sit outside upon the sand."

"Why, Silver," said the captain, "if you had pleased to be an honest man, you might have been sitting in your galley. It's your own doing. You're either my ship's cook – and then you were treated handsome – or Cap'n Silver, a common mutineer and pirate, and then you can go hang!"

"Well, well, cap'n," returned the sea-cook, sitting down as he was bidden on the sand, "you'll have to give me a hand up again, that's all. A sweet pretty place you have of it here. Ah, there's Jim! The top of the morning to you, Jim. Doctor, here's my service. Why, there you all are together like a happy family, in a manner of speaking."

"If you have anything to say, my man, better say it," said the captain.

"Right you were, Cap'n Smollett," replied Silver. "Dooty is dooty, to be sure. Well now, you look here, that was a good lay of yours last night. I don't deny it was a good lay. Some of you pretty handy with a handspike-end. And I'll not deny neither but what some of my people was shook – maybe all was shook; maybe I was shook myself; maybe that's why I'm here for terms. But you mark me, cap'n, it won't do twice, by thunder! We'll have to do sentry-go and ease off a point or so on the rum. Maybe you think we were all a sheet in the wind's eye. But I'll tell you I was sober; I was on'y dog tired; and if I'd awoke a second sooner, I'd 'a caught you at the act, I would. He wasn't dead when I got round to him, not he."

"Well?" says Captain Smollett as cool as can be.

All that Silver said was a riddle to him, but you would never have guessed it from his tone. As for me, I began to have an inkling. Ben Gunn's last words came back to my mind. I began to suppose that he had paid the buccaneers a visit while they all lay drunk together round their fire, and I reckoned up with glee that we had only fourteen enemies to deal with.

"Well, here it is," said Silver. "We want that treasure, and we'll have it – that's our point! You would just as soon save your lives, I reckon; and that's yours. You have a chart, haven't you?"

"That's as may be," replied the captain.

"Oh, well, you have, I know that," returned Long John. "You needn't be so husky with a man; there ain't a particle of service in that, and you may lay to it. What I mean is, we want your chart. Now, I never meant you no harm, myself."

"That won't do with me, my man," interrupted the captain. "We know exactly what you meant to do, and we don't care, for now, you see, you can't do it."

And the captain looked at him calmly and proceeded to fill a pipe.

"If Abe Gray – " Silver broke out.

"Avast there!" cried Mr. Smollett. "Gray told me nothing, and I asked him nothing; and what's more, I would see you and him and this whole island blown clean out of the water into blazes first. So there's my mind for you, my man, on that."

This little whiff of temper seemed to cool Silver down. He had been growing nettled before, but now he pulled himself together.

"Like enough," said he. "I would set no limits to what gentlemen might consider shipshape, or might not, as the case were. And seein' as how you are about to take a pipe, cap'n, I'll make so free as do likewise."

And he filled a pipe and lighted it; and the two men sat silently smoking for quite a while, now looking each other in the face, now stopping their tobacco, now leaning forward to spit. It was as good as the play to see them.

"Now," resumed Silver, "here it is. You give us the chart to get the treasure by, and drop shooting poor seamen and stoving of their heads in while asleep. You do that, and we'll offer you a choice. Either you come aboard along of us, once the treasure shipped, and then I'll give you my affy-davy, upon my word of honour, to clap you somewhere safe ashore. Or if that ain't to your fancy, some of my hands being rough and having old scores on account of hazing, then you can stay here, you can. We'll divide stores with you, man for man; and I'll give my affy-davy, as before to speak the first ship I sight, and send 'em here to pick you up. Now, you'll own that's talking. Handsomer you couldn't look to get, now you. And I hope" – raising his voice – "that all hands in this here block house will overhaul my words, for what is spoke to one is spoke to all."

Captain Smollett rose from his seat and knocked out the ashes of his pipe in the palm of his left hand.

"Is that all?" he asked.

"Every last word, by thunder!" answered John. "Refuse that, and you've seen the last of me but musket-balls."

"Very good," said the captain. "Now you'll hear me. If you'll come up one by one, unarmed, I'll engage to clap you all in irons and take you home to a fair trial in England. If you won't, my name is Alexander Smollett, I've flown my sovereign's colours, and I'll see you all to Davy Jones. You can't find the treasure. You can't sail the ship – there's not a man among you fit to sail the ship. You can't fight us – Gray, there, got away from five of you. Your ship's in irons, Master Silver; you're on a lee shore, and so you'll find. I stand here and tell you so; and they're the last good words you'll get from me, for in the name of heaven, I'll put a bullet in your back when next I meet you. Tramp, my lad. Bundle out of this, please, hand over hand, and double quick."

Silver's face was a picture; his eyes started in his head with wrath. He shook the fire out of his pipe.

"Give me a hand up!" he cried.

"Not I," returned the captain.

"Who'll give me a hand up?" he roared.

Not a man among us moved. Growling the foulest imprecations, he crawled along the sand till he got hold of the porch and could hoist himself again upon his crutch. Then he spat into the spring.

"There!" he cried. "That's what I think of ye. Before an hour's out, I'll stove in your old block house like a rum puncheon. Laugh, by thunder, laugh! Before an hour's out, ye'll laugh upon the other side. Them that die'll be the lucky ones."

And with a dreadful oath he stumbled off, ploughed down the sand, was helped across the stockade, after four or five failures, by the man with the flag of truce, and disappeared in an instant afterwards among the trees.

CHAPTER TWENTY ONE

The Attack

As soon as Silver disappeared, the captain, who had been closely watching him, turned towards the interior of the house and found not a man of us at his post but Gray. It was the first time we had ever seen him angry.

"Quarters!" he roared. And then, as we all slunk back to our places, "Gray," he said, "I'll put your name in the log; you've stood by your duty like a seaman. Mr. Trelawney, I'm surprised at you, sir. Doctor, I thought you had worn the king's coat! If that was how you served at Fontenoy, sir, you'd have been better in your berth."

The doctor's watch were all back at their loopholes, the rest were busy loading the spare muskets, and everyone with a red face, you may be certain, and a flea in his ear, as the saying is.

The captain looked on for a while in silence. Then he spoke.

"My lads," said he, "I've given Silver a broadside. I pitched it in red-hot on purpose; and before the hour's out, as he said, we shall be boarded. We're outnumbered, I needn't tell you that, but we fight in shelter; and a minute ago I should have said we fought with discipline. I've no manner of doubt that we can drub them, if you choose."

Then he went the rounds and saw, as he said, that all was clear.

On the two short sides of the house, east and west, there were only two loopholes; on the south side where the porch was, two again; and on the north side, five. There was a round score of muskets for the seven of us; the firewood had been built into four piles – tables, you might say – one about the middle of each side, and on each of these tables some ammunition and four loaded muskets were laid ready to the hand of the defenders. In the middle, the cutlasses lay ranged.

"Toss out the fire," said the captain; "the chill is past, and we mustn't have smoke in our eyes."

The iron fire-basket was carried bodily out by Mr. Trelawney, and the embers smothered among sand.

"Hawkins hasn't had his breakfast. Hawkins, help yourself, and back to your post to eat it," continued Captain Smollett. "Lively, now, my lad; you'll want it before you've done. Hunter, serve out a round of brandy to all hands."

And while this was going on, the captain completed, in his own mind, the plan of the defence.

"Doctor, you will take the door," he resumed. "See, and don't expose yourself; keep within, and fire through the porch. Hunter, take the east side, there. Joyce, you stand by the west, my man. Mr. Trelawney, you are the best shot – you and Gray will take this long north side, with the five loopholes; it's there the danger is. If they can get up to it and fire in upon us through our own ports, things would begin to look dirty. Hawkins, neither you nor I are much account at the shooting; we'll stand by to load and bear a hand."

As the captain had said, the chill was past. As soon as the sun had climbed above our girdle of trees, it fell with all its force upon the clearing and drank up the vapours at a draught. Soon the sand was baking and the resin melting in the logs of the block house. Jackets and coats were flung aside, shirts thrown open at the neck and rolled up to the shoulders; and we stood there, each at his post, in a fever of heat and anxiety.

An hour passed away.

"Hang them!" said the captain. "This is as dull as the doldrums. Gray, whistle for a wind."

And just at that moment came the first news of the attack.

"If you please, sir," said Joyce, "if I see anyone, am I to fire?"

"I told you so!" cried the captain.

"Thank you, sir," returned Joyce with the same quiet civility.

Nothing followed for a time, but the remark had set us all on the alert, straining ears and eyes – the musketeers with their pieces balanced in their hands, the captain out in the middle of the block house with his mouth very tight and a frown on his face.

So some seconds passed, till suddenly Joyce whipped up his musket and fired. The report had scarcely died away ere it was repeated and repeated from without in a scattering volley, shot behind shot, like a string of geese, from every side of the enclosure. Several bullets struck the log-house, but not one entered; and as the smoke cleared away and vanished, the stockade and the woods around it looked as quiet and empty as before. Not a bough waved, not the gleam of a musket-barrel betrayed the presence of our foes.

"Did you hit your man?" asked the captain.

"No, sir," replied Joyce. "I believe not, sir."

"Next best thing to tell the truth," muttered Captain Smollett. "Load his gun, Hawkins. How many should say there were on your side, doctor?"

"I know precisely," said Dr. Livesey. "Three shots were fired on this side. I saw the three flashes – two close together – one farther to the west."

"Three!" repeated the captain. "And how many on yours, Mr. Trelawney?"

But this was not so easily answered. There had come many from the north – seven by the squire's computation, eight or nine according to Gray. From the east and west only a single shot had been fired. It was plain, therefore, that the attack would be developed from the north and that on the other three sides we were only to be annoyed by a show of hostilities. But Captain Smollett made no change in his arrangements. If the mutineers succeeded in crossing the stockade, he argued, they would take possession of any unprotected loophole and shoot us down like rats in our own stronghold.

Nor had we much time left to us for thought. Suddenly, with a loud huzza, a little cloud of pirates leaped from the woods on the north side and ran straight on the stockade. At the same moment, the fire was once more opened from the woods, and a rifle ball sang through the doorway and knocked the doctor's musket into bits.

The boarders swarmed over the fence like monkeys. Squire and Gray fired again and yet again; three men fell, one forwards into the enclosure, two back on the outside. But of these, one was evidently more frightened than hurt, for he was on his feet again in a crack and instantly disappeared among the trees.

Two had bit the dust, one had fled, four had made good their footing inside our defences, while from the shelter of the woods seven or eight men, each evidently supplied with several muskets, kept up a hot though useless fire on the log-house.

The four who had boarded made straight before them for the building, shouting as they ran, and the men among the trees shouted back to encourage them. Several shots were fired, but such was the hurry of the marksmen that not one appears to have taken effect. In a moment, the four pirates had swarmed up the mound and were upon us.

The head of Job Anderson, the boatswain, appeared at the middle loophole.

"At 'em, all hands – all hands!" he roared in a voice of thunder.

At the same moment, another pirate grasped Hunter's musket by the muzzle, wrenched it from his hands, plucked it through the loophole, and with one stunning blow, laid the poor fellow senseless on the floor. Meanwhile a third, running unharmed all around the house, appeared suddenly in the doorway and fell with his cutlass on the doctor.

Our position was utterly reversed. A moment since we were firing, under cover, at an exposed enemy; now it was we who lay uncovered and could not return a blow.

The log-house was full of smoke, to which we owed our comparative safety. Cries and confusion, the flashes and reports of pistol-shots, and one loud groan rang in my ears.

"Out, lads, out, and fight 'em in the open! Cutlasses!" cried the captain.

I snatched a cutlass from the pile, and someone, at the same time snatching another, gave me a cut across the knuckles which I hardly felt. I dashed out of the door into the clear sunlight. Someone was close behind, I knew not whom. Right in front, the doctor was pursuing his assailant down the hill, and just as my eyes fell upon him, beat down his guard and sent him sprawling on his back with a great slash across the face.

"Round the house, lads! Round the house!" cried the captain; and even in the hurly-burly, I perceived a change in his voice.

Mechanically, I obeyed, turned eastwards, and with my cutlass raised, ran round the corner of the house. Next moment I was face to face with Anderson. He roared aloud, and his hanger went up above his head, flashing in the sunlight. I had not time to be afraid, but as the blow still hung impending, leaped in a trice upon one side, and missing my foot in the soft sand, rolled headlong down the slope.

When I had first sallied from the door, the other mutineers had been already swarming up the palisade to make an end of us. One man, in a red night-cap, with his cutlass in his mouth, had even got upon the top and thrown a leg across. Well, so short had been the interval that when I found my feet again all was in the same posture, the fellow with the red night-cap still half-way over, another still just showing his head above the top of the stockade. And yet, in this breath of time, the fight was over and the victory was ours.

Gray, following close behind me, had cut down the big boatswain ere he had time to recover from his last blow. Another had been shot at a loophole in the very act of firing into the house and now lay in agony, the pistol still smoking in his hand. A third, as I had seen, the doctor had disposed of at a blow. Of the four who had scaled the palisade, one only remained unaccounted for, and he, having left his cutlass on the field, was now clambering out again with the fear of death upon him.

"Fire – fire from the house!" cried the doctor. "And you, lads, back into cover."

But his words were unheeded, no shot was fired, and the last boarder made good his escape and disappeared with the rest into the wood. In three seconds nothing remained of the attacking party but the five who had fallen, four on the inside and one on the outside of the palisade.

The doctor and Gray and I ran full speed for shelter. The survivors would soon be back where they had left their muskets, and at any moment the fire might recommence.

The house was by this time somewhat cleared of smoke, and we saw at a glance the price we had paid for victory. Hunter lay beside his loophole, stunned; Joyce by his, shot through the head, never to move again; while right in the centre, the squire was supporting the captain, one as pale as the other.

"The captain's wounded," said Mr. Trelawney.

"Have they run?" asked Mr. Smollett.

"All that could, you may be bound," returned the doctor; "but there's five of them will never run again."

"Five!" cried the captain. "Come, that's better. Five against three leaves us four to nine. That's better odds than we had at starting. We were seven to nineteen then, or thought we were, and that's as bad to bear."[1]

1 The mutineers were soon only eight in number, for the man shot by Mr. Trelawney on board the schooner died that same evening of his wound. But this was, of course, not known till after by the faithful party.

PART FIVE

My Sea Adventure

CHAPTER TWENTY TWO

How My Sea Adventure Began

THERE WAS NO RETURN of the mutineers – not so much as another shot out of the woods. They had "got their rations for that day," as the captain put it, and we had the place to ourselves and a quiet time to overhaul the wounded and get dinner. Squire and I cooked outside in spite of the danger, and even outside we could hardly tell what we were at, for horror of the loud groans that reached us from the doctor's patients.

Out of the eight men who had fallen in the action, only three still breathed – that one of the pirates who had been shot at the loophole, Hunter, and Captain Smollett; and of these, the first two were as good as dead; the mutineer indeed died under the doctor's knife, and Hunter, do what we could, never recovered consciousness in this world. He lingered all day, breathing loudly like the old buccaneer at home in his apoplectic fit, but the bones of his chest had been crushed by the blow and his skull fractured in falling, and some time in the following night, without sign or sound, he went to his Maker.

As for the captain, his wounds were grievous indeed, but not dangerous. No organ was fatally injured. Anderson's ball – for it was Job that shot him first – had broken his shoulder-blade and touched the lung, not badly; the second had only torn and displaced some muscles in the calf. He was sure to recover, the doctor said, but in the meantime, and for weeks to come, he must not walk nor move his arm, nor so much as speak when he could help it.

My own accidental cut across the knuckles was a flea-bite. Doctor Livesey patched it up with plaster and pulled my ears for me into the bargain.

After dinner the squire and the doctor sat by the captain's side awhile in consultation; and when they had talked to their hearts' content, it being then a little past noon, the doctor took up his hat and pistols, girt on a cutlass, put the chart in his pocket, and with a musket over his shoulder crossed the palisade on the north side and set off briskly through the trees.

Gray and I were sitting together at the far end of the block house, to be out of earshot of our officers consulting; and Gray took his pipe out of his mouth and fairly forgot to put it back again, so thunder-struck he was at this occurrence.

"Why, in the name of Davy Jones," said he, "is Dr. Livesey mad?"

"Why no," says I. "He's about the last of this crew for that, I take it."

"Well, shipmate," said Gray, "mad he may not be; but if *he's* not, you mark my words, *I* am."

"I take it," replied I, "the doctor has his idea; and if I am right, he's going now to see Ben Gunn."

I was right, as appeared later; but in the meantime, the house being stifling hot and the little patch of sand inside the palisade ablaze with midday sun, I began to get another thought into my head, which was not by any means so right. What I began to do was to envy the doctor walking in the cool shadow of the woods with the birds about him and the pleasant smell of the pines, while I sat grilling, with my clothes stuck to the hot resin, and so much blood about me and so many poor dead bodies lying all around that I took a disgust of the place that was almost as strong as fear.

All the time I was washing out the block house, and then washing up the things from dinner, this disgust and envy kept growing stronger and stronger, till at last, being near a bread-bag, and no one then observing me, I took the first step towards my escapade and filled both pockets of my coat with biscuit.

I was a fool, if you like, and certainly I was going to do a foolish, over-bold act; but I was determined to do it with all the precautions in my power. These biscuits, should anything befall me, would keep me, at least, from starving till far on in the next day.

The next thing I laid hold of was a brace of pistols, and as I already had a powder-horn and bullets, I felt myself well supplied with arms.

As for the scheme I had in my head, it was not a bad one in itself. I was to go down the sandy spit that divides the anchorage on the east from the open sea, find the white rock I had observed last evening, and ascertain whether it was there or not that Ben Gunn had hidden his boat, a thing quite worth doing, as I still believe. But as I was certain I should not be allowed to leave the enclosure, my only plan was to take French leave and slip out when nobody was watching, and that was so bad a way of doing it as made the thing itself wrong. But I was only a boy, and I had made my mind up.

Well, as things at last fell out, I found an admirable opportunity. The squire and Gray were busy helping the captain with his bandages, the coast was clear, I made a bolt for it over the stockade and into the thickest of the trees, and before my absence was observed I was out of cry of my companions.

This was my second folly, far worse than the first, as I left but two sound men to guard the house; but like the first, it was a help towards saving all of us.

I took my way straight for the east coast of the island, for I was determined to go down the sea side of the spit to avoid all chance of observation from the anchorage. It was already late in the afternoon, although still warm and sunny. As I continued to thread the tall woods, I could hear from far before me not only the continuous thunder of the surf, but a certain tossing of foliage and grinding of boughs which showed me the sea breeze had set in higher than usual. Soon cool draughts of air began to reach me, and a few steps farther I came forth into the open borders of the grove, and saw the sea lying blue and sunny to the horizon and the surf tumbling and tossing its foam along the beach.

I have never seen the sea quiet round Treasure Island. The sun might blaze overhead, the air be without a breath, the surface smooth and blue, but still these great rollers would be running along all the external coast, thundering and thundering by day and night; and I scarce believe there is one spot in the island where a man would be out of earshot of their noise.

I walked along beside the surf with great enjoyment, till, thinking I was now got far enough to the south, I took the cover of some thick bushes and crept warily up to the ridge of the spit.

Behind me was the sea, in front the anchorage. The sea breeze, as though it had the sooner blown itself out by its unusual violence, was already at an end; it had been succeeded by light, variable airs from the south and south-east, carrying great banks of fog; and the anchorage, under lee of Skeleton Island, lay still and leaden as when first we entered it. The *Hispaniola*, in that unbroken mirror, was exactly portrayed from the truck to the waterline, the Jolly Roger hanging from her peak.

Alongside lay one of the gigs, Silver in the stern-sheets – him I could always recognize – while a couple of men were leaning over the stern bulwarks, one of them with a red cap – the very rogue that I had seen some hours before stride-legs upon the palisade. Apparently they were talking and laughing, though at that distance – upwards of a mile – I could, of course, hear no word of what was said. All at once there began the most horrid, unearthly screaming, which at first startled me badly,

though I had soon remembered the voice of Captain Flint and even thought I could make out the bird by her bright plumage as she sat perched upon her master's wrist.

Soon after, the jolly-boat shoved off and pulled for shore, and the man with the red cap and his comrade went below by the cabin companion.

Just about the same time, the sun had gone down behind the Spy-glass, and as the fog was collecting rapidly, it began to grow dark in earnest. I saw I must lose no time if I were to find the boat that evening.

The white rock, visible enough above the brush, was still some eighth of a mile further down the spit, and it took me a goodish while to get up with it, crawling, often on all fours, among the scrub. Night had almost come when I laid my hand on its rough sides. Right below it there was an exceedingly small hollow of green turf, hidden by banks and a thick underwood about knee-deep, that grew there very plentifully; and in the centre of the dell, sure enough, a little tent of goat-skins, like what the gipsies carry about with them in England.

I dropped into the hollow, lifted the side of the tent, and there was Ben Gunn's boat – home-made if ever anything was home-made; a rude, lop-sided framework of tough wood, and stretched upon that a covering of goat-skin, with the hair inside. The thing was extremely small, even for me, and I can hardly imagine that it could have floated with a full-sized man. There was one thwart set as low as possible, a kind of stretcher in the bows, and a double paddle for propulsion.

I had not then seen a coracle, such as the ancient Britons made, but I have seen one since, and I can give you no fairer idea of Ben Gunn's boat than by saying it was like the first and the worst coracle ever made by man. But the great advantage of the coracle it certainly possessed, for it was exceedingly light and portable.

Well, now that I had found the boat, you would have thought I had had enough of truantry for once, but in the meantime I had taken another notion and become so obstinately fond of it that I would have carried it out, I believe, in the teeth of Captain Smollett himself. This was to slip out under cover of the night, cut the *Hispaniola* adrift, and let her go ashore where she fancied. I had quite made up my mind that the mutineers, after their repulse of the morning, had nothing nearer their hearts than to up anchor and away to sea; this, I thought, it would be a fine thing to prevent, and now that I had seen how they left their watchmen unprovided with a boat, I thought it might be done with little risk.

Down I sat to wait for darkness, and made a hearty meal of biscuit. It was a night out of ten thousand for my purpose. The fog had now buried all heaven. As the last rays of daylight dwindled and disappeared, absolute blackness settled down on Treasure Island. And when, at last, I shouldered the coracle and groped my way stumblingly out of the hollow where I had supped, there were but two points visible on the whole anchorage.

One was the great fire on shore, by which the defeated pirates lay carousing in the swamp. The other, a mere blur of light upon the darkness, indicated the position of the anchored ship. She had swung round to the ebb – her bow was now towards me – the only lights on board were in the cabin, and what I saw was merely a reflection on the fog of the strong rays that flowed from the stern window.

The ebb had already run some time, and I had to wade through a long belt of swampy sand, where I sank several times above the ankle, before I came to the edge of the retreating water, and wading a little way in, with some strength and dexterity, set my coracle, keel downwards, on the surface.

CHAPTER TWENTY THREE

The Ebb-tide Runs

THE CORACLE – as I had ample reason to know before I was done with her – was a very safe boat for a person of my height and weight, both buoyant and clever in a seaway; but she was the most cross-grained, lop-sided craft to manage. Do as you pleased, she always made more leeway than anything else, and turning round and round was the manoeuvre she was best at. Even Ben Gunn himself has admitted that she was "queer to handle till you knew her way."

Certainly I did not know her way. She turned in every direction but the one I was bound to go; the most part of the time we were broadside on, and I am very sure I never should have made the ship at all but for the tide. By good fortune, paddle as I pleased, the tide was still sweeping me down; and there lay the *Hispaniola* right in the fairway, hardly to be missed.

First she loomed before me like a blot of something yet blacker than darkness, then her spars and hull began to take shape, and the next moment, as it seemed (for, the farther I went, the brisker grew the current of the ebb), I was alongside of her hawser and had laid hold.

The hawser was as taut as a bowstring, and the current so strong she pulled upon her anchor. All round the hull, in the blackness, the rippling current bubbled and chattered like a little mountain stream. One cut with my sea-gully and the *Hispaniola* would go humming down the tide.

So far so good, but it next occurred to my recollection that a taut hawser, suddenly cut, is a thing as dangerous as a kicking horse. Ten to one, if I were so foolhardy as to cut the *Hispaniola* from her anchor, I and the coracle would be knocked clean out of the water.

This brought me to a full stop, and if fortune had not again particularly favoured me, I should have had to abandon my design. But the light airs which had begun blowing from the south-east and south had hauled round after nightfall into the south-west. Just while I was meditating, a puff came, caught the *Hispaniola*, and forced her up into the current; and to my great joy, I felt the hawser slacken in my grasp, and the hand by which I held it dip for a second under water.

With that I made my mind up, took out my gully, opened it with my teeth, and cut one strand after another, till the vessel swung only by two. Then I lay quiet, waiting to sever these last when the strain should be once more lightened by a breath of wind.

All this time I had heard the sound of loud voices from the cabin, but to say truth, my mind had been so entirely taken up with other thoughts that I had scarcely given ear. Now, however, when I had nothing else to do, I began to pay more heed.

One I recognized for the coxswain's, Israel Hands, that had been Flint's gunner in former days. The other was, of course, my friend of the red night-cap. Both men were plainly the worse of drink, and they were still drinking, for even while I was listening, one of them, with a drunken cry, opened the stern window and threw out something, which I divined to be an empty bottle. But they were not only tipsy; it was plain that they were furiously angry. Oaths flew like hailstones, and every now and then there came forth such an explosion as I thought was sure to end in blows. But each time the quarrel passed off and the voices grumbled lower for a while, until the next crisis came and in its turn passed away without result.

On shore, I could see the glow of the great camp-fire burning warmly through the shore-side trees. Someone was singing, a dull, old, droning sailor's song, with a droop and a quaver at the end of every verse, and seemingly no end to it at all but the patience of the singer. I had heard it on the voyage more than once and remembered these words:

"But one man of her crew alive,
What put to sea with seventy-five."

And I thought it was a ditty rather too dolefully appropriate for a company that had met such cruel losses in the morning. But, indeed, from what I saw, all these buccaneers were as callous as the sea they sailed on.

At last the breeze came; the schooner sidled and drew nearer in the dark; I felt the hawser slacken once more, and with a good, tough effort, cut the last fibres through.

The breeze had but little action on the coracle, and I was almost instantly swept against the bows of the *Hispaniola*. At the same time, the schooner began to turn upon her heel, spinning slowly, end for end, across the current.

I wrought like a fiend, for I expected every moment to be swamped; and since I found I could not push the coracle directly off, I now shoved straight astern. At length I was clear of my dangerous neighbour, and just as I gave the last impulsion, my hands came across a light cord that was trailing overboard across the stern bulwarks. Instantly I grasped it.

Why I should have done so I can hardly say. It was at first mere instinct, but once I had it in my hands and found it fast, curiosity began to get the upper hand, and I determined I should have one look through the cabin window.

I pulled in hand over hand on the cord, and when I judged myself near enough, rose at infinite risk to about half my height and thus commanded the roof and a slice of the interior of the cabin.

By this time the schooner and her little consort were gliding pretty swiftly through the water; indeed, we had already fetched up level with the camp-fire. The ship was talking, as sailors say, loudly, treading the innumerable ripples with an incessant weltering splash; and until I got my eye above the window-sill I could not comprehend why the watchmen had taken no alarm. One glance, however, was sufficient; and it was only one glance that I durst take from that unsteady skiff. It showed me Hands and his companion locked together in deadly wrestle, each with a hand upon the other's throat.

I dropped upon the thwart again, none too soon, for I was near overboard. I could see nothing for the moment but these two furious, encrimsoned faces swaying together under the smoky lamp, and I shut my eyes to let them grow once more familiar with the darkness.

The endless ballad had come to an end at last, and the whole diminished company about the camp-fire had broken into the chorus I had heard so often:

"Fifteen men on the dead man's chest –
Yo-ho-ho, and a bottle of rum!
Drink and the devil had done for the rest –
Yo-ho-ho, and a bottle of rum!"

I was just thinking how busy drink and the devil were at that very moment in the cabin of the *Hispaniola*, when I was surprised by a sudden lurch of the coracle. At the same moment, she yawed sharply and seemed to change her course. The speed in the meantime had strangely increased.

I opened my eyes at once. All round me were little ripples, combing over with a sharp, bristling sound and slightly phosphorescent. The *Hispaniola* herself, a few yards in whose wake I was still being whirled along, seemed to stagger in her course, and I saw her spars toss a little against the blackness of the night; nay, as I looked longer, I made sure she also was wheeling to the southward.

I glanced over my shoulder, and my heart jumped against my ribs. There, right behind me, was the glow of the camp-fire. The current had turned at right angles, sweeping round along with it the tall schooner and the little dancing coracle; ever quickening, ever bubbling higher, ever muttering louder, it went spinning through the narrows for the open sea.

Suddenly the schooner in front of me gave a violent yaw, turning, perhaps, through twenty degrees; and almost at the same moment one shout followed another from on board; I could hear feet pounding on the companion ladder and I knew that the two drunkards had at last been interrupted in their quarrel and awakened to a sense of their disaster.

I lay down flat in the bottom of that wretched skiff and devoutly recommended my spirit to its Maker. At the end of the straits, I made sure we must fall into some bar of raging breakers, where all my troubles would be ended speedily; and though I could, perhaps, bear to die, I could not bear to look upon my fate as it approached.

So I must have lain for hours, continually beaten to and fro upon the billows, now and again wetted with flying sprays, and never ceasing to expect death at the next plunge. Gradually weariness grew upon me; a numbness, an occasional stupor, fell upon my mind even in the midst of my terrors, until sleep at last supervened and in my sea-tossed coracle I lay and dreamed of home and the old Admiral Benbow.

CHAPTER TWENTY FOUR

The Cruise of the Coracle

IT WAS BROAD DAY when I awoke and found myself tossing at the south-west end of Treasure Island. The sun was up but was still hid from me behind the great bulk of the Spy-glass, which on this side descended almost to the sea in formidable cliffs.

Haulbowline Head and Mizzen-mast Hill were at my elbow, the hill bare and dark, the head bound with cliffs forty or fifty feet high and fringed with great masses of fallen rock. I was scarce a quarter of a mile to seaward, and it was my first thought to paddle in and land.

That notion was soon given over. Among the fallen rocks the breakers spouted and bellowed; loud reverberations, heavy sprays flying and falling, succeeded one another from second to second; and I saw myself, if I ventured nearer, dashed to death upon the rough shore or spending my strength in vain to scale the beetling crags.

Nor was that all, for crawling together on flat tables of rock or letting themselves drop into the sea with loud reports I beheld huge slimy monsters – soft snails, as it were, of incredible bigness – two or three score of them together, making the rocks to echo with their barkings.

I have understood since that they were sea lions, and entirely harmless. But the look of them, added to the difficulty of the shore and the high running of the surf, was more than enough to disgust me of that landing-place. I felt willing rather to starve at sea than to confront such perils.

In the meantime I had a better chance, as I supposed, before me. North of Haulbowline Head, the land runs in a long way, leaving at low tide a long stretch of yellow sand. To the north of that, again, there comes another cape – Cape of the Woods, as it was marked upon the chart – buried in tall green pines, which descended to the margin of the sea.

I remembered what Silver had said about the current that sets northward along the whole west coast of Treasure Island, and seeing from my position that I was already under its influence, I preferred to leave Haulbowline Head behind me and reserve my strength for an attempt to land upon the kindlier-looking Cape of the Woods.

There was a great, smooth swell upon the sea. The wind blowing steady and gentle from the south, there was no contrariety between that and the current, and the billows rose and fell unbroken.

Had it been otherwise, I must long ago have perished; but as it was, it is surprising how easily and securely my little and light boat could ride. Often, as I still lay at the bottom and kept no more than an eye above the gunwale, I would see a big blue summit heaving close above me; yet the coracle would but bounce a little, dance as if on springs, and subside on the other side into the trough as lightly as a bird.

I began after a little to grow very bold and sat up to try my skill at paddling. But even a small change in the disposition of the weight will produce violent changes in the behaviour of a coracle. And I had hardly moved before the boat, giving up at once her gentle dancing movement, ran straight down a slope of water so steep that it made me giddy, and struck her nose, with a spout of spray, deep into the side of the next wave.

I was drenched and terrified, and fell instantly back into my old position, whereupon the coracle seemed to find her head again and led me as softly as before among the billows. It was plain she was not to be interfered with, and at that rate, since I could in no way influence her course, what hope had I left of reaching land?

I began to be horribly frightened, but I kept my head, for all that. First, moving with all care, I gradually baled out the coracle with my sea-cap; then, getting my eye once more above the gunwale, I set myself to study how it was she managed to slip so quietly through the rollers.

I found each wave, instead of the big, smooth glossy mountain it looks from shore or from a vessel's deck, was for all the world like any range of hills on dry land, full of peaks and smooth places and valleys. The coracle, left to herself, turning from side to side, threaded, so to speak, her way through these lower parts and avoided the steep slopes and higher, toppling summits of the wave.

"Well, now," thought I to myself, "it is plain I must lie where I am and not disturb the balance; but it is plain also that I can put the paddle over the side and from time to time, in smooth places, give her a shove or two towards land." No sooner thought upon than done. There I lay on my elbows in the most trying attitude, and every now and again gave a weak stroke or two to turn her head to shore.

It was very tiring and slow work, yet I did visibly gain ground; and as we drew near the Cape of the Woods, though I saw I must infallibly miss that point, I had still made some hundred yards of easting. I was, indeed, close in. I could see the cool green tree-tops swaying together in the breeze, and I felt sure I should make the next promontory without fail.

It was high time, for I now began to be tortured with thirst. The glow of the sun from above, its thousandfold reflection from the waves, the sea-water that fell and dried upon me, caking my very lips with salt, combined to make my throat burn and my brain ache. The sight of the trees so near at hand had almost made me sick with longing, but the current had soon carried me past the point, and as the next reach of sea opened out, I beheld a sight that changed the nature of my thoughts.

Right in front of me, not half a mile away, I beheld the *Hispaniola* under sail. I made sure, of course, that I should be taken; but I was so distressed for want of water that I scarce knew whether to be glad or sorry at the thought, and long before I had come to a conclusion, surprise had taken entire possession of my mind and I could do nothing but stare and wonder.

The *Hispaniola* was under her main-sail and two jibs, and the beautiful white canvas shone in the sun like snow or silver. When I first sighted her, all her sails were drawing; she was lying a course about north-west, and I presumed the men on board were going round the island on their way back to the anchorage. Presently she began to fetch more and more to the westward, so that I thought they had sighted me and were going about in chase. At last, however, she fell right into the wind's eye, was taken dead aback, and stood there awhile helpless, with her sails shivering.

"Clumsy fellows," said I; "they must still be drunk as owls." And I thought how Captain Smollett would have set them skipping.

Meanwhile the schooner gradually fell off and filled again upon another tack, sailed swiftly for a minute or so, and brought up once more dead in the wind's eye. Again and again was this repeated. To and fro, up and down, north, south, east, and west, the *Hispaniola* sailed by swoops and dashes, and at each repetition ended as she had begun, with idly flapping canvas. It became plain to me that nobody was steering. And if so, where were the men? Either they were dead drunk or had deserted her, I thought, and perhaps if I could get on board I might return the vessel to her captain.

The current was bearing coracle and schooner southward at an equal rate. As for the latter's sailing, it was so wild and intermittent, and she hung each time so long in irons, that she certainly gained nothing, if she did not even lose. If only I dared to sit up and paddle, I made sure that I could overhaul her. The scheme had an air of adventure that inspired me, and the thought of the water breaker beside the fore companion doubled my growing courage.

Up I got, was welcomed almost instantly by another cloud of spray, but this time stuck to my purpose and set myself, with all my strength and caution, to paddle after the unsteered *Hispaniola*. Once I shipped a sea so heavy that I had to stop and bail, with my heart fluttering like a bird, but gradually I got into the way of the thing and guided my coracle among the waves, with only now and then a blow upon her bows and a dash of foam in my face.

I was now gaining rapidly on the schooner; I could see the brass glisten on the tiller as it banged about, and still no soul appeared upon her decks. I could not choose but suppose she was deserted. If not, the men were lying drunk below, where I might batten them down, perhaps, and do what I chose with the ship.

For some time she had been doing the worse thing possible for me – standing still. She headed nearly due south, yawing, of course, all the time. Each time she fell off, her sails partly filled, and these brought her in a moment right to the wind again. I have said this was the worst thing possible for me, for helpless as she looked in this situation, with the canvas cracking like cannon and the blocks trundling and banging on the deck, she still continued to run away from me, not only with the speed of the current, but by the whole amount of her leeway, which was naturally great.

But now, at last, I had my chance. The breeze fell for some seconds, very low, and the current gradually turning her, the *Hispaniola* revolved slowly round her centre and at last presented me her stern, with the cabin window still gaping open and the lamp over the table still burning on into the day. The main-sail hung drooped like a banner. She was stock-still but for the current.

For the last little while I had even lost, but now redoubling my efforts, I began once more to overhaul the chase.

I was not a hundred yards from her when the wind came again in a clap; she filled on the port tack and was off again, stooping and skimming like a swallow.

My first impulse was one of despair, but my second was towards joy. Round she came, till she was broadside on to me – round still till she had covered a half and then two thirds and then three quarters of the distance that separated us. I could see the waves boiling white under her forefoot. Immensely tall she looked to me from my low station in the coracle.

And then, of a sudden, I began to comprehend. I had scarce time to think – scarce time to act and save myself. I was on the summit of one swell when the schooner came stooping over the next. The bowsprit was over my head. I sprang to my feet and leaped, stamping the coracle under water. With one hand I caught the jib-boom, while my foot was lodged between the stay and the brace; and as I still clung there panting, a dull blow told me that the schooner had charged down upon and struck the coracle and that I was left without retreat on the *Hispaniola*.

CHAPTER TWENTY FIVE

I Strike the Jolly Roger

I HAD SCARCE gained a position on the bowsprit when the flying jib flapped and filled upon the other tack, with a report like a gun. The schooner trembled to her keel under the reverse, but next moment, the other sails still drawing, the jib flapped back again and hung idle.

This had nearly tossed me off into the sea; and now I lost no time, crawled back along the bowsprit, and tumbled head foremost on the deck.

I was on the lee side of the forecastle, and the mainsail, which was still drawing, concealed from me a certain portion of the after-deck. Not a soul was to be seen. The planks, which had not been swabbed since the mutiny, bore the print of many feet, and an empty bottle, broken by the neck, tumbled to and fro like a live thing in the scuppers.

Suddenly the *Hispaniola* came right into the wind. The jibs behind me cracked aloud, the rudder slammed to, the whole ship gave a sickening heave and shudder, and at the same moment the main-boom swung inboard, the sheet groaning in the blocks, and showed me the lee after-deck.

There were the two watchmen, sure enough: red-cap on his back, as stiff as a handspike, with his arms stretched out like those of a crucifix and his teeth showing through his open lips; Israel Hands propped against the bulwarks, his chin on his chest, his hands lying open before him on the deck, his face as white, under its tan, as a tallow candle.

For a while the ship kept bucking and sidling like a vicious horse, the sails filling, now on one tack, now on another, and the boom swinging to and fro till the mast groaned aloud under the strain. Now and again too there would come a cloud of light sprays over the bulwark and a heavy blow of the ship's bows against the swell; so much heavier weather was made of it by this great rigged ship than by my home-made, lop-sided coracle, now gone to the bottom of the sea.

At every jump of the schooner, red-cap slipped to and fro, but – what was ghastly to behold – neither his attitude nor his fixed teeth-disclosing grin was anyway disturbed by this rough usage. At every jump too, Hands appeared still more to sink into himself and settle down upon the deck, his feet sliding ever the farther out, and the whole body canting towards the stern, so that his face became, little by little, hid from me; and at last I could see nothing beyond his ear and the frayed ringlet of one whisker.

At the same time, I observed, around both of them, splashes of dark blood upon the planks and began to feel sure that they had killed each other in their drunken wrath.

While I was thus looking and wondering, in a calm moment, when the ship was still, Israel Hands turned partly round and with a low moan writhed himself back to the position in which I had seen him first. The moan, which told of pain and deadly weakness, and the way in which his jaw hung open went right to my heart. But when I remembered the talk I had overheard from the apple barrel, all pity left me.

I walked aft until I reached the main-mast.

"Come aboard, Mr. Hands," I said ironically.

He rolled his eyes round heavily, but he was too far gone to express surprise. All he could do was to utter one word, "Brandy."

It occurred to me there was no time to lose, and dodging the boom as it once more lurched across the deck, I slipped aft and down the companion stairs into the cabin.

It was such a scene of confusion as you can hardly fancy. All the lockfast places had been broken open in quest of the chart. The floor was thick with mud where ruffians had sat down to drink or consult after wading in the marshes round their camp. The bulkheads, all painted in clear white and beaded round with gilt, bore a pattern of dirty hands. Dozens of empty bottles clinked together in corners to the rolling of the ship. One of the doctor's medical books lay open on the table, half of the leaves gutted out, I suppose, for pipelights. In the midst of all this the lamp still cast a smoky glow, obscure and brown as umber.

I went into the cellar; all the barrels were gone, and of the bottles a most surprising number had been drunk out and thrown away. Certainly, since the mutiny began, not a man of them could ever have been sober.

Foraging about, I found a bottle with some brandy left, for Hands; and for myself I routed out some biscuit, some pickled fruits, a great

bunch of raisins, and a piece of cheese. With these I came on deck, put down my own stock behind the rudder head and well out of the coxswain's reach, went forward to the water-breaker, and had a good deep drink of water, and then, and not till then, gave Hands the brandy.

He must have drunk a gill before he took the bottle from his mouth.

"Aye," said he, "by thunder, but I wanted some o' that!"

I had sat down already in my own corner and begun to eat.

"Much hurt?" I asked him.

He grunted, or rather, I might say, he barked.

"If that doctor was aboard," he said, "I'd be right enough in a couple of turns, but I don't have no manner of luck, you see, and that's what's the matter with me. As for that swab, he's good and dead, he is," he added, indicating the man with the red cap. "He warn't no seaman anyhow. And where mought you have come from?"

"Well," said I, "I've come aboard to take possession of this ship, Mr. Hands; and you'll please regard me as your captain until further notice."

He looked at me sourly enough but said nothing. Some of the colour had come back into his cheeks, though he still looked very sick and still continued to slip out and settle down as the ship banged about.

"By the by," I continued, "I can't have these colours, Mr. Hands; and by your leave, I'll strike 'em. Better none than these."

And again dodging the boom, I ran to the colour lines, handed down their cursed black flag, and chucked it overboard.

"God save the king!" said I, waving my cap. "And there's an end to Captain Silver!"

He watched me keenly and slyly, his chin all the while on his breast.

"I reckon," he said at last, "I reckon, Cap'n Hawkins, you'll kind of want to get ashore now. S'pose we talks."

"Why, yes," says I, "with all my heart, Mr. Hands. Say on." And I went back to my meal with a good appetite.

"This man," he began, nodding feebly at the corpse " – O'Brien were his name, a rank Irelander – this man and me got the canvas on her, meaning for to sail her back. Well, *he's* dead now, he is – as dead as bilge; and who's to sail this ship, I don't see. Without I gives you a hint, you ain't that man, as far's I can tell. Now, look here, you gives me food and drink and a old scarf or ankecher to tie my wound up, you do, and I'll tell you how to sail her, and that's about square all round, I take it."

"I'll tell you one thing," says I: "I'm not going back to Captain Kidd's anchorage. I mean to get into North Inlet and beach her quietly there."

"To be sure you did," he cried. "Why, I ain't sich an infernal lubber after all. I can see, can't I? I've tried my fling, I have, and I've lost, and it's you has the wind of me. North Inlet? Why, I haven't no ch'ice, not I! I'd help you sail her up to Execution Dock, by thunder! So I would."

Well, as it seemed to me, there was some sense in this. We struck our bargain on the spot. In three minutes I had the *Hispaniola* sailing easily before the wind along the coast of Treasure Island, with good hopes of turning the northern point ere noon and beating down again as far as North Inlet before high water, when we might beach her safely and wait till the subsiding tide permitted us to land.

Then I lashed the tiller and went below to my own chest, where I got a soft silk handkerchief of my mother's. With this, and with my aid, Hands bound up the great bleeding stab he had received in the thigh, and after he had eaten a little and had a swallow or two more of the brandy, he began to pick up visibly, sat straighter up, spoke louder and clearer, and looked in every way another man.

The breeze served us admirably. We skimmed before it like a bird, the coast of the island flashing by and the view changing every minute. Soon we were past the high lands and bowling beside low, sandy country, sparsely dotted with dwarf pines, and soon we were beyond that again and had turned the corner of the rocky hill that ends the island on the north.

I was greatly elated with my new command, and pleased with the bright, sunshiny weather and these different prospects of the coast. I had now plenty of water and good things to eat, and my conscience, which had smitten me hard for my desertion, was quieted by the great conquest I had made. I should, I think, have had nothing left me to desire but for the eyes of the coxswain as they followed me derisively about the deck and the odd smile that appeared continually on his face. It was a smile that had in it something both of pain and weakness – a haggard old man's smile; but there was, besides that, a grain of derision, a shadow of treachery, in his expression as he craftily watched, and watched, and watched me at my work.

CHAPTER TWENTY SIX

Israel Hands

The wind, serving us to a desire, now hauled into the west. We could run so much the easier from the north-east corner of the island to the mouth of the North Inlet. Only, as we had no power to anchor and dared not beach her till the tide had flowed a good deal farther, time hung on our hands. The coxswain told me how to lay the ship to; after a good many trials I succeeded, and we both sat in silence over another meal.

"Cap'n," said he at length with that same uncomfortable smile, "here's my old shipmate, O'Brien; s'pose you was to heave him overboard. I ain't partic'lar as a rule, and I don't take no blame for settling his hash, but I don't reckon him ornamental now, do you?"

"I'm not strong enough, and I don't like the job; and there he lies, for me," said I.

"This here's an unlucky ship, this *Hispaniola*, Jim," he went on, blinking. "There's a power of men been killed in this *Hispaniola* – a sight o' poor seamen dead and gone since you and me took ship to Bristol. I never seen sich dirty luck, not I. There was this here O'Brien now – he's dead, ain't he? Well now, I'm no scholar, and you're a lad as can read and figure, and to put it straight, do you take it as a dead man is dead for good, or do he come alive again?"

"You can kill the body, Mr. Hands, but not the spirit; you must know that already," I replied. "O'Brien there is in another world, and may be watching us."

"Ah!" says he. "Well, that's unfort'nate – appears as if killing parties was a waste of time. Howsomever, sperrits don't reckon for much, by what I've seen. I'll chance it with the sperrits, Jim. And now, you've spoke up free, and I'll take it kind if you'd step down into that there cabin and get me a – well, a – shiver my timbers! I can't hit the name on 't; well, you get me a bottle of wine, Jim – this here brandy's too strong for my head."

Now, the coxswain's hesitation seemed to be unnatural, and as for the notion of his preferring wine to brandy, I entirely disbelieved it. The whole story was a pretext. He wanted me to leave the deck – so much was plain; but with what purpose I could in no way imagine. His eyes never met mine; they kept wandering to and fro, up and down, now with a look to the sky, now with a flitting glance upon the dead O'Brien. All the time he kept smiling and putting his tongue out in the most guilty, embarrassed manner, so that a child could have told that he was bent on some deception. I was prompt with my answer, however, for I saw where my advantage lay and that with a fellow so densely stupid I could easily conceal my suspicions to the end.

"Some wine?" I said. "Far better. Will you have white or red?"

"Well, I reckon it's about the blessed same to me, shipmate," he replied; "so it's strong, and plenty of it, what's the odds?"

"All right," I answered. "I'll bring you port, Mr. Hands. But I'll have to dig for it."

With that I scuttled down the companion with all the noise I could, slipped off my shoes, ran quietly along the sparred gallery, mounted the forecastle ladder, and popped my head out of the fore companion. I knew he would not expect to see me there, yet I took every precaution possible, and certainly the worst of my suspicions proved too true.

He had risen from his position to his hands and knees, and though his leg obviously hurt him pretty sharply when he moved – for I could hear him stifle a groan – yet it was at a good, rattling rate that he trailed himself across the deck. In half a minute he had reached the port scuppers and picked, out of a coil of rope, a long knife, or rather a short dirk, discoloured to the hilt with blood. He looked upon it for a moment, thrusting forth his under jaw, tried the point upon his hand, and then, hastily concealing it in the bosom of his jacket, trundled back again into his old place against the bulwark.

This was all that I required to know. Israel could move about, he was now armed, and if he had been at so much trouble to get rid of me, it was plain that I was meant to be the victim. What he would do afterwards – whether he would try to crawl right across the island from North Inlet to the camp among the swamps or whether he would fire Long Tom, trusting that his own comrades might come first to help him – was, of course, more than I could say.

Yet I felt sure that I could trust him in one point, since in that our interests jumped together, and that was in the disposition of the schooner. We both desired to have her stranded safe enough, in a sheltered place, and so that, when the time came, she could be got off again with as little labour and danger as might be; and until that was done I considered that my life would certainly be spared.

While I was thus turning the business over in my mind, I had not been idle with my body. I had stolen back to the cabin, slipped once more into my shoes, and laid my hand at random on a bottle of wine, and now, with this for an excuse, I made my reappearance on the deck.

Hands lay as I had left him, all fallen together in a bundle and with his eyelids lowered as though he were too weak to bear the light. He looked up, however, at my coming, knocked the neck off the bottle like a man who had done the same thing often, and took a good swig, with his favourite toast of "Here's luck!" Then he lay quiet for a little, and then, pulling out a stick of tobacco, begged me to cut him a quid.

"Cut me a junk o' that," says he, "for I haven't no knife and hardly strength enough, so be as I had. Ah, Jim, Jim, I reckon I've missed stays! Cut me a quid, as'll likely be the last, lad, for I'm for my long home, and no mistake."

"Well," said I, "I'll cut you some tobacco, but if I was you and thought myself so badly, I would go to my prayers like a Christian man."

"Why?" said he. "Now, you tell me why."

"Why?" I cried. "You were asking me just now about the dead. You've broken your trust; you've lived in sin and lies and blood; there's a man you killed lying at your feet this moment, and you ask me why! For God's mercy, Mr. Hands, that's why."

I spoke with a little heat, thinking of the bloody dirk he had hidden in his pocket and designed, in his ill thoughts, to end me with. He, for his part, took a great draught of the wine and spoke with the most unusual solemnity.

"For thirty years," he said, "I've sailed the seas and seen good and bad, better and worse, fair weather and foul, provisions running out, knives going, and what not. Well, now I tell you, I never seen good come o' goodness yet. Him as strikes first is my fancy; dead men don't bite; them's my views – amen, so be it. And now, you look here," he added, suddenly changing his tone, "we've had about enough of this foolery. The tide's made good enough by now. You just take my orders, Cap'n Hawkins, and we'll sail slap in and be done with it."

All told, we had scarce two miles to run; but the navigation was delicate, the entrance to this northern anchorage was not only narrow and shoal, but lay east and west, so that the schooner must be nicely handled to be got in. I think I was a good, prompt subaltern, and I am very sure that Hands was an excellent pilot, for we went about and about and dodged in, shaving the banks, with a certainty and a neatness that were a pleasure to behold.

Scarcely had we passed the heads before the land closed around us. The shores of North Inlet were as thickly wooded as those of the southern anchorage, but the space was longer and narrower and more like, what in truth it was, the estuary of a river. Right before us, at the southern end, we saw the wreck of a ship in the last stages of dilapidation. It had been a great vessel of three masts but had lain so long exposed to the injuries of the weather that it was hung about with great webs of dripping seaweed, and on the deck of it shore bushes had taken root and now flourished thick with flowers. It was a sad sight, but it showed us that the anchorage was calm.

"Now," said Hands, "look there; there's a pet bit for to beach a ship in. Fine flat sand, never a cat's paw, trees all around of it, and flowers a-blowing like a garding on that old ship."

"And once beached," I inquired, "how shall we get her off again?"

"Why, so," he replied: "you take a line ashore there on the other side at low water, take a turn about one of them big pines; bring it back, take a turn around the capstan, and lie to for the tide. Come high water, all hands take a pull upon the line, and off she comes as sweet as natur'. And now, boy, you stand by. We're near the bit now, and she's too much way on her. Starboard a little – so – steady – starboard – larboard a little – steady – steady!"

So he issued his commands, which I breathlessly obeyed, till, all of a sudden, he cried, "Now, my hearty, luff!" And I put the helm hard up, and the *Hispaniola* swung round rapidly and ran stem on for the low, wooded shore.

The excitement of these last manoeuvres had somewhat interfered with the watch I had kept hitherto, sharply enough, upon the coxswain. Even then I was still so much interested, waiting for the ship to touch, that I had quite forgot the peril that hung over my head and stood craning over the starboard bulwarks and watching the ripples spreading wide before the bows. I might have fallen without a struggle for my life had not a sudden disquietude seized upon me and made me turn my head. Perhaps I had heard a creak or seen his shadow moving with the tail of my eye; perhaps it was an instinct like a cat's; but, sure enough, when I looked round, there was Hands, already half-way towards me, with the dirk in his right hand.

We must both have cried out aloud when our eyes met, but while mine was the shrill cry of terror, his was a roar of fury like a charging bully's. At the same instant, he threw himself forward and I leapt sideways towards the bows. As I did so, I let go of the tiller, which sprang sharp to leeward, and I think this saved my life, for it struck Hands across the chest and stopped him, for the moment, dead.

Before he could recover, I was safe out of the corner where he had me trapped, with all the deck to dodge about. Just forward of the main-mast I stopped, drew a pistol from my pocket, took a cool aim, though he had already turned and was once more coming directly after me, and drew the trigger. The hammer fell, but there followed neither flash nor sound; the priming was useless with sea-water. I cursed myself for my neglect. Why had not I, long before, reprimed and reloaded my only weapons? Then I should not have been as now, a mere fleeing sheep before this butcher.

Wounded as he was, it was wonderful how fast he could move, his grizzled hair tumbling over his face, and his face itself as red as a red ensign with his haste and fury. I had no time to try my other pistol, nor indeed much inclination, for I was sure it would be useless. One thing I saw plainly: I must not simply retreat before him, or he would speedily hold me boxed into the bows, as a moment since he had so nearly boxed me in the stern. Once so caught, and nine or ten inches of the blood-stained dirk would be my last experience on this side of eternity. I placed my palms against the main-mast, which was of a goodish bigness, and waited, every nerve upon the stretch.

Seeing that I meant to dodge, he also paused; and a moment or two passed in feints on his part and corresponding movements upon mine. It was such a game as I had often played at home about the rocks of Black Hill Cove, but never before, you may be sure, with such a wildly beating heart as now. Still, as I say, it was a boy's game, and I thought I could hold my own at it against an elderly seaman with a wounded thigh. Indeed my courage had begun to rise so high that I allowed myself a few darting thoughts on what would be the end of the affair, and while I saw certainly that I could spin it out for long, I saw no hope of any ultimate escape.

Well, while things stood thus, suddenly the *Hispaniola* struck, staggered, ground for an instant in the sand, and then, swift as a blow, canted over to the port side till the deck stood at an angle of forty-five degrees and about a puncheon of water splashed into the scupper holes and lay, in a pool, between the deck and bulwark.

We were both of us capsized in a second, and both of us rolled, almost together, into the scuppers, the dead red-cap, with his arms still spread out, tumbling stiffly after us. So near were we, indeed, that my head came against the coxswain's foot with a crack that made my teeth rattle. Blow and all, I was the first afoot again, for Hands had got involved with the dead body. The sudden canting of the ship had made the deck no place for running on; I had to find some new way of escape, and that upon the instant, for my foe was almost touching me. Quick as thought, I sprang into the mizzen shrouds, rattled up hand over hand, and did not draw a breath till I was seated on the cross-trees.

I had been saved by being prompt; the dirk had struck not half a foot below me as I pursued my upward flight; and there stood Israel Hands with his mouth open and his face upturned to mine, a perfect statue of surprise and disappointment.

Now that I had a moment to myself, I lost no time in changing the priming of my pistol, and then, having one ready for service, and to make assurance doubly sure, I proceeded to draw the load of the other and recharge it afresh from the beginning.

My new employment struck Hands all of a heap; he began to see the dice going against him, and after an obvious hesitation, he also hauled himself heavily into the shrouds, and with the dirk in his teeth, began slowly and painfully to mount. It cost him no end of time and groans to haul his wounded leg behind him, and I had quietly finished my arrangements before he was much more than a third of the way up. Then, with a pistol in either hand, I addressed him.

"One more step, Mr. Hands," said I, "and I'll blow your brains out! Dead men don't bite, you know," I added with a chuckle.

He stopped instantly. I could see by the working of his face that he was trying to think, and the process was so slow and laborious that, in my new-found security, I laughed aloud. At last, with a swallow or two, he spoke, his face still wearing the same expression of extreme perplexity. In order to speak he had to take the dagger from his mouth, but in all else he remained unmoved.

"Jim," says he, "I reckon we're fouled, you and me, and we'll have to sign articles. I'd have had you but for that there lurch, but I don't have no luck, not I; and I reckon I'll have to strike, which comes hard, you see, for a master mariner to a ship's younker like you, Jim."

I was drinking in his words and smiling away, as conceited as a cock upon a wall, when, all in a breath, back went his right hand over his shoulder. Something sang like an arrow through the air; I felt a blow

and then a sharp pang, and there I was pinned by the shoulder to the mast. In the horrid pain and surprise of the moment – I scarce can say it was by my own volition, and I am sure it was without a conscious aim – both my pistols went off, and both escaped out of my hands. They did not fall alone; with a choked cry, the coxswain loosed his grasp upon the shrouds and plunged head first into the water.

CHAPTER TWENTY SEVEN

"Pieces of Eight"

OWING TO THE cant of the vessel, the masts hung far out over the water, and from my perch on the cross-trees I had nothing below me but the surface of the bay. Hands, who was not so far up, was in consequence nearer to the ship and fell between me and the bulwarks. He rose once to the surface in a lather of foam and blood and then sank again for good. As the water settled, I could see him lying huddled together on the clean, bright sand in the shadow of the vessel's sides. A fish or two whipped past his body. Sometimes, by the quivering of the water, he appeared to move a little, as if he were trying to rise. But he was dead enough, for all that, being both shot and drowned, and was food for fish in the very place where he had designed my slaughter.

I was no sooner certain of this than I began to feel sick, faint, and terrified. The hot blood was running over my back and chest. The dirk, where it had pinned my shoulder to the mast, seemed to burn like a hot iron; yet it was not so much these real sufferings that distressed me, for these, it seemed to me, I could bear without a murmur; it was the horror I had upon my mind of falling from the cross-trees into that still green water, beside the body of the coxswain.

I clung with both hands till my nails ached, and I shut my eyes as if to cover up the peril. Gradually my mind came back again, my pulses quieted down to a more natural time, and I was once more in possession of myself.

It was my first thought to pluck forth the dirk, but either it stuck too hard or my nerve failed me, and I desisted with a violent shudder. Oddly enough, that very shudder did the business. The knife, in fact, had come the nearest in the world to missing me altogether; it held me by a mere pinch of skin, and this the shudder tore away. The blood ran down the faster, to be sure, but I was my own master again and only tacked to the mast by my coat and shirt.

These last I broke through with a sudden jerk, and then regained the deck by the starboard shrouds. For nothing in the world would I have again ventured, shaken as I was, upon the overhanging port shrouds from which Israel had so lately fallen.

I went below and did what I could for my wound; it pained me a good deal and still bled freely, but it was neither deep nor dangerous, nor did it greatly gall me when I used my arm. Then I looked around me, and as the ship was now, in a sense, my own, I began to think of clearing it from its last passenger – the dead man, O'Brien.

He had pitched, as I have said, against the bulwarks, where he lay like some horrible, ungainly sort of puppet, life-size, indeed, but how different from life's colour or life's comeliness! In that position I could easily have my way with him, and as the habit of tragical adventures had worn off almost all my terror for the dead, I took him by the waist as if he had been a sack of bran and with one good heave, tumbled him overboard. He went in with a sounding plunge; the red cap came off and remained floating on the surface; and as soon as the splash subsided, I could see him and Israel lying side by side, both wavering with the tremulous movement of the water. O'Brien, though still quite a young man, was very bald. There he lay, with that bald head across the knees of the man who had killed him and the quick fishes steering to and fro over both.

I was now alone upon the ship; the tide had just turned. The sun was within so few degrees of setting that already the shadow of the pines upon the western shore began to reach right across the anchorage and fall in patterns on the deck. The evening breeze had sprung up, and though it was well warded off by the hill with the two peaks upon the east, the cordage had begun to sing a little softly to itself and the idle sails to rattle to and fro.

I began to see a danger to the ship. The jibs I speedily doused and brought tumbling to the deck, but the main-sail was a harder matter. Of course, when the schooner canted over, the boom had swung outboard, and the cap of it and a foot or two of sail hung even under water. I thought this made it still more dangerous; yet the strain was so heavy that I half feared to meddle. At last I got my knife and cut the halyards. The peak dropped instantly, a great belly of loose canvas floated broad upon the water, and since, pull as I liked, I could not budge the downhall, that was the extent of what I could accomplish. For the rest, the *Hispaniola* must trust to luck, like myself.

By this time the whole anchorage had fallen into shadow – the last rays, I remember, falling through a glade of the wood and shining bright as jewels on the flowery mantle of the wreck. It began to be chill; the tide was rapidly fleeting seaward, the schooner settling more and more on her beam-ends.

I scrambled forward and looked over. It seemed shallow enough, and holding the cut hawser in both hands for a last security, I let myself drop softly overboard. The water scarcely reached my waist; the sand was firm and covered with ripple marks, and I waded ashore in great spirits, leaving the *Hispaniola* on her side, with her main-sail trailing wide upon the surface of the bay. About the same time, the sun went fairly down and the breeze whistled low in the dusk among the tossing pines.

At least, and at last, I was off the sea, nor had I returned thence empty-handed. There lay the schooner, clear at last from buccaneers and ready for our own men to board and get to sea again. I had nothing nearer my fancy than to get home to the stockade and boast of my achievements. Possibly I might be blamed a bit for my truantry, but the recapture of the *Hispaniola* was a clenching answer, and I hoped that even Captain Smollett would confess I had not lost my time.

So thinking, and in famous spirits, I began to set my face homeward for the block house and my companions. I remembered that the most easterly of the rivers which drain into Captain Kidd's anchorage ran from the two-peaked hill upon my left, and I bent my course in that direction that I might pass the stream while it was small. The wood was pretty open, and keeping along the lower spurs, I had soon turned the corner of that hill, and not long after waded to the mid-calf across the watercourse.

This brought me near to where I had encountered Ben Gunn, the maroon; and I walked more circumspectly, keeping an eye on every side. The dusk had come nigh hand completely, and as I opened out the cleft between the two peaks, I became aware of a wavering glow against the sky, where, as I judged, the man of the island was cooking his supper before a roaring fire. And yet I wondered, in my heart, that he should show himself so careless. For if I could see this radiance, might it not reach the eyes of Silver himself where he camped upon the shore among the marshes?

Gradually the night fell blacker; it was all I could do to guide myself even roughly towards my destination; the double hill behind me and the Spy-glass on my right hand loomed faint and fainter; the stars were few and pale; and in the low ground where I wandered I kept tripping among bushes and rolling into sandy pits.

Suddenly a kind of brightness fell about me. I looked up; a pale glimmer of moonbeams had alighted on the summit of the Spy-glass, and soon after I saw something broad and silvery moving low down behind the trees, and knew the moon had risen.

With this to help me, I passed rapidly over what remained to me of my journey, and sometimes walking, sometimes running, impatiently drew near to the stockade. Yet, as I began to thread the grove that lies before it, I was not so thoughtless but that I slacked my pace and went a trifle warily. It would have been a poor end of my adventures to get shot down by my own party in mistake.

The moon was climbing higher and higher, its light began to fall here and there in masses through the more open districts of the wood, and right in front of me a glow of a different colour appeared among the trees. It was red and hot, and now and again it was a little darkened – as it were, the embers of a bonfire smouldering.

For the life of me I could not think what it might be.

At last I came right down upon the borders of the clearing. The western end was already steeped in moonshine; the rest, and the block house itself, still lay in a black shadow chequered with long silvery streaks of light. On the other side of the house an immense fire had burned itself into clear embers and shed a steady, red reverberation, contrasted strongly with the mellow paleness of the moon. There was not a soul stirring nor a sound beside the noises of the breeze.

I stopped, with much wonder in my heart, and perhaps a little terror also. It had not been our way to build great fires; we were, indeed, by the captain's orders, somewhat niggardly of firewood, and I began to fear that something had gone wrong while I was absent.

I stole round by the eastern end, keeping close in shadow, and at a convenient place, where the darkness was thickest, crossed the palisade.

To make assurance surer, I got upon my hands and knees and crawled, without a sound, towards the corner of the house. As I drew nearer, my heart was suddenly and greatly lightened. It is not a pleasant noise in itself, and I have often complained of it at other times, but just then it was like music to hear my friends snoring together so loud and peaceful in their sleep. The sea-cry of the watch, that beautiful "All's well," never fell more reassuringly on my ear.

In the meantime, there was no doubt of one thing; they kept an infamous bad watch. If it had been Silver and his lads that were now creeping in on them, not a soul would have seen daybreak. That was what it was, thought I, to have the captain wounded; and again I blamed myself sharply for leaving them in that danger with so few to mount guard.

By this time I had got to the door and stood up. All was dark within, so that I could distinguish nothing by the eye. As for sounds, there was the steady drone of the snorers and a small occasional noise, a flickering or pecking that I could in no way account for.

With my arms before me I walked steadily in. I should lie down in my own place (I thought with a silent chuckle) and enjoy their faces when they found me in the morning.

My foot struck something yielding – it was a sleeper's leg; and he turned and groaned, but without awaking.

And then, all of a sudden, a shrill voice broke forth out of the darkness:

"Pieces of eight! Pieces of eight! Pieces of eight! Pieces of eight! Pieces of eight!" and so forth, without pause or change, like the clacking of a tiny mill.

Silver's green parrot, Captain Flint! It was she whom I had heard pecking at a piece of bark; it was she, keeping better watch than any human being, who thus announced my arrival with her wearisome refrain.

I had no time left me to recover. At the sharp, clipping tone of the parrot, the sleepers awoke and sprang up; and with a mighty oath, the voice of Silver cried, "Who goes?"

I turned to run, struck violently against one person, recoiled, and ran full into the arms of a second, who for his part closed upon and held me tight.

"Bring a torch, Dick," said Silver when my capture was thus assured.

And one of the men left the log-house and presently returned with a lighted brand.

PART SIX

Captain Silver

CHAPTER TWENTY EIGHT

In the Enemy's Camp

The red glare of the torch, lighting up the interior of the block house, showed me the worst of my apprehensions realized. The pirates were in possession of the house and stores: there was the cask of cognac, there were the pork and bread, as before, and what tenfold increased my horror, not a sign of any prisoner. I could only judge that all had perished, and my heart smote me sorely that I had not been there to perish with them.

There were six of the buccaneers, all told; not another man was left alive. Five of them were on their feet, flushed and swollen, suddenly called out of the first sleep of drunkenness. The sixth had only risen upon his elbow; he was deadly pale, and the blood-stained bandage round his head told that he had recently been wounded, and still more recently dressed. I remembered the man who had been shot and had run back among the woods in the great attack, and doubted not that this was he.

The parrot sat, preening her plumage, on Long John's shoulder. He himself, I thought, looked somewhat paler and more stern than I was used to. He still wore the fine broadcloth suit in which he had fulfilled his mission, but it was bitterly the worse for wear, daubed with clay and torn with the sharp briers of the wood.

"So," said he, "here's Jim Hawkins, shiver my timbers! Dropped in, like, eh? Well, come, I take that friendly."

And thereupon he sat down across the brandy cask and began to fill a pipe.

"Give me a loan of the link, Dick," said he; and then, when he had a good light, "That'll do, lad," he added; "stick the glim in the wood heap; and you, gentlemen, bring yourselves to! You needn't stand up for Mr.

Hawkins; *he'll* excuse you, you may lay to that. And so, Jim" – stopping the tobacco – "here you were, and quite a pleasant surprise for poor old John. I see you were smart when first I set my eyes on you, but this here gets away from me clean, it do."

To all this, as may be well supposed, I made no answer. They had set me with my back against the wall, and I stood there, looking Silver in the face, pluckily enough, I hope, to all outward appearance, but with black despair in my heart.

Silver took a whiff or two of his pipe with great composure and then ran on again.

"Now, you see, Jim, so be as you *are* here," says he, "I'll give you a piece of my mind. I've always liked you, I have, for a lad of spirit, and the picter of my own self when I was young and handsome. I always wanted you to jine and take your share, and die a gentleman, and now, my cock, you've got to. Cap'n Smollett's a fine seaman, as I'll own up to any day, but stiff on discipline. 'Dooty is dooty,' says he, and right he is. Just you keep clear of the cap'n. The doctor himself is gone dead again you – 'ungrateful scamp' was what he said; and the short and the long of the whole story is about here: you can't go back to your own lot, for they won't have you; and without you start a third ship's company all by yourself, which might be lonely, you'll have to jine with Cap'n Silver."

So far so good. My friends, then, were still alive, and though I partly believed the truth of Silver's statement, that the cabin party were incensed at me for my desertion, I was more relieved than distressed by what I heard.

"I don't say nothing as to your being in our hands," continued Silver, "though there you are, and you may lay to it. I'm all for argyment; I never seen good come out o' threatening. If you like the service, well, you'll jine; and if you don't, Jim, why, you're free to answer no – free and welcome, shipmate; and if fairer can be said by mortal seaman, shiver my sides!"

"Am I to answer, then?" I asked with a very tremulous voice. Through all this sneering talk, I was made to feel the threat of death that overhung me, and my cheeks burned and my heart beat painfully in my breast.

"Lad," said Silver, "no one's a-pressing of you. Take your bearings. None of us won't hurry you, mate; time goes so pleasant in your company, you see."

"Well," says I, growing a bit bolder, "if I'm to choose, I declare I have a right to know what's what, and why you're here, and where my friends are."

"Wot's wot?" repeated one of the buccaneers in a deep growl. "Ah, he'd be a lucky one as knowed that!"

"You'll perhaps batten down your hatches till you're spoke to, my friend," cried Silver truculently to this speaker. And then, in his first gracious tones, he replied to me, "Yesterday morning, Mr. Hawkins," said he, "in the dog-watch, down came Doctor Livesey with a flag of truce. Says he, 'Cap'n Silver, you're sold out. Ship's gone.' Well, maybe we'd been taking a glass, and a song to help it round. I won't say no. Leastways, none of us had looked out. We looked out, and by thunder, the old ship was gone! I never seen a pack o' fools look fishier; and you may lay to that, if I tells you that looked the fishiest. 'Well,' says the doctor, 'let's bargain.' We bargained, him and I, and here we are: stores, brandy, block house, the firewood you was thoughtful enough to cut, and in a manner of speaking, the whole blessed boat, from cross-trees to kelson. As for them, they've tramped; I don't know where's they are."

He drew again quietly at his pipe.

"And lest you should take it into that head of yours," he went on, "that you was included in the treaty, here's the last word that was said: 'How many are you,' says I, 'to leave?' 'Four,' says he; 'four, and one of us wounded. As for that boy, I don't know where he is, confound him,' says he, 'nor I don't much care. We're about sick of him.' These was his words.

"Is that all?" I asked.

"Well, it's all that you're to hear, my son," returned Silver.

"And now I am to choose?"

"And now you are to choose, and you may lay to that," said Silver.

"Well," said I, "I am not such a fool but I know pretty well what I have to look for. Let the worst come to the worst, it's little I care. I've seen too many die since I fell in with you. But there's a thing or two I have to tell you," I said, and by this time I was quite excited; "and the first is this: here you are, in a bad way – ship lost, treasure lost, men lost, your whole business gone to wreck; and if you want to know who did it – it was I! I was in the apple barrel the night we sighted land, and I heard you, John, and you, Dick Johnson, and Hands, who is now at the bottom of the sea, and told every word you said before the hour was out. And as for the schooner, it was I who cut her cable, and it was I that killed the men you had aboard of her, and it was I who brought her where you'll never see her more, not one of you. The laugh's on my side; I've had the top of this business from the first; I no more fear you than I fear a fly. Kill me, if you please, or spare me. But one thing I'll say, and no more; if you spare me, bygones are bygones, and when you fellows are in court for piracy, I'll save you all I can. It is for you to choose. Kill another and do yourselves no good, or spare me and keep a witness to save you from the gallows."

I stopped, for, I tell you, I was out of breath, and to my wonder, not a man of them moved, but all sat staring at me like as many sheep. And while they were still staring, I broke out again, "And now, Mr. Silver," I said, "I believe you're the best man here, and if things go to the worst, I'll take it kind of you to let the doctor know the way I took it."

"I'll bear it in mind," said Silver with an accent so curious that I could not, for the life of me, decide whether he were laughing at my request or had been favourably affected by my courage.

"I'll put one to that," cried the old mahogany-faced seaman – Morgan by name – whom I had seen in Long John's public-house upon the quays of Bristol. "It was him that knowed Black Dog."

"Well, and see here," added the sea-cook. "I'll put another again to that, by thunder! For it was this same boy that faked the chart from Billy Bones. First and last, we've split upon Jim Hawkins!"

"Then here goes!" said Morgan with an oath.

And he sprang up, drawing his knife as if he had been twenty.

"Avast, there!" cried Silver. "Who are you, Tom Morgan? Maybe you thought you was cap'n here, perhaps. By the powers, but I'll teach you better! Cross me, and you'll go where many a good man's gone before you, first and last, these thirty year back – some to the yard-arm, shiver my timbers, and some by the board, and all to feed the fishes. There's never a man looked me between the eyes and seen a good day a'terwards, Tom Morgan, you may lay to that."

Morgan paused, but a hoarse murmur rose from the others.

"Tom's right," said one.

"I stood hazing long enough from one," added another. "I'll be hanged if I'll be hazed by you, John Silver."

"Did any of you gentlemen want to have it out with *me*?" roared Silver, bending far forward from his position on the keg, with his pipe still glowing in his right hand. "Put a name on what you're at; you ain't dumb, I reckon. Him that wants shall get it. Have I lived this many years, and a son of a rum puncheon cock his hat athwart my hawse at the latter end of it? You know the way; you're all gentlemen o' fortune, by your account. Well, I'm ready. Take a cutlass, him that dares, and I'll see the colour of his inside, crutch and all, before that pipe's empty."

Not a man stirred; not a man answered.

"That's your sort, is it?" he added, returning his pipe to his mouth. "Well, you're a gay lot to look at, anyway. Not much worth to fight, you

ain't. P'r'aps you can understand King George's English. I'm cap'n here by 'lection. I'm cap'n here because I'm the best man by a long sea-mile. You won't fight, as gentlemen o' fortune should; then, by thunder, you'll obey, and you may lay to it! I like that boy, now; I never seen a better boy than that. He's more a man than any pair of rats of you in this here house, and what I say is this: let me see him that'll lay a hand on him – that's what I say, and you may lay to it."

There was a long pause after this. I stood straight up against the wall, my heart still going like a sledge-hammer, but with a ray of hope now shining in my bosom. Silver leant back against the wall, his arms crossed, his pipe in the corner of his mouth, as calm as though he had been in church; yet his eye kept wandering furtively, and he kept the tail of it on his unruly followers. They, on their part, drew gradually together towards the far end of the block house, and the low hiss of their whispering sounded in my ear continuously, like a stream. One after another, they would look up, and the red light of the torch would fall for a second on their nervous faces; but it was not towards me, it was towards Silver that they turned their eyes.

"You seem to have a lot to say," remarked Silver, spitting far into the air. "Pipe up and let me hear it, or lay to."

"Ax your pardon, sir," returned one of the men; "you're pretty free with some of the rules; maybe you'll kindly keep an eye upon the rest. This crew's dissatisfied; this crew don't vally bullying a marlin-spike;

this crew has its rights like other crews, I'll make so free as that; and by your own rules, I take it we can talk together. I ax your pardon, sir, acknowledging you for to be captaing at this present; but I claim my right, and steps outside for a council."

And with an elaborate sea-salute, this fellow, a long, ill-looking, yellow-eyed man of five and thirty, stepped coolly towards the door and disappeared out of the house. One after another the rest followed his example, each making a salute as he passed, each adding some apology. "According to rules," said one. "Forecastle council," said Morgan. And so with one remark or another all marched out and left Silver and me alone with the torch.

The sea-cook instantly removed his pipe.

"Now, look you here, Jim Hawkins," he said in a steady whisper that was no more than audible, "you're within half a plank of death, and what's a long sight worse, of torture. They're going to throw me off. But, you mark, I stand by you through thick and thin. I didn't mean to; no, not till you spoke up. I was about desperate to lose that much blunt, and be hanged into the bargain. But I see you was the right sort. I says to myself, you stand by Hawkins, John, and Hawkins'll stand by you. You're his last card, and by the living thunder, John, he's yours! Back to back, says I. You save your witness, and he'll save your neck!"

I began dimly to understand.

"You mean all's lost?" I asked.

"Aye, by gum, I do!" he answered. "Ship gone, neck gone – that's the size of it. Once I looked into that bay, Jim Hawkins, and seen no schooner – well, I'm tough, but I gave out. As for that lot and their council, mark me, they're outright fools and cowards. I'll save your life – if so be as I can – from them. But, see here, Jim – tit for tat – you save Long John from swinging."

I was bewildered; it seemed a thing so hopeless he was asking – he, the old buccaneer, the ringleader throughout.

"What I can do, that I'll do," I said.

"It's a bargain!" cried Long John. "You speak up plucky, and by thunder, I've a chance!"

He hobbled to the torch, where it stood propped among the firewood, and took a fresh light to his pipe.

"Understand me, Jim," he said, returning. "I've a head on my shoulders, I have. I'm on squire's side now. I know you've got that ship safe somewheres. How you done it, I don't know, but safe it is. I guess Hands and O'Brien turned soft. I never much believed in neither of *them*. Now you mark me. I ask no questions, nor I won't let others. I know when a game's up, I do; and I know a lad that's staunch. Ah, you that's young – you and me might have done a power of good together!"

He drew some cognac from the cask into a tin cannikin.

"Will you taste, messmate?" he asked; and when I had refused: "Well, I'll take a drain myself, Jim," said he. "I need a caulker, for there's trouble on hand. And talking o' trouble, why did that doctor give me the chart, Jim?"

My face expressed a wonder so unaffected that he saw the needlessness of further questions.

"Ah, well, he did, though," said he. "And there's something under that, no doubt – something, surely, under that, Jim – bad or good."

And he took another swallow of the brandy, shaking his great fair head like a man who looks forward to the worst.

CHAPTER TWENTY NINE

The Black Spot Again

THE COUNCIL of buccaneers had lasted some time, when one of them re-entered the house, and with a repetition of the same salute, which had in my eyes an ironical air, begged for a moment's loan of the torch. Silver briefly agreed, and this emissary retired again, leaving us together in the dark.

"There's a breeze coming, Jim," said Silver, who had by this time adopted quite a friendly and familiar tone.

I turned to the loophole nearest me and looked out. The embers of the great fire had so far burned themselves out and now glowed so low and duskily that I understood why these conspirators desired a torch. About half-way down the slope to the stockade, they were collected in a group; one held the light, another was on his knees in their midst, and I saw the blade of an open knife shine in his hand with varying colours in the moon and torchlight. The rest were all somewhat stooping, as though watching the manoeuvres of this last. I could just make out that he had a book as well as a knife in his hand, and was still wondering how anything so incongruous had come in their possession when the kneeling figure rose once more to his feet and the whole party began to move together towards the house.

"Here they come," said I; and I returned to my former position, for it seemed beneath my dignity that they should find me watching them.

"Well, let 'em come, lad – let 'em come," said Silver cheerily. "I've still a shot in my locker."

The door opened, and the five men, standing huddled together just inside, pushed one of their number forward. In any other circumstances it would have been comical to see his slow advance, hesitating as he set down each foot, but holding his closed right hand in front of him.

"Step up, lad," cried Silver. "I won't eat you. Hand it over, lubber. I know the rules, I do; I won't hurt a depytation."

Thus encouraged, the buccaneer stepped forth more briskly, and having passed something to Silver, from hand to hand, slipped yet more smartly back again to his companions.

The sea-cook looked at what had been given him.

"The black spot! I thought so," he observed. "Where might you have got the paper? Why, hillo! Look here, now; this ain't lucky! You've gone and cut this out of a Bible. What fool's cut a Bible?"

"Ah, there!" said Morgan. "There! Wot did I say? No good'll come o' that, I said."

"Well, you've about fixed it now, among you," continued Silver. "You'll all swing now, I reckon. What soft-headed lubber had a Bible?"

"It was Dick," said one.

"Dick, was it? Then Dick can get to prayers," said Silver. "He's seen his slice of luck, has Dick, and you may lay to that."

But here the long man with the yellow eyes struck in.

"Belay that talk, John Silver," he said. "This crew has tipped you the black spot in full council, as in dooty bound; just you turn it over, as in dooty bound, and see what's wrote there. Then you can talk."

"Thanky, George," replied the sea-cook. "You always was brisk for business, and has the rules by heart, George, as I'm pleased to see. Well, what is it, anyway? Ah! 'Deposed' – that's it, is it? Very pretty wrote, to be sure; like print, I swear. Your hand o' write, George? Why, you was gettin' quite a leadin' man in this here crew. You'll be cap'n next, I shouldn't wonder. Just oblige me with that torch again, will you? This pipe don't draw."

"Come, now," said George, "you don't fool this crew no more. You're a funny man, by your account; but you're over now, and you'll maybe step down off that barrel and help vote."

"I thought you said you knowed the rules," returned Silver contemptuously. "Leastways, if you don't, I do; and I wait here – and I'm still your cap'n, mind – till you outs with your grievances and I reply; in the meantime, your black spot ain't worth a biscuit. After that, we'll see."

"Oh," replied George, "you don't be under no kind of apprehension; *we're* all square, we are. First, you've made a hash of this cruise – you'll be a bold man to say no to that. Second, you let the enemy out o' this here trap for nothing. Why did they want out? I dunno, but it's pretty plain they wanted it. Third, you wouldn't let us go at them upon the march. Oh, we see through you, John Silver; you want to play booty, that's what's wrong with you. And then, fourth, there's this here boy."

"Is that all?" asked Silver quietly.

"Enough, too," retorted George. "We'll all swing and sun-dry for your bungling."

"Well now, look here, I'll answer these four p'ints; one after another I'll answer 'em. I made a hash o' this cruise, did I? Well now, you all know what I wanted, and you all know if that had been done that we'd 'a been aboard the *Hispaniola* this night as ever was, every man of us alive, and fit, and full of good plum-duff, and the treasure in the hold of her, by thunder! Well, who crossed me? Who forced my hand, as was the lawful cap'n? Who tipped me the black spot the day we landed and began this dance? Ah, it's a fine dance – I'm with you there – and looks mighty like a hornpipe in a rope's end at Execution Dock by London town, it does. But who done it? Why, it was Anderson, and Hands, and you, George Merry! And you're the last above board of that same meddling crew; and you have the Davy Jones's insolence to up and stand for cap'n over me – you, that sank the lot of us! By the powers! But this tops the stiffest yarn to nothing."

Silver paused, and I could see by the faces of George and his late comrades that these words had not been said in vain.

"That's for number one," cried the accused, wiping the sweat from his brow, for he had been talking with a vehemence that shook the house. "Why, I give you my word, I'm sick to speak to you. You've neither sense nor memory, and I leave it to fancy where your mothers was that let you come to sea. Sea! Gentlemen o' fortune! I reckon tailors is your trade."

"Go on, John," said Morgan. "Speak up to the others."

"Ah, the others!" returned John. "They're a nice lot, ain't they? You say this cruise is bungled. Ah! By gum, if you could understand how bad it's bungled, you would see! We're that near the gibbet that my neck's stiff with thinking on it. You've seen 'em, maybe, hanged in chains, birds about 'em, seamen p'inting 'em out as they go down with the tide. 'Who's that?' says one. 'That! Why, that's John Silver. I knowed him well,' says another. And you can hear the chains a-jangle as you go about and reach for the other buoy. Now, that's about where we are, every mother's son of us, thanks to him, and Hands, and Anderson, and other ruination fools of you. And if you want to know about number four, and that boy, why, shiver my timbers, isn't he a hostage? Are we a-going to waste a hostage? No, not us; he might be our last chance, and I shouldn't wonder. Kill that boy? Not me, mates! And number three? Ah, well, there's a deal to say to number three. Maybe you don't count it nothing to have a real college doctor to see you every day – you, John, with your head broke – or you, George Merry, that had the ague shakes upon you not six hours agone, and has your eyes the colour of lemon peel to this same moment on the clock? And maybe, perhaps, you didn't know there was a consort coming either? But there is, and not so long till then; and we'll see who'll be glad to have a hostage when it comes to that. And as for number two, and why I made a bargain – well, you came crawling on your knees to me to make it – on your knees you came, you was that downhearted – and you'd have starved too if I hadn't – but that's a trifle! You look there – that's why!"

And he cast down upon the floor a paper that I instantly recognized – none other than the chart on yellow paper, with the three red crosses, that I had found in the oilcloth at the bottom of the captain's chest. Why the doctor had given it to him was more than I could fancy.

But if it were inexplicable to me, the appearance of the chart was incredible to the surviving mutineers. They leaped upon it like cats upon a mouse. It went from hand to hand, one tearing it from another; and by the oaths and the cries and the childish laughter with which they accompanied their examination, you would have thought, not only they were fingering the very gold, but were at sea with it, besides, in safety.

"Yes," said one, "that's Flint, sure enough. J. F., and a score below, with a clove hitch to it; so he done ever."

"Mighty pretty," said George. "But how are we to get away with it, and us no ship."

Silver suddenly sprang up, and supporting himself with a hand against the wall: "Now I give you warning, George," he cried. "One more word of your sauce, and I'll call you down and fight you. How? Why, how do I know? You had ought to tell me that – you and the rest, that lost me my schooner, with your interference, burn you! But not you, you can't; you hain't got the invention of a cockroach. But civil you can speak, and shall, George Merry, you may lay to that."

"That's fair enow," said the old man Morgan.

"Fair! I reckon so," said the sea-cook. "You lost the ship; I found the treasure. Who's the better man at that? And now I resign, by thunder! Elect whom you please to be your cap'n now; I'm done with it."

"Silver!" they cried. "Barbecue forever! Barbecue for cap'n!"

"So that's the toon, is it?" cried the cook. "George, I reckon you'll have to wait another turn, friend; and lucky for you as I'm not a revengeful man. But that was never my way. And now, shipmates, this black spot? 'Tain't much good now, is it? Dick's crossed his luck and spoiled his Bible, and that's about all."

"It'll do to kiss the book on still, won't it?" growled Dick, who was evidently uneasy at the curse he had brought upon himself.

"A Bible with a bit cut out!" returned Silver derisively. "Not it. It don't bind no more'n a ballad-book."

"Don't it, though?" cried Dick with a sort of joy. "Well, I reckon that's worth having too."

"Here, Jim – here's a cur'osity for you," said Silver, and he tossed me the paper.

It was around about the size of a crown piece. One side was blank, for it had been the last leaf; the other contained a verse or two of Revelation – these words among the rest, which struck sharply home upon my mind: "Without are dogs and murderers." The printed side had been blackened with wood ash, which already began to come off and soil my fingers; on the blank side had been written with the same material the one word "Depposed." I have that curiosity beside me at this moment, but not a trace of writing now remains beyond a single scratch, such as a man might make with his thumb-nail.

That was the end of the night's business. Soon after, with a drink all round, we lay down to sleep, and the outside of Silver's vengeance was to put George Merry up for sentinel and threaten him with death if he should prove unfaithful.

It was long ere I could close an eye, and heaven knows I had matter enough for thought in the man whom I had slain that afternoon, in my own most perilous position, and above all, in the remarkable game that I saw Silver now engaged upon – keeping the mutineers together with one hand and grasping with the other after every means, possible and impossible, to make his peace and save his miserable life. He himself slept peacefully and snored aloud, yet my heart was sore for him, wicked as he was, to think on the dark perils that environed and the shameful gibbet that awaited him.

CHAPTER THIRTY

On Parole

I WAS WAKENED – indeed, we were all wakened, for I could see even the sentinel shake himself together from where he had fallen against the door-post – by a clear, hearty voice hailing us from the margin of the wood:

"Block house, ahoy!" it cried. "Here's the doctor."

And the doctor it was. Although I was glad to hear the sound, yet my gladness was not without admixture. I remembered with confusion my insubordinate and stealthy conduct, and when I saw where it had brought me – among what companions and surrounded by what dangers – I felt ashamed to look him in the face.

He must have risen in the dark, for the day had hardly come; and when I ran to a loophole and looked out, I saw him standing, like Silver once before, up to the mid-leg in creeping vapour.

"You, doctor! Top o' the morning to you, sir!" cried Silver, broad awake and beaming with good nature in a moment. "Bright and early, to be sure; and it's the early bird, as the saying goes, that gets the rations. George, shake up your timbers, son, and help Dr. Livesey over the ship's side. All a-doin' well, your patients was – all well and merry."

So he pattered on, standing on the hilltop with his crutch under his elbow and one hand upon the side of the log-house – quite the old John in voice, manner, and expression.

"We've quite a surprise for you too, sir," he continued. "We've a little stranger here – he! he! A noo boarder and lodger, sir, and looking fit and taut as a fiddle; slep' like a supercargo, he did, right alongside of John – stem to stem we was, all night."

Dr. Livesey was by this time across the stockade and pretty near the cook, and I could hear the alteration in his voice as he said, "Not Jim?"

"The very same Jim as ever was," says Silver.

The doctor stopped outright, although he did not speak, and it was some seconds before he seemed able to move on.

"Well, well," he said at last, "duty first and pleasure afterwards, as you might have said yourself, Silver. Let us overhaul these patients of yours."

A moment afterwards he had entered the block house and with one grim nod to me proceeded with his work among the sick. He seemed under no apprehension, though he must have known that his life, among these treacherous demons, depended on a hair; and he rattled on to his patients as if he were paying an ordinary professional visit in a quiet English family. His manner, I suppose, reacted on the men, for they behaved to him as if nothing had occurred, as if he were still ship's doctor and they still faithful hands before the mast.

"You're doing well, my friend," he said to the fellow with the bandaged head, "and if ever any person had a close shave, it was you; your head must be as hard as iron. Well, George, how goes it? You're a pretty colour, certainly; why, your liver, man, is upside down. Did you take that medicine? Did he take that medicine, men?"

"Aye, aye, sir, he took it, sure enough," returned Morgan.

"Because, you see, since I am mutineers' doctor, or prison doctor as I prefer to call it," says Doctor Livesey in his pleasantest way, "I make it a point of honour not to lose a man for King George (God bless him!) and the gallows."

The rogues looked at each other but swallowed the home-thrust in silence.

"Dick don't feel well, sir," said one.

"Don't he?" replied the doctor. "Well, step up here, Dick, and let me see your tongue. No, I should be surprised if he did! The man's tongue is fit to frighten the French. Another fever."

"Ah, there," said Morgan, "that comed of sp'iling Bibles."

"That comes – as you call it – of being arrant asses," retorted the doctor, "and not having sense enough to know honest air from poison, and the dry land from a vile, pestiferous slough. I think it most probable – though of course it's only an opinion – that you'll all have the deuce to pay before you get that malaria out of your systems. Camp in a bog, would you? Silver, I'm surprised at you. You're less of a fool than many, take you all round; but you don't appear to me to have the rudiments of a notion of the rules of health.

"Well," he added after he had dosed them round and they had taken his prescriptions, with really laughable humility, more like charity schoolchildren than blood-guilty mutineers and pirates – "well, that's done for today. And now I should wish to have a talk with that boy, please."

And he nodded his head in my direction carelessly.

George Merry was at the door, spitting and spluttering over some bad-tasted medicine; but at the first word of the doctor's proposal he swung round with a deep flush and cried "No!" and swore.

Silver struck the barrel with his open hand.

"Si-lence!" he roared and looked about him positively like a lion. "Doctor," he went on in his usual tones, "I was a-thinking of that, knowing as how you had a fancy for the boy. We're all humbly grateful for your kindness, and as you see, puts faith in you and takes the drugs down like that much grog. And I take it I've found a way as'll suit all. Hawkins, will you give me your word of honour as a young gentleman – for a young gentleman you are, although poor born – your word of honour not to slip your cable?"

I readily gave the pledge required.

"Then, doctor," said Silver, "you just step outside o' that stockade, and once you're there I'll bring the boy down on the inside, and I reckon you can yarn through the spars. Good day to you, sir, and all our dooties to the squire and Cap'n Smollett."

The explosion of disapproval, which nothing but Silver's black looks had restrained, broke out immediately the doctor had left the house. Silver was roundly accused of playing double – of trying to make a separate peace for himself, of sacrificing the interests of his accomplices and victims, and, in one word, of the identical, exact thing that he was doing. It seemed to me so obvious, in this case, that I could not imagine how he was to turn their anger. But he was twice the man the rest were, and his last night's victory had given him a huge preponderance on their minds. He called them all the fools and dolts you can imagine, said it was necessary I should talk to the doctor, fluttered the chart in their faces, asked them if they could afford to break the treaty the very day they were bound a-treasure-hunting.

"No, by thunder!" he cried. "It's us must break the treaty when the time comes; and till then I'll gammon that doctor, if I have to ile his boots with brandy."

And then he bade them get the fire lit, and stalked out upon his crutch, with his hand on my shoulder, leaving them in a disarray, and silenced by his volubility rather than convinced.

"Slow, lad, slow," he said. "They might round upon us in a twinkle of an eye if we was seen to hurry."

Very deliberately, then, did we advance across the sand to where the doctor awaited us on the other side of the stockade, and as soon as we were within easy speaking distance Silver stopped.

"You'll make a note of this here also, doctor," says he, "and the boy'll tell you how I saved his life, and were deposed for it too, and you may lay to that. Doctor, when a man's steering as near the wind as me – playing chuck-farthing with the last breath in his body, like – you wouldn't think it too much, mayhap, to give him one good word? You'll please bear in mind it's not my life only now – it's that boy's into the bargain; and you'll speak me fair, doctor, and give me a bit o' hope to go on, for the sake of mercy."

Silver was a changed man once he was out there and had his back to his friends and the block house; his cheeks seemed to have fallen in, his voice trembled; never was a soul more dead in earnest.

"Why, John, you're not afraid?" asked Dr. Livesey.

"Doctor, I'm no coward; no, not I – not *so* much!" and he snapped his fingers. "If I was I wouldn't say it. But I'll own up fairly, I've the shakes upon me for the gallows. You're a good man and a true; I never seen a better man! And you'll not forget what I done good, not any more than you'll forget the bad, I know. And I step aside – see here – and leave you and Jim alone. And you'll put that down for me too, for it's a long stretch, is that!"

So saying, he stepped back a little way, till he was out of earshot, and there sat down upon a tree-stump and began to whistle, spinning round now and again upon his seat so as to command a sight, sometimes of me and the doctor and sometimes of his unruly ruffians as they went to and fro in the sand between the fire – which they were busy rekindling – and the house, from which they brought forth pork and bread to make the breakfast.

"So, Jim," said the doctor sadly, "here you are. As you have brewed, so shall you drink, my boy. Heaven knows, I cannot find it in my heart to blame you, but this much I will say, be it kind or unkind: when Captain Smollett was well, you dared not have gone off; and when he was ill and couldn't help it, by George, it was downright cowardly!"

I will own that I here began to weep. "Doctor," I said, "you might spare me. I have blamed myself enough; my life's forfeit anyway, and I should have been dead by now if Silver hadn't stood for me; and doctor, believe this, I can die – and I dare say I deserve it – but what I fear is torture. If they come to torture me – "

"Jim," the doctor interrupted, and his voice was quite changed, "Jim, I can't have this. Whip over, and we'll run for it."

"Doctor," said I, "I passed my word."

"I know, I know," he cried. "We can't help that, Jim, now. I'll take it on my shoulders, holus bolus, blame and shame, my boy; but stay here, I cannot let you. Jump! One jump, and you're out, and we'll run for it like antelopes."

"No," I replied; "you know right well you wouldn't do the thing yourself – neither you nor squire nor captain; and no more will I. Silver trusted me; I passed my word, and back I go. But, doctor, you did not let me finish. If they come to torture me, I might let slip a word of where the ship is, for I got the ship, part by luck and part by risking, and she lies in North Inlet, on the southern beach, and just below high water. At half tide she must be high and dry."

"The ship!" exclaimed the doctor.

Rapidly I described to him my adventures, and he heard me out in silence.

"There is a kind of fate in this," he observed when I had done. "Every step, it's you that saves our lives; and do you suppose by any chance that we are going to let you lose yours? That would be a poor return, my boy.

You found out the plot; you found Ben Gunn – the best deed that ever you did, or will do, though you live to ninety. Oh, by Jupiter, and talking of Ben Gunn! Why, this is the mischief in person. Silver!" he cried. "Silver! I'll give you a piece of advice," he continued as the cook drew near again; "don't you be in any great hurry after that treasure."

"Why, sir, I do my possible, which that ain't," said Silver. "I can only, asking your pardon, save my life and the boy's by seeking for that treasure; and you may lay to that."

"Well, Silver," replied the doctor, "if that is so, I'll go one step further: look out for squalls when you find it."

"Sir," said Silver, "as between man and man, that's too much and too little. What you're after, why you left the block house, why you given me that there chart, I don't know, now, do I? And yet I done your bidding with my eyes shut and never a word of hope! But no, this here's too much. If you won't tell me what you mean plain out, just say so and I'll leave the helm."

"No," said the doctor musingly; "I've no right to say more; it's not my secret, you see, Silver, or, I give you my word, I'd tell it you. But I'll go as far with you as I dare go, and a step beyond, for I'll have my wig sorted by the captain or I'm mistaken! And first, I'll give you a bit of hope; Silver, if we both get alive out of this wolf-trap, I'll do my best to save you, short of perjury."

Silver's face was radiant. "You couldn't say more, I'm sure, sir, not if you was my mother," he cried.

"Well, that's my first concession," added the doctor. "My second is a piece of advice: keep the boy close beside you, and when you need help, halloo. I'm off to seek it for you, and that itself will show you if I speak at random. Good-bye, Jim."

And Dr. Livesey shook hands with me through the stockade, nodded to Silver, and set off at a brisk pace into the wood.

CHAPTER THIRTY ONE

The Treasure-hunt – Flint's Pointer

"Jim," said Silver when we were alone, "if I saved your life, you saved mine; and I'll not forget it. I seen the doctor waving you to run for it – with the tail of my eye, I did; and I seen you say no, as plain as hearing. Jim, that's one to you. This is the first glint of hope I had since the attack failed, and I owe it you. And now, Jim, we're to go in for this here treasure-hunting, with sealed orders too, and I don't like it; and you and me must stick close, back to back like, and we'll save our necks in spite o' fate and fortune."

Just then a man hailed us from the fire that breakfast was ready, and we were soon seated here and there about the sand over biscuit and fried junk. They had lit a fire fit to roast an ox, and it was now grown so hot that they could only approach it from the windward, and even there not without precaution. In the same wasteful spirit, they had cooked, I suppose, three times more than we could eat; and one of them, with an empty laugh, threw what was left into the fire, which blazed and roared again over this unusual fuel. I never in my life saw men so careless of the morrow; hand to mouth is the only word that can describe their way of doing; and what with wasted food and sleeping sentries, though they were bold enough for a brush and be done with it, I could see their entire unfitness for anything like a prolonged campaign.

Even Silver, eating away, with Captain Flint upon his shoulder, had not a word of blame for their recklessness. And this the more surprised me, for I thought he had never shown himself so cunning as he did then.

"Aye, mates," said he, "it's lucky you have Barbecue to think for you with this here head. I got what I wanted, I did. Sure enough, they have the ship. Where they have it, I don't know yet; but once we hit the treasure, we'll have to jump about and find out. And then, mates, us that has the boats, I reckon, has the upper hand."

Thus he kept running on, with his mouth full of the hot bacon; thus he restored their hope and confidence, and, I more than suspect, repaired his own at the same time.

"As for hostage," he continued, "that's his last talk, I guess, with them he loves so dear. I've got my piece o' news, and thanky to him for that; but it's over and done. I'll take him in a line when we go treasure-hunting, for we'll keep him like so much gold, in case of accidents, you mark, and in the meantime. Once we got the ship and treasure both and off to sea like jolly companions, why then we'll talk Mr. Hawkins over, we will, and we'll give him his share, to be sure, for all his kindness."

It was no wonder the men were in a good humour now. For my part, I was horribly cast down. Should the scheme he had now sketched prove feasible, Silver, already doubly a traitor, would not hesitate to adopt it. He had still a foot in either camp, and there was no doubt he would prefer wealth and freedom with the pirates to a bare escape from hanging, which was the best he had to hope on our side.

Nay, and even if things so fell out that he was forced to keep his faith with Dr. Livesey, even then what danger lay before us! What a moment that would be when the suspicions of his followers turned to certainty and he and I should have to fight for dear life – he a cripple and I a boy – against five strong and active seamen!

Add to this double apprehension the mystery that still hung over the behaviour of my friends, their unexplained desertion of the stockade, their inexplicable cession of the chart, or harder still to understand, the doctor's last warning to Silver, "Look out for squalls when you find it," and you will readily believe how little taste I found in my breakfast and with how uneasy a heart I set forth behind my captors on the quest for treasure.

We made a curious figure, had anyone been there to see us – all in soiled sailor clothes and all but me armed to the teeth. Silver had two guns slung about him – one before and one behind – besides the great cutlass at his waist and a pistol in each pocket of his square-tailed coat. To complete his strange appearance, Captain Flint sat perched upon his shoulder and gabbling odds and ends of purposeless sea-talk. I had a line about my waist and followed obediently after the sea-cook, who held the loose end of the rope, now in his free hand, now between his powerful teeth. For all the world, I was led like a dancing bear.

The other men were variously burthened, some carrying picks and shovels – for that had been the very first necessary they brought

ashore from the *Hispaniola* – others laden with pork, bread, and brandy for the midday meal. All the stores, I observed, came from our stock, and I could see the truth of Silver's words the night before. Had he not struck a bargain with the doctor, he and his mutineers, deserted by the ship, must have been driven to subsist on clear water and the proceeds of their hunting. Water would have been little to their taste; a sailor is not usually a good shot; and besides all that, when they were so short of eatables, it was not likely they would be very flush of powder.

Well, thus equipped, we all set out – even the fellow with the broken head, who should certainly have kept in shadow – and straggled, one after another, to the beach, where the two gigs awaited us. Even these bore trace of the drunken folly of the pirates, one in a broken thwart, and both in their muddy and unbailed condition. Both were to be carried along with us for the sake of safety; and so, with our numbers divided between them, we set forth upon the bosom of the anchorage.

As we pulled over, there was some discussion on the chart. The red cross was, of course, far too large to be a guide; and the terms of the note on the back, as you will hear, admitted of some ambiguity. They ran, the reader may remember, thus:

Tall tree, Spy-glass shoulder, bearing a point to the N. of N.N.E.
Skeleton Island E.S.E. and by E.
Ten feet.

A tall tree was thus the principal mark. Now, right before us the anchorage was bounded by a plateau from two to three hundred feet high, adjoining on the north the sloping southern shoulder of the Spy-glass and rising again towards the south into the rough, cliffy eminence called the Mizzen-mast Hill. The top of the plateau was dotted thickly with pine-trees of varying height. Every here and there, one of a different species rose forty or fifty feet clear above its neighbours, and which of these was the particular "tall tree" of Captain Flint could only be decided on the spot, and by the readings of the compass.

Yet, although that was the case, every man on board the boats had picked a favourite of his own ere we were half-way over, Long John alone shrugging his shoulders and bidding them wait till they were there.

We pulled easily, by Silver's directions, not to weary the hands prematurely, and after quite a long passage, landed at the mouth of the second river – that which runs down a woody cleft of the Spy-glass. Thence, bending to our left, we began to ascend the slope towards the plateau.

At the first outset, heavy, miry ground and a matted, marish vegetation greatly delayed our progress; but by little and little the hill began to steepen and become stony under foot, and the wood to change its character and to grow in a more open order. It was, indeed, a most pleasant portion of the island that we were now approaching. A heavy-scented broom and many flowering shrubs had almost taken the place of grass. Thickets of green nutmeg-trees were dotted here and there with the red columns and the broad shadow of the pines; and the first mingled their spice with the aroma of the others. The air, besides, was fresh and stirring, and this, under the sheer sunbeams, was a wonderful refreshment to our senses.

The party spread itself abroad, in a fan shape, shouting and leaping to and fro. About the centre, and a good way behind the rest, Silver and I followed – I tethered by my rope, he ploughing, with deep pants, among the sliding gravel. From time to time, indeed, I had to lend him a hand, or he must have missed his footing and fallen backward down the hill.

We had thus proceeded for about half a mile and were approaching the brow of the plateau when the man upon the farthest left began to cry aloud, as if in terror. Shout after shout came from him, and the others began to run in his direction.

"He can't 'a found the treasure," said old Morgan, hurrying past us from the right, "for that's clean a-top."

Indeed, as we found when we also reached the spot, it was something very different. At the foot of a pretty big pine and involved in a green creeper, which had even partly lifted some of the smaller bones, a human skeleton lay, with a few shreds of clothing, on the ground. I believe a chill struck for a moment to every heart.

"He was a seaman," said George Merry, who, bolder than the rest, had gone up close and was examining the rags of clothing. "Leastways, this is good sea-cloth."

"Aye, aye," said Silver; "like enough; you wouldn't look to find a bishop here, I reckon. But what sort of a way is that for bones to lie? 'Tain't in natur.'"

Indeed, on a second glance, it seemed impossible to fancy that the body was in a natural position. But for some disarray (the work, perhaps, of the birds that had fed upon him or of the slow-growing creeper that had gradually enveloped his remains) the man lay perfectly straight – his feet pointing in one direction, his hands, raised above his head like a diver's, pointing directly in the opposite.

"I've taken a notion into my old numbskull," observed Silver. "Here's the compass; there's the tip-top p'int o' Skeleton Island, stickin' out like a tooth. Just take a bearing, will you, along the line of them bones."

It was done. The body pointed straight in the direction of the island, and the compass read duly E.S.E. and by E.

"I thought so," cried the cook; "this here is a p'inter. Right up there is our line for the Pole Star and the jolly dollars. But, by thunder! If it don't make me cold inside to think of Flint. This is one of *his* jokes, and no mistake. Him and these six was alone here; he killed 'em, every man; and this one he hauled here and laid down by compass, shiver my timbers! They're long bones, and the hair's been yellow. Aye, that would be Allardyce. You mind Allardyce, Tom Morgan?"

"Aye, aye," returned Morgan; "I mind him; he owed me money, he did, and took my knife ashore with him."

"Speaking of knives," said another, "why don't we find his'n lying round? Flint warn't the man to pick a seaman's pocket; and the birds, I guess, would leave it be."

"By the powers, and that's true!" cried Silver.

"There ain't a thing left here," said Merry, still feeling round among the bones; "not a copper doit nor a baccy box. It don't look nat'ral to me."

"No, by gum, it don't," agreed Silver; "not nat'ral, nor not nice, says you. Great guns! Messmates, but if Flint was living, this would be a hot spot for you and me. Six they were, and six are we; and bones is what they are now."

"I saw him dead with these here deadlights," said Morgan. "Billy took me in. There he laid, with penny-pieces on his eyes."

"Dead – aye, sure enough he's dead and gone below," said the fellow with the bandage; "but if ever sperrit walked, it would be Flint's. Dear heart, but he died bad, did Flint!"

"Aye, that he did," observed another; "now he raged, and now he hollered for the rum, and now he sang. 'Fifteen Men' were his only song, mates; and I tell you true, I never rightly liked to hear it since. It was main hot, and the windy was open, and I hear that old song comin' out as clear as clear – and the death-haul on the man already."

"Come, come," said Silver; "stow this talk. He's dead, and he don't walk, that I know; leastways, he won't walk by day, and you may lay to that. Care killed a cat. Fetch ahead for the doubloons."

We started, certainly; but in spite of the hot sun and the staring daylight, the pirates no longer ran separate and shouting through the wood, but kept side by side and spoke with bated breath. The terror of the dead buccaneer had fallen on their spirits.

CHAPTER THIRTY TWO

The Treasure-hunt – The Voice Among the Trees

PARTLY FROM THE damping influence of this alarm, partly to rest Silver and the sick folk, the whole party sat down as soon as they had gained the brow of the ascent.

The plateau being somewhat tilted towards the west, this spot on which we had paused commanded a wide prospect on either hand. Before us, over the tree-tops, we beheld the Cape of the Woods fringed with surf; behind, we not only looked down upon the anchorage and Skeleton Island, but saw – clear across the spit and the eastern lowlands – a great field of open sea upon the east. Sheer above us rose the Spyglass, here dotted with single pines, there black with precipices. There was no sound but that of the distant breakers, mounting from all round, and the chirp of countless insects in the brush. Not a man, not a sail, upon the sea; the very largeness of the view increased the sense of solitude.

Silver, as he sat, took certain bearings with his compass.

"There are three 'tall trees'" said he, "about in the right line from Skeleton Island. 'Spy-glass shoulder,' I take it, means that lower p'int there. It's child's play to find the stuff now. I've half a mind to dine first."

"I don't feel sharp," growled Morgan. "Thinkin' o' Flint – I think it were – as done me."

"Ah, well, my son, you praise your stars he's dead," said Silver.

"He were an ugly devil," cried a third pirate with a shudder; "that blue in the face too!"

"That was how the rum took him," added Merry. "Blue! Well, I reckon he was blue. That's a true word."

Ever since they had found the skeleton and got upon this train of thought, they had spoken lower and lower, and they had almost got to whispering by now, so that the sound of their talk hardly interrupted the silence of the wood. All of a sudden, out of the middle of the trees in front of us, a thin, high, trembling voice struck up the well-known air and words:

"Fifteen men on the dead man's chest –
Yo-ho-ho, and a bottle of rum!"

I never have seen men more dreadfully affected than the pirates. The colour went from their six faces like enchantment; some leaped to their feet, some clawed hold of others; Morgan grovelled on the ground.

"It's Flint, by – – !" cried Merry.

The song had stopped as suddenly as it began – broken off, you would have said, in the middle of a note, as though someone had laid his hand upon the singer's mouth. Coming through the clear, sunny atmosphere among the green tree-tops, I thought it had sounded airily and sweetly; and the effect on my companions was the stranger.

"Come," said Silver, struggling with his ashen lips to get the word out; "this won't do. Stand by to go about. This is a rum start, and I can't name the voice, but it's someone skylarking – someone that's flesh and blood, and you may lay to that."

His courage had come back as he spoke, and some of the colour to his face along with it. Already the others had begun to lend an ear to this encouragement and were coming a little to themselves, when the same voice broke out again – not this time singing, but in a faint distant hail that echoed yet fainter among the clefts of the Spy-glass.

"Darby M'Graw," it wailed – for that is the word that best describes the sound – "Darby M'Graw! Darby M'Graw!" again and again and again; and then rising a little higher, and with an oath that I leave out: "Fetch aft the rum, Darby!"

The buccaneers remained rooted to the ground, their eyes starting from their heads. Long after the voice had died away they still stared in silence, dreadfully, before them.

"That fixes it!" gasped one. "Let's go."

"They was his last words," moaned Morgan, "his last words above board."

Dick had his Bible out and was praying volubly. He had been well brought up, had Dick, before he came to sea and fell among bad companions.

Still Silver was unconquered. I could hear his teeth rattle in his head, but he had not yet surrendered.

"Nobody in this here island ever heard of Darby," he muttered; "not one but us that's here." And then, making a great effort: "Shipmates," he cried, "I'm here to get that stuff, and I'll not be beat by man or devil. I never was feared of Flint in his life, and, by the powers, I'll face him dead. There's seven hundred thousand pound not a quarter of a mile from here. When did ever a gentleman o' fortune show his stern to that much dollars for a boozy old seaman with a blue mug – and him dead too?"

But there was no sign of reawakening courage in his followers, rather, indeed, of growing terror at the irreverence of his words.

"Belay there, John!" said Merry. "Don't you cross a sperrit."

And the rest were all too terrified to reply. They would have run away severally had they dared; but fear kept them together, and kept them close by John, as if his daring helped them. He, on his part, had pretty well fought his weakness down.

"Sperrit? Well, maybe," he said. "But there's one thing not clear to me. There was an echo. Now, no man ever seen a sperrit with a shadow; well then, what's he doing with an echo to him, I should like to know? That ain't in natur', surely?"

This argument seemed weak enough to me. But you can never tell what will affect the superstitious, and to my wonder, George Merry was greatly relieved.

"Well, that's so," he said. "You've a head upon your shoulders, John, and no mistake. 'Bout ship, mates! This here crew is on a wrong tack, I do believe. And come to think on it, it was like Flint's voice, I grant you, but not just so clear-away like it, after all. It was liker somebody else's voice now – it was liker – "

"By the powers, Ben Gunn!" roared Silver.

"Aye, and so it were," cried Morgan, springing on his knees. "Ben Gunn it were!"

"It don't make much odds, do it, now?" asked Dick. "Ben Gunn's not here in the body any more'n Flint."

But the older hands greeted this remark with scorn.

"Why, nobody minds Ben Gunn," cried Merry; "dead or alive, nobody minds him."

It was extraordinary how their spirits had returned and how the natural colour had revived in their faces. Soon they were chatting together, with intervals of listening; and not long after, hearing no further sound, they shouldered the tools and set forth again, Merry walking first with Silver's compass to keep them on the right line with Skeleton Island. He had said the truth: dead or alive, nobody minded Ben Gunn.

Dick alone still held his Bible, and looked around him as he went, with fearful glances; but he found no sympathy, and Silver even joked him on his precautions.

"I told you," said he – "I told you you had sp'iled your Bible. If it ain't no good to swear by, what do you suppose a sperrit would give for it? Not that!" and he snapped his big fingers, halting a moment on his crutch.

But Dick was not to be comforted; indeed, it was soon plain to me that the lad was falling sick; hastened by heat, exhaustion, and the shock of his alarm, the fever, predicted by Dr. Livesey, was evidently growing swiftly higher.

It was fine open walking here, upon the summit; our way lay a little downhill, for, as I have said, the plateau tilted towards the west. The pines, great and small, grew wide apart; and even between the clumps of nutmeg and azalea, wide open spaces baked in the hot sunshine. Striking, as we did, pretty near north-west across the island, we drew, on the one hand, ever nearer under the shoulders of the Spy-glass, and on the other, looked ever wider over that western bay where I had once tossed and trembled in the coracle.

The first of the tall trees was reached, and by the bearings proved the wrong one. So with the second. The third rose nearly two hundred feet into the air above a clump of underwood – a giant of a vegetable, with a red column as big as a cottage, and a wide shadow around in which a company could have manoeuvred. It was conspicuous far to sea both on the east and west and might have been entered as a sailing mark upon the chart.

But it was not its size that now impressed my companions; it was the knowledge that seven hundred thousand pounds in gold lay somewhere buried below its spreading shadow. The thought of the money, as they drew nearer, swallowed up their previous terrors. Their eyes burned in their heads; their feet grew speedier and lighter; their whole soul was bound up in that fortune, that whole lifetime of extravagance and pleasure, that lay waiting there for each of them.

Silver hobbled, grunting, on his crutch; his nostrils stood out and quivered; he cursed like a madman when the flies settled on his hot and shiny countenance; he plucked furiously at the line that held me to him and from time to time turned his eyes upon me with a deadly look. Certainly he took no pains to hide his thoughts, and certainly I read them like print. In the immediate nearness of the gold, all else had been forgotten: his promise and the doctor's warning were both things of the past, and I could not doubt that he hoped to seize upon the treasure, find and board the *Hispaniola* under cover of night, cut every honest throat about that island, and sail away as he had at first intended, laden with crimes and riches.

Shaken as I was with these alarms, it was hard for me to keep up with the rapid pace of the treasure-hunters. Now and again I stumbled, and it was then that Silver plucked so roughly at the rope and launched at me his murderous glances. Dick, who had dropped behind us and now brought up the rear, was babbling to himself both prayers and curses as his fever kept rising. This also added to my wretchedness, and to crown all, I was haunted by the thought of the tragedy that had once been acted on that plateau, when that ungodly buccaneer with the blue face – he who died at Savannah, singing and shouting for drink – had there, with his own hand, cut down his six accomplices. This grove that was now so peaceful must then have rung with cries, I thought; and even with the thought I could believe I heard it ringing still.

We were now at the margin of the thicket.

"Huzza, mates, all together!" shouted Merry; and the foremost broke into a run.

And suddenly, not ten yards further, we beheld them stop. A low cry arose. Silver doubled his pace, digging away with the foot of his crutch like one possessed; and next moment he and I had come also to a dead halt.

Before us was a great excavation, not very recent, for the sides had fallen in and grass had sprouted on the bottom. In this were the shaft of a pick broken in two and the boards of several packing-cases strewn around. On one of these boards I saw, branded with a hot iron, the name *Walrus* – the name of Flint's ship.

All was clear to probation. The *cache* had been found and rifled; the seven hundred thousand pounds were gone!

CHAPTER THIRTY THREE

The Fall of a Chieftain

THERE NEVER WAS such an overturn in this world. Each of these six men was as though he had been struck. But with Silver the blow passed almost instantly. Every thought of his soul had been set full-stretch, like a racer, on that money; well, he was brought up, in a single second, dead; and he kept his head, found his temper, and changed his plan before the others had had time to realize the disappointment.

"Jim," he whispered, "take that, and stand by for trouble."

And he passed me a double-barrelled pistol.

At the same time, he began quietly moving northward, and in a few steps had put the hollow between us two and the other five. Then he looked at me and nodded, as much as to say, "Here is a narrow corner," as, indeed, I thought it was. His looks were not quite friendly, and I was so revolted at these constant changes that I could not forbear whispering, "So you've changed sides again."

There was no time left for him to answer in. The buccaneers, with oaths and cries, began to leap, one after another, into the pit and to dig with their fingers, throwing the boards aside as they did so. Morgan found a piece of gold. He held it up with a perfect spout of oaths. It was a two-guinea piece, and it went from hand to hand among them for a quarter of a minute.

"Two guineas!" roared Merry, shaking it at Silver. "That's your seven hundred thousand pounds, is it? You're the man for bargains, ain't you? You're him that never bungled nothing, you wooden-headed lubber!"

"Dig away, boys," said Silver with the coolest insolence; "you'll find some pig-nuts and I shouldn't wonder."

"Pig-nuts!" repeated Merry, in a scream. "Mates, do you hear that? I tell you now, that man there knew it all along. Look in the face of him and you'll see it wrote there."

"Ah, Merry," remarked Silver, "standing for cap'n again? You're a pushing lad, to be sure."

But this time everyone was entirely in Merry's favour. They began to scramble out of the excavation, darting furious glances behind them. One thing I observed, which looked well for us: they all got out upon the opposite side from Silver.

Well, there we stood, two on one side, five on the other, the pit between us, and nobody screwed up high enough to offer the first blow. Silver never moved; he watched them, very upright on his crutch, and looked as cool as ever I saw him. He was brave, and no mistake.

At last Merry seemed to think a speech might help matters.

"Mates," says he, "there's two of them alone there; one's the old cripple that brought us all here and blundered us down to this; the other's that cub that I mean to have the heart of. Now, mates – "

He was raising his arm and his voice, and plainly meant to lead a charge. But just then – crack! crack! crack! – three musket-shots flashed out of the thicket. Merry tumbled head foremost into the excavation; the man with the bandage spun round like a teetotum and fell all his length upon his side, where he lay dead, but still twitching; and the other three turned and ran for it with all their might.

Before you could wink, Long John had fired two barrels of a pistol into the struggling Merry, and as the man rolled up his eyes at him in the last agony, "George," said he, "I reckon I settled you."

At the same moment, the doctor, Gray, and Ben Gunn joined us, with smoking muskets, from among the nutmeg-trees.

"Forward!" cried the doctor. "Double quick, my lads. We must head 'em off the boats."

And we set off at a great pace, sometimes plunging through the bushes to the chest.

I tell you, but Silver was anxious to keep up with us. The work that man went through, leaping on his crutch till the muscles of his chest were fit to burst, was work no sound man ever equalled; and so thinks the doctor. As it was, he was already thirty yards behind us and on the verge of strangling when we reached the brow of the slope.

"Doctor," he hailed, "see there! No hurry!"

Sure enough there was no hurry. In a more open part of the plateau, we could see the three survivors still running in the same direction as they had started, right for Mizzenmast Hill. We were already between them and the boats; and so we four sat down to breathe, while Long John, mopping his face, came slowly up with us.

"Thank ye kindly, doctor," says he. "You came in in about the nick, I guess, for me and Hawkins. And so it's you, Ben Gunn!" he added. "Well, you're a nice one, to be sure."

"I'm Ben Gunn, I am," replied the maroon, wriggling like an eel in his embarrassment. "And," he added, after a long pause, "how do, Mr. Silver? Pretty well, I thank ye, says you."

"Ben, Ben," murmured Silver, "to think as you've done me!"

The doctor sent back Gray for one of the pick-axes deserted, in their flight, by the mutineers, and then as we proceeded leisurely downhill to where the boats were lying, related in a few words what had taken place. It was a story that profoundly interested Silver; and Ben Gunn, the half-idiot maroon, was the hero from beginning to end.

Ben, in his long, lonely wanderings about the island, had found the skeleton – it was he that had rifled it; he had found the treasure; he had dug it up (it was the haft of his pick-axe that lay broken in the excavation); he had carried it on his back, in many weary journeys, from the foot of the tall pine to a cave he had on the two-pointed hill at the north-east angle of the island, and there it had lain stored in safety since two months before the arrival of the *Hispaniola.*

When the doctor had wormed this secret from him on the afternoon of the attack, and when next morning he saw the anchorage deserted, he had gone to Silver, given him the chart, which was now useless – given him the stores, for Ben Gunn's cave was well supplied with goats' meat salted by himself – given anything and everything to get a chance of moving in safety from the stockade to the two-pointed hill, there to be clear of malaria and keep a guard upon the money.

"As for you, Jim," he said, "it went against my heart, but I did what I thought best for those who had stood by their duty; and if you were not one of these, whose fault was it?"

That morning, finding that I was to be involved in the horrid disappointment he had prepared for the mutineers, he had run all the way to the cave, and leaving the squire to guard the captain, had taken Gray and the maroon and started, making the diagonal across the island to be at hand beside the pine. Soon, however, he saw that our party had the start of him; and Ben Gunn, being fleet of foot, had been dispatched in front to do his best alone. Then it had occurred to him to work upon the superstitions of his former shipmates, and he was so far successful that Gray and the doctor had come up and were already ambushed before the arrival of the treasure-hunters.

"Ah," said Silver, "it were fortunate for me that I had Hawkins here. You would have let old John be cut to bits, and never given it a thought, doctor."

"Not a thought," replied Dr. Livesey cheerily.

And by this time we had reached the gigs. The doctor, with the pick-axe, demolished one of them, and then we all got aboard the other and set out to go round by sea for North Inlet.

This was a run of eight or nine miles. Silver, though he was almost killed already with fatigue, was set to an oar, like the rest of us, and we were soon skimming swiftly over a smooth sea. Soon we passed out of the straits and doubled the south-east corner of the island, round which, four days ago, we had towed the *Hispaniola.*

As we passed the two-pointed hill, we could see the black mouth of Ben Gunn's cave and a figure standing by it, leaning on a musket. It was the squire, and we waved a handkerchief and gave him three cheers, in which the voice of Silver joined as heartily as any.

Three miles farther, just inside the mouth of North Inlet, what should we meet but the *Hispaniola*, cruising by herself? The last flood had lifted her, and had there been much wind or a strong tide current, as in the southern anchorage, we should never have found her more, or found her stranded beyond help. As it was, there was little amiss beyond the wreck of the main-sail. Another anchor was got ready and dropped in a fathom and a half of water. We all pulled round again to Rum Cove, the nearest point for Ben Gunn's treasure-house; and then Gray, single-handed, returned with the gig to the *Hispaniola*, where he was to pass the night on guard.

A gentle slope ran up from the beach to the entrance of the cave. At the top, the squire met us. To me he was cordial and kind, saying nothing of my escapade either in the way of blame or praise. At Silver's polite salute he somewhat flushed.

"John Silver," he said, "you're a prodigious villain and imposter – a monstrous imposter, sir. I am told I am not to prosecute you. Well, then, I will not. But the dead men, sir, hang about your neck like mill-stones."

"Thank you kindly, sir," replied Long John, again saluting.

"I dare you to thank me!" cried the squire. "It is a gross dereliction of my duty. Stand back."

And thereupon we all entered the cave. It was a large, airy place, with a little spring and a pool of clear water, overhung with ferns. The floor was sand. Before a big fire lay Captain Smollett; and in a far corner, only duskily flickered over by the blaze, I beheld great heaps of coin and quadrilaterals built of bars of gold. That was Flint's treasure that we had come so far to seek and that had cost already the lives of seventeen men from the *Hispaniola*. How many it had cost in the amassing, what blood and sorrow, what good ships scuttled on the deep, what brave men walking the plank blindfold, what shot of cannon, what shame and lies and cruelty, perhaps no man alive could tell. Yet there were still three upon that island – Silver, and old Morgan, and Ben Gunn – who had each taken his share in these crimes, as each had hoped in vain to share in the reward.

"Come in, Jim," said the captain. "You're a good boy in your line, Jim, but I don't think you and me'll go to sea again. You're too much of the born favourite for me. Is that you, John Silver? What brings you here, man?"

"Come back to my dooty, sir," returned Silver.

"Ah!" said the captain, and that was all he said.

What a supper I had of it that night, with all my friends around me; and what a meal it was, with Ben Gunn's salted goat and some delicacies and a bottle of old wine from the *Hispaniola*. Never, I am sure, were people gayer or happier. And there was Silver, sitting back almost out of the firelight, but eating heartily, prompt to spring forward when anything was wanted, even joining quietly in our laughter – the same bland, polite, obsequious seaman of the voyage out.

CHAPTER THIRTY FOUR

And Last

The next morning we fell early to work, for the transportation of this great mass of gold near a mile by land to the beach, and thence three miles by boat to the *Hispaniola*, was a considerable task for so small a number of workmen. The three fellows still abroad upon the island did not greatly trouble us; a single sentry on the shoulder of the hill was sufficient to ensure us against any sudden onslaught, and we thought, besides, they had had more than enough of fighting.

Therefore the work was pushed on briskly. Gray and Ben Gunn came and went with the boat, while the rest during their absences piled treasure on the beach. Two of the bars, slung in a rope's end, made a good load for a grown man – one that he was glad to walk slowly with. For my part, as I was not much use at carrying, I was kept busy all day in the cave packing the minted money into bread-bags.

It was a strange collection, like Billy Bones's hoard for the diversity of coinage, but so much larger and so much more varied that I think I never had more pleasure than in sorting them. English, French, Spanish, Portuguese, Georges, and Louises, doubloons and double guineas and moidores and sequins, the pictures of all the kings of Europe for the last hundred years, strange Oriental pieces stamped with what looked like wisps of string or bits of spider's web, round pieces and square pieces, and pieces bored through the middle, as if to wear them round your neck – nearly every variety of money in the world must, I think, have found a place in that collection; and for number, I am sure they were like autumn leaves, so that my back ached with stooping and my fingers with sorting them out.

Day after day this work went on; by every evening a fortune had been stowed aboard, but there was another fortune waiting for the morrow; and all this time we heard nothing of the three surviving mutineers.

At last – I think it was on the third night – the doctor and I were strolling on the shoulder of the hill where it overlooks the lowlands of the isle, when, from out the thick darkness below, the wind brought us a noise between shrieking and singing. It was only a snatch that reached our ears, followed by the former silence.

"Heaven forgive them," said the doctor; "'tis the mutineers!"

"All drunk, sir," struck in the voice of Silver from behind us.

Silver, I should say, was allowed his entire liberty, and in spite of daily rebuffs, seemed to regard himself once more as quite a privileged and friendly dependent. Indeed, it was remarkable how well he bore these slights and with what unwearying politeness he kept on trying to ingratiate himself with all. Yet, I think, none treated him better than a dog, unless it was Ben Gunn, who was still terribly afraid of his old quartermaster, or myself, who had really something to thank him for; although for that matter, I suppose, I had reason to think even worse of him than anybody else, for I had seen him meditating a fresh treachery upon the plateau. Accordingly, it was pretty gruffly that the doctor answered him.

"Drunk or raving," said he.

"Right you were, sir," replied Silver; "and precious little odds which, to you and me."

"I suppose you would hardly ask me to call you a humane man," returned the doctor with a sneer, "and so my feelings may surprise you, Master Silver. But if I were sure they were raving – as I am morally certain one, at least, of them is down with fever – I should leave this camp, and at whatever risk to my own carcass, take them the assistance of my skill."

"Ask your pardon, sir, you would be very wrong," quoth Silver. "You would lose your precious life, and you may lay to that. I'm on your side now, hand and glove; and I shouldn't wish for to see the party weakened, let alone yourself, seeing as I know what I owes you. But these men down there, they couldn't keep their word – no, not supposing they wished to; and what's more, they couldn't believe as you could."

"No," said the doctor. "You're the man to keep your word, we know that."

Well, that was about the last news we had of the three pirates. Only once we heard a gunshot a great way off and supposed them to be hunting. A council was held, and it was decided that we must desert them on the island – to the huge glee, I must say, of Ben Gunn, and with the strong approval of Gray. We left a good stock of powder and shot, the bulk of the salt goat, a few medicines, and some other necessaries, tools, clothing, a spare sail, a fathom or two of rope, and by the particular desire of the doctor, a handsome present of tobacco.

That was about our last doing on the island. Before that, we had got the treasure stowed and had shipped enough water and the remainder of the goat meat in case of any distress; and at last, one fine morning, we weighed anchor, which was about all that we could manage, and stood out of North Inlet, the same colours flying that the captain had flown and fought under at the palisade.

The three fellows must have been watching us closer than we thought for, as we soon had proved. For coming through the narrows, we had to lie very near the southern point, and there we saw all three of them kneeling together on a spit of sand, with their arms raised in supplication. It went to all our hearts, I think, to leave them in that wretched state; but we could not risk another mutiny; and to take them home for the gibbet would have been a cruel sort of kindness. The doctor hailed them and told them of the stores we had left, and where they were to find them. But they continued to call us by name and appeal to us, for God's sake, to be merciful and not leave them to die in such a place.

At last, seeing the ship still bore on her course and was now swiftly drawing out of earshot, one of them – I know not which it was – leapt to his feet with a hoarse cry, whipped his musket to his shoulder, and sent a shot whistling over Silver's head and through the main-sail.

After that, we kept under cover of the bulwarks, and when next I looked out they had disappeared from the spit, and the spit itself had almost melted out of sight in the growing distance. That was, at least, the end of that; and before noon, to my inexpressible joy, the highest rock of Treasure Island had sunk into the blue round of sea.

We were so short of men that everyone on board had to bear a hand – only the captain lying on a mattress in the stern and giving his orders, for though greatly recovered he was still in want of quiet. We laid her head for the nearest port in Spanish America, for we could not risk the voyage home without fresh hands; and as it was, what with baffling winds and a couple of fresh gales, we were all worn out before we reached it.

It was just at sundown when we cast anchor in a most beautiful land-locked gulf, and were immediately surrounded by shore boats full of Negroes and Mexican Indians and half-bloods selling fruits and vegetables and offering to dive for bits of money. The sight of so many good-humoured faces (especially the blacks), the taste of the tropical fruits, and above all the lights that began to shine in the town made a most charming contrast to our dark and bloody sojourn on the island; and the doctor and the squire, taking me along with them, went ashore to pass the early part of the night. Here they met the captain of an English man-of-war, fell in talk with him, went on board his ship, and, in short, had so agreeable a time that day was breaking when we came alongside the *Hispaniola*.

Ben Gunn was on deck alone, and as soon as we came on board he began, with wonderful contortions, to make us a confession. Silver was gone. The maroon had connived at his escape in a shore boat some hours ago, and he now assured us he had only done so to preserve our lives, which would certainly have been forfeit if "that man with the one leg had stayed aboard." But this was not all. The sea-cook had not gone empty-handed. He had cut through a bulkhead unobserved and had removed one of the sacks of coin, worth perhaps three or four hundred guineas, to help him on his further wanderings.

I think we were all pleased to be so cheaply quit of him.

Well, to make a long story short, we got a few hands on board, made a good cruise home, and the *Hispaniola* reached Bristol just as Mr. Blandly was beginning to think of fitting out her consort. Five men only of those who had sailed returned with her. "Drink and the devil had done for the rest," with a vengeance, although, to be sure, we were not quite in so bad a case as that other ship they sang about:

With one man of her crew alive,
What put to sea with seventy-five.

All of us had an ample share of the treasure and used it wisely or foolishly, according to our natures. Captain Smollett is now retired from the sea. Gray not only saved his money, but being suddenly smit with the desire to rise, also studied his profession, and he is now mate and part owner of a fine full-rigged ship, married besides, and the father of a family. As for Ben Gunn, he got a thousand pounds, which he spent or lost in three weeks, or to be more exact, in nineteen days, for he was back begging on the twentieth. Then he was given a lodge to keep, exactly as he had feared upon the island; and he still lives, a great favourite, though something of a butt, with the country boys, and a notable singer in church on Sundays and saints' days.

Of Silver we have heard no more. That formidable seafaring man with one leg has at last gone clean out of my life; but I dare say he met his old Negress, and perhaps still lives in comfort with her and Captain Flint. It is to be hoped so, I suppose, for his chances of comfort in another world are very small.

The bar silver and the arms still lie, for all that I know, where Flint buried them; and certainly they shall lie there for me. Oxen and wain-ropes would not bring me back again to that accursed island; and the worst dreams that ever I have are when I hear the surf booming about its coasts or start upright in bed with the sharp voice of Captain Flint still ringing in my ears: "Pieces of eight! Pieces of eight!"

THE ISLAND OF DR MOREAU

CONTENTS

INTRODUCTION

On February the First 1887, the *Lady Vain* was lost by collision with a derelict when about the latitude 1° S. and longitude 107° W.

On January the Fifth, 1888 – that is eleven months and four days after – my uncle, Edward Prendick, a private gentleman, who certainly went aboard the *Lady Vain* at Callao, and who had been considered drowned, was picked up in latitude 5° 3' S. and longitude 101° W. in a small open boat of which the name was illegible, but which is supposed to have belonged to the missing schooner *Ipecacuanha*. He gave such a strange account of himself that he was supposed demented. Subsequently he alleged that his mind was a blank from the moment of his escape from the *Lady Vain*. His case was discussed among psychologists at the time as a curious instance of the lapse of memory consequent upon physical and mental stress. The following narrative was found among his papers by the undersigned, his nephew and heir, but unaccompanied by any definite request for publication.

The only island known to exist in the region in which my uncle was picked up is Noble's Isle, a small volcanic islet and uninhabited. It was visited in 1891 by *H. M. S. Scorpion*. A party of sailors then landed, but found nothing living thereon except certain curious white moths, some hogs and rabbits, and some rather peculiar rats. So that this narrative is without confirmation in its most essential particular. With that understood, there seems no harm in putting this strange story before the public in accordance, as I believe, with my uncle's intentions. There is at least this much in its behalf: my uncle passed out of human knowledge about latitude 5° S. and longitude 105° E., and reappeared in the same part of the ocean after a space of eleven months. In some way he must have lived during the interval. And it seems that a schooner called the *Ipecacuanha* with a drunken captain, John Davies, did start from Africa with a puma and certain other animals aboard in January, 1887, that the vessel was well known at several ports in the South Pacific, and that it finally disappeared from those seas (with a considerable amount of copra aboard), sailing to its unknown fate from Bayna in December, 1887, a date that tallies entirely with my uncle's story.

CHARLES EDWARD PRENDICK.

(The Story written by Edward Prendick.)

CHAPTER ONE

In the Dingey of the "*Lady Vain*"

I DO NOT PROPOSE to add anything to what has already been written concerning the loss of the *Lady Vain*. As everyone knows, she collided with a derelict when ten days out from Callao. The longboat, with seven of the crew, was picked up eighteen days after by H. M. gunboat *Myrtle*, and the story of their terrible privations has become quite as well known as the far more horrible *Medusa* case. But I have to add to the published story of the *Lady Vain* another, possibly as horrible and far stranger. It has hitherto been supposed that the four men who were in the dingey perished, but this is incorrect. I have the best of evidence for this assertion: I was one of the four men.

But in the first place I must state that there never were four men in the dingey, – the number was three. Constans, who was "seen by the captain to jump into the gig,"[1] luckily for us and unluckily for himself did not reach us. He came down out of the tangle of ropes under the stays of the smashed bowsprit, some small rope caught his heel as he let go, and he hung for a moment head downward, and then fell and struck a block or spar floating in the water. We pulled towards him, but he never came up.

I say luckily for us he did not reach us, and I might almost say luckily for himself; for we had only a small beaker of water and some soddened ship's biscuits with us, so sudden had been the alarm, so unprepared the ship for any disaster. We thought the people on the launch would be better provisioned (though it seems they were not), and we tried to hail them. They could not have heard us, and the next morning when the drizzle cleared, – which was not until past mid-

1 *Daily News*, March 17, 1887.

day, – we could see nothing of them. We could not stand up to look about us, because of the pitching of the boat. The two other men who had escaped so far with me were a man named Helmar, a passenger like myself, and a seaman whose name I don't know, – a short sturdy man, with a stammer.

We drifted famishing, and, after our water had come to an end, tormented by an intolerable thirst, for eight days altogether. After the second day the sea subsided slowly to a glassy calm. It is quite impossible for the ordinary reader to imagine those eight days. He has not, luckily for himself, anything in his memory to imagine with. After the first day we said little to one another, and lay in our places in the boat and stared at the horizon, or watched, with eyes that grew larger and more haggard every day, the misery and weakness gaining upon our companions. The sun became pitiless. The water ended on the fourth day, and we were already thinking strange things and saying them with our eyes; but it was, I think, the sixth before Helmar gave voice to the thing we had all been thinking. I remember our voices were dry and thin, so that we bent towards one another and spared our words. I stood out against it with all my might, was rather for scuttling the boat and perishing together among the sharks that followed us; but when Helmar said that if his proposal was accepted we should have drink, the sailor came round to him.

I would not draw lots however, and in the night the sailor whispered to Helmar again and again, and I sat in the bows with my clasp-knife in my hand, though I doubt if I had the stuff in me to fight; and in the morning I agreed to Helmar's proposal, and we handed halfpence to find the odd man. The lot fell upon the sailor; but he was the strongest of us and would not abide by it, and attacked Helmar with his hands. They grappled together and almost stood up. I crawled along the boat to them, intending to help Helmar by grasping the sailor's leg; but the sailor stumbled with the swaying of the boat, and the two fell upon the gunwale and rolled overboard together. They sank like stones. I remember laughing at that, and wondering why I laughed. The laugh caught me suddenly like a thing from without.

I lay across one of the thwarts for I know not how long, thinking that if I had the strength I would drink sea-water and madden myself to die quickly. And even as I lay there I saw, with no more interest than if it had been a picture, a sail come up towards me over the sky-line. My mind must have been wandering, and yet I remember all that happened, quite distinctly. I remember how my head swayed with the seas, and the horizon with the sail above it danced up and down; but I also remember as distinctly that I had a persuasion that I was dead, and that I thought what a jest it was that they should come too late by such a little to catch me in my body.

For an endless period, as it seemed to me, I lay with my head on the thwart watching the schooner (she was a little ship, schooner-rigged fore and aft) come up out of the sea. She kept tacking to and fro in a widening compass, for she was sailing dead into the wind. It never entered my head to attempt to attract attention, and I do not remember anything distinctly after the sight of her side until I found myself in a little cabin aft. There's a dim half-memory of being lifted up to the gangway, and of a big round countenance covered with freckles and surrounded with red hair staring at me over the bulwarks. I also had a disconnected impression of a dark face, with extraordinary eyes, close to mine; but that I thought was a nightmare, until I met it again. I fancy I recollect some stuff being poured in between my teeth; and that is all.

CHAPTER TWO

The Man who was Going Nowhere

THE CABIN in which I found myself was small and rather untidy. A youngish man with flaxen hair, a bristly straw-coloured moustache, and a dropping nether lip, was sitting and holding my wrist. For a minute we stared at each other without speaking. He had watery grey eyes, oddly void of expression. Then just overhead came a sound like an iron bedstead being knocked about, and the low angry growling of some large animal. At the same time the man spoke. He repeated his question, – "How do you feel now?"

I think I said I felt all right. I could not recollect how I had got there. He must have seen the question in my face, for my voice was inaccessible to me.

"You were picked up in a boat, starving. The name on the boat was the *Lady Vain*, and there were spots of blood on the gunwale."

At the same time my eye caught my hand, so thin that it looked like a dirty skin-purse full of loose bones, and all the business of the boat came back to me.

"Have some of this," said he, and gave me a dose of some scarlet stuff, iced.

It tasted like blood, and made me feel stronger.

"You were in luck," said he, "to get picked up by a ship with a medical man aboard." He spoke with a slobbering articulation, with the ghost of a lisp.

"What ship is this?" I said slowly, hoarse from my long silence.

"It's a little trader from Arica and Callao. I never asked where she came from in the beginning, – out of the land of born fools, I guess. I'm a passenger myself, from Arica. The silly ass who owns her, – he's captain too, named Davies, – he's lost his certificate, or something. You know the kind of man, – calls the thing the *Ipecacuanha*, of all silly, infernal names; though when there's much of a sea without any wind, she certainly acts according."

(Then the noise overhead began again, a snarling growl and the voice of a human being together. Then another voice, telling some "Heaven-forsaken idiot" to desist.)

"You were nearly dead," said my interlocutor. "It was a very near thing, indeed. But I've put some stuff into you now. Notice your arm's sore? Injections. You've been insensible for nearly thirty hours."

I thought slowly. (I was distracted now by the yelping of a number of dogs.) "Am I eligible for solid food?" I asked.

"Thanks to me," he said. "Even now the mutton is boiling."

"Yes," I said with assurance; "I could eat some mutton."

"But," said he with a momentary hesitation, "you know I'm dying to hear of how you came to be alone in that boat. *Damn that howling*!" I thought I detected a certain suspicion in his eyes.

He suddenly left the cabin, and I heard him in violent controversy with some one, who seemed to me to talk gibberish in response to him. The matter sounded as though it ended in blows, but in that I thought my ears were mistaken. Then he shouted at the dogs, and returned to the cabin.

"Well?" said he in the doorway. "You were just beginning to tell me."

I told him my name, Edward Prendick, and how I had taken to Natural History as a relief from the dulness of my comfortable independence.

He seemed interested in this. "I've done some science myself. I did my Biology at University College, – getting out the ovary of the earthworm and the radula of the snail, and all that. Lord! It's ten years ago. But go on! go on! tell me about the boat."

He was evidently satisfied with the frankness of my story, which I told in concise sentences enough, for I felt horribly weak; and when it was finished he reverted at once to the topic of Natural History and his own biological studies. He began to question me closely about Tottenham Court Road and Gower Street. "Is Caplatzi still flourishing? What a shop that was!" He had evidently been a very ordinary medical student, and drifted incontinently to the topic of the music halls. He told me some anecdotes.

"Left it all," he said, "ten years ago. How jolly it all used to be! But I made a young ass of myself, – played myself out before I was twenty-one. I daresay it's all different now. But I must look up that ass of a cook, and see what he's done to your mutton."

The growling overhead was renewed, so suddenly and with so much savage anger that it startled me. "What's that?" I called after him, but the door had closed. He came back again with the boiled mutton, and I was so excited by the appetising smell of it that I forgot the noise of the beast that had troubled me.

After a day of alternate sleep and feeding I was so far recovered as to be able to get from my bunk to the scuttle, and see the green seas trying to keep pace with us. I judged the schooner was running before the wind. Montgomery – that was the name of the flaxen-haired man – came in again as I stood there, and I asked him for some clothes. He lent me some duck things of his own, for those I had worn in the boat had been thrown overboard. They were rather loose for me, for he was large and long in his limbs. He told me casually that the captain was three-parts drunk in his own cabin. As I assumed the clothes, I began asking him some questions about the destination of the ship. He said the ship was bound to Hawaii, but that it had to land him first.

"Where?" said I.

"It's an island, where I live. So far as I know, it hasn't got a name."

He stared at me with his nether lip dropping, and looked so wilfully stupid of a sudden that it came into my head that he desired to avoid my questions. I had the discretion to ask no more.

CHAPTER THREE

The Strange Face

WE LEFT THE CABIN and found a man at the companion obstructing our way. He was standing on the ladder with his back to us, peering over the combing of the hatchway. He was, I could see, a misshapen man, short, broad, and clumsy, with a crooked back, a hairy neck, and a head sunk between his shoulders. He was dressed in dark-blue serge, and had peculiarly thick, coarse, black hair. I heard the unseen dogs growl furiously, and forthwith he ducked back, – coming into contact with the hand I put out to fend him off from myself. He turned with animal swiftness.

In some indefinable way the black face thus flashed upon me shocked me profoundly. It was a singularly deformed one. The facial part projected, forming something dimly suggestive of a muzzle, and the huge half-open mouth showed as big white teeth as I had ever seen in a human mouth. His eyes were blood-shot at the edges, with scarcely a rim of white round the hazel pupils. There was a curious glow of excitement in his face.

"Confound you!" said Montgomery. "Why the devil don't you get out of the way?"

The black-faced man started aside without a word. I went on up the companion, staring at him instinctively as I did so. Montgomery stayed at the foot for a moment. "You have no business here, you know," he said in a deliberate tone. "Your place is forward."

The black-faced man cowered. "They – won't have me forward." He spoke slowly, with a queer, hoarse quality in his voice.

"Won't have you forward!" said Montgomery, in a menacing voice. "But I tell you to go!" He was on the brink of saying something further, then looked up at me suddenly and followed me up the ladder.

I had paused half way through the hatchway, looking back, still astonished beyond measure at the grotesque ugliness of this black-faced creature. I had never beheld such a repulsive and extraordinary face before, and yet – if the contradiction is credible – I experienced at the same time an odd feeling that in some way I *had* already encountered exactly the features and gestures that now amazed me. Afterwards it occurred to me that probably I had seen him as I was lifted aboard; and yet that scarcely satisfied my suspicion of a previous acquaintance. Yet how one could have set eyes on so singular a face and yet have forgotten the precise occasion, passed my imagination.

Montgomery's movement to follow me released my attention, and I turned and looked about me at the flush deck of the little schooner. I was already half prepared by the sounds I had heard for what I saw. Certainly I never beheld a deck so dirty. It was littered with scraps of carrot, shreds of green stuff, and indescribable filth. Fastened by chains to the mainmast were a number of grisly staghounds, who now began leaping and barking at me, and by the mizzen a huge puma was cramped in a little iron cage far too small even to give it turning room. Farther under the starboard bulwark were some big hutches containing a number of rabbits, and a solitary llama was squeezed in a mere box of a cage forward. The dogs were muzzled by leather straps. The only human being on deck was a gaunt and silent sailor at the wheel.

The patched and dirty spankers were tense before the wind, and up aloft the little ship seemed carrying every sail she had. The sky was clear, the sun midway down the western sky; long waves, capped by the breeze with froth, were running with us. We went past the steersman to the taffrail, and saw the water come foaming under the stern and the bubbles go dancing and vanishing in her wake. I turned and surveyed the unsavoury length of the ship.

"Is this an ocean menagerie?" said I.

"Looks like it," said Montgomery.

"What are these beasts for? Merchandise, curios? Does the captain think he is going to sell them somewhere in the South Seas?"

"It looks like it, doesn't it?" said Montgomery, and turned towards the wake again.

Suddenly we heard a yelp and a volley of furious blasphemy from the companion hatchway, and the deformed man with the black face came up hurriedly. He was immediately followed by a heavy red-haired man in a white cap. At the sight of the former the staghounds, who had all tired of barking at me by this time, became furiously excited, howling and leaping against their chains. The black hesitated before them, and this gave the red-haired man time to come up with him and deliver a tremendous blow between the shoulder-blades. The poor devil went down like a felled ox, and rolled in the dirt among the furiously excited dogs. It was lucky for him that they were muzzled. The red-haired man gave a yawp of exultation and stood staggering, and as it seemed to me in serious danger of either going backwards down the companion hatchway or forwards upon his victim.

So soon as the second man had appeared, Montgomery had started forward. "Steady on there!" he cried, in a tone of remonstrance. A couple of sailors appeared on the forecastle. The black-faced man, howling in a singular voice rolled about under the feet of the dogs. No one attempted to help him. The brutes did their best to worry him, butting their muzzles at him. There was a quick dance of their lithe grey-figured bodies over the clumsy, prostrate figure. The sailors forward shouted, as though it was admirable sport. Montgomery gave an angry exclamation, and went striding down the deck, and I followed him. The black-faced man scrambled up and staggered forward, going and leaning over the bulwark by the main shrouds, where he remained, panting and glaring over his shoulder at the dogs. The red-haired man laughed a satisfied laugh.

"Look here, Captain," said Montgomery, with his lisp a little accentuated, gripping the elbows of the red-haired man, "this won't do!"

I stood behind Montgomery. The captain came half round, and regarded him with the dull and solemn eyes of a drunken man. "Wha' won't do?" he said, and added, after looking sleepily into Montgomery's face for a minute, "Blasted Sawbones!"

With a sudden movement he shook his arms free, and after two ineffectual attempts stuck his freckled fists into his side pockets.

"That man's a passenger," said Montgomery. "I'd advise you to keep your hands off him."

"Go to hell!" said the captain, loudly. He suddenly turned and staggered towards the side. "Do what I like on my own ship," he said.

I think Montgomery might have left him then, seeing the brute was drunk; but he only turned a shade paler, and followed the captain to the bulwarks.

"Look you here, Captain," he said; "that man of mine is not to be ill-treated. He has been hazed ever since he came aboard."

For a minute, alcoholic fumes kept the captain speechless. "Blasted Sawbones!" was all he considered necessary.

I could see that Montgomery had one of those slow, pertinacious tempers that will warm day after day to a white heat, and never again cool to forgiveness; and I saw too that this quarrel had been some time growing. "The man's drunk," said I, perhaps officiously; "you'll do no good."

Montgomery gave an ugly twist to his dropping lip. "He's always drunk. Do you think that excuses his assaulting his passengers?"

"My ship," began the captain, waving his hand unsteadily towards the cages, "was a clean ship. Look at it now!" It was certainly anything but clean. "Crew," continued the captain, "clean, respectable crew."

"You agreed to take the beasts."

"I wish I'd never set eyes on your infernal island. What the devil – want beasts for on an island like that? Then, that man of yours – understood he was a man. He's a lunatic; and he hadn't no business aft. Do you think the whole damned ship belongs to you?"

"Your sailors began to haze the poor devil as soon as he came aboard."

"That's just what he is – he's a devil! an ugly devil! My men can't stand him. *I* can't stand him. None of us can't stand him. Nor *you* either!"

Montgomery turned away. "*You* leave that man alone, anyhow," he said, nodding his head as he spoke.

But the captain meant to quarrel now. He raised his voice. "If he comes this end of the ship again I'll cut his insides out, I tell you. Cut out his blasted insides! Who are you, to tell me what I'm to do? I tell you I'm captain of this ship, – captain and owner. I'm the law here, I tell you, – the law and the prophets. I bargained to take a man and his attendant to and from Arica, and bring back some animals. I never bargained to carry a mad devil and a silly Sawbones, a – "

Well, never mind what he called Montgomery. I saw the latter take a step forward, and interposed. "He's drunk," said I. The captain began some abuse even fouler than the last. "Shut up!" I said, turning on him sharply, for I had seen danger in Montgomery's white face. With that I brought the downpour on myself.

However, I was glad to avert what was uncommonly near a scuffle, even at the price of the captain's drunken ill-will. I do not think I have ever heard quite so much vile language come in a continuous stream from any man's lips before, though I have frequented eccentric company enough. I found some of it hard to endure, though I am a mild-tempered man; but, certainly, when I told the captain to "shut up" I had forgotten that I was merely a bit of human flotsam, cut off from my resources and with my fare unpaid; a mere casual dependant on the bounty, or speculative enterprise, of the ship. He reminded me of it with considerable vigour; but at any rate I prevented a fight.

CHAPTER FOUR

At the Schooner's Rail

THAT NIGHT land was sighted after sundown, and the schooner hove to. Montgomery intimated that was his destination. It was too far to see any details; it seemed to me then simply a low-lying patch of dim blue in the uncertain blue-grey sea. An almost vertical streak of smoke went up from it into the sky. The captain was not on deck when it was sighted. After he had vented his wrath on me he had staggered below, and I understand he went to sleep on the floor of his own cabin. The mate practically assumed the command. He was the gaunt, taciturn individual we had seen at the wheel. Apparently he was in an evil temper with Montgomery. He took not the slightest notice of either of us. We dined with him in a sulky silence, after a few ineffectual efforts on my part to talk. It struck me too that the men regarded my companion and his animals in a singularly unfriendly manner. I found Montgomery very reticent about his purpose with these creatures, and about his destination; and though I was sensible of a growing curiosity as to both, I did not press him.

We remained talking on the quarter deck until the sky was thick with stars. Except for an occasional sound in the yellow-lit forecastle and a movement of the animals now and then, the night was very still. The puma lay crouched together, watching us with shining eyes, a black heap in the corner of its cage. Montgomery produced some cigars. He talked to me of London in a tone of half-painful reminiscence, asking all kinds of questions about changes that had taken place. He spoke like a man who had loved his life there, and had been suddenly and irrevocably cut off from it. I gossiped as well as I could of this and that. All the time the strangeness of him was shaping itself in my mind; and as I talked I peered at his odd, pallid face in the dim light of the binnacle lantern behind me. Then I looked out at the darkling sea, where in the dimness his little island was hidden.

This man, it seemed to me, had come out of Immensity merely to save my life. To-morrow he would drop over the side, and vanish again out of my existence. Even had it been under commonplace circumstances, it would have made me a trifle thoughtful; but in the first place was the singularity of an educated man living on this unknown little island, and coupled with that the extraordinary nature of his luggage. I found myself repeating the captain's question. What did he want with the beasts? Why, too, had he pretended they were not his when I had remarked about them at first? Then, again, in his personal attendant there was a bizarre quality which had impressed me profoundly. These circumstances threw a haze of mystery round the man. They laid hold of my imagination, and hampered my tongue.

Towards midnight our talk of London died away, and we stood side by side leaning over the bulwarks and staring dreamily over the silent, starlit sea, each pursuing his own thoughts. It was the atmosphere for sentiment, and I began upon my gratitude.

"If I may say it," said I, after a time, "you have saved my life."

"Chance," he answered. "Just chance."

"I prefer to make my thanks to the accessible agent."

"Thank no one. You had the need, and I had the knowledge; and I injected and fed you much as I might have collected a specimen. I was bored and wanted something to do. If I'd been jaded that day, or hadn't liked your face, well – it's a curious question where you would have been now!"

This damped my mood a little. "At any rate," I began.

"It's a chance, I tell you," he interrupted, "as everything is in a man's life. Only the asses won't see it! Why am I here now, an outcast from civilisation, instead of being a happy man enjoying all the pleasures of London? Simply because eleven years ago – I lost my head for ten minutes on a foggy night."

He stopped. "Yes?" said I.

"That's all."

We relapsed into silence. Presently he laughed. "There's something in this starlight that loosens one's tongue. I'm an ass, and yet somehow I would like to tell you."

"Whatever you tell me, you may rely upon my keeping to myself – if that's it."

He was on the point of beginning, and then shook his head, doubtfully.

"Don't," said I. "It is all the same to me. After all, it is better to keep your secret. There's nothing gained but a little relief if I respect your confidence. If I don't – well?"

He grunted undecidedly. I felt I had him at a disadvantage, had caught him in the mood of indiscretion; and to tell the truth I was not curious to learn what might have driven a young medical student out of London. I have an imagination. I shrugged my shoulders and turned away. Over the taffrail leant a silent black figure, watching the stars. It was Montgomery's strange attendant. It looked over its shoulder quickly with my movement, then looked away again.

It may seem a little thing to you, perhaps, but it came like a sudden blow to me. The only light near us was a lantern at the wheel. The creature's face was turned for one brief instant out of the dimness of the stern towards this illumination, and I saw that the eyes that glanced at me shone with a pale-green light. I did not know then that a reddish luminosity, at least, is not uncommon in human eyes. The thing came to me as stark inhumanity. That black figure with its eyes of fire struck down through all my adult thoughts and feelings, and for a moment the forgotten horrors of childhood came back to my mind. Then the effect passed as it had come. An uncouth black figure of a man, a figure of no particular import, hung over the taffrail against the starlight, and I found Montgomery was speaking to me.

"I'm thinking of turning in, then," said he, "if you've had enough of this."

I answered him incongruously. We went below, and he wished me good-night at the door of my cabin.

That night I had some very unpleasant dreams. The waning moon rose late. Its light struck a ghostly white beam across my cabin, and made an ominous shape on the planking by my bunk. Then the staghounds woke, and began howling and baying; so that I dreamt fitfully, and scarcely slept until the approach of dawn.

CHAPTER FIVE

The Man who had Nowhere to Go

IN THE EARLY MORNING (it was the second morning after my recovery, and I believe the fourth after I was picked up), I awoke through an avenue of tumultuous dreams, – dreams of guns and howling mobs, – and became sensible of a hoarse shouting above me. I rubbed my eyes and lay listening to the noise, doubtful for a little while of my whereabouts. Then came a sudden pattering of bare feet, the sound of heavy objects being thrown about, a violent creaking and the rattling of chains. I heard the swish of the water as the ship was suddenly brought round, and a foamy yellow-green wave flew across the little round window and left it streaming. I jumped into my clothes and went on deck.

As I came up the ladder I saw against the flushed sky – for the sun was just rising – the broad back and red hair of the captain, and over his shoulder the puma spinning from a tackle rigged on to the mizzen spanker-boom.

The poor brute seemed horribly scared, and crouched in the bottom of its little cage.

"Overboard with 'em!" bawled the captain. "Overboard with 'em! We'll have a clean ship soon of the whole bilin' of 'em."

He stood in my way, so that I had perforce to tap his shoulder to come on deck. He came round with a start, and staggered back a few paces to stare at me. It needed no expert eye to tell that the man was still drunk.

"Hullo!" said he, stupidly; and then with a light coming into his eyes, "Why, it's Mister – Mister?"

"Prendick," said I.

"Prendick be damned!" said he. "Shut-up, – that's your name. Mister Shut-up."

It was no good answering the brute; but I certainly did not expect his next move. He held out his hand to the gangway by which Montgomery stood talking to a massive grey-haired man in dirty-blue flannels, who had apparently just come aboard.

"That way, Mister Blasted Shut-up! that way!" roared the captain.

Montgomery and his companion turned as he spoke.

"What do you mean?" I said.

"That way, Mister Blasted Shut-up, – that's what I mean! Overboard, Mister Shut-up, – and sharp! We're cleaning the ship out, – cleaning the whole blessed ship out; and overboard you go!"

I stared at him dumfounded. Then it occurred to me that it was exactly the thing I wanted. The lost prospect of a journey as sole passenger with this quarrelsome sot was not one to mourn over. I turned towards Montgomery.

"Can't have you," said Montgomery's companion, concisely.

"You can't have me!" said I, aghast. He had the squarest and most resolute face I ever set eyes upon.

"Look here," I began, turning to the captain.

"Overboard!" said the captain. "This ship aint for beasts and cannibals and worse than beasts, any more. Overboard you go, Mister Shut-up. If they can't have you, you goes overboard. But, anyhow, you go – with your friends. I've done with this blessed island for evermore, amen! I've had enough of it."

"But, Montgomery," I appealed.

He distorted his lower lip, and nodded his head hopelessly at the grey-haired man beside him, to indicate his powerlessness to help me.

"I'll see to *you*, presently," said the captain.

Then began a curious three-cornered altercation. Alternately I appealed to one and another of the three men, – first to the grey-haired man to let me land, and then to the drunken captain to keep me aboard. I even bawled entreaties to the sailors. Montgomery said never a word, only shook his head. "You're going overboard, I tell you," was the captain's refrain. "Law be damned! I'm king here." At last I must confess my voice suddenly broke in the middle of a vigorous threat. I felt a gust of hysterical petulance, and went aft and stared dismally at nothing.

Meanwhile the sailors progressed rapidly with the task of unshipping the packages and caged animals. A large launch, with two standing lugs, lay under the lee of the schooner; and into this the strange assortment of goods were swung. I did not then see the hands from the island that were receiving the packages, for the hull of the launch was hidden from me by the side of the schooner. Neither Montgomery nor his companion took the slightest notice of me, but busied themselves in assisting and directing the four or five sailors who were unloading the goods. The captain went forward interfering rather than assisting. I was alternately despairful and desperate. Once or twice as I stood waiting there for things to accomplish themselves, I could not resist an impulse to laugh at my miserable quandary. I felt all the wretcheder for the lack of a breakfast. Hunger and a lack of blood-corpuscles take all the manhood from a man. I perceived pretty clearly that I had not the stamina either to resist what the captain chose to do to expel me, or to force myself upon Montgomery and his companion. So I waited passively upon fate; and the work of transferring Montgomery's possessions to the launch went on as if I did not exist.

Presently that work was finished, and then came a struggle. I was hauled, resisting weakly enough, to the gangway. Even then I noticed the oddness of the brown faces of the men who were with Montgomery in the launch; but the launch was now fully laden, and was shoved off hastily. A broadening gap of green water appeared under me, and I pushed back with all my strength to avoid falling headlong. The hands in the launch shouted derisively, and I heard Montgomery curse at them; and then the captain, the mate, and one of the seamen helping him, ran me aft towards the stern.

The dingey of the *Lady Vain* had been towing behind; it was half full of water, had no oars, and was quite unvictualled. I refused to go aboard her, and flung myself full length on the deck. In the end, they swung me into her by a rope (for they had no stern ladder), and then they cut me adrift. I drifted slowly from the schooner. In a kind of stupor I watched all hands take to the rigging, and slowly but surely she came round to the wind; the sails fluttered, and then bellied out as the wind came into them. I stared at her weather-beaten side heeling steeply towards me; and then she passed out of my range of view.

I did not turn my head to follow her. At first I could scarcely believe what had happened. I crouched in the bottom of the dingey, stunned, and staring blankly at the vacant, oily sea. Then I realised that I was in that little hell of mine again, now half swamped; and looking back over the gunwale, I saw the schooner standing away from me, with the red-haired captain mocking at me over the taffrail, and turning towards the island saw the launch growing smaller as she approached the beach.

Abruptly the cruelty of this desertion became clear to me. I had no means of reaching the land unless I should chance to drift there. I was still weak, you must remember, from my exposure in the boat; I was empty and very faint, or I should have had more heart. But as it was I suddenly began to sob and weep, as I had never done since I was a little child. The tears ran down my face. In a passion of despair I struck with my fists at the water in the bottom of the boat, and kicked savagely at the gunwale. I prayed aloud for God to let me die.

CHAPTER SIX

The Evil-Looking Boatmen

But the islanders, seeing that I was really adrift, took pity on me. I drifted very slowly to the eastward, approaching the island slantingly; and presently I saw, with hysterical relief, the launch come round and return towards me. She was heavily laden, and I could make out as she drew nearer Montgomery's white-haired, broad-shouldered companion sitting cramped up with the dogs and several packing-cases in the stern sheets. This individual stared fixedly at me without moving or speaking. The black-faced cripple was glaring at me as fixedly in the bows near the puma. There were three other men besides, – three strange brutish-looking fellows, at whom the staghounds were snarling savagely. Montgomery, who was steering, brought the boat by me, and rising, caught and fastened my painter to the tiller to tow me, for there was no room aboard.

I had recovered from my hysterical phase by this time and answered his hail, as he approached, bravely enough. I told him the dingey was nearly swamped, and he reached me a piggin. I was jerked back as the rope tightened between the boats. For some time I was busy baling.

It was not until I had got the water under (for the water in the dingey had been shipped; the boat was perfectly sound) that I had leisure to look at the people in the launch again.

The white-haired man I found was still regarding me steadfastly, but with an expression, as I now fancied, of some perplexity. When my eyes met his, he looked down at the staghound that sat between his knees. He was a powerfully-built man, as I have said, with a fine forehead and rather heavy features; but his eyes had that odd drooping of the skin above the lids which often comes with advancing years, and the fall of his heavy mouth at the corners gave him an expression of pugnacious resolution. He talked to Montgomery in a tone too low for me to hear.

From him my eyes travelled to his three men; and a strange crew they were. I saw only their faces, yet there was something in their faces – I knew not what – that gave me a queer spasm of disgust. I looked steadily at them, and the impression did not pass, though I failed to see what had occasioned it. They seemed to me then to be brown men; but their limbs were oddly swathed in some thin, dirty, white stuff down even to the fingers and feet: I have never seen men so wrapped up before, and women so only in the East. They wore turbans too, and thereunder peered out their elfin faces at me, – faces with protruding lower-jaws and bright eyes. They had lank black hair, almost like horsehair, and seemed as they sat to exceed in stature any race of men I have seen. The white-haired man, who I knew was a good six feet in height, sat a head below any one of the three. I found afterwards that really none were taller than myself; but their bodies were abnormally long, and the thigh-part of the leg short and curiously twisted. At any rate, they were an amazingly ugly gang, and over the heads of them under the forward lug peered the black face of the man whose eyes were luminous in the dark. As I stared at them, they met my gaze; and then first one and then another turned away from my direct stare, and looked at me in an odd, furtive manner. It occurred to me that I was perhaps annoying them, and I turned my attention to the island we were approaching.

It was low, and covered with thick vegetation, – chiefly a kind of palm, that was new to me. From one point a thin white thread of vapour rose slantingly to an immense height, and then frayed out like a down feather. We were now within the embrace of a broad bay flanked on either hand by a low promontory. The beach was of dull-grey sand, and sloped steeply up to a ridge, perhaps sixty or seventy feet above the sea-level, and irregularly set with trees and undergrowth. Half way up was a square enclosure of some greyish stone, which I found subsequently was built partly of coral and partly of pumiceous lava. Two thatched roofs peeped from within this enclosure. A man stood awaiting us at the water's edge. I fancied while we were still far off that I saw some other and very grotesque-looking creatures scuttle into the bushes upon the slope; but I saw nothing of these as we drew nearer. This man was of a moderate size, and with a black negroid face. He had a large, almost lipless, mouth, extraordinary lank arms, long thin feet, and bow-legs, and stood with his heavy face thrust forward staring at us. He was dressed like Montgomery and his white-haired companion, in jacket and trousers of blue serge. As we came still nearer, this individual began to run to and fro on the beach, making the most grotesque movements.

At a word of command from Montgomery, the four men in the launch sprang up, and with singularly awkward gestures struck the lugs. Montgomery steered us round and into a narrow little dock excavated in the beach. Then the man on the beach hastened towards us. This dock, as I call it, was really a mere ditch just long enough at this phase of the tide to take the longboat. I heard the bows ground in the sand, staved the dingey off the rudder of the big boat with my piggin, and freeing the painter, landed. The three muffled men, with the clumsiest movements, scrambled out upon the sand, and forthwith set to landing the cargo, assisted by the man on the beach. I was struck especially by the curious movements of the legs of the three swathed and bandaged boatmen, – not stiff they were, but distorted in some odd way, almost as if they were jointed in the wrong place. The dogs were still snarling, and strained at their chains after these men, as the white-haired man landed with them. The three big fellows spoke to one another in odd guttural tones, and the man who had waited for us on the beach began chattering to them excitedly – a foreign language, as I fancied – as they laid hands on some bales piled near the stern. Somewhere I had heard such a voice before, and I could not think where. The white-haired man stood, holding in a tumult of six dogs, and bawling orders over their din. Montgomery, having unshipped the rudder, landed likewise, and all set to work at unloading. I was too faint, what with my long fast and the sun beating down on my bare head, to offer any assistance.

Presently the white-haired man seemed to recollect my presence, and came up to me.

"You look," said he, "as though you had scarcely breakfasted." His little eyes were a brilliant black under his heavy brows. "I must apologise for that. Now you are our guest, we must make you comfortable, – though you are uninvited, you know." He looked keenly into my face. "Montgomery says you are an educated man, Mr. Prendick; says you know something of science. May I ask what that signifies?"

I told him I had spent some years at the Royal College of Science, and had done some researches in biology under Huxley. He raised his eyebrows slightly at that.

"That alters the case a little, Mr. Prendick," he said, with a trifle more respect in his manner. "As it happens, we are biologists here. This is a biological station – of a sort." His eye rested on the men in white who were busily hauling the puma, on rollers, towards the walled yard. "I and Montgomery, at least," he added. Then, "When you will be able to get away, I can't say. We're off the track to anywhere. We see a ship once in a twelve-month or so."

He left me abruptly, and went up the beach past this group, and I think entered the enclosure. The other two men were with Montgomery, erecting a pile of smaller packages on a low-wheeled truck. The llama was still on the launch with the rabbit hutches; the staghounds were still lashed to the thwarts. The pile of things completed, all three men laid hold of the truck and began shoving the ton-weight or so upon it after the puma. Presently Montgomery left them, and coming back to me held out his hand.

"I'm glad," said he, "for my own part. That captain was a silly ass. He'd have made things lively for you."

"It was you," said I, "that saved me again."

"That depends. You'll find this island an infernally rum place, I promise you. I'd watch my goings carefully, if I were you. *He* – " He hesitated, and seemed to alter his mind about what was on his lips. "I wish you'd help me with these rabbits," he said.

His procedure with the rabbits was singular. I waded in with him, and helped him lug one of the hutches ashore. No sooner was that done than he opened the door of it, and tilting the thing on one end turned its living contents out on the ground. They fell in a struggling heap one on the top of the other. He clapped his hands, and forthwith they went off with that hopping run of theirs, fifteen or twenty of them I should think, up the beach.

"Increase and multiply, my friends," said Montgomery. "Replenish the island. Hitherto we've had a certain lack of meat here."

As I watched them disappearing, the white-haired man returned with a brandy-flask and some biscuits. "Something to go on with, Prendick," said he, in a far more familiar tone than before. I made no ado, but set to work on the biscuits at once, while the white-haired man helped Montgomery to release about a score more of the rabbits. Three big hutches, however, went up to the house with the puma. The brandy I did not touch, for I have been an abstainer from my birth.

CHAPTER SEVEN

The Locked Door

THE READER will perhaps understand that at first everything was so strange about me, and my position was the outcome of such unexpected adventures, that I had no discernment of the relative strangeness of this or that thing. I followed the llama up the beach, and was overtaken by Montgomery, who asked me not to enter the stone enclosure. I noticed then that the puma in its cage and the pile of packages had been placed outside the entrance to this quadrangle.

I turned and saw that the launch had now been unloaded, run out again, and was being beached, and the white-haired man was walking towards us. He addressed Montgomery.

"And now comes the problem of this uninvited guest. What are we to do with him?"

"He knows something of science," said Montgomery.

"I'm itching to get to work again – with this new stuff," said the white-haired man, nodding towards the enclosure. His eyes grew brighter.

"I daresay you are," said Montgomery, in anything but a cordial tone.

"We can't send him over there, and we can't spare the time to build him a new shanty; and we certainly can't take him into our confidence just yet."

"I'm in your hands," said I. I had no idea of what he meant by "over there."

"I've been thinking of the same things," Montgomery answered. "There's my room with the outer door – "

"That's it," said the elder man, promptly, looking at Montgomery; and all three of us went towards the enclosure. "I'm sorry to make a mystery, Mr. Prendick; but you'll remember you're uninvited. Our little establishment here contains a secret or so, is a kind of Blue-Beard's chamber, in fact. Nothing very dreadful, really, to a sane man; but just now, as we don't know you – "

"Decidedly," said I, "I should be a fool to take offence at any want of confidence."

He twisted his heavy mouth into a faint smile – he was one of those saturnine people who smile with the corners of the mouth down, – and bowed his acknowledgment of my complaisance. The main entrance to the enclosure was passed; it was a heavy wooden gate, framed in iron and locked, with the cargo of the launch piled outside it, and at the corner we came to a small doorway I had not previously observed. The white-haired man produced a bundle of keys from the pocket of his greasy blue jacket, opened this door, and entered. His keys, and the elaborate locking-up of the place even while it was still under his eye, struck me as peculiar. I followed him, and found myself in a small apartment, plainly but not uncomfortably furnished and with its inner door, which was slightly ajar, opening into a paved courtyard. This inner door Montgomery at once closed. A hammock was slung across the darker corner of the room, and a small unglazed window defended by an iron bar looked out towards the sea.

This the white-haired man told me was to be my apartment; and the inner door, which "for fear of accidents," he said, he would lock on the other side, was my limit inward. He called my attention to a convenient deck-chair before the window, and to an array of old books, chiefly, I found, surgical works and editions of the Latin and Greek classics (languages I cannot read with any comfort), on a shelf near the hammock. He left the room by the outer door, as if to avoid opening the inner one again.

"We usually have our meals in here," said Montgomery, and then, as if in doubt, went out after the other. "Moreau!" I heard him call, and for the moment I do not think I noticed. Then as I handled the books on the shelf it came up in consciousness: Where had I heard the name of Moreau before? I sat down before the window, took out the biscuits that still remained to me, and ate them with an excellent appetite. Moreau!

Through the window I saw one of those unaccountable men in white, lugging a packing-case along the beach. Presently the window-frame hid him. Then I heard a key inserted and turned in the lock behind me. After a little while I heard through the locked door the noise of the staghounds, that had now been brought up from the beach. They were not barking, but sniffing and growling in a curious fashion. I could hear the rapid patter of their feet, and Montgomery's voice soothing them.

I was very much impressed by the elaborate secrecy of these two men regarding the contents of the place, and for some time I was thinking of that and of the unaccountable familiarity of the name of Moreau;

but so odd is the human memory that I could not then recall that well-known name in its proper connection. From that my thoughts went to the indefinable queerness of the deformed man on the beach. I never saw such a gait, such odd motions as he pulled at the box. I recalled that none of these men had spoken to me, though most of them I had found looking at me at one time or another in a peculiarly furtive manner, quite unlike the frank stare of your unsophisticated savage. Indeed, they had all seemed remarkably taciturn, and when they did speak, endowed with very uncanny voices. What was wrong with them? Then I recalled the eyes of Montgomery's ungainly attendant.

Just as I was thinking of him he came in. He was now dressed in white, and carried a little tray with some coffee and boiled vegetables thereon. I could hardly repress a shuddering recoil as he came, bending amiably, and placed the tray before me on the table. Then astonishment paralysed me. Under his stringy black locks I saw his ear; it jumped upon me suddenly close to my face. The man had pointed ears, covered with a fine brown fur!

"Your breakfast, sair," he said.

I stared at his face without attempting to answer him. He turned and went towards the door, regarding me oddly over his shoulder. I followed him out with my eyes; and as I did so, by some odd trick of unconscious cerebration, there came surging into my head the phrase, "The Moreau Hollows" – was it? "The Moreau – " Ah! It sent my memory back ten years. "The Moreau Horrors!" The phrase drifted loose in my mind for a moment, and then I saw it in red lettering on a little buff-coloured pamphlet, to read which made one shiver and creep. Then I remembered distinctly all about it. That long-forgotten pamphlet came back with startling vividness to my mind. I had been a mere lad then, and Moreau was, I suppose, about fifty, – a prominent and masterful physiologist, well-known in scientific circles for his extraordinary imagination and his brutal directness in discussion.

Was this the same Moreau? He had published some very astonishing facts in connection with the transfusion of blood, and in addition was known to be doing valuable work on morbid growths. Then suddenly his career was closed. He had to leave England. A journalist obtained access to his laboratory in the capacity of laboratory-assistant, with the deliberate intention of making sensational exposures; and by the help of a shocking accident (if it was an accident), his gruesome pamphlet became notorious. On the day of its publication a wretched dog, flayed and otherwise mutilated, escaped from Moreau's house. It was in the silly season, and a prominent editor, a cousin of the temporary laboratory-assistant, appealed to the conscience of the nation. It was not the first time that conscience has turned against the methods of research. The doctor was simply howled out of the country. It may be that he deserved to be; but I still think that the tepid support of his fellow-investigators and his desertion by the great body of scientific workers was a shameful thing. Yet some of his experiments, by the journalist's account, were wantonly cruel. He might perhaps have purchased his social peace by abandoning his investigations; but he apparently preferred the latter, as most men would who have once fallen under the overmastering spell of research. He was unmarried, and had indeed nothing but his own interest to consider.

I felt convinced that this must be the same man. Everything pointed to it. It dawned upon me to what end the puma and the other animals – which had now been brought with other luggage into the enclosure behind the house – were destined; and a curious faint odour, the halitus of something familiar, an odour that had been in the background of my consciousness hitherto, suddenly came forward into the forefront of my thoughts. It was the antiseptic odour of the dissecting-room. I heard the puma growling through the wall, and one of the dogs yelped as though it had been struck.

Yet surely, and especially to another scientific man, there was nothing so horrible in vivisection as to account for this secrecy; and by some odd leap in my thoughts the pointed ears and luminous eyes of Montgomery's attendant came back again before me with the sharpest definition. I stared before me out at the green sea, frothing under a freshening breeze, and let these and other strange memories of the last few days chase one another through my mind.

What could it all mean? A locked enclosure on a lonely island, a notorious vivisector, and these crippled and distorted men?

CHAPTER EIGHT

The Crying of the Puma

Montgomery interrupted my tangle of mystification and suspicion about one o'clock, and his grotesque attendant followed him with a tray bearing bread, some herbs and other eatables, a flask of whiskey, a jug of water, and three glasses and knives. I glanced askance at this strange creature, and found him watching me with his queer, restless eyes. Montgomery said he would lunch with me, but that Moreau was too preoccupied with some work to come.

"Moreau!" said I. "I know that name."

"The devil you do!" said he. "What an ass I was to mention it to you! I might have thought. Anyhow, it will give you an inkling of our – mysteries. Whiskey?"

"No, thanks; I'm an abstainer."

"I wish I'd been. But it's no use locking the door after the steed is stolen. It was that infernal stuff which led to my coming here, – that, and a foggy night. I thought myself in luck at the time, when Moreau offered to get me off. It's queer – "

"Montgomery," said I, suddenly, as the outer door closed, "why has your man pointed ears?"

"Damn!" he said, over his first mouthful of food. He stared at me for a moment, and then repeated, "Pointed ears?"

"Little points to them," said I, as calmly as possible, with a catch in my breath; "and a fine black fur at the edges?"

He helped himself to whiskey and water with great deliberation. "I was under the impression – that his hair covered his ears."

"I saw them as he stooped by me to put that coffee you sent to me on the table. And his eyes shine in the dark."

By this time Montgomery had recovered from the surprise of my question. "I always thought," he said deliberately, with a certain accentuation of his flavouring of lisp, "that there *was* something the matter with his ears, from the way he covered them. What were they like?"

I was persuaded from his manner that this ignorance was a pretence. Still, I could hardly tell the man that I thought him a liar. "Pointed," I said; "rather small and furry, – distinctly furry. But the whole man is one of the strangest beings I ever set eyes on."

A sharp, hoarse cry of animal pain came from the enclosure behind us. Its depth and volume testified to the puma. I saw Montgomery wince.

"Yes?" he said.

"Where did you pick up the creature?"

"San Francisco. He's an ugly brute, I admit. Half-witted, you know. Can't remember where he came from. But I'm used to him, you know. We both are. How does he strike you?"

"He's unnatural," I said. "There's something about him – don't think me fanciful, but it gives me a nasty little sensation, a tightening of my muscles, when he comes near me. It's a touch – of the diabolical, in fact."

Montgomery had stopped eating while I told him this. "Rum!" he said. "I can't see it." He resumed his meal. "I had no idea of it," he said, and masticated. "The crew of the schooner must have felt it the same. Made a dead set at the poor devil. You saw the captain?"

Suddenly the puma howled again, this time more painfully. Montgomery swore under his breath. I had half a mind to attack him about the men on the beach. Then the poor brute within gave vent to a series of short, sharp cries.

"Your men on the beach," said I; "what race are they?"

"Excellent fellows, aren't they?" said he, absentmindedly, knitting his brows as the animal yelled out sharply.

I said no more. There was another outcry worse than the former. He looked at me with his dull grey eyes, and then took some more whiskey. He tried to draw me into a discussion about alcohol, professing to have saved my life with it. He seemed anxious to lay stress on the fact that I owed my life to him. I answered him distractedly.

Presently our meal came to an end; the misshapen monster with the pointed ears cleared the remains away, and Montgomery left me alone in the room again. All the time he had been in a state of ill-concealed irritation at the noise of the vivisected puma. He had spoken of his odd want of nerve, and left me to the obvious application.

I found myself that the cries were singularly irritating, and they grew in depth and intensity as the afternoon wore on. They were painful at first, but their constant resurgence at last altogether upset my balance. I flung aside a crib of Horace I had been reading, and began to clench my fists, to bite my lips, and to pace the room. Presently I got to stopping my ears with my fingers.

The emotional appeal of those yells grew upon me steadily, grew at last to such an exquisite expression of suffering that I could stand it in that confined room no longer. I stepped out of the door into the slumberous heat of the late afternoon, and walking past the main entrance – locked again, I noticed – turned the corner of the wall.

The crying sounded even louder out of doors. It was as if all the pain in the world had found a voice. Yet had I known such pain was in the next room, and had it been dumb, I believe – I have thought since – I could have stood it well enough. It is when suffering finds a voice and sets our nerves quivering that this pity comes troubling us. But in spite of the brilliant sunlight and the green fans of the trees waving in the soothing sea-breeze, the world was a confusion, blurred with drifting black and red phantasms, until I was out of earshot of the house in the chequered wall.

CHAPTER NINE

The Thing in the Forest

I STRODE THROUGH the undergrowth that clothed the ridge behind the house, scarcely heeding whither I went; passed on through the shadow of a thick cluster of straight-stemmed trees beyond it, and so presently found myself some way on the other side of the ridge, and descending towards a streamlet that ran through a narrow valley. I paused and listened. The distance I had come, or the intervening masses of thicket, deadened any sound that might be coming from the enclosure. The air was still. Then with a rustle a rabbit emerged, and went scampering up the slope before me. I hesitated, and sat down in the edge of the shade.

The place was a pleasant one. The rivulet was hidden by the luxuriant vegetation of the banks save at one point, where I caught a triangular patch of its glittering water. On the farther side I saw through a bluish haze a tangle of trees and creepers, and above these again the luminous blue of the sky. Here and there a splash of white or crimson marked the blooming of some trailing epiphyte. I let my eyes wander over this scene for a while, and then began to turn over in my mind again the strange peculiarities of Montgomery's man. But it was too hot to think elaborately, and presently I fell into a tranquil state midway between dozing and waking.

From this I was aroused, after I know not how long, by a rustling amidst the greenery on the other side of the stream. For a moment I could see nothing but the waving summits of the ferns and reeds. Then suddenly upon the bank of the stream appeared something – at first I could not distinguish what it was. It bowed its round head to the water, and began to drink. Then I saw it was a man, going on all-fours like a beast. He was clothed in bluish cloth, and was of a copper-coloured hue, with black hair. It seemed that grotesque ugliness was an invariable character of these islanders. I could hear the suck of the water at his lips as he drank.

I leant forward to see him better, and a piece of lava, detached by my hand, went pattering down the slope. He looked up guiltily, and his eyes met mine. Forthwith he scrambled to his feet, and stood wiping his clumsy hand across his mouth and regarding me. His legs were scarcely half the length of his body. So, staring one another out of countenance, we remained for perhaps the space of a minute. Then, stopping to look back once or twice, he slunk off among the bushes to the right of me, and I heard the swish of the fronds grow faint in the distance and die away. Long after he had disappeared, I remained sitting up staring in the direction of his retreat. My drowsy tranquillity had gone.

I was startled by a noise behind me, and turning suddenly saw the flapping white tail of a rabbit vanishing up the slope. I jumped to my feet. The apparition of this grotesque, half-bestial creature had suddenly populated the stillness of the afternoon for me. I looked around me rather nervously, and regretted that I was unarmed. Then I thought that the man I had just seen had been clothed in bluish cloth, had not been naked as a savage would have been; and I tried to persuade myself from that fact that he was after all probably a peaceful character, that the dull ferocity of his countenance belied him.

Yet I was greatly disturbed at the apparition. I walked to the left along the slope, turning my head about and peering this way and that among the straight stems of the trees. Why should a man go on all-fours and drink with his lips? Presently I heard an animal wailing again, and taking it to be the puma, I turned about and walked in a direction diametrically opposite to the sound. This led me down to the stream, across which I stepped and pushed my way up through the undergrowth beyond.

I was startled by a great patch of vivid scarlet on the ground, and going up to it found it to be a peculiar fungus, branched and corrugated like a foliaceous lichen, but deliquescing into slime at the touch; and then in the shadow of some luxuriant ferns I came upon an unpleasant thing, – the dead body of a rabbit covered with shining flies, but still warm and with the head torn off. I stopped aghast at the sight of the scattered blood. Here at least was one visitor to the island disposed of! There were no traces of other violence about it. It looked as though it had been suddenly snatched up and killed; and as I stared at the little furry body came the difficulty of how the thing had been done. The vague dread that had been in my mind since I had seen the inhuman face of the man at the stream grew distincter as I stood there. I began to realise the hardihood of my expedition among these unknown people. The thicket about me became altered to my imagination. Every shadow became something more than a shadow, – became an ambush; every rustle became a threat. Invisible things seemed watching me. I resolved to go back to the enclosure on the beach. I suddenly turned away and thrust myself violently, possibly even frantically, through the bushes, anxious to get a clear space about me again.

I stopped just in time to prevent myself emerging upon an open space. It was a kind of glade in the forest, made by a fall; seedlings were already starting up to struggle for the vacant space; and beyond, the dense growth of stems and twining vines and splashes of fungus and flowers closed in again. Before me, squatting together upon the fungoid ruins of a huge fallen tree and still unaware of my approach, were three grotesque human figures. One was evidently a female; the other two were men. They were naked, save for swathings of scarlet cloth about the middle; and their skins were of a dull pinkish-drab colour, such as I had seen in no savages before. They had fat, heavy, chinless faces, retreating foreheads, and a scant bristly hair upon their heads. I never saw such bestial-looking creatures.

They were talking, or at least one of the men was talking to the other two, and all three had been too closely interested to heed the rustling of my approach. They swayed their heads and shoulders from side to side. The speaker's words came thick and sloppy, and though I could hear them distinctly I could not distinguish what he said. He seemed to me to be reciting some complicated gibberish. Presently his articulation became shriller, and spreading his hands he rose to his feet. At that the others began to gibber in unison, also rising to their feet, spreading their hands and swaying their bodies in rhythm with their chant. I noticed then the abnormal shortness of their legs, and their lank, clumsy feet. All three began slowly to circle round, raising and stamping their feet and waving their arms; a kind of tune crept into their rhythmic recitation, and a refrain, – "Aloola," or "Balloola," it sounded like. Their eyes began to sparkle, and their ugly faces to brighten, with an expression of strange pleasure. Saliva dripped from their lipless mouths.

Suddenly, as I watched their grotesque and unaccountable gestures, I perceived clearly for the first time what it was that had offended me, what had given me the two inconsistent and conflicting impressions of utter strangeness and yet of the strangest familiarity. The three creatures engaged in this mysterious rite were human in shape, and yet human beings with the strangest air about them of some familiar animal. Each of these creatures, despite its human form, its rag of clothing, and the rough humanity of its bodily form, had woven into it – into its movements, into the expression of its countenance, into its whole presence – some now irresistible suggestion of a hog, a swinish taint, the unmistakable mark of the beast.

I stood overcome by this amazing realisation and then the most horrible questionings came rushing into my mind. They began leaping in the air, first one and then the other, whooping and grunting. Then one slipped, and for a moment was on all-fours, – to recover, indeed, forthwith. But that transitory gleam of the true animalism of these monsters was enough.

I turned as noiselessly as possible, and becoming every now and then rigid with the fear of being discovered, as a branch cracked or a leaf rustled, I pushed back into the bushes. It was long before I grew bolder, and dared to move freely. My only idea for the moment was to get away from these foul beings, and I scarcely noticed that I had emerged upon a faint pathway amidst the trees. Then suddenly traversing a little glade, I saw with an unpleasant start two clumsy legs among the trees, walking with noiseless footsteps parallel with my course, and perhaps thirty yards away from me. The head and upper part of the body were hidden by a tangle of creeper. I stopped abruptly, hoping the creature did not see me. The feet stopped as I did. So nervous was I that I controlled an impulse to headlong flight with the utmost difficulty. Then looking hard, I distinguished through the interlacing network the head and body of the brute I had seen drinking. He moved his head. There was an emerald flash in his eyes as he glanced at me from the shadow of the trees, a half-luminous colour that vanished as he turned his head again. He was motionless for a moment, and then with a noiseless tread began running through the green confusion. In another moment he had vanished behind some bushes. I could not see him, but I felt that he had stopped and was watching me again.

What on earth was he, – man or beast? What did he want with me? I had no weapon, not even a stick. Flight would be madness. At any rate the Thing, whatever it was, lacked the courage to attack me. Setting my teeth hard, I walked straight towards him. I was anxious not to show the fear that seemed chilling my backbone. I pushed through a tangle of tall white-flowered bushes, and saw him twenty paces beyond, looking over his shoulder at me and hesitating. I advanced a step or two, looking steadfastly into his eyes.

"Who are you?" said I.

He tried to meet my gaze. "No!" he said suddenly, and turning went bounding away from me through the undergrowth. Then he turned and stared at me again. His eyes shone brightly out of the dusk under the trees.

My heart was in my mouth; but I felt my only chance was bluff, and walked steadily towards him. He turned again, and vanished into the dusk. Once more I thought I caught the glint of his eyes, and that was all.

For the first time I realised how the lateness of the hour might affect me. The sun had set some minutes since, the swift dusk of the tropics was already fading out of the eastern sky, and a pioneer moth fluttered silently by my head. Unless I would spend the night among the unknown dangers of the mysterious forest, I must hasten back to the enclosure. The thought of a return to that pain-haunted refuge was extremely disagreeable, but still more so was the idea of being overtaken in the open by darkness and all that darkness might conceal. I gave one more look into the blue shadows that had swallowed up this odd creature, and then retraced my way down the slope towards the stream, going as I judged in the direction from which I had come.

I walked eagerly, my mind confused with many things, and presently found myself in a level place among scattered trees. The colourless clearness that comes after the sunset flush was darkling; the blue sky above grew momentarily deeper, and the little stars one by one pierced the attenuated light; the interspaces of the trees, the gaps in the further vegetation, that had been hazy blue in the daylight, grew black and mysterious. I pushed on. The colour vanished from the world. The tree-tops rose against the luminous blue sky in inky silhouette, and all below that outline melted into one formless blackness. Presently the trees grew thinner, and the shrubby undergrowth more abundant. Then there was a desolate space covered with a white sand, and then another expanse of tangled bushes. I did not remember crossing the sand-opening before. I began to be tormented by a faint rustling upon my right hand. I thought at first it was fancy, for whenever I stopped there was silence, save for the evening breeze in the tree-tops. Then when I turned to hurry on again there was an echo to my footsteps.

I turned away from the thickets, keeping to the more open ground, and endeavouring by sudden turns now and then to surprise something in the act of creeping upon me. I saw nothing, and nevertheless my sense of another presence grew steadily. I increased my pace, and after some time came to a slight ridge, crossed it, and turned sharply, regarding it steadfastly from the further side. It came out black and clear-cut against the darkling sky; and presently a shapeless lump heaved up momentarily against the sky-line and vanished again. I felt assured now that my tawny-faced antagonist was stalking me once more; and coupled with that was another unpleasant realisation, that I had lost my way.

For a time I hurried on hopelessly perplexed, and pursued by that stealthy approach. Whatever it was, the Thing either lacked the courage to attack me, or it was waiting to take me at some disadvantage. I kept studiously to the open. At times I would turn and listen; and presently I had half persuaded myself that my pursuer had abandoned the chase, or was a mere creation of my disordered imagination. Then I heard the sound of the sea. I quickened my footsteps almost into a run, and immediately there was a stumble in my rear.

I turned suddenly, and stared at the uncertain trees behind me. One black shadow seemed to leap into another. I listened, rigid, and heard nothing but the creep of the blood in my ears. I thought that my nerves were unstrung, and that my imagination was tricking me, and turned resolutely towards the sound of the sea again.

In a minute or so the trees grew thinner, and I emerged upon a bare, low headland running out into the sombre water. The night was calm and clear, and the reflection of the growing multitude of the stars shivered in the tranquil heaving of the sea. Some way out, the wash upon an irregular band of reef shone with a pallid light of its own. Westward I saw the zodiacal light mingling with the yellow brilliance of the evening star. The coast fell away from me to the east, and westward it was hidden by the shoulder of the cape. Then I recalled the fact that Moreau's beach lay to the west.

A twig snapped behind me, and there was a rustle. I turned, and stood facing the dark trees. I could see nothing – or else I could see too much. Every dark form in the dimness had its ominous quality, its peculiar suggestion of alert watchfulness. So I stood for perhaps a minute, and then, with an eye to the trees still, turned westward to cross the headland; and as I moved, one among the lurking shadows moved to follow me.

My heart beat quickly. Presently the broad sweep of a bay to the westward became visible, and I halted again. The noiseless shadow halted a dozen yards from me. A little point of light shone on the further bend of the curve, and the grey sweep of the sandy beach lay faint under the starlight. Perhaps two miles away was that little point of light. To get to the beach I should have to go through the trees where the shadows lurked, and down a bushy slope.

I could see the Thing rather more distinctly now. It was no animal, for it stood erect. At that I opened my mouth to speak, and found a hoarse phlegm choked my voice. I tried again, and shouted, "Who is there?" There was no answer. I advanced a step. The Thing did not move, only gathered itself together. My foot struck a stone. That gave me an idea. Without taking my eyes off the black form before me, I stooped and picked up this lump of rock; but at my motion the Thing turned abruptly as a dog might have done, and slunk obliquely into the further darkness. Then I recalled a schoolboy expedient against big dogs, and twisted the rock into my handkerchief, and gave this a turn round my wrist. I heard a movement further off among the shadows, as if the Thing was in retreat. Then suddenly my tense excitement gave way; I broke into a profuse perspiration and fell a-trembling, with my adversary routed and this weapon in my hand.

It was some time before I could summon resolution to go down through the trees and bushes upon the flank of the headland to the beach. At last I did it at a run; and as I emerged from the thicket upon the sand, I heard some other body come crashing after me. At that I completely lost my head with fear, and began running along the sand. Forthwith there came the swift patter of soft feet in pursuit. I gave a wild cry, and redoubled my pace. Some dim, black things about three or four times the size of rabbits went running or hopping up from the beach towards the bushes as I passed.

So long as I live, I shall remember the terror of that chase. I ran near the water's edge, and heard every now and then the splash of the feet that gained upon me. Far away, hopelessly far, was the yellow light. All the night about us was black and still. Splash, splash, came the pursuing feet, nearer and nearer. I felt my breath going, for I was quite out of training; it whooped as I drew it, and I felt a pain like a knife at my side. I perceived the Thing would come up with me long before I reached the enclosure, and, desperate and sobbing for my breath, I wheeled round upon it and struck at it as it came up to me, – struck with all my strength. The stone came out of the sling of the handkerchief as I did so. As I turned, the Thing, which had been running on all-fours, rose to its feet, and the missile fell fair on its left temple. The skull rang loud, and the animal-man blundered into me, thrust me back with its hands, and went staggering past me to fall headlong upon the sand with its face in the water; and there it lay still.

I could not bring myself to approach that black heap. I left it there, with the water rippling round it, under the still stars, and giving it a wide berth pursued my way towards the yellow glow of the house; and presently, with a positive effect of relief, came the pitiful moaning of the puma, the sound that had originally driven me out to explore this mysterious island. At that, though I was faint and horribly fatigued, I gathered together all my strength, and began running again towards the light. I thought I heard a voice calling me.

CHAPTER TEN

The Crying of the Man

As I DREW NEAR the house I saw that the light shone from the open door of my room; and then I heard coming from out of the darkness at the side of that orange oblong of light, the voice of Montgomery shouting, "Prendick!" I continued running. Presently I heard him again. I replied by a feeble "Hullo!" and in another moment had staggered up to him.

"Where have you been?" said he, holding me at arm's length, so that the light from the door fell on my face. "We have both been so busy that we forgot you until about half an hour ago." He led me into the room and sat me down in the deck chair. For awhile I was blinded by the light. "We did not think you would start to explore this island of ours without telling us," he said; and then, "I was afraid – But – what – Hullo!"

My last remaining strength slipped from me, and my head fell forward on my chest. I think he found a certain satisfaction in giving me brandy.

"For God's sake," said I, "fasten that door."

"You've been meeting some of our curiosities, eh?" said he.

He locked the door and turned to me again. He asked me no questions, but gave me some more brandy and water and pressed me to eat. I was in a state of collapse. He said something vague about his forgetting to warn me, and asked me briefly when I left the house and what I had seen.

I answered him as briefly, in fragmentary sentences. "Tell me what it all means," said I, in a state bordering on hysterics.

"It's nothing so very dreadful," said he. "But I think you have had about enough for one day." The puma suddenly gave a sharp yell of pain. At that he swore under his breath. "I'm damned," said he, "if this place is not as bad as Gower Street, with its cats."

"Montgomery," said I, "what was that thing that came after me? Was it a beast or was it a man?"

"If you don't sleep to-night," he said, "you'll be off your head to-morrow."

I stood up in front of him. "What was that thing that came after me?" I asked.

He looked me squarely in the eyes, and twisted his mouth askew. His eyes, which had seemed animated a minute before, went dull. "From your account," said he, "I'm thinking it was a bogle."

I felt a gust of intense irritation, which passed as quickly as it came. I flung myself into the chair again, and pressed my hands on my forehead. The puma began once more.

Montgomery came round behind me and put his hand on my shoulder. "Look here, Prendick," he said, "I had no business to let you drift out into this silly island of ours. But it's not so bad as you feel, man. Your nerves are worked to rags. Let me give you something that will make you sleep. *That* – will keep on for hours yet. You must simply get to sleep, or I won't answer for it."

I did not reply. I bowed forward, and covered my face with my hands. Presently he returned with a small measure containing a dark liquid. This he gave me. I took it unresistingly, and he helped me into the hammock.

When I awoke, it was broad day. For a little while I lay flat, staring at the roof above me. The rafters, I observed, were made out of the timbers of a ship. Then I turned my head, and saw a meal prepared for me on the table. I perceived that I was hungry, and prepared to clamber out of the hammock, which, very politely anticipating my intention, twisted round and deposited me upon all-fours on the floor.

I got up and sat down before the food. I had a heavy feeling in my head, and only the vaguest memory at first of the things that had happened over night. The morning breeze blew very pleasantly through the unglazed window, and that and the food contributed to the sense of animal comfort which I experienced. Presently the door behind me – the door inward towards the yard of the enclosure – opened. I turned and saw Montgomery's face.

"All right," said he. "I'm frightfully busy." And he shut the door.

Afterwards I discovered that he forgot to re-lock it. Then I recalled the expression of his face the previous night, and with that the memory of all I had experienced reconstructed itself before me. Even as that fear came back to me came a cry from within; but this time it was not the cry of a puma. I put down the mouthful that hesitated upon my lips, and listened. Silence, save for the whisper of the morning breeze. I began to think my ears had deceived me.

After a long pause I resumed my meal, but with my ears still vigilant. Presently I heard something else, very faint and low. I sat as if frozen in my attitude. Though it was faint and low, it moved me more profoundly than all that I had hitherto heard of the abominations behind the wall. There was no mistake this time in the quality of the dim, broken sounds; no doubt at all of their source. For it was groaning, broken by sobs and gasps of anguish. It was no brute this time; it was a human being in torment!

As I realised this I rose, and in three steps had crossed the room, seized the handle of the door into the yard, and flung it open before me.

"Prendick, man! Stop!" cried Montgomery, intervening.

A startled deerhound yelped and snarled. There was blood, I saw, in the sink, - brown, and some scarlet - and I smelt the peculiar smell of carbolic acid. Then through an open doorway beyond, in the dim light of the shadow, I saw something bound painfully upon a framework, scarred, red, and bandaged; and then blotting this out appeared the face of old Moreau, white and terrible. In a moment he had gripped me by the shoulder with a hand that was smeared red, had twisted me off my feet, and flung me headlong back into my own room. He lifted me as though I was a little child. I fell at full length upon the floor, and the door slammed and shut out the passionate intensity of his face. Then I heard the key turn in the lock, and Montgomery's voice in expostulation.

"Ruin the work of a lifetime," I heard Moreau say.

"He does not understand," said Montgomery. and other things that were inaudible.

"I can't spare the time yet," said Moreau.

The rest I did not hear. I picked myself up and stood trembling, my mind a chaos of the most horrible misgivings. Could it be possible, I thought, that such a thing as the vivisection of men was carried on here? The question shot like lightning across a tumultuous sky; and suddenly the clouded horror of my mind condensed into a vivid realisation of my own danger.

CHAPTER ELEVEN

The Hunting of the Man

IT CAME BEFORE my mind with an unreasonable hope of escape that the outer door of my room was still open to me. I was convinced now, absolutely assured, that Moreau had been vivisecting a human being. All the time since I had heard his name, I had been trying to link in my mind in some way the grotesque animalism of the islanders with his abominations; and now I thought I saw it all. The memory of his work on the transfusion of blood recurred to me. These creatures I had seen were the victims of some hideous experiment. These sickening scoundrels had merely intended to keep me back, to fool me with their display of confidence, and presently to fall upon me with a fate more horrible than death, – with torture; and after torture the most hideous degradation it is possible to conceive, – to send me off a lost soul, a beast, to the rest of their Comus rout.

I looked round for some weapon. Nothing. Then with an inspiration I turned over the deck chair, put my foot on the side of it, and tore away the side rail. It happened that a nail came away with the wood, and projecting, gave a touch of danger to an otherwise petty weapon. I heard a step outside, and incontinently flung open the door and found Montgomery within a yard of it. He meant to lock the outer door! I raised this nailed stick of mine and cut at his face; but he sprang back. I hesitated a moment, then turned and fled, round the corner of the house. "Prendick, man!" I heard his astonished cry, "don't be a silly ass, man!"

Another minute, thought I, and he would have had me locked in, and as ready as a hospital rabbit for my fate. He emerged behind the corner, for I heard him shout, "Prendick!" Then he began to run after me, shouting things as he ran. This time running blindly, I went northeastward in a direction at right angles to my previous expedition. Once, as I went running headlong up the beach, I glanced over my shoulder and saw his attendant with him. I ran furiously up the slope, over it, then turning eastward along a rocky valley fringed on either side with jungle I ran for perhaps a mile altogether, my chest straining, my heart beating in my ears; and then hearing nothing of Montgomery or his man, and feeling upon the verge of exhaustion, I doubled sharply back towards the beach as I judged, and lay down in the shelter of a canebrake. There I remained for a long time, too fearful to move, and indeed too fearful even to plan a course of action. The wild scene about me lay sleeping silently under the sun, and the only sound near me was the thin hum of some small gnats that had discovered me. Presently I became aware of a drowsy breathing sound, the soughing of the sea upon the beach.

After about an hour I heard Montgomery shouting my name, far away to the north. That set me thinking of my plan of action. As I interpreted it then, this island was inhabited only by these two vivisectors and their animalised victims. Some of these no doubt they could press into their service against me if need arose. I knew both Moreau and Montgomery carried revolvers; and, save for a feeble bar of deal spiked with a small nail, the merest mockery of a mace, I was unarmed.

So I lay still there, until I began to think of food and drink; and at that thought the real hopelessness of my position came home to me. I knew no way of getting anything to eat. I was too ignorant of botany to discover any resort of root or fruit that might lie about me; I had no means of trapping the few rabbits upon the island. It grew blanker the more I turned the prospect over. At last in the desperation of my position, my mind turned to the animal men I had encountered. I tried to find some hope in what I remembered of them. In turn I recalled each one I had seen, and tried to draw some augury of assistance from my memory.

Then suddenly I heard a staghound bay, and at that realised a new danger. I took little time to think, or they would have caught me then, but snatching up my nailed stick, rushed headlong from my hiding-place towards the sound of the sea. I remember a growth of thorny plants, with spines that stabbed like pen-knives. I emerged bleeding and with torn clothes upon the lip of a long creek opening northward. I went straight into the water without a minute's hesitation, wading up the creek, and presently finding myself kneedeep in a little stream. I scrambled out at last on the westward bank, and with my heart beating loudly in my ears, crept into a tangle of ferns to await the issue. I heard the dog (there was only one) draw nearer, and yelp when it came to the thorns. Then I heard no more, and presently began to think I had escaped.

The minutes passed; the silence lengthened out, and at last after an hour of security my courage began to return to me. By this time I was no longer very much terrified or very miserable. I had, as it were, passed the limit of terror and despair. I felt now that my life was practically lost, and that persuasion made me capable of daring anything. I had even a certain wish to encounter Moreau face to face; and as I had waded into the water, I remembered that if I were too hard pressed at least one path of escape from torment still lay open to me, – they could not very well prevent my drowning myself. I had half a mind to drown myself then; but an odd wish to see the whole adventure out, a queer, impersonal, spectacular interest in myself, restrained me. I stretched my limbs, sore and painful from the pricks of the spiny plants, and stared around me at the trees; and, so suddenly that it seemed to jump out of the green tracery about it, my eyes lit upon a black face watching me. I saw that it was the simian creature who had met the launch upon the beach. He was clinging to the oblique stem of a palm-tree. I gripped my stick, and stood up facing him. He began chattering. "You, you, you," was all I could distinguish at first. Suddenly he dropped from the tree, and in another moment was holding the fronds apart and staring curiously at me.

I did not feel the same repugnance towards this creature which I had experienced in my encounters with the other Beast Men. "You," he said, "in the boat." He was a man, then, – at least as much of a man as Montgomery's attendant, – for he could talk.

"Yes," I said, "I came in the boat. From the ship."

"Oh!" he said, and his bright, restless eyes travelled over me, to my hands, to the stick I carried, to my feet, to the tattered places in my coat, and the cuts and scratches I had received from the thorns. He seemed puzzled at something. His eyes came back to my hands. He held his own hand out and counted his digits slowly, "One, two, three, four, five – eigh?"

I did not grasp his meaning then; afterwards I was to find that a great proportion of these Beast People had malformed hands, lacking sometimes even three digits. But guessing this was in some way a greeting, I did the same thing by way of reply. He grinned with immense satisfaction. Then his swift roving glance went round again; he made a swift movement – and vanished. The fern fronds he had stood between came swishing together.

I pushed out of the brake after him, and was astonished to find him swinging cheerfully by one lank arm from a rope of creepers that looped down from the foliage overhead. His back was to me.

"Hullo!" said I.

He came down with a twisting jump, and stood facing me.

"I say," said I, "where can I get something to eat?"

"Eat!" he said. "Eat Man's food, now." And his eye went back to the swing of ropes. "At the huts."

"But where are the huts?"

"Oh!"

"I'm new, you know."

At that he swung round, and set off at a quick walk. All his motions were curiously rapid. "Come along," said he.

I went with him to see the adventure out. I guessed the huts were some rough shelter where he and some more of these Beast People lived. I might perhaps find them friendly, find some handle in their minds to take hold of. I did not know how far they had forgotten their human heritage.

My ape-like companion trotted along by my side, with his hands hanging down and his jaw thrust forward. I wondered what memory he might have in him. "How long have you been on this island?" said I.

"How long?" he asked; and after having the question repeated, he held up three fingers.

The creature was little better than an idiot. I tried to make out what he meant by that, and it seems I bored him. After another question or two he suddenly left my side and went leaping at some fruit that hung from a tree. He pulled down a handful of prickly husks and went on eating the contents. I noted this with satisfaction, for here at least was a hint for feeding. I tried him with some other questions, but his chattering, prompt responses were as often as not quite at cross purposes with my question. Some few were appropriate, others quite parrot-like.

I was so intent upon these peculiarities that I scarcely noticed the path we followed. Presently we came to trees, all charred and brown, and so to a bare place covered with a yellow-white incrustation, across which a drifting smoke, pungent in whiffs to nose and eyes, went drifting. On our right, over a shoulder of bare rock, I saw the level blue of the sea. The path coiled down abruptly into a narrow ravine between two tumbled and knotty masses of blackish scoriae. Into this we plunged.

It was extremely dark, this passage, after the blinding sunlight reflected from the sulphurous ground. Its walls grew steep, and approached each other. Blotches of green and crimson drifted across my eyes. My conductor stopped suddenly. "Home!" said he, and I stood in a floor of a chasm that was at first absolutely dark to me. I heard some strange noises, and thrust the knuckles of my left hand into my eyes. I became aware of a disagreeable odor, like that of a monkey's cage ill-cleaned. Beyond, the rock opened again upon a gradual slope of sunlit greenery, and on either hand the light smote down through narrow ways into the central gloom.

CHAPTER TWELVE

The Sayers of the Law

THEN SOMETHING COLD touched my hand. I started violently, and saw close to me a dim pinkish thing, looking more like a flayed child than anything else in the world. The creature had exactly the mild but repulsive features of a sloth, the same low forehead and slow gestures.

As the first shock of the change of light passed, I saw about me more distinctly. The little sloth-like creature was standing and staring at me. My conductor had vanished. The place was a narrow passage between high walls of lava, a crack in the knotted rock, and on either side interwoven heaps of sea-mat, palm-fans, and reeds leaning against the rock formed rough and impenetrably dark dens. The winding way up the ravine between these was scarcely three yards wide, and was disfigured by lumps of decaying fruit-pulp and other refuse, which accounted for the disagreeable stench of the place.

The little pink sloth-creature was still blinking at me when my Ape-man reappeared at the aperture of the nearest of these dens, and beckoned me in. As he did so a slouching monster wriggled out of one of the places, further up this strange street, and stood up in featureless silhouette against the bright green beyond, staring at me. I hesitated, having half a mind to bolt the way I had come; and then, determined to go through with the adventure, I gripped my nailed stick about the middle and crawled into the little evil-smelling lean-to after my conductor.

It was a semi-circular space, shaped like the half of a bee-hive; and against the rocky wall that formed the inner side of it was a pile of variegated fruits, cocoa-nuts among others. Some rough vessels of lava and wood stood about the floor, and one on a rough stool. There was no fire. In the darkest corner of the hut sat a shapeless mass of darkness that grunted "Hey!" as I came in, and my Ape-man stood in the dim light of the doorway and held out a split cocoa-nut to me as I crawled into the other corner and squatted down. I took it, and began gnawing it, as serenely as possible, in spite of a certain trepidation and the nearly intolerable closeness of the den. The little pink sloth-creature stood in the aperture of the hut, and something else with a drab face and bright eyes came staring over its shoulder.

"Hey!" came out of the lump of mystery opposite. "It is a man."

"It is a man," gabbled my conductor, "a man, a man, a five-man, like me."

"Shut up!" said the voice from the dark, and grunted. I gnawed my cocoa-nut amid an impressive stillness.

I peered hard into the blackness, but could distinguish nothing.

"It is a man," the voice repeated. "He comes to live with us?"

It was a thick voice, with something in it – a kind of whistling overtone – that struck me as peculiar; but the English accent was strangely good.

The Ape-man looked at me as though he expected something. I perceived the pause was interrogative. "He comes to live with you," I said.

"It is a man. He must learn the Law."

I began to distinguish now a deeper blackness in the black, a vague outline of a hunched-up figure. Then I noticed the opening of the place was darkened by two more black heads. My hand tightened on my stick.

The thing in the dark repeated in a louder tone, "Say the words." I had missed its last remark. "Not to go on all-fours; that is the Law," it repeated in a kind of sing-song.

I was puzzled.

"Say the words," said the Ape-man, repeating, and the figures in the doorway echoed this, with a threat in the tone of their voices.

I realised that I had to repeat this idiotic formula; and then began the insanest ceremony. The voice in the dark began intoning a mad litany, line by line, and I and the rest to repeat it. As they did so, they swayed from side to side in the oddest way, and beat their hands upon their knees; and I followed their example. I could have imagined I was already dead and in another world. That dark hut, these grotesque dim figures, just flecked here and there by a glimmer of light, and all of them swaying in unison and chanting,

"Not to go on all-fours; that is the Law. Are we not Men?

"Not to suck up Drink; that is the Law. Are we not Men?

"Not to eat Fish or Flesh; that is the Law. Are we not Men?

"Not to claw the Bark of Trees; that is the Law. Are we not Men?

"Not to chase other Men; that is the Law. Are we not Men?"

And so from the prohibition of these acts of folly, on to the prohibition of what I thought then were the maddest, most impossible, and most indecent things one could well imagine. A kind of rhythmic fervour fell on all of us; we gabbled and swayed faster and faster, repeating this amazing Law. Superficially the contagion of these brutes was upon me, but deep down within me the laughter and disgust struggled together. We ran through a long list of prohibitions, and then the chant swung round to a new formula.

"*His* is the House of Pain.

"*His* is the Hand that makes.

"*His* is the Hand that wounds.

"*His* is the Hand that heals."

And so on for another long series, mostly quite incomprehensible gibberish to me about *Him*, whoever he might be. I could have fancied it was a dream, but never before have I heard chanting in a dream.

"*His* is the lightning flash," we sang. "*His* is the deep, salt sea."

A horrible fancy came into my head that Moreau, after animalising these men, had infected their dwarfed brains with a kind of deification of himself. However, I was too keenly aware of white teeth and strong claws about me to stop my chanting on that account.

"*His* are the stars in the sky."

At last that song ended. I saw the Ape-man's face shining with perspiration; and my eyes being now accustomed to the darkness, I saw more distinctly the figure in the corner from which the voice came. It was the size of a man, but it seemed covered with a dull grey hair almost like a Skye-terrier. What was it? What were they all? Imagine yourself surrounded by all the most horrible cripples and maniacs it is possible to conceive, and you may understand a little of my feelings with these grotesque caricatures of humanity about me.

"He is a five-man, a five-man, a five-man – like me," said the Ape-man.

I held out my hands. The grey creature in the corner leant forward.

"Not to run on all-fours; that is the Law. Are we not Men?" he said.

He put out a strangely distorted talon and gripped my fingers. The thing was almost like the hoof of a deer produced into claws. I could have yelled with surprise and pain. His face came forward and peered at my nails, came forward into the light of the opening of the hut and I saw with a quivering disgust that it was like the face of neither man nor beast, but a mere shock of grey hair, with three shadowy over-archings to mark the eyes and mouth.

"He has little nails," said this grisly creature in his hairy beard. "It is well."

He threw my hand down, and instinctively I gripped my stick.

"Eat roots and herbs; it is His will," said the Ape-man.

"I am the Sayer of the Law," said the grey figure. "Here come all that be new to learn the Law. I sit in the darkness and say the Law."

"It is even so," said one of the beasts in the doorway.

"Evil are the punishments of those who break the Law. None escape."

"None escape," said the Beast Folk, glancing furtively at one another.

"None, none," said the Ape-man, – "none escape. See! I did a little thing, a wrong thing, once. I jabbered, jabbered, stopped talking. None could understand. I am burnt, branded in the hand. He is great. He is good!"

"None escape," said the grey creature in the corner.

"None escape," said the Beast People, looking askance at one another.

"For every one the want that is bad," said the grey Sayer of the Law. "What you will want we do not know; we shall know. Some want to follow things that move, to watch and slink and wait and spring; to kill and bite, bite deep and rich, sucking the blood. It is bad. 'Not to chase other Men; that is the Law. Are we not Men? Not to eat Flesh or Fish; that is the Law. Are we not Men?'"

"None escape," said a dappled brute standing in the doorway.

"For every one the want is bad," said the grey Sayer of the Law. "Some want to go tearing with teeth and hands into the roots of things, snuffing into the earth. It is bad."

"None escape," said the men in the door.

"Some go clawing trees; some go scratching at the graves of the dead; some go fighting with foreheads or feet or claws; some bite suddenly, none giving occasion; some love uncleanness."

"None escape," said the Ape-man, scratching his calf.

"None escape," said the little pink sloth-creature.

"Punishment is sharp and sure. Therefore learn the Law. Say the words."

And incontinently he began again the strange litany of the Law, and again I and all these creatures began singing and swaying. My head reeled with this jabbering and the close stench of the place; but I kept on, trusting to find presently some chance of a new development.

"Not to go on all-fours; that is the Law. Are we not Men?"

We were making such a noise that I noticed nothing of a tumult outside, until some one, who I think was one of the two Swine Men I had seen, thrust his head over the little pink sloth-creature and shouted something excitedly, something that I did not catch. Incontinently those at the opening of the hut vanished; my Ape-man rushed out; the thing that had sat in the dark followed him (I only observed that it was big and clumsy, and covered with silvery hair), and I was left alone. Then before I reached the aperture I heard the yelp of a staghound.

In another moment I was standing outside the hovel, my chair-rail in my hand, every muscle of me quivering. Before me were the clumsy backs of perhaps a score of these Beast People, their misshapen heads half hidden by their shoulder-blades. They were gesticulating excitedly. Other half-animal faces glared interrogation out of the hovels. Looking in the direction in which they faced, I saw coming through the haze under the trees beyond the end of the passage of dens the dark figure and awful white face of Moreau. He was holding the leaping staghound back, and close behind him came Montgomery revolver in hand.

For a moment I stood horror-struck. I turned and saw the passage behind me blocked by another heavy brute, with a huge grey face and twinkling little eyes, advancing towards me. I looked round and saw to the right of me and a half-dozen yards in front of me a narrow gap in the wall of rock through which a ray of light slanted into the shadows.

"Stop!" cried Moreau as I strode towards this, and then, "Hold him!"

At that, first one face turned towards me and then others. Their bestial minds were happily slow. I dashed my shoulder into a clumsy monster who was turning to see what Moreau meant, and flung him forward into another. I felt his hands fly round, clutching at me and missing me. The little pink sloth-creature dashed at me, and I gashed down its ugly face with the nail in my stick and in another minute was scrambling up a steep side pathway, a kind of sloping chimney, out of the ravine. I heard a howl behind me, and cries of "Catch him!" "Hold him!" and the grey-faced creature appeared behind me and jammed his huge bulk into the cleft. "Go on! go on!" they howled. I clambered up the narrow cleft in the rock and came out upon the sulphur on the westward side of the village of the Beast Men.

That gap was altogether fortunate for me, for the narrow chimney, slanting obliquely upward, must have impeded the nearer pursuers. I ran over the white space and down a steep slope, through a scattered growth of trees, and came to a low-lying stretch of tall reeds, through which I pushed into a dark, thick undergrowth that was black and succulent under foot. As I plunged into the reeds, my foremost pursuers emerged from the gap. I broke my way through this undergrowth for some minutes. The air behind me and about me was soon full of threatening cries. I heard the tumult of my pursuers in the gap up the slope, then the crashing of the reeds, and every now and then the crackling crash of a branch. Some of the creatures roared like excited beasts of prey. The staghound yelped to the left. I heard Moreau and Montgomery shouting in the same direction. I turned sharply to the right. It seemed to me even then that I heard Montgomery shouting for me to run for my life.

Presently the ground gave rich and oozy under my feet; but I was desperate and went headlong into it, struggled through kneedeep, and so came to a winding path among tall canes. The noise of my pursuers passed away to my left. In one place three strange, pink, hopping animals, about the size of cats, bolted before my footsteps. This pathway ran up hill, across another open space covered with white incrustation, and plunged into a canebrake again. Then suddenly it turned parallel with the edge of a steep-walled gap, which came without warning, like the ha-ha of an English park, – turned with an unexpected abruptness. I was still running with all my might, and I never saw this drop until I was flying headlong through the air.

I fell on my forearms and head, among thorns, and rose with a torn ear and bleeding face. I had fallen into a precipitous ravine, rocky and thorny, full of a hazy mist which drifted about me in wisps, and with a narrow streamlet from which this mist came meandering down the centre. I was astonished at this thin fog in the full blaze of daylight; but I had no time to stand wondering then. I turned to my right, downstream, hoping to come to the sea in that direction, and so have my way open to drown myself. It was only later I found that I had dropped my nailed stick in my fall.

Presently the ravine grew narrower for a space, and carelessly I stepped into the stream. I jumped out again pretty quickly, for the water was almost boiling. I noticed too there was a thin sulphurous scum drifting upon its coiling water. Almost immediately came a turn in the ravine, and the indistinct blue horizon. The nearer sea was flashing the sun from a myriad facets. I saw my death before me; but I was hot and panting, with the warm blood oozing out on my face and running pleasantly through my veins. I felt more than a touch of exultation too, at having distanced my pursuers. It was not in me then to go out and drown myself yet. I stared back the way I had come.

I listened. Save for the hum of the gnats and the chirp of some small insects that hopped among the thorns, the air was absolutely still. Then came the yelp of a dog, very faint, and a chattering and gibbering, the snap of a whip, and voices. They grew louder, then fainter again. The noise receded up the stream and faded away. For a while the chase was over; but I knew now how much hope of help for me lay in the Beast People.

CHAPTER THIRTEEN

A Parley

I TURNED AGAIN and went on down towards the sea. I found the hot stream broadened out to a shallow, weedy sand, in which an abundance of crabs and long-bodied, many-legged creatures started from my footfall. I walked to the very edge of the salt water, and then I felt I was safe. I turned and stared, arms akimbo, at the thick green behind me, into which the steamy ravine cut like a smoking gash. But, as I say, I was too full of excitement and (a true saying, though those who have never known danger may doubt it) too desperate to die.

Then it came into my head that there was one chance before me yet. While Moreau and Montgomery and their bestial rabble chased me through the island, might I not go round the beach until I came to their enclosure, – make a flank march upon them, in fact, and then with a rock lugged out of their loosely-built wall, perhaps, smash in the lock of the smaller door and see what I could find (knife, pistol, or what not) to fight them with when they returned? It was at any rate something to try.

So I turned to the westward and walked along by the water's edge. The setting sun flashed his blinding heat into my eyes. The slight Pacific tide was running in with a gentle ripple. Presently the shore fell away southward, and the sun came round upon my right hand. Then suddenly, far in front of me, I saw first one and then several figures emerging from the bushes, – Moreau, with his grey staghound, then Montgomery, and two others. At that I stopped.

They saw me, and began gesticulating and advancing. I stood watching them approach. The two Beast Men came running forward to cut me off from the undergrowth, inland. Montgomery came, running also, but straight towards me. Moreau followed slower with the dog.

At last I roused myself from my inaction, and turning seaward walked straight into the water. The water was very shallow at first. I was thirty yards out before the waves reached to my waist. Dimly I could see the intertidal creatures darting away from my feet.

"What are you doing, man?" cried Montgomery.

I turned, standing waist deep, and stared at them. Montgomery stood panting at the margin of the water. His face was bright-red with exertion, his long flaxen hair blown about his head, and his dropping nether lip showed his irregular teeth. Moreau was just coming up, his face pale and firm, and the dog at his hand barked at me. Both men had heavy whips. Farther up the beach stared the Beast Men.

"What am I doing? I am going to drown myself," said I.

Montgomery and Moreau looked at each other. "Why?" asked Moreau.

"Because that is better than being tortured by you."

"I told you so," said Montgomery, and Moreau said something in a low tone.

"What makes you think I shall torture you?" asked Moreau.

"What I saw," I said. "And those – yonder."

"Hush!" said Moreau, and held up his hand.

"I will not," said I. "They were men: what are they now? I at least will not be like them."

I looked past my interlocutors. Up the beach were M'ling, Montgomery's attendant, and one of the white-swathed brutes from the boat. Farther up, in the shadow of the trees, I saw my little Ape-man, and behind him some other dim figures.

"Who are these creatures?" said I, pointing to them and raising my voice more and more that it might reach them. "They were men, men like yourselves, whom you have infected with some bestial taint, – men whom you have enslaved, and whom you still fear.

"You who listen," I cried, pointing now to Moreau and shouting past him to the Beast Men, – "You who listen! Do you not see these men still fear you, go in dread of you? Why, then, do you fear them? You are many – "

"For God's sake," cried Montgomery, "stop that, Prendick!"

"Prendick!" cried Moreau.

They both shouted together, as if to drown my voice; and behind them lowered the staring faces of the Beast Men, wondering, their deformed hands hanging down, their shoulders hunched up. They seemed, as I fancied, to be trying to understand me, to remember, I thought, something of their human past.

I went on shouting, I scarcely remember what, – that Moreau and Montgomery could be killed, that they were not to be feared: that was the burden of what I put into the heads of the Beast People. I saw the green-eyed man in the dark rags, who had met me on the evening of my arrival, come out from among the trees, and others followed him, to hear me better. At last for want of breath I paused.

"Listen to me for a moment," said the steady voice of Moreau; "and then say what you will."

"Well?" said I.

He coughed, thought, then shouted: "Latin, Prendick! bad Latin, schoolboy Latin; but try and understand. *Hi non sunt homines; sunt animalia qui nos habemus* – vivisected. A humanising process. I will explain. Come ashore."

I laughed. "A pretty story," said I. "They talk, build houses. They were men. It's likely I'll come ashore."

"The water just beyond where you stand is deep – and full of sharks."

"That's my way," said I. "Short and sharp. Presently."

"Wait a minute." He took something out of his pocket that flashed back the sun, and dropped the object at his feet. "That's a loaded revolver," said he. "Montgomery here will do the same. Now we are going up the beach until you are satisfied the distance is safe. Then come and take the revolvers."

"Not I! You have a third between you."

"I want you to think over things, Prendick. In the first place, I never asked you to come upon this island. If we vivisected men, we should import men, not beasts. In the next, we had you drugged last night, had we wanted to work you any mischief; and in the next, now your first panic is over and you can think a little, is Montgomery here quite up to the character you give him? We have chased you for your good. Because this island is full of inimical phenomena. Besides, why should we want to shoot you when you have just offered to drown yourself?"

"Why did you set – your people onto me when I was in the hut?"

"We felt sure of catching you, and bringing you out of danger. Afterwards we drew away from the scent, for your good."

I mused. It seemed just possible. Then I remembered something again. "But I saw," said I, "in the enclosure – "

"That was the puma."

"Look here, Prendick," said Montgomery, "you're a silly ass! Come out of the water and take these revolvers, and talk. We can't do anything more than we could do now."

I will confess that then, and indeed always, I distrusted and dreaded Moreau; but Montgomery was a man I felt I understood.

"Go up the beach," said I, after thinking, and added, "holding your hands up."

"Can't do that," said Montgomery, with an explanatory nod over his shoulder. "Undignified."

"Go up to the trees, then," said I, "as you please."

"It's a damned silly ceremony," said Montgomery.

Both turned and faced the six or seven grotesque creatures, who stood there in the sunlight, solid, casting shadows, moving, and yet so incredibly unreal. Montgomery cracked his whip at them, and forthwith they all turned and fled helter-skelter into the trees; and when Montgomery and Moreau were at a distance I judged sufficient, I waded ashore, and picked up and examined the revolvers. To satisfy myself against the subtlest trickery, I discharged one at a round lump of lava, and had the satisfaction of seeing the stone pulverised and the beach splashed with lead. Still I hesitated for a moment.

"I'll take the risk," said I, at last; and with a revolver in each hand I walked up the beach towards them.

"That's better," said Moreau, without affectation. "As it is, you have wasted the best part of my day with your confounded imagination." And with a touch of contempt which humiliated me, he and Montgomery turned and went on in silence before me.

The knot of Beast Men, still wondering, stood back among the trees. I passed them as serenely as possible. One started to follow me, but retreated again when Montgomery cracked his whip. The rest stood silent – watching. They may once have been animals; but I never before saw an animal trying to think.

CHAPTER FOURTEEN

Doctor Moreau Explains

"AND NOW, PRENDICK, I will explain," said Doctor Moreau, so soon as we had eaten and drunk. "I must confess that you are the most dictatorial guest I ever entertained. I warn you that this is the last I shall do to oblige you. The next thing you threaten to commit suicide about, I shan't do, – even at some personal inconvenience."

He sat in my deck chair, a cigar half consumed in his white, dexterous-looking fingers. The light of the swinging lamp fell on his white hair; he stared through the little window out at the starlight. I sat as far away from him as possible, the table between us and the revolvers to hand. Montgomery was not present. I did not care to be with the two of them in such a little room.

"You admit that the vivisected human being, as you called it, is, after all, only the puma?" said Moreau. He had made me visit that horror in the inner room, to assure myself of its inhumanity.

"It is the puma," I said, "still alive, but so cut and mutilated as I pray I may never see living flesh again. Of all vile – "

"Never mind that," said Moreau; "at least, spare me those youthful horrors. Montgomery used to be just the same. You admit that it is the puma. Now be quiet, while I reel off my physiological lecture to you."

And forthwith, beginning in the tone of a man supremely bored, but presently warming a little, he explained his work to me. He was very simple and convincing. Now and then there was a touch of sarcasm in his voice. Presently I found myself hot with shame at our mutual positions.

The creatures I had seen were not men, had never been men. They were animals, humanised animals, – triumphs of vivisection.

"You forget all that a skilled vivisector can do with living things," said Moreau. "For my own part, I'm puzzled why the things I have done here have not been done before. Small efforts, of course, have been made, – amputation, tongue-cutting, excisions. Of course you know a squint may be induced or cured by surgery? Then in the case of excisions you have all kinds of secondary changes, pigmentary disturbances, modifications of the passions, alterations in the secretion of fatty tissue. I have no doubt you have heard of these things?"

"Of course," said I. "But these foul creatures of yours – "

"All in good time," said he, waving his hand at me; "I am only beginning. Those are trivial cases of alteration. Surgery can do better things than that. There is building up as well as breaking down and changing. You have heard, perhaps, of a common surgical operation resorted to in cases where the nose has been destroyed: a flap of skin is cut from the forehead, turned down on the nose, and heals in the new position. This is a kind of grafting in a new position of part of an animal upon itself. Grafting of freshly obtained material from another animal is also possible, – the case of teeth, for example. The grafting of skin and bone is done to facilitate healing: the surgeon places in the middle of the wound pieces of skin snipped from another animal, or fragments of bone from a victim freshly killed. Hunter's cock-spur – possibly you have heard of that – flourished on the bull's neck; and the rhinoceros rats of the Algerian zouaves are also to be thought of, – monsters manufactured by transferring a slip from the tail of an ordinary rat to its snout, and allowing it to heal in that position."

"Monsters manufactured!" said I. "Then you mean to tell me – "

"Yes. These creatures you have seen are animals carven and wrought into new shapes. To that, to the study of the plasticity of living forms, my life has been devoted. I have studied for years, gaining in knowledge as I go. I see you look horrified, and yet I am telling you nothing new. It all lay in the surface of practical anatomy years ago, but no one had the temerity to touch it. It is not simply the outward form of an animal which I can change. The physiology, the chemical rhythm of the creature, may also be made to undergo an enduring modification, – of which vaccination and other methods of inoculation with living or dead matter are examples that will, no doubt, be familiar to you. A similar operation is the transfusion of blood, – with which subject, indeed, I began. These are all familiar cases. Less so, and probably far more extensive, were the operations of those mediaeval practitioners who made dwarfs and beggar-cripples, show-monsters, – some vestiges of whose art still remain in the preliminary manipulation of the young mountebank or contortionist. Victor Hugo gives an account of them in 'L'Homme qui Rit.' – But perhaps my meaning grows plain now. You begin to see that it is a possible thing to transplant tissue from one part of an animal to another, or from one animal to another; to alter its chemical reactions and methods of growth; to modify the articulations of its limbs; and, indeed, to change it in its most intimate structure.

"And yet this extraordinary branch of knowledge has never been sought as an end, and systematically, by modern investigators until I took it up! Some such things have been hit upon in the last resort of surgery; most of the kindred evidence that will recur to your mind has been demonstrated as it were by accident, – by tyrants, by criminals, by the breeders of horses and dogs, by all kinds of untrained clumsy-handed men working for their own immediate ends. I was the first man to take up this question armed with antiseptic surgery, and with a really scientific knowledge of the laws of growth. Yet one would imagine it must have been practised in secret before. Such creatures as the Siamese Twins – And in the vaults of the Inquisition. No doubt their chief aim was artistic torture, but some at least of the inquisitors must have had a touch of scientific curiosity."

"But," said I, "these things – these animals talk!"

He said that was so, and proceeded to point out that the possibility of vivisection does not stop at a mere physical metamorphosis. A pig may be educated. The mental structure is even less determinate than the bodily. In our growing science of hypnotism we find the promise of a possibility of superseding old inherent instincts by new suggestions, grafting upon or replacing the inherited fixed ideas. Very much indeed of what we call moral education, he said, is such an artificial modification and perversion of instinct; pugnacity is trained into courageous self-sacrifice, and suppressed sexuality into religious emotion. And the great difference between man and monkey is in the larynx, he continued, – in the incapacity to frame delicately different sound-symbols by which thought could be sustained. In this I failed to agree with him, but with a certain incivility he declined to notice my objection. He repeated that the thing was so, and continued his account of his work.

I asked him why he had taken the human form as a model. There seemed to me then, and there still seems to me now, a strange wickedness for that choice.

He confessed that he had chosen that form by chance. "I might just as well have worked to form sheep into llamas and llamas into sheep. I suppose there is something in the human form that appeals to the artistic turn of mind more powerfully than any animal shape can. But I've not confined myself to man-making. Once or twice – " He was silent, for a minute perhaps. "These years! How they have slipped by! And here I have wasted a day saving your life, and am now wasting an hour explaining myself!"

"But," said I, "I still do not understand. Where is your justification for inflicting all this pain? The only thing that could excuse vivisection to me would be some application – "

"Precisely," said he. "But, you see, I am differently constituted. We are on different platforms. You are a materialist."

"*I am not* a materialist," I began hotly.

"In my view – in my view. For it is just this question of pain that parts us. So long as visible or audible pain turns you sick; so long as your own pains drive you; so long as pain underlies your propositions about sin, – so long, I tell you, you are an animal, thinking a little less obscurely what an animal feels. This pain – "

I gave an impatient shrug at such sophistry.

"Oh, but it is such a little thing! A mind truly opened to what science has to teach must see that it is a little thing. It may be that save in this little planet, this speck of cosmic dust, invisible long before the nearest star could be attained – it may be, I say, that nowhere else does this thing called pain occur. But the laws we feel our way towards – Why, even on this earth, even among living things, what pain is there?"

As he spoke he drew a little penknife from his pocket, opened the smaller blade, and moved his chair so that I could see his thigh. Then, choosing the place deliberately, he drove the blade into his leg and withdrew it.

"No doubt," he said, "you have seen that before. It does not hurt a pinprick. But what does it show? The capacity for pain is not needed in the muscle, and it is not placed there, – is but little needed in the skin, and only here and there over the thigh is a spot capable of feeling pain. Pain is simply our intrinsic medical adviser to warn us and stimulate us. Not all living flesh is painful; nor is all nerve, not even all sensory nerve. There's no taint of pain, real pain, in the sensations of the optic nerve. If you wound the optic nerve, you merely see flashes of light, – just as disease of the auditory nerve merely means a humming in our ears. Plants do not feel pain, nor the lower animals; it's possible that such animals as the starfish and crayfish do not feel pain at all. Then with men, the more intelligent they become, the more intelligently they will see after their own welfare, and the less they will need the goad to keep them out of danger. I never yet heard of a useless thing that was not ground out of existence by evolution sooner or later. Did you? And pain gets needless.

"Then I am a religious man, Prendick, as every sane man must be. It may be, I fancy, that I have seen more of the ways of this world's Maker than you, – for I have sought his laws, in *my* way, all my life, while you, I understand, have been collecting butterflies. And I tell you, pleasure and pain have nothing to do with heaven or hell. Pleasure and pain – bah! What is your theologian's ecstasy but Mahomet's houri in the dark? This store which men and women set on pleasure and pain, Prendick, is the mark of the beast upon them, – the mark of the beast from which they came! Pain, pain and pleasure, they are for us only so long as we wriggle in the dust.

"You see, I went on with this research just the way it led me. That is the only way I ever heard of true research going. I asked a question, devised some method of obtaining an answer, and got a fresh question. Was this possible or that possible? You cannot imagine what this means to an investigator, what an intellectual passion grows upon him! You cannot imagine the strange, colourless delight of these intellectual desires! The thing before you is no longer an animal, a fellow-creature, but a problem! Sympathetic pain, – all I know of it I remember as a thing I used to suffer from years ago. I wanted – it was the one thing I wanted – to find out the extreme limit of plasticity in a living shape."

"But," said I, "the thing is an abomination – "

"To this day I have never troubled about the ethics of the matter," he continued. "The study of Nature makes a man at last as remorseless as Nature. I have gone on, not heeding anything but the question I was pursuing; and the material has – dripped into the huts yonder. It is nearly eleven years since we came here, I and Montgomery and six Kanakas. I remember the green stillness of the island and the empty ocean about us, as though it was yesterday. The place seemed waiting for me.

"The stores were landed and the house was built. The Kanakas founded some huts near the ravine. I went to work here upon what I had brought with me. There were some disagreeable things happened at first. I began with a sheep, and killed it after a day and a half by a slip of the scalpel. I took another sheep, and made a thing of pain and fear and left it bound up to heal. It looked quite human to me when I had finished it; but when I went to it I was discontented with it. It remembered me, and was terrified beyond imagination; and it had no more than the wits of a sheep. The more I looked at it the clumsier it seemed, until at last I put the monster out of its misery. These animals without courage, these fear-haunted, pain-driven things, without a spark of pugnacious energy to face torment, – they are no good for man-making.

"Then I took a gorilla I had; and upon that, working with infinite care and mastering difficulty after difficulty, I made my first man. All the week, night and day, I moulded him. With him it was chiefly the brain that needed moulding; much had to be added, much changed. I thought him a fair specimen of the negroid type when I had finished him, and he lay bandaged, bound, and motionless before me. It was only when his life was assured that I left him and came into this room again, and found Montgomery much as you are. He had heard some of the cries as the thing grew human, – cries like those that disturbed *you* so. I didn't take him completely into my confidence at first. And the Kanakas too, had realised something of it. They were scared out of their wits by the sight of me. I got Montgomery over to me – in a way; but I and he had the hardest job to prevent the Kanakas deserting. Finally they did; and so we lost the yacht. I spent many days educating the brute, – altogether I had him for three or four months. I taught him the rudiments of English; gave him ideas of counting; even made the thing read the alphabet. But at that he was slow, though I've met with idiots slower. He began with a clean sheet, mentally; had no memories left in his mind of what he had been. When his scars were quite healed, and he was no longer anything but painful and stiff, and able to converse a little, I took him yonder and introduced him to the Kanakas as an interesting stowaway.

"They were horribly afraid of him at first, somehow, – which offended me rather, for I was conceited about him; but his ways seemed so mild, and he was so abject, that after a time they received him and took his education in hand. He was quick to learn, very imitative and adaptive, and built himself a hovel rather better, it seemed to me, than their own shanties. There was one among the boys a bit of a missionary, and he taught the thing to read, or at least to pick out letters, and gave him some rudimentary ideas of morality; but it seems the beast's habits were not all that is desirable.

"I rested from work for some days after this, and was in a mind to write an account of the whole affair to wake up English physiology. Then I came upon the creature squatting up in a tree and gibbering at two of the Kanakas who had been teasing him. I threatened him, told him the inhumanity of such a proceeding, aroused his sense of shame, and came home resolved to do better before I took my work back to England. I have been doing better. But somehow the things drift back again: the stubborn beast-flesh grows day by day back again. But I mean to do better things still. I mean to conquer that. This puma –

"But that's the story. All the Kanaka boys are dead now; one fell overboard of the launch, and one died of a wounded heel that he poisoned in some way with plant-juice. Three went away in the yacht, and I suppose and hope were drowned. The other one – was killed. Well, I have replaced them. Montgomery went on much as you are disposed to do at first, and then –

"What became of the other one?" said I, sharply, – "the other Kanaka who was killed?"

"The fact is, after I had made a number of human creatures I made a Thing – " He hesitated.

"Yes?" said I.

"It was killed."

"I don't understand," said I; "do you mean to say – "

"It killed the Kanaka – yes. It killed several other things that it caught. We chased it for a couple of days. It only got loose by accident – I never meant it to get away. It wasn't finished. It was purely an experiment. It was a limbless thing, with a horrible face, that writhed along the ground in a serpentine fashion. It was immensely strong, and in infuriating pain. It lurked in the woods for some days, until we hunted it; and then it wriggled into the northern part of the island, and we divided the party to close in upon it. Montgomery insisted upon coming with me. The man had a rifle; and when his body was found, one of the barrels was curved into the shape of an S and very nearly bitten through. Montgomery shot the thing. After that I stuck to the ideal of humanity – except for little things."

He became silent. I sat in silence watching his face.

"So for twenty years altogether – counting nine years in England – I have been going on; and there is still something in everything I do that defeats me, makes me dissatisfied, challenges me to further effort. Sometimes I rise above my level, sometimes I fall below it; but always I fall short of the things I dream. The human shape I can get now, almost with ease, so that it is lithe and graceful, or thick and strong; but often there is trouble with the hands and the claws, – painful things, that I dare not shape too freely. But it is in the subtle grafting and reshaping one must needs do to the brain that my trouble lies. The intelligence is often oddly low, with unaccountable blank ends, unexpected gaps. And least satisfactory of all is something that I cannot touch, somewhere – I cannot determine where – in the seat of the emotions. Cravings, instincts, desires that harm humanity, a strange hidden reservoir to burst forth suddenly and inundate the whole being of the creature with anger, hate, or fear. These creatures of mine seemed strange and uncanny to you so soon as you began to observe them; but to me, just after I make them, they seem to be indisputably human beings. It's afterwards, as I observe them, that the persuasion fades. First one animal trait, then another, creeps to the surface and stares out at me. But I will conquer yet! Each time I dip a living creature into the bath of burning pain, I say, 'This time I will burn out all the animal; this time I will make a rational creature of my own!' After all, what is ten years? Men have been a hundred thousand in the making." He thought darkly. "But I am drawing near the fastness. This puma of mine – " After a silence, "And they revert. As soon as my hand is taken from them the beast begins to creep back, begins to assert itself again." Another long silence.

"Then you take the things you make into those dens?" said I.

"They go. I turn them out when I begin to feel the beast in them, and presently they wander there. They all dread this house and me. There is a kind of travesty of humanity over there. Montgomery knows about it, for he interferes in their affairs. He has trained one or two of them to our service. He's ashamed of it, but I believe he half likes some of those beasts. It's his business, not mine. They only sicken me with a sense of failure. I take no interest in them. I fancy they follow in the lines the Kanaka missionary marked out, and have a kind of mockery of a rational life, poor beasts! There's something they call the Law. Sing hymns about 'all thine.' They build themselves their dens, gather fruit, and pull herbs – marry even. But I can see through it all, see into their very souls, and see there nothing but the souls of beasts, beasts that perish, anger and the lusts to live and gratify themselves. – Yet they're odd; complex, like everything else alive. There is a kind of upward striving in them, part vanity, part waste sexual emotion, part waste curiosity. It only mocks me. I have some hope of this puma. I have worked hard at her head and brain –

"And now," said he, standing up after a long gap of silence, during which we had each pursued our own thoughts, "what do you think? Are you in fear of me still?"

I looked at him, and saw but a white-faced, white-haired man, with calm eyes. Save for his serenity, the touch almost of beauty that resulted from his set tranquillity and his magnificent build, he might have passed muster among a hundred other comfortable old gentlemen. Then I shivered. By way of answer to his second question, I handed him a revolver with either hand.

"Keep them," he said, and snatched at a yawn. He stood up, stared at me for a moment, and smiled. "You have had two eventful days," said he. "I should advise some sleep. I'm glad it's all clear. Good-night." He thought me over for a moment, then went out by the inner door.

I immediately turned the key in the outer one. I sat down again; sat for a time in a kind of stagnant mood, so weary, emotionally, mentally, and physically, that I could not think beyond the point at which he had left me. The black window stared at me like an eye. At last with an effort I put out the light and got into the hammock. Very soon I was asleep.

CHAPTER FIFTEEN

Concerning the Beast Folk

I WOKE EARLY. Moreau's explanation stood before my mind, clear and definite, from the moment of my awakening. I got out of the hammock and went to the door to assure myself that the key was turned. Then I tried the window-bar, and found it firmly fixed. That these man-like creatures were in truth only bestial monsters, mere grotesque travesties of men, filled me with a vague uncertainty of their possibilities which was far worse than any definite fear.

A tapping came at the door, and I heard the glutinous accents of M'ling speaking. I pocketed one of the revolvers (keeping one hand upon it), and opened to him.

"Good-morning, sair," he said, bringing in, in addition to the customary herb-breakfast, an ill-cooked rabbit. Montgomery followed him. His roving eye caught the position of my arm and he smiled askew.

The puma was resting to heal that day; but Moreau, who was singularly solitary in his habits, did not join us. I talked with Montgomery to clear my ideas of the way in which the Beast Folk lived. In particular, I was urgent to know how these inhuman monsters were kept from falling upon Moreau and Montgomery and from rending one another. He explained to me that the comparative safety of Moreau and himself was due to the limited mental scope of these monsters. In spite of their increased intelligence and the tendency of their animal instincts to reawaken, they had certain fixed ideas implanted by Moreau in their minds, which absolutely bounded their imaginations. They were really hypnotised; had been told that certain things were impossible, and that certain things were not to be done, and these prohibitions were woven into the texture of their minds beyond any possibility of disobedience or dispute.

Certain matters, however, in which old instinct was at war with Moreau's convenience, were in a less stable condition. A series of propositions called the Law (I had already heard them recited) battled in their minds with the deep-seated, ever-rebellious cravings of their animal natures. This Law they were ever repeating, I found, and ever breaking. Both Montgomery and Moreau displayed particular solicitude to keep them ignorant of the taste of blood; they feared the inevitable suggestions of that flavour. Montgomery told me that the Law, especially among the feline Beast People, became oddly weakened about nightfall; that then the animal was at its strongest; that a spirit of adventure sprang up in them at the dusk, when they would dare things they never seemed to dream about by day. To that I owed my stalking by the Leopard-man, on the night of my arrival. But during these earlier days of my stay they broke the Law only furtively and after dark; in the daylight there was a general atmosphere of respect for its multifarious prohibitions.

And here perhaps I may give a few general facts about the island and the Beast People. The island, which was of irregular outline and lay low upon the wide sea, had a total area, I suppose, of seven or eight square miles.{2}[2] It was volcanic in origin, and was now fringed on three sides by coral reefs; some fumaroles to the northward, and a hot spring, were the only vestiges of the forces that had long since originated it. Now and then a faint quiver of earthquake would be sensible, and sometimes the ascent of the spire of smoke would be rendered tumultuous by gusts of steam; but that was all. The population of the island, Montgomery informed me, now numbered rather more than sixty of these strange creations of Moreau's art, not counting the smaller monstrosities which lived in the undergrowth and were without human form. Altogether he had made nearly a hundred and twenty; but many had died, and others – like the writhing Footless Thing of which he had told me – had come by violent ends. In answer to my question, Montgomery said that they actually bore offspring, but that these generally died. When they lived, Moreau took them and stamped the human form upon them. There was no evidence of the inheritance of their acquired human characteristics. The females were less numerous than the males, and liable to much furtive persecution in spite of the monogamy the Law enjoined.

It would be impossible for me to describe these Beast People in detail; my eye has had no training in details, and unhappily I cannot sketch. Most striking, perhaps, in their general appearance was the

2 This description corresponds in every respect to Noble's Isle. – C. E. P.

disproportion between the legs of these creatures and the length of their bodies; and yet – so relative is our idea of grace – my eye became habituated to their forms, and at last I even fell in with their persuasion that my own long thighs were ungainly. Another point was the forward carriage of the head and the clumsy and inhuman curvature of the spine. Even the Ape-man lacked that inward sinuous curve of the back which makes the human figure so graceful. Most had their shoulders hunched clumsily, and their short forearms hung weakly at their sides. Few of them were conspicuously hairy, at least until the end of my time upon the island.

The next most obvious deformity was in their faces, almost all of which were prognathous, malformed about the ears, with large and protuberant noses, very furry or very bristly hair, and often strangely-coloured or strangely-placed eyes. None could laugh, though the Ape-man had a chattering titter. Beyond these general characters their heads had little in common; each preserved the quality of its particular species: the human mark distorted but did not hide the leopard, the ox, or the sow, or other animal or animals, from which the creature had been moulded. The voices, too, varied exceedingly. The hands were always malformed; and though some surprised me by their unexpected human appearance, almost all were deficient in the number of the digits, clumsy about the finger-nails, and lacking any tactile sensibility.

The two most formidable Animal Men were my Leopard-man and a creature made of hyena and swine. Larger than these were the three bull-creatures who pulled in the boat. Then came the silvery-hairy-man, who was also the Sayer of the Law, M'ling, and a satyr-like creature of ape and goat. There were three Swine-men and a Swine-woman, a mare-rhinoceros-creature, and several other females whose sources I did not ascertain. There were several wolf-creatures, a bear-bull, and a Saint-Bernard-man. I have already described the Ape-man, and there was a particularly hateful (and evil-smelling) old woman made of vixen and bear, whom I hated from the beginning. She was said to be a passionate votary of the Law. Smaller creatures were certain dappled youths and my little sloth-creature. But enough of this catalogue.

At first I had a shivering horror of the brutes, felt all too keenly that they were still brutes; but insensibly I became a little habituated to the idea of them, and moreover I was affected by Montgomery's attitude towards them. He had been with them so long that he had come to regard them as almost normal human beings. His London days seemed a glorious, impossible past to him. Only once in a year or so did he go to Arica to deal with Moreau's agent, a trader in animals there. He hardly met the finest type of mankind in that seafaring village of Spanish mongrels. The men aboard-ship, he told me, seemed at first just as strange to him as the Beast Men seemed to me, – unnaturally long in the leg, flat in the face, prominent in the forehead, suspicious, dangerous, and cold-hearted. In fact, he did not like men: his heart had warmed to me, he thought, because he had saved my life. I fancied even then that he had a sneaking kindness for some of these metamorphosed brutes, a vicious sympathy with some of their ways, but that he attempted to veil it from me at first.

M'ling, the black-faced man, Montgomery's attendant, the first of the Beast Folk I had encountered, did not live with the others across the island, but in a small kennel at the back of the enclosure. The creature was scarcely so intelligent as the Ape-man, but far more docile, and the most human-looking of all the Beast Folk; and Montgomery had trained it to prepare food, and indeed to discharge all the trivial domestic offices that were required. It was a complex trophy of Moreau's horrible skill, – a bear, tainted with dog and ox, and one of the most elaborately made of all his creatures. It treated Montgomery with a strange tenderness and devotion. Sometimes he would notice it, pat it, call it half-mocking, half-jocular names, and so make it caper with extraordinary delight; sometimes he would ill-treat it, especially after he had been at the whiskey, kicking it, beating it, pelting it with stones or lighted fusees. But whether he treated it well or ill, it loved nothing so much as to be near him.

I say I became habituated to the Beast People, that a thousand things which had seemed unnatural and repulsive speedily became natural and ordinary to me. I suppose everything in existence takes its colour from the average hue of our surroundings. Montgomery and Moreau were too peculiar and individual to keep my general impressions of humanity well defined. I would see one of the clumsy bovine-creatures who worked the launch treading heavily through the undergrowth, and find myself asking, trying hard to recall, how he differed from some really human yokel trudging home from his mechanical labours; or I would meet the Fox-bear woman's vulpine, shifty face, strangely human in its speculative cunning, and even imagine I had met it before in some city byway.

Yet every now and then the beast would flash out upon me beyond doubt or denial. An ugly-looking man, a hunch-backed human savage to all appearance, squatting in the aperture of one of the dens, would stretch his arms and yawn, showing with startling suddenness scissor-edged incisors and sabre-like canines, keen and brilliant as knives. Or in some narrow pathway, glancing with a transitory daring into the eyes of some lithe, white-swathed female figure, I would suddenly see (with a spasmodic revulsion) that she had slit-like pupils, or glancing down note the curving nail with which she held her shapeless wrap about her. It is a curious thing, by the bye, for which I am quite unable to account, that these weird creatures – the females, I mean – had in the earlier days of my stay an instinctive sense of their own repulsive clumsiness, and displayed in consequence a more than human regard for the decency and decorum of extensive costume.

CHAPTER SIXTEEN

How the Beast Folk Taste Blood

MY INEXPERIENCE as a writer betrays me, and I wander from the thread of my story.

After I had breakfasted with Montgomery, he took me across the island to see the fumarole and the source of the hot spring into whose scalding waters I had blundered on the previous day. Both of us carried whips and loaded revolvers. While going through a leafy jungle on our road thither, we heard a rabbit squealing. We stopped and listened, but we heard no more; and presently we went on our way, and the incident dropped out of our minds. Montgomery called my attention to certain little pink animals with long hind-legs, that went leaping through the undergrowth. He told me they were creatures made of the offspring of the Beast People, that Moreau had invented. He had fancied they might serve for meat, but a rabbit-like habit of devouring their young had defeated this intention. I had already encountered some of these creatures, – once during my moonlight flight from the Leopard-man, and once during my pursuit by Moreau on the previous day. By chance, one hopping to avoid us leapt into the hole caused by the uprooting of a wind-blown tree; before it could extricate itself we managed to catch it. It spat like a cat, scratched and kicked vigorously with its hind-legs, and made an attempt to bite; but its teeth were too feeble to inflict more than a painless pinch. It seemed to me rather a pretty little creature; and as Montgomery stated that it never destroyed the turf by burrowing, and was very cleanly in its habits, I should imagine it might prove a convenient substitute for the common rabbit in gentlemen's parks.

We also saw on our way the trunk of a tree barked in long strips and splintered deeply. Montgomery called my attention to this. "Not to claw bark of trees, *that* is the Law," he said. "Much some of them care for it!" It was after this, I think, that we met the Satyr and the Ape-man. The

Satyr was a gleam of classical memory on the part of Moreau, – his face ovine in expression, like the coarser Hebrew type; his voice a harsh bleat, his nether extremities Satanic. He was gnawing the husk of a pod-like fruit as he passed us. Both of them saluted Montgomery.

"Hail," said they, "to the Other with the Whip!"

"There's a Third with a Whip now," said Montgomery. "So you'd better mind!"

"Was he not made?" said the Ape-man. "He said – he said he was made."

The Satyr-man looked curiously at me. "The Third with the Whip, he that walks weeping into the sea, has a thin white face."

"He has a thin long whip," said Montgomery.

"Yesterday he bled and wept," said the Satyr. "You never bleed nor weep. The Master does not bleed or weep."

"Ollendorffian beggar!" said Montgomery, "you'll bleed and weep if you don't look out!"

"He has five fingers, he is a five-man like me," said the Ape-man.

"Come along, Prendick," said Montgomery, taking my arm; and I went on with him.

The Satyr and the Ape-man stood watching us and making other remarks to each other.

"He says nothing," said the Satyr. "Men have voices."

"Yesterday he asked me of things to eat," said the Ape-man. "He did not know."

Then they spoke inaudible things, and I heard the Satyr laughing.

It was on our way back that we came upon the dead rabbit. The red body of the wretched little beast was rent to pieces, many of the ribs stripped white, and the backbone indisputably gnawed.

At that Montgomery stopped. "Good God!" said he, stooping down, and picking up some of the crushed vertebrae to examine them more closely. "Good God!" he repeated, "what can this mean?"

"Some carnivore of yours has remembered its old habits," I said after a pause. "This backbone has been bitten through."

He stood staring, with his face white and his lip pulled askew. "I don't like this," he said slowly.

"I saw something of the same kind," said I, "the first day I came here."

"The devil you did! What was it?"

"A rabbit with its head twisted off."

"The day you came here?"

"The day I came here. In the undergrowth at the back of the enclosure, when I went out in the evening. The head was completely wrung off."

He gave a long, low whistle.

"And what is more, I have an idea which of your brutes did the thing. It's only a suspicion, you know. Before I came on the rabbit I saw one of your monsters drinking in the stream."

"Sucking his drink?"

"Yes."

"'Not to suck your drink; that is the Law.' Much the brutes care for the Law, eh? when Moreau's not about!"

"It was the brute who chased me."

"Of course," said Montgomery; "it's just the way with carnivores. After a kill, they drink. It's the taste of blood, you know. – What was the brute like?" he continued. "Would you know him again?" He glanced about us, standing astride over the mess of dead rabbit, his eyes roving among the shadows and screens of greenery, the lurking-places and ambuscades of the forest that bounded us in. "The taste of blood," he said again.

He took out his revolver, examined the cartridges in it and replaced it. Then he began to pull at his dropping lip.

"I think I should know the brute again," I said. "I stunned him. He ought to have a handsome bruise on the forehead of him."

"But then we have to *prove* that he killed the rabbit," said Montgomery. "I wish I'd never brought the things here."

I should have gone on, but he stayed there thinking over the mangled rabbit in a puzzle-headed way. As it was, I went to such a distance that the rabbit's remains were hidden.

"Come on!" I said.

Presently he woke up and came towards me. "You see," he said, almost in a whisper, "they are all supposed to have a fixed idea against eating anything that runs on land. If some brute has by any accident tasted blood – "

We went on some way in silence. "I wonder what can have happened," he said to himself. Then, after a pause again: "I did a foolish thing the other day. That servant of mine – I showed him how to skin and cook a rabbit. It's odd – I saw him licking his hands – It never occurred to me."

Then: "We must put a stop to this. I must tell Moreau."

He could think of nothing else on our homeward journey.

Moreau took the matter even more seriously than Montgomery, and I need scarcely say that I was affected by their evident consternation.

"We must make an example," said Moreau. "I've no doubt in my own mind that the Leopard-man was the sinner. But how can we prove it? I wish, Montgomery, you had kept your taste for meat in hand, and gone without these exciting novelties. We may find ourselves in a mess yet, through it."

"I was a silly ass," said Montgomery. "But the thing's done now; and you said I might have them, you know."

"We must see to the thing at once," said Moreau. "I suppose if anything should turn up, M'ling can take care of himself?"

"I'm not so sure of M'ling," said Montgomery. "I think I ought to know him."

In the afternoon, Moreau, Montgomery, myself, and M'ling went across the island to the huts in the ravine. We three were armed; M'ling carried the little hatchet he used in chopping firewood, and some coils of wire. Moreau had a huge cowherd's horn slung over his shoulder.

"You will see a gathering of the Beast People," said Montgomery. "It is a pretty sight!"

Moreau said not a word on the way, but the expression of his heavy, white-fringed face was grimly set.

We crossed the ravine down which smoked the stream of hot water, and followed the winding pathway through the canebrakes until we reached a wide area covered over with a thick, powdery yellow substance which I believe was sulphur. Above the shoulder of a weedy bank the sea glittered. We came to a kind of shallow natural amphitheatre, and here the four of us halted. Then Moreau sounded the horn, and broke the sleeping stillness of the tropical afternoon. He must have had strong lungs. The hooting note rose and rose amidst its echoes, to at last an ear-penetrating intensity.

"Ah!" said Moreau, letting the curved instrument fall to his side again.

Immediately there was a crashing through the yellow canes, and a sound of voices from the dense green jungle that marked the morass through which I had run on the previous day. Then at three or four points on the edge of the sulphurous area appeared the grotesque forms of the Beast People hurrying towards us. I could not help a creeping horror, as I perceived first one and then another trot out from the trees or reeds and come shambling along over the hot dust. But Moreau and Montgomery stood calmly enough; and, perforce, I stuck beside them.

First to arrive was the Satyr, strangely unreal for all that he cast a shadow and tossed the dust with his hoofs. After him from the brake came a monstrous lout, a thing of horse and rhinoceros, chewing a straw as it came; then appeared the Swine-woman and two Wolf-women; then the Fox-bear witch, with her red eyes in her peaked red face, and then others, – all hurrying eagerly. As they came forward they began to cringe towards Moreau and chant, quite regardless of one another, fragments of the latter half of the litany of the Law, – "His is the Hand that wounds; His is the Hand that heals," and so forth. As soon as they had approached within a distance of perhaps thirty yards they halted, and bowing on knees and elbows began flinging the white dust upon their heads.

Imagine the scene if you can! We three blue-clad men, with our misshapen black-faced attendant, standing in a wide expanse of sunlit yellow dust under the blazing blue sky, and surrounded by this circle of crouching and gesticulating monstrosities, – some almost human save in their subtle expression and gestures, some like cripples, some so strangely distorted as to resemble nothing but the denizens of our wildest dreams; and, beyond, the reedy lines of a canebrake in one direction, a dense tangle of palm-trees on the other, separating us from the ravine with the huts, and to the north the hazy horizon of the Pacific Ocean.

"Sixty-two, sixty-three," counted Moreau. "There are four more."

"I do not see the Leopard-man," said I.

Presently Moreau sounded the great horn again, and at the sound of it all the Beast People writhed and grovelled in the dust. Then, slinking out of the canebrake, stooping near the ground and trying to join the dust-throwing circle behind Moreau's back, came the Leopard-man. The last of the Beast People to arrive was the little Ape-man. The earlier animals, hot and weary with their grovelling, shot vicious glances at him.

"Cease!" said Moreau, in his firm, loud voice; and the Beast People sat back upon their hams and rested from their worshipping.

"Where is the Sayer of the Law?" said Moreau, and the hairy-grey monster bowed his face in the dust.

"Say the words!" said Moreau.

Forthwith all in the kneeling assembly, swaying from side to side and dashing up the sulphur with their hands, – first the right hand and a puff of dust, and then the left, – began once more to chant their strange litany. When they reached, "Not to eat Flesh or Fish, that is the Law," Moreau held up his lank white hand.

"Stop!" he cried, and there fell absolute silence upon them all.

I think they all knew and dreaded what was coming. I looked round at their strange faces. When I saw their wincing attitudes and the furtive dread in their bright eyes, I wondered that I had ever believed them to be men.

"That Law has been broken!" said Moreau.

"None escape," from the faceless creature with the silvery hair. "None escape," repeated the kneeling circle of Beast People.

"Who is he?" cried Moreau, and looked round at their faces, cracking his whip. I fancied the Hyena-swine looked dejected, so too did the Leopard-man. Moreau stopped, facing this creature, who cringed towards him with the memory and dread of infinite torment.

"Who is he?" repeated Moreau, in a voice of thunder.

"Evil is he who breaks the Law," chanted the Sayer of the Law.

Moreau looked into the eyes of the Leopard-man, and seemed to be dragging the very soul out of the creature.

"Who breaks the Law – " said Moreau, taking his eyes off his victim, and turning towards us (it seemed to me there was a touch of exultation in his voice).

"Goes back to the House of Pain," they all clamoured, – "goes back to the House of Pain, O Master!"

"Back to the House of Pain, – back to the House of Pain," gabbled the Ape-man, as though the idea was sweet to him.

"Do you hear?" said Moreau, turning back to the criminal, "my friend – Hullo!"

For the Leopard-man, released from Moreau's eye, had risen straight from his knees, and now, with eyes aflame and his huge feline tusks flashing out from under his curling lips, leapt towards his tormentor. I am convinced that only the madness of unendurable fear could have prompted this attack. The whole circle of threescore monsters seemed to rise about us. I drew my revolver. The two figures collided. I saw Moreau reeling back from the Leopard-man's blow. There was a furious yelling and howling all about us. Every one was moving rapidly. For a moment I thought it was a general revolt. The furious face of the Leopard-man flashed by mine, with M'ling close in pursuit. I saw the yellow eyes of the Hyena-swine blazing with excitement, his attitude as if he were half resolved to attack me. The Satyr, too, glared at me over the Hyena-swine's hunched shoulders. I heard the crack of Moreau's pistol, and saw the pink flash dart across the tumult. The whole crowd seemed to swing round in the direction of the glint of fire, and I too was swung round by the magnetism of the movement. In another second I was running, one of a tumultuous shouting crowd, in pursuit of the escaping Leopard-man.

That is all I can tell definitely. I saw the Leopard-man strike Moreau, and then everything spun about me until I was running headlong. M'ling was ahead, close in pursuit of the fugitive. Behind, their tongues already lolling out, ran the Wolf-women in great leaping strides. The Swine folk followed, squealing with excitement, and the two Bull-men in their swathings of white. Then came Moreau in a cluster of the Beast People, his wide-brimmed straw hat blown off, his revolver in hand, and his lank white hair streaming out. The Hyena-swine ran beside me, keeping pace with me and glancing furtively at me out of his feline eyes, and the others came pattering and shouting behind us.

The Leopard-man went bursting his way through the long canes, which sprang back as he passed, and rattled in M'ling's face. We others in the rear found a trampled path for us when we reached the brake. The chase lay through the brake for perhaps a quarter of a mile, and then plunged into a dense thicket, which retarded our movements exceedingly, though we went through it in a crowd together, – fronds flicking into our faces, ropy creepers catching us under the chin or gripping our ankles, thorny plants hooking into and tearing cloth and flesh together.

"He has gone on all-fours through this," panted Moreau, now just ahead of me.

"None escape," said the Wolf-bear, laughing into my face with the exultation of hunting. We burst out again among rocks, and saw the quarry ahead running lightly on all-fours and snarling at us over his shoulder. At that the Wolf Folk howled with delight. The Thing was still clothed, and at a distance its face still seemed human; but the carriage of its four limbs was feline, and the furtive droop of its shoulder was distinctly that of a hunted animal. It leapt over some thorny yellow-flowering bushes, and was hidden. M'ling was halfway across the space.

Most of us now had lost the first speed of the chase, and had fallen into a longer and steadier stride. I saw as we traversed the open that the pursuit was now spreading from a column into a line. The Hyena-swine still ran close to me, watching me as it ran, every now and then puckering its muzzle with a snarling laugh. At the edge of the rocks the Leopard-man, realising that he was making for the projecting cape upon which he had stalked me on the night of my arrival, had doubled in the undergrowth; but Montgomery had seen the manoeuvre, and turned him again. So, panting, tumbling against rocks, torn by brambles, impeded by ferns and reeds, I helped to pursue the Leopard-man who had broken the Law, and the Hyena-swine ran, laughing savagely, by my side. I staggered on, my head reeling and my heart beating against my ribs, tired almost to death, and yet not daring to lose sight of the chase lest I should be left alone with this horrible companion. I staggered on in spite of infinite fatigue and the dense heat of the tropical afternoon.

At last the fury of the hunt slackened. We had pinned the wretched brute into a corner of the island. Moreau, whip in hand, marshalled us all into an irregular line, and we advanced now slowly, shouting to one another as we advanced and tightening the cordon about our victim. He lurked noiseless and invisible in the bushes through which I had run from him during that midnight pursuit.

"Steady!" cried Moreau, "steady!" as the ends of the line crept round the tangle of undergrowth and hemmed the brute in.

"Ware a rush!" came the voice of Montgomery from beyond the thicket.

I was on the slope above the bushes; Montgomery and Moreau beat along the beach beneath. Slowly we pushed in among the fretted network of branches and leaves. The quarry was silent.

"Back to the House of Pain, the House of Pain, the House of Pain!" yelped the voice of the Ape-man, some twenty yards to the right.

When I heard that, I forgave the poor wretch all the fear he had inspired in me. I heard the twigs snap and the boughs swish aside before the heavy tread of the Horse-rhinoceros upon my right. Then suddenly through a polygon of green, in the half darkness under the luxuriant growth, I saw the creature we were hunting. I halted. He was crouched together into the smallest possible compass, his luminous green eyes turned over his shoulder regarding me.

It may seem a strange contradiction in me, – I cannot explain the fact, – but now, seeing the creature there in a perfectly animal attitude, with the light gleaming in its eyes and its imperfectly human face distorted with terror, I realised again the fact of its humanity. In another moment other of its pursuers would see it, and it would be overpowered and captured, to experience once more the horrible tortures of the enclosure. Abruptly I slipped out my revolver, aimed between its terror-struck eyes, and fired. As I did so, the Hyena-swine saw the Thing, and flung itself upon it with an eager cry, thrusting thirsty teeth into its neck. All about me the green masses of the thicket were swaying and cracking as the Beast People came rushing together. One face and then another appeared.

"Don't kill it, Prendick!" cried Moreau. "Don't kill it!" and I saw him stooping as he pushed through under the fronds of the big ferns.

In another moment he had beaten off the Hyena-swine with the handle of his whip, and he and Montgomery were keeping away the excited carnivorous Beast People, and particularly M'ling, from the still quivering body. The hairy-grey Thing came sniffing at the corpse under my arm. The other animals, in their animal ardour, jostled me to get a nearer view.

"Confound you, Prendick!" said Moreau. "I wanted him."

"I'm sorry," said I, though I was not. "It was the impulse of the moment." I felt sick with exertion and excitement. Turning, I pushed my way out of the crowding Beast People and went on alone up the slope towards the higher part of the headland. Under the shouted directions of Moreau I heard the three white-swathed Bull-men begin dragging the victim down towards the water.

It was easy now for me to be alone. The Beast People manifested a quite human curiosity about the dead body, and followed it in a thick knot, sniffing and growling at it as the Bull-men dragged it down the beach. I went to the headland and watched the bull-men, black against the evening sky as they carried the weighted dead body out to sea; and like a wave across my mind came the realisation of the unspeakable aimlessness of things upon the island. Upon the beach among the rocks beneath me were the Ape-man, the Hyena-swine, and several other of the Beast People, standing about Montgomery and Moreau. They were all still intensely excited, and all overflowing with noisy expressions of their loyalty to the Law; yet I felt an absolute assurance in my own mind that the Hyena-swine was implicated in the rabbit-killing. A strange persuasion came upon me, that, save for the grossness of the line, the grotesqueness of the forms, I had here before me the whole balance of human life in miniature, the whole interplay of instinct, reason, and fate in its simplest form. The Leopard-man had happened to go under: that was all the difference. Poor brute!

Poor brutes! I began to see the viler aspect of Moreau's cruelty. I had not thought before of the pain and trouble that came to these poor victims after they had passed from Moreau's hands. I had shivered only at the days of actual torment in the enclosure. But now that seemed to me the lesser part. Before, they had been beasts, their instincts fitly adapted to their surroundings, and happy as living things may be. Now they stumbled in the shackles of humanity, lived in a fear that never died, fretted by a law they could not understand; their mock-human existence, begun in an agony, was one long internal struggle, one long dread of Moreau – and for what? It was the wantonness of it that stirred me.

Had Moreau had any intelligible object, I could have sympathised at least a little with him. I am not so squeamish about pain as that. I could have forgiven him a little even, had his motive been only hate. But he was so irresponsible, so utterly careless! His curiosity, his mad, aimless investigations, drove him on; and the Things were thrown out to live a year or so, to struggle and blunder and suffer, and at last to die painfully. They were wretched in themselves; the old animal hate moved them to trouble one another; the Law held them back from a brief hot struggle and a decisive end to their natural animosities.

In those days my fear of the Beast People went the way of my personal fear for Moreau. I fell indeed into a morbid state, deep and enduring, and alien to fear, which has left permanent scars upon my mind. I must confess that I lost faith in the sanity of the world when I saw it suffering the painful disorder of this island. A blind Fate, a vast pitiless mechanism, seemed to cut and shape the fabric of existence and I, Moreau (by his passion for research), Montgomery (by his passion for drink), the Beast People with their instincts and mental restrictions, were torn and crushed, ruthlessly, inevitably, amid the infinite complexity of its incessant wheels. But this condition did not come all at once: I think indeed that I anticipate a little in speaking of it now.

CHAPTER SEVENTEEN

A Catastrophe

Scarcely six weeks passed before I had lost every feeling but dislike and abhorrence for this infamous experiment of Moreau's. My one idea was to get away from these horrible caricatures of my Maker's image, back to the sweet and wholesome intercourse of men. My fellow-creatures, from whom I was thus separated, began to assume idyllic virtue and beauty in my memory. My first friendship with Montgomery did not increase. His long separation from humanity, his secret vice of drunkenness, his evident sympathy with the Beast People, tainted him to me. Several times I let him go alone among them. I avoided intercourse with them in every possible way. I spent an increasing proportion of my time upon the beach, looking for some liberating sail that never appeared, – until one day there fell upon us an appalling disaster, which put an altogether different aspect upon my strange surroundings.

It was about seven or eight weeks after my landing, – rather more, I think, though I had not troubled to keep account of the time, – when this catastrophe occurred. It happened in the early morning – I should think about six. I had risen and breakfasted early, having been aroused by the noise of three Beast Men carrying wood into the enclosure.

After breakfast I went to the open gateway of the enclosure, and stood there smoking a cigarette and enjoying the freshness of the early morning. Moreau presently came round the corner of the enclosure and greeted me. He passed by me, and I heard him behind me unlock and enter his laboratory. So indurated was I at that time to the abomination of the place, that I heard without a touch of emotion the puma victim begin another day of torture. It met its persecutor with a shriek, almost exactly like that of an angry virago.

Then suddenly something happened, – I do not know what, to this day. I heard a short, sharp cry behind me, a fall, and turning saw an awful face rushing upon me, – not human, not animal, but hellish, brown, seamed with red branching scars, red drops starting out upon it, and the lidless eyes ablaze. I threw up my arm to defend myself from the blow that flung me headlong with a broken forearm; and the great monster, swathed in lint and with red-stained bandages fluttering about it, leapt over me and passed. I rolled over and over down the beach, tried to sit up, and collapsed upon my broken arm. Then Moreau appeared, his massive white face all the more terrible for the blood that trickled from his forehead. He carried a revolver in one hand. He scarcely glanced at me, but rushed off at once in pursuit of the puma.

I tried the other arm and sat up. The muffled figure in front ran in great striding leaps along the beach, and Moreau followed her. She turned her head and saw him, then doubling abruptly made for the bushes. She gained upon him at every stride. I saw her plunge into them, and Moreau, running slantingly to intercept her, fired and missed as she disappeared. Then he too vanished in the green confusion. I stared after them, and then the pain in my arm flamed up, and with a groan I staggered to my feet. Montgomery appeared in the doorway, dressed, and with his revolver in his hand.

"Great God, Prendick!" he said, not noticing that I was hurt, "that brute's loose! Tore the fetter out of the wall! Have you seen them?" Then sharply, seeing I gripped my arm, "What's the matter?"

"I was standing in the doorway," said I.

He came forward and took my arm. "Blood on the sleeve," said he, and rolled back the flannel. He pocketed his weapon, felt my arm about painfully, and led me inside. "Your arm is broken," he said, and then, "Tell me exactly how it happened – what happened?"

I told him what I had seen; told him in broken sentences, with gasps of pain between them, and very dexterously and swiftly he bound my arm meanwhile. He slung it from my shoulder, stood back and looked at me.

"You'll do," he said. "And now?"

He thought. Then he went out and locked the gates of the enclosure. He was absent some time.

I was chiefly concerned about my arm. The incident seemed merely one more of many horrible things. I sat down in the deck chair, and I must admit swore heartily at the island. The first dull feeling of injury in my arm had already given way to a burning pain when Montgomery reappeared. His face was rather pale, and he showed more of his lower gums than ever.

"I can neither see nor hear anything of him," he said. "I've been thinking he may want my help." He stared at me with his expressionless eyes. "That was a strong brute," he said. "It simply wrenched its fetter out of the wall." He went to the window, then to the door, and there turned to me. "I shall go after him," he said. "There's another revolver I can leave with you. To tell you the truth, I feel anxious somehow."

He obtained the weapon, and put it ready to my hand on the table; then went out, leaving a restless contagion in the air. I did not sit long after he left, but took the revolver in hand and went to the doorway.

The morning was as still as death. Not a whisper of wind was stirring; the sea was like polished glass, the sky empty, the beach desolate. In my half-excited, half-feverish state, this stillness of things oppressed me. I tried to whistle, and the tune died away. I swore again, – the second time that morning. Then I went to the corner of the enclosure and stared inland at the green bush that had swallowed up Moreau and Montgomery. When would they return, and how? Then far away up the beach a little grey Beast Man appeared, ran down to the water's edge and began splashing about. I strolled back to the doorway, then to the corner again, and so began pacing to and fro like a sentinel upon duty. Once I was arrested by the distant voice of Montgomery bawling, "Coo-ee – Moreau!" My arm became less painful, but very hot. I got feverish and thirsty. My shadow grew shorter. I watched the distant figure until it went away again. Would Moreau and Montgomery never return? Three sea-birds began fighting for some stranded treasure.

Then from far away behind the enclosure I heard a pistol-shot. A long silence, and then came another. Then a yelling cry nearer, and another dismal gap of silence. My unfortunate imagination set to work to torment me. Then suddenly a shot close by. I went to the corner, startled, and saw Montgomery, – his face scarlet, his hair disordered, and the knee of his trousers torn. His face expressed profound consternation. Behind him slouched the Beast Man, M'ling, and round M'ling's jaws were some queer dark stains.

"Has he come?" said Montgomery.

"Moreau?" said I. "No."

"My God!" The man was panting, almost sobbing. "Go back in," he said, taking my arm. "They're mad. They're all rushing about mad. What can have happened? I don't know. I'll tell you, when my breath comes. Where's some brandy?"

Montgomery limped before me into the room and sat down in the deck chair. M'ling flung himself down just outside the doorway and began panting like a dog. I got Montgomery some brandy-and-water.

He sat staring in front of him at nothing, recovering his breath. After some minutes he began to tell me what had happened.

He had followed their track for some way. It was plain enough at first on account of the crushed and broken bushes, white rags torn from the puma's bandages, and occasional smears of blood on the leaves of the shrubs and undergrowth. He lost the track, however, on the stony ground beyond the stream where I had seen the Beast Man drinking, and went wandering aimlessly westward shouting Moreau's name. Then M'ling had come to him carrying a light hatchet. M'ling had seen nothing of the puma affair; had been felling wood, and heard him calling. They went on shouting together. Two Beast Men came crouching and peering at them through the undergrowth, with gestures and a furtive carriage that alarmed Montgomery by their strangeness. He hailed them, and they fled guiltily. He stopped shouting after that, and after wandering some time farther in an undecided way, determined to visit the huts.

He found the ravine deserted.

Growing more alarmed every minute, he began to retrace his steps. Then it was he encountered the two Swine-men I had seen dancing on the night of my arrival; blood-stained they were about the mouth, and intensely excited. They came crashing through the ferns, and stopped with fierce faces when they saw him. He cracked his whip in some trepidation, and forthwith they rushed at him. Never before had a Beast Man dared to do that. One he shot through the head; M'ling flung himself upon the other, and the two rolled grappling. M'ling got his brute under and with his teeth in its throat, and Montgomery shot that too as it struggled in M'ling's grip. He had some difficulty in inducing M'ling to come on with him. Thence they had hurried back to me. On the way, M'ling had suddenly rushed into a thicket and driven out an under-sized Ocelot-man, also blood-stained, and lame through a wound in the foot. This brute had run a little way and then turned savagely at bay, and Montgomery – with a certain wantonness, I thought – had shot him.

"What does it all mean?" said I.

He shook his head, and turned once more to the brandy.

CHAPTER EIGHTEEN

The Finding of Moreau

When I saw Montgomery swallow a third dose of brandy, I took it upon myself to interfere. He was already more than half fuddled. I told him that some serious thing must have happened to Moreau by this time, or he would have returned before this, and that it behoved us to ascertain what that catastrophe was. Montgomery raised some feeble objections, and at last agreed. We had some food, and then all three of us started.

It is possibly due to the tension of my mind, at the time, but even now that start into the hot stillness of the tropical afternoon is a singularly vivid impression. M'ling went first, his shoulder hunched, his strange black head moving with quick starts as he peered first on this side of the way and then on that. He was unarmed; his axe he had dropped when he encountered the Swine-man. Teeth were *his* weapons, when it came to fighting. Montgomery followed with stumbling footsteps, his hands in his pockets, his face downcast; he was in a state of muddled sullenness with me on account of the brandy. My left arm was in a sling (it was lucky it was my left), and I carried my revolver in my right. Soon we traced a narrow path through the wild luxuriance of the island, going northwestward; and presently M'ling stopped, and became rigid with watchfulness. Montgomery almost staggered into him, and then stopped too. Then, listening intently, we heard coming through the trees the sound of voices and footsteps approaching us.

"He is dead," said a deep, vibrating voice.

"He is not dead; he is *not* dead," jabbered another.

"We saw, we saw," said several voices.

"Hullo!" suddenly shouted Montgomery, "Hullo, there!"

"Confound you!" said I, and gripped my pistol.

There was a silence, then a crashing among the interlacing vegetation, first here, then there, and then half-a-dozen faces appeared, – strange faces, lit by a strange light. M'ling made a growling noise in his throat. I recognised the Ape-man: I had indeed already identified his voice, and two of the white-swathed brown-featured creatures I had seen in Montgomery's boat. With these were the two dappled brutes and that grey, horribly crooked creature who said the Law, with grey hair streaming down its cheeks, heavy grey eyebrows, and grey locks pouring off from a central parting upon its sloping forehead, – a heavy, faceless thing, with strange red eyes, looking at us curiously from amidst the green.

For a space no one spoke. Then Montgomery hiccoughed, "Who – said he was dead?"

The Monkey-man looked guiltily at the hairy-grey Thing. "He is dead," said this monster. "They saw."

There was nothing threatening about this detachment, at any rate. They seemed awestricken and puzzled.

"Where is he?" said Montgomery.

"Beyond," and the grey creature pointed.

"Is there a Law now?" asked the Monkey-man. "Is it still to be this and that? Is he dead indeed?"

"Is there a Law?" repeated the man in white. "Is there a Law, thou Other with the Whip?"

"He is dead," said the hairy-grey Thing. And they all stood watching us.

"Prendick," said Montgomery, turning his dull eyes to me. "He's dead, evidently."

I had been standing behind him during this colloquy. I began to see how things lay with them. I suddenly stepped in front of Montgomery and lifted up my voice: – "Children of the Law," I said, "he is not dead!" M'ling turned his sharp eyes on me. "He has changed his shape; he has changed his body," I went on. "For a time you will not see him. He is – there," I pointed upward, "where he can watch you. You cannot see him, but he can see you. Fear the Law!"

I looked at them squarely. They flinched.

"He is great, he is good," said the Ape-man, peering fearfully upward among the dense trees.

"And the other Thing?" I demanded.

"The Thing that bled, and ran screaming and sobbing, – that is dead too," said the grey Thing, still regarding me.

"That's well," grunted Montgomery.

"The Other with the Whip – " began the grey Thing.

"Well?" said I.

"Said he was dead."

But Montgomery was still sober enough to understand my motive in denying Moreau's death. "He is not dead," he said slowly, "not dead at all. No more dead than I am."

"Some," said I, "have broken the Law: they will die. Some have died. Show us now where his old body lies, – the body he cast away because he had no more need of it."

"It is this way, Man who walked in the Sea," said the grey Thing.

And with these six creatures guiding us, we went through the tumult of ferns and creepers and tree-stems towards the northwest. Then came a yelling, a crashing among the branches, and a little pink homunculus rushed by us shrieking. Immediately after appeared a monster in headlong pursuit, blood-bedabbled, who was amongst us almost before he could stop his career. The grey Thing leapt aside. M'ling, with a snarl, flew at it, and was struck aside. Montgomery fired and missed, bowed his head, threw up his arm, and turned to run. I fired, and the Thing still came on; fired again, point-blank, into its ugly face. I saw its features vanish in a flash: its face was driven in. Yet it passed me, gripped Montgomery, and holding him, fell headlong beside him and pulled him sprawling upon itself in its death-agony.

I found myself alone with M'ling, the dead brute, and the prostrate man. Montgomery raised himself slowly and stared in a muddled way at the shattered Beast Man beside him. It more than half sobered him. He scrambled to his feet. Then I saw the grey Thing returning cautiously through the trees.

"See," said I, pointing to the dead brute, "is the Law not alive? This came of breaking the Law."

He peered at the body. "He sends the Fire that kills," said he, in his deep voice, repeating part of the Ritual. The others gathered round and stared for a space.

At last we drew near the westward extremity of the island. We came upon the gnawed and mutilated body of the puma, its shoulder-bone smashed by a bullet, and perhaps twenty yards farther found at last what we sought. Moreau lay face downward in a trampled space in a canebrake. One hand was almost severed at the wrist and his silvery hair was dabbled in blood. His head had been battered in by the fetters of the puma. The broken canes beneath him were smeared with blood. His revolver we could not find. Montgomery turned him over. Resting at intervals, and with the help of the seven Beast People (for he was a heavy man), we carried Moreau back to the enclosure. The night was darkling. Twice we heard unseen creatures howling and shrieking past our little band, and once the little pink sloth-creature appeared and stared at us, and vanished again. But we were not attacked again. At the gates of the enclosure our company of Beast People left us, M'ling going with the rest. We locked ourselves in, and then took Moreau's mangled body into the yard and laid it upon a pile of brushwood. Then we went into the laboratory and put an end to all we found living there.

CHAPTER NINETEEN

Montgomery's "Bank Holiday"

When this was accomplished, and we had washed and eaten, Montgomery and I went into my little room and seriously discussed our position for the first time. It was then near midnight. He was almost sober, but greatly disturbed in his mind. He had been strangely under the influence of Moreau's personality: I do not think it had ever occurred to him that Moreau could die. This disaster was the sudden collapse of the habits that had become part of his nature in the ten or more monotonous years he had spent on the island. He talked vaguely, answered my questions crookedly, wandered into general questions.

"This silly ass of a world," he said; "what a muddle it all is! I haven't had any life. I wonder when it's going to begin. Sixteen years being bullied by nurses and schoolmasters at their own sweet will; five in London grinding hard at medicine, bad food, shabby lodgings, shabby clothes, shabby vice, a blunder, – I didn't know any better, – and hustled off to this beastly island. Ten years here! What's it all for, Prendick? Are we bubbles blown by a baby?"

It was hard to deal with such ravings. "The thing we have to think of now," said I, "is how to get away from this island."

"What's the good of getting away? I'm an outcast. Where am *I* to join on? It's all very well for *you*, Prendick. Poor old Moreau! We can't leave him here to have his bones picked. As it is – And besides, what will become of the decent part of the Beast Folk?"

"Well," said I, "that will do to-morrow. I've been thinking we might make the brushwood into a pyre and burn his body – and those other things. Then what will happen with the Beast Folk?"

"*I* don't know. I suppose those that were made of beasts of prey will make silly asses of themselves sooner or later. We can't massacre the lot – can we? I suppose that's what *your* humanity would suggest? But they'll change. They are sure to change."

He talked thus inconclusively until at last I felt my temper going.

"Damnation!" he exclaimed at some petulance of mine; "can't you see I'm in a worse hole than you are?" And he got up, and went for the brandy. "Drink!" he said returning, "you logic-chopping, chalky-faced saint of an atheist, drink!"

"Not I," said I, and sat grimly watching his face under the yellow paraffine flare, as he drank himself into a garrulous misery.

I have a memory of infinite tedium. He wandered into a maudlin defence of the Beast People and of M'ling. M'ling, he said, was the only thing that had ever really cared for him. And suddenly an idea came to him.

"I'm damned!" said he, staggering to his feet and clutching the brandy bottle.

By some flash of intuition I knew what it was he intended. "You don't give drink to that beast!" I said, rising and facing him.

"Beast!" said he. "You're the beast. He takes his liquor like a Christian. Come out of the way, Prendick!"

"For God's sake," said I.

"Get – out of the way!" he roared, and suddenly whipped out his revolver.

"Very well," said I, and stood aside, half-minded to fall upon him as he put his hand upon the latch, but deterred by the thought of my useless arm. "You've made a beast of yourself, – to the beasts you may go."

He flung the doorway open, and stood half facing me between the yellow lamp-light and the pallid glare of the moon; his eye-sockets were blotches of black under his stubbly eyebrows.

"You're a solemn prig, Prendick, a silly ass! You're always fearing and fancying. We're on the edge of things. I'm bound to cut my throat to-morrow. I'm going to have a damned Bank Holiday to-night." He turned and went out into the moonlight. "M'ling!" he cried; "M'ling, old friend!"

Three dim creatures in the silvery light came along the edge of the wan beach, – one a white-wrapped creature, the other two blotches of blackness following it. They halted, staring. Then I saw M'ling's hunched shoulders as he came round the corner of the house.

"Drink!" cried Montgomery, "drink, you brutes! Drink and be men! Damme, I'm the cleverest. Moreau forgot this; this is the last touch. Drink, I tell you!" And waving the bottle in his hand he started off at a kind of quick trot to the westward, M'ling ranging himself between him and the three dim creatures who followed.

I went to the doorway. They were already indistinct in the mist of the moonlight before Montgomery halted. I saw him administer a dose of the raw brandy to M'ling, and saw the five figures melt into one vague patch.

"Sing!" I heard Montgomery shout, – "sing all together, 'Confound old Prendick!' That's right; now again, 'Confound old Prendick!'"

The black group broke up into five separate figures, and wound slowly away from me along the band of shining beach. Each went howling at his own sweet will, yelping insults at me, or giving whatever other vent this new inspiration of brandy demanded. Presently I heard Montgomery's voice shouting, "Right turn!" and they passed with their shouts and howls into the blackness of the landward trees. Slowly, very slowly, they receded into silence.

The peaceful splendour of the night healed again. The moon was now past the meridian and travelling down the west. It was at its full, and very bright riding through the empty blue sky. The shadow of the wall lay, a yard wide and of inky blackness, at my feet. The eastward sea was a featureless grey, dark and mysterious; and between the sea and the shadow the grey sands (of volcanic glass and crystals) flashed and shone like a beach of diamonds. Behind me the paraffine lamp flared hot and ruddy.

Then I shut the door, locked it, and went into the enclosure where Moreau lay beside his latest victims, – the staghounds and the llama and some other wretched brutes, – with his massive face calm even after his terrible death, and with the hard eyes open, staring at the dead white moon above. I sat down upon the edge of the sink, and with my eyes upon that ghastly pile of silvery light and ominous shadows began to turn over my plans. In the morning I would gather some provisions in the dingey, and after setting fire to the pyre before me, push out into the desolation of the high sea once more. I felt that for Montgomery there was no help; that he was, in truth, half akin to these Beast Folk, unfitted for human kindred.

I do not know how long I sat there scheming. It must have been an hour or so. Then my planning was interrupted by the return of Montgomery to my neighbourhood. I heard a yelling from many throats, a tumult of exultant cries passing down towards the beach, whooping and howling, and excited shrieks that seemed to come to a stop near the water's edge. The riot rose and fell; I heard heavy blows and the splintering smash of wood, but it did not trouble me then. A discordant chanting began.

My thoughts went back to my means of escape. I got up, brought the lamp, and went into a shed to look at some kegs I had seen there.

Then I became interested in the contents of some biscuit-tins, and opened one. I saw something out of the tail of my eye, – a red figure, – and turned sharply.

Behind me lay the yard, vividly black-and-white in the moonlight, and the pile of wood and faggots on which Moreau and his mutilated victims lay, one over another. They seemed to be gripping one another in one last revengeful grapple. His wounds gaped, black as night, and the blood that had dripped lay in black patches upon the sand. Then I saw, without understanding, the cause of my phantom, – a ruddy glow that came and danced and went upon the wall opposite. I misinterpreted this, fancied it was a reflection of my flickering lamp, and turned again to the stores in the shed. I went on rummaging among them, as well as a one-armed man could, finding this convenient thing and that, and putting them aside for to-morrow's launch. My movements were slow, and the time passed quickly. Insensibly the daylight crept upon me.

The chanting died down, giving place to a clamour; then it began again, and suddenly broke into a tumult. I heard cries of, "More! more!" a sound like quarrelling, and a sudden wild shriek. The quality of the sounds changed so greatly that it arrested my attention. I went out into the yard and listened. Then cutting like a knife across the confusion came the crack of a revolver.

I rushed at once through my room to the little doorway. As I did so I heard some of the packing-cases behind me go sliding down and smash together with a clatter of glass on the floor of the shed. But I did not heed these. I flung the door open and looked out.

Up the beach by the boathouse a bonfire was burning, raining up sparks into the indistinctness of the dawn. Around this struggled a mass of black figures. I heard Montgomery call my name. I began to run at once towards this fire, revolver in hand. I saw the pink tongue of Montgomery's pistol lick out once, close to the ground. He was down. I shouted with all my strength and fired into the air. I heard some one cry, "The Master!" The knotted black struggle broke into scattering units, the fire leapt and sank down. The crowd of Beast People fled in sudden panic before me, up the beach. In my excitement I fired at their retreating backs as they disappeared among the bushes. Then I turned to the black heaps upon the ground.

Montgomery lay on his back, with the hairy-grey Beast-man sprawling across his body. The brute was dead, but still gripping Montgomery's throat with its curving claws. Near by lay M'ling on his face and quite still, his neck bitten open and the upper part of the smashed brandy-bottle in his hand. Two other figures lay near the fire, – the one motionless, the other groaning fitfully, every now and then raising its head slowly, then dropping it again.

I caught hold of the grey man and pulled him off Montgomery's body; his claws drew down the torn coat reluctantly as I dragged him away. Montgomery was dark in the face and scarcely breathing. I splashed sea-water on his face and pillowed his head on my rolled-up coat. M'ling was dead. The wounded creature by the fire – it was a Wolf-brute with a bearded grey face – lay, I found, with the fore part of its body upon the still glowing timber. The wretched thing was injured so dreadfully that in mercy I blew its brains out at once. The other brute was one of the Bull-men swathed in white. He too was dead. The rest of the Beast People had vanished from the beach.

I went to Montgomery again and knelt beside him, cursing my ignorance of medicine. The fire beside me had sunk down, and only charred beams of timber glowing at the central ends and mixed with a grey ash of brushwood remained. I wondered casually where Montgomery had got his wood. Then I saw that the dawn was upon us. The sky had grown brighter, the setting moon was becoming pale and opaque in the luminous blue of the day. The sky to the eastward was rimmed with red.

Suddenly I heard a thud and a hissing behind me, and, looking round, sprang to my feet with a cry of horror. Against the warm dawn great tumultuous masses of black smoke were boiling up out of the enclosure, and through their stormy darkness shot flickering threads of blood-red flame. Then the thatched roof caught. I saw the curving charge of the flames across the sloping straw. A spurt of fire jetted from the window of my room.

I knew at once what had happened. I remembered the crash I had heard. When I had rushed out to Montgomery's assistance, I had overturned the lamp.

The hopelessness of saving any of the contents of the enclosure stared me in the face. My mind came back to my plan of flight, and turning swiftly I looked to see where the two boats lay upon the beach. They were gone! Two axes lay upon the sands beside me; chips and splinters were scattered broadcast, and the ashes of the bonfire were blackening and smoking under the dawn. Montgomery had burnt the boats to revenge himself upon me and prevent our return to mankind!

A sudden convulsion of rage shook me. I was almost moved to batter his foolish head in, as he lay there helpless at my feet. Then suddenly his hand moved, so feebly, so pitifully, that my wrath vanished.

He groaned, and opened his eyes for a minute. I knelt down beside him and raised his head. He opened his eyes again, staring silently at the dawn, and then they met mine. The lids fell.

"Sorry," he said presently, with an effort. He seemed trying to think. "The last," he murmured, "the last of this silly universe. What a mess – "

I listened. His head fell helplessly to one side. I thought some drink might revive him; but there was neither drink nor vessel in which to bring drink at hand. He seemed suddenly heavier. My heart went cold. I bent down to his face, put my hand through the rent in his blouse. He was dead; and even as he died a line of white heat, the limb of the sun, rose eastward beyond the projection of the bay, splashing its radiance across the sky and turning the dark sea into a weltering tumult of dazzling light. It fell like a glory upon his death-shrunken face.

I let his head fall gently upon the rough pillow I had made for him, and stood up. Before me was the glittering desolation of the sea, the awful solitude upon which I had already suffered so much; behind me the island, hushed under the dawn, its Beast People silent and unseen. The enclosure, with all its provisions and ammunition, burnt noisily, with sudden gusts of flame, a fitful crackling, and now and then a crash. The heavy smoke drove up the beach away from me, rolling low over the distant tree-tops towards the huts in the ravine. Beside me were the charred vestiges of the boats and these five dead bodies.

Then out of the bushes came three Beast People, with hunched shoulders, protruding heads, misshapen hands awkwardly held, and inquisitive, unfriendly eyes and advanced towards me with hesitating gestures.

CHAPTER TWENTY

The Alone with the Beast Folk

I FACED THESE PEOPLE, facing my fate in them, single-handed now, – literally single-handed, for I had a broken arm. In my pocket was a revolver with two empty chambers. Among the chips scattered about the beach lay the two axes that had been used to chop up the boats. The tide was creeping in behind me. There was nothing for it but courage. I looked squarely into the faces of the advancing monsters. They avoided my eyes, and their quivering nostrils investigated the bodies that lay beyond me on the beach. I took half-a-dozen steps, picked up the blood-stained whip that lay beneath the body of the Wolf-man, and cracked it. They stopped and stared at me.

"Salute!" said I. "Bow down!"

They hesitated. One bent his knees. I repeated my command, with my heart in my mouth, and advanced upon them. One knelt, then the other two.

I turned and walked towards the dead bodies, keeping my face towards the three kneeling Beast Men, very much as an actor passing up the stage faces the audience.

"They broke the Law," said I, putting my foot on the Sayer of the Law. "They have been slain, – even the Sayer of the Law; even the Other with the Whip. Great is the Law! Come and see."

"None escape," said one of them, advancing and peering.

"None escape," said I. "Therefore hear and do as I command." They stood up, looking questioningly at one another.

"Stand there," said I.

I picked up the hatchets and swung them by their heads from the sling of my arm; turned Montgomery over; picked up his revolver still loaded in two chambers, and bending down to rummage, found half-a-dozen cartridges in his pocket.

"Take him," said I, standing up again and pointing with the whip; "take him, and carry him out and cast him into the sea."

They came forward, evidently still afraid of Montgomery, but still more afraid of my cracking red whip-lash; and after some fumbling and hesitation, some whip-cracking and shouting, they lifted him gingerly, carried him down to the beach, and went splashing into the dazzling welter of the sea.

"On!" said I, "on! Carry him far."

They went in up to their armpits and stood regarding me.

"Let go," said I; and the body of Montgomery vanished with a splash. Something seemed to tighten across my chest.

"Good!" said I, with a break in my voice; and they came back, hurrying and fearful, to the margin of the water, leaving long wakes of black in the silver. At the water's edge they stopped, turning and glaring into the sea as though they presently expected Montgomery to arise therefrom and exact vengeance.

"Now these," said I, pointing to the other bodies.

They took care not to approach the place where they had thrown Montgomery into the water, but instead, carried the four dead Beast People slantingly along the beach for perhaps a hundred yards before they waded out and cast them away.

As I watched them disposing of the mangled remains of M'ling, I heard a light footfall behind me, and turning quickly saw the big Hyena-swine perhaps a dozen yards away. His head was bent down, his bright eyes were fixed upon me, his stumpy hands clenched and held close by his side. He stopped in this crouching attitude when I turned, his eyes a little averted.

For a moment we stood eye to eye. I dropped the whip and snatched at the pistol in my pocket; for I meant to kill this brute, the most formidable of any left now upon the island, at the first excuse. It may seem treacherous, but so I was resolved. I was far more afraid of him than of any other two of the Beast Folk. His continued life was I knew a threat against mine.

I was perhaps a dozen seconds collecting myself. Then cried I, "Salute! Bow down!"

His teeth flashed upon me in a snarl. "*Who* are you that I should – "

Perhaps a little too spasmodically I drew my revolver, aimed quickly and fired. I heard him yelp, saw him run sideways and turn, knew I had missed, and clicked back the cock with my thumb for the next shot. But he was already running headlong, jumping from side to side, and I dared not risk another miss. Every now and then he looked back at me over his shoulder. He went slanting along the beach, and vanished beneath the driving masses of dense smoke that were still pouring out from the burning enclosure. For some time I stood staring after him. I turned to my three obedient Beast Folk again and signalled them to drop the body they still carried. Then I went back to the place by the fire where the bodies had fallen and kicked the sand until all the brown blood-stains were absorbed and hidden.

I dismissed my three serfs with a wave of the hand, and went up the beach into the thickets. I carried my pistol in my hand, my whip thrust with the hatchets in the sling of my arm. I was anxious to be alone, to think out the position in which I was now placed. A dreadful thing that I was only beginning to realise was, that over all this island there was now no safe place where I could be alone and secure to rest or sleep. I had recovered strength amazingly since my landing, but I was still inclined to be nervous and to break down under any great stress. I felt that I ought to cross the island and establish myself with the Beast People, and make myself secure in their confidence. But my heart failed me. I went back to the beach, and turning eastward past the burning enclosure, made for a point where a shallow spit of coral sand ran out towards the reef. Here I could sit down and think, my back to the sea and my face against any surprise. And there I sat, chin on knees, the sun beating down upon my head and unspeakable dread in my mind, plotting how I could live on against the hour of my rescue (if ever rescue came). I tried to review the whole situation as calmly as I could, but it was difficult to clear the thing of emotion.

I began turning over in my mind the reason of Montgomery's despair. "They will change," he said; "they are sure to change." And Moreau, what was it that Moreau had said? "The stubborn beast-flesh grows day by day back again." Then I came round to the Hyena-swine. I felt sure that if I did not kill that brute, he would kill me. The Sayer of the Law was dead: worse luck. They knew now that we of the Whips could be killed even as they themselves were killed. Were they peering at me already out of the green masses of ferns and palms over yonder, watching until I came within their spring? Were they plotting against me? What was the Hyena-swine telling them? My imagination was running away with me into a morass of unsubstantial fears.

My thoughts were disturbed by a crying of sea-birds hurrying towards some black object that had been stranded by the waves on the beach near the enclosure. I knew what that object was, but I had not the heart to go back and drive them off. I began walking along the beach in the opposite direction, designing to come round the eastward corner of the island and so approach the ravine of the huts, without traversing the possible ambuscades of the thickets.

Perhaps half a mile along the beach I became aware of one of my three Beast Folk advancing out of the landward bushes towards me. I was now so nervous with my own imaginings that I immediately drew my revolver. Even the propitiatory gestures of the creature failed to disarm me. He hesitated as he approached.

"Go away!" cried I.

There was something very suggestive of a dog in the cringing attitude of the creature. It retreated a little way, very like a dog being sent home, and stopped, looking at me imploringly with canine brown eyes.

"Go away," said I. "Do not come near me."

"May I not come near you?" it said.

"No; go away," I insisted, and snapped my whip. Then putting my whip in my teeth, I stooped for a stone, and with that threat drove the creature away.

So in solitude I came round by the ravine of the Beast People, and hiding among the weeds and reeds that separated this crevice from the sea I watched such of them as appeared, trying to judge from their gestures and appearance how the death of Moreau and Montgomery and the destruction of the House of Pain had affected them. I know now the folly of my cowardice. Had I kept my courage up to the level of the dawn, had I not allowed it to ebb away in solitary thought, I might have grasped the vacant sceptre of Moreau and ruled over the Beast People. As it was I lost the opportunity, and sank to the position of a mere leader among my fellows.

Towards noon certain of them came and squatted basking in the hot sand. The imperious voices of hunger and thirst prevailed over my dread. I came out of the bushes, and, revolver in hand, walked down towards these seated figures. One, a Wolf-woman, turned her head and stared at me, and then the others. None attempted to rise or salute me. I felt too faint and weary to insist, and I let the moment pass.

"I want food," said I, almost apologetically, and drawing near.

"There is food in the huts," said an Ox-boar-man, drowsily, and looking away from me.

I passed them, and went down into the shadow and odours of the almost deserted ravine. In an empty hut I feasted on some specked and half-decayed fruit; and then after I had propped some branches and sticks about the opening, and placed myself with my face towards it and my hand upon my revolver, the exhaustion of the last thirty hours claimed its own, and I fell into a light slumber, hoping that the flimsy barricade I had erected would cause sufficient noise in its removal to save me from surprise.

CHAPTER TWENTY ONE

The Reversion of the Beast Folk

In this way I became one among the Beast People in the Island of Doctor Moreau. When I awoke, it was dark about me. My arm ached in its bandages. I sat up, wondering at first where I might be. I heard coarse voices talking outside. Then I saw that my barricade had gone, and that the opening of the hut stood clear. My revolver was still in my hand.

I heard something breathing, saw something crouched together close beside me. I held my breath, trying to see what it was. It began to move slowly, interminably. Then something soft and warm and moist passed across my hand. All my muscles contracted. I snatched my hand away. A cry of alarm began and was stifled in my throat. Then I just realised what had happened sufficiently to stay my fingers on the revolver.

"Who is that?" I said in a hoarse whisper, the revolver still pointed.

"I – Master."

"Who are you?"

"They say there is no Master now. But I know, I know. I carried the bodies into the sea, O Walker in the Sea! the bodies of those you slew. I am your slave, Master."

"Are you the one I met on the beach?" I asked.

"The same, Master."

The Thing was evidently faithful enough, for it might have fallen upon me as I slept. "It is well," I said, extending my hand for another licking kiss. I began to realise what its presence meant, and the tide of my courage flowed. "Where are the others?" I asked.

"They are mad; they are fools," said the Dog-man. "Even now they talk together beyond there. They say, 'The Master is dead. The Other with the Whip is dead. That Other who walked in the Sea is as we are. We have no Master, no Whips, no House of Pain, any more. There is an end. We love the Law, and will keep it; but there is no Pain, no Master, no Whips for ever again.' So they say. But I know, Master, I know."

I felt in the darkness, and patted the Dog-man's head. "It is well," I said again.

"Presently you will slay them all," said the Dog-man.

"Presently," I answered, "I will slay them all, – after certain days and certain things have come to pass. Every one of them save those you spare, every one of them shall be slain."

"What the Master wishes to kill, the Master kills," said the Dog-man with a certain satisfaction in his voice.

"And that their sins may grow," I said, "let them live in their folly until their time is ripe. Let them not know that I am the Master."

"The Master's will is sweet," said the Dog-man, with the ready tact of his canine blood.

"But one has sinned," said I. "Him I will kill, whenever I may meet him. When I say to you, '*That is he*,' see that you fall upon him. And now I will go to the men and women who are assembled together."

For a moment the opening of the hut was blackened by the exit of the Dog-man. Then I followed and stood up, almost in the exact spot where I had been when I had heard Moreau and his staghound pursuing me. But now it was night, and all the miasmatic ravine about me was black; and beyond, instead of a green, sunlit slope, I saw a red fire, before which hunched, grotesque figures moved to and fro. Farther were the thick trees, a bank of darkness, fringed above with the black lace of the upper branches. The moon was just riding up on the edge of the ravine, and like a bar across its face drove the spire of vapour that was for ever streaming from the fumaroles of the island.

"Walk by me," said I, nerving myself; and side by side we walked down the narrow way, taking little heed of the dim Things that peered at us out of the huts.

None about the fire attempted to salute me. Most of them disregarded me, ostentatiously. I looked round for the Hyena-swine, but he was not there. Altogether, perhaps twenty of the Beast Folk squatted, staring into the fire or talking to one another.

"He is dead, he is dead! the Master is dead!" said the voice of the Ape-man to the right of me. "The House of Pain – there is no House of Pain!"

"He is not dead," said I, in a loud voice. "Even now he watches us!"

This startled them. Twenty pairs of eyes regarded me.

"The House of Pain is gone," said I. "It will come again. The Master you cannot see; yet even now he listens among you."

"True, true!" said the Dog-man.

They were staggered at my assurance. An animal may be ferocious and cunning enough, but it takes a real man to tell a lie.

"The Man with the Bandaged Arm speaks a strange thing," said one of the Beast Folk.

"I tell you it is so," I said. "The Master and the House of Pain will come again. Woe be to him who breaks the Law!"

They looked curiously at one another. With an affectation of indifference I began to chop idly at the ground in front of me with my hatchet. They looked, I noticed, at the deep cuts I made in the turf.

Then the Satyr raised a doubt. I answered him. Then one of the dappled things objected, and an animated discussion sprang up round the fire. Every moment I began to feel more convinced of my present security. I talked now without the catching in my breath, due to the intensity of my excitement, that had troubled me at first. In the course of about an hour I had really convinced several of the Beast Folk of the truth of my assertions, and talked most of the others into a dubious state. I kept a sharp eye for my enemy the Hyena-swine, but he never appeared. Every now and then a suspicious movement would startle me, but my confidence grew rapidly. Then as the moon crept down from the zenith, one by one the listeners began to yawn (showing the oddest teeth in the light of the sinking fire), and first one and then another retired towards the dens in the ravine; and I, dreading the silence and darkness, went with them, knowing I was safer with several of them than with one alone.

In this manner began the longer part of my sojourn upon this Island of Doctor Moreau. But from that night until the end came, there was but one thing happened to tell save a series of innumerable small unpleasant details and the fretting of an incessant uneasiness. So that I prefer to make no chronicle for that gap of time, to tell only one cardinal incident of the ten months I spent as an intimate of these half-humanised brutes. There is much that sticks in my memory that I could write, – things that I would cheerfully give my right hand to forget; but they do not help the telling of the story.

In the retrospect it is strange to remember how soon I fell in with these monsters' ways, and gained my confidence again. I had my quarrels with them of course, and could show some of their teeth-marks still; but they soon gained a wholesome respect for my trick of throwing stones and for the bite of my hatchet. And my Saint-Bernard-man's loyalty was of infinite service to me. I found their simple scale of honour was based mainly on the capacity for inflicting trenchant wounds. Indeed, I may say – without vanity, I hope – that I held something like pre-eminence among them. One or two, whom in a rare access of high spirits I had scarred rather badly, bore me a grudge; but it vented itself chiefly behind my back, and at a safe distance from my missiles, in grimaces.

The Hyena-swine avoided me, and I was always on the alert for him. My inseparable Dog-man hated and dreaded him intensely. I really believe that was at the root of the brute's attachment to me. It was soon evident to me that the former monster had tasted blood, and gone the way of the Leopard-man. He formed a lair somewhere in the forest, and became solitary. Once I tried to induce the Beast Folk to hunt him, but I lacked the authority to make them co-operate for one end. Again and again I tried to approach his den and come upon him unaware; but always he was too acute for me, and saw or winded me and got away. He too made every forest pathway dangerous to me and my ally with his lurking ambuscades. The Dog-man scarcely dared to leave my side.

In the first month or so the Beast Folk, compared with their latter condition, were human enough, and for one or two besides my canine friend I even conceived a friendly tolerance. The little pink sloth-creature displayed an odd affection for me, and took to following me about. The Monkey-man bored me, however; he assumed, on the strength of his five digits, that he was my equal, and was for ever jabbering at me, – jabbering the most arrant nonsense. One thing about him entertained me a little: he had a fantastic trick of coining new words. He had an idea, I believe, that to gabble about names that meant nothing was the proper use of speech. He called it "Big Thinks" to distinguish it from "Little Thinks," the sane every-day interests of life. If ever I made a remark he did not understand, he would praise it very much, ask me to say it again, learn it by heart, and go off repeating it, with a word wrong here or there, to all the milder of the Beast People. He thought nothing of what was plain and comprehensible. I invented some very curious "Big Thinks" for his especial use. I think now that he was the silliest creature I ever met; he had developed in the most wonderful way the distinctive silliness of man without losing one jot of the natural folly of a monkey.

This, I say, was in the earlier weeks of my solitude among these brutes. During that time they respected the usage established by the Law, and behaved with general decorum. Once I found another rabbit torn to pieces, – by the Hyena-swine, I am assured, – but that was all. It was about May when I first distinctly perceived a growing difference in their speech and carriage, a growing coarseness of articulation, a growing disinclination to talk. My Monkey-man's jabber multiplied in volume but grew less and less comprehensible, more and more simian. Some of the others seemed altogether slipping their hold upon speech, though they still understood what I said to them at that time. (Can you imagine language, once clear-cut and exact, softening and guttering, losing shape and import, becoming mere lumps of sound again?) And they walked erect with an increasing difficulty. Though they evidently felt ashamed of themselves, every now and then I would come upon one or another running on toes and finger-tips, and quite unable to recover the vertical attitude. They held things more clumsily; drinking by suction, feeding by gnawing, grew commoner every day. I realised more keenly than ever what Moreau had told me about the "stubborn beast-flesh." They were reverting, and reverting very rapidly.

Some of them – the pioneers in this, I noticed with some surprise, were all females – began to disregard the injunction of decency, deliberately for the most part. Others even attempted public outrages upon the institution of monogamy. The tradition of the Law was clearly losing its force. I cannot pursue this disagreeable subject.

My Dog-man imperceptibly slipped back to the dog again; day by day he became dumb, quadrupedal, hairy. I scarcely noticed the transition from the companion on my right hand to the lurching dog at my side.

As the carelessness and disorganisation increased from day to day, the lane of dwelling places, at no time very sweet, became so loathsome that I left it, and going across the island made myself a hovel of boughs amid the black ruins of Moreau's enclosure. Some memory of pain, I found, still made that place the safest from the Beast Folk.

It would be impossible to detail every step of the lapsing of these monsters, – to tell how, day by day, the human semblance left them; how they gave up bandagings and wrappings, abandoned at last every stitch of clothing; how the hair began to spread over the exposed limbs; how their foreheads fell away and their faces projected; how the quasi-human intimacy I had permitted myself with some of them in the first month of my loneliness became a shuddering horror to recall.

The change was slow and inevitable. For them and for me it came without any definite shock. I still went among them in safety, because no jolt in the downward glide had released the increasing charge of explosive animalism that ousted the human day by day. But I began to fear that soon now that shock must come. My Saint-Bernard-brute followed me to the enclosure every night, and his vigilance enabled me to sleep at times in something like peace. The little pink sloth-thing became shy and left me, to crawl back to its natural life once more among the tree-branches. We were in just the state of equilibrium that would remain in one of those "Happy Family" cages which animal-tamers exhibit, if the tamer were to leave it for ever.

Of course these creatures did not decline into such beasts as the reader has seen in zoological gardens, – into ordinary bears, wolves, tigers, oxen, swine, and apes. There was still something strange about each; in each Moreau had blended this animal with that. One perhaps was ursine chiefly, another feline chiefly, another bovine chiefly; but each was tainted with other creatures, – a kind of generalised animalism appearing through the specific dispositions. And the dwindling shreds of the humanity still startled me every now and then, – a momentary recrudescence of speech perhaps, an unexpected dexterity of the fore-feet, a pitiful attempt to walk erect.

I too must have undergone strange changes. My clothes hung about me as yellow rags, through whose rents showed the tanned skin. My hair grew long, and became matted together. I am told that even now my eyes have a strange brightness, a swift alertness of movement.

At first I spent the daylight hours on the southward beach watching for a ship, hoping and praying for a ship. I counted on the *Ipecacuanha* returning as the year wore on; but she never came. Five times I saw sails, and thrice smoke; but nothing ever touched the island. I always had a bonfire ready, but no doubt the volcanic reputation of the island was taken to account for that.

It was only about September or October that I began to think of making a raft. By that time my arm had healed, and both my hands were at my service again. At first, I found my helplessness appalling. I had never done any carpentry or such-like work in my life, and I spent day after day in experimental chopping and binding among the trees. I had no ropes, and could hit on nothing wherewith to make ropes; none of the abundant creepers seemed limber or strong enough, and with all my litter of scientific education I could not devise any way of making them so. I spent more than a fortnight grubbing among the black ruins of the enclosure and on the beach where the boats had been burnt, looking for nails and other stray pieces of metal that might prove of service. Now and then some Beast-creature would watch me, and go leaping off when I called to it. There came a season of thunder-storms and heavy rain, which greatly retarded my work; but at last the raft was completed.

I was delighted with it. But with a certain lack of practical sense which has always been my bane, I had made it a mile or more from the sea; and before I had dragged it down to the beach the thing had fallen to pieces. Perhaps it is as well that I was saved from launching it; but at the time my misery at my failure was so acute that for some days I simply moped on the beach, and stared at the water and thought of death.

I did not, however, mean to die, and an incident occurred that warned me unmistakably of the folly of letting the days pass so, – for each fresh day was fraught with increasing danger from the Beast People.

I was lying in the shade of the enclosure wall, staring out to sea, when I was startled by something cold touching the skin of my heel, and starting round found the little pink sloth-creature blinking into my face. He had long since lost speech and active movement, and the lank hair of the little brute grew thicker every day and his stumpy claws more askew. He made a moaning noise when he saw he had attracted my attention, went a little way towards the bushes and looked back at me.

At first I did not understand, but presently it occurred to me that he wished me to follow him; and this I did at last, – slowly, for the day was hot. When we reached the trees he clambered into them, for he could travel better among their swinging creepers than on the ground. And suddenly in a trampled space I came upon a ghastly group. My Saint-Bernard-creature lay on the ground, dead; and near his body crouched the Hyena-swine, gripping the quivering flesh with its misshapen claws, gnawing at it, and snarling with delight. As I approached, the monster lifted its glaring eyes to mine, its lips went trembling back from its red-stained teeth, and it growled menacingly. It was not afraid and not ashamed; the last vestige of the human taint had vanished. I advanced a step farther, stopped, and pulled out my revolver. At last I had him face to face.

The brute made no sign of retreat; but its ears went back, its hair bristled, and its body crouched together. I aimed between the eyes and fired. As I did so, the Thing rose straight at me in a leap, and I was knocked over like a ninepin. It clutched at me with its crippled hand, and struck me in the face. Its spring carried it over me. I fell under the hind part of its body; but luckily I had hit as I meant, and it had died even as it leapt. I crawled out from under its unclean weight and stood up trembling, staring at its quivering body. That danger at least was over; but this, I knew was only the first of the series of relapses that must come.

I burnt both of the bodies on a pyre of brushwood; but after that I saw that unless I left the island my death was only a question of time. The Beast People by that time had, with one or two exceptions, left the ravine and made themselves lairs according to their taste among the thickets of the island. Few prowled by day, most of them slept, and the island might have seemed deserted to a new-comer; but at night the air was hideous with their calls and howling. I had half a mind to make a massacre of them; to build traps, or fight them with my knife. Had I possessed sufficient cartridges, I should not have hesitated to begin the killing. There could now be scarcely a score left of the dangerous carnivores; the braver of these were already dead. After the death of this poor dog of mine, my last friend, I too adopted to some extent the practice of slumbering in the daytime in order to be on my guard at night. I rebuilt my den in the walls of the enclosure, with such a narrow opening that anything attempting to enter must necessarily make a considerable noise. The creatures had lost the art of fire too, and recovered their fear of it. I turned once more, almost passionately now, to hammering together stakes and branches to form a raft for my escape.

I found a thousand difficulties. I am an extremely unhandy man (my schooling was over before the days of Slöjd); but most of the requirements of a raft I met at last in some clumsy, circuitous way or other, and this time I took care of the strength. The only insurmountable obstacle was that I had no vessel to contain the water I should need if I floated forth upon these untravelled seas. I would have even tried pottery, but the island contained no clay. I used to go moping about the island trying with all my might to solve this one last difficulty. Sometimes I would give way to wild outbursts of rage, and hack and splinter some unlucky tree in my intolerable vexation. But I could think of nothing.

And then came a day, a wonderful day, which I spent in ecstasy. I saw a sail to the southwest, a small sail like that of a little schooner; and forthwith I lit a great pile of brushwood, and stood by it in the heat of it, and the heat of the midday sun, watching. All day I watched that sail, eating or drinking nothing, so that my head reeled; and the Beasts came and glared at me, and seemed to wonder, and went away. It was still distant when night came and swallowed it up; and all night I toiled to keep my blaze bright and high, and the eyes of the Beasts shone out of the darkness, marvelling. In the dawn the sail was nearer, and I saw it was the dirty lug-sail of a small boat. But it sailed strangely. My eyes were weary with watching, and I peered and could not believe them. Two men were in the boat, sitting low down, – one by the bows, the other at the rudder. The head was not kept to the wind; it yawed and fell away.

As the day grew brighter, I began waving the last rag of my jacket to them; but they did not notice me, and sat still, facing each other. I went to the lowest point of the low headland, and gesticulated and shouted. There was no response, and the boat kept on her aimless course, making slowly, very slowly, for the bay. Suddenly a great white bird flew up out of the boat, and neither of the men stirred nor noticed it; it circled round, and then came sweeping overhead with its strong wings outspread.

Then I stopped shouting, and sat down on the headland and rested my chin on my hands and stared. Slowly, slowly, the boat drove past towards the west. I would have swum out to it, but something – a cold, vague fear – kept me back. In the afternoon the tide stranded the boat, and left it a hundred yards or so to the westward of the ruins of the enclosure. The men in it were dead, had been dead so long that they fell to pieces when I tilted the boat on its side and dragged them out. One had a shock of red hair, like the captain of the *Ipecacuanha*, and a dirty white cap lay in the bottom of the boat.

As I stood beside the boat, three of the Beasts came slinking out of the bushes and sniffing towards me. One of my spasms of disgust came upon me. I thrust the little boat down the beach and clambered on board her. Two of the brutes were Wolf-beasts, and came forward with quivering nostrils and glittering eyes; the third was the horrible nondescript of bear and bull. When I saw them approaching those wretched remains, heard them snarling at one another and caught the gleam of their teeth, a frantic horror succeeded my repulsion. I turned my back upon them, struck the lug and began paddling out to sea. I could not bring myself to look behind me.

I lay, however, between the reef and the island that night, and the next morning went round to the stream and filled the empty keg aboard with water. Then, with such patience as I could command, I collected a quantity of fruit, and waylaid and killed two rabbits with my last three cartridges. While I was doing this I left the boat moored to an inward projection of the reef, for fear of the Beast People.

CHAPTER TWENTY TWO

The Man Alone

IN THE EVENING I started, and drove out to sea before a gentle wind from the southwest, slowly, steadily; and the island grew smaller and smaller, and the lank spire of smoke dwindled to a finer and finer line against the hot sunset. The ocean rose up around me, hiding that low, dark patch from my eyes. The daylight, the trailing glory of the sun, went streaming out of the sky, was drawn aside like some luminous curtain, and at last I looked into the blue gulf of immensity which the sunshine hides, and saw the floating hosts of the stars. The sea was silent, the sky was silent. I was alone with the night and silence.

So I drifted for three days, eating and drinking sparingly, and meditating upon all that had happened to me, – not desiring very greatly then to see men again. One unclean rag was about me, my hair a black tangle: no doubt my discoverers thought me a madman.

It is strange, but I felt no desire to return to mankind. I was only glad to be quit of the foulness of the Beast People. And on the third day I was picked up by a brig from Apia to San Francisco. Neither the captain nor the mate would believe my story, judging that solitude and danger had made me mad; and fearing their opinion might be that of others, I refrained from telling my adventure further, and professed to recall nothing that had happened to me between the loss of the *Lady Vain* and the time when I was picked up again, – the space of a year.

I had to act with the utmost circumspection to save myself from the suspicion of insanity. My memory of the Law, of the two dead sailors, of the ambuscades of the darkness, of the body in the canebrake, haunted me; and, unnatural as it seems, with my return to mankind came, instead of that confidence and sympathy I had expected, a strange enhancement of the uncertainty and dread I had experienced during my stay upon the island. No one would believe me; I was almost as queer to men as I had been to the Beast People. I may have caught something of the natural wildness of my companions. They say that terror is a disease, and anyhow I can witness that for several years now a restless fear has dwelt in my mind, – such a restless fear as a half-tamed lion cub may feel.

My trouble took the strangest form. I could not persuade myself that the men and women I met were not also another Beast People, animals half wrought into the outward image of human souls, and that they would presently begin to revert, – to show first this bestial mark and then that. But I have confided my case to a strangely able man, – a man who had known Moreau, and seemed half to credit my story; a mental specialist, – and he has helped me mightily, though I do not expect that the terror of that island will ever altogether leave me. At most times it lies far in the back of my mind, a mere distant cloud, a memory, and a faint distrust; but there are times when the little cloud spreads until it obscures the whole sky. Then I look about me at my fellow-men; and I go in fear. I see faces, keen and bright; others dull or dangerous; others, unsteady, insincere, – none that have the calm authority of a reasonable soul. I feel as though the animal was surging up through them; that presently the degradation of the Islanders will be played over again on a larger scale. I know this is an illusion; that these seeming men and women about me are indeed men and women, – men and women for ever, perfectly reasonable creatures, full of human desires and tender solicitude, emancipated from instinct and the slaves of no fantastic Law, – beings altogether different from the Beast Folk. Yet I shrink from them, from their curious glances, their inquiries and assistance, and long to be away from them and alone. For that reason I live near the broad free downland, and can escape thither when this shadow is over my soul; and very sweet is the empty downland then, under the wind-swept sky.

When I lived in London the horror was well-nigh insupportable. I could not get away from men: their voices came through windows; locked doors were flimsy safeguards. I would go out into the streets to fight with my delusion, and prowling women would mew after me; furtive, craving men glance jealously at me; weary, pale workers go coughing by me with tired eyes and eager paces, like wounded deer dripping blood; old people, bent and dull, pass murmuring to themselves; and, all unheeding, a ragged tail of gibing children. Then I would turn aside into some chapel, – and even there, such was my disturbance, it seemed that the preacher gibbered "Big Thinks," even as the Ape-man had done; or into some library, and there the intent faces over the books seemed but patient creatures waiting for prey. Particularly nauseous were the blank, expressionless faces of people in trains and omnibuses; they seemed no more my fellow-creatures than dead bodies would be, so that I did not dare to travel unless I was assured of being alone. And even it seemed that I too was not a reasonable creature, but only an animal tormented with some strange disorder in its brain which sent it to wander alone, like a sheep stricken with gid.

This is a mood, however, that comes to me now, I thank God, more rarely. I have withdrawn myself from the confusion of cities and multitudes, and spend my days surrounded by wise books, – bright windows in this life of ours, lit by the shining souls of men. I see few strangers, and have but a small household. My days I devote to reading and to experiments in chemistry, and I spend many of the clear nights in the study of astronomy. There is – though I do not know how there is or why there is – a sense of infinite peace and protection in the glittering hosts of heaven. There it must be, I think, in the vast and eternal laws of matter, and not in the daily cares and sins and troubles of men, that whatever is more than animal within us must find its solace and its hope. I hope, or I could not live.

And so, in hope and solitude, my story ends.

EDWARD PRENDICK.

NOTE. The substance of the chapter entitled "Doctor Moreau explains," which contains the essential idea of the story, appeared as a middle article in the *Saturday Review* in January, 1895. This is the only portion of this story that has been previously published, and it has been entirely recast to adapt it to the narrative form.

READ THE MOST POPULAR ENGAGE CLASSICS

20,000 Leagues Under the Sea by Jules Verne
A Christmas Carol by Charles Dickens
A Fighting Man of Mars by Edgar Rice Burroughs
A Portrait of the Artist as a Young Man by James Joyce
A Princess of Mars by Edgar Rice Burroughs
A Room with a View by E. M. Forster
A Study in Scarlet by Arthur Conan Doyle
A Tale of Two Cities by Jules Verne
Aesop's Fables by Aesop
Alice in Wonderland by Lewis Carroll
Anna Karenina by Leo Tolstoy
Anne of Avonlea by Lucy Maud Montgomery
Anne of Green Gables by Lucy Maud Montgomery
Around the World in 80 Days by Jules Verne
As a Man Thinketh by James Allen
Black Beauty by Anna Sewell
Bleak House by Charles Dickens
Candide by Voltaire
Common Sense by Thomas Paine
Crime and Punishment by Fyodor Dostoevsky
Don Quixote by Miguel de Cervantes
Dracula by Bram Stoker
Dubliners by James Joyce
Emily of New Moon by Lucy Maud Montgomery
Emma by Jane Austen
Far from the Madding Crowd by Thomas Hardy
Frankenstein by Mary Shelley
From the Earth to the Moon by Jules Verne
Great Expectations by Charles Dickens
Grimm's Fairy Tales by Jakob and Wilhelm Grimm
Gulliver's Travels by Jonathan Swift
Hamlet by William Shakespeare
Hard Times by Charles Dickens
Heart of Darkness by Joseph Conrad
Howards End by E. M. Forster
Jane Eyre by Charlotte Brontë
Journey to the Center of the Earth by Jules Verne
Kidnapped by Robert Louis Stevenson
Kim by Rudyard Kipling
Les Misérables by Victor Hugo

ENGAGE CLASSICS

Leviathan BY THOMAS HOBBES
Little Men BY LOUISA MAY ALCOTT
Little Women BY LOUISA MAY ALCOTT
Macbeth BY WILLIAM SHAKESPEARE
Madame Bovary BY GUSTAVE FLAUBERT
Mansfield Park BY JANE AUSTEN
Meditations BY MARCUS AURELIUS
Middlemarch BY GEORGE ELIOT
Moby Dick BY HERMAN MELVILLE
Moll Flanders BY DANIEL DEFOE
My Ántonia BY WILLA CATHER
Nicomachean Ethics BY ARISTOTLE
North and South BY ELIZABETH GASKELL
Northanger Abbey BY JANE AUSTEN
Notes from the Underground BY FYODOR DOSTOYEVSKY
Oliver Twist BY CHARLES DICKENS
On Liberty BY JOHN STUART MILL
On War BY CARL VON CLAUSEWITZ
Orthodoxy BY GILBERT K. CHESTERTON
Paradise Lost BY JOHN MILTON
Persuasion BY JANE AUSTEN
Plato: Five Dialogues BY PLATO
Plutarch's Lives BY PLUTARCH
Politics BY ARISTOTLE
Pollyanna BY ELEANOR H. PORTER
Pride & Prejudice BY JANE AUSTEN
Raggedy Ann Stories BY JOHNNY GRUELLE
Robinson Crusoe BY DANIEL DEFOE
Second Treatise Of Government BY JOHN LOCKE
Self-Reliance, Nature, and Other Essays BY RALPH WALDO EMERSON
Sense & Sensibility BY JANE AUSTEN
Sons and Lovers BY D. H. LAWRENCE
Swann's Way, In Search of Lost Time BY MARCEL PROUST
Tarzan of the Apes BY EDGAR RICE BURROUGHS
Tess of the d'Urbervilles BY THOMAS HARDY
The Adventures of Huckleberry Finn BY MARK TWAIN
The Adventures of Sherlock Holmes BY ARTHUR CONAN DOYLE
The Adventures of Tom Sawyer BY MARK TWAIN
The Age of Innocence BY EDITH WHARTON
The Art of War BY SUN TZU
The Awakening BY KATE CHOPIN
The Beautiful and the Damned BY F. SCOTT FITZGERALD
The Brothers Karamazov BY FYODOR DOSTOEVSKY

ENGAGE CLASSICS

The Call of the Wild BY JACK LONDON
The Chessmen of Mars BY EDGAR RICE BURROUGHS
The Communist Manifesto BY KARL MARX & FRIEDRICH ENGELS
The Corpus Hermeticum BY HERMES TRISMEGISTUS
The Count of Monte Cristo BY ALEXANDRE DUMAS
The Divine Comedy - Inferno BY DANTE
The Divine Comedy - Purgatorio BY DANTE
The Divine Comedy - Paradiso BY DANTE
The Everlasting Man BY GILBERT K. CHESTERTON
The First Men in the Moon BY H. G. WELLS
The Gods of Mars BY EDGAR RICE BURROUGHS
The Histories BY HERODOTUS
The History of the Peloponnesian War BY THUCYDIDES
The Hound of the Baskervilles BY ARTHUR CONAN DOYLE
The Hunchback of Notre-Dame BY VICTOR HUGO
The Idiot BY FYODOR DOSTOEVSKY
The Iliad BY HOMER
The Importance of Being Earnest BY OSCAR WILDE
The Innocents Abroad BY MARK TWAIN
The Invisible Man BY H. G. WELLS
The Island of Doctor Moreau BY H. G. WELLS
The Jungle BY UPTON SINCLAIR
The Jungle Book BY RUDYARD KIPLING
The Kama Sutra BY VĀTSYĀYANA
The Kybalion BY THREE INITIATES
The Last of the Mohicans BY JAMES FENIMORE COOPER
The Legend of Sleepy Hollow BY WASHINGTON IRVING
The Life and Opinions of Tristram Shandy BY LAURENCE STERNE
The Lost World BY ARTHUR CONAN DOYLE
The Man Who Was Thursday BY GILBERT K. CHESTERTON
The Master Mind of Mars BY EDGAR RICE BURROUGHS
The Mayor of Casterbridge BY THOMAS HARDY
The Memoirs of Sherlock Holmes BY ARTHUR CONAN DOYLE
The Merry Adventures of Robin Hood BY HOWARD PYLE
The Metamorphosis BY FRANZ KAFKA
The Mill on the Floss BY GEORGE ELIOT
The Murder on the Links BY AGATHA CHRISTIE
The Mysterious Affair at Styles BY AGATHA CHRISTIE
The Nature of Things BY TITUS LUCRETIUS CARUS
The Odyssey BY HOMER
The Old Curiosity Shop BY CHARLES DICKENS
The Origin of Species BY CHARLES DARWIN
The Picture of Dorian Gray BY OSCAR WILDE

ENGAGE CLASSICS

The Pilgrim's Progress BY JOHN BUNYAN
The Portrait of a Lady BY HENRY JAMES
The Prince BY NICCOLÒ MACHIAVELLI
The Prince and the Pauper BY MARK TWAIN
The Problems of Philosophy BY BERTRAND RUSSELL
The Prophet BY KAHLIL GIBRAN
The Republic BY PLATO
The Return of the Native BY THOMAS HARDY
The Scarlet Letter BY NATHANIEL HAWTHORNE
The Science of Getting Rich BY WALLACE D. WATTLES
The Secret Garden BY FRANCES HODGSON BURNETT
The Sign of the Four BY ARTHUR CONAN DOYLE
The Souls of Black Folk BY W. E. B. DU BOIS
The Strange Case of Dr. Jekyll & Mr. Hyde BY ROBERT LOUIS STEVENSON
The Swiss Family Robinson BY JOHANN DAVID WYSS
The Tale of Peter Rabbit BY BEATRIX POTTER
The Tenant of Wildfell Hall BY ANNE BRONTË
The Three Musketeers BY ALEXANDRE DUMAS
The Time Machine BY H. G. WELLS
The Valley of Fear BY ARTHUR CONAN DOYLE
The War of the Worlds BY H. G. WELLS
The Warlord of Mars BY EDGAR RICE BURROUGHS
The Wealth of Nations BY ADAM SMITH
The Wind in the Willows BY KENNETH GRAHAME
The Wizard of Oz BY L. FRANK BAUM
The Woman in White BY WILKIE COLLINS
This Side of Paradise BY F. SCOTT FITZGERALD
Through the Looking-Glass BY LEWIS CARROLL
Thuvia, Maid of Mars BY EDGAR RICE BURROUGHS
Tom Jones BY HENRY FIELDING
Treasure Island BY ROBERT LOUIS STEVENSON
Twelve Years a Slave BY SOLOMON NORTHUP
Ulysses BY JAMES JOYCE
Uncle Tom's Cabin BY HARRIET BEECHER STOWE
Utilitarianism BY JOHN STUART MILL
Vanity Fair BY WILLIAM MAKEPEACE THACKERAY
Villette BY CHARLOTTE BRONTË
Walden BY HENRY DAVID THOREAU
War and Peace BY LEO TOLSTOY
What's Wrong with the World BY GILBERT K. CHESTERTON
White Fang BY JACK LONDON
Wuthering Heights BY EMILY BRONTË

www.ingramcontent.com/pod-product-compliance
Lightning Source LLC
Chambersburg PA
CBHW020944310726
48980CB00001B/49
9781774762301